GUILD OF

FOUR

by C.R. Guardian

Copyright ©2024 Line By Lion Publications
www.pixelandpen.studio
ISBN   9781948807708
Cover Design by Jordan Mizell
Editing by Priscilla VanDerWheele-Smith and Dani J. Caile

LINE BY LION
PUBLICATIONS

To she who traveled many perilous roads in life with me. It was your meticulous eye that scoured the pages for errors and loopholes. Thank you, Priscilla, for giving my writing purpose and transforming it from mere scribbles into something meaningful.

Chapter One

You Dropped This

IN the early 1400s, there were four guilds of assassins in Europe. The Clubs took care of the peasants and their squabbles. The Diamonds made merchants answer for their greed. The Hearts dealt death to the corrupt within the church. And the Spades weeded out dishonest knights and soldiers. These guilds also protected the honest, fair, and virtuous in each subdivision. They remain active to this day with a far greater reach.

May 8, 2016
2:54 PM EDT
Baltimore, Maryland

BOMBS would detonate in thirteen minutes.

Nigel sneezed on the face of his watch. He polished it with the edge of his shirt and shivered with anticipation. Spring allergies would not ruin this moment. He reclined against the steep roof of the three-story Victorian they'd rented the month prior. The mansion provided the perfect vantage of the civic center down the street. Nigel blew his nose until he could smell the blooming lilacs scattered throughout the neighborhood. Soon, the air would smell of smoke. The need to breathe it in displaced all other desire.

He glanced at his watch. *Twelve minutes.*

His compatriots were lined up down the roof, all shifting due to the nerve-wracking suspense. He looked from Cassandra, his fiancé, to Tyler, his best friend, to Jared, his explosives supplier. *This moment requires a declamation.* Nigel stood and announced, "This will finally get our message out."

None replied. Their eyes were transfixed on the civic center.

I need to get in their line of sight. He went to do so. Shingles on the old house broke away and he lost his footing on the precarious roof. He fell, sliding rapidly toward the edge. Shingles tore at his palms as he struggled wildly to slow his descent.

Cassandra swiftly stuck out a foot.

He caught her leg. They inched a few yards further before they halted. "Thanks, babe." Nigel laughed awkwardly, his heart sledgehammering a hole through his chest. "That was—" He swallowed hard. "Invigorating." At least now he had their attention.

"You okay, cookie?" Cassandra said, forcing a look of support through her expression of relief.

"I'm fine." He took a few seconds to regain his resolve. Standing carefully, he said, "If this were a book, we'd be protagonists. We arrive on page one to deliver a message that will become the foundation of chapters to follow." He looked to his fiancé for support. "Can you feel it, Cass? Can you feel the readers of the future absorbing our message, devouring the words of true change?"

Cassandra nodded, but watched his feet, clearly concerned with his perch at the edge of the roof.

"We," he continued, "are the beginning. The main characters who will travel from arc to arc, dedicating our lives to shifting the status quo." Gesturing in the direction of the civic center, he went on. "This is the hook. The shocking moment that pins a reader's eyes to the page." Nigel held out a fist to his best friend. "Tyler, tell me you're hooked."

"Oh, I'm hooked, brother," Tyler said, cautiously leaning forward to bump his fist against Nigel's.

They explosively opened their fists.

Nigel nearly lost his balance again.

"Can you please sit or kneel, cookie?" Cassandra pleaded. "It would mean the world to me if you did."

He waved a hand dismissively and continued ever onward. "Today, we introduce a storyline they can't ignore, scattering ashy breadcrumbs they can't help but follow. We create intrigue with this first step by inciting the glorious incident in this perfectly assembled *mise en scène*."

"You talk too much," Jared interrupted. "Who wants a beer?"

"You're leaving?" said Tyler, flabbergasted. "You'll miss the fireworks."

"That would worry me," Jared said, "if I thought Nigel here couldn't paint me a pretty word picture when I got back." He crawled across the roof. "Knowing that will greet me when I return, maybe I'll grab a couple." He slipped through the rooftop window that led into the attic.

"Forget him," Nigel said. "He doesn't get what we're doing here." Nobody really got him. He was used to being the smartest person in the room. "Besides, he's served his purpose." He gestured again in the direction of the civic center. "That being to provide us with the vehicle in which we detonate explosives under three decorated generals of the U.S. of A's military. I wish we were there to see their unsuspecting faces turn to horror; their bodies turn to mist when the stage erupts beneath their feet." He spread his arms wide. "They speak today on behalf of homeless veterans. However, their deaths will serve as a sacrifice that spreads a greater message to—"

"You dropped this," a man's voice announced from somewhere below.

Nigel shifted to look over the side of the roof.

On the front sidewalk stood a figure wearing a white bomb disposal uniform, his face concealed within a gas mask. He set down a familiar metal crate. Nigel recognized the pink bow Cassandra tied hours before attached to its lid. "I'll just leave this here, then," the man said.

"That's our bomb!" Nigel said. "What the fuck?" His confusion was replaced by the sudden and intense need to sneeze. It escaped hard and jarring. A shingle broke. He fell. This time, his fiancé was too far away to offer her foot. He slid off the roof, barely catching the gutter's lip with his right hand.

"I'm coming, cookie!" The sound of denim sliding across shingles announced Cassandra's approach. "I'm here."

A second sneeze seized Nigel's body. The gutter bent. It broke away. Cassandra's hand appeared, missing his by a mere inch. Down he plummeted, his hands reaching back to break his fall. Metal crunched as his body crashed into the package left by the strange man. The feeling of his spine wrapped around metal wickedly wrenched his stomach.

The man in the bomb disposal uniform stared down at him through the mask. "You're not the smartest *cookie* in the batch, are you?" The mask didn't muffle the voice at all. The man shook his head before walking away.

Jared threw open the front door and ran to stand over Nigel.

They locked eyes.

Wincing, Nigel managed to get out, "Broke something."

Jared chuckled. "Oh, I'm sure you did from that height." He knelt. "Don't worry. You can't die. You're the *protagonist*." Regaining his feet, Jared walked away nonchalantly.

Surely, if the bomb were about to go off, he'd be running.

~ Six of Spades ~

ACROSS the street, Powder Keg leaned against a tree and looked through his gas mask at the other two terrorists perched precariously on the roof's edge. He sighed heavily, fogging up the mask's lens. "The foolishness of youth."

"The world is better off without them," Jared said.

"Thanks for the heads-up on this one."

"You know I hate terrorists killing innocents to make a point."

Powder Keg held out a fat envelope. "For your trouble."

"Don't do it for the money," Jared said. Didn't stop him from taking it.

Powder Keg glanced at the occupants atop the house. They were struggling to make their way to a window.

Their leader, lying prone atop the bomb, sneezed so hard the building shattered. The outside of the house became the inside. The roof rose with the blast, throwing those on top into the air. It then gave a splintered sigh, a crumpled groan, and caved in with a roar. An open maw of fire and smoke devoured the young terrorists, silencing their screams.

Powder Keg glanced at the tree next to him. The remains of a mailbox protruded from the trunk. *Should have used the tree as cover.* "That could have been me." He walked away from the inferno, down a few blocks to a black F-150.

As he got into the truck's cab, his leg vibrated with the buzz of his phone. The lens of his gas mask lit up with one word: Acehole. *What's he want?* "Answer," Powder Keg commanded the phone.

"PK, where you at on this fine day?"

"Baltimore." He started the truck. "What do you have for me?" There was a long pause. "Ace?"

"Promise you won't turn it down."

"That depends." Powder Keg heard sirens and watched as a fire engine, followed by two police cars, sped around the bend. He glanced in the rearview mirror to see them pull up to what remained of the house. "Pausing for suspense?"

"Sorry," Ace said. "It's loud as fuck on your end."

"The sound of a job well done," said Powder Keg.

"I'm sure." Ace cleared his throat. "I've chosen a new recruit. I need you to test him."

"Thanatos said the recruit was a woman."

"We're going with someone else."

"Regardless, it's not happening. I don't test recruits." Powder Keg started the truck and began down the street.

"What if I told you Thanatos agreed to test him?"

Powder Keg laughed until the lens of his mask steamed up.

"Fine. That's a lie," admitted Ace. "He doesn't even know we're passing on Shuriken."

"That'll go over well."

"She'll be there next time."

"Planning on more of us dying?" An ambulance nearly went on two wheels rounding the corner ahead. Powder Keg pulled to the side of the road, allowing ample space for it to pass. When no answer came, he asked, "Is the recruit a demolitions expert?"

"Could be," said Ace.

Powder Keg returned to the road. "I didn't ask if he *could* be."

"Not likely," Ace yielded. "At least I don't believe he's an explosives guru. Although, to be fair, it is in his blood."

That's cryptic. "I have no business testing him if he's not."

Ace groaned. "You won't even consider it?"

Powder Keg sighed deeply. "Send me the file and I'll look it over."

"Deal."

"It's almost definitely a no."

"I'll take it," Ace said. "That's more than Thanatos will concede after I break the news about Shuriken." There was a slight pause. "Sent. Please think about it."

Across the lens of the mask flashed, Call Ended. A PDF icon took its place.

"Open File," commanded Powder Keg.

It opened. Across the top, the file read: Hunter, Chase.

Not possible. Powder Keg became a furnace inside a cocoon of fabric. Breathing in, breathing out, he tried to calm himself. *There must be hundreds of people with that name.* He gave the command, "Scroll down." *Thousands, even.*

A picture rose before his eyes of a young man in his late twenties with blond hair and a strong upper body. The furnace blazed anew at the sight of him. The recruit knelt in a cemetery with a hand atop a newly-chiseled gravestone. This was not some other Hunter, Chase.

"Over my dead body."

Chapter Two

Good Mourning

May 9, 2016
10:33 AM CDT
Kansas City, Missouri

CHASE Hunter stood staring at his uncle Frank's recliner, the vacuum whirring stationary beside him. *I've cleaned around this so many times yet can't bring myself to sit in your chair.*

Starting with the living room was a mistake. Chase lost all desire to tidy up the rest of the house. He tugged the vacuum's plug from the wall.

Someone cleared their throat behind him.

Startled, he turned.

Sitting on his couch was a white man and a Hispanic woman, each in their early thirties. The man stood.

Chase tripped over the vacuum in an attempt to retreat backward and fell on his ass. He scooted along the floor until his back met the wall. "Take what you want."

The man was six and a half feet tall and built like a water buffalo. His size and pale skin reminded Chase of a Nordic warrior; the resemblance was strengthened by a thick beard and long, blond hair.

He's taller than me by four inches. Chase was strong; his upper body built. Generally, he could take anyone who wanted to fight. This often meant nobody dared. But this man was a formidable beast.

"You scared the poor thing," said the woman on the couch. She had tan skin and thick, dark hair, spilling in waves over her shoulders. Judging by how small she appeared on the couch, she couldn't be more than five feet tall. A black folder rested on her lap. "It's okay, Chase," she said, before nodding at the oxen of a man standing beside her. "He, too, spring-cleans in the nude."

Blood rushed painfully into Chase's cheeks. He slapped a hand over his genitals. He had two options: run or fight. They were between him and the front door. *My bat is against the nightstand upstairs.* He glanced at the stairwell. *Shotgun and GLOCK in Frank's room.* His heart throbbed as though he'd drunk a dozen energy drinks. He breathed long and hard before saying, "Leave or I'm calling the police." *Shit!* His phone was upstairs, too. *They don't know that.*

"We did knock," the man replied.

"He knocked," the woman said. "I walked in."

I need to keep them talking while I think of a way out. "And I don't answer, so you pick my lock?"

"Door was open," they said in unison.

Chase remembered turning the deadbolt. "No, it wasn't." *I can't just sit here.* He pointed at the door. When they looked, he bolted for the stairs. *Forget the bat, get the GLOCK.* He kept his eyes on them while ascending.

They didn't pursue. They simply watched with curiosity.

Upon reaching the top of the stairs, he found a woman

standing inside the doorway to his room.

With the eyes of a fox, she peered at him through brown ringlets of hair. "To be fair," she said, holding out a pair of his jeans, "the door was open by the time they arrived."

Chase nearly swallowed his tongue. He stumbled backward until his foot caught air. Down the stairs he rolled, shoulder, hip, and head all protesting when he found the bottom.

Rubbing his head, in a daze, he watched the three approach.

The man peered upstairs. "What are you doing here, Vixen?"

"Funny you should ask, Beast," Vixen replied. "I was wondering the same about you two."

The other woman placed a hand on the man's shoulder. "We were told the approach was ours."

"That's absurd," Vixen said. "The approach is always mine."

Beast cleared his throat. "This probably isn't a mid-recruitment discussion."

Recruitment? Chase glared at each intruder in turn. "Who are you people and what the fuck?"

"Unlike these two," Vixen said, "I had the courtesy to find you some clothes before introducing myself." She threw the jeans to him.

Chase made a point not to catch them. He was, however, happy when one of the legs fell over his crotch. "Then who the hell are you?"

"Vixen. The one who locked your pick." She laughed. "I mean, picked your lock. Sorry. Something is clearly wrong here." She turned to the others. "You feel that, too?"

"It's definitely not right." Chase shot back before they could reply. "There are three strangers in my house, one of whom admitted to breaking and entering."

Beast strode to the dining room table, pulled a chair out for himself, and gestured at the seat across from him. "Sit with me."

Chase glared, not moving.

"I get it," the man said, his voice softening. "You don't trust us. We'll come to you."

Chase slapped a palm against the wood floor. The nerves in his hand needled his fingers. "Stay where you are." He became fully aware of the cadence of his heart beating against his temples. He felt dizzy and warm. The heat at the center of his chest was so intense, he believed his blood might boil. He took a breath. "Lockpicker, would you throw me my bat?"

Vixen said, "You didn't do so well catching the jeans."

He gave her a look to say he wasn't in the mood. "If you want an ounce of trust from me, toss down an olive branch."

Vixen disappeared into his room. She returned and underhand-tossed him the bat.

Chase caught it. Confusion washed over him. "I didn't expect that. I don't really have a follow up."

"We're not here to hurt you," Beast said.

"Then what are you here for?" asked Chase.

"To talk."

The two women approached.

Chase pointed the bat at Vixen. "Not you."

The other woman proceeded forward with the black folder. He spied a prosthetic leg through a split in her long skirt. Not a peg leg either. The natural way she walked suggested it was state of the art.

He freed the folder from her fingertips.

Her dark green eyes narrowed slightly.

Chase's eyes flitted from her to the table. He tightened his grip on the bat.

She backed away, the corner of her lip rising in a half-smile.

That's hardly comforting. At least she'd retreated a few feet.

Chase perused the folder's contents. Inside was a picture of someone—likely a man by the build—opening the door to an F-150. Chase knew the truck by the dent along the bumper. He'd put it there years before when he accidentally backed into an HVAC van. That F-150, dented bumper and all, had blown to hell three weeks prior with his uncle Frank inside. A timestamp confirmed the picture was taken the day of the murder.

Chase closed the folder. "If you were detectives, you wouldn't pick the lock." He pointed the folder at Beast. "Why do you have a picture of my uncle's truck? And who's the man in the hoodie?"

Beast gestured again to the chair. "Sit and we'll discuss it."

"I'm comfortable right here," Chase said. "Besides, for all I know, you're working for my uncle's killer. I'll come closer and you'll break my neck."

"I'd be wary, too," Beast said, the chair creaking when he leaned back. "We—" The man's finger twitched to and from the woman sitting with him. "—are Griffin. Individually, she is Eagle, and I, Beast." He nodded at the top of the stairs. "As you know, she's Vixen."

Chase scoffed.

"How about this," said Beast. "Before you tell us all to go to hell, I'll provide our real names ... *if* you take a seat."

Eagle produced another folder from a leather binder and

set it on the table. "Of course," she said, sounding mildly annoyed. "If I were you, I'd put my pants on first."

Chase glanced at where she dropped the second folder. "More pictures?"

"Pants," Eagle repeated.

Chase nodded at Vixen. "Stay where you are." The words were meant to sound commanding but came out like a plea.

She smirked but gave no impression of advancing.

Chase swallowed, untangling the knot his vocal cords had tied. He clenched the folder between his teeth and stood. Shaking, he placed one foot in a jean leg. The bat slipped from his grip and he knelt quickly to catch it. *They're coming!* In a panic, he bolted upright, the bat swinging in a vertical arc. His eyes darted around the room and—

They hadn't moved.

His pulse assaulted every vein in waves, embarrassment lending vigor to the barrage. His teeth had bitten clean through the folder and pictures within.

Vixen tipped her head to the side and raised an eyebrow.

Eagle gestured at the living room. "If our intent was to kill, we'd have struck while you stood staring at that chair."

The warmth in Chase's chest took up residence behind his eyes. He spit out the folder and threaded the other foot through the jeans. "That *recliner* was my uncle's." The pictures fell to rest on the floor. Indentations from Chase's teeth had pierced the hoodie-wearing man.

It was silent. Then Vixen said, "She didn't know. Please forgive the offense."

"I'll pardon the misunderstanding." Chase drew up the zipper. "What I'll not forgive is the intrusion."

Beast shifted in the chair and gave Eagle an awkward glance. "Vixen's right. Something is off." He cleared his throat hard. "How many people have you killed, Chase?"

How many have I ... "What?"

"This is a mistake." Eagle grabbed the folder from the table. "We should go."

His answers were walking out the door. "Wait." Chase's hand darted as if to snatch the folder from afar. "I haven't killed *anyone*."

Vixen sat on the top step. "When approaching killers, we must make an impact. Nothing makes quite the impression as a stranger appearing in your home."

Chase felt lost. "Why approach killers *at all*?"

"In this case," Eagle said, setting down the folder, "to offer an opportunity."

Chase wanted more than anything to get closer. *This could be a ploy.* He sized them up again. *One's on a prosthetic; another's too big to be quick.* He looked up the stairs. *She's far enough away. I could be halfway down the block before they caught up.* He hurled the bat at Beast and went for the folder.

Without moving from the chair, Beast caught the bat.

Chase lurched to a stop and cringed, raising a shoulder to protect his face. He expected the weapon to return the way it left, but instead, he heard it set peacefully on the tabletop.

Beast sighed. "If it'll calm your rabbiting ass down, my name's Alexander."

Chase peeked one eye over his shoulder to see Eagle's eyes widen.

Beast nodded to her.

She relaxed. "Erica." She glowered at Chase. "Now *sit*."

Chase could read people. Not as well as his uncle, maybe, but the gift was there. Eagle, or Erica, appeared the type of person who had little patience for bullshit. Her eyes hadn't lied when they grew in surprise nor had they lied when they relaxed. She trusted Beast, or Alexander. Chase noticed their matching rings. *Beast and Eagle. Together they are Griffin.* "Are you married?"

Beast ran a finger along the wedding band. "That a problem?"

Chase took a step forward. "No." He took a few more. "How long?"

Eagle's expression softened. "Couple years now."

Chase approached the folder. He felt better about them. Not sure why, but he did. "This doesn't mean I trust you." He pointed at their chairs in turn. "Pull the seats forward. Pin yourselves in."

Beast followed the instruction.

Eagle's eyes nearly rolled into the back of her head, yet her chair scooted forward. She placed an elbow on the table, dropping her chin into her palm. "Happy?"

Chase shrugged. He turned to Vixen. "Name?"

She pursed her lips.

"Whatever," Chase said, retrieving his bat from the table. "Stay where you are or my *rabbiting ass* goes out the door." He opened the folder and studied the picture cradled within. It was of an old black man with white hair, thin lips, and a short nose. "Am I supposed to know this man?"

"That's Bryant Kettleman," Beast answered. "He tried to blow up a residential building fifteen years ago. The bomb squad responsible for stopping him was led by your uncle

Frank."

Chase sat. "Really?"

"After three years in prison, he gave up the names of four Kansas City arsonists. His sentence was reduced, then he was paroled early for good behavior." Beast crossed his arms and nodded at the picture. "That happened to be two days before your uncle was killed. The parole officer assigned hasn't heard from Mr. Kettleman since. He believes he fled the state, possibly the country."

Chase pushed the folder away. "He's gone?"

"For now," said Eagle.

"We'll help you get him," Beast assured.

"Let me get this straight." Chase was more than a little suspicious of their desire to help him catch Frank's killer. "You broke into my house to tell me you're eager to catch ... Mr. Kettleman, was it?"

"Not catch," Vixen said. "Assassinate."

Chase turned. "You're going to kill him?"

Eagle said, "You'd rather we put him in a corner? Demand he think about what he's done?"

"No," Chase admitted. "I want him dead more than you do. I'm wondering how much this'll cost me."

"We won't charge anything," Beast said, "because it'll be you pulling the trigger."

"We already established I'm not a killer." Chase put the pieces together. "You said recruitment earlier. This is more than a trigger needing pulled?"

Beast nodded. "We're part of a brotherhood of assassins." He pushed back his chair.

Chase smacked the bat against the floor. "Don't unpin

yourself after saying something like that." He looked at Eagle. She'd be candid. "Am I supposed to believe this shit?"

"Believe what you want." She, too, pushed back her chair. "I'm out."

Chase raised the bat. "Keep moving and I'll break that pretty prosthetic of—" His face met the table, the bat torn from his grip. Pain blossomed at the front and back of his head. He tried to move, but his scalp screamed for him to stop. He glanced to his right and saw Beast's body. The pain at the back of his head made sense. Beast had a fistful of his hair. *I mistook how fast he could be.* The pulsating of his heart threatened to punch a hole through his jugular. *Why didn't I run when I had the chance?*

Eagle appeared to his left. She rested her cheek against the table so her green eyes could meet his hazels. "My husband doesn't take well to people threatening me," she smiled. "Especially aggressors wielding bats." She straightened. "A story for another time, perhaps."

Chase released a breath he'd not meant to hold. "Sorry."

Beast let go. A loud crack resounded.

Chase tensed in anticipation of being hit. When pain didn't follow, he lifted his head to see the bat broken in two.

Beast tossed the pieces aside, the smaller of them skittering across the floor. "Forgive the harsh reaction."

Vixen clapped. "This is why I do the approach."

Eagle shot her an icy stare. "You're not helping."

Chase sat up. "I'm sorry for threatening you."

"Believe me," said Vixen, "you're lucky Beast didn't let you swing. Eagle would have put three bullets through you before you saw her move."

Eagle's eyes drifted shut. "Still not helpful." Her eyes

opened to focus on Chase. "Join us. Avenge your uncle's death. That's the offer."

Chase studied her stoic expression, then Beast's blue eyes. "You're serious?"

"We are." Beast's smile returned. "We are card holders of the Guild of Four. A Guild of the people, for the people."

Chase eyed the larger piece of bat. "I don't know what that means." He rose. *I have the killer's name.* He could go from here on his own. Provide the name to the proper authorities. "Now, if you'll excuse me, I need to finish vacuuming." *This time with clothes on.* He retreated until the backs of his knees met the couch. "Please show yourselves out."

"You feel responsible," Eagle said.

Chase squinted. "What's that?"

"You feel you should have been there. That somehow you could have saved him. You should have been prepared."

Chase shook his head.

"It happened before," Beast spoke up. "Your parents were killed when you were an infant. Someone blew up their car. We might be able to find that person as well."

"How do you know all this?" asked Chase.

Beast shrugged. "It's our business to know the pasts of those we recruit."

There were so many questions. Why had his uncle been murdered? Had his parents' killer returned? And if so, why all these years later? "It can't be coincidence that my uncle was blown up, too," Chase said, pointing at the folders. "How do we know it's this guy?"

"We don't," admitted Beast. "We'll figure it out together."

Frank wouldn't want this for me. So why am I considering it?

Eagle's prosthetic caught the light as she started for the door. "You prayed lightning wouldn't strike the same family twice." She opened it. "Truth is, lightning strikes the same places all the time. The difference here is we have the resources to direct its hot touch back at those responsible." She gestured outside. "You're considering telling us not to go because it's time for you to strike back."

Chase often dreamed of his uncle's truck exploding. The dreams were vivid. He would try to run, try to scream for Frank to get out. But his feet were cemented, his voice mute. Rather than waking during these night terrors, he'd force himself to watch. He felt he deserved to endure it. *Does Frank haunt me because he wants vengeance?*

Chase stared at the oak floorboards. "Frank took me in when my parents died. Then he was taken as well. It's like I'm meant to suffer. Why I'm telling you, I don't know." A lump grew in his throat and he forced his eyes to meet Eagle's. "People say you're supposed to feel something when someone you love is in danger. That you know their soul has left the world." He swallowed. "I was at the bank when my uncle died. I didn't feel a thing. He was torn apart by shrapnel and I didn't shiver."

"People say a lot of shit," Eagle said. "But that's all it is, Chase. Shit."

Beast collected the folders. "We're offering you a way to do something about it. We can't bring your family back, but we sure as hell can put their killer in the ground."

Chase forced a laugh. "Alive or dead, my uncle would never approve of me becoming a murderer to kill a murderer. Even if it was his own."

Eagle looked to Beast. "That's our answer."

Beast sighed heavily. "Sounds like it is."

"Sorry," Chase said.

Beast walked to the door. "Enjoy your spring cleaning."

Eagle nodded at Chase and they left, leaving the door open as it had been when they first arrived.

Chase took a deep breath and held it until he couldn't. It escaped in a rush, leaving him dizzy. "That was strange." He dropped backward over the arm of the couch to lie staring at the ceiling.

The banister creaked.

How did I forget she was there? He lifted his head to peek over the couch.

Vixen was descending. "I didn't hear it."

"Hear what?"

"Your answer," she said, her eyebrows knit together. "I never heard a 'no.'"

"Frank would want me to move on, not to obsess over his death. He'd tell me, 'That's the past, this is now.'"

"What do you want?" She leaned on the back of the couch. "Because all I'm hearing is what he wouldn't."

Chase shrugged.

Vixen leaned forward to get a better look at him. "Your parents died a long time ago," she said. "That was in the past. Have you gotten over them?"

"Not exactly." He dropped his head against the couch cushion. "And I never really knew them. Frank raised me. He was my father." He looked at the recliner. "His murder will never fade from memory." His eyes returned to her. "Nothing will fix that."

Vixen crawled over the back of the couch and laid on him. Dark ringlets of hair fell to frame his face, blocking out the rest of the world. Her arms burrowed under him and she hugged him tight. Her body was warm, her breasts firm against his chest.

Chase swallowed hard. Although bewildered, he returned the hug and closed his eyes. Her skin was soft and comforting, and her hair smelled of pomegranate.

She tucked her head into the crook of his neck, her lips brushing his ear, and said, "Assassinating this man is a carrot. The Guild offers new members one unsanctioned kill when they join. Doesn't matter who, doesn't matter why." She lifted her head.

He opened his eyes to stare deep into hers. They were the color of honey. He was ensnared by them.

Vixen glanced at his lips. "We won't go after him without you."

If I pass on this, I'll regret it. He knew that, years from now, when Frank's death still weighed heavily, he'd long to return to this moment. *But—* "My uncle wouldn't want this." *He's dead.* Chase closed his eyes and sighed. *I need justice.* The police never caught his parents' killer. How were they supposed to catch Frank's?

He opened his eyes and gazed at her. *She is gorgeous.* He imagined an angel offering him a fiery blade of justice. *Or she's the devil wrapped in a perfect body, asking me to sign away my soul.* "Can I sleep on it?"

She pulled an arm out from under him and cupped his cheek in her palm. "I'm not going to waste my time over a maybe." She placed her lips to his.

What in heaven's name? He melted, his ribcage straining the liquid of his heart.

When their lips parted, she ran a knuckle along his eyebrow. "What's it going to be, Hunter?"

He knew he wore a dumb-ass expression, but couldn't steal his gaze from her to pull himself together. He managed the word, "Okay."

She smiled sweetly. "I need to hear a yes."

He nodded. "Yes."

Vixen planted a short kiss on his bottom lip. She pushed against his chest to get up, then strode to the door. "I'll see you tomorrow at noon."

Chase didn't watch her leave. He stared at the ceiling, dumbfounded by the morning's events. By the time he shifted to get one last look, she was gone.

He licked his lips, tasting pomegranate lip gloss.

I guess I'm an assassin now.

Chapter Three

Slice of Heaven

THE four Guilds managed themselves by requiring each kill be sanctioned before being carried out. Only contracts that could further the Guild's influence and reputation were sanctioned. Ten percent of payment earned would go to the Guild, while the rest went to the assassin. The split was generously in the Guild members' favors to keep them loyal. Therefore, an assassin carrying out unsanctioned kills was swiftly dealt with.

May 9, 2016
11:47 PM MDT
Colorado Springs, Colorado

CHRISTOPH turned up the heat as he drove. Somehow, Colorado Springs missed the memo that spring had arrived, and the air was still crisp and cold. It had even snowed heavily a week or so before.

It was quiet tonight. The only sounds were of his tires on the road and a faint rattling coming from somewhere in his engine. *Sounds expensive.* There would be plenty of time to worry about that later, whereas his time with Tyra was rapidly coming to an end. He missed her already and she was still in the car with him.

His eyes dropped to Tyra's hand resting on his leg, her fingernails a dark crimson. *I love that color on her.*

The street lights all died at once. "What in the hell?"

Tyra squeezed his leg. "We're the only lights on the road. Turn them off or someone will notice."

He shook his head. "I won't be able to see a damned thing if I—"

"Please, don't fight," she said. "Not tonight."

Christoph sighed and turned off the headlights. He had to squint to see the road ahead. "What's so special about tonight?"

"Besides all the fucked-up shit we did?"

He couldn't argue there. She let him do things to her he never imagined possible.

He squeezed her hand. "You know I love you, right?" he assured her. When she smiled with all but her eyes, he added, "You mean everything to me."

She sat back and stared ahead. "If you can't see, you should drive slower."

He brought the car to a crawl. The final quarter-mile was silent besides the rattling in his engine.

She opened the door while he was still driving.

"Tyra!" Christoph yelled.

"Here's fine," she said, stepping out before the car could come to a stop.

He pushed the brake the final centimeter. "Are you crazy?"

She made her way around the front of the car. It jolted slightly, though he hadn't seen her bump into it. A clinking sound came from the back. He looked in the rearview mirror but saw nothing. *My car is falling apart.*

Tyra knocked on his window. "I need one last kiss."

He brought the window down. The smell of firewood burning in hearths made the street feel as warm and inviting as her lips. "Only one?"

"I could do with more." She leaned in and they kissed hard, tongues tangling together.

He broke the kiss. "One's all ya get."

"You'd stop me?" She frowned, leaning in for a second. Her fingers wrapped around his head, weaving into his hair to hold him. The kiss that followed was more passionate than their first. It went on so long he wondered if she meant it to be their last. He knew this couldn't go on forever, no matter how much he wanted it to. She was married.

But why not forever? "What was that kiss for?" he said, while wishing he'd yelled: *Run away with me!*

She was crying. "I love you."

"Tyra, what's wrong?"

A tear sped down her cheek. "Goodbye."

This can't be it. He reached through the window and took her hand. "I'll see you tomorrow?"

"Christoph, he's already suspicious. He'd kill us both if he found out."

That's it. "I can't let you go. Not back to him."

She raised her shoulder to wipe the tear dripping from her chin. "I know you can't."

"Then come away with me," he insisted. "Tonight."

She stared at his hand, considering. Her body shivered from the cold. No, not the cold. She was sobbing to the point of shaking.

She kissed his knuckles. "Bye, my love." She let go and ran up the winding sidewalk. He lost her in the dark for a second before she appeared under the light of the bi-parting swing-gate access door. She typed in the code and the thin light above the door transitioned from red to green. Stepping through, she disappeared from sight.

"No, no, no." His breathing quickened. *I can't lose her.* He felt the onset of a panic attack. *Not like this.*

He stared through the gate at the well-lit greenhouse. Tyra's husband had hired Christoph's company to build it. There was no reason he needed a two-story greenhouse. For what he "needed," a simple twelve by eight would have sufficed and could have been built in one day. He insisted on larger.

Every day Christoph and his men worked, Tyra brought out cookies, sandwiches, and lemonade for lunch. On the final day, her husband failed to come home for the walk-through. Tyra admitted to Christoph her husband would never use the greenhouse. It was never about having fresh tomatoes and cucumbers during the winter. It was about appearances. Her husband wanted to be seen as the man who had everything. She opened up further, confessing her husband forced her to perform sexual favors on his bosses to secure promotions. It was after this admission that Christoph leaned in and kissed her for the first time. She began crying and he consoled her well into the night.

I'll find a way to convince her. He squeezed the steering wheel. *I have to.* He did a U-turn and flipped the headlights on.

A white man in his late forties, early fifties stood in front of the car.

Christoph's foot slammed against the brake.

The person did not flinch nor did he look intent on stepping away. An unlit cigarette was pressed between his lips. There was a metallic clink when he threw back the lid to a Zippo lighter and snapped his fingers against the flint wheel. A flame scratched to life and danced before his eyes.

"What in the—" Christoph stuck his head out the window. "I could've killed you." The smell of warm rubber took up residence in his nostrils. "Please move."

The tip of the cigarette glowed red. The man smiled a terrifying, disturbing smile and exhaled. Smoke gave birth to eerie shadow demons that crawled up his face.

"Seriously?" Christoph noticed the man wore black gloves and a leather jacket with the crimson Harley Davidson logo clear upon the breast. *Maybe his motorcycle ran out of gas or something.* "Do you need a ride?" The irritation he felt was poorly hidden in his voice. When there was no response, Christoph placed his hand against the center of the steering wheel. *Tyra wouldn't appreciate me blaring the horn.* He withdrew his hand and put the car in reverse. He backed up several feet, turned, and put the car into drive. Upon circumnavigating the human obstruction, he raised his middle finger.

The man nodded, smoke lifting from his nostrils.

Not sure what that was. Christoph chuckled nervously. *Probably the neighborhood drunk.*

He barely made it thirty yards before the car lurched to a stop. "This car!" But the car was still running. He tried to accelerate. His tires spun, the smell of burnt rubber returning home. "What now?" Christoph threw the car into park, leaned back in his seat, and sighed. A red glow drew his eyes to the rearview mirror. He pushed against the brake and the rest of the man glowed as red as his cigarette.

What's his deal?

The man walked to the open window and rested the hand holding the cigarette atop the door. He blew smoke through the window. "Car trouble?"

Christoph waved the smoke away, coughing. "Why do I—" Cough. "—feel you're responsible?" Cough, cough.

"I'm not sure," the man replied. "You don't know me at all."

"Sorry, that was rude." Christoph unbuckled his seatbelt and tried to open the door. It wouldn't budge.

"No need to apologize." The man leaned in. "Name's Ace, and you were right to assume."

What? "Why?" Christoph stuck his head out the window and looked at the back of his car. He couldn't see anything.

Ace dropped his arm and wrapped it around Christoph's throat.

The fight or flight response flared in warning. *Retreat!* Christoph decided. He tried to back into his car. Before he could break free, something hit his head. Stars lit the corners of his vision. He jerked away in desperation. Gloved knuckles came into view and struck the bridge of his nose. There was more under the glove than fist; knuckles don't clink like metal.

Fight! Christoph struck out blindly.

Ace caught his fist and twisted down and back.

Flight! "Fuck!" *Run!* Christoph doubled over sideways. It was a failed attempt to gain a reprieve from the excruciating pain. His blood pumped too hard through veins too thin, as though it were maple syrup being blown through stirring straws.

When Christoph was on the verge of passing out, Ace let go.

Christoph coughed and gulped in air, swallowing more than breathing. His head spun; his stomach turned.

Ace flicked Christoph's forehead. "You've been sleeping with a married woman."

Her husband hired a hit man. Christoph's vision was murky but returning. He locked eyes with the aggressor. "I was only being friendly. She took her car to the shop and asked for a ride home."

Ace lunged forward and grabbed Christoph by the hair. "Lying won't save you." He tightened his hold and twisted. "Especially a lie as sorry as that."

Christoph's face met the steering wheel. The horn went off, a big F you to Tyra's desire for quiet. He nearly blacked out as the stars in his vision multiplied. The bridge of his nose felt on fire. "Who are you?"

"The question isn't who, but why?" Ace corrected. "Half of her husband's firm have been between her legs. How do you think he made partner so young?"

"I know this already. He's a monster." Christoph saw the glow of the cigarette through watery vision. *Now or never. Fight!* He wrenched his hand free and clawed at his assailant's face. The red glow smeared across his vision.

Ace avoided the hit entirely.

Christoph's cheek took a blow from the metal knuckles.

Ace laughed. "One stupid decision after another. Do you ever tire of making the wrong move?"

Warm smoke caressed Christoph's face. He couldn't smell the cigarette, but that wasn't surprising with the amount of blood he felt running from his nostrils. Unfortunately, he could taste the smoke. He'd been breathing through his mouth ever since the second blow.

"What do you want?"

"She fucks a lot of men. Why kill you?"

Christoph screamed, trying the door again. *If I open it, even a little, I might hit him hard enough he'll back off.* It was still jammed.

"Think about it, Christoph."

"I don't know." Christoph pushed harder.

Ace stepped back and the door broke free.

Christoph hadn't expected it to open so fast. He fell forward, barely catching the door to steady himself. He looked up in time to see Ace kick. The door slammed against the side of Christoph's face and shoulder.

Ace prepared to kick again.

Christoph put out a hand to stop the door. He heard more than felt bones crunch and snap. Crippling pain followed in the form of miniature explosions radiating up his arm. He saw Ace reel back for another kick and retreated into the car. He sat up in time for the door to slam shut. He cradled his wrist against his chest and sobbed like a child.

Ace slapped Christoph's cheek through the window. "Money," he said, grabbing Christoph's hair again. "She may screw a lot of men into bliss for her husband. But you—" Ace laughed, sending the word 'you' spinning. "You, she makes love to for herself. The moment this relationship became serious, it would cost money. More money than my client was willing to part with." He tightened his grip. "Understand?"

What money? "I haven't stolen anything."

Ace put his cigarette inches from Christoph's lip. "No?" He pulled Christoph's face forward to extinguish the cigarette against searing flesh.

"Son of a *BITCH*," Christoph yelled, jerking his head side to side. He felt hairs being pulled out but was more concerned about the smoldering embers eating through his lip. "I didn't steal." He licked the burn. "Please stop." His tongue darted out again. "I'll do anything."

Ace brushed Christoph's upper lip with a fingertip and blew on the wound. "I know," he confessed. "That's not what this is about."

"Then what?" Christoph said, lowering his voice. "Why?"

Ace smiled. "That communal slice of heaven between her thighs put in a lot of time. Time spent gaining her husband a high position in the firm."

"Why are you working for him?" Christoph said. "He forced her to do those things. He's allowing other men to rape his wife. You should be *killing him*."

Ace let out a raspy laugh. "That's not how this works. And her husband doesn't have a fucking clue about the two of you." He loosened his grip on Christoph's hair.

Wait... what? "Then why would he kill me?" Christoph said. "I don't understand."

"Clearly." Ace tapped the cigarette burn on Christoph's upper lip. "The husband is not the client." He twisted the hair and jerked Christoph's head back.

Christoph yelled out in pain. He clawed at the fingers digging into his scalp.

"Oh, nooo, please stop," said Ace, his voice resonating

with amusement. "You're hurting me ever so badly." The man released.

Christoph attempted to crawl into the passenger-side seat. *If I can get to the other door, I can make a break for —*

A hand grabbed the back of his shirt and tugged, pulling him into the driver's seat. An arm encircled his throat, held, tightened.

"Let me go!" Christoph scratched at the arm.

"Were you raised by cats?" Ace flexed, cutting off Christoph's ability to breathe. "Stop and I'll loosen."

Christoph went limp. "Yer lyin'," he choked.

The arm relaxed. "What's that now?"

"She didn't hire you."

Ace relaxed further. "Only you two knew of the affair. Did you hire me?"

Christoph took one heavy breath and shook his head. "Why would she?"

"When Tyra married a lawyer, there was a prenuptial agreement. If she divorced him, she'd get nothing. She knows in a few years, he'll be at the top because of her. No longer will he use her to get ahead." He placed his lip against Christoph's ear. "If she left him now, she'd give up a house bought with the spoils of her body. All those years of filling that slice of heaven between her legs with old men would be for naught."

"I can't leave her to this life."

"Not up to you," said Ace.

"I can't give up."

"She's aware." Ace rubbed the side of his lip along the curve of Christoph's earlobe. "She's nearly left him a hundred times for you."

Christoph felt an odd sense of achievement. It was buried

in a truckload of dread, but there all the same. "She thought of leaving him?"

Ace nodded against the side of Christoph's face. "Then she realized the cost. A life of luxury you could never provide. A life she earned."

Something pinched his neck. Christoph winced. The sensation of a needle followed. He slapped and jerked away.

Ace let go and stepped back.

Christoph twirled to see a syringe in the man's hand. "What is that?"

"I'm not sure exactly," Ace said. "Something I borrowed from Widow." He put a cap over the needle and dropped it in a pocket. "You asked who I was." He patted the pocket. "This is my answer."

Christoph wanted to ask what that meant, but his mouth refused. His hand fell to his side, it, too, losing the ability to carry out simple commands. His world grew into a shadowed mess. Whatever coursed through his veins was rapidly paralyzing him. He could no longer draw a full breath. His lungs failed to answer the demand for oxygen.

"I kill with elaborate traps," Ace said as he reached past Christoph. "You built this one yourself."

Christoph watched as the 'P' on his console switched to 'D.' *Car is in drive, but still not moving.*

"There we go," Ace said, patting Christoph's chest with a hand. "Let's end that emotional suffering."

There was the sound of a window breaking followed by the roar of flame. What little breath Christoph could manage filled his lungs with the smoke of burning fabric.

Christoph knew he should continue fighting back or

fleeing to safety, but the desire to do either was fading, numbing, muting. He wondered why the smoke wasn't bothering him. *It doesn't matter anymore.* The world walked away, leaving him to die alone in darkness. His last thoughts were of Tyra, his love for her enduring even until death.

~ Ace of Spades ~

ACE stepped away from the car and waved away the smoke from the Molotov cocktail. He was certain securing the woven steel cable to the car would catch Christoph's attention. But Tyra assured him Christoph would be watching her and the headlights would be off. She was correct. It had been surprisingly easy to secure without detection.

Ace's phone rang with a ringing tone. He missed the days when you didn't have to hear everyone's choice of music erupting from their phones.

He took it from his pocket and saw Tyra's number. *She's not happy.* He answered the call. "It's taken care of."

"What did you do?" Her voice was shaking. "I couldn't see anything and then there was fire."

Ace pulled a remote from his pocket. He'd taken it from Zettabyte's lab. He turned the knob and the streetlights lit up. "Better?"

She screamed and began crying hysterically.

"I was to make sure he never returned. No amount of convincing was going to keep that man from coming back to *save* you. Death doesn't leave room for convincing. It is permanent. He's no longer your concern. You are welcome."

She said something else, but her crying made it impossible

to translate.

"Stop wailing," Ace demanded. "Why call an assassins' guild if this wasn't the end game?"

She pulled it together enough to choke out, "I said scare him!"

"I did that, too."

"You're a monster." She breathed in sharply.

"Funny, that's what he called your husband."

"I'm calling your Guild and telling them what you did."

"Honey, are you actually threatening me when I'm standing right outside?" Ace saw the curtain move in one of the mansion windows and waved. "The Guild turned you down for this type of work. I called back because I was bored. They don't care I'm here." That was a lie. He'd have some serious explaining to do if she called that number again. "If you call to complain or fail to pay up, I'll return to scare *you*, too. Maybe enjoy myself a slice of that communal pie."

"I'm calling the police."

"You do that. Forget not the part where you hired me." Ace hung up.

Where were we? Ace reached for the woven steel cable. His hand jerked the final few inches to the metal. *I should turn this off.* He ran a finger along the cuff of the glove until he felt a button. Once pressed, the attraction between the cable and his hand ceased. He'd taken the electromagnetic glove from Golem's workshop. It had done nicely to keep the car door shut.

He could feel the cold of the cable through the glove as he unhooked it and put a shoulder to the trunk. The car inched forward, met the edge of the hill, and began moving faster.

"Off you go." Ace stood and watched the car pick up

speed. Before long, it was careening down the road. It leapt across an intersection, barely missing a blue sedan, and sped past a sign warning: DEAD END

Ace dropped the cable to the pavement. His phone rang but he waited to answer. He wanted to watch his work play out. He didn't want to miss the car colliding with the four-foot thick, red brick wall standing proudly at the end of the road.

Another ring.

You're nearly there, baby.

Ring ...

The car jerked to the side as though the steering wheel had turned. The forward momentum forced the vehicle to flip.

Ring ...

Flame and metal decorated the air as the car rolled once—twice—and slid after the third. It came to rest within a couple feet of the brick wall.

Ring ...

"Damn." Ace spat on the road. "So close." He put a black clove cigarette to his lips and waited for the phone to stop ringing. *She needs to let it go.* He blew the smoke toward the crash, admiring the mangled mess of fire and steel. "That'll 'bout do it."

His phone began ringing again.

Ace didn't look at who was calling when he answered, "I swear, bitch, I will cut you open and watch you bleed out."

A deep voice with a thick Jamaican accent replied, "Don' tink you be gettin' close to try."

Great. "Thanatos," Ace said with as much excitement in his voice as he could muster. "Brother."

"Yu noh famaly o' mine."

"I thought you were my ex. She's been driving me crazy.

Threatening to—"

"Mi don' care."

"Fine. What's up?" Ace knelt to admire his handiwork. Four high-impact circle-screws, each a foot long, had been fed into the road earlier that night. The cable was then threaded through the circles of the screws, and doubled around and back under itself before continuing on to the next screw. A hook had been secured in the fourth. He was glad he'd put in so many because the first two screws were pulled up entirely. He realized Thanatos hadn't replied. "Did I lose you?" He heard the sound of a sniper rifle being taken apart. "If you're wrapping something up, you can call me back."

"Mi a goin' decide today."

Ace locked the phone between his ear and shoulder and bent to undo the hook from the cable. "About that." Ace could hear metal rubbing on metal. "You're busy. We'll talk later."

"Mi do two tings atta same time."

Ace stifled a laugh and undid the first loop of cable. He fed it back through the circle screw. "I decided on the boy from Missouri."

"What bway?" Thanatos sounded angry. "What of da woman from Virginiya, or 'im from Texaus?"

"I decided to go another way." Ace grinned, knowing full well this would get the sniper's blood boiling. "An irresistible option presented itself." He pulled the first circle screw out of the ground and placed it on the road.

"Da woman," Thanatos insisted. "Shi da wan."

"She'll be around next time." Ace hoped this would end the conversation. He repeated the process for the second circle screw, feeding the cable through. "As Ace, I have the right to bypass your decision."

"Wi noh talkin' dis tru?"

"It's too late. He was approached this morning." Ace's lungs warmed with smoke. "Don't worry. He's worth it."

"Mi say, 'im bettah be."

Ace undid the third loop and began turning the circle screw. It must have been pulled up slightly as well because it didn't take long. "I'll be taking over who assesses him." He

waited for a response but there was only quiet. *He's pissed.* "If he passes the first few, I want you to test him."

"Ell noh," Thanatos growled. "Eh sniper is notta test. Tiz only death."

There it is. The only thing he says that sounds remotely English. "Know I may call on you anyway."

"Mi turn yu down den, as mi a doin' now." Thanatos ended the call.

Ace pocketed the phone and looked at the inferno raging below. He undid the final length of cable and looped it into a circle. He set it to the side and tried the next screw. It hadn't budged when the car was brought to a halt, nor did it want to now. "You're going to be a little bastard, aren't ya?"

Sirens pierced the night.

"Excellent response time." Ace placed the nearly finished cigarette to his lips. "Come on, you." He clamped down on the screw and put all his strength into loosening it. When it finally gave, he twisted until it came free of the asphalt. He stood and watched the first police car speed around the corner below and stop.

An officer got out and gave the burning car a wide birth as he circled it. It was clear the officer was looking for survivors.

You won't find one. Ace stared at the wreckage. "When a

man dies over a woman, rarely is much left of him." Smoke curled around the words as they were spoken. He popped his neck loudly, breathed in once more, and tossed the spent cigarette into the gutter. He blew into the sky. A plume of smoke spiraled to join the thick trail lifting from the roaring wreckage.

The woman moved the curtain again to peek out.

She'll be my undoing if I don't do something about her. He stretched and started toward the house. "Might have to sample that slice of heaven before I go."

Chapter Four

Through an Open Window

May 10, 2016
1:03 PM CDT
Kansas City, Missouri

CHASE stood in the kitchen, aiming his uncle's shotgun at the clock. "Thought she'd be here by noon." *Maybe they decided I'm not assassin material.* Wouldn't surprise him, considering his horrible performance the day before.

His grip tightened. He'd never been a gun person. But whether he entered the police academy as planned or became an assassin, he'd need to awaken that part of himself.

A hand flashed into view from his right, catching the barrel. His feet kicked out from under him and his back met the floor.

Vixen stood over him. Practiced hands emptied shotgun shells onto his chest. "Good morning." She placed the weapon on the counter.

"It's noon," he groaned. "But come on in. Make yourself at home."

With a bare foot, she cleared the shells from his chest and pressed toes to his ribs. "You have a smart mouth." Her toes flexed. "That's good."

"I aim to impress."

"I'm serious," said Vixen. "Quick wit serves to disarm your opponent."

"Yes, this is me winning."

She laughed, lowering to straddle his chest. "Where was this humor yesterday?"

His eyes trailed over her body, ears warming. She wore black tights, a leather jacket, and a hair tie around each wrist. "What are you doing?"

"Nervous?" she asked.

"No," he lied.

"You know what else throws off your opponent?" She pressed her lips to his. They were warm, full, and altogether perfect. Her hair fell to block out everything but the memory of them on the couch.

He closed his eyes, returning the kiss. *My ass was handed to me by a girl and I'm loving it.*

When their lips parted, she straightened fast and slapped him across the face.

He blinked. *Loving it less.* He put a hand to his cheek and felt the radiating sting. "Why?" He squinted, anticipating another slap.

"Did you expect it?"

"No." He stretched his jaw. "Worth it."

She patted his chest. "Your world's bottom up and you crack jokes." She kissed him again, this time hardly more than a peck. She looked around. "You finished cleaning."

He raised an eyebrow. "You never know when visitors might stop by uninvited."

She leaned back and stretched.

A sharp pain shot across his ribcage. That was likely her intent. Another way to toy with him. He didn't care how painfully she straddled him, as long as she continued doing so.

She tapped his lip. "You're enjoying this."

Chase crossed his arms behind his head. "Been a while since a woman pinned me down."

"I'm sure she wasn't asking you to become an assassin."

He chuckled. "No, but I'm not entirely sure how I made the cut this time."

She squeezed his arm. "Technically, you haven't yet. Let's get to work." She stood and offered her hand to help him up.

He stayed on the ground. "I haven't?"

"There's a testing period." Vixen explained. "You'll have seven opponents, each allowed two hours to kill you. They often use the first hour to prepare and the second to test your ability to survive."

"Survive against seasoned assassins?" Chase suppressed the impulse to laugh. "You might tell a person that *before* they agree to join." He went to pass by her.

She grabbed his arm. "I'll train you."

"Thanks, but you'd be starting from scratch."

"Good," Vixen said. "I don't have to train around bad habits." She let go of him. "Now, hit me."

"No."

She slapped his face. "Hit me."

"Stop it." He tried to step around her while pushing her out of his way.

She sidestepped gracefully and her hands shot out, one grabbing his wrist, the other his elbow. She used his momentum to twirl him around, then let go.

His shoulder went through drywall. Fortunately, this anchored his body upright. *Fine, let's do this.* He attempted to launch at her.

She bent backward, and her foot slammed into his chest.

His back met the wall, widening the indentation left by his shoulder. When he went to move, he found her foot pressed to his chest, pinning him in.

I need to slow her down. He punched her calf.

She winced. Her leg dropped.

"Good move," she said. "Follow through next time."

He swung a fist, watched for her to block, then grabbed her wrist. He pulled her forward, bringing his knee into her side.

She crumpled, swaying backward and sucking in air. "Nice kidney shot." She sucked in again and groaned, "More of that."

"No," he argued. "I don't want to keep hurting you." He ran up the stairs and into his room.

"We're going to need to spar if you're going to survive this," she said from below. "Are we sparring or are you going into these tests blind?" This time, heavy footsteps betrayed her approach.

"How were you able to sneak up on me earlier?" asked Chase.

"Because I needed to physically disarm you, requiring stealth." She leaned against the frame of his doorway. "Now I want you to know I'm here. A louder approach is meant to disarm you emotionally, allowing you to feel in control."

"It's not working." He grabbed a backpack from the closet. "I have about as much control over you as a fly over a windshield." He found a baseball inside, twirled, and flung it at her.

Vixen's hand arced, seizing the ball from the air. She underhand-tossed it back to him.

Chase caught it and pressed it to his chest. "Fly." He pointed the ball at her. "Windshield." He dropped the ball and returned to the closet. He grabbed clothing by the fistfuls, tossing them to the bed. A shirt snagged on a hanger. He pulled harder. The fabric tore. He threw the shirt, hanger and all, across the room.

"What are you doing, Chase?"

"I can't survive seasoned assassins, Vixen." He balled up his fists. "There's no way that's going to happen. So, I'm leaving before they arrive at my doorstep."

"That's why I'm here," said Vixen. "To train you before they appear."

"I told you yesterday, I'm no killer. So, if professional killers are thrown at me, how can I prevail against them?"

"If you do live, you can avenge your uncle."

"Don't get me wrong," said Chase. "That's a tasty carrot. But it's dangling from a stick that *will* bludgeon me to death."

"A fair concern," agreed Vixen. "I'll call my boss and tell him you're out." She retrieved her phone from a pocket and left the room.

"Really?" Chase watched her go. "Just like that?"

Her voice came from outside the room. "He's turning us down." She started down the stairs. "What do you mean, 'who'? Chase Hunter."

He went to the door, but stayed out of sight to give her the illusion of privacy.

"Come again?" she said.

Chase could hear the mumbling of another voice, but couldn't make out what was said.

Vixen let out an exasperated breath. "Of course, I'm pissed, Ace. You said sending multiple people for the approach was a mistake. That sounded like bull at the time, but now I know you're full of shit." More mumbling. "He's not cut out for—"

The mumbling cut her off.

She groaned. "You're missing my point. If I'm forced to do this, he'll never make it to testing."

More mumbling.

"Don't question my loyalty," she said, her agitation growing by the second.

Mumbling.

Vixen exhaled slowly. "Would striking you constitute as an offense? Because I'll gladly fly home and plant my foot up your ass."

Chase stepped out to see her.

She was facing away from him, her hair pulled up tight between her fingers. She twisted her hair into a bun and let go. Long curls flooded over her shoulders. "Whatever. Don't tell me. Even if it *is* relevant to his training." She turned.

Chase thought about ducking out of sight, but knew it was too late. He smiled awkwardly.

She studied him. "I'm hanging up now, Ace." She ended the call. "You sure you've never killed anyone?"

"I think I'd remember that."

"You're not a spy, a secret agent, or a sleeper?"

"Could you have snuck up on me if I were?"

"Why, then, are you so damned important?"

I. Don't. Know! "Please clue me in when you figure it out. Because I'm as confused as you are and twice as anxious about all of this." He placed a hand on the banister. "I'm a regular guy. There are only two remotely interesting things about me: I almost went to the Olympics for artistic gymnastics. And, by some miracle, I survived a car bombing when I was six." He sat at the top of the stairs. "I take it your boss didn't like me backing out?"

"He didn't accept it."

"I don't follow."

She took a deep breath and pursed her lips to one side. "Turns out you can't refuse because you were approached by too many of us." Her eyes dropped to look at her phone as though ashamed. "If you went to the police, you'd have three faces to describe in detail." Another hair fell askew. This time, she didn't tuck it back into place. "Part of my job is to be the only face. Hiding one of us is easier than hiding three."

"Then why were there three?" Chase asked, heat pulsing up from his neck.

"I don't know," admitted Vixen.

Chase sighed heavily. "So, I'm fucked if I don't agree to this, is what you're saying."

"I'm afraid so."

He ran a palm from his eyes to his chin and glared at her. "Do I need to sign something?"

Her expression shifted skeptical. "Are you agreeing?"

"I clearly don't have a choice," Chase said. "May I add a condition or two?"

"Listening."

"Let me finish mourning my uncle's death." He lifted four fingers. "Four days." He thought about it and added a thumb. "Five."

"That enough time?"

"To pack, flee the country, and hide?" He pretended to mull it over. "Yeah, then another sixty years to live my life. Seventy, if I remain in good health."

She shook her head. "You're dead if you run."

"I'm dead if I don't." Chase shrugged.

"Wherever you go, we'll find you, be it Mexico, China, or the Arctic."

"Plenty of places left."

"And we'll follow." Vixen inched forward.

Chase looked at the ceiling, running his fingers through his hair. "This is so messed up."

"I agree."

He dropped his gaze. "Then let me go."

"I can't do that," she said with a hint of pity.

"Then you'll have to stop me from leaving." He stood.

"You won't get far." Vixen's fingers gripped the banister and her toe pressed against the bottom step. "With me here, the furthest you'll get is the mailbox."

"If I get to the street, do I win something?"

A smile returned to her lips. "There's that disarming charm."

"Clearly not disarming enough." He nodded at her whitened knuckles. "You're preparing to pounce."

"I can't say why things played out this way, but I'm here to help you live through whatever comes. Right now, protecting you means convincing you to stay. Whether you believe in yourself or not, I can train you to survive." Vixen wrinkled her nose before pleading. "Please don't force me to be your final test."

She clearly didn't want to kill him. He knew, however, if he ran, she wouldn't hesitate. *I move on with her or die by her hand.* "All right."

"What's the remark this time?" she said, doubtful. "I give you time to board a shuttle for space?"

"You're my only option." The front door demanded he make a break for it. Yet, his feet remained planted and his eyes stayed with her. "Until yesterday, I didn't question who I was. Then I went and accepted your invitation into a guild of assassins." The window of his room whispered in his mind, *jump and flee.* Instead, he nodded. "Now all I have are questions."

She sighed heavily but smiled. "Then let's find some answers along the way."

"Along the way of what, exactly?" he chuckled nervously. "Testing me?"

"Training you for the tests to come." She started up the stairs. "Let's begin with rule one: Trust people to your detriment. A lesson showing its truth today." She threw the phone over the banister. It skittered along the ground, stopping under his couch.

Something was clearly wrong with that logic. "Then I can't trust you."

She patted him on the cheek. "No, you shouldn't trust me. But you won't survive without training." She walked past him. "Second rule: Never drop your guard."

"I'm raising my guard."

Her right foot came back, mule-kicking him hard in the stomach.

He fell a few steps, stumbled, and rolled to the base of the stairs. He moaned in pain and confusion. He felt the side of his head for blood. His fingers came away clean. "And that was for ...?"

"Letting down your guard." The corner of her lip rose. "Don't be careless when your opponent has the upper ground."

He picked himself up. "You're making me hate my stairs."

"Yet, you're still on them." She grasped the banister and jumped. Her body twirled.

This time, he expected an offensive and sprang into a backflip the moment her feet left the step.

Vixen dropped a few steps up. "The Olympics for artistic gymnastics ..." she said, tasting the words on her tongue. Her eyes surveyed him from head to toe as though appraising him for the first time. "This'll be fun." She descended the steps, pulling her hair into a ponytail. She secured it with a hair tie and turned so her side faced his front. "Let's see how you fare on even ground." She brought her hands up to peer between them.

He mirrored her stance. "I've never fought someone like you."

"I can tell." She lunged, grabbing both his wrists. Before he could pull away, she twisted them painfully. Her foot met his chest and she pulled him close.

He jerked backward.

Her foot pushed and she let go.

His body slammed into the wall. He put a foot against it and slumped. *My turn.*

She swung an open palm at his face.

He ducked under it and kicked off the wall. His arms wrapped around her midsection, scooping her over his shoulder. She was surprisingly light, allowing him to charge easily toward the opposite wall.

Her spatial awareness was finely honed for her feet came up at precisely the right moment. Her knees buckled slightly when her toes met the wall before she sprang.

They were thrown in reverse. He let go of her, bent backward, and put his palms to the floorboards. Her shoulders thumped to the floor and he rose into a handstand. As his face passed over hers, he winked at her expression of surprise and dropped his legs to stand.

"Clever." She rolled onto her stomach and got up. "Don't expect me to fall for it again."

"Don't repeat what works?"

"Clever makes an impact. If your opponent is surprised by something, they'll look for a way around it." She popped her back, then stretched.

Chase decided to be the first to strike. He punched with his left fist while swinging hard with the right.

She dodged the left and caught the right by the wrist. She dropped, slid around behind him, and wrenched his arm upward.

His nerves screamed for release. He threw himself back to flatten her chest against him. Air flooded out of her lungs and warmed the back of his neck. He shot forward and down, put his left hand to the floor, then pushed off with his feet. His body went upside down.

Her legs wrapped around him and she clung on. Her added weight forced them to fall.

They landed, his body forcing the remaining air from her lungs. Pain blurred his vision. His arm threatened to pop out of socket. *I need to retreat.* He untangled his legs from hers and rolled away. His palm pushed off the floor, his feet planted, and he shot up.

Vixen choked in a breath and slapped the floor with both hands. Her hair tie must have snapped because curls haloed her head. She remained down for longer than usual.

"I think you broke my rib," she said.

His shoulder was sore. "Finding it hard to feel sorry for you," he said, moving his arm out in a circle, testing the damage done. There was full rotation and the pain was regressing. *I'm fine.*

She still laid there attempting to draw a full breath.

I might not totally suck. He reached out a hand. "Need help?"

She slapped his hand away, rising on her own. She reached toward the ceiling. "No broken ribs." Her arms dropped. "You're less fun than I'd imagined." She resumed a fighting stance. "But you're a quick study."

"Yeah?"

She lunged.

"Shit!" He threw out his arms to grab her.

She dropped into a roll, rose on her hands, and shot a foot back to connect with his knee.

He crumpled, redirecting into a roll of his own. They both popped up as one, her open palm already on a collision course.

He bounced back, barely avoiding it. *She's way faster than me.*

As if to prove the point, she took a quick step and struck him in the nose.

Pain radiated into his cheeks. Tears obscured his vision.

She rocked on her heels. "It's fun again."

He wiped his nose with a finger. "Sure." It came away red. He tilted his head back and squeezed the bridge. "How am I supposed to pass these tests?" His voice was nasally. "I can barely survive you."

She approached.

He swung.

She avoided the hit and threw her hands behind her head. "Whoa, killer. I'm simply checking on you."

"Check from there." Blood tickled his upper lip.

"Don't be a child." Vixen walked up, placing a hand to his face.

"Beware. I'll blow a bloody snot bubble if you try anything."

"What a lovely image." She gently massaged his chin, cheek, and nose.

It hurt but he dared not recoil. "Your assessment?"

"You have a lot to learn, but—"

"About my face."

"Handsome with plenty of character."

"Not for much longer if we continue this."

She smiled. "You'll have some bruises, but nothing's broken ... yet."

"Yet? Are you trying to break me?"

"No." She drew her hands away. "Your opponents will." She went to the window and brushed the curtain aside. "One could be here now."

He tensed. "You've beaten me to a pulp knowing an assassin could be walking up my porch?"

"You're hardly a pulp." She locked hands against wrists

behind her back and faced him. "You probably won't see one today. You may not see one for months. But they will come, so take this opportunity to prepare." She brought her hands around, curling her fingers as though intent on clawing out his eyes. "Hit me."

"You don't think I've been trying to? Every punch gets turned against me."

"Your mind won't allow it. *Mommy* and *daddy* told you no hitting girls."

"They died long before that advice. My uncle said not to hit anyone until they've struck twice."

"I've done that and more."

He stepped forward, fists rising. "This is true."

"Then *hit* me."

He punched.

She sidestepped, struck him in the cheek with her palm, and passed by.

He took a blow to the back of his head, sparks dancing across his vision. He twirled, threw his head back to avoid one hit, sidestepped another, and ducked under the third. *I'm getting the hang of this.*

That self-assurance disintegrated when her next volley connected with his ear, nose, and throat.

He choked, stumbling backward, a hand protectively gripping his Adam's apple. *Dammit!* Ringing erupted in his ears. He'd been in fights before, but nothing compared to this. *Then again, I've never fought a woman.*

She took advantage of his wavering concentration, striking him hard along the side of his chin.

He felt his vision blur in one direction while his body

swayed in the other. He took a knee.

She sported a grin. "You good?"

Chase lifted. "Give me a minu—"

She grabbed his shoulders and brought up her knee.

The room drowned in darkness.

CHASE awoke, his forehead burning. He rolled over and stroked his head, realizing it had taken the brunt of his fall. The final ghostly shadows occupying his peripheral receded.

Vixen knelt beside him. "You can't pass out during testing." She slapped his forehead. "Sure way to die." She stood, offering her hand. "Try again."

He took the hand. When she went to lift him, he locked onto her grip, twirled around on the floor, and planted his feet against her stomach.

She tried to wrench free but was already doubling over.

He pushed off the floor with his shoulders, let go of her hand, and his legs launched her into the air.

Vixen came within an inch of the ceiling then dropped, arms flailing.

Chase rolled out of the way and cringed when her body made a sickening thud. He braced, expecting a reactive assault.

None followed.

He glanced over his shoulder to see her lying face down, calm and quiet. "Faker." A minute passed before concern grabbed his guts and twisted. "Vixen?"

She didn't move.

He pursed his lips. *This could be my chance to leave. Or I could finish her off.* He looked to the kitchen knives. *I'm not a killer.* His eyes returned to see her body rise and fall with each breath. *Isn't that why she's here, though? To mold me into one?*

She moaned.

He thought of the knives. *Psychopath me needs to chill.* Cautiously, he approached her on all fours, as though nearing a wounded wolverine. "Vixen?" He shook her.

Her eyelids wrinkled and snapped opened.

Hairs rose along his arms and neck. "I don't expect you're the forgiving type."

"Get off me."

"Not on you."

Her eyes narrowed into slits.

"Sorry." He withdrew a few feet and rose on one knee.

Air hissed through her teeth when she sat up. She examined her right elbow. It was red and swollen.

He repeated what she'd said earlier: "You'll have some bruises, but nothing's broken ... *yet.*" When she failed to reply, he added, "I hope."

"Because you're concerned for my wellbeing or because you fear what I'll do to you if something is?"

"Can't it be both?"

She stood slowly.

He got up as well, staring at her body. He realized she was aware and shot his eyes up to meet hers. "Sooo," he said. "How severe will my punishment be?"

"I'm actually good for the day." She rubbed a red spot spreading across her forehead. "You?"

Thank heaven. "Definitely." He went to the fridge for a water. He heard footsteps quicken, turning too late to counter the kick to his cheek. He stumbled, choking.

She closed the distance, kicking again.

He grabbed her ankle.

Vixen went airborne, her other foot flashing over the first to pop him in the ear.

The ringing returned.

He dropped her ankle and retreated further into the kitchen.

This time when she neared, Chase rushed forward to wrap his arms around her midsection. He squeezed and twirled her around, pops erupting along her spine. He released on the third spin.

Her foot met the floor but her body continued spiraling. She tripped, fell, and sprawled awkwardly. "That's what I'm talking about."

He could barely hear her over the singing bells in his head. He stretched his jaw to pop his ears.

She got up. "Saved me a trip to the chiropractor."

He brought up his fists, shaking his head.

She sighed. "Stop it with the fists. Fingers are brittle bastards. Only ball your hands for body shots to the stomach, kidneys, or liver. If you keep swinging at my face, I'll drop my forehead to break your fingers." She brought her hands back up. "Swing slowly and I'll walk you through it."

He eyed her cautiously. *She sounds sincere, but—* He swung fast and hard.

She dodged, grabbed his wrist, and pulled him forward, extending a foot to trip him.

Again, he found himself on the floor.

She kicked his leg. "If I say we're taking something slow, take it slow. Don't, and I'll put you down."

He got up. "You said I can't trust you."

"Give it a break, Hunter. You don't need trust to learn."
She brought her hands up. "Slowly punch me in the face. When I
drop my forehead, push against it."

Chase considered charging, but followed her instruction
instead.

She pushed her forehead against his knuckles. "Feel that
pressure on your fingers and along the back of your hand?"

"Yeah."

"That's where you'll break. You'd fall to twenty-percent
efficiency for several minutes as excruciating pain paralyzes
you, then only return to fifty percent when you finally get your
shit together."

He shook his head. "I've been in a few fights and haven't
sprained a wrist."

"You fought untrained morons, not professionals who can
take a hit while returning damage." Vixen ran a finger over the
muscles in her palm. "I've felt your hands. Years spent as a
gymnast have left them hard and strong. That's a gift." She
resumed her fighting stance. "But they'll still break under the
right pressure."

He brought his hands up, mimicking her.

She struck fast.

He batted her hand to the side. *What happened to going slow?*

She stepped, struck.

He caught her palm and pulled her close.

She used the momentum to knee him in the abdomen,
twirl around, and elbow him in the chin.

A flurry of stars glittered on a canvas of night. He shook
his head. A dot of light split the darkness, spreading to shred the
black.

She was stretching from side to side.

His eyes trailed up her leg. *When did I fall?*

She rolled her shoulders. "I'd help you up, but you lost that privilege." She shifted her weight to the leg closest to him.

He spun and pushed off the floor. When his face came around, he glimpsed her palm as it caught him in the forehead.

Her other hand grabbed the back of his neck and pulled.

He flexed every muscle in his body to keep from being woman-handled. However, this only turned him into a statue for her to anchor onto.

Her knee made a critical impact inside the ribcage arch on his right.

A sharp pain radiated outward. He felt instantly exhausted, unable to draw breath. He gasped several times in panic before choking down some air. He realized he was on the floor. His arm wrapped around his leg, pulling his knee to his chest. "What was that?"

Vixen stepped in front of him. "Direct hit to the liver. If you hadn't flexed, it would be far worse." She shrugged. "Then again, if you hadn't become a pillar, I wouldn't have hit you so hard."

A tear streaked across his cheek. "You're saying this could be worse?"

She laughed. "Much." She walked to the fridge. "Water?"

"God, yes!"

She threw him a bottle and got one for herself.

Drinking hurt. He poured some water on his face. "Why am I tired? Why was I hugging my leg?"

"Most people drop like that. It relieves pressure. Like when you go fetal if you're kicked in the balls." She downed the water. "A liver shot saps everything away. You want to fight on; your body refuses. Learn to block it." She dropped the bottle in the bin. "To pull off a good liver shot, you must learn how the liver moves. Imagine the rook on a chess board. It can go forward, backward, up, down, left, and right. It cannot go diagonally. Hit hard at an upward angle and imagine the rook flying out your opponent's shoulder." She tapped under her ribs on both sides. "The kidneys are here. Any hit to them is nearly as bad."

He took another drink, this one easier than the last. "Up 'til now, I've learned more about taking a hit than throwing one."

"I'd argue that's more important for what's coming. Now, relax the mind and the body will follow." She gestured for him to rise.

He grudgingly stood to face her.

Vixen slapped his water bottle out of his grip and took his hands. She lifted them in front of his face, parting them slightly.

He winced, anticipating a hit.

She wrinkled her nose. "I'm sorry. I've been ... aggressive."

He forced a laugh. "The word you're looking for is 'vicious.'"

She raked her teeth across her bottom lip. "Perhaps, but this is a baptism by fire. You have a lot to learn." She parted his hands further. "You need to be able to see around your hands. Avoid focusing too much on the person you're fighting. You have to be able to see your surroundings as fully as possible. That's extremely important if your opponent is joined by another."

Another? "I'll have to fight two of you at once?"

"No. Never," she promised. "It's simply good advice." She let go of his hands. "Imagine your surroundings as both enemy and friend. Use it to throw off your opponent, while knowing they're doing the same to trip you up, box you in, and crush you when you're careless." She slapped at his face.

He backed away.

"Listen to me," she said, "and you might survive." She struck again.

He dodged successfully, retreating a few more steps.

"I said 'listen.'" She swung a third time.

He batted it away. "I am." This time, when he stepped back, his spine aligned with the corner of the wall.

Vixen slapped his cheek. "No." She stabbed a finger into his chest. "You're not." She stepped back. "If you were, you wouldn't be pinned to the wall."

Blood boiled up his neck, flooding his cheeks. *I want to feel insulted, but she's right. I let her block me in.* "Sorry."

"Don't apologize." She gestured for him to pass. "Just adjust your mindset."

He walked out and turned to face her, hands up.

She shook her head. "Listen for a bit."

He dropped his arms.

"If I were your first test, you'd be dead. You make the same mistakes over and over."

"I'm not like you. The only reason I'm continuing is because I have no other option. I run, I'm dead. I join, I'm dead." He threw his hands up. "What's the point?"

"So, what, then? Give up?" She rushed him.

He dodged to the right, to the left, and faltered back.

She pressed forward.

He rolled to the side.

It continued like this for several minutes. He'd strike, she'd parry. She'd kick, he'd block. He'd push, she'd pull.

Then it all went wrong.

She batted down a hit of his, came in close, and grabbed his shoulders.

He flexed every muscle, waiting for her to strike his liver.

Instead, Vixen wrapped her left leg around the outside of his, straightened, and pushed. The back of his knee crumpled against the back of hers. They fell with her on top.

Did not see that coming. "That was clever."

"Find a way around it." She struck him in the throat.

He choked, unable to breathe. He attempted to roll away.

Vixen tightened her legs, holding him still, her hands free to strike his chest, throat, and chin.

He conjured an image of a tiger clawing open its prey. *I can't take much more of this.* He grabbed the front of her jacket, yanking her one way while he rolled the other. He coughed until breath came easily. "You could have collapsed my throat." He grabbed the countertop to help him up.

She stood. "I connected with the side of your throat, not the center. I'm not trying to kill you." She looked at the zipper on her jacket. It must have broken when he threw her off him. She grabbed where it had separated, pulling to unzip it in both directions.

She was wearing a silky top. A purple, sleeveless, V-neck blouse. The way it molded to her form, it might as well have been part of her. She put the jacket on the arm of the couch.

His eyes trailed over the rise and fall of her all-too-perfect breasts. His chest warmed and his stomach somersaulted. He forced his eyes to the ceiling, the table, the curtains.

She stepped into his line of sight.

His eyes returned to her chest. *Come on.* He forced them up. "Can you put the jacket back on?"

"You broke it." She followed his eyes on their next wayward glance. "They're just breasts."

"Yep, that's all they are. Perfectly shaped, firm breasts." He took a deep breath, dropping his gaze to the floor.

"Firm?" She laughed. "You're ridiculous."

"I'd know," said Chase. "We've been grappling."

It was her turn to look around sheepishly. "I can't believe you find me that distracting."

"Right. You're completely unaware of how gorgeous you are." He stared into those beautiful eyes glazed in honey. "No offense, but you are the most distracting woman I've ever met."

"Why would I take offense?" She began toward him, her hips mesmerizing in their sway. "You're not so bad yourself."

He retreated a step but let her approach. "I'm not remotely in your league."

"What league?" She ran a finger across his cheek. "You have eyes stolen from a wolf and an Olympian's torso." She squeezed his arm. "You could tear me apart, yet refrain." She closed her eyes, inhaling deep through her nostrils. "And you smell of cinnamon." Her eyes drifted open. "You don't think I'm distracted, too?"

He wasn't sure how to respond, so he didn't.

She patted his chest. "If you're going to be one of us, you have to fight your urges. Distraction should be a weapon in your arsenal, not that of your opponent's. To feign distraction causes your adversary to approach when they should flee."

"Makes sense."

She nodded. "I'll kiss you now for flattering me. Then we'll get back to work and forget it ever happened."

This is a trap. Yet, he dared not pass up another kiss.

Vixen's mouth pressed to his.

He licked her upper lip. To his surprise, she let him in. Their tongues did some sparring of their own, one tangling over the other. His arms encircled her, fingers pressing into the small of her back.

She broke the kiss. "Oookidokey." She looked bewildered. "I should not—" She swallowed and cleared her throat. "Um." Her eyes focused on his lips. "Yep."

"I'm sorry if I—"

Her lips captured his words, her body shifting to fill the void between them.

A furnace blazed in his chest, the heat warming his neck to the base of his skull. It was spreading, molten droplets racing down his spine.

Their lips parted and she hummed contentedly.

He kissed the tip of her nose. "What was that about fighting urges?"

"Hell." She laughed. "I don't remember." Her lips collapsed against his again.

His arms locked and lifted her.

She jumped, wrapping her legs around his waist.

They were interrupted by a song playing beneath his couch.

Vixen broke the kiss and pressed her forehead to his. "Probably good this was interrupted." She dropped her feet to the floor, stepped out of his embrace, and retrieved the phone.

"Still training, Ace." She sat on the backs of her heels. "No, we have a long way to go. I'll be here a few more—"

"That's enough training," the voice said, loud enough for Chase to hear.

"I'll come back tomor—"

"No."

"He won't survive if—"

"Question me again." The voice was angry.

Vixen's face grew red. "Let me finish a sentence." The voice remained silent. "He's not like the others." She stood. "He's never killed anyone."

"Know your place."

She took the phone away from her ear and glared at it. "He did not just hang up." Her head shook slightly. "Apparently, we're done."

"It's all right."

"No, it's not."

Chase nodded to the laptop on his coffee table. "I'll train on my own."

"Research how to take a hit." She pointed at the kitchen knives. "Then look up how to avoid being cut open."

"I'll walk you out while you give hints."

"Use your strength," Vixen said, opening the door. "The first test hits like a truck. Prepare for a beating."

"And to avoid getting cut open?"

"Run like a madman until you find an opening to strike. Only strike when you're absolutely certain it won't cost you blood. You'll still lose more than you care to."

"Run from knives." He chuckled. "Got it."

"No, you really don't." Vixen stormed off the porch and around the side of the house until she came to the lean-to woodshed built into its side. She retrieved tennis shoes that were cradled by the firewood.

The top of the lean-to stopped directly under his window.

"That's how you got in."

"How'd you think?"

He shrugged. "Wings?"

She grinned, shaking her head before starting toward the street. "Don't stop to think when you get hit. It only prolongs pain."

When they neared a Ford Mustang, she reached inside the toe of her shoe and pulled out a key. "Remember when I hit your jaw?"

"Why would I remember something so jarring and emasculating?"

She smirked. "It connects with the skull, next to a whole lot of important shit. Jacks with the nerves, *jarring* the opponent. Hit hard enough, they'll take a nap." She unlocked the door. "Your muscles will save your life by absorbing damage. It's as if you were sculpted for this. Use it."

"Thanks for training me."

She patted his chest. "After today, you should no longer fear being struck. That's huge." She got in, started the car, and rolled down the window. "Research your ass off: How to breathe during a fight, when to flex, and how to target openings in your opponent's defense."

"Anything else?"

"Try not to let this keep you up tonight. Head to bed early. You'll need to be wide awake if your first opponent arrives tomorrow. But sleep with one eye open. They won't wait for the sun." She gripped the steering wheel. "You've got this."

He nodded. "Sleep, but don't sleep." He stepped back. "I've got this."

"You just might," she said, smiling as the window rose

and she drove away.

His eyes searched the street for an attacker. When none approached, he ran ten fingers through his hair to grip the back of his head and sighed heavily. "I've got this."

Chapter Five

If I Were Here for You

IN time, the guilds combined their efforts and lost their anonymity, becoming known as The Guild of Four.

May 10, 2016
7:05 PM CDT
Houston, Texas

~ Seven of Spades ~

KARA left work, her laptop bag strung over a shoulder and her hands full of case documents. The day had gone from bad to worse. The judge ruled against her at every turn. On top of that, she'd have to work from home late into the night.

I should have listened to Paul. Her husband said that morning not to go in. He'd felt something bad was about to happen. *He was right. This was the worst day I've had in years.* But, with a case like this, she didn't have the luxury of time off.

It was sweet of him to worry. Peculiar, really. Her line of work invited enemies, but this was the first time he'd ever voiced concern.

The oddest sensation tickled at the hairs of her neck when she reached her car. The kind you get when someone's watching you. After placing the files atop the car and turning slowly, she looked into the shadows. *Those lights weren't out this morning.* As her eyes adjusted, part of the dark solidified into a man, leaning against the wall.

She squinted, cocking her head to the side. "Waiting for someone?"

"You could—say that." He started toward her.

He probably wants me to drop the case. She didn't have time for this today. There was always some family member or friend of the accused trying to convince her of something. They'd say: "He's a good person. He'd never pull a gun on an officer," or "She wasn't that drunk. The victim jumped in front of her car." or her absolute favorite, "You actually think someone so smart would do something so unbelievably stupid?"

The answers to all of the above were: "We have video evidence of him doing just that"; "Her blood alcohol was two times the legal limit while driving fifteen over"; and "Intelligent people break the law because they think they're too smart to get caught."

A pasty-skinned man in his late thirties stepped from the shadows. His hair was spiked green with blue tips. He wore no shirt, just a pair of coveralls with a seemingly uncountable number of pockets. Each pocket was of a different size and color. Despite the crazy hair and outfit, he wasn't ugly. In fact, his face was attractive with striking features, while his chest and arms were toned.

Why would such a man paint himself into a clown?

He smiled.

Something inside warned her to leave. *Go now!* She jumped into the car and brought the seatbelt across her chest. Before she could buckle up, she remembered—*the files.*

She looked out and saw him lean against a car close by. His eyes were dark and cold. She'd seen eyes like those before. They belonged to someone accustomed to ending lives.

He glanced at the top of her car. "Would you like me—to gather them for you—Attorney Wetherton?"

"No." She forced down the urge to drive away without the files.

"It's really—no trouble," he said. "No trouble—at all."

Why does he talk like that? "Don't bother yourself." She stepped out, keeping an eye on him while pulling the files off the car. The bottom folder slipped and paper spilled across concrete.

She ran sweaty palms against her pants before stooping to pick them up.

The man knelt beside her.

He ran a finger along a blue folder. "Color-coordinated?"

"Yeah." She met his eyes, not sure what to make of him.

"Color-coordinated—my case files, too." He placed the paperwork into piles before grabbing her blue folder. "Evidence or witnesses?"

"Evidence." Her eyes trailed over his coveralls. *Can't judge a book, I suppose.* "You were a lawyer?"

"For a time." He placed the appropriate files in the blue folder.

He's not very old. "You couldn't have been a lawyer long."

He shook his head. "No—not long. It's a rather—boring story, really."

Something told her it wasn't boring at all.

When he leaned forward to grab another file, something gleamed in his pocket.

She adjusted to get a better look. *Knives?* She scooted away. "I have mace and a gun."

His dark eyes locked on her. "Thanks—for sharing."

She stood. "I don't want to hurt you."

"Your gun—is in your car." He pointed and rose with her files in hand. "As for pepper spray." He tilted his head slightly, licking his bottom lip. "I use it—to spice spaghetti." A slender knife in a smaller pocket shifted.

She backed up until she felt the frame of her car door. Dropping into the seat, she grabbed her keys from the ignition. Her small bottle of mace hung from one of the rings.

"I'd say don't." He placed a hand on the open door. "But you'll do—what you do."

She hated that he wasn't bothered by her threat. *Why didn't I listen to my husband?*

One of his hands entered a pocket.

She pointed the mace at him. "I need your hands where I can see them."

His hand remained where it was.

She reached into her glovebox and found the gun. "I will shoot you." She brought the gun up beside the mace, both aimed at his face.

His knuckles moved within the pocket. "Guns aren't as powerful—as you'd think."

"Guns are objectively powerful." Her finger slid over the trigger. "Hundreds of people are shot every day by them." She nodded at his hand. "Do knives make you powerful?"

Cold, unwavering eyes absorbed her gaze.

Her hands began shaking.

He tilted his head. "Relax."

"Step back and I might."

He leaned forward. "My name's—Pockets."

"I would have guessed Knives."

"Long story." The hand began lifting from the pocket.

"Lower—the gun."

Her eyes closed, head turned, and mace pushed forward.

Pockets jumped back, slamming the car door.

Mace spewed forth, splashing against the window. Kara's eyes lit on fire and her lungs filled with bees. Gasping, she threw the mace. She'd never used pepper spray before. She had never felt its clutch around her throat, its thumbs digging into her eyes. Every breath brought choking, every exhalation coughing. *I have to get out!* She pushed over the middle console, into the passenger seat, and found the door handle. Her body spilled out, collapsing onto concrete. She breathed deep, choking on what spray still clung to her throat.

"Are you quite—all right?" she heard Pockets say.

As if he actually cares. Through teary vision, she saw him walk around the car holding her folders, the files back inside. She wiped her eyes with the sleeve of her shirt.

"I guessed—the colors," he said. "There weren't many—left to collect." He placed the folders at his feet before backing away. "Arguments and—closing statement went in white. Yellow—got miscellaneous notes. What was left—went in red. All were marked for—"

"My eyes only," she said, blinking furiously. She aimed the gun.

Pockets tilted his head to the right. "I'm not here—for

you."

"You said that. I don't care."

He eyed the gun. "You are practiced—are you not?" This was said more as a statement than a question. "How many bullets—at center mass to drop me?"

"Five." She lowered the gun to aim at his chest.

His head swiveled to the left. "I saw a man take fifty—and yet kill those shooting him." The way his head swayed back to the right conjured up the image of a serpent. "He died, as well—eventually. But the tale remains—relevant."

She aimed at his head.

Appearing not at all worried, he said, "Headshots aren't—easy."

"From this close, I like my chances." Her hand grew tired from the gun's weight. "I will kill you."

"Are you so sure—of your abilities?" He weaved his head back and forth and smiled widely, completing the portrait of the snake. "Splitting my skull—" Head swiveling left. "—with a bullet—" Swiveling right. "—would prove—" Left. "—quite effective." Right.

A chime alerted them to the elevator car approaching their floor.

"This was—fun." Pockets winked and walked away. "Another time—perhaps."

She rose to watch him return to the shadows. As perplexed as she was by his retreat, she decided to put distance between them. She tucked the gun in the back of her skirt and picked up the folders. Rounding the car, she found the ground empty. *He really did gather all the files.* She glanced at his dark outline. *What a peculiar man.* She opened the door to the back of her car and put the folders on the seat. The car smelled of pepper spray. *Maybe I should give it some time to air out.* She glanced to the shadows. *He seems content sitting in the dark.*

The bell to the elevator chimed twice to signal its arrival.

Kara opened the driver's side door and stepped away. The fumes were worse there. *That's decided.* She turned, leaned against the car, and faced the elevator. Michael, one of her assistant attorneys, stepped out, his eyes peering into a laptop bag.

He pulled out a red folder and opened it. The Bluetooth in his ear blinked green. "I got it here. She left later than expected, but I—" His eyes rose, locking on hers. The red folder dropped into the bag. "Call ya back." The Bluetooth blinked. "Hey, Kara."

"Michael?"

He squinted at her. "Have you been crying?"

Pockets stepped out of the shadows. "I spied—with my little eyes—a red folder."

Michael looked at him. "Who the fuck?"

She began toward Michael. "I only left one red folder behind, containing the locations of lead witnesses. It was locked in my office safe." She stopped a few feet from him. "Explain."

"You gave me the combination," he reminded her. "It was a while ago, but—"

Pockets laughed. "That's not—an answer." He pulled out a long, slender knife and began twirling it around his fingers.

"Is that a knife?" Michael looked from Pockets to Kara. "Who is this?"

She reached for the bag. "Why do you have it?"

Michael jerked away. "You think I'd put their lives at risk?"

"I didn't." She became suddenly aware of the gun tucked in the back of her skirt. She retrieved it.

"Kara." He threw his hands up. "Are you *fucking* insane?"

"I'm taking the folder."

He backed away. "Jesus, I'll return it."

"No."

"You're being ridiculous. There was something off about their testimony. I needed their location to talk about—"

"It's true—what they say," Pockets interrupted. "Some lawyers are serpents—in suits."

"Stay out of this," she said. "Their testimony is solid, Michael. You said so yourself." She failed to piece together why he'd betray her. It made no sense. He was one of her brightest ... *Intelligent people break the law because they think they're too smart to get caught.* "Who's paying you?"

Michael began crying. "I'm in deep, Kara. You have to help me." His hands fell, one dropping into the laptop bag. "I'll do anything."

"Fine." She reached out a hand. "First, give me the folder."

"I will." Michael's hand rose from the bag.

Pockets snapped his fingers and threw the knife.

Michael yelped in pain, his hand slapping his bicep. Between his fingers appeared a crimson flow. His eyes filled with rage and the bag fell to concrete. The hand that had been inside held a gun.

Kara pulled her trigger. It caught. "What?" *The safety ...*

Michael took the gun in his other hand.

"Whoa," Pockets yelled, stepping closer. "It's getting—tense."

"Screw you," Michael said, pointing the gun at Kara.

"Grab another knife and I take off her head."

She backed away quickly, hands and fingers shaking wildly. Her gun fell and clattered at her feet.

Michael took three quick steps and put his gun to her forehead. "You were going to shoot me?"

"Don't." She put her hands behind her head. "Please."

"Point it—at me," Pockets said. "As of now, I'm—your only threat." He had a blade dangling from his fingertips.

Michael turned, pointing his gun at Pockets. "I told you if you grabbed another knife, I'd take off her head. Drop it!"

Pockets smirked. "Take the folder and go—before you do something altogether—stupid."

"I said, drop it!"

"If that's—what you want." Pockets cocked a foot back and dropped the knife. As the hilt neared the ground, his foot snapped forward.

Warmth sprayed Kara's face. She blinked, wiping a hand across her eyes, fingers coming away red. *Blood?*

Protruding from the back of Michael's neck was an inch of sharp metal. He wavered for a second, his gun dropping to concrete. His body deflated and crumpled. Blood gushed from his throat, choking him. Drowning him. His eyes glanced at her, face twisting in perplexed anger.

She knelt, picked up his gun, and placed a hand on his shoulder. "You're going to be fine."

His eyes narrowed.

Pockets walked up. "No, Kara—he won't be." He reached for his knife.

Her hands balled into fists. "Don't you touch him." Her fingernails dug into her palms. She picked up Michael's gun and pointed it at Pockets, making certain the safety was disengaged.

"I'll need—her back."

"Her?"

He pointed at the knife buried in her dying colleague's throat and said, "Trisha."

A gurgling came from Michael's throat, his body trembling.

"No," Kara said, nodding the gun up and down to remind the murderer it was there.

Pockets weaved his head to the left. "It's not nice—to leave an animal suffering." With blinding speed, he shot forward.

Kara jolted in surprise. Her gun hand twisted backward, then forward, and she was disarmed.

Pockets deftly disassembled the gun, tossing parts in opposite directions. "Thank you." He knelt and twisted "Trisha" before pulling "her" free.

Michael's throat opened wide and in a matter of seconds he went still.

Kara shook uncontrollably. "What did you do?"

"Come along, Andrea," Pockets said, retrieving the other knife from Michael's arm. "It's time—for us to go."

"What ... did you ... do?" Kara repeated in a way Pockets would understand.

Pockets shrugged, dropping "Trisha" back into his coveralls. With "Andrea" in hand, he stood.

I'm next. "Please, don't kill me."

With the blade Pockets began digging under his fingernails, cleaning out what appeared to be old blood and replacing it with new. "If I were here for you—"

"I'd be dead," she realized.

He nodded slowly, weaving his head to the right and dropping "Andrea" alongside her sister blade.

Kara stood taller and said, "If you're not going to kill me, then I'm making a citizen's arrest."

Pockets smirked. "You'd sound more confident—with that in hand." He pointed at the gun she'd dropped earlier.

Although bewildered by him suggesting she retrieve her gun, she did just that and pointed it at him. "Get on your knees and put your hands on the back of your head."

His body shook as though chuckling, but no sound escaped.

"On ... your ... knees," she demanded. "We'll wait for the police to sort all this out."

"No, Kara—we'll not."

"I can't let you go."

"You can." He turned his back on her. "And you will."

She gritted her teeth and rubbed her finger along the trigger. As much as she wanted to stop him, she couldn't bring herself to pull.

Pockets reached the stairs and started down, a hand rising to wave with a knife between two fingers.

Kara pulled out her phone. She dialed 911 and placed it to her ear. *How am I going to explain this?*

"911, what's your emergency?" came a woman's voice.

Kara feared to answer.

"Hello?" the voice tried again. "If you're hurt and cannot respond verbally, please push any number on your phone."

Kara took a deep breath. "There's been a murder. I tried to apprehend the killer, but he escaped on foot."

"Please state your name and location."

"Kara Wetherton. 1201 Franklin, Houston, Texas."

"Can you describe the assailant, and in which direction he fled?"

Kara stared at Michael's body. *That could have been me if Pockets hadn't intervened.*

She decided to lie, but knew there were cameras on the exits. *Most people that come and go are dressed nicely.* "I only saw him from behind," she said. "He was tall and wore a black suit." *I'll have to explain why my eyes are bloodshot.* "He caught me off guard with mace."

"The direction in which he fled?"

"The East stairs. I can't say after that."

"You're certain the victim is dead?"

She stared at the motionless body. Saw eyes which held no light. "The victim's name is Michael Johnson. He bled out a few minutes ago." Kara walked away. "I don't know what he was mixed up in, but he had confidential files from my office on his person."

"Are you wounded?"

"No. Shaken."

"As far as you know, is the assailant wounded?"

"I don't believe so."

"Officers are on their way. Anything else you think we should know?"

Plenty. "No." Kara leaned against her car trunk. "I don't believe so."

"Sounds like you've had a rough day," the operator said. "But I need you to remain where you are. They'll take your statement when they arrive. Leave everything as-is."

"I'll wait." Kara forced herself to look at Michael. *I should have listened to my husband.*

Chapter Six

Pockets Full of Knives

May 11, 2016
11:29 AM CDT
Kansas City, Missouri

CHASE took Vixen's advice and went to bed three hours early the night before. However, the thought of her kiss stealing his breath in turn stole away his ability to sleep. For as badly as he wished the impending tests were what kept him awake, it was actually, wholly, the thought of her lips and body pressed to his. Throughout the night, his mind repeatedly reminded him to rest, which made rest more impossible. And when he finally did slip into sleep, he'd wake from rolling onto bruises. The number of places that hurt far outnumbered those that did not. He could not stay comfortable for more than five minutes at a time. Yet, somehow, that morning he felt refreshed and ready for the day.

Although he hated not being able to choose, the idea of fighting for his life was invigorating. It felt like a new beginning, albeit a possible ending.

At least his thoughts were no longer consumed by his uncle's murder.

Chase dropped his legs off the side of the bed and scanned the bruises on his knuckles, arms, and legs. *How am I going to fight when I'm already beaten up?* Maybe they wouldn't come today. *Might not for months, she said.* Rising from the bed, he began to stretch. Lightning forked across his chest, ricocheting off ribs to decimate his abdomen. "Ouch." He fell back, curling into a ball until the pain subsided.

Ten minutes passed before he got up and went to the bathroom. He ran water over his hands and brought it to his face. The image in the mirror made him wince. "I make a handsome blueberry." So many shades of blue, red, and purple. It occurred to him the local art department might accept models. *I'd be a challenging nude.*

Feeling a tad masochistic, he touched each bruise in turn, testing the pain they produced. Vixen said the first opponent would hit like a truck. *If I hurt this bad from practice, then I'll need protection for the actual test.* He left the bathroom and went to his uncle's room. His hand hovered over the knob, unable to commit. He hadn't been inside since the funeral. *I bet he's watching right now, disappointed.* Three minutes passed. *Or, he'd want me to survive.* Chase felt the latter more likely. He opened the door and stepped inside.

Shame remained outside, watching.

The air inside was stagnant. *I'm sorry I waited so long to visit you.* A tear rimmed his eyelid. He blinked it away and opened a window. *That's better.* He went to the closet and lifted out the box he'd placed there the morning of the funeral. Inside was his uncle's off-duty GLOCK 30, work boots, and protective vest.

After upending the box on the bed, he picked up the vest. It was heavy in his hands with large pockets hard to the touch. He placed it on, snapping the clasps, shifting the weight, and adjusting the straps until it felt right. *This'll chafe like crazy.*

A car door shut outside the house. *They're here.* He thought he was ready. *I'm a fool.* He wasn't prepared; not in the slightest.

Stop and think for a moment ...

1. Relax.

2. Breathe.

3. Pick up the damn GLOCK.

He relaxed, drew a breath, and curled his fingers around the weapon.

Someone knocked downstairs.

"I'm not letting you in to shoot me in the face." He checked the gun clip. Empty. *Where'd he keep the bullets?* Chase searched, finding a belt and holster in the second drawer. He put them on before continuing the search for ammunition.

Nothing.

Seriously? He holstered the GLOCK. *The assassin won't know it's empty.* No sooner had he left his uncle's room than the door swung shut behind him. His spine erected and he found himself standing on tiptoes, a scream caged behind pursed lips. "What in God's name?!" A breeze drifted from his room down the hall. *Someone opened my window, creating a vacuum, slamming this door... . I need to start locking that freaking window.* He approached his bedroom door, the gun held out before him.

A hand clasped his. Vixen followed. "Morning," she said, pulling the gun to point past her shoulder, twisting it from his grip, and pressing the barrel to his forehead.

He waited for his breath and heartbeat to return before

saying, "I nearly pissed myself." He pulled his head away from the GLOCK. "What if I'd shot you?"

"Don't be silly, this gun's too light to be loaded." She raised an eyebrow. "You *did* know it was empty, right?"

"Yeah, but didn't think they would."

"Smart." She handed him the gun. "You could definitely use that to your advantage. Bullets?"

Chase shook his head.

"Probably good," she said. "You suck with guns."

"I hunt quail. They're small and they fly."

"Two things. Quail don't fight back and the gun has to stay in your hands to be effective. In your case, the empty gun will confuse your opponent." She leaned against the wall. "You can only pull it off once. If used correctly, it'll save your life. Used wrong, you're dead."

"You think it'll keep him from rushing me?"

"No, but he'll waste time trying to steal it. Once he does, use his confusion to strike." Her eyes trailed over the vest. "Is that plated?" Her hands caressed it as though it were precious. "Your uncle's, I assume?"

"Yeah." Chase glanced at her hands. "Does plated mean bulletproof?"

"Resistant. The plates protect you from higher calibers, arrows, knives, and shrapnel." She looked him over. "Very effective, but it'll weigh you down."

"Slower is fine if it'll protect me from being gutted by the knife guy."

"Like a wall built around your organs." She stepped back. "Don't get cocky, of course. Every wall has its weakness. Gaps a knife can pass through. Once he realizes you have it on, he'll aim for your throat." Vixen placed a finger to her lip. "You'll need to hide its outline."

"I have a winter coat."

"Perfect."

He retrieved the coat, threw it on, and returned with arms spread. "This work?"

She nodded.

He unzipped the coat.

Her head shook. "Keep it on or you won't pull this off."

"I'll be a sweaty mess. It's seventy degrees outside."

She glanced downstairs. "Comfort or survival, Hunter?" Her eyes returned, fingers rising up her torso in a zipping gesture.

"When you put it that way." The zipper met his throat. "Better a sweaty mess than a bloody one."

She laughed.

The sound was heaven. His heart warmed. Then something occurred to him, freezing it solid. "You were told not to train me." His eyes focused on the front door. "And you keep glancing downstairs as if we're about to be joined by another."

"I hate being in the dark. I'm here for answers. I won't get them unless I'm in the field during testing."

"Testing." His back met the wall. "It's today."

"What?"

He'd seen her confused. Her current expression was a cheap imitation. "You wouldn't stop by just in case, Vixen. You can't be that bored to drive here and—"

"Fly here," she said. "I was on a jet home to New York when I got word. It's too soon for someone as unqualified as you."

I'm going to die. "New York. That's cool." He forced a smile. *These are the last breaths I'll take.* "Do you like it there?" *The last beautiful woman I'll ever lay eyes on.* "I hear it's a wonderful city."

"Hunter, stop."

"I'm not ready, Vixen." *I'm dead, I'm dead, I'm dead.* Chase bolted down the stairs, grabbed his phone and keys off the counter, and burst through the front door. "What am I doing?" He looked around for an immediate threat, but there was none. *I can still run.* Fumbling with the keys, he ran to his Chevy Cavalier. *Pull it together.* Seconds felt like hours before the car door opened.

Vixen was close behind. "I'm coming."

He got in and unlocked her door. "You want to see me die that badly?"

She got in. "Chill. You can survive this."

"Easy for you to say. The heavy hitter won't be swinging at you."

"He tested me, too, and I was less qualified than you. Maybe that's why I'm so invested." Her eyes went wide and she stiffened. "Watch out!"

A horn blared. Brakes screeched.

Chase jerked round to see a black F-150 swerve, barely missing them. He hadn't realized they'd gotten in the car, let alone that he started it and backed out. "Mother Teresa, that was hella close." He stared as the truck sped away as if possessed by demons.

Chase's hands shook, energy coursing through every vein. A horse galloped circles around his neck. The fabric of his shirt felt abrasive. Daylight glared and the scent from the car freshener burnt the hairs of his nostrils. "I'm having a panic attack." Inhalation overlapped exhalation.

"Hold still." She put a finger to his carotid. "You've never had an adrenaline rush?"

"Is that what this is?"

"Senses overloading."

"Near to shorting out."

"That's her. What a wickedly amazing bitch."

"I almost died attempting to escape death?"

"Escape?" She laughed. "If that's your intent, you shouldn't bring your phone."

Chase flung it out the window and started down the road.

Vixen shrugged. "He'll still find you."

"Oh, *my* God! Stop talking." Every breath took thought.

"Did you just tell me to shut up?"

"My heart's hosting a rock band at the moment. You saying I'm screwed doesn't drown out the drum solo."

"You have to admit this situation is strange. There was a more qualified recruit, yet he chose you. Then he cut our training short. Why would—"

"Keep talking and I'll crash on purpose."

"I wanted you to have the best chance possible."

The light ahead was red. Chase stopped, throwing the car into park, and turned to face her. "Stop pretending to give a shit about my well-being."

"I'm not pretending, Hunter."

"I'm sure. You're the only *fucking* assassin that wants people to live? Is that it?"

She settled into her seat, looking away. "It's green."

He looked in the rear-view mirror to see a red van pull up behind him, the driver a large, black man. "That your heavy hitter?"

She remained silent, eyes forward.

"Great." Chase put the car in drive. "Now you're silent?"

At the next red light, Chase eyed the mirror to see the man return the stare. *What's he waiting for?* A cold sweat broke across Chase's brow. He swallowed. His eyes returned forward. *Green light.* He stomped on the pedal. *I have an idea.* He took a sharp turn down the road leading to the city pool.

The van didn't follow.

Chase laughed nervously. "Thought he was a friend of yours."

"Couldn't tell you if he were," she confessed, voice flat.

"Good on you for keeping your eyes open."

He felt proud of the achievement, albeit a small one. He followed the road down a hill to an abandoned parking lot ahead. The pool would stay closed for a few more weeks, making it the perfect oasis to gather his thoughts. "I need to get out and shake this feeling off," he said, parking. "I'll only be a minute."

She shrugged.

Before he could open his door, a black Ford Focus entered the parking lot.

He narrowed his eyes. *Could be nothing.*

The car slowed.

Or something.

Without stopping, a white man wearing only coveralls stepped out. The Focus continued, bouncing over a parking block and uprooting a handicap sign.

Chase looked in his mirror at the man approaching the back of his Cavalier. He sported a colorful, spiked Mohawk and was reaching a hand into one of the coverall's many pockets.

Chase looked at Vixen. "Do I get out and introduce myself?"

She ducked in her chair. "I wouldn't."

Chase's eyes returned to the mirror.

The man winked, his hand jerked, and a tire burst.

Chase threw the car in reverse and stomped on the pedal. Despite the flat, the car lurched.

The assassin jumped atop the trunk, slapped the roof, and yelled gleefully.

"Athletic prick." Chase slammed on the brake, throwing the man from the car. His eyes still on the mirror, he shifted the car to drive, turned the wheel, and punched the gas.

"Chase!" Vixen yelled.

He threw his eyes forward in time to see a red blur. The Cavalier slammed to a halt, partly due to his assault on the brake pedal, but mostly because two vehicles had become suddenly, uncomfortably intimate.

His vision filled with white. It punched him square in the jaw, sending his head reeling. Chase's heart throbbed loud in his chest. It was all he could hear. He pushed the white away. A fit of choking coughing overtook him, each breath filling his lungs with some sort of dust. Something smelled like it was burning.

Chase reached for Vixen. "You all right?"

"There can't be—" She coughed. "Why are there two?"

"Two?" Her meaning struck like a sledgehammer to the gut. "Are you fucking serious?" He pushed what remained of the airbag away. "When I asked if this scenario were possible, two words left your mouth: No and never."

Something metal struck his window, the glass becoming a

web of fissures.

Chase grabbed the gun from its holster, pressing it through the fractal. Around the barrel shards crumbled.

The spiky-haired assassin threw up his hands. In each, he held a knuckled blade. "Of course—he's a gun person." The man's head swiveled to the right.

Chase stepped out, glancing at the vehicle he'd hit. *The red van from before.*

Its door opened. The black man jumped out, bald and larger than expected. A white, sleeveless shirt clung to solid muscle. His hands were wrapped in straps of leather.

Chase did his best to keep calm. However, the adrenaline from before was compounding. He ran an inventory of their stats to refocus his mind. Both men were around forty. Coveralls was built for speed, 150 pounds of lean muscle and shorter than him by a few inches. Sleeveless was taller by a few, weighed down by 400 pounds and sculpted by the gods to hit like a Mack Truck. The immediate threat was the man with an outfit full of metal projectiles.

He pointed the gun at Coveralls. "Return the knives home." *There certainly are enough pockets to choose from.* He hadn't counted but there must have been more than fifty sewn into the coveralls.

The two assassins exchanged looks of bewilderment. When Vixen rounded the car, their confusion multiplied.

The black man pointed at her. "Why you here?"

"Me?" She gestured at coveralls. "What about Pockets?"

"I believe—Noose asked first," Pockets said. "Are we—chaperoning the recruits now?"

Noose straightened, turning to Pockets. "Why *are* you

here?"

"I'm within—my time."

Noose looked to Vixen, shrugging. "I'm at a loss."

Chase took advantage of their confusion, running hard across the parking lot to the grass plot across from the pool. A place nearby could provide cover. *If I can get there, I'll stand a chance.* He dared not look back, not even when three simultaneous pops jolted the back of his vest. Adrenaline carried him fast from concrete to grass. The tall, wire fence was eighty yards ahead.

Fast steps announced a pursuer, someone without a metal vest to slow them down. *I'm dead if I don't reach it first.*

He could hear breathing now.

Go faster. His feet sped so quickly, one tripped the other. He stumbled the final two steps and began climbing the fence. At any moment, his pursuer would grab and throw him down. Surprisingly, Chase scaled the fence and dropped on the other side unmolested.

The fence rattled.

He rolled, thinking he'd be the landing pad.

Someone thumped down behind. "Keep running," came Vixen's voice.

"Thank God." He twirled around.

His actual opponents were sixty yards off. A moment of relief twisted into an unnerving vine, thorns stabbing into his heart. "They're walking?" *That doesn't bode well.*

"They think you'll die quickly," Vixen said, helping him up. "You will if you stand here gawking."

"I take it they didn't get the lecture on being cocky."

"Maybe not, but you did. Yet, here you stand."

"This way." Chase walked to a metal panel on the ground. Lifting it, he revealed the hidden stairwell.

"A storm shelter's not ideal."

"Not a storm shelter," he assured her, descending. "They tore down the top half of the grade school. The basement classrooms remain."

"Still not ideal."

"Scared?"

She scowled.

Chase opened the door at the bottom. Something foul crawled up his nostrils and died. A mouse ran across what he could see of the trashed hallway.

Vixen followed him in. "What's that smell?"

"No idea."

"Why are we here?"

"I attended class here when I was little. I know its halls." Chase stepped over a fallen chair. "Your friends do not." Natural light sprayed out from a room deeper in. *I'm guessing the ceiling collapsed there.* He pointed. "Besides that room, the rest should be dark. Plenty of places to hide."

"Then get to it," Vixen said, tugging three times at the back of his vest. "You want these?"

He turned to see knives. "Yes, please."

"If you collect them, Pockets will get pissed. He'll start making mistakes." She placed them in his palm. "Don't tell anyone I'm helping you."

"I won't. But why are you?"

"I don't know." Vixen shook her head. "Something is terribly off about all of this." Pointing ahead of them, she said, "Kevin hates to be underground, especially when it's dark."

"Kevin?"

"I meant 'Pockets.'"

Kevin ... Knowing his real name made Pockets seem less terrifying. "What a name for an assassin." Chase placed the knives in a pouch along the side of the vest. "Sounds like an indie band guitarist."

She slapped his arm.

He laughed. "I'm not going to say it to his face. At least not until I've passed my tests. Not even then, probably."

Vixen nodded as though he'd answered correctly.

Chase looked at the doorway. "What's the other dude's name? Jacob?"

"Izach."

"That's not as reassuring. Is it 'Noose' because he hangs people?"

"Sometimes, but he's been known to strangle people with his bare hands."

Chase raised his eyebrows, blinking slowly.

"Exactly," she said. "Hide."

"Right." He walked into a spiderweb. "Ah, hells no." He brushed it away and flicked a spider from his arm. "I hate spiders."

"Then be glad Widow isn't testing you."

"I don't know what that means, but I'm glad for it." He scratched his arm. "I feel like they're all over me."

"This used to be a school." Vixen chuckled. "Pretend they're little students with eight hands attending a sewing class."

"Weavers 101," Chase added, smiling. "Sad to report that didn't help." It had.

Chase mapped out the tripping hazards. There were fallen beams and boards, doors, chairs, tables, and more. *They'll come in useful.* He knew his opponents would think similarly.

There were footsteps on stairs, descending.

Chase's eyebrows rose.

Pockets appeared. "Something—died in here."

Noose followed. "Many things, I'd imagine."

Pockets glared at the hallway. "Nope, I can't." He turned, returning to the surface.

Vixen winked at Chase.

Noose pulled Pockets back by the arm. "Don't be a pussy."

"I'm not—doing this," Pockets insisted.

Vixen looked at Chase. "I'd advise you to knock this one out," she said, pointing at Noose, "and chill with the spiders for an hour while Pockets paces topside."

Pockets threw up his arms. "Why are you—advising him at all?"

"You shouldn't be here either," said Vixen.

Noose nodded at Pockets. "I saw his time. We're both scheduled for now." He stepped past Vixen, unwrapping the leather strip from his hand. "How 'bout you get to knocking me out, kid?"

Chase backed away. "No, thanks."

Vixen sidestepped, placing a hand on Noose's chest. "Two assassins simultaneously testing one recruit. This doesn't bother you?"

"Not really." Noose brushed her hand away. "Turns out, Pockets and I both took our time getting here. The boy only has 40 minutes to survive. Since pussy pocket there's afraid of the dark, it'll just be me anyway."

Pockets struck Noose in the shoulder. "I was stuck—in a collapsed mine—for a week, asshole."

Noose shrugged.

Pockets sighed. "Fine." Two knives were lifted from his coveralls. "I'm going to kill you—if we get buried alive."

Vixen stepped back. "I'm sorry, Chase."

I need to run. Chase backed another step. *I need to run now.* He took off down the hallway, skirting around a fallen stack of chairs. A knife hit his vest moments before he turned down another hall. Darkness consumed him and he slowed, squinting to make out the rooms on either side. *This won't work if I can't remember the layout down here.* The room to his left felt familiar. He turned sharply into it. His hips collided with the side of a table; his chest smacked down atop it. He groaned, crawled over it, and pushed past chairs on his way to the back of the room. He crouched behind what felt like a podium.

Footsteps came his way.

Something clanked against the ground and Pockets said, "I hate you—right now."

"I'm comfortable with that," Noose replied.

Chase smiled and stole a moment to find the knife in his vest and pulled it free.

Pockets muttered under his breath while shuffling his feet along the floor.

He's feeling ahead.

A chair was kicked aside near the doorway and a figure appeared in the darkness, long spikes along the head. *If I go now, I can take down Pockets.* Chase felt the weight of the knife in his hand, yet remained still. *Or I can slip behind them in the dark.* He secured the blade in a pocket on his vest and watched.

Pockets continued on, followed shortly by the dark bulk of Noose.

Chase waited for a solid minute before rising on heels. His elbow bumped something and it fell, shattering loudly.

Noose let out a bellow of laughter.

If I escape this room quietly, they'll waste time here. Chase ran, reached a table, and rolled over it. His feet met the floor, sprung, and across the hall he flew. The landing was less graceful for within the door appeared a stack of chairs, its dark outline looming. He slammed into it and the stack toppled. The chairs crashed with him among them, alerting the others to his clever escape. Chase moaned and licked his lip to find a deep gash. "That hurt," he growled, rolling to his back to see Noose's figure framed by the doorway.

Both assassins were laughing.

Two knives rubbed together to Noose's left. "Stealth is not—your strong suit."

"I don't know," Noose chuckled. "What if he intends to die quickly?"

"I appear to be," Chase admitted, grabbing a chair and standing.

"What's that you got?" Noose said, shifting.

Chase aimed the legs forward and forward he charged. He caught Noose in the chest and the large man stumbled. Chase gave a final push and let go.

Noose toppled into the room adjacent. There came a thump, table legs screeching, and a crash.

Pockets blocked the darker side of the hallway. He thrust a knife into Chase's vest. "Why aren't you—a bleeding mess," he said, twisting the knife. "An armored coat?"

That was a short-lived secret. Chase didn't stop to think about it. He ran for the light. Darkness had served him miserably. To avoid his opponents' attacks, he'd need to see them clearly. And now that his secret was out, he'd need to—*Drop!* He fell into a roll. A knife whizzed overhead, clattering in the naturally lit room. Chase could see better now where the ceiling had collapsed, what remained showing obvious water damage. At the intersecting hallways, he popped up and sideways flipped in the direction of the exit. While airborne, a blade nicked the vest and smacked the wall beyond him. He rolled again and came up on a knee to see Vixen chewing at her lip. *She's worried.*

Chase turned.

Pockets nonchalantly walked into view. A knife was tossed into the air. He took a step and caught the knife behind his back.

Chase pulled the gun free of its holster.

"Almost forgot." Pockets smiled. "—about that." His head weaved toward the naturally lit room. His body followed as he sidestepped into it.

"Come out," Chase said, glancing at the dark hallway. *Noose can't be far behind.*

A large knife inched out, the assassin's eye peering at Chase through the reflection. "Beatrice, what—do you think? Should I—go out?"

Who's he talking to? "Beatrice?"

The knife waved, the reflected eye bobbing up and down. "I was in that mine—a long time. Took to naming knives—after women I'd made love to."

"That's an impressive number of pockets."

The assassin's eye squinted as the rest of the reflection

bounced in silent laughter. "Only the knives at my hip—are named after lovers. The rest are women—I respect. Some are strong—characters from books. Others, colleagues and—friends."

Vixen spoke up. "Am I in there somewhere?"

"Most definitely," Pockets said, the reflection of his eye shifting to look at her. "Mesmerizing is the blade—bearing your name." The eye returned to stare at Chase. "That armor—weighs you down."

"I'll take heavy over holey." Chase pointed the gun at the reflection. "You obviously agree, hidden as you are."

"On the contrary," said Pockets. "You brought a gun—to a knife fight."

"Rock beats scissors every time." Chase stepped forward.

"Scizzors—is another monster entirely." The knife disappeared into the room. "Survive us—and you'll meet him."

What? Chase turned to Vixen for clarification.

She glared, jerking her head at the room where Pockets hid.

Chase sidestepped for a better angle. "Final warning."

"People—and their guns." Pockets sounded disgusted. "So confident—they've already won. So confident—they die."

"Step out with your lady friends and we'll see if the confidence is misplaced." Chase hoped for the opposite. *Even if he stays, Noose is elsewhere.*

Pockets thought similarly, singing loudly, "Oh, where—oh, where can my—Noosey be?" The head in the reflection swiveled. "The Lord took him—away from me."

"If the good Lord returns him, I'm putting two in his chest."

"You'll do—what you do," Pockets said. "In fact—why haven't you?" The knife appeared again, eye blinking in the reflection. "Go ahead. Shoot—through the wall. It's thin enough."

"I don't think the point of these tests is to kill off Guild members."

"Wouldn't be the first time—a recruit killed one of us." The knife disappeared. "Or the last—I'm sure." Pockets twirled into the hallway and threw out a hand.

There was a glint of light on metal.

Chase bounced back, yet the blade thumped in the vest below his throat.

Pockets smiled. "That's Tiffany."

"She's not my type." Chase pulled the knife from his vest and hurled it back at the assassin.

Pockets snapped it out of the air, twirled, and let go.

Thump.

Chase glanced to see the knife back where it had been.

"Oh, that Tiffany," Pockets winked. "What—a tease."

"You're toying with me," said Chase.

"I'm waiting for you—to pull the trigger."

Chase raised the gun. "You think I won't?"

Pockets shrugged, pulling out another knife. "Trisha, well—she's clumsy." The blade dangled from his fingertips. "Trips a lot." He cocked a foot back. "Falls down." The knife dropped and Pockets kicked.

Yikes. Chase ducked, the blade missing his face by a foot. He jerked upright to see the assassin had closed the distance.

Pockets grabbed the gun, bent to the side, and swiped a knife at Chase's wrist.

Chase let go, deciding an empty gun a better loss than his hand.

Pockets eyed the gun suspiciously. "It isn't—"

Chase charged, shoulders low.

Pockets harrumphed, his body pinned to the wall.

The gun clattered at their feet.

A knee slammed into Chase's inner thigh, his groin the likely target. Chase grabbed Pockets by the abdomen, lifted, and launched the man up and back. The assassin's spine met the floor with a thud. Chase twisted round and collapsed.

Pockets threw his hands up to catch Chase's weight, but took a knee to the stomach. Air rushed from his lungs.

Chase's fingers wrapped around the assassin's throat, squeezing.

Pockets scratched at Chase's arms to no avail, his eyes wide, wild, panicked.

A leather strap swept through Chase's vision, tightening around his neck.

"Strangling's my game, kid," Noose said.

Chase didn't let go. The tighter Noose pulled, the stronger Chase gripped. At least until a knife left a pocket. Chase let go, grabbing instead for the knife directed at his bicep. Only the tip of the blade entered his flesh before he clamped onto the hilt.

Pockets jerked his hand away, the knife hurtling down the hall.

The leather around Chase's throat cut off all airflow. His vision blurred; his lungs pleaded for oxygen. *Find a way around it.* He threw his head back.

To avoid the hit, the big man raised his body, chest, and head.

Darkness flooded over Chase.

CHASE woke choking and coughing, in the middle of an argument.

"—cut our training short," Vixen yelled.

"How short?" Noose said. "He couldn't get out of a simple chokehold."

Chase coughed and tried to stand. The leather strap was still around his neck. It tightened to hold him in place.

"Stop struggling for a sec," Noose growled. "The adults are talking."

"What—do we do?" Pockets said. "We can't test him."

"I don't see why not," Noose disagreed.

"Why not?" Vixen twirled her finger in a circle. "Fighting multiple Guild members would be hard enough *with* suitable training. He can't tie his shoes in our world. We're asking him to make sailors' knots in a hurricane."

"Leave if you want," Noose said to Pockets. "I was ordered to test him. That's what I'm gonna do."

Chase gripped at the strap as it tightened.

"Chase," Vixen yelled. "Get up!"

"Yes," Noose said. "Let me help you with that." He pulled the leather strap to bring Chase to his feet.

Chase swung a fist at Noose's balls. When the large man dropped forward to avoid the hit, Chase swung his head back to connect with the assassin's chin.

Noose grunted, stumbled, and lost his grip on the leather.

Chase pivoted to place his feet against the wall and launched off.

Noose flung backward. He let go of Chase completely to stop himself from colliding with Pockets.

Released, Chase dropped and rolled away from them, coughing until breath came freely.

Noose regained his balance and hit Pockets in the chest with the back of his hand. "If you're not going to test him, get out of my way."

Pockets produced from a coveralls pocket a narrow blade. Attached to its hilt was a long, thin chain. "Chase—you'll either live a legend—or die tragically." He dropped the blade to dangle at his side. "What's it going to be?"

Likely die. Chase shook his head. *Keep them talking.* "What's her name?"

"Your—chaperon."

Vixen tilted her head. "That's supposed to be me?"

Pockets kicked the blade to spin around his body. "She's hypnotic—in her sway." It whistled left, then right, and left again.

Noose backed away. "Watch it with that."

Chase hunched down, not sure what was happening. *Maybe he'll chainsaw me with it?* That didn't seem likely since the assassin didn't approach.

Pockets caught the chain on his elbow, shifted his weight, and shot his hand forward. The blade flew like an arrow loosed from a bow.

Chase fell backward, the blade passing over him. It passed again, returning to its master.

The blade whistled, spiraling around Pockets. The assassin

jumped sideways, the blade swiping in a downward arc.

Chase rolled, hearing metal slap concrete behind him. He twirled a leg around, put his palm to the floor, and pushed. His body rose quickly, his eyes catching a glimpse of metal as it crossed behind him. "Holy!" He twirled around, watching the blade return.

Noose was leaning against the wall. He obviously didn't want to be in front of his Guild brother during the chain-blade's song.

Chase dodged again, the blade cutting a small groove in the vest. *Wait a minute.* There was a slight change to the whistle before release. He crouched, listening.

The wait wasn't long. A sharp chirp cut through the blade's melody.

Chase lunged backward, his hands slapping at the air around him. A chain entered his left palm and his fingers closed around it. The moment his feet met the ground, he spun 360 degrees, wrapping the chain around his back. He launched into a back flip, tugging. The chain grew taught for an instant, then fell slack. He landed, the weapon now his.

Pockets looked annoyed.

Noose, on the other hand, wore an amused smile. "He's like a squirrel on cocaine."

"He's fun, isn't he?" Vixen said from the entrance.

Pockets allowed a smile to traipse from one corner of his mouth to the other. "I suppose." He held out a hand to Chase. "Give her back—and we'll keep playing."

Chase kissed the blade, opened a pouch in the vest, and dropped the chain-blade inside. "Vixen is safer with me."

Pockets closed his fist. "I have more—where she came

from."

"None as graceful, I'm sure."

Vixen smiled.

Pockets reached into a pocket, lifting out another chain-blade, this one double-tipped. "Perhaps not. But Widow here—has a nasty bite."

Noose stepped away from the wall. "Let me get behind him first."

I can't take both of them.

Fortunately, he didn't have to.

Pockets ignored Noose, twirling the chain-blade around himself.

He's used to testing on his own. That gave Chase an idea. *Neither know how to do this together.* He withdrew the Vixen chain-blade from the pouch. "Let's dance."

Pockets smirked, letting Widow fly.

Chase charged, dodging right, rolling left, lunging forward along the ground.

Meanwhile, the blade snapped the air to his left, cut the wall at his right, and slapped down behind.

Chase bounced up, wrapped the stolen chain around the spiky-haired assassin's throat, and twisted Pockets to face Noose. As suspected, Noose was already swinging a fist. And, as suspected, black knuckles struck the pasty skin of Chase's captive.

Pockets went limp.

Chase let him fall, grabbing the second chain-blade from loose fingers.

Noose swung again.

With an unconscious man lying between them, Chase

easily avoided the strike. He did two backward somersaults, landed, and placed both chain-blades in the pouch.

Noose put two fingers against his fallen comrade's neck. "Your acrobatics are fun and all, but fascinating is you managing to knock each of us unconscious within fifteen minutes. My head met a table. His, my fist."

That explains Noose's disappearance.

Noose stepped over the fallen assassin, popping knuckles in meaty fists.

Pockets groaned.

Chase backed away. *I should try my luck again in the shadows.* He turned and ran. Before he could make it to the dark hallway, something wrapped around his legs. He managed to bounce twice before falling. Two steel balls connected by wire were wrapped around his ankles. He bent to undo them, but Noose was too close, the wire too tight.

Chase shifted, planting his feet against the wall. He glanced at an open room across from him and kicked. The dust on the ground carried him. Once inside, he threw his feet up to slam its wooden door shut. Pieces crumbled, hinges snapped, and the door fell to land atop him. Dust from the decayed wood filled his lungs. Pushing backward on his hands, he retreated, sneezing, coughing, and choking with each breath.

Noose appeared in the doorway, laughing. He wiped a tear from his eye. "I haven't laughed like this since—" A short laugh. "Ever."

Chase went to work loosening the wire around his ankles. He did this slowly, hoping to appear tightly bound.

Noose brushed a finger against a broken hinge. "How did that even happen?"

Chase spit out a splinter.

Noose bent to pick up the door. "Let's finish this, kid."

Chase finally freed his legs. He waited until the door was blocking Noose's vision, then put a foot through it. The door fell again, this time with Chase's leg sticking through the other side.

Noose backed up two steps and dropped, his hands clutching his crotch.

Did not mean to hit him there. Chase pulled his foot free of the door and backed out from under it.

Pockets appeared, burying a hand in his coveralls.

I need a shield. Chase jumped up, his eyes scanning the room. A second door was on the opposite end. *Or a way out.* It was stuck tight. He tugged. It held. Chase's eyes darted back.

Pockets stepped over a groaning Noose, his fingers freeing a knife from its prison.

Chase ducked and the knife hit the door above his head. He backed up a step, held his breath, and lunged at the center of the door. He passed through, decayed wood exploding around him. He crawled quickly the moment he got his hands and knees under him. He yelped in pain when something cut into the palm of his left hand. Glass. *I'm in the room from before.* He bit his lip when he pulled out the shard. *Would have been nice to know there was an exit to this room.* He shook his hand vigorously. At least now he knew the path out.

Someone slammed into a desk behind him.

"You had to choose—a dark playground," Pockets griped.

Chase slowed to silence his creep.

A knife skittered off a desk to his right. Another slammed into a chair deeper in the room.

He's throwing blindly.

A knife hit the floor directly in front of him, another struck his vest.

And doing it well. Chase gave up stealth, speeding toward the exit. He prepared to cross under the table he thought was there but his head thumped against wood. The table had been overturned. He rubbed his head. *If you hadn't knocked out Noose earlier, I'd be angry with you.* A knife struck the table.

"Where—are you?" Pockets yelled from behind. A chair slammed into Chase's back.

Chase cried out, more from being startled than the pain. He leapt over the table, escaping into the darker depths of the hallway.

"Noose," Pockets yelled, kicking desks and throwing chairs. "Get off—your big, black ass."

Chase's hand ran along the wall until he found where the hallway intersected and turned right.

Pockets, Noose, or both shuffled feet along the floor behind him.

Chase quickened his pace, his hand counting one, two, three doors down. *One more should do.* He found the doorway missing its door. He slipped inside and pressed his back to the wall, listening for followers.

Noose's voice came not far off: "Didn't expect a kick in the nuts."

Pockets chuckled. "Classic."

"It's not funny," Noose said as they neared.

Chase held his breath.

"You punched me—in the face," reminded Pockets. "Am I complaining?"

"Bitch, you're doing it right now."

"Wait up," Pockets said, directly outside the door. "Do

you have—your phone?"

The hallway lit up with someone's camera light. "Now, I feel stupid for not thinking of that before."

Chase's eyes went wide. He could see Pockets bathed in light. Fortunately, the man wasn't looking at him. There was no way to sneak deeper into the room without drawing attention.

"We're idiots," Pockets agreed, the light doubling outside the room.

Noose chuckled. "We should be the ones being tested."

"We are—in a way." Pockets smirked. "He realized something—before we did."

"And what's that?"

"We've never fought—together. And therefore—we suck at it."

"About that," said Noose. "Watch it with the spinning blade shit."

Pockets winked. "We'll see." His eyes narrowed and he sidestepped toward the room. "It's an amazing   thing —peripheral vision." His hand snapped out fast. Too fast. Chase tried to wrench free.

Pockets wasn't strong enough to overpower Chase. He didn't have to nor did he try. He only held until Noose could follow up.

Noose locked onto the vest, tugging.

Chase stumbled into the hallway, his hand darting into the pouch to pull out a knife. He swiped it around to cut Noose's arm.

Noose released before the knife could wound him.

Chase couldn't escape down either side of the hall. Pockets covered one, Noose the other. He darted back into the room, praying there was a second door to this one as well. Leather struck the side of his throat, wrapping three times. Chase was only allowed one more step before he was jerked back. Two more tugs brought Chase stumbling to slam into Noose's chest.

"Hold him." Pockets placed his phone on the ground, the flashlight facing the ceiling. "Should I carve our initials—into his forehead?"

Chase grabbed at the leather around his throat, feeling a metal ball attached to its end. Their shadows played on the ceiling, shifting wildly. He strained for breath and his eyes darted for a way out. *I'm screwed.* He tried to calm his mind.

Pockets stepped forward, knife in hand.

Panic was taking over. Chase had forgotten how many times the leather wrapped around him. His finger brushed along it, counting. *Left to right, one, two, three times.* He threw out both legs, planted his feet against Pockets's chest, and launched into an arc.

Pockets flew one way, Noose stumbled the other, Chase twirled in the air.

Noose tugged, only to grant speed to Chase's spiral. "Son of bitch," he growled.

Chase broke free of the leather. He landed, turned, and sprinted at Pockets who was still fighting to regain balance. Chase put a foot against the wall, sprang, and twirled through the air again.

"Watch it," Noose yelled too late.

Chase's legs caught Pockets around the throat. The two of them spun, crashing to the ground. Chase adjusted, open-palmed Pockets in the chin, and was up and running at a charging Noose.

Chase dropped into a roll, coming up to strike the man in

the kidney.

Noose crumpled, stumbled back, and looked further down the hallway.

Chase glowered, realizing he'd failed to blackout Pockets. He turned sharply, redirecting to barely avoid a chain-blade to the face.

The blade returned to Pockets. It was blunt, heavy, and appeared more for breaking bones than piercing flesh. Pockets twirled it around twice, caught the chain on his elbow, and let it fly.

Chase fell flat, letting it pass over him.

Pockets snapped his arm back, returning the blade to spin around him. He jumped sideways, twisting. The blade flew under Pockets, appeared in an arc above him, and swiped down.

There was no avoiding it. Chase braced.

Thwack.

A plate in the vest became pinned between the heavy blade and his rib cage. It felt like a boulder rolling over him. He coughed, pain radiating, ribs raging. *Damn, that hurt.* He raised his arm and took a deep breath as Vixen had done at his house. *No broken ribs.* "You're as acrobatic as I am," Chase said, trying to distract the man. He turned, planting his feet against the wall. He looked at Noose. "Don't you think?"

The big man shook his head. "That's his only trick."

Pockets chuckled. "It really — kind of is."

Chase kicked off the wall, sliding backward into the room. He twirled, pressing his palm to the ground to gain footing. His body rose in a burst, already running to the back of the room. *Please be a door.*

Light from a phone flooded into the room.

To Chase's horror, there was no exit except the entrance he'd slid through. He turned slowly, eyes scanning. A metal chair offered itself up as the assassins neared. He bolted forward, planted a foot on it, and spiraled over the heads of both opponents. He felt Noose try to grab his ankle, but the spin made getting a grip difficult. Fortunately, Chase was able to land, roll, and spring into a sprint. His heart tap-danced behind his eyes, his energy low, his breathing labored. *I can't take much more of this.* He had left the room and was down the hall when something tangled up his legs. Reduced to hopping, he bounced around fallen chairs on his way to the converging hallways.

Stomping thundered from behind.

Chase glanced back to see Noose charging. Chase bounced harder. He took a shoulder to the back of the vest and fell, sprawling. He rolled onto his back, chest heaving.

Noose slowed, turned, smiled.

Chase moaned, lifting himself on an elbow. "How many of those do you have?" he said, gesturing at the wire around his tangled legs.

Noose shrugged. "Couple more."

Chase rested his head on the ground, relieved he could catch his breath. "Just finish this."

"That's the spirit," Noose said. "Give in."

"I could—poke more holes in him," Pockets suggested. "One—or two." He threw a knife.

Chase flinched, but the knife only stuck in his vest. *Why keep toying with me?* Chase sat up, pulled the knife free, and dropped it in the pouch. There was a satisfying clink as it nestled among the others.

Pockets half-closed his eyes.

Chase forced a smile. "Play nice and I'll return them after class."

Noose grunted a laugh and brought out two rubber handles with a wire stretched between them. He pressed a button and pulled. The wire lengthened another five inches. "Let's finish this."

Chase kicked with tangled legs.

Noose grabbed Chase's feet, pulled them up, and kicked him square in the balls.

Light flashed across Chase's vision. Crippling pain vibrated in waves, crashing into his abdomen with the force of a tsunami. He closed tear-filled eyes, curled up, and prayed for death. He was twelve the last time he'd taken a hit to the testicles so severely. He had landed wrong on a balance beam. No, this was worse. His stomach and abdomen were kickboxing and neither were interested in backing out of the fight. Chase opened his eyes in time to see a black fist. His head was raised, so the impact slammed his skull to the ground. Darkness swept over him. Only a few murky specks of vision remained.

Noose knelt over him.

Chase brought his knees to his chest, rocked his body, and slammed his forehead into the large man's face.

Noose roared in pain, shuffling back.

The hit didn't improve the fact that Chase was already blacking out. *Fight through it.* Chase threw out his feet, felt them strike Noose's knees, and pushed off. He slid across the ground.

Noose uttered something. It was incoherent, but the tone bore anger.

Chase brought his knees over his head, placed fingers to the ground at his shoulders, and pushed. His body launched upward. His feet planted. He shook his head, regaining a sliver of vision.

Pockets laughed from behind. "Rule 32: Don't underestimate—the recruit."

Chase didn't have time to untangle the wire from his ankles, but he needed to flee. Desperately. He began bouncing toward the literal light at the end of the tunnel.

A knife slid across his calf and stuck in a desk a few feet ahead.

Chase couldn't stop, couldn't look to see how bad it was. *Keep going.* He called upon his final reserve of energy, pulling together all he had to remain upright, pulling together everything to escape. There wasn't much left in that tank. *Keep jumping.* He was slowing considerably, his legs pleading for rest. *Once I see Vixen, I'll get a boost. I can make it.* He was nearly there. Just ... two ... more ... lunges.

Something hard and heavy hit him in the back of the head. His legs gave out, dropping him to the ground. *Don't stop!* He couldn't do more than crawl. He did his best, grabbing the corner of the wall and pulling himself forward.

Vixen had come further in, her hands to her mouth, her eyes wide.

She really does care. Chase was right. A surge of energy washed over him. His excitement was short-lived, for whatever hit him before struck him again. *Roll.* He did, glimpsing Noose standing over him with a stepping stool in hand.

"You're one slippery bastard," Noose said.

The bouncing had loosened the wire around Chase's ankles. He kicked his feet, twirled, and rose with hands ready. His fingers closed on the stool as it fell.

Noose jerked the stool from Chase's grip and swung again.

Chase found himself on the ground, blinking blood out of his eye. He put a finger to his eyebrow, pulling it away when searing pain responded. There was a large split in the skin. Through tears, blood, and a silhouette of mental fog, Chase could feel his body being lifted by the vest. He grabbed a knife from the pouch and struck out blindly.

"Fucking hell," Noose yelled.

Chase dropped, managing to get his feet under him. Without missing a beat, he shot away. He made it ten yards when his calf exploded. His body dropped hard against a chair. He choked in a breath, pushed off, and landed on his back. His eyes trailed down to see a blade sticking from his leg, a chain spreading from it to Pockets. "Are you serious?"

Pockets smirked.

Noose ran past them to cut off Chase's exit.

Chase threw his knife at Pockets, but the assassin merely snapped it out of the air.

Chase glared. "I'll get one to stick in your scrawny—" Leather crossed his vision, tightening around his throat. "Fuck this."

Chase knew he couldn't pull Noose, but Pockets was lighter. *This'll hurt.* He brought his leg back, grabbing the knife in his calf.

Noose tightened his hold, whispering, "Just die, kid."

Chase gritted his teeth, pulled the knife free, and twirled the chain around his wrist. "Raaaooohhh, my God!" It was far worse than when it went in. Injecting acid into his vein would have been less painful.

Pockets narrowed his eyes.

Chase's body began shaking. He jerked his head away from Noose.

Noose replied by pulling on the leather.

Chase went limp.

Pockets, his grip tight around the chain, was pulled along with them. He fell, sprawling at Chase's feet. Thirty or so knives spilled across the floor.

Chase kicked Pockets hard in the face, his hand grabbing the knife closest to him. He jerked forward.

Noose pulled, this time, harder than before.

Chase's eyes threatened to bounce from their sockets. He swiped the knife back, cutting through the leather. Air filled his lungs. The large assassin toppled backward, crashing into what sounded like chairs.

Chase threw the knife at Pockets, knowing he'd catch it.

Sure enough, Pockets took a hand from the chain to do so.

Chase put a palm to the ground, kicked out his feet, and rose, spinning. The chain wrapped around his torso, successfully tearing it from the assassin's grip.

Pockets punched the wall and regained his feet. "You're one—defiant wasp."

Chase eyed a fallen locker behind Pockets. "You're the one with stingers." He jumped, kicking both feet forward.

Pockets took the feet to his sternum. His calves met the locker, his knees buckled, and he fell.

Chase, on the other hand, was thrown backward, his shoulders colliding with Noose's stomach.

Noose wrapped an arm around Chase's throat, squeezing. "Come cut this bastard open," Noose said when Pockets regained his feet.

"Meet—Goldilocks," Pockets said, producing three golden blades. One was large, another mid-sized, and the last small. "One's too big," he said, dropping it back in the pocket. "Another—not quite right." This one he threw to stick in the vest. "But baby bear, here." He snapped his wrist and the smallest blade sank into the gap between the plates. "You'll find—he's just right."

Chase could feel it needling him, but it hadn't pierced the skin. He stretched his neck, saying, "You didn't throw it hard enough."

"Just needs—a little help," Pockets said, pulling out the largest of the Goldilocks. He threw it in such a way that the hilt of the larger blade slammed into that of the smaller.

Chase screamed as metal hammered down, splitting flesh, and sinking into the muscle of his abdomen.

Noose sucked air through teeth. "Sounds like that hurt something fierce. How 'bout another?"

Pockets obliged, bringing out a black, serrated blade. "How about—we get that vest off first?"

Chase pulled a knife from the pouch and stabbed it into the bicep of the arm holding him. He swiped the blade around again.

"Son of a bitch," Noose roared, throwing Chase against the wall. He stood and backed away.

Mind muddled, Chase grabbed a chair and pulled himself up to sit.

"This is your fault," Noose yelled at Pockets. "You keep giving him weapons. I'm bleeding from three places because of you. I'm done playing games."

"Are you—snapping your fingers?"

"Damn straight." His index finger met his thumb and snapped. Noose's eyes met Chase's. "That sound means death, boy."

Chase gritted his teeth, his finger tapping the blade stuck inside his abdomen. This one he didn't dare pull out. He looked between the two assassins. Neither was smiling. *Move or die.*

Pockets lunged forward with a knife in each hand.

Chase ducked under him and fell to the ground. He got on all fours and jumped up to run. He made it three steps before pain and fatigue forced his legs to give. His muscles spasmed in their appeal for rest, yet he crawled for the room lit by natural light. *I'm not getting out of this.* There was nothing left to burn inside.

He stopped two feet from the room, reaching for sunlight as though it held some sort of power.

"Sorry, kid," Noose said, stepping into the light and kneeling. "We'll make it quick." He looked beyond Chase. "Grab his ankles." Noose took Chase by the shoulders and turned him over.

Pockets followed the order.

Chase kicked with the ferocity of an earthworm.

Noose lifted Chase, wrapping the uninjured arm around his throat.

Chase pushed off with his legs, trying to ram his head into Noose's throat.

The large assassin simply straightened.

Pockets leaned backward, pulling Chase's body taught.

I'm being drawn and quartered. Chase's breath was cut off. He clawed at Noose's arm, digging fingernails into flesh.

Noose made an uncomfortable grunt, but continued to

hold.

A dark rim invaded Chase's vision. Hope abandoned him, fleeing down the cursed hallway. He glanced over to see Vixen frowning, her eyes full of anger and fear. The frame of black closed around her as Chase began to lose consciousness. He was hanging on by a fraying thread. *It's hopeless.* He couldn't roll, couldn't use his legs to launch, and Noose wasn't letting go, no matter how deep the fingernails dug.

"Lights out," Noose whispered in his ear.

Just give in, his body pleaded. *Let darkness embrace you in sleep eternal.* Chase stretched his neck, turning his head into the crook of Noose's arm. A thin passage of air was opened up, clearing his vision a little to stare up at the collapsed ceiling. The breath was a small victory clouded by impending defeat.

Someone was there, standing at the lip of the hole. Whoever it was wore a billowy, white bomb disposal uniform. His uncle's uniform had been green. *When we die, our clothes turn white.* The person wore a gas mask. *That's new.*

His uncle had come for him. Chase gave in, allowing the dark frame to consume his remaining vision. He didn't know what dying would feel like. He'd never done it before. But it surprised him that it was accompanied by concussions of tumultuous thunder that shook the very air around him.

Chapter Seven

Web of Lies

EUROPEANS painted faces of warriors hiding in shadow upon thick paper, playing them one against the other. A card depicting a knife-wielding assassin would be played against an archer. A shadowed creature thrown down against a robed woman crushing herbs with mortar and pestle. As this practice spread, cards took on faces of the more renowned assassins.

May 11, 2016
12:32 PM EDT
Ann Arbor, Michigan

~ Eight of Spades ~

SHARON grabbed a freshly baked chocolate chip cookie and bit into it. *Still too hot.* She zipped up her jacket and walked to the mailbox, taking a moment to wave at two neighbors as they jogged by. *How are they not freezing their asses off?* She was new to Michigan. Tampa would be in the mid- to high-eighties this time of year. But in this cold corner of hell, it was barely sixty degrees.

She retrieved her mail. It seemed a boring assortment until she rifled through the weekly circular and found an envelope inside. It bore no return address or stamp. The only marking was her name scrawled in cursive across its face.

Curiosity got the best of her. She tore it open to find the edge of a picture inside. *A secret admirer?* She screamed when the picture left its enclosure. The envelope fell from her fingertips. Half of the picture stared back at her from the sidewalk. She closed her eyes to see the image cauterized on the inside of her eyelids: A gory scene of a man she knew all too well, his head resting against a wall, hands resting in his lap, a hole blown through his chest.

How did they find me?

Her eyes shot open, darting about for who may have delivered the photo. Kids played a few houses down. The joggers neared the end of the road. Across the street, an old man worked on an old Ford. Nothing out of the ordinary. Besides, of course, the terrifying picture.

Sharon's hands shook so badly, the rest of the mail joined the envelope at her feet. She tried to swallow, but her throat was dryer than the burnt cookies waiting inside.

A white utility van with blackout windows entered the street. Her eyes followed until it turned the corner and disappeared.

I need to get far, far away from here. Then again, she thought she'd already run far enough to escape those who killed her employer.

She stole up her sidewalk and ducked inside her house. Before the door could close, she twisted round to watch for pursuers. *No one.* She took a deep breath, pushed the door shut, and closed her eyes. The image of death greeted her in the darkness. Her eyes snapped open.

Calm down. Get the car keys. Everything will be fine. She slapped her neck. Something bit her. Jerking around, she saw an African American woman wearing all black. The only aspects not dark about her were four diamond stud earrings, a gold wedding band, and an empty syringe held between the fingers of her right hand.

"What did—Who—How ..." Sharon's words trailed into mist as she became lightheaded. Her consciousness drained out the tips of her fingers and toes. Her body fell back, met the wall, slid. "Why?"

The dark woman knelt. "We'll talk soon."

Sharon blinked, dropped chin to sternum, and yielded to the encroaching, numb blanket of silence.

SHARON'S eyes drifted open to see the chandelier above her dining room table. Her wrists were cold, her feet colder. *Am I restrained?* She tried to move and that realization became confirmed. Eyes widening, she glanced down to see iron manacles binding her wrists to a two-foot-long metal bar. She found herself sitting on a dining room chair with gloves covering her hands. Wires sprouted from the fingertips and were strung across the table to a laptop. Her first thought was to tear off the gloves, but the bar and manacles prevented her hands from touching.

Behind her, someone began whistling a familiar song. She was too scared and confused to match the music to whichever movie it belonged.

When Sharon attempted to turn toward the whistler, it became clear her ankles, too, were trapped. A thick wire ran from the bar between her wrists through to her legs. Between her knees, she saw at her feet a rectangular, glass box. No, not at her feet—encasing them, each foot bare and stuck in a separate padded hole. Inside the box, her ankles were cuffed together. The cable she'd followed with her eyes ran through the cuffs and into the bottom of the glass box.

The whistling ceased. Then a woman said, "Do you see them?"

Sharon dropped her head back to look upside down.

It was the dark woman from before. She held a cookie.

Sharon narrowed her eyes at the intruder. "You can't drug and imprison someone in their own home."

"That would be a no." She nodded at Sharon's feet. "Keep studying the box."

Sharon looked again and noticed the wire trailing along the bottom of the cage. "You're a psychopath who locks feet in—" She choked on the final words. Three of the largest spiders she'd ever seen fought for space behind a black divider. Her eyes shot across to see three more at the opposite end, trapped by another divider. Tilting her head, she saw more thin black walls between the spiders and her bare feet. Sharon was hard to rattle, but at that moment, she was a bead in a rainstick.

"I'm Widow," the dark woman said, walking to the table and sitting at the laptop. "I have a few base questions."

Sharon brought her knees up, lifting the box from the ground to better see the spiders.

Widow raised an eyebrow at her. "Set it down slowly or

you'll regret the consequences."

"Screw you," Sharon said, thrusting her feet down to slam the box against the floor.

The first divider at each side snapped open. The spiders now had a larger area in which to roam. Among themselves, they fought for personal space.

Sharon's eyes flew wide. "For *fuck* sake."

"Warned you." Placing the cookie on the table, Widow returned her attention to the laptop. "Here's your second warning." She stroked the wires. "A fly struggling in a web succeeds only in attracting the spider." While typing, she asked, "What color is the wall?"

"What?"

"The color." Widow pointed with her thumb at the wall. "That's the first baseline question."

"Blue."

"Do you live at 133rd Birchwood Drive?"

"Bitch, you're in my house. You know I live on Meadowlark."

"That's a no?"

"No," yelled Sharon. "Get this off me."

"This time, I need you to lie," Widow said, typing. "Are you human?"

"Yes."

Widow blinked slowly at her. "I said lie."

"Look, bitch." Sharon went to stand, but was only able to rise a few inches with the metal bar manacled to her wrists. "When I get out of this, I'm going to rip you apart."

Widow glanced at Sharon's feet, smiling at the cage.

Sharon did the same. At each end, another divider had

snapped. "Nooo, no, no, nooo."

"Sit down, love," Widow said. "This won't take long. If you answer fully and accurately, you'll soon be free of the box."

Sharon locked eyes with the woman. She gritted her teeth for a few seconds before sitting. "Get on with it."

"Does this cookie have nuts in it?"

Sharon looked at the cookie. "What?"

Widow picked it up. "Are there nuts in this cookie?"

"I hate nuts."

"Good, I'm beyond allergic." Widow took a bite. "Did you know the man in the picture you found in your mailbox?"

"No."

Widow pushed a key.

Sharon felt two simultaneous pops. "Fuck! Yes. The answer's yes."

"Were you aiding him in luring unsuspecting women to his home where he'd murder them?"

"I helped get him women. I didn't know he was killing them."

Widow's little finger snapped a key.

With each pop of the box, Sharon's heart thumped. "You bitch! You're psychotic."

"Maybe," the woman admitted. "But what of you?"

"What of me?"

"You convinced women to cheat while their husbands were overseas fighting for your country, assuring them their husbands were doing the same with the women in their camp. You sent wandering sheep bleating into a dragon's lair." Widow ran a finger over an earring, tightening the stud. "Is there no form of psychosis in your actions?" She frowned. "Are you not deranged?"

Sharon opened her mouth to protest, but uttered not a sound.

"What's wrong?" Widow tenderly stroked the corner of a key with her pinky finger. "Feeling vulnerable? I'm sure those women felt powerless when you led them to a slaughter."

"No."

Widow tilted her wrist up and spiraled her pinky finger down toward the keyboard.

Sharon looked at the laptop. "Won't you kill me regardless, pass or fail?"

"No, love." Her pinky left the key. "I don't kill people."

"Oh! You scared me." Sharon let out a long breath. "Unhook this crap and I promise not to press charges." She shook her head. "I'm glad he's dead. He made me sick."

"Yet, you took his money."

"I feared he'd kill me, too."

Widow slapped the key.

POP. POP.

Sharon screamed. Only one set of dividers remained between her and the spiders. "You said you don't kill people."

"I don't." Widow leaned to look at the box. "They do."

The sweat on Sharon's palms made the gloves seem tighter. She stretched her fingers and eyed the cables running from her fingertips. Surely if she disconnected them from the laptop, the command wouldn't reach the final divider. *Right?*

"One last question," Widow said, narrowing her eyes. "Would you go to the police and confess if I untangled you from this web of wires?"

Of course not. "Anything you want."

Widow's finger moved to the ENTER key.

Sharon jerked back her hands, yanking the wires from the laptop a second before the key was smashed.

PoPoP

Sharon's lungs emptied, rattling the chandelier with a scream that could be heard across the block. She slammed the box over and over. "Shatter, damn you!"

The spiders became frenzied. One clung to Sharon's ankle for purchase. Teeth sank into flesh.

She screamed, her feet kicking, her knees rocking the table. The laptop jolted and she glimpsed pictures of women. Only a few were fully visible. She knew their faces well. *That's not important right now.* She slammed her feet down again, crushing part of a spider under her heel. Pale blue blood splattered on the glass. What remained of the arachnid fought to survive. Into the arch of her foot, fangs dug deeper. Another lost a leg, which enraged it further.

A scream erupted from her throat, so loud and high it made the dog bark next door. She hated that dog, but today it might deliver salvation.

Her legs felt as though they were set over a roasting pit. "Get them off me," she yelled, twirling her body back and forth in panic. "Somebody, heeelllp!" She rocked her chair and fell onto her left side. Wires followed.

A few spiders fell from her ankles, only to be replaced by those who had remained at the far-right wall.

Sharon wiggled her feet vigorously. In response, the spiders latched on with fangs to secure their hold.

Widow placed the laptop on the floor so Sharon could see the collage of women's faces.

Sharon shook her head.

Widow knelt behind the screen. "I'll leave this with you." She tapped a key, then left through the patio sliding doors. The faces played across the scene. With each face, a caption appeared noting the names of family members they'd left behind.

Sharon's body began jolting involuntarily, her muscles convulsing. Her heart drummed. Her blood felt thick as tomato soup rushing through her veins. It thrummed heavily in her throat, making it near impossible to breathe.

"Help," she managed to yell.

People began calling back. Someone was pounding into her door over and over. For an instant, she felt hope. Then a murky red flooded her vision. *It's too late. I'm going to die in my dining room.* Darkness invaded.

The sound of wood splintering was muffled somewhere far, far away.

Sharon lay dying on the floor of her new home, paid for by her betrayal of women to a serial killer. The poetic justice was not lost on her. *That can't be my last thought.* The darkness devoured all but a pinprick of light. *My last thought should be ... adorable rabbits.*

All went black, but one image remained: A rabbit suspended in a web of spiders.

Chapter Eight

Time's Up

May 11, 2016
12:33 PM CDT
Kansas City, Missouri

VIXEN shook Pockets awake.

He brought a knife to her throat.

"Kevin," she said, putting a hand to the blade. She felt the tip of another knife pressed to her kidney.

Pockets tucked the knives away, his eyes darting from her to the halls around. "What happened?"

I've been asking that myself. "I think a bomb went off topside."

He placed a hand to the back of his head. "What—hit me?"

"That locker." Vixen pointed behind him.

Pockets craned his neck to see. "Where's—the recruit's body?"

"He's not a corpse, if that's what you're asking."

Surprise spread from his chin up. "He's alive?"

Vixen looked at Chase perched against a wall. "Barely."

Chase opened one eye. "Thanks to you ... Kevin." He smiled, then grimaced and put a hand over his abdomen.

Pockets looked from Chase to Vixen. "Why is he—thanking me?"

She nodded at a pile of ventilation and stone. "When the ceiling fell, Noose let go to protect himself. You kept pulling on Chase's ankles. Otherwise, he'd be buried, too."

Pockets sat up and followed her gaze.

She stood and walked to the debris. "Chase shouldn't be lifting anything. So, it's up to you and me to get Noose out. I've already called our Kansas City contacts to pick us up."

Pockets rushed to pick up one end of a concrete slab. "Is Noose alive under there?"

"Heard groaning a bit ago, so I'm hopeful."

Together Pockets and Vixen lifted, grunting as they crab-walked three feet to drop the slab.

A slab had fallen at a perfect angle over Noose's upper half, holding back most of the larger debris. That's not to say the big man was without injury. Bone projected from his right leg, his head bled, and his right arm twisted strangely.

"He's one—lucky bastard," said Pockets, as they continued removing wreckage. "Speaking of—lucky. How long was I—out?" asked Pockets.

"Not long," said Vixen.

Pockets threw a block of cement aside and shook his head.

She followed his gaze to see Chase running a fingernail along the knife in his abdomen. "I don't know how he survived against two of us."

"My thoughts—precisely."

Chase inhaled deeply, winced, and took his hand away

from the wound. "You talk like you give a shit."

Pockets winked at him. "Notice—the knife in the gap."

"What? This?" Chase said, gesturing in a circle over the wound. "I failed to notice that."

Pockets shook in a silent chuckle. "Could have put that—through your throat."

Vixen grabbed a metal pole from the debris and drew a circle around Chase's abdomen. "Judging by how much hilt is showing, he only hammered the knife into your muscle."

Chase's eyes narrowed. "You missed on purpose?"

"I didn't—miss," Pockets said. "When you had the gun—I wanted to kill you. I hate—fools and their guns." He grinned. "When I found it empty—I knew."

"Knew what?" Chase asked.

"That you'd make a perfect addition to the Guild," Vixen said as she brushed wires off the ventilation shaft. "During testing, it's not so much about killing a recruit as it is deciding whether they'd make a decent card holder. Doesn't mean they take it easy if they like you. Just means they test you to an impossible degree if they don't."

Pockets tossed a piece of metal over his shoulder. "We determine—what you're capable of surviving. Then—we test those limits, pushing you—until time is up."

Chase shook his head. "If that bomb didn't go off when it did, I'd be dead."

"Noose chose—to kill you," Pockets said. "I've never—tested alongside another Guild member. I didn't know—if I could defy his decision." Pockets nodded at the ceiling. "Crawling—for the light. Leading us to a bomb." He gestured at Noose's unconscious body. "Brilliant."

"Sorry to disappoint," Chase said. "That wasn't me."

Pockets glanced at Vixen, dumbfounded. "You?"

Her eyes went wide. "Nooo."

"It was someone in a bomb uniform." Chase groaned. "I thought it was my uncle, come to take me to the next world. Only, this person's uniform was white and he wore a gas mask."

Pockets looked at Vixen, his forehead wrinkling. "Why would Powder Keg try to kill the recruit?"

She shrugged. "A third tester, maybe?"

"Who's Powder Keg?" Chase said, eyes closed.

"The bomb maker—of our Guild chapter," Pockets said.

Chase's eyes snapped open. "Explosives kill my uncle. Now they interrupt my testing. That's some coincidental bullshit, right there."

"Believe what you want," said Vixen. "I don't understand anything that's happening around you."

"Am I—missing something?" asked Pockets.

"Ahhh," Noose groaned, startling them all.

Vixen dropped to put a hand against his chest. "Don't move."

Noose tried to sit up. "Whaaat the shiiit?"

"Where do you hurt?" Vixen asked.

"Nobody told us the recruit was a goddamn bomber," said Noose.

"We think it was Powder Keg," said Vixen.

Noose rested his head against a slab of concrete. "Three assassins sent to test one recruit. Now, that's fucked up."

"Powder Keg—did come with me to Kansas City," Pockets informed. "Said we'd share the flight. That he had—a hit."

What is going on? "We'll figure it out later," Vixen said.

"Right now, we need to focus on getting Noose out. Grab that end." Her fingers locked on the ventilation shaft.

Pockets took hold and together they lifted.

"Son of a bitch, drop it," Noose yelled. "I said, drop it!"

They let go.

What happened?

Pockets knelt to look under the ventilation shaft. "A metal rod—has pierced his thigh."

"I asked where you hurt, jackass," Vixen said. "We wouldn't have lifted it."

"Hard to pinpoint everywhere," Noose growled, rolling his head along the concrete. "I feel nauseated."

"The doctor's coming. And an Officer Clark is on his way to 'investigate' the explosion." She took out her phone and began texting. "I'll tell him to grab a metal saw."

"Officer Clark?" Chase asked. "Trevor Clark?"

Vixen nodded. "That's the name and number I have for our contact."

Chase thumped his head against the wall. "My uncle said he's a good cop," then muttered, "Can't believe he's dirty."

"He's not," Vixen said. "You'll understand one day. We have doctors and officers all over the world, hoping to make a better planet. Those we kill are not good people." As if on cue, an ambulance siren wailed. "And that 'dirty' doctor is going to patch you up."

"Who is—our doctor here?"

"Allison Beck," Vixen replied. "She's young. Her bio says she's pre-med, studying to become a critical care surgeon."

"Good. I'll need a surgeon," Noose said. "And a tetanus shot." He closed his eyes. "Maybe three."

Vixen slapped his cheek. "I wouldn't nap if I were you. If you're concussed, you may not wake up."

He groaned long and low and opened his eyes.

The siren drew close, then cut off.

Noose opened one eye to look at Chase. "You're lucky, kid."

"Don't feel like it," Chase admitted.

"No?" Pockets said. "You—survived my knives, him—crushing your windpipe, and a bomb—going off overhead. You did good." He nodded. "Better than."

"Hey, hey," announced a woman's voice.

Vixen turned to see a tall Caucasian woman and a round Indian man, both wearing scrubs. *Who is—*

"Who's—the dude?" Pockets said, voicing her concern.

"Lahar's an EMT," Allison said, stepping into the hallway. "He's trustworthy."

"Better be," Noose said, moaning loudly when he sat up.

Allison rushed forward with a medical bag. "I'm going to ask that you stop moving."

Lahar followed, a pole stretcher under one arm and a trauma bag over the other.

Allison checked Noose's pulse, her eyes trailing over his wrecked body. "He needs a hospital." She looked at Chase, eying his abdomen. "As does he." She squinted. "Is that a knife?"

"Yeah. I'll be wanting—her back," Pockets said. He looked at Chase. "She—and her sisters."

Chase chuckled, then winced and closed his eyes.

Vixen put a hand on the doctor's shoulder. "Can you get them to a hospital without questions?"

"I don't know," Allison admitted.

"If need be—we'll pay more people."

"Then, yeah." Allison nodded. "I have a few more nurses I trust."

A police siren blared, nearing fast.

Lahar straightened when the siren cut off.

Vixen held up a hand. "The officer is with us. His precinct thinks he's responding to the explosion."

Lahar looked back at the entrance. "Will we get in trouble for cutting the fence?"

Allison glared at him. "He's not gonna care about the fence."

Vixen nodded. "Like the two of you, he's more concerned with concealing our existence than he is a hole in the fence."

"Won't the hole make it harder to cover up, though?" said Lahar.

"I'm telling you," Allison said, "he's not gonna care."

The first words out of Officer Clark's mouth were "Who cut the fence?"

"Knew he'd be mad," Lahar said.

"No, it's smart." Clark stepped into the hallway holding a saw. "Makes the explosion easier to pin on vandals." He wrinkled his nose. "You didn't tell me someone died down here."

"That's just—the way it smells," Pockets said. "Cut Noose free."

Clark went to work.

Allison checked Chase's knife wounds. "Let's take him to the ambulance."

Chase shook his head. "I want to make sure Noose is all

right."

"It's not a thick rod," Clark said. "He'll be fine."

"Huh," Noose grunted. "Says the man *without* a metal pole inside him."

"Well," Clark said. "It's not great. But you'll live."

Noose took Vixen's hand. "Call Max."

She took out her phone. "Number?"

He gave it, she dialed, and put the phone to her ear.

After a few rings, there was an answer. "This is Maximus."

"Hey, Max," Vixen said. "Your husband was in an accident. He's fine, but—"

"I'll come right away," Max interrupted. "What hospital? What city?" A muffled yell followed: "Girls!"

Noose took the phone. "Babe, don't scare them."

Max said something she couldn't make out.

"I get that," Noose said. "I'll be home soon. I needed you to know it wouldn't be in time to tuck the gremlins in. And that I won't be able to lift them for a while."

"Promise me, you're okay, Izach," Vixen overheard Max say.

"Promise," Noose replied. "Give them kisses and a cuddle." He smiled. "I love you too, Marshmallow." He hung up and handed the phone back to Vixen. Then he looked beyond her. "What?"

She turned to see Chase smiling weakly.

He straightened. "Just didn't expect you to be—"

"A homosexual?" Noose snapped.

Chase shook his head. "A father."

"Oh." Noose looked around at everyone staring at him. "A father who wants to get home to his kids, but has a pole sticking out of him."

"Right," said Officer Clark, kneeling to saw through the rod.

"He's right," Pockets said. "We need to—get moving." He grabbed the pole stretcher.

Lahar dropped his end of the stretcher and his trauma bag and backed away, his hands up.

"My knives—are no longer in play," said Pockets.

"Sorry," Lahar's voice cracked. "I'm nervous." He leaned down, expanding the stretcher until it was flat.

Pockets gestured at Chase. "Get on."

Chase looked to Noose.

"He'll be fine," Vixen said. "Go."

Face twisting in pain, Chase inched over until he was on the stretcher.

Lahar knelt. "One ... two ... and—" He and Pockets lifted, then started for the exit.

Chase's eyes met Vixen's. She smiled at him just before he disappeared up the stairs.

Noose waited until their footsteps could no longer be heard before saying to Vixen, "Kid worries more for my well-being than his own."

"He's something else," Vixen agreed.

"Something," Noose admitted. "Not one of us."

Chapter Nine

Killer Wheels

GROUPS of cards became packs. Within each pack were five common figures. The first and most obvious was that of the Cloak, the elite members of the Guild. The Cloaks were known for killing off nobles or members of the royal family without detection. The artwork on their cards portrayed powerful, winged spirits or angels, a sword in each hand. This titan could kill off all other cards.

May 11, 2016
08:01 PM CDT
Manhattan, Kansas

~ Ace of Spades ~

ACE stood outside a phone store that sat atop a hill. Late night traffic thrummed as he gazed down at the intersection below. His watch ticked against his wrist when he brought a clove cigarette to his lips, its tip hissing red as he drew breath. He hummed when the smoke escaped the side of his mouth.

He dropped the lighter into his pocket and pulled out his phone. The screen lit to show an aerial view of a car dealership. Sure enough, his mark was pulling out of the parking lot. *Same time, every time.* He let smoke escape through his teeth. *People with enemies should really change their routine.*

The drone was programmed to follow the tracker he'd placed on the car. All Ace had to do was sit back and watch his mark draw near. He leaned against the Ford Expedition he'd stolen from the dealership the night before. The phone vibrated. *Vixen. She's persistent.* He declined her call for the sixteenth time in eight hours. *Well, so am I.*

As Ace saw it, Vixen was the love of his life; his heart, the clay in her hands. Sure, she was twenty years his junior, but everything about her awoke him inside. *Then she kissed Chase.* Ace's grip tightened on the phone. *And she returned to him, deliberately disobeying my direct order.* His chest blazed like a kiln, hardening his heart. *How did he survive two assassins?*

Powder Keg ruined everything. Chase shouldn't have survived.

"He was dead."

The phone vibrated again, alerting him to a voicemail.

Ace threw the phone across the parking lot. *I was too sure my trap would go off without a hitch.* He hadn't expected the need for a third assassin; therefore, he didn't line up the next test. Chase was injured and weak, and he couldn't strike. All his assassins were scheduled solid for a month and he wasn't allowed to test the recruits as Ace. Calling in someone from another card suit to test Chase could jeopardize everything.

Stop thinking about it. His watch always made him feel better. He stared into it. It was framed in white gold with a scratch across the window. The plate between the gears and hands had been removed so he could see the mechanism at work. Timing was everything to him, down to the very turning of each gear. He held it to his ear, closed his eyes, and listened to the pieces moving inside. The warmth in his chest dissipated. He took a deep breath and went to recover the phone. *It's going to be fine. One of these tests is bound to kill him.* He picked it up to find the screen cracked, but the display functional. *I just need to be more creative with who I throw at him.*

"Move your car," came a man's voice.

"I'm waiting for a friend," Ace said, turning to see a young Caucasian man in his mid-twenties wearing a polo. "I'm from out of town and thought I'd meet him here." It wasn't a complete lie. He was from out of town and waiting for someone.

The young man pointed at a handicapped sign. "They don't have disabled parking where you're from?"

Ace took a long drag from his cigarette. "They do."

"Then why park here?"

"What's your name?"

"Quillium." He folded his arms. "Now, move your car." The young man's eyes caught Ace off guard. They seemed to stare to the soul.

Let's see how he takes the truth. "This is the perfect place for me to park in order to kill my mark."

"Go kill *Mark* somewhere else," Quillium said, unflinching.

"His name's not Mark. He is a mark. Like a target or a hit."

The young man's expression remained the same. "I'd hate

for the police to give you a ticket right before you kill someone."

This kid's not backing down. Ace noticed the wedding ring on his finger. *How about a direct threat?* "I'm sure your wife would appreciate you coming home. Leave me alone or I'll aim to kill another tonight."

Quillium cocked an eyebrow, his eyes boring deeper into Ace. It was as though he could see everything Ace had ever done or ever would do.

"I'll kill you where you stand," Ace pressed.

"I believe you."

He really does. It was eerie, but Ace found it curious. Quillium knew he was in danger, yet there he stood, fearless.

Ace flicked the spent clove at the young man's feet. "You've got balls." Another cigarette rose, a flame sparked, and smoke warmed his throat. "My name's Ace," he said, smoke escaping between the words.

"Just move your car, man," Quillium said, irritation rippling his calm.

"When an assassin has the perfect vantage, there's no moving him." Ace checked the phone. The drone and his mark were still a ways off, but he needed to prepare. *Time to end this conversation.* "There are two parking places here for the handicapped. I'll move when the unlikely happens and two vehicles with disabled people arrive simultaneously."

When there was no response, Ace glanced at Quillium. The young man was looking through the window at a woman inside.

"Well?" Ace said.

Quillium met Ace's eyes and frowned. "We're closing anyway." He opened the door for the coworker. "We good?"

"Yep, everything is done," the woman said, a bike helmet gripped in her right hand. She put her free hand out to shake Ace's. "I'm Ruby."

"Sorry," Ace said, lifting both hands to show one held a cigarette, the other a phone.

"Right, sorry." Ruby laughed. She smacked Quillium's arm. "I'm biking home tonight, so I don't need a ride."

"Cool," Quillium said, locking the doors.

Ruby fastened the helmet to her head and glanced at the Expedition. "That's a handicapped space, sir."

Ace feigned confusion. "Is it?"

Quillium raised an eyebrow. "He needs a jump from my car. Then he'll be on his way."

Earlier he wouldn't back down. Now he's helping?

Ruby knelt to undo the bike chain. "It's supposed to rain tomorrow."

"I'll pick you up," Quillium said, his eyes remaining on Ace.

She mounted the bike. "See ya then," she said and waved at Ace. "Nice to meet you."

Ace nodded once and watched Ruby speed away. "Nice gal." When Quillium failed to reply, Ace sucked on the clove, nodding slowly as smoke seeped out the side of his lip. "Must be a friend for you to protect her."

Quillium glared and pressed a button on his keys.

Lights flashed on a Ford Taurus. A Richard King Ford dealership badge was stuck to the back.

"That your car?" asked Ace.

"Nope," Quillium said, walking toward it. "I just happen to have the keys and feel like committing a felony."

"Hey, that's what I did," Ace said, tapping the Expedition. "Small world. Can't believe both of us stole a car from Dick King."

Quillium turned. "He has some powerful friends."

"You know him?"

"I worked at his dealership for a year. He's an egotistical asshole with the police in his pocket."

"Glad you hate him." Ace sucked on the cigarette until the remaining tobacco smoldered to ash. He blew a thick trail of smoke in the air. "He dies tonight. What's the weapon of choice, you ask?" He gestured enthusiastically at the Expedition and spoke in the voice of a game show host: "A brand new carrr! 2017 Ford Expedition, great for the largest of families. Perfect for—"

"Carrying large weapons and dead bodies?"

Ace narrowed his eyes. *I like this kid.* He looked him over. *I was around his age when I killed for the first time.* "Wanna watch?"

For a long while, Quillium stood quietly beside the Taurus, eyes delving into the soul.

It took everything Ace had to look away. "You see, I like to set up one thing after another. Then I watch as the dominoes fall." His mark must have gotten stuck in traffic, because he was farther off than expected. "The final domino crushes them."

"You do the same with your cigarettes."

"What's that, now?"

"Each, a domino creating a picture of cancer." Quillium walked over to look at the phone. "You believe smoking gives you control over how you die. But cancer isn't tamed. It's chaos. Only a fool thinks otherwise."

Well, that took an interesting turn. Ace decided to change the subject. "I take it you didn't like working for Mr. King."

Quillium forced a laughed. "Worst job I've ever had."

"Never much cared for car salesmen." Ace nodded. "You two have a difference of opinion?"

"I didn't take kindly to being struck."

Ace lifted his phone. "Hope you beat his ass."

"Unfortunately, no. I held back my inner demons that day. I sued him instead. His lawyers were better."

"Shame." Ace looked at the screen. "Rich men could use some smacking around on occasion. Deflates their ego."

"Trust me," Quillium said, "next time someone pushes me around, I won't hold them back."

Ace raised an eyebrow. "Them?"

"My demons." Quillium pointed at the phone. "If that's a live feed, he's not far away."

Time to work. "It's been nice chatting with you, but I have less than two minutes to prepare. Feel free to watch, but no more distractions, thank you."

Quillium looked at the Expedition. "Who hired you?"

"That qualifies as a distraction." Ace reached through the broken window and pulled out a remote control.

Quillium looked at the remote. "You're serious, aren't you?"

Ace looked at the young man. "You know I am. You saw through me the moment we met." He looked back at the remote. "But, for some reason, I don't scare you. I don't know what I want to do more: kill you or hire you." He pressed a button and the Expedition roared to life. "I won't kill you because you intrigue me. And our current recruit is still alive, so I can't count this as an approach."

"Glad I'm safe from both. I'd make a horrible hitman and an ugly corpse." He looked the remote over. "You're going to drive the Expedition like an RC car?"

"That's the plan." Ace pressed a button. The Expedition clicked and the gear shifted into drive. Ace released the brake and nudged the joystick. The car inched forward. "I'll drive it down the hill and ram it up Dick's ass."

Quillium looked at the road. "The street we're on is empty, but how will you avoid southbound traffic?"

Ace pretended to ignore him, his eyes focusing on the Lincoln Navigator pulling onto Seth Child Road. With Richard two blocks away, Ace glanced at the stoplight down the hill and hovered a finger over the button to turn the light red. He pressed and the light turned yellow, then red.

Richard's Lincoln Navigator pulled to a stop at the intersection.

Quillium reached for the remote. "You're going to hurt more than just him."

Ace pulled it away. "One moment you're on board. The next, you're grabbing at me."

Quillium reached again. "Innocent people are going to die."

Ace pulled a gun and pointed it at Quillium. "I'm changing my mind on the not killing you."

Quillium's eyes flickered. His hand snapped forward. Before Ace could react, the gun was in his face, the trigger clicking.

Kid's fast. Ace glanced over. "Not afraid to kill."

"Who the fuck?" Quillium said, voice deeper than before. He pulled the trigger again. The young man's eyes shifted back to the way they were. He studied the gun in his hand. "Sorry, but Chaos doesn't abide guns being pointed at my face."

"Let's just say, I've never been more relieved to have a fingerprint sensor on my gun." Ace nodded slowly while watching the young man's eyes. *He was a completely different person.* "Inner demons, indeed." He held out a hand. "The gun, please."

Quillium threw the weapon into the grass. "You think I'm stupid?"

"Far from it." Stepping out of the way, Ace pushed the joystick. The Expedition lurched forward.

Quillium jumped backward.

Ace felt the mirror pass within an inch of his arm. The Ford sped down the hill. "Let's test that Lincoln's safety rating."

Richard clearly saw it coming because the Lincoln accelerated. It was too late to avoid the accident for the Ford smashed into the back of the Navigator with a crunch. The Lincoln spun to face the opposite direction.

Quillium sighed in relief. "You missed everyone else."

"For now," Ace said.

The driver door swung open and an unharmed Richard King jumped out to assess the damage. The distance did not mute the curses he hurled at the empty Expedition. The moment Mr. King realized the vehicle was empty, he stared up the hill.

Ace waved before placing his thumb and middle finger together over a red button decorated with a black skull. "Go to hell, your majesty." He snapped his fingers, so the middle struck the skull.

At 26,000 feet per second, the impact of an explosion took out everything around the expedition. Richard was turned into soup. Quillium and Ace were thrown to the pavement of the parking lot. The store windows shattered.

"That'll 'bout do it," Ace said. He got to his feet and threw the remote onto the pavement. "Five-star crash rating, my ass." He looked at Quillium. "See ya."

The young man stood slowly. "What have we done?"

Ace went and picked up his gun. "*We* didn't do anything."

"I could have stopped you."

"You tried."

"Not hard enough."

"Your friend Chaos tried to shoot me."

Quillium's eyes finally met Ace's. "You've made me an accomplice."

"You're not wrong." Ace took the pack of cloves from his pocket only to find it empty. Tossing it beside the remote, he fished out a second pack from the inner pocket of his leather jacket. He put the clove to his lips and lit it. *Just another domino standing in line.* Smoke erupted from his nostrils. "You need to get out of here."

Quillium's eyebrows rose. "We have to call the police."

Ace pointed at the cloud of smoke. "Explosions tend to do that on their own."

"Holy shit," Quillium said. "I have motive." He ran to his car. In seconds, he was driving down a back road, away from the scene.

Wish I had more time to get to know his demons. Ace's phone vibrated. "Vixen again." He declined the call.

His mind returned to Chase surviving his trap. *I need to find a cleverer way of ensnaring him.* He smiled when his phone resumed buzzing. *Vixen.* She had never tested a recruit, so she'd turn the assignment down. *Unless I gave her something in return. Something too good to pass up.*

Chapter Ten

The Smell of Gunpowder in the Evening

May 12, 2016
01:02 AM EDT
New York City, New York

VIXEN'S phone announced, "This user's voicemail box is full."

Of course, it is. She hung up and stepped into her apartment. It had been a long flight home. Ace refusing to answer his phone made it feel all the longer. She looked at her call log. *57 outbound calls to that piece of shit.* Once inside, she climbed the stairs to her room, closed the door, and collapsed into bed. *Did I reengage the alarm?* She thought about it. *Did I have to disarm it when I came in?* She thought she might have ... *No, I didn't.* That wasn't shocking. She had a bad habit of forgetting to set it when she came and went. *I'm too tired to care.*

She gazed at the ceiling, attempting to quiet the many thoughts utilizing her skull as a bouncy house. She'd disobeyed

Ace, followed Chase to his testing, and watched Powder Keg drop a ceiling on Noose. All she'd accomplished by going was to reap another bountiful harvest of questions.

She tried Ace one last time. Yet again, he sent her to voicemail. His mailbox was filled with her messages already. Leaving another would be pointless.

I should really get some sleep. She rose and took off her blouse and bra. *Seriously, why two assassins?* Her shoes clunked to the ground. *Was Powder Keg a third test or there with his own agenda?* She pulled off her jeans. *Why do I care so much?* Balling up her clothes, she threw them in the general direction of the hamper.

The light was still on.

She covered her eyes with the crook of her arm. "I don't wanna." She remembered why she bought the apartment in the first place. She scrolled through the apps on her phone until she came to the one that controlled damn near everything. The lights went out. *Much better.* She dropped the phone on the opposite side of the pillow.

She pulled the covers out from under her, settled underneath, and closed her eyes. *How had Chase survived?* "I'm going to sleep," she reminded herself. She took a deep breath and let it escape. *Was he meant to?* "Uuugh, shut up!" The thoughts seemed outside of her now. Her imagination gave them form. She could hear them breathing, walking. She imagined one sitting in her rocking chair. They wouldn't let her be. *Why had Ace cut their training short?* She tossed. *Why won't he pick up his phone and explain himself?* She turned. *And the bomb...* She sat up in bed.

Something tickled her nose. Smoke. She breathed in deep. *From the bomb?* She smelled her arm. *It's not me. Maybe I smell it because I'm thinking about it.* She convinced herself that was the case.

"Dammit," she said, looking at the moonlight spilling in through her open door. *Screw it.* She decided to ignore it. As tired as she was, a little light wouldn't keep her from—*I definitely closed my door.* Her eyes widened. *And the smell of smoke is too strong to be imaginary.*

One hand pulled blankets to cover her breasts while the other retrieved the GLOCK 26 concealed under her pillow. She pointed the gun at a dimly lit, billowy silhouette of a man sitting in her rocking chair. "Powder Keg."

"Hello, dear," he said. It always surprised her how clear his voice came through the military-grade gas mask. He'd explained before that he installed a voice amplifier of his own design. It barely inhibited his voice, if at all.

She lowered the gun. "Why are you here?"

He turned on the lamp beside the rocking chair. Besides the gas mask, he wore the usual white bomb uniform, black gloves, and boots. "I'm not here to harm you," he assured.

"If I thought you were, the gun would be aimed at your mask." She fought the urge to pick it back up.

He leaned forward, peering out from behind the lens. "I'm here to apologize for almost killing you."

"Noose deserves that apology, followed by Pockets and the recruit."

A thunderous chuckle broke through the mask. "Pockets maybe. Noose would kill me on sight." He stood from the chair. "And the recruit is why I'm here." His hand rose from his side.

As though instinct ruled over her, the gun was back in hand.

"You're jumpy," he said. "I would be, too, if a bomb were under my bed."

Her eyes narrowed. "You're surprisingly quiet, I'll give you that. Sneaking into my room is one thing. Tucking bombs under my bed without me noticing, in that bulky ass uniform ..." She tilted her head. "Nobody's that good."

"Far from it, dear," he said, returning to sit in the rocking chair. "I was here before you arrived. I was waiting on your balcony when you came in. You were too distracted or weary to notice the alarm was disengaged." He nodded at the open door. "I didn't know where we'd talk. There's a bomb under your couch as well."

He's lying. Just in case he wasn't, she took her finger off the trigger. The gun remained aimed at his face. Swallowing anger and fear, she decided this was an opportunity for answers. "Were you a *third* tester?"

"No," he admitted.

"There were four of us down there. Why violate the laws of our Guild?"

"I didn't expect you to be there." He leaned back in the rocking chair. "Mind you, that wouldn't have stopped me from carrying out judgment."

"Judgment." She forced a short laugh. "That was nearly an execution of three brotherhood assassins and a recruit." She paused, letting that sink in. "Successful or no, that's punishable by death." She returned her finger to the trigger, wanting to make clear she wasn't afraid to carry out a judgment of her own. "I don't think there's anything under my bed."

Powder Keg sat silently.

"Answer me," she said.

"Was there a question?"

"You didn't answer the original. Why?"

"Because two assassins were sent to test one recruit at the same damn time, Vixen."

"I'm certain that was an error in scheduling."

"It wasn't." Powder Keg rocked in the chair. "I overheard Ace tell Noose when the test would begin. Then Ace told him, 'Whether or not you believe Chase fits, do everything in your power to kill him.' Then he called Pockets immediately after, repeating the same time of testing, same spiel, same everything."

Vixen shook her head. "Ace wouldn't do that."

"No?" said Powder Keg. "I'll prove it to you—if you don't shoot me for moving my hand to my mask."

"Are you actually going to take it off?"

He laughed loudly. "Hell, no." He pressed something at the base of his mask. It lit up with a faint blue. "Don't worry. I can't shoot lasers from this."

I'm so confused. "Then what are you doing?"

"Playback bookmark seven hundred and twenty-three."

B723 appeared in red across the mask. Ace's voice came, quiet, distant, muffled.

"Activate external speaker," Powder Keg commanded.

Ace's voice erupted: "Even if you like him, do your best to kill him." Ace paused. "Thanks, Noose. Report to me after."

"End playback," Powder Keg said. The red numbers dissolved.

Vixen raised an eyebrow. "Despite how cool I suddenly think your mask is, that recording is out of context. You can't just—"

"Playback bookmark seven hundred and twenty-four."

The red glow of B724 illuminated Powder Keg's face within.

"He's special is all," Ace said. "Do everything in your power to kill him." There was a pause. "No, I'm simply asking you to test him more thoroughly than you've ever tested a recruit before." Another pause. "No, Pockets, I'm not saying you generally hold back or that you suck at testing. I wish only to prove to Thanatos that Chase is more worthy than the chick from Virginia." Another pause. "I'm sorry. I forgot she was your find." A longer pause. "Then you should want him out, so we can bring her in." A short pause. "Fine, that's your prerogative. Test him as you will."

"End playback," Powder Keg said, B724 fading.

I bet Ace took Noose's phone call. She couldn't think about that now. "The explanation was there," she said. "Chase was tested thoroughly to prove he was more qualified than Shuriken."

"Sure." Powder Keg rocked. "Still proves they were sent at the same time."

"That I didn't hear."

"Playback bookmark—"

"Fine, I believe you," said Vixen. "The same explanation applies."

Powder Keg stopped rocking. "The boy was dead before the tests began, Vixen. That was Ace's intent. Not some bullshit about him being more qualified."

Why am I arguing when I fear the same? She bit the inside of her lip to keep her expression firm. "Pockets mentioned you two shared a flight. Did you intend to bomb the testing?"

"As a last resort," Powder Keg admitted, pressing under

his mask. The dim, blue light went out. "I hoped Ace would fail and the recruit would survive on his own, despite the odds stacked against him. I knew I couldn't intervene without breaking the rules. I was determined not to." He pinched the glove over his knuckle. "I followed at a distance before watching you all delve into the ground. At first there was talking at the base of the stairs, then silence. I grew frustrated and found a hole further across the grass."

"You were above us the whole time?"

"I was." He looked at her. "I wanted to come down and stop them. Tell them it wasn't right."

"I tried," she said. "Noose was adamant. Now I know it's because he was ordered to. He probably suspected Ace sent two assassins on purpose. And Pockets likely thought it was to thoroughly prove Chase was the right pick. Neither mentioned the order feeling off until they thought you were the third."

"Noose was a soldier," Powder Keg explained. "Can't fault him for following the orders of a superior."

"I suppose that's true." Vixen put the gun down and laid on her side. "And Pockets?"

"Like you said," Powder Keg said. "He thought it a more thorough test." He rocked back in the chair. "I waited over the hole, listening. There'd be drawn-out silence, then fighting, a cry of pain, more fighting, then silence. It drove me insane not being able to see. There was a moment I had to back off because Pockets entered the room directly below me."

She smiled. "Chase had an empty gun pointed at him."

Powder Keg chuckled behind the mask. "That's my boy."

"Your boy?"

"What can I say?" he said. "I'm invested now."

She pressed her lips to the side. "You said you were determined not to intervene. Why did you?"

Powder Keg stopped rocking. "The recruit appeared right below me. He was a gazelle being torn apart by lions. I didn't think about it. I planted a precision explosive over Noose and, before I could stop myself, I set it off."

She was confused. "Even with a precision explosive, how could you know Chase would be free of the blast?"

Powder Keg nodded his head left then right. "True, the explosion could have killed him. But he would have been certainly dead without it." He stood. "And I was hopeful Noose could survive the ceiling collapse." His eyes watched her from behind the mask. "Two assassins, Laura. That does not happen."

"Vixen," she corrected.

"I came to say sorry, and I have." He went to leave. "Sleep well ... *Vixen*."

She jolted. "Wait."

He stopped in the doorway. "Pull the trigger or don't. That's up to you."

"No, it's not that." She tucked the gun back under her pillow. There were many things she needed to ask. "I don't buy that you sacrificed yourself for a recruit. I think you saved Chase because you had to. Maybe you feel guilty about something or maybe you have to be the one who kills him."

"What are you accusing me of?"

"Are you the bomber who killed his family?"

He bowed his head and sighed long and slow.

"That a yes?" she pressed. "Because I told him you weren't. Was it an unsanctioned hit? Maybe you hated them. I don't know. Or were they bad people and the hit was sanctioned?" She paused to let him reply. His silence ushered her on a different path. "Maybe you feel guilty because it was an accident. His uncle Frank was on the bomb squad. Maybe he traced evidence from similar explosions to you. Found something that would draw you out of the shadows. Draw the Guild out of the shadows with you. I could see that forcing your hand. Is guilt what forced you to save Chase?" Silence. "What about him made you throw away your life?"

He adjusted as though nervous. "Do you know why Ace cut your training short?"

She wanted to stay on point, but also needed that answer. "No."

"You kissed Chase."

"Why would that upset him?" she said. "I kiss everyone."

"Not like that you don't."

"Like what?"

"There are cameras set up for surveillance in every recruit's home. You know this."

"I do, but they're only observed before the approach. A way to be sure we have the right person and to know where and when they let their guard down."

"Ace is obsessed with this recruit. He hasn't stopped watching." Powder Keg leaned against the doorframe. "I was walking down the hall when Ace swore like a madman and began throwing things. Seconds later, he burst from his office, phone pressed to his ear. Didn't take long to figure out he was yelling at you to cut the training short and come home."

She furrowed her brow. "Why does he care?"

"Are you that blind, Laura? The only person he's equally obsessed with is you." Powder Keg left, closing the door behind him.

"Wait," Vixen called, but his footsteps descended the stairs. "Powder Keg?"

She heard the alarm pad beep as though the code were being input, then the front door closed. It chimed twice shortly after to confirm the alarm was armed.

She remembered Powder Keg's threat of a bomb. After dropping to catch herself on palms, she peeked under the bed. An orange origami butterfly sat within reach, words written along the wing. She snatched it up, unfolding to read:

Made you look.

~ Powder Keg

Chapter Eleven

Eagle's Eye

THE second figure bore the likeness of a leader, weapons forward, commanding troops to war. It stood for the assassin who took requests for action and distributed them among Guild members.

May 12, 2016
12:12 PM EDT
Montpelier, Vermont

~ Ten of Spades ~

GAZING down the scope of her custom-built sniper rifle, Eagle snapped her fingers, committing to the kill. Through the scope, she could see the checkmark scar on the congressman's neck. Calm washed over her. The math was done, the minute of angle adjusted for a six-hundred-and-seventy-yard shot.

Beast stood on the rooftop beside her. "Heavy, warm wind

coming in from the west."

She adjusted, lined up her shot again, and placed her finger over the trigger. Her target's wife leaned in, obstructing the view.

Eagle took her finger from the trigger. *Move it or lose it.* Patience was her greatest weapon, but the woman had leaned forward three times already. "God wants this lady to die."

"Need me to check the wind speed again?" Beast held up the Kestrel weather station. "Yes? No?"

"I'm good."

The woman sat back.

Eagle let out a long breath and returned her finger to the trigger.

"Wind shifted."

Groaning, she took her eye from the scope. "We're going to be spotted if this keeps up."

"We're fine." He held the Kestrel out for her to read.

"Thank you." She returned her eye to the scope, finger to the trigger. With the wind changing often, she aimed to strike the man square in the chest. She recalled a lecture from Thanatos. *Bullet dis size cleave anybawdy in twine.* "Down you go." She squeezed.

The man's wife leaned forward, her face bursting like a melon struck by an anvil. The intended target jolted, his chest a gaping cavity.

Eagle cursed.

"Miss?" asked Beast.

"No," she said, looking at him. "My kill count increased by two."

Beast thinned his lips. "Whoops."

A police car pulled up below them.

"Of course," Eagle complained. "Told you this was taking too long."

"Supervisor or concerned tenant?"

"Supervisor."

"On it." Beast turned and ran, leaving her to pack up.

Eagle picked up the bullet casing from the ground and peeked over the edge of the building.

People looked back, pointing.

That's not good. She took the sniper rifle apart, snapping the pieces into empty segments of her prosthetic, completing it. She made her way to the opposite side of the roof.

Earlier, Beast had tied a duffel bag with sixty pounds of sand to a long, thick rope. He'd let it drop to the ground so he could measure how much rope was needed. He cut the rope and secured a handle, then wrapped it around the railing.

The door to the roof opened. Beast walked out first, winking at her. "I'm not sure what they saw," he said to those following him. "There's nobody here."

She jumped, barely glimpsing the uniform of the officer following her husband. The duffel bag counterweight passed her. Soon her feet came to rest gently on solid ground. She let go of the handle. It zipped upward and the duffel bag plunged.

Beast appeared, pointing straight ahead and yelling, "There's a skinny white dude running up the alley!" He vanished for a bit.

She counted how long it might take the officers to get back to the door and glanced up. *Five, four, three, two—*

Beast reappeared. He jumped. The duffel bag rose fast; his feet stomped down hard. "Got everything?"

Eagle nodded.

They walked over and hid behind an air conditioning unit.

Police ran past, clearly following the "supervisor's" word about the man fleeing on foot.

"I think we're good." Beast said. "The officers said there were reports of suspicious behavior. They were doing a routine drive-by when they heard the shot."

She rose. "I messed this one up, Alex."

He wrapped his arm around her. "Wasn't your fault. The wind and—"

"Stop," interrupted a man's voice directly behind them. "Put your hands behind your head and get on your knees. Both of you."

"Hold that thought," Beast said. His hands went to the back of his head as he turned. "Hello, officer."

Eagle turned as well to see a young man in uniform. *He's about to wet himself.*

"Um, get on the ground," said the officer.

"There a problem?" Beast said.

"Just get down."

"Of course." Beast began to kneel. Before his knee could touch the ground, he lunged.

The young officer reached one hand for his gun, the other for his radio.

Too late, rookie.

Beast had the young man by the throat, head-butted him, and thrust him against the building.

The officer went limp.

Beast's thumb rose to the young man's carotid. "He'll live." He let go.

The officer crumpled.

Beast returned to Eagle, wrapping an arm around her

middle and continuing their conversation as though nothing had occurred. "And that lady kept leaning in. I don't know how you're so patient. You're perfect, you know that?"

"I blew an innocent woman's face off."

"Hush now," he whispered before kissing the side of her head. "You're perfect." He looked around the corner. "We're clear 'til the next corner."

Eagle followed. The phone in her pocket vibrated. She pulled it out and answered. "Not a great time, sir."

"Job well done," Ace replied. "I thought Thanatos accepted the job, but whatever works. Explains why Beast turned down the hit I sent him."

She rolled her eyes. "We need to clear out of our current location, sir. And quietly."

"The client said you took out the wife as well."

"Couldn't be helped," she said. "Respectfully, I need to end this call, sir."

Beast peeked around the next corner. "The car's not far. I'll open your door. When I believe you're clear, I'll nod."

"Love you," she said.

He kissed her and left.

She returned her attention to Ace. "Sir, are we in trouble for killing the woman?"

"No, she fully supported the part her husband played in human trafficking. Killing the wife sends a message to those who might follow in his footsteps. Tells them their families aren't immune to the consequences of their actions."

God, he's long-winded today. "It was an accident, sir."

Ace laughed. "They don't know that. They'll run scared."

"There's a Chinese proverb snipers live by." She looked at Beast. He shook his head. *Not yet.* "Kill one man, terrorize a thousand."

"I love it."

"If we're not in trouble, sir, may I ask why you're calling?" She peered out to see an officer standing in the doorway of the apartment building.

The officer spoke into his radio: "Derick, I'm going to need you to respond."

She ducked behind the wall.

"Just texted you," Ace said.

There was a chime in Eagle's ear. She read the message. Thanatos had warned her Ace might request she test the recruit. "I respectfully decline, sir."

"That's an order, soldier," Ace replied. "Do everything in your power to take him out, and I mean everythi—"

"Sorry, sir," Eagle interrupted. "But no."

"I'm your Ace," he said. "I'm not asking."

Although she'd prepared many rejections, she went with the most direct. "I decline this assignment as I have the right to. I'm not in the army anymore. I don't have to shoot when a higher rank gives the order. According to Guild law, I can turn down anything I'm morally against."

"Well, now, that's not—"

"Thanatos made perfectly clear a sniper is not a test. We are only death. A sniper has never been called upon to test anyone. In fact, there is a law against it placed by the founder of the snipers in our Guild."

Ace cut in, "I doubt that's—"

"In the early 16th century, da Vinci laid down the law for how the weapon would be used, stating, 'Use it not as a test, but as a weapon of death.' You're free to look it up if you'd like. Since I'm escaping a crime scene at the moment, I can't do it for you. May I respectfully decline this assignment and be on my way, sir?" She let it rest, waiting for his response.

None came.

She raised an eyebrow. "May I go, *sir*?"

Ace let out a heavy sigh. "I'll find someone better suited to test the recruit."

"Sir. Yes, sir." She realized he'd already hung up.

Beast nodded.

Eagle walked briskly to the car and jumped into the passenger seat. Vibrating erupted from her pocket as she closed the door. "What now?" She took out the phone and answered. "Thanatos."

Beast pulled around a police car. An officer looked in at them. Beast nodded. The officer nodded back.

"Girl," Thanatos said, "know ya be answerin' correctly. Eh sniper is notta test. Tiz only death."

"That's what I told him," Eagle assured. "He has a hard-on for this recruit."

"Worry nah. Change is a comin'," Thanatos said. "You on da right side."

"I know I am."

Thanatos hung up.

Beast squeezed her knee. "I take it Ace wanted to have a long chat in the middle of our daring escape."

Nodding, she placed a hand over his. "Hopefully, we won't have to bother with him much longer. Change is on its way, whatever that means."

"Cryptic."

Eagle looked back to see police cars blocking off the street. "Whatever comes, we'll rise above it."

His thumb stroked her knee. "We always do."

Chapter Twelve

No Need to Explain

May 12, 2016
01:02 PM EDT
New York City, New York
Guild of Four Spade Suit Headquarters

VIXEN drove her crimson 2016 Mustang Shelby GT500 Convertible into the garage of the largest bank in New York City. She delved deep into the garage's sub-levels, met a dead end, and pulled into the handicapped space. The lowest level was missing an elevator so the spot would never be utilized. Upon pressing a button built into her steering wheel, a section of wall shifted back and slid aside. A room large enough to fit a tank appeared. She pulled in and pressed the button again. The wall closed behind her.

The screen in her dash shifted from GPS navigation to request a password. She typed in "Nyx" and the wall ahead shifted back and to the side. A hidden parking lot appeared before her.

Vixen drove in and pulled into her spot. She always felt strange parking in her space. Each space had a painted portrait of the card correlating with the assassin who owned it. Hers was the only one with a character painted in her likeness. In the portrait, she sat on a throne of thorns wearing a black dress. One hand rested on the throne with a black crown dangling from her fingertips. The other hand held a large strawberry. Juice or blood—she wasn't sure which—flowed from the fruit, trickling off her wrist.

Nightshade, her best friend inside and outside the Guild, was the artist. When she asked him why he'd painted a strawberry in her hand, he shrugged and said, "I think it's supposed to symbolize a heart. I didn't ask. Ace said that's how he wanted it and if I painted it any other way, he'd offer me only the worst assignments."

Everyone else had chosen their artwork. She wanted a pocket watch with a "Q" at its center. It would blur across the space as though swinging hypnotically.

Like many of his decisions, Ace had made this one for her. She'd wanted her office to be near the front. Instead, it was next to his at the back. She'd asked to become a certified Guild pilot. He refused, stating it a waste of time and resources. She'd mentioned buying a car only to leave the office to find a GT500 parked in her space. She loved her car, but that wasn't the point. It should have been her decision to buy it.

This controlling behavior annoyed her to no end. The only thing that aggravated her more was his current mismanagement of Chase's testing. *He has to explain himself.*

She stepped out to see Widow's black Alfa Romeo 4C Spider convertible. Widow's portrait was Vixen's favorite. It was painted to look like an aging card, the edges worn and cracked. Atop a web, spanning the entire space, sat a black spider in the shape of an eight. A red hourglass was at the center of the bottom oval, while the top oval had fangs. Where the two ovals touched, eight black legs spread across the card. The shadows and webbing gave it a three-dimensional look, making it eerily lifelike.

The Joker space was vacant a car. *Mica promised he'd be here today.* Nightshade had changed his portrait again. The last time she'd looked, the Joker was human, held batons between his fingers, and wore a jester's hat. Now the Joker sported the hooves, hindquarters, and horns of the god Pan. Instead of batons between his fingers, he held syringes. Crushed under a hoof was the jester's hat, tattered and worn. Painted twice in a state of decay was the word JOKER, upside down at the top right of the card and right side up along the bottom left, completely backward from the usual card setup.

There were tattoos along the Joker's wrists. Vixen knelt to read them. Along one wrist read "Vérité," while the other read "Yquity." *Truth and Justice. He thinks he's the judge, jury, and executioner.* She thought about that. *I guess, to an extent, we all do. He's just honest about it.* She stood, her eyes glued to the portrait as a whole.

She became permeated in the aroma of clove cigarettes. There was only one person she knew who allowed those bad habits to dangle perpetually from his bottom lip. He often had another lit seconds before vampirically draining the current one of its glowing soul. Before she could turn to greet him, his arms wrapped around her.

She squirmed. "Why do you do that, Ace?"

He squeezed. "I'm proud to be the only one who can sneak up on you."

You didn't. "I meant, hugging me from behind." She pulled from his embrace to stand at the center of Nightshade's space. She faced Ace before dusting ashes from her shoulder.

He looked down at the parking space. With a flick of his fingers, his spent cigarette hit the concrete and he crushed it with the toe of his shoe. A black scar smeared across Nightshade's portrait. "The Fool changed it again," Ace said, before pulling a nearly empty pack of cloves from his pocket. "He looks like a demented goat in this one."

She shrugged. "I like it." She gestured at her own. "If you want demented, move my car."

"Yours is beautiful." He stepped forward, reaching for her hand.

She pushed him away as convincingly playful as possible. "Where is Nightshade?"

"I sent him to exchange currency," Ace explained. "You two might as well be conjoined twins when he's around. I wanted you to myself."

Of course, you did.

She'd always thought Ace hated Nightshade. He consistently said things like "Nightshade is disturbing", "He's not good for you", or "Can't you see he's screwed in the head?" Powder Keg opened her eyes when he pointed out Ace's obsession with her. It wasn't Nightshade Ace despised. It was the unshakable friendship she and Nightshade shared. She couldn't believe how blind she'd been to his envy. How would he respond to her betraying his trust by helping Chase during testing? *How will he punish me for the kiss?* "Ace, about the last few days."

"No explanation needed."

"You're not mad?"

He shrugged. "I'm not happy, but I've thought about it and I think it'll play to our advantage."

"Advantage?"

"Let's talk inside."

She looked at the Joker's space. "I'll be right in."

"His art will still be here when we're through." He placed an arm around her waist and began leading her to the sliding glass doors. "What we need to discuss is more important."

Why do I feel like this is a trap? They walked into the hallway and neared the door that led to the hole. She had never been to it, but knew the name summed it up: a hole chiseled from cold concrete, ten feet deep with walls separated by three feet. It was a punishment suited for Guild members who stepped out of line. *Does my disobedience qualify?* Her stomach turned.

Ace's arm flexed across her spine. "Why do you pull away?"

She hadn't realized she was. "I'm a bit ..." She swallowed, her eyes widening at the hallway to the hole. "I think I'll—"

"What is it?" Ace followed her eyes. "You think your actions are worthy of that?"

"I didn't," she said, this time consciously backing out of his reach.

He laughed loudly, walking past the terrifying hallway.

Her entire body settled. Yet, the feeling of being trapped remained, itching at the back of her skull for escape. "I've never disobeyed you before."

"No, you haven't." He stopped at the conference room.

"But I'm a forgiving man. And you'll make it up to me." He gestured to the door.

She walked in. "I can cover a hit or two of yours." She brought out her phone to check her schedule. "I'm free in parts of November." Her eyes rose to see he'd closed the glass doors behind them.

His thumb swiped over a sensor and the glass frosted, plunging the conference room into privacy mode. "That's not quite what I had in mind."

Her eyes narrowed at him and the door. "I'm not sure what you think is going to happen, but—"

"Your mind today," he interrupted. "Who do you think I am?"

"I don't know anymore, Ace," she admitted. "You cut my training short for no reason, sent two assassins to test one recruit, and refused to pick up when I called for answers. I've never felt more at odds with you. You've lost your mind with this recruit."

He gestured at the table. "Sit and I'll explain."

She walked around the table, arriving at the Queen of Spades etched into the glass. "Please do," she said, taking her seat.

He pulled his chair out, sat, and leaned forward. "I've been watching Chase for a while. He has far more potential than you know. He's more qualified than even he knows. The only time he reveals the extent of his proficiency is when he's pushed to breaking."

"I'd believe you meant only to push if you'd sent one assassin with the order to do all in their power to kill him." She leaned back. "But you sent two, leading me to believe your intent scales more toward the breaking."

Ace's finger ran along the Ace of Spades etched into the glass in front of him. "I'll admit I got a tad overzealous." He tapped the A. "Thanatos has been on my ass for recruiting Chase over another. But I'm telling you: He's worth it. A bomb waiting to go off." He winked.

"I don't think Noose would find that funny."

Ace laughed. "He needed a vacation."

"I'm sure he would've preferred the Caymans over a hospital."

He shrugged. "Testing a recruit isn't easy money. He knew the risks going in."

Enough small talk. What does he want? "You said you had something in mind for me."

"Huh?"

"Something I could do to make amends."

"Right, right." Ace stood and walked behind her. "Chase trusts you."

"I told him not to."

"Yet, he does."

"I believe so." She tried to swivel her chair to face him.

He stopped her by leaning over the top, hands dropping to massage her shoulders. "And he clearly likes you."

"Surrre?" She slapped his hand. "Why are you—"

"And he believes you like him?"

"I think so."

"And you kissed him, planting the seed for future growth."

She slapped his hand again. "Could you stop?"

His hands ceased rubbing, allowing her to swivel so their

eyes could meet. "I have a challenge for you."

"Challenge?"

"Test Chase."

"I'm the training, not the test."

"Come on." Ace sat in the chair belonging to Scizzors, the Guild's Jack of Spades. "It'll be the easiest ten grand you've ever made."

"I'm already being paid twenty to train him, which *is* the easiest money I'll ever make since you won't let me spend time with him."

He nodded. "On that, I've reversed my thinking. Return to train him. Make him trust you, like you, ... love you." He grinned. "Then, when you feel he won't expect it, test him."

"If I were to test him, which I'm not agreeing to do, it's not like I'm able to choose when to spring the trap. You love leading people into snares, but that's all about timing. If a moment comes and I know he trusts me completely, I can't fluidly test him when Guild law gums up the works."

"Guild law technically allows the tester to set their own time."

She raised an eyebrow. "Only the Ace and the King are allowed to do that."

"Wrong," he said. "The law doesn't actually specify by whom the time is set."

"That seems like an important rule to leave out."

He chuckled softly. "Right? It was left implied, but implied does not a commandment make."

"None of this sounds right," said Vixen.

Ace shrugged. "You're welcome to read it. Zetta pointed out the error three years ago. I didn't alert the other Aces because I knew the oversight might one day come in handy."

"You're taking advantage of an oversight?"

"Not I."

She looked at the etching of the Queen of Spades and bit the inside of her lip. *This is wrong on so many levels.* If she nurtured the trust Chase had in her, he'd walk right into the trap's teeth. *I could attack while he's wary.*

"I can tell you're thinking about it. Let's sweeten the pot." Ace leaned back in the chair, crossing his arms. "Do this and I'll let you train to become a Guild pilot."

Her eyes snapped up. *Now that's something I didn't expect.* "Don't joke."

"I'm not."

Her eyes narrowed.

His narrowed mockingly. "I'll even process the paperwork."

This still feels wrong, but that license would double the contracts I can take. "I'll attack when I get back."

He shook his head. "He'll be suspicious after the last tests." He tapped the table with his knuckle. "No, I need you to wait until he's putty in your hands. Keep training him, but say you're disobeying the Guild to do so." He snapped his fingers. "Give Chase one of Zettabyte's toys—the one that disrupts cameras and microphones. Tell him it'll allow you to train him without the Guild knowing. Say we've been watching."

"I hear you have been."

"Yeah, no, that's true." He raked his bottom lip through his teeth. "I have plenty riding on him. I've lost my head a few times, but no more. I need to back off and let the pieces fall on their own."

"Me being one of the falling pawns?"

"Pawn?" His brow wrinkled. "No, sweetheart. If we're going with a chess reference, it's never been more fitting that you hold the Queen card. It's the piece that moves more freely than the others. All the more reason to allow you the loophole to set your own time."

"Chase is a good person," said Vixen.

"I know," Ace laughed. "What's up with that?"

"He won't see me coming if I bait him into trusting me."

"Loving you."

She blinked at him. "You realize *love* takes more than training alone."

"I do."

"You're jealous of my friendship with Nightshade. How will you react when I court Chase?"

"If it's on my order, there's no reason to fear reprisal."

"Zetta's disrupter will cause the image to go fuzzy and the microphones to pick up interference. Everything Chase and I do will be left to your imagination."

"I'm a grown man, Vixen. Not some boy watching channels he's not supposed to, peering at static, hoping to glimpse a breast."

"Don't kid yourself. You'll watch. And every time I'm there, you'll misinterpret what you're glimpsing."

He looked away, his finger picking at the Jack of Spades etching. "Do what you have to."

"I'm not saying I'll sleep with Chase," said Vixen. "I'm saying you'll believe I am regardless."

"And I'm fine with that," Ace said. He was clearly not. "He's more important than my sanity."

"Comments like that feel like you're selling more than me on this."

He made a fist over the Jack of Spades. "Vixen."

"I'm done," she promised. "I've made my point. You only listen when your temper rises. Now you can't blame me when you develop an ulcer."

He relaxed his fist and hinted at a smile. "It's refreshing how well you know me."

"Tell me something," she said. "What happens if Chase falls for your trap? If he dies?"

"Then he's not as qualified as I believed him to be. I'll concede to Thanatos and we'll recruit his first choice."

"And you're fine placing your pride in the hands of a recruit? In the hands of a man who never killed anyone in his life? Who, until recently, believed he'd follow in his uncle's shoes and become a cop? A man happy to color within the lines of the law?"

Ace's eyes wandered around the room before he knocked twice on the glass table. "I am."

She felt her mouth stray open. "You believe that much in him? Have you met him?"

"From a distance."

"Then you're aware he cares for others over himself. He held back during training, not wanting to hurt me. No matter how badly I punished him for it, he failed to commit full strength to his attacks. Then Pockets appeared. Chase turned to me and said, 'Should I get out and say hi?'"

"Well, he'll learn to—"

"I'm not done," she said. "After the bomb went off, our medical staff arrived to take him to the ambulance. He refused to go at first because he wanted to make sure Noose was going to be all right." She stood for emphasis. "Chase was bleeding out, a knife *protruding* from his abdomen, yet he held up the ambulance for ten minutes while we cut Noose out of the debris."

"Are you done?"

She threw her arms out and dropped into her chair. "I could go on."

"Please don't." He smiled. "I know Chase better than you'll ever realize."

"'From a distance.'"

"Yes," said Ace. "He'll surprise you. Surprises me every day."

Her arms dangled off the sides of her chair. "Fine."

"You'll do it?"

"Yeah," she said, her eyes straying to look at the Queen of Hearts etching. "I'll do it." *And Chase had better surprise me.*

He clapped his hands and rubbed them together. "Right on." He jumped from the chair and strode toward the frosted glass doors. "The sooner, the better. I know you have that pharmaceutical salesman to kill today, but fly out after."

She needed to remind him of something. "You lined up hit after hit for me, going on for weeks. I thought it was to keep me from training him."

"Oh, right." He stopped in the doorway. "Everyone's booked so we can't just pass them off." He tapped the frosted glass with his knuckle. "That's my bad. But it'll give him time to heal."

"He'll need it."

"Then it's settled." Ace swept his finger over the sensor

and the frost vanished. "Once you've tested him, I'll tell the pilots you're ready for your wings." He winked, nearly skipping out of the room in his revelry.

Vixen sat in silence, her eyes returning to the Queen of Spades etching. *Feels like I traded my soul for a pilot's license.*

Chapter Thirteen

Jump

ANOTHER common figure was that of a beautiful woman. Her arms were often outstretched while standing among graves. She represented each chapter's Guild matron who trained recruits before testing, nursed them to health after, and prepared their bodies for burial if they died during the test.

May 12, 2016
03:28 PM EDT
New York City, New York

~ Queen of Spades ~

JOHN combed his hair and beard while appraising his reflection in the window. *Lookin' good.* He stepped into the clinic lobby and breathed in the chemically purified air. "That's the stuff."

An elderly woman looked up from a book, her eyebrow cocked.

He winked. "Smells so strongly of disinfectant. Any bacterium with an extra coil of plasmid would think twice about making an entrance, am I right?"

"I'm sorry?"

"No, I am," he said with mock apology. "Smart jokes don't land well." Although this was whispered under his breath, the glare she shot him made it obvious she'd caught every word.

She went back to reading a romance novel. At least he assumed it was a romance novel. The picture on the front was of a shirtless man riding a horse; a woman sat snugly behind him with her hands in the air.

Stupid old woman reading stupid trash about ruggedly stupid studs riding stupid steeds. For once he decided to think the insult over hiding it in hushed tones.

He reached the counter and smiled when a young nurse looked up from data entry. His eyes dropped to her large chest. "I like the way you pull off scrubs."

She crossed her arms over her ample bosom. "Excuse me?"

"Sorry. I have a hard time keeping my mouth shut around gorgeous women."

The elderly woman barked a laugh.

He leaned on an elbow and pivoted to point at the old cow. "Be a dear and bury your nose back in that horse shit." He turned back to the voluptuous young lady. "Your type gets me in all sorts of trouble." He grinned. "I'm imagining us in a coat closet somewhere, but I'm eager to hear your fantasy."

Her upper lip wrinkled. "Sign in and sit down."

"I'm not a patient." He lifted his briefcase. "John Shoemaker from Pharmakon Pharmaceuticals. Is Dr. Lessing about?"

"She'll be back from lunch shortly. Take a seat and fill these out." She handed him a clipboard with forms to sign.

"I'll answer these questions if you answer a few of mine," he said.

She sighed loudly. "I'd love to, buuut ..." She slid the window divider closed and returned her attention to the computer.

She enjoys playing games. John ran a hand over his beard as his eyes returned to her breasts. *Those gals should be allowed to breathe, not be caged behind fabric, all plump and lonely.*

She paused typing. "Stop staring at my breasts."

"What's that?" He tapped on the glass. "Can't hear you through the divider."

"Funny, I hear you just fine."

Palming the glass, he slid it open and leaned in so she couldn't close it on him. "I'm trying to get a read on you. I find you mysterious."

"The only mystery here is why you don't realize you're repulsive."

The elderly woman laughed so hard she began coughing.

The nurse stood. "Excuse me. Someone actually needs my attention."

He watched her go to the elderly woman. *Nurturing too. She's the whole package.*

"Mr. Shoemaker?" a woman said from behind him.

He turned and let his eyes measure up the sexiest woman in all the universe. Dark ringlets of hair cascaded against the sweetest pair of tits he'd ever had the pleasure of appraising. They weren't large like the young nurse's, but they were clearly firm and full and in need of his attention. If only her blouse didn't leave so much to the imagination. "Damn!"

"Pardon me?"

"Anyone ever call you a vixen?"

She smirked. "By what definition? Do you find me ill-tempered or attractive?"

"Gorgeous," John said. "I could happily drop dead after this encounter."

"Wouldn't that be something?" She winked.

He realized she'd said his name earlier. "Please say I've never met you. If I've forgotten a creature so divine, I deserve to be pushed from the top of this building."

"I'd never push you." She laughed and extended a hand. "I'm Dr. Lessing and I'm pleased to meet you."

His eyes widened as he received her perfect hand in his. *How many times will I put my foot in my mouth today?* "I apologize for everything I've said. My tongue might be the noose that hangs me."

"I doubt a noose will be your end, Mr. Shoemaker."

"Tell that to your nurse." He noticed the young woman from before returning to her desk.

Dr. Lessing gestured at a door with a sign that read STAIRS. "We can talk in here if she's making you uncomfortable."

"The stairwell?"

"My office is being used by another doctor. That shouldn't stop us from discussing business."

"Yeah, sure. That's cool." John walked through the door and placed his briefcase on the first step.

She looked at it. "Pharmakon Pharmaceuticals? Pharmakon is Greek for both the cure and the illness." She grinned. "Which are you selling?"

He laughed. "The cure, I assure you." *She's funny.* His eyes dropped to her chest, then to his briefcase. He opened it to take out the first package. "This is what they're replacing Zohydro with. Better for severe pain with half the risk of addiction."

She nodded slowly. "I'm surprised you're worried about drug abuse. Didn't someone from your company hand out opiates to homeless veterans?"

Not this. "I might have heard something about that."

"What was his excuse, again?"

"The DEA made it hard for vets to get their meds."

"So, handing drugs to people on the street was justified?"

He loosened his tie. "Yeah. When they're forcing vets to make the trek across town to get medical treatment once a month. Especially when those people are homeless. Have you ever been to a VA health facility?"

She nodded. "I have."

"Then you know they're few and far between and packed to the brim with people. And that was before the Fed's ruling. Now, they turn away more people than they treat."

"So, you pass out tranquilizers like candy because you're the cure?"

"Yeah. I mean, that was the excuse he gave. But they suspended that guy."

"Didn't stop you when you came back though, did it?" she asked.

He took a deep breath and let it out. *She knows.* "No."

"Not even when you heard people were overdosing."

"I can't stop helping the many because of the few who receive drugs from both the VA and me."

"You're not a doctor, John. You're handing drugs to people who don't need them."

"Some may not need them for pain, but they need them to sleep," said John. "PTSD is a real problem."

"I don't disagree," said the doctor. "However, you admitted giving highly addictive medications out for illnesses other than those they're generally prescribed to combat."

John took the package from her, threw it in the briefcase, and slammed the lid shut. "I see we're not doing business today. Thanks for your time." He extended his hand.

She took it. "Sorry to waste yours."

He tried to pull away, but she held tight.

Her expression turned thoughtful.

"Let go," he said, looking at their hands.

"I feel a quick heartbeat between your thumb and index finger. I know we disagree on some things, but may I try something to confirm my diagnosis?"

"You got me worked up, is all." He tried a second time to pull away.

"Not just fast," Dr. Lessing said. "Irregular."

"That's not good."

"Shhh." She brought his hand up in front of his face. "I'm counting." A minute of silence went by. "I'm a doctor and you trust I'll help you."

"I suppose. Why?"

"I need you to trust me so I can slow your heartbeat." With her free hand, she pointed at his wrist. "Stare right here."

"Oookay."

"This is a vision test. Do all I say," said the doctor. She tapped his wrist. "Hold your hand there and gaze into your wrist. Imagine you see all the way to the bone. Trust I'm doing this for your wellbeing."

John nodded and stared at his wrist, trying to imagine the bone appearing.

She came around beside him and slowly brought her free hand up between John's wrist and his face. "I'm putting my hand here and you're slowly closing your eyes." The doctor began to drop her hand.

John's eyes fluttered, his vision blurring as he continued focusing on his wrist, the bones clear in his imagination.

"Focus on your wrist," she began, her voice growing calm. "As you look at your wrist, you notice a force pulling your hand toward your face. It's magnetic and you can't stop your hand from touching your face." The way she repeated things in slightly different ways made him feel like he was drifting out to sea. "As it comes, you'll notice your eyes beginning to lose focus." Her words washed over him, sending him drifting further away from shore. "Your eyes begin to lose focus and when your fingers brush your face, you sleep."

John's hand touched his face and darkness swept over him. There was a soft, distant feeling of his body moving.

Snap.

He opened his eyes and heard the last of a statement.

"... you will wake," she said. "But you will be cemented to the floor. So, now you are cemented where you stand." She snapped her fingers. "You notice your surroundings but they'll not scare you. You feel like this is exactly where you're meant to be at this exact moment in your life."

Looking around, John saw he was on the edge of the roof. He glanced down at the street eighteen stories below. He usually hated heights, but this felt like the perfect place to perch. He didn't know how much time had passed since he'd been with her in the stairwell. Surprisingly, he didn't care.

"I'm a doctor and you trust me. If you trust me, nod up and down." She was to his right, nodding. "I'm a doctor so you trust me. Nod if you understand."

John smiled, nodded, and stared down at the people below.

"You are not afraid," she said. "When you look from a height of over one hundred feet, your eyes cannot truly focus, causing the stomach to turn ever so slightly. There's no reason to fear it. It's purely biological." The doctor stood next to him looking down. "You are relaxed and have perfect balance. You have perfect balance. I want you to face me now and look at my forehead. Your feet will become unstuck and you will look at me. Look right here at my forehead."

John turned and looked where the doctor was pointing.

The doctor went on. "You can see right through my head; right through to my brain and to the back of my skull. I'm going to take your arm and it's going to feel wet and heavy, like a moist towel." She did, and it did. "And when I drop it you are going to sleep. That's right," she said and snapped. "Sleep."

Darkness took John again. He could feel the thoughts going through his mind as if they were commands. *Everything she says will make me go deeper. Down, deeper into sleep. I will focus deeper on her voice, and everything she says will instantly* (snap), *and completely* (snap), *become my reality* (snap). *On the count of three* (snap), *and on that number alone I will awake* (snap). *One ... Two ... Three ...* (snap).

He woke, eyes staring deep into her skull.

"I'm a doctor and all that I say is truth," she said. "Nod your head if you agree."

She's my doctor. I believe in her. John nodded.

"Place your feet against the side of the roof," she commanded, "and stare down at all the beautiful people."

John turned, placing his feet at the very edge and looking at the people below.

"Nod if you believe they are beautiful," she said.

They're the most beautiful people I've ever seen. John nodded.

"As you look down, you feel a sense of wonder," she continued. "You know you are safe, for if you fall, those beautiful people will catch you. You know that if you jump, they will embrace you. If you believe this, nod your head."

They will love and protect me. John nodded his head.

"You feel a sense of foreboding," she went on. "This sense of foreboding is warning you not to leave this rooftop by the stairs. You know that if you take the stairs, the vibrations could force your irregular heartbeat to kill you. You feel your heart could stop beating and you'll die alone in the stairs. This is a fear that scares you to your core. You fear you'll die alone in an empty stairwell and nothing scares you more than dying alone. Nod your head if you agree."

Nothing scares me more. John nodded his head.

"You look at the beautiful people," she said. "If you think they are beautiful, nod your head."

They are. John nodded.

"You know they'll catch you if you fall. Nod if you agree."

They will. He nodded.

She stood beside him to look down. "If you leave by the stairs, your heart could explode without warning. If you left by the stairs, it would take you longer to get to all those beautiful people. If you agree, nod your head."

Too long. John nodded. *They're waiting for me.* He could feel the doctor looking at him, but couldn't pull his eyes away from the beautiful people.

She went on. "People fear heights because they fear the inherent desire to jump. This fear will not cripple you. This fear is lifted and you desire to jump. You feel this desire now. If you agree, nod your head."

John nodded, a desire to jump urging his toes to inch off the rooftop. Two birds were playing freely in the breeze.

"So many beautiful people waiting for you," said the doctor. "When I snap my fingers, you'll join them. When I snap my fingers, you'll leap from this building and spread your arms. When I snap my fingers, you'll fly to join all those beautiful people. Your heaven is no longer up here with me. Your heaven is waiting for you below. When I snap my fingers, you will fly to your heaven. Your heaven is with all those beautiful people, and they are waiting. If you agree, nod your head."

I'll show them I can fly. John nodded his head, feet inching forward. The wonderful feeling he had from standing on the rooftop dissipated. All he had to do to find that solace again was to join the beautiful people below. *My heaven is with them.*

The doctor snapped her fingers.

Spreading his arms, John nodded and from the building, he dove. He could feel the wind rushing against him, could see the beautiful people look up. They pointed, screamed, and rushed out of his way.

They're yelling for me to join them. He closed his eyes and felt the wind against his face. *The beautiful people are preparing for me a place to land. My heaven is there with all the beauti—*

Chapter Fourteen

Interrupted Mending

June 6, 2016
05:13 PM CDT
Kansas City, Missouri

IT took a week for Chase's wounds to stop waking him in the night. The doctor, Allison, checked on him multiple times, removing stitches and renewing his medications. Another week passed before the only remaining stitches were inside of him; those knitting his muscle together.

Allison told him to wait a month before doing minor exercises, strongly suggested he not lift anything heavy for two months, and demanded he steer clear of intensive core strengthening for three.

He'd thought the Guild would throw another test at him right away. Yet, the first three weeks had passed without a peep. Even Vixen hadn't returned to train. He'd expected as much. She'd broken the rules for him. Seeking answers was her excuse, but when Noose and Pockets closed in for the kill, her concern for him was absolute.

He'd spent most of the wait researching martial arts, finding ways to meld in his acrobatics. The second focus of his research was the many ways people kill one another. Knowledge would be his greatest defense. While he was injured, he believed preparation would be his only offense. If he couldn't take a hit, he'd need to avoid one. If he couldn't grapple, he'd need an alternative to survive.

He'd burnt through a quarter of his inheritance fortifying the house. Cameras and microphones were wired throughout and he'd hid short-range and long-range Tasers in the furniture. All of the lights, locks, windows, and doors could be operated from a remote in his pocket. Wherever his opponent was, he could lock them inside or outside with a push of a button to slow their approach. The greatest lesson he'd learned from the first test was every second mattered. Even if he barred the opponent a few minutes, he'd be a few minutes free of fighting. A few minutes could be used to secure a more optimal position.

The bomber from his first tests saved his life. That, combined with his uncle's past profession, made explosives intriguing. Chase didn't want to hurt anyone. His furtive study focused on blasts that could disable motor functions. His uncle Frank had books on the subject of bomb creation and disposal and the internet was ripe with information.

When Officer Clark returned Chase's car fully repaired from the accident, Chase asked where he could get the chemicals needed to make some explosives. Within days, his basement was full of them. He had shelves covered with canisters and corked vials, each labeled for the chemical mixtures they possessed. He even had a Super Soaker full of acrolein, a liquid as disabling as Mace. It had been three days since he made it and the room still smelt of burnt cooking grease.

Chase's most recent project was producing flash bombs. He had eleven. He was placing two of them on a shelf when something thumped above him. He brought the remote from his pocket and pressed the light bulb at its center. As one, the lights in his house winked out.

He grabbed the most expensive of his purchases from the table and put it on. The military-grade helmet could stop a rifle round, had a built-in gas mask, and included dual-mounted displays for cycling through camera feeds. Because the lights were off, the cameras should have switched instantly to night vision. However, something was wrong. Static was all he saw, white noise all he heard.

So much for knowing where they are. He slapped the side of the helmet, hoping it was a hiccup.

Nothing.

He took the helmet off and listened. Footsteps crossed the floor directly above him and stopped. *Maybe they don't know about the basement.* He could only hope. *Just in case.* He pushed a button on the remote and a level three, bullet-resistant glass door slammed shut at the base of the stairs.

Judging by the quickened footsteps, he'd given away his position. He'd forgotten how loud the door was when using the remote. *Should have walked the three feet and closed it myself.* He looked at the window, his only escape. Quickly, he put on the helmet, grabbed a lighter, and went to the shelves with the smoke bombs. *Which would work best?*

Footsteps on stairs rushed his decision.

He grabbed one and scratched a flame to life. His hand shook badly and the flame blinked out. He took a breath then brought forth another spark, lit the fuse, and prepared to throw it.

Too late. A woman's outline stood on the other side of the door.

He pulled out the fuse and took off the helmet. "Vixen?"

"Hi." Her voice was muffled behind the glass.

He went to the door. "Didn't expect to be seeing you."

She shook her head. "As far as the Guild knows, you're not." Her knuckle rapped on the glass. "May I come into your fortress of solitude?"

"Depends. Are you my next opponent?"

"Would I have tromped around upstairs if I were?" she smirked. "Besides, I don't test recruits."

He wasn't sure he could trust her, but opened the door anyway. Next, he pressed the bulb at the center of the remote to get a better look at her.

Her hair was up in a bun. She wore a blue, sleeveless blouse and tight jeans. After entering the room, her eyes immediately scanned the shelves and workbench. "I see you've upgraded a few things." Her eyes focused beyond him. "Why two water boilers?"

Shrugging, he followed her gaze. "I haven't a clue. Only the newer of the two makes any noise. I'm guessing the older was too heavy for Frank to remove on his own. He wasn't one to ask for help."

"Are they both connected?"

"I don't know. As long as everything works, I'm not worried about it." Returning his eyes to her, he saw her reexamining the shelves. "Do you hate it?"

"Are you kidding?" She twirled a finger in a circle. "This is amazing."

"I've kept busy."

She took a vial from the shelf. "Understatement of the year."

"Don't open that unless you feel like vomiting," he warned.

She chuckled. "I know what chloropicrin is." The vial was returned to the shelf. "According to our records, Allison visited." Turning and smirking, she added, "Often."

"Jealous?"

"Have to admit ..." She hoisted herself up onto the workbench and pointed the toes of her shoes at him. "I've dreamt of our last kiss."

I'm not that lucky. "Sure, you did." He ran a hand over the wound on his arm. "Allison wanted to be sure I was healing. She confirmed what you told me about Pockets."

"That being?"

"He struck perfectly." He tapped the scar on his arm. "If the knife had been a few inches over, it would have severed tendons or punctured my artery. Same story with my calf."

"Your abdomen?"

"Likewise," Chase said. "She did several scans, determining the wound was deep enough to damage muscle, but that no organs were harmed." He ran a hand across his ribs. "Radiograph proved my lungs were fine and my ribs unbroken."

Vixen smiled sweetly. "Good to hear."

"She said Pockets would have made an excellent surgeon with how sharp and sterile his blades were."

Vixen nodded. "He was a lawyer, actually."

Not a chance. "With that speech impediment?"

"Being trapped in a mine with little oxygen will damage a person."

Right. "How *did* that happen?"

The workbench creaked as she leaned back on elbows. "Class action lawsuit for fifteen wrongful deaths. A major mining company was accused of improper methane monitoring in Arizona, but they had records to prove they operated within regulations. A witness had proof the records were falsified, but he died in a car accident before he could testify. Other damning evidence was thrown out by the judge."

Chase furrowed his brow. "If they won, why toss Pockets in a mine?"

"Kevin wouldn't let it go." She swung her feet out and up to cross them underneath her. "Felt responsible for the families. He dug deeper and found evidence the judge had been bribed. Then he made the mistake of filing the case for judicial misconduct with the clerk."

"Ah," Chase said, putting the pieces together. "Clerk was on the payroll."

She shrugged. "Kevin got home early to celebrate his anniversary and found his wife on the kitchen floor, her throat sliced open."

Chase sat straight down on the concrete floor and shook his head.

Vixen continued. "He remembers something hitting him as he knelt over her and then waking up in the mine."

"How'd he get out?"

She leaned forward on her hands. "He'd sent a copy to a colleague of the evidence he'd found proving judicial misconduct. The news picked it up and Pockets went from being the most likely suspect in his wife's murder to the obvious victim." She gestured at the wall. "The day after his wife was murdered, the mining company reported a collapsed section. Was too convenient to be ignored so rescuers eventually dug Kevin out."

Chase stood. "Hope those bastards got what was coming." He placed the smoke bomb back on the shelf.

"Only the judge and the briber got any time."

Chase spun on one foot. "Are you *fucking* kidding me?"

"Kevin became Pockets and hunted them all down. He killed thirteen people before they caught him." Vixen dropped her legs off the side of the workbench. Her body followed. "We ghosted him out of police custody and finished off the rest. Technically, he's still in hiding."

"Why take the risk of testing recruits if it could land him in prison?"

"He believes we're the alternative to a corrupt legal system. If he were caught, we'd simply ghost him out again."

"Crazy." Chase stood. "I can't imagine becoming a lawyer only to end up losing my wife and becoming an assassin."

She picked up the helmet. "He's not wasting his law degree. He's saved us a lot of money by reading complicated contracts. Some businesses make the wording as difficult as possible so we'll screw up how the target is supposed to die. Then they'll argue we broke contract and demand a partial refund."

That makes no sense. "Why would you demand anything of an organization you know kills people?"

"It's business," she said then chuckled softly. "One time, a client said they wanted a guy poisoned, but the contract stipulated he be publicly decapitated. Scizzors dipped his barbed tail in Nightshade's dart frog extract, wrapped it around the guy's throat in a coffee shop, and pulled. The business paid us twenty percent more, they were so impressed."

"He has a tail?"

"Well, not exactly." She put the helmet down. "You'll see when he tests you."

"What?" Chase nearly fell into the shelf behind him. "I'm fighting a guy that rips heads off?"

"Don't worry about it." She tapped the helmet. "This is expensive."

Chase was still stunned. "I think I should be."

"Should be what?"

"Worried."

"You're still on that?" She put the helmet on. "Scizzors is a teddy bear," her voice came, muffled.

"Your childhood must've been messed up if your teddy bears walked around decapitating people."

"My parents didn't believe in giving children toys."

"While I appreciate the glimpse into why you are who you are, that wasn't my point."

Vixen took off the helmet and winked at him as she set it down. She approached him.

Chase backed into the shelf. "Why are you here?" He placed a hand back to steady one of the vials that rocked from his impact.

"To train you."

"I'm not gonna be much fun," he said. "Allison told me no heavy lifting for months."

She patted his chest. "We'll be fine." She admired the shelves and door one last time before heading for the stairs. "This sure is something."

Chase watched her go before opening a drawer and retrieving a Taser. He placed it in his back pocket and followed. "How about you lecture and I absorb your wisdom?" He came around the corner to see her heading up to his room. "Stairs aren't my friend. We can talk down here."

"I have jet lag."

"Oh." He started after her. "Let me swap out the sheets. I'd hate for you to roll around in my filth."

She ignored him and went in.

"It'll just take me—" He shut up when he found her tucked into the covers. "Sweet dreams, I guess. I'll be in the basement mixing chemicals if you need me."

She patted the bed. "Join me."

He stopped cold, heat climbing the hairs of his neck. Thoughts of her had haunted him every day she'd been away. She was seductive and beautiful, which begged the question: How does she assassinate? Movies portrayed hitwomen as poisoners or seducers who lured men into bed for the kill.

"Are you coming?" She yawned.

"I'm not tired." He looked away. "You know where to find me."

She appeared disappointed. "Are you afraid of me?"

"Are you kidding?" said Chase. "You disobeyed your leadership by following me to testing." He leaned against the door until it thumped against the wall. "Can't help but wonder if you need to prove your loyalty. And the last time you showed up, I was attacked. Today you've led me upstairs, away from my bombs. Oh, and you're an assassin."

"Feeling vulnerable, Hunter?" Vixen said. "Is that why there's a stun gun tucked in your back pocket?"

He reached behind him and brushed its handle with a finger.

She rose onto her elbows. "You also moved the furniture around. How many bombs are within reach right now?" She slid a hand under his pillow, pulling out another of his Tasers. "Judging by the types of bombs you've created, the weapons are meant to incapacitate while you flee."

"I thought I hid them better." He slid down the door to sit. "Felt I was more prepared."

"You did and you are," she admitted. "But, like you said, you allowed me to tempt you upstairs. What's rule number one?"

"Trust people to your detriment."

She threw the blankets off and perched on the side of the bed. "And rule two?"

He cocked his left leg and placed his hand over the remote in his pocket. "Don't drop your guard."

"Yet, you're on your ass." She sprung.

Chase kicked off the floor and darted for the stairs. He pressed the corresponding button on his remote. The bedroom door slammed shut, its lock thumping into place. He pressed two others and the locks to his front and back doors made a *thunk, thunk*.

Vixen jiggled the handle and slapped the door. "This is new."

"All the doors and windows are. Even the one you use to get in my room." He pressed a button and heard the window thwap shut.

"Clever," she said, knocking on the door. "Now let me

out."

"Find a way around it." Smiling, he started down the stairs. "Or take that nap. I know how tired you are from your trip." He chuckled. "Jet lag, my ass."

"Hunter, if you care for your room, do not leave me in here."

"It's all replaceable." He continued to the basement and put on the gas mask he'd left on the table. His smile widened when the sound of pounding came from above.

Finding the containers of hydroxylammonium chloride and sodium nitrite, he sat on his stool and went to work. He poured two parts of the first followed by one part of the second into a five-liter Erlenmeyer flask. The mixture began bubbling immediately so he stoppered it using a rubber cork with a tube running through it. The other end of the tube was fed into a chemist's 24- by 18-inch gas jar. He placed the flask over a burner and put the heat on low, quickening the chemical reaction. After a few minutes, he put a wooden toothpick under the flask to ignite it. Once he blew out the flame, he stuck the smoldering stick in the gas jar. The flame bloomed anew. *Good. It's working.* He shook the toothpick and tossed it to the floor.

There was a momentary silence in the thumping coming from upstairs. He tilted his head, listening. Something crashed then the thumping began again. He shook his head, a feeling of pride radiating from within his chest. *She's not getting through that door.*

He transferred the tube from the gas jar to a receiving bag. Leaning back, he watched it slowly begin to inflate. His favorite subject in school had been chemistry. He loved watching chemicals communicate with one another. They were much like people. Some didn't get along and had harsh reactions to being near one another. Others made love, giving birth to new chemicals. And some did nothing at all, simply ignoring each other before separating.

When the bag was nearly full, he realized he no longer heard Vixen slamming the door. *She finally gave up?*

He prepared another two parts hydroxylammonium chloride and one part sodium nitrite and set them aside separately. He lifted the first receiving bag, preparing to tie it off—

Someone grabbed his shirt from behind. The stool collapsed out from under him and his back met concrete. He'd been holding the receiving bag and accidentally tightened his fist around it as he fell, releasing the gas directly into the face of an irate Vixen.

She stood over him, the hanger pole from his closet gripped in her free hand. She began chuckling, shook her head, and cleared her throat. "That wasn't funny, locking me—" More chuckling. Another clearing of her throat. "Locking me in your room." Her voice was lower than usual. "You forgot the drywall." She laughed and backed away, lifting the iron bar in front of her face. "Why am I holding a stripper pole?"

"You're breathing nitrous oxide, Vixen." His voice was muffled behind the gas mask. He pointed to the house, just in case she couldn't understand him. "Get out of here before you inhale more."

She dropped the bar and stumbled away from him, grinning ear-to-ear and babbling, "I'd like to dance for you."

Chase quickly turned off the burner and followed her into the house. Vixen's blouse was on the floor, followed by her bra, shoes, and socks. He snatched up her shirt and ran around the corner to find her jeans meeting her ankles. Before she could take off the final article of clothing, he yelled, "Vixen, you're naked."

She turned.

Careful to look away, he held out her blouse for her. "Put your clothes on."

"You think I'm pretty."

"I do, but I'm not going to take advantage of you."

"I think *you're* pretty."

"Thanks," he said, smiling and shaking her blouse. "Please put this on."

She took the blouse.

He waited a bit before looking.

Her top was inside out, but at least she was covered.

She pointed at his face. "Woohoo, scary." She laughed softly before sitting on the floor.

He took off the gas mask and threw it on the couch. "Better?"

"I feel weird. Weird numb. Colors spinning."

He sat beside her, wrapping an arm around her back to brace her. "You'll be all right?"

"Yeah," she said, blinking. "Yeah." She giggled like a school girl and rested her head against his shoulder. "Yeah, yeah." Her hand clamped over her head. "Owy owy ow."

"Headache?"

"Mmmhmmm," she hummed. "I'm sorry."

"About what?" he asked.

She nestled her forehead into the crook of his neck. "The hole in your wall."

Her words from earlier echoed in his mind: *You forgot the*

drywall. "That's why you were holding the bar from my closet."

She chuckled. "Might be."

He gave her a squeeze. "Starting to wake up?"

"I didn't take a nap."

He laughed. "I meant from the gas."

"Oh, ha ha, yeah."

"Still numb?"

"Mmmm."

"May I ask how the next four assassins kill?"

"Why?"

He shrugged. "Fighting two of your brothers was unexpected. I'd like to be prepared if I have to fight four. I almost died in the first thirty minutes last time."

"Against four of us, you wouldn't last thirty seconds." She rested a hand on his leg. "I don't know how you survived two."

"I'm that good," he joked, placing a hand over hers. "It's not like I left with knives sticking out of me or anything."

"You're supposed to take a few hits. Survival is the point of the tests. And you passed ..." She poked his arm. "Admirably."

"Thanks." He patted her hand. "You ready to stand?"

"I think I'll sit a little longer, if that's all right. Or lie down." Shifting her body, she dropped her head into his lap.

He ran his fingers through her hair.

"You can do that all day," Vixen said, then jolted upright. "Oooh!" She pointed at the cookie jar on his counter. "Do you have cookies?"

"That's full of nuts actually."

"Nuts?" She laughed, dropping her head back into his lap. "Why are there nuts in your cookie jar when I want a chocolate chip cookie?"

"My uncle was allergic," Chase explained. "We couldn't have them in the house. I love peanuts, almonds, and cashews. Since he died, I've been trying to look on the bright side of things. So, now I have nuts in the house."

"That makes sense." She squeezed his thigh. "After my mother died, I ran away from home. Crazy to think I could have eaten pistachios to make my world brighter."

"It's not really working," he admitted. "I'd rather he be here instead."

"We are who we are because of them." She looked up at him. "Death is part of life. Especially if you become one of us."

"I guess that's true." He wrinkled his nose. "Sorry I locked you in the room."

"Don't be," she said. "That was perfect."

Taking the remote from his pocket, he handed it to her. "Lights, windows, doors, and locks."

She pushed buttons and thumps, clicks, and whirs followed. Lights went on and off, lock bolts shifted, doors opened or closed. "I have an app on my phone for my lights," she said. She brought up his lights and left them on before handing him the remote.

He took it from her. "So, less impressive than I thought."

"Not at all," said Vixen. "You set this up on your own."

"The cameras are all static, otherwise I'd show you how that helmet downstairs works."

"That's my fault." Her hand extended toward her jeans though they were far out of reach.

"Want me to get them?"

She nodded. "Yes, please."

He leaned her against the wall and retrieved them for her.

Adjusting, she placed her back against the wall and produced a small disc from a pocket. "When you were setting up cameras, did you come across any others?"

"Others?" He looked around. "No."

"Yeah, they're experts at hiding them." She put the disc on the ground in front of her. A green light lit at its center then faded. "The Guild cannot know I'm here. That gadget interrupts all cameras and microphones within 500 yards."

He picked it up, turning it over to see the word "Zettabyte" scribbled in black marker. "This thing has a zettabyte of memory?" He turned it back over. "How advanced are you people?"

She took it from him and looked herself. "Zettabyte is an assassin in our Guild. She's a hacker."

"I was gonna say. That's unbelievable." He rested his head against the wall. "Did you find out anything about the explosion? Was I the target?"

She met his eyes. "You swear you'll keep this between us?"

"'Course."

"An assassin put himself on the chopping block to save your life. He didn't think you being tested by two assassins was fair."

"I knew being tested by two of your people at once couldn't have been an accident."

"No. Which is why I'm here." She put the disc on the ground and pushed it with her foot. "And why I brought that to conceal my disobedience." She reached out her hands. "I'm good to stand now."

He helped her regain her feet before picking up the disc. "Thanks for returning to help. And for the answers."

"Trust me and I'll get you through this."

"What about rule number one?"

"It says trust people to your detriment as a warning, not a command."

"You made fun of me for trusting you in my room."

"That was before I realized you rigged the doors to slam shut with the push of a button. You trusted me to an extent, while secretly preparing for a strike. You reacted perfectly when I did." She gestured at the wall. "Take Allison, for example. We need doctors. Therefore, we rely on a few in every major city. However, we don't allow ourselves to fully trust them. We always plan a way around if things go sideways. As you did with the doors." She smiled and ran a hand along his arm. "Your mistake was believing I'd be caged for more than ten minutes."

"You surprised the hell out of me," said Chase.

"As did you, deflating a bag of laughing gas in my face," said Vixen.

"That was a *happy* accident."

"My headache says otherwise."

"You weren't the intended target, I promise."

"Maybe not, but it worked." She reached behind his back to take the Taser from his pocket. Holding it in front of her, she pulled the trigger. It *pop, pop, popped* and she released. "As would this on all but Scizzors." She placed the Taser in his palm. "A few bombs should drop him, though."

"That's more terrifying than helpful."

"He only looks and sounds terrifying." Her hand rose to cover a yawn.

"You weren't lying about the jet lag."

She yawned again. "I doubt you gassing me helped."

Wrapping a hand around her shoulders, Chase led her to the stairs. "After I assess the damage you did to my closet wall, I say we take that nap."

Vixen nodded slowly. "I made a mess."

Chapter Fifteen

Pervert Fishing

THE fourth figure was of a man wielding a bow in one hand and a sword in the other with up to seven other weapons tucked into his belt. This assassin was known as the Johannes Factotum, representing the Guild member with medial knowledge of all types of combat and weaponry. These assassins aided new members in finding a specialization. Although a powerful card, it could be beaten in strange ways.

June 6, 2016
11:57 PM EDT
Dover, Delaware

~ Jack of Spades and Three of Spades ~

TAYLA'S fingertips traced her belt until they tripped over the hammers of her guns, one holstered at each hip. They were aptly named "Fangs" for the lethal load they carried. She took a deep breath to press back her nerves. This would be her first time shadowing one of the assassins. She was along to observe, but had been told to bring her guns regardless. Glancing into the dark alleyway, she saw her mentor adjust his cloak.

"You're free to sit this out," Scizzors said. He stepped into the light cast by streetlamps. He was a large, slumped-over man with pale skin. A massive cloak hid him head to toe. Along the head, the cloak bulked up on each side. "Can't have you shaking like a scared pup when we get in there. Everyone's eyes need to be on me."

"Little chance anybody will care about me when that cloak comes off."

A deep chuckle rumbled in his throat. "Why look like me if you can't scare the shit out of everybody?"

She smirked, remembering what Widow told her. Somewhere in Florida, there was an actual wanted poster stating: "Billy-Goat Headed Alligator Man. Extreme Caution Advised: Decapitates Victims." The caution was followed by a rough drawing of a hideous monster.

Tayla checked her reflection in a store window. She adjusted her trench coat to hide her Fangs. "How do I look?"

"Let's admire ourselves later," said Scizzors. His hood was pulled back enough for her to see a vicious underbite with sharp, jagged teeth poking above scarred lips. "You can tell me honestly if you're not ready for this, Viper."

Tayla was still unaccustomed to her assassin tag, even if it was familiar. Her brothers called her Viper because of a split at the tip of her tongue. Now, the name served to hide her identity. "I'm ready," she assured him.

He started across the street.

Tayla followed close behind.

Scizzors stopped in front of the bar and adjusted his gauntlet. "The eyes I sent to follow our target told me he frequents this bar. He's a rich kid who likes to play doctor with little girls."

"He cuts them open?"

"Not a surgeon," Scizzors corrected. "Gynecologist."

She scrunched up her face in disgust.

"My thoughts exactly." His lips cracked as they warped into a wicked smile. "Now let's commence the part of the evening where I scare the ever-loving shit out of people." He opened the door and gestured for Tayla to lead the way.

Once inside, she separated from him, walking to a wall adjacent from the bartender. Her fingers ran along her trench coat until she found the bulge of her Fangs hidden within. She leaned against the wall and looked around.

Scizzors stopped at the middle of the bar, the hood of his cloak shifting as he sought his prey. People grew quiet when they caught a glimpse inside the hood.

Once he gives them more than a glimpse, they'll know monsters go bump in the night. Tayla had heard bits and pieces of his story from him and the other Spades. Kids bullied him when he was younger for his extreme underbite. As Scizzors grew, his spine curved and he became hunched over, inviting harsher treatment from his peers. By twenty, he gave up on looking normal and invested every penny in the opposite goal. Long ram horns were surgically inserted into his skull and accentuated with a tribal tattoo covering his bald head. Jagged implants set beneath the skin made his skull more beastly. She wasn't sure if he sharpened his teeth, had customized dentures, or wore cosmetic snap-ins. Whatever he did, his smile resembled that of a deep ocean anglerfish. And the scariest trick of all was that of his long, blue tentacles protruding from his back. She rubbed her arm where they had touched her during testing. She swore she could still feel their bite. On his belt he wore a six-foot whip made of metal links: his "barbed tail." He called it that due to the final foot which was lined with small hooks. In a fight, he'd loop that whip around the gauntlet. He was every bit the terrifying devil his bullies had made him out to be. He didn't just accept this role; he relished it.

She couldn't help but marvel at him. Instead of letting his abnormality crush him, he twisted it into his greatest asset.

Scizzors cleared his throat. In a deep, raspy, pirate's voice, he asked, "Where be the boy who owes me boss 'is moneys?"

Tayla swallowed a laugh. She'd never heard him do the voice.

A few of the bar's patrons made for the door, likely because they owed someone a sizable sum.

The bartender placed a baseball bat on the countertop. "We don't need trouble here, sir. Find your *boy* somewhere else."

Scizzors reached into the cloak at his neck. A humming emanated from him.

People had been taking video. Now, they began tapping and shaking their phones. As Tayla watched, a few of the phones went black. She joined in their bewilderment.

The bottom of Scizzors's cloak glowed a dim blue.

The glow brightened until the floor beneath Scizzors reflected a radiant azure. *The tentacles aren't just offensive. They're short-range EMPs, too.*

Scizzors walked to the counter, standing two feet from a red-headed young man. "Aiden, we need be talkin' outside so the gruff, grizzly man won't club skulls in wit' his wee wittle bat."

The young man swiveled on his barstool, a frosted mug of beer in hand. "I don't owe shit to anybody." He laughed when he got a better look at Scizzors. "Are you seeing this, Brett?" He smacked a well-built man beside him. "This joker's wearing a robe in public. Who you supposed to be, asshole? Friar Tuck?"

Brett swallowed his beer before chuckling. "You wander off from a Renaissance festival?"

Scizzors gripped the cloak at the back of his neck with his left hand. "How 'bout we remove them smiles?" The cloak came away.

Aiden launched backward, throwing his beer at Scizzors and knocking Brett off the barstool.

A woman shriveled into her seat when she spotted the living nightmare, stifling a horrified gasp.

Brett stood, nursing an elbow with his hand. "You're on your own, man."

Aiden's head jerked around, his eyes wide. "You fucking serious?"

"Can't fight this one for you."

Brett was clearly the muscle that allowed rich boy Aiden to run his mouth in bars.

The bar's bouncer came out of the bathroom, drying his hands on his tee. When his eyes locked on Scizzors, he grabbed an expandable tactical baton. He flipped his wrist. With a *tickitytack*, the cudgel went from seven inches to sixteen.

Tayla had wondered why the bar had no security. Here he

stood, taller and wider than Scizzors. Her hands slipped inside the trench coat, preparing to bare her Fangs if the command came.

Instead, Scizzors unhooked the barbed tail from his belt with the gauntleted hand. "What's wrong, Aiden? Ye look a wee peaked, boy."

The bouncer stepped forward, baton ready. "I'm going to need you to leave."

"Yer protectin' a pedo here."

The bouncer looked at Aiden. "What?"

Surprisingly, Aiden's eyes found a way to grow wider.

The bartender shook his head. "That's a horrible accusation to hurl about."

"Get out." The bouncer lifted the baton and approached.

With astonishing grace, Scizzors unraveled the tail, arced it through the air, and let it snap.

The baton thumped to the ground. The bouncer took a knee, holding a hand to his thigh. Blood beaded between his fingers before streaking down over knuckles.

Scizzors pointed at Aiden. "No one need hurt over yer sins, boy."

The bartender upended a whiskey bottle, his Adam's apple dancing violently as he downed it all. He was clearly preparing to do something requiring courage ... something stupid. He dropped the bottle and his hands disappeared behind the counter. Up they came with a shotgun.

Tayla bared her Fangs and pulled their triggers.

The bartender took a bullet to each arm and howled. The shotgun dipped and fired, more bullets tearing grooves in the counter than not. The last few sprayed wild. A woman screamed in pain as a pellet pierced her cheek.

"Wichser," Scizzors cursed, his hand slapping over Tayla's shoulder.

Aiden took the opportunity to bolt for the door, the front of his britches wet with urine.

Scizzors shook his head, turning hard and swinging the tail back. "Verpiss dich," he roared, snapping it forward. The barbs dug into Aiden's leg and jerked backward.

Aiden collapsed, screaming as blood stained his jeans where barbs tore more than fabric.

Tayla caught the eyes of the monster who was Scizzors. They were reptilian: green and yellow with hints of red.

He shot her a look.

Through the contact lenses was pure, malicious animosity. She felt as though she were staring into the eyes of a starved crocodile. The hair stood on her arms. The eyes narrowed and locked on Aiden.

"Yer end is now," said Scizzors, pulling until the barbs ripped free.

A bottle shattered against one of the ram horns, beer and glass showering the tattoo.

Scizzors let out an exasperated roar as he turned to find who'd thrown it.

The bouncer stood defiant, blood drying on his hand. He pointed a Beretta M9 in Tayla's direction. "Put your guns down, miss."

Tayla smiled, a Fang pointed at each of the bouncer's arms.

Scizzors gestured for her to lower her weapons.

"Come on," she groaned. "Really?"

He repeated the gesture. "None need killin' besides this

one here."

"Shoot them," Aiden yelled.

"Nah, we be leavin' now," Scizzors said, nodding to Tayla. "Be a dear, get me cloak."

Tayla furrowed her brow. "We're walking away?"

"Get me cloak."

She followed his instruction. The cloak required far more strength to lift than expected. *What's this made of?* She rested it over her shoulder to carry its weight and glared at the bouncer. "You're damn lucky the big man stopped me."

"Just get out," the bouncer demanded.

She smirked while backing away. "We're going."

Scizzors tilted his head toward her and whispered, "Make a wall when I give the order."

"What?"

"My cloak is lined with five layers of STF-treated Kevlar."

That'll work. She got a better grip to ready herself for the order.

Aiden bounced on his good leg for the door.

Scizzors rolled his eyes and produced a barbed dart from his pocket. "Where ya goin'?" He shot his hand forward.

Aiden yelled and hit the floor again, reaching back to feel the blade stuck in his leg. He began crying.

"Stop struggling," Scizzors said, pulling out another barbed knife. "I have more when ya start crawlin'."

"Hey!" The bouncer raised the gun.

"Wall," Scizzors said as his tail whipped back.

Tayla threw up her hands, spreading the cloak seconds before two loud bangs rang out. The cloak barely swayed on impact. *Impressive.* She looked back in time to see the barbed tail wrap around Aiden's throat.

The young man grabbed at it, attempting to pull it free. The barbs ripped holes in his throat and dug into his fingertips.

Tayla heard the bouncer closing the distance and dropped the cloak. With lightning speed, she pulled her Fangs and put two bullets in each of his arms and one in his right leg.

The bouncer struck the ground, his gun sliding within an inch of her feet.

"Viper," Scizzors chided.

She turned to see him glaring at her. "What?"

He shook his head, returning his attention to Aiden. "Imagine I'm the father of every baby girl you've touched," he said, abandoning the voice from before.

The young man pleaded between sobs.

"Apology not accepted." Scizzors took a step forward. He snapped two fingers together with the hand not covered by a gauntlet.

Aiden let out a long breath, dropping his head to the ground as though submitting to the inevitable.

Scizzors flung his weight backward, jerking the tail away.

Tayla—and every other person in the bar—tore their gaze from the gruesome sight. There was no missing the grotesque sound of flesh ripping open or the gurgling when Aidan tried to breathe through an open windpipe. She closed her eyes and imagined being somewhere else. Anywhere but there. She'd had those barbs wrapped around her legs during testing. She shook at the thought of them tearing through her carotid.

Scizzors wrapped the bloody tail around his gauntlet and started for the door. "Bring me cloak."

Tayla gladly knelt to collect it, intending to use the cloak as a visual shield between her and the head separated from its body. But when she passed, her eyes were magnetized to the disturbing picture of death. Vomit climbed her throat. "Oh, God." She swallowed and followed Scizzors out. There would be no shaking that image from her mind.

They arrived in the alleyway before Scizzors broke her trance, saying, "You good?"

She looked up to see blood dotting his face. His shirt was drenched in it. "I think so," she lied.

He nodded curtly. "I'll have some notes about you getting innocent people hurt. Be prepared to answer Ace if he brings it up."

She barely registered his warning. Aiden's head in a pool of blood flashed across her vision. It would be forever branded at the back of her mind. She forced a smile, nodded, and underlined the mental note she'd made the day she passed his test:

Never ever cross this monster!

Chapter Sixteen

Balls of Steel

June 7, 2016
07:32 AM CDT
Kansas City, Missouri

CHASE jolted awake to a hand on his face. His fingers curled around the Taser under his pillow. He relaxed when he saw Vixen smiling at him.

"Morning," she said softly. "It would appear we took more than a nap."

"How long were we out?"

Her thumb stroked his cheek. "Fourteen hours of the deepest sleep I've ever had."

"Might have something to do with my gassing you."

"Or you're just that comforting." She itched her chest and looked down. "Is my blouse inside out?"

"Yeah. You took it off after being gassed."

"Oh, right." She laughed. "Are my bra and jeans still down there?"

"I think so." He rose on an elbow and stared at her lips. "You're beautiful."

"Don't you dare kiss me until I've brushed my—"

He pressed his lips to hers.

Her hands flattened against his chest as though to push him away, then gripped his shirt to pull him closer. When their lips parted, she hummed contentedly.

He smiled. "I've been craving another kiss since our last. Though, I confess, my dreams have us doing far more."

Vixen grinned. "Mine, too."

"I doubt that very much," said Chase.

She pinched his arm. "Don't put yourself down. You're a handsome gentleman."

"I thought you'd be more into bad boys."

"Why?" she asked. "Do I look like a woman who enjoys verbal abuse?"

He laughed. "You seem to enjoy physical abuse."

"Trust me. If you ever struck me outside of training, I'd kill you."

"You have no need to fear that," he promised.

"I know," she said before kissing the tip of his nose. "There's a police officers' barbecue tomorrow night to raise funds for new vehicles. Would you go with me?"

"You want me to go somewhere crawling with police?"

"Trevor will be there."

"Who?"

"Officer Clark."

"I'd rather not, if that's all right."

Sweat broke out across his brow. He felt stupid for asking. "No, that makes sense. My uncle would have wanted me to go, though, so you'll be by yourself a few hours if you're still here."

"I can entertain myself by searching out your hidden

weapons."

"As long as you put them all back." Chase hid his embarrassment by looking at the closet. Clothing was piled on the ground and covered in chunks of drywall. "Or you could do something about that chaos."

Vixen must have noticed the red in his cheeks, because she said, "I'll go if it means that much to you."

"No, you're right. Better safe than sorry." Smiling widely, he leaned in and brushed his nose against hers. "You spoke of dreams earlier."

This time she did push him away. "If we're going into that, I must insist I shower first."

"I'll join you."

Her eyes narrowed, but she smirked.

Downstairs, the front door opened. The stun gun was in hand and Chase was halfway to the flash bomb concealed in a dresser drawer before he realized he'd gotten out of bed.

"Chase?" came Allison's voice. "I called."

Shit! "Be down in a minute." He felt himself uncoil and took a deep breath. He tossed Vixen the stun gun.

Vixen tucked it under his pillow, whispering, "Does she come this early every time?"

He grinned. "You are jealous, aren't you?"

She pursed her lips to the side and shrugged. "Does she like you?"

She really is. "She's just checking on me."

"Uh-huh."

He shook his head. "It's her job, ya crazy." He walked out and started down the stairs.

Allison approached. "How you feeling today?"

"I'm doing great."

"No heavy lifting or rapid movements, I hope."

"I was yanked off a stool yesterday."

Her eyes widened. "You passed another test? I'm so proud of you!"

"No, it was ..." he stopped, remembering Vixen wasn't supposed to be there. "I fell, is all. Embarrassing really."

Her eyes glanced over. "Oh, dear. I'm sorry."

"For?" He followed her gaze to Vixen's discarded bra and jeans. "That's, um ... I, uh ... I like to wear those sometimes ... for fun."

"Okay." Her expression was one of complete bewilderment. "I'm sorry, but neither of those would fit you." A smile spread across her lips. "You know, if you had sex last night, that would fall under rapid movements and heavy lifting."

Vixen began laughing. "What's with everyone calling me heavy?"

Allison's eyes went wide. "Is that who I think it is?"

Chase turned to watch Vixen walk from his room.

"I'm taking a shower," she said, removing her blouse as she went. "You're welcome to join me."

There was no hiding his blush when he caught the perfect side profile of her breast. His eyes returned to Allison. "Thanks for stopping by."

"Yeah," Allison replied, eyes glued to where Vixen had been. "She's, um." She nodded slowly.

"You have no idea." He walked past her to open the door.

Allison snapped out of her trance. "Are you two ..." Her eyes narrowed at the ceiling. "I'll come back later."

For some reason, he doubted he'd ever see her again. "See you then." He waited for her to clear the driveway before shutting the door and sprinting for the stairs. "Was that safe when you're not supposed to—" He crested the final step and saw too late Vixen charging him with her blouse back on.

Her arms wrapped around his waist. His right bicep crashed into the banister at the top of the steps. It took a minute for Chase to realize it was the wood of the banister he felt and heard break, not bone. He wrapped his arms around her, lifted, and walked her a few steps from the precarious banister before her hands locked on his knees and pulled. He dropped to kneel.

Once down, she elbowed him twice in the ribs.

He dropped her and pushed her away. "This is not how I imagined finding you when I ran up here."

Scurrying back, she said, "Nudity shouldn't drop your guard, Hunter. Otherwise, you open yourself to every bare-breasted woman hiding a knife behind her back."

"Apparently my life's been dull. Every naked woman I've encountered had something besides murder on her mind."

"Dull indeed," said Vixen. She had a leather satchel tied around each bicep.

He pointed at one. "What are those?"

She lunged.

Chase rolled out of her way, then rose to see her snap a hand back. Something struck him in the throat. He coughed. It wasn't until he heard it rolling along the wood floor that he saw the metal ball escape down the hall. "Where were?" He swallowed hard. "Where were you hiding those?"

"I left them in your bed before I met you in the basement." Vixen said, crossing her arms to pull a metal ball from each satchel.

His first instinct was to run. Instead, he rushed her, head down, shoulders forward.

Vixen tried to avoid him but he collided with her side, sending her reeling into the frame of his bedroom door.

He pushed off the wall, pivoting to land atop her. Before he could lock her down, she rotated round to face him and, with each hand, slapped the sides of his head. Each palm must have contained a metal ball because his bell was rung so loudly that pangs of pain bounced around his skull. When she slapped again, he shot his head back and rolled off of her. On all fours, he galloped down the hallway. One ball smacked the back of his neck, the other hit the wall beyond him. He jumped, twisting with palms prepared to catch a third or fourth.

None followed.

Vixen was nowhere to be seen.

That's just perfect. He approached his bedroom, assuming she'd ducked inside.

A foot connected with the side of his leg as he passed the bathroom. His knee met the floor.

She was on his back before he could readjust, her arm tightening around his throat.

Black dots bled into his vision. Once gaining his feet, he went to drop, intending to land on her, but she planted her feet and walked backward, bending him at a strange angle.

She's so strong. The dark invaded his vision. Wrenching to the side, he lost more vision. *I can't shake her.*

As he began to lose consciousness, he heard her whisper in his ear, "Turn your head into the crook of my arm."

He did, regaining some vision. Before he could rejoice, she

tightened, dropping him. He blinked to gain back a shred of sight and looked for Vixen. "You enjoy playing hide and seek?"

"What?" she said from the kitchen downstairs.

He crawled to the top of the steps.

She closed the fridge door, a water in each hand.

"How'd you get down there so fast?" Chase said.

"You've been lying there a while. One would think you slept long enough last night, but apparently you fancied a nap."

"That's not embarrassing at all."

"Turning your head allows only a few seconds to follow through. Think fast or you're screwed."

"Dead, you mean."

"Oh, yeah." She threw him a water. "We should have covered chokeholds on day one."

"Noose's reaction to my passing out makes sense now."

"It does." She smiled. "There are many reasons for these tests and he felt you weren't prepared in the least."

"What are they?"

"What are what?"

"The reasons," Chase said. "If there are many, I want to hear them. Because if I'd had bullets, Pockets would be dead."

She wrinkled her nose adorably and whispered, "Takes more than bullets to slow that sharp-edged crazer down."

"He could have been seriously injured." He threw a hand up. "People were seriously injured, almost killed." He ran a hand across the wound on his abdomen. "That felt chaotic and without any purpose besides taking me out. It put me, you, and those testing me directly in harm's way. It maimed two of us. What could possibly justify that?"

Vixen counted on a finger. "One, to learn from real-life

experience how someone might avoid dying by your hand. Your life depended on escape. This was not simulated risk, it was real. Your life was on the line. Therefore, you put everything into it. You left no stone unturned. So too will be the life of the person you hunt in the future. They will employ every possible tactic at their disposal to stay alive. To learn how you'd get away gives you a direct glimpse into how they might. Find a way around it." She counted the next finger. "Two, the one testing you hones their skills."

"You mean, the two testing me."

Vixen bit her bottom lip. "In this case, that's fair." She shrugged as though embarrassed and continued. "The *testers* were also in your shoes once. Now they hunt targets for their career. They show you what you can become by relentlessly applying pressure. Just as you learn from a test, so do they with every new method you employ to evade their snares." She counted on another finger. "Three, it helps you decide what you're good at. Aiding in you deciding how to take out your future targets. It fleshes out your strengths and weaknesses. What type of assassin will you become? Up close and personal, distant executioner, or a hybrid of some sort?" She twirled the next finger in the air. "Four is huge: It helps you escape in the future if the tide turns on you. Some prey you pursue will bite back if they get even the slightest whiff of you coming. Escape, reassess, and strike again with ways you've learned here from those who have done the same to you."

Chase shook his head. "I guess that makes sense."

She ignored him and stuck out her thumb. "And five is the reason you nearly died: It allows our people to assess the skills and character of those we recruit. If they feel you are not a good fit, it is better to take you out then and there. Not let you loose on the world only to give us a bad name. We are few. One of us can bring shame to us all. It's extraordinary you escaped Noose's clutches once he decided you were a threat to the Guild. You might not like him right now, but he is loyal to the core. He loves this Guild as much as he loves his husband and children, and he loves them more than you will ever comprehend. If he chose to kill you, he did so believing it was absolutely the right thing to do. And, in all honesty, you should count your lucky stars that you are alive after he decided you should not be, because I guarantee a few of those stars were obliterated when they stood between you and Noose."

"Trust me, I know." Chase took a drink of water and adjusted to sit up. "Surviving at all was sheer luck."

Vixen laughed and ascended the steps. "Perhaps, but you did plenty. Not everything was dumb luck, although it definitely played its hand." She threw her empty water bottle at him.

When he reached to catch it, Chase failed to see her open palm follow to catch him in the jaw. Fortunately, her being lower than he took away most of the impact, allowing him to remain clear-sighted. He planted a foot at the center of her chest and kicked.

Because she grabbed his calf, she managed to stumble only a few steps.

He, on the other hand, lost his balance entirely. His back slammed and raked along the stairs until she stopped his slide by sitting atop his chest. The breath was knocked from his lungs. He lay gasping under her weight, hands struggling to bat away a flurry of punches. "Stop," he choked. "I can't—" He gasped.

"Catch my—"

She tightened her legs around him to further inhibit his ability to breathe.

She'll kill me if I don't find a way around this. Allowing her a few solid strikes to his face, he dropped his hands to grip the stairs and pushed off.

Vixen slid off him, bounced to the base of the stairs, and snapped a hand forward.

He barely managed to close his eyes before a ball struck his nose. "How many of those do you have?"

Vixen shook her arms and the satchels rattled. "A few in each." She crossed her arms to grab two more. "Run."

He rushed forward, grabbed her fists, and toppled her over.

She got her right hand free and went to slam a fisted metal ball into his chin.

He threw his head back and backhanded her wrist.

Vixen's hand jerked and the ball smacked the floor beside her ear. She closed her eyes, clearly anticipating the ball hitting her face.

Chase grabbed the satchel on her right arm and yanked it down.

Vixen gripped the satchel before he could pull it off. She jerked it out of his grip and swung. The two metal balls inside popped the shoulder where Pockets had stuck him with a knife.

Chase wrinkled his nose and threw a hand over the spot. The muscle was tender to the touch. He wasn't certain the internal stitches were dissolved yet. "Why hit there?"

"You strike where your opponent is weakest," said Vixen.

He should have guessed she'd spout something like that.

Should have realized she'd never hold back, even if it meant prolonging his healing.

This time when she swung the satchel, he twisted to the side and punched her as hard as he could in the bicep. Her arm dropped. She massaged it. "You suck," she said, rubbing vigorously.

"*I* suck?" He grabbed the bag of metal balls and threw it under the dining room table. "Give up the other or I'll stay here all day."

Vixen glared, then smirked. "Fine," she said, undoing the leather straps and throwing the second satchel at the couch. "I really do need to shower."

"Feel free." Chase stood and helped her up. "If the hot water knob sticks, just whack it a few times."

"You could join me for real this time."

"I'm not falling for that again."

"Suit yourself," she said when she reached the top of the stairs. Her fingers curled the bottom of her blouse and pulled it up as she disappeared around the corner.

This is for sure a trap. He followed, ready this time for an assault. He came around the corner, his arms ready to grab her.

Sure enough, she jumped and kicked out, intending to catch him in the chest to throw him off balance. Instead, he grabbed her by the ankles and twirled her body through the air, but lost his grip.

Chase let out a panicked "No!"

Vixen's hips broke through what remained of the cracked banister, her right foot entrapped within the metal banister threads. She slid, her body swung down, and she smacked hard against the side of the stairwell. The threads were close enough that she remained suspended by her ensnared ankle.

The apologies poured forth, "I'm so sorry. Are you all right? I'm such an idiot." Chase ran down the steps to see a solitary tear trace a line down her forehead. "What hurts?"

One hand rubbed the back of her head while the other gestured at her foot. "Maybe start by getting me down."

Putting his hands under her shoulders, he lifted and rested her weight against his chest. "Do you trust me?"

"Why?"

"I'm going to lift you over my head."

"Thought the doc said no *heavy* lifting."

At least she's cracking jokes. He gripped her sides firmly. "Are you ready?"

"Yes, please."

"Can you move your leg?" He straightened his arms.

"I don't think it's broken." She ran her foot up the banister threads and it came free.

He placed her down.

"Mother of—" She brought her knee to her chest and cradled the ankle in her fingertips. "Definitely sprained, though."

"I'm so, so, so sorry." He picked her back up in his arms. "I'll take you to my bed."

"Don't go near the stairs," she yelled. "No more stairs."

"Couch?"

"Yes, please."

He walked her over and gently set her down. "Are you all right?"

"I'm fine." She pressed on the sprain. Her face contorted. "I will be, I mean."

Chase put one of the couch pillows under her neck. The other he placed under her knees. "Better?"

"Yes, thank you." She laid back.

"How's your head?"

She put a hand back and felt what was likely a massive lump. "I'll live." Shaking her head at him, she added, "You sure know how to show a girl a good time."

"It's not hard," he laughed. "Just spoil them." He rounded the couch and lifted her legs by the calves. He sat and placed her left ankle against his knee. The right ankle he cradled in his palm. *She'll either strike me when I start this or she'll pull away.* He moved his hands above the sprain and began massaging. To his surprise, she neither struck nor withdrew. When he moved his hands down the ankle, she scrunched her face, but didn't move to stop him.

During his gymnastics training, it was like his body was pit against him. Every opportunity to hurt itself, it took it. His right ankle still popped funny when he woke in the morning. That, and he could pull his left wrist back further than should be possible. He'd had plenty of physical therapy to know what he did now was painfully uncomfortable. But she would feel better after.

He repeated in his head what his athletic trainer had said: *Firm pressure, gentle strokes.* He circled her ankle with all ten fingers until her eyebrows stopped furrowing in pain.

Moaning softly, she closed her eyes. "I've never understood how a person could have 'magic fingers' until this very moment." Her flesh warmed at his touch and her knees separated. "You should move those fingers up my leg."

His cheeks felt like they might melt from his face. "What?"

Opening one eye to look at him, she smirked. "You really aren't a bad boy."

He returned his attention to her ankle. *Firm pressure, gentle strokes.* "You're not afraid of the Guild seeing?"

"We have the signal disrupter from Zettabyte."

His mind returned to his fear of her killing men through seduction. *But we slept in the same bed last night and I'm still alive.* He bit his bottom lip, his hands now massaging her calf. "What if someone shows up to test me?"

"I'm already taking that risk by being here. Our being naked wouldn't make my punishment any harsher."

"Might make my survival a bit more difficult, being without armor and all that."

"I feel a Taser under my left elbow, and I'm pretty sure I saw a canister of some sort under the couch. I think you're at least somewhat prepared." She spread her legs wider. "Any other excuses before those hands do their magic elsewhere?"

His fingers now massaged the outside of her thighs. "The curtains are closed," he stated, more to himself than to her. "I'm afraid to leave them open because of bullets eager to bathe in brain matter."

She laughed. "It's cute you think a curtain will stop that from happening." Taking his hand, she redirected his fingers to stroke her inner thighs.

He could feel the heat radiating. "I should really just focus on your sprain." He ran his hands along her skin and returned to her ankle. *Firm, gentle strokes.* "From what you saw during my first test, what should I work on most?"

There was a short silence before she brought her knees together. "From what I could see—" She cleared her throat. "You need to use your surroundings more often."

"Okay." He forced himself to look at her.

She was frowning.

"I'll do better," he promised.

"Pockets said you found interesting applications for the tables and chairs." A slight smile appeared at the corner of her mouth. "Something about you goring Noose like a bull?"

He grinned. "That was a highlight."

"It made an impact, for sure. Work on further discovering your creativity. You obviously have a talent for finding clever ways to manipulate your surroundings. Nurture that gift."

"Let's practice then," he said, tapping her legs. "Let me up."

Vixen didn't move. "I'm offering myself to you here. I thought you found me beautiful?"

"You're gorgeous," Chase assured her. "More than any other woman I know."

"Then why not take me? Earlier, you were eager to jump in the shower." She leveled her stare at him. "What changed?"

Why am I fighting this? "Something feels wrong." Something did.

"It's because I attacked you both times, isn't it?" She smiled. "My ankle's all twisted up. That's not going to happen now."

He raised an eyebrow. "You could kill me in ten different ways with both legs and an arm missing."

"Good point," she said. "Is that why? Because I promise I won't strike you." Leaning forward, she stroked his neck. "Unless you like it rough."

"Not particularly," he admitted. "I seriously have no idea why I'm not tearing your underwear off."

"Let me help." She gripped the sides of her panties.

"Ssstooop."

"It's just sex," she chided, but left them on.

"With you, Vixen, it could never be '*just sex*.'" He realized what he'd said and shook his head. "This isn't a conversation I thought I'd be on the other side of."

"What are you saying?"

"I like you." He swallowed the lump hugging his voice box. "More than like you." He swallowed harder. "Even when you're kicking my ass, I'm thankful you're *here* kicking my ass."

"That's the strangest thing I've ever heard."

He felt his heart snap and nodded one long nod. "You're right." Gently, he lifted her legs and scooted out from under them. "Who are my next opponents and how do they kill?"

She rose from the couch.

"Get off your ankle," he said. "Seriously."

Vixen limped toward him and brought up her fists.

What is she doing? His hands rose as well. "Please go sit dow—"

Her hand swiped.

Chase slapped it aside only to see her sprained ankle snap up. He snatched her leg by the calf and cupped her ankle in his palm.

Her eyes looked at the hand cradling her. "Even as I attack, you protect me. Noose was right. You're not one of us."

"What's that supposed to mean?"

She jumped and the other foot caught him in the chest.

The ankle was torn from his grip as he stumbled to the side. He regained his fighting stance before noticing her attack landed her on the floor. "Stop this. You need to rest." He went to help her.

She slapped him hard across the face.

"What's wrong with you?" He struck down, blocking her good foot from barreling into his crotch. Then he caught her sprained foot as she rose, cupped her ankle, returned it to the floor.

She scooted away from him. "Stop protecting me."

"You need to sit down."

She rose and limped backward. "You *need* to practice if you're so worried about your next opponents." Again, she kicked with her sprained foot.

He skirted to the side, he caught her leg under his arm, and gripped her thigh. His other hand grabbed her bottom and he walked her backward.

She bounced on her good leg to stay upright.

He pushed when her knee met the arm of the couch. "Stay," he demanded.

She disobeyed. "I'm not a dog." She came off the couch. This time she nearly fell when she put her weight on the ankle.

"Vixen, please," he groaned, feeling the pain for her. "You're going to cause irreversible damage if you keep this up."

Once more, she kicked with the wounded leg.

He went to cup her ankle, but her body contorted and the foot was pulled back. Next thing he knew, she'd grabbed him under the arms. He expected a heavy hit and leaned backward.

Digging in her fingernails, she raked lines down his flesh as he pulled away.

He turned his arms this way and that to see crimson dots pool to become long, thin lines. His eyes rose to meet hers. "Are you kidding me?"

"You're repeating tactics, Hunter," she said. "You become predictable. Keep your eyes on the clavicle, because it responds to every move your opponent makes. If it sways back, there's a kick coming. If it tilts on the right, a punch is coming from the right. If you focus only on what is striking you or on where you are striking, your eyes will give away everything." Sure enough, her clavicle swayed back and the sprained ankle kicked.

He refused not to catch and cradle it in his hands.

She came in close, bending at the knee. Both hands struck the underside of his arms. She pinched.

He crossed his arms and brought them down to break her hold.

Her fingernails came away red.

"Hell's kittens, Vixen," he cursed, grabbing her by the shoulder. He swept a leg to dislodge the only foot she had planted and pushed.

She collapsed backward onto the couch.

He placed a hand on the underside of his arm. There was stinging pain at his touch. "Is my next opponent a cat?" He turned his back to her, knowing she'd attack. When the springs of the couch squeaked, he dodged left, twisted, and grabbed her out of the air. He twirled, intending to throw her back onto the couch, only, he'd grabbed her awkwardly and his hand slipped from her arm.

Vixen flew past the couch to land hard on the wood floor. She coughed.

That had to hurt. He wanted badly to help her, but knew she'd only punish him for doing so.

Vixen rolled onto her stomach, coughing twice more before rising on hands. He imagined an injured wolf eying its hunter. That's not to say the fight was over. Most animals when pinned and injured are far more unpredictable and dangerous.

Better to diffuse the situation. "Are you angry with me?"

"You're asking a girl you rejected if she's a little miffed?"

"Why be mad if it's *'just sex'* to you?"

She opened her mouth, then worked her jaw a few times. Her face twisted and her eyes avoided his. "I can't go through with this."

"With what?"

She started limping for the door. "I've got to go."

"You're barely dressed, Vixen."

She shrugged and left the door open as she went.

Of course, not. He shook his head. *Why would that stop her?*

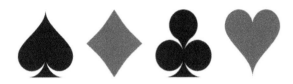

Chapter Seventeen

Bad Roommate

ANOTHER common figure was of a king's jester. If the cards landed one way, this figure could kill off any other card. If they landed another, the figure would make the dealt hand worthless.

At the beginning, there were four fools, one for each chapter of the Guild. But in the mid-1860s, games gained popularity that allowed only two. The jesters were called "trumps," "tricksters," "fools," and "tigers." The game Euchre invented a card called the "Imperial Bower," later known as the "Joker." In the early 1900s, this card became a staple in every deck due to the rising popularity of Poker. As a result, the Guild of Four agreed to adopt the rule. They didn't replace the fools that died in the Clubs and Diamonds. These cardholders no longer belonged to any suit and were able to float from one territory to another without the laws of card transfer hindering them.

As the name implied, the assassins chosen for the Joker role were often strange, slightly crazy, and always interesting.

Jokers were most admired for their ability to calm a situation with humor. For this reason, they also became the liaisons for the Guild, solving small disagreements between assassins and resolving larger issues between suits.

June 7, 2016
09:14 AM EDT
New York City, New York

~ JOKER ~

MICA walked into the kitchen and took the eggs from the fridge. He started a burner and laid a pan over the top of it. It was a bright and beautiful day and he had a lot to get to before his flight.

A young woman came out of his roommate's room. She was gorgeous despite the disheveled, curly hair and smeared makeup.

"Morning, beautiful stranger," Mica said as he broke two eggs into the pan. "Would you like some breakfast on this remarkable day?"

"I'm sorry." She glanced around then blinked quickly at the window. Her confused, mascara-streaked expression finally landed on him. "I don't know how I got here."

He shook his head. "That's not great. Do you remember how much you had to drink?" It was concerning how many women left his roommate's room in the morning completely lost and bewildered.

"That's the thing," said the young woman. "I only had a cranberry martini."

"Oh." *Not okay!* The others said they'd had plenty. "I'm sure Andrew will be up soon if you want to discuss it with him. Sounds like some dots need to be connected."

Her eyes had trouble focusing on him. She was gripping her wrist tightly. "I don't know who that is." With growing distress, she stumbled to the door. "I have a headache. I'm sorry. Thank you for breakfast." She left barefoot, the door remaining ajar after her exit.

Mica flipped the eggs violently, causing the yokes to break. *He'd better freaking explain himself.* He threw the spatula at the sink and went to close the door.

"Smells great in here," Andrew said from the hallway to their rooms. He wore only an undershirt and boxers.

"Enlighten me." Mica ran a hand over his mouth and glared at the other man. "Why have three women left here confused as fuck with how they arrived?"

"Bitches are crazy, man," he said, sitting in Mica's lazy chair.

"I don't buy that bullshit."

"I'm not required to sell you anything." He turned on the television and brought the footrest up. "My room. My bed. My bitches."

Mica chuckled. "Are they, now?"

"Yup." He turned the channel until wrestling came on and stuck a hand down the front of his underwear to itch himself.

Mica felt his lip curl with disdain. "I need something from my room."

"I'm not stopping you." Andrew stopped itching. His hand remained where it was.

Mica went to the hallway, looked back to see if Andrew

was watching, and dipped through his roommate's open door. He checked coat pockets, pant pockets, and finally the man's wallet. A small, plastic bag was inside, containing a white powder. Mica took the bag and quickly left Andrew's room to enter his own.

He mixed the powder into the water on his nightstand and stirred it with a finger. As the water spiraled, he grabbed a briefcase from under his bed. He turned it over and pressed his thumb to a fingerprint sensor. There was a thump. He opened the lid to see the many vials hidden within. He reached into the top pocket lining and pulled out multiple tests. While shuffling through them, he heard his roommate yell something.

"What?" Mica yelled back.

"Eggs are burning, bro," Andrew repeated.

"Thanks!" He found what he was looking for and dipped his finger in the water again. Finger dripping, he ran it over the test strip. "I'll be right there." He blew on the paper. The first line lit up pink. That confirmed the test was working. He blew longer and waited. "This fuckwit be a dead fuckwit." He blew again to be sure a second pink line wouldn't show.

Nothing.

He blew again and watched for even the slightest second line to appear.

Still nothing.

Andrew ran into the room. "Bro! The kitchen is full of smoke."

"Take it off the burner, then," said Mica, glaring. "I'll be there shortly."

"What are you doing?"

"I'm diabetic," Mica lied. "Just checking my blood."

"That's some creepy vampire shit."

"You're right, Andrew." Mica raised an eyebrow at him. "Diabetics are for sure vampires." He stood and began walking toward Andrew, waving the test in the air to continue drying it. "Just hiding among the populace, struggling with our glucose, waiting to strike."

Andrew stepped backward. "Don't wave that around, jackass."

"What's wrong?" Mica said. "Scared you might catch my vampirism?"

Andrew took a few more steps. "It's gross, man. Fuck off."

Mica pointed past him. "Then go get the pan off the burner, dumbass."

Andrew turned and sprinted toward the kitchen. "They're your fucking eggs, bro."

Idiot. Mica closed his door and looked at the test strip. "An idiot who drugs his dates." He pulled out his phone to call Ace. As it rang, he ran a finger through the coins atop his dresser.

"Nightshade," Ace answered. "I'm busy watching a car sink into the Hudson. Make it quick."

Mica finished counting the coins. "I owe the Guild twenty percent of a dollar seventy-five."

"Thirty-five cents?" Ace said with more than a hint of annoyance. "May I ask why?"

"I was hired by a client to do a job."

"You only charged a dollar and some change?" Now there was anger in the voice.

"It's nearly two dollars." *Better explain myself.* "As for the client ... I'm paying myself."

"What?" Ace growled. "Don't call me over personal

vendettas."

"So, I'm good to go?"

"If this gets in the way of you testing the recruit tomorrow, I'll pull out your teeth through your ass."

"I swear, this'll only take a second. Just wanted to clear it with the territory first." Mica waited for a definitive answer. "Hello?" The call ended. "Yes, Nightshade," Mica said, mocking Ace's voice. "Happy hunting, kid. Jolly ho-hum diddly-dee, you don't owe me a twenty-percent marksman's fee." He went to the bed and closed the briefcase. It rattled as he picked it up and headed for the kitchen.

Andrew had returned to the recliner. The windows were open, but the smell of burnt eggs still dominated the air. The sink was a mess of blackened debris. Mica picked up the pan and ran water over it. The desire to throw it at his roommate's head was truly, terribly, tremendously tempting. *Stick to the plan.*

Andrew shifted in the recliner. "Smells like shit in here, now."

"Let me make it up to you," Mica said, placing the briefcase on the counter. "I'll make my famous scrambled eggs."

Andrew laughed. "You're going to cook for me?"

"Sure." Mica forced a smile. "I need to use the eggs before they expire." He finished washing the pan and placed it back on the burner. He retrieved eggs, milk, cheese, and butter from the fridge and began. Two tablespoons of butter began to melt in the pan as he stirred up the other ingredients. He poured the rest into the pan and glanced up to see Andrew watching from the other side of the counter.

"Go relax," said Mica. "I'll bring you a plate when I'm done."

The man eyed the briefcase. "What's this for?"

"I have special salt in there."

"Special salt?" Andrew touched the top of the briefcase.

Mica slapped his roommate's hand away. "Best salt in the world. So good, it'll make you cry."

Andrew wrinkled his forehead. "There are different flavors of salt?"

Mica closed his eyes and sighed to sell it. "It's better than crack." He rounded the counter.

The anticipation on the man's face was priceless.

Mica opened the briefcase and ran his fingers over the many vials hidden within. "Let us see," he said, looking over the labels. "There you are." He pulled out the black vial labeled NaCN.

Andrew stood taller to peer inside the case. "What's aconite?"

For a man who drugs women, he sure doesn't know his poisons. "An extract from a plant called monkshood."

"What's conium and belladonna?"

"More plants," Mica said honestly, smiling from ear to ear. *Probably best that I don't say hemlock and deadly nightshade.*

Andrew wrinkled his brow. "You a gardener?"

"You know," Mica said, further preparing the eggs, "I thought about that handle for a while, before I settled on another."

Andrew sat on a stool on the other side of the counter. "Handle?"

Mica sprinkled the white powder from the black vial over his masterpiece. "Almost done."

Andrew leaned forward to see the meal coming along.

"Sorry about earlier."

Mica snapped two fingers together and said, "Already forgotten." He plated half the eggs and passed them to his roommate. "Breakfast is served."

Andrew took a bite, chewed, and scrunched up his face as he swallowed.

"Good, isn't it?" Mica said, propping himself against the counter on open palms. "It really hits the spot." He chuckled at the faces Andrew was making. Chuckles turned to deep-bellied laughter when Andrew kept taking bites.

Andrew coughed bits of food onto Mica's chest.

Mica brought his laughing under control. "What's wrong, Andy? Bitter?" He smiled broadly. "I might have gone a little overboard."

"Did you spike this?" Andrew pushed the plate across the counter. It crashed at Mica's feet.

"Funny word choice," Mica said, running a finger through the eggs dotting his shirt. "It's almost like it popped into your head because you have a nasty habit of doing the same to women's drinks." He reached the hand across the counter and wiped it down Andrew's face.

"I have a black belt, bro!" Andrew grabbed Mica's wrist, his grip tight. "I'll kick your ass."

"I don't care what McDojo you went to, bro fucker." Mica winked. "I've already won this fight." He reached into his pocket and pulled out the test he'd done. "To prove your innocence there should be two pink lines here. I see only one." He slapped it to the counter.

Mica could feel the young man's heart throbbing between the thumb and index finger gripping his wrist.

Andrew coughed. "What are—?" A fit of short, quick breaths interrupted him.

Mica reached into his pocket and pulled out the bag with white residue. He slapped it on top of the test. "You're going to start convulsing. You'll lose the ability to breathe altogether in roughly two minutes."

Andrew vomited against Mica's arm. His grip tightened and he began spasming. He let go of Mica and clawed at his collar as though it were too tight against his throat. He choked and landed against the counter, sliding sideways until he fell. He landed hard, his body wracked with convulsions.

Mica walked around to look at him. "Eyes itch, yet?" He knelt and watched as vomit foamed in Andrew's throat. "As you breathe in through your nose, you might notice the smell of almonds. If you don't, you're not defective or anything. Not everybody does because, well, they can't breathe." He lifted the front of his ex-roommate's undershirt and wiped the vomit from his arm. "Your body has a lot of other things to focus on besides breathing right now. A desperate fight against the effects of lactic acidosis being its primary concern."

Andrew grabbed hold of Mica's ankle, his grasp weak.

Mica let out a satisfied sigh. "Black belt, eh? Not worth much at the moment, is it?" Mica pressed harder against Andrew's forehead. "Then again, it wouldn't really matter what that black belt was in. No martial art will teach you how to defend against sodium cyanide." He pulled his ankle out of Andrew's fingers. "Next stop on the death train: heartbeat cessation."

Andrew's eyes froze in a blank stare and his throat gurgled softly.

Mica went to the remote and changed the channel. "Sorry, Vixen. I know you wanted me to work on my interpersonal skills." Mica looked at Andrew. "Turns out, I'm just not a people person."

Chapter Eighteen

Imported Walnut Salt

June 8, 2016
03:09 PM CDT
Kansas City, Missouri

VIXEN drove up to the airport gate. *Why's Ace here?*

He was out front talking to Nightshade and Thanatos.

She began backing out slowly.

Ace looked at her and curtly shook his head.

Pressing gently on the brake, she whispered through a grit-teeth smile, "Shit, shit, shit." She rolled down the window and stuck out her head. "Thanks for bringing me my overnight bag, Thanatos," she lied, hoping it would explain her sudden appearance.

Nightshade began walking to her, but Ace stopped him. They talked for a bit, then Ace approached alone. As he neared, it became apparent that he hadn't slept. He rapped a knuckle on the passenger-side window.

Taking a deep breath, she unlocked the door.

"Vixen," Ace said, once inside. "Why aren't you with Chase, securing the bond?"

"Are you feeling well?" she asked. "You look sick?"

"Answer the question."

"Let me grab my overnight bag from Thanatos and I'll tell you all about it."

"Right. This overnight bag?" Ace reached behind her seat, his hand returning with a backpack. Once unzipped and upturned, three sets of clothing dumped onto his lap along with her GLOCK 26. Staring coldly at her, he took the gun in hand. "Even if you had forgotten it, you wouldn't spend Guild money to have it returned to you. And, before you lie to me again, Thanatos already told me you asked him to pick you up."

Eying the gun, Vixen bit the inside of her lip and shrugged.

"Did he hurt you?" Ace asked.

"I was training him. He's supposed to hurt me." She pointed at her ankle. "I severely sprained my ankle. Something could be broken, but I want my doctor at home to look at it. Our doctor here is smitten with the recruit."

"All the more reason to go to her. Tell her to back off before she damages your ability to build trust with Chase." He turned away. "How's the sex?"

"I wouldn't know."

He tapped the GLOCK's barrel against the window a few times. "Another lie." He made a fist with his other hand. "I saw blurry shadows before the lights went out the night you returned. Didn't see blurry anything until you woke the next day. I know, because I watched for those *fucking* blurry shadows."

No wonder he looks sick and exhausted. "Nothing happened,

Ace."

He glowered at her.

She shook her head. "I told you not to read into static. We went to bed and slept. Cuddling, sure. Sex? He's a gentleman. He didn't even undress."

Ace's eyes darted about the car before returning to her. "Why not?"

"A second ago, you looked on the verge of killing someone because I *may* have slept with him. Now you're mad I didn't?"

Ace put the gun in the overnight bag and stuffed clothes in after it. "Go to the doctor, then return to Chase." He handed her the bag. "I'm not your pimp. I'm not telling you to fuck him. But don't take it off the menu because you fear my jealousy." He scraped his foot along the gravel outside the door. "By the way, you're taking Nightshade along. There are more of us here than our car drop could handle without raising eyebrows."

"This is Kansas City. You're telling me we only have one dealership working for us?"

"We lost the other due to someone taking an F-150 a while back and never returning it."

"A while back?"

He nodded. "When all this began."

"Powder Keg," she realized.

"Most likely." He got out.

"I offered," she admitted.

He dropped his head to look at her. "Offered?"

She picked at the steering wheel. "I told Chase to take me on the couch." Her eyes met his. "He refused."

"Nobody can refuse you."

"That's sweet of you." She wriggled slightly in her seat as

the burn of Chase's rejection blossomed anew. "But painfully untrue."

"Didn't peg him as gay."

"Not in the least," she said. "He wanted to. Still, he said no."

"He said no," Ace said, looking baffled, "to *you*?"

She glared at him, hoping he'd get the hint and drop it.

He rolled his eyes. "Try again."

"You don't fear me falling in love?"

"I know where your loyalty lies. Sex won't change that." Placing a knee on the seat, he leaned in until his face was inches from hers. "If, however, you make me question that ...?" His eyes bored into hers. "This job has many dangers. You are immune to none of them." He leaned further and kissed her. "Good luck today." He gestured for Nightshade to come.

That asshole just threatened me. Vixen placed a finger to her lips. *Then sealed it with a fucking kiss.*

Nightshade ran past Ace and leapt in. "Hey, lovely. This seat taken?"

She chewed at the inside of her cheek while watching Ace stride away. "Where do you want to be dropped off?"

"Take me to him."

"If I pull up with you in the car, you suppose that wouldn't be wildly suspicious?"

"Good point." He twiddled his thumbs for a second. "I'll show up with gifts. Wine or something. Give the recruit's drink a little kick."

"He'll set a bomb off in your face the moment you show it to him."

"So, it's true." Nightshade laughed. "He's a bomber. How

exciting!"

"More a chemist. You'd like him." Thoughts of Chase's shelves filled with gasses and explosives brought a smile to her face. Remembering him gassing her widened the grin.

Nightshade smirked. "You like this guy."

Her smile wilted. "No."

"Your cheeks are red. You *dooo* like him!" He did a little jig in his seat. "That's fantastic." Then he stopped. "I can't poison someone you've taken a fancy to."

The thought of Chase dying was horrible. Worse was the idea of carrying it out herself. *But if I don't, Ace might question my loyalty, cut me from the deck via accident, and kill Chase after all.* "Ace wants me to test him and Chase won't pass if I stick the knife in." She frowned. "If you don't kill him, I'll have to."

"That's ridiculous." Nightshade laughed. "You don't test people."

She gave him a grave look to prove her seriousness.

"What? Ace is such a dick."

She pulled onto the highway. "What time do you start?"

"Five."

That'll line up nicely. She nodded. "I've thought of an approach."

"We're not talking about this," he said.

She shot him another look.

"All right." Nightshade buckled up. "What's your plan?"

"Put a gas canister in his car when I'm distracting him. He's attending a police officers' barbecue at six and asked me to be his date."

"That's your idea? Poison him at a cop event?"

"You asked."

05:42 PM CDT

CHASE sat in his car, watching men and women laughing and carrying on. He wasn't sure he belonged. These people knew him before he'd been recruited. They knew him as Frank's nephew. Many thought of him as Frank's son. Every one of them believed he'd join the Police Academy. What would they think of him joining a guild of assassins? *They'd put me behind bars, no matter our history.*

He shifted uncomfortably. He'd worn the vest just in case he was attacked. The vest fit strangely now that he'd made some adjustments to incorporate his new found skillset. He doubted he'd be tested during a police banquet, but he also suspected assassins wouldn't wait out a barbecue if they had a strict two-hour window.

He nearly jumped out of his skin when a hand slapped the top of his car.

Trevor's face appeared in his window. "You coming?"

"Scared the crap out of me."

"Why?" Trevor said, then laughed. "That's right. You're being hunted."

"Thanks for securing the stuff I needed, by the way." Chase got out of his car.

"What are friends for?" Trevor said, then smiled. "You paid me far more than it was all worth, so I should be thanking you."

Chase shrugged. "Thought it was only right with you

risking your neck to procure them in the first place." He looked at the other officers. "What if they smell it on me?"

"All I smell is aftershave."

"You know what I mean." Chase sighed heavily. "I've joined the dark side. They're bound to see through me."

"They're cops, not psychics." Trevor put a hand on Chase's shoulder. "They'll be glad to see you. Most haven't since the funeral. If they smell anything on you, it should be beer, brisket, and barbequed ribs. Here, let's get you something to eat."

Chase followed Trevor into the crowd. His friend was right. Nobody would suspect he was training to be an assassin. Most people greeted him with a handshake and asked how he'd fared since Frank's passing. Others full-on hugged him. Some cried on his shoulder, lamenting Frank's absence from the festivities. Within fifteen minutes, Chase was exhausted from answering the same questions, the top one being: "When are you joining the Academy to take Frank's place?" He ate quickly before excusing himself. It was just too much.

He stopped in his tracks and smiled ear to ear when he saw Vixen sitting on the hood of his car, smiling at him. "I thought you didn't want to come."

Vixen shrugged. "I told you I'd be here if you wanted me." She nodded beyond him. "Looks to me like you need some company besides Officer Clark."

Chase turned to see Trevor hitting on one of the women officers. He thought her name might be Katie. *Or Cathy?* It didn't matter. He turned back to his date. "Hungry?"

"Not really," she said. "You look like you're running away. Would you rather we leave?"

"Now that I have you," Chase said, smiling, "the comments should change from my uncle to 'Who's this lovely lady?'"

She grew quiet and her eyes met the ground.

He hadn't seen that reaction from her yet. To break the silence, he asked, "How's the ankle?"

"Not happy, but if you lend me your weight, I'll walk with you." She got off his car and motioned for him to come forward.

He lent her his shoulder and she placed her weight against him.

She limped at his side. "Do they have popcorn?"

"I think over by the bounce house."

"I feel the vest." She dropped a hand to squeeze one of the plates. "It feels different."

"Yeah, don't squeeze too hard."

Her hand rose to scruff his hair. "What did you do?"

He shook his head, starting toward the popcorn vendor.

"Tell me," she pleaded.

Chase chose to remain silent about the alterations. "I don't know what you're talking about." He smiled.

"At least you don't have to worry about being attacked here."

"Why's that?"

She gestured around at the officers.

Chase shook his head. "Nice test. You told me it wouldn't matter where I was. The assassin would come for me if it was their time. They'd have to be stealthy and smart, but I'm sure they'd follow through all the same."

Her smile faded for an instant before returning. "I'm glad you're paying attention."

"Either that or die, right?"

This time, Vixen's smile left entirely. She nodded methodically. "That or die."

"Then, in that case, keep an eye out for your friends."

"That's your job, Hunter," she said. "I'm here to train you. If they show, I can't say a word."

Doesn't mean I won't be watching your eyes for signs of recognition. "Right." He ran a finger along her forehead to secure stray hairs behind her ear.

She blushed again and removed herself from him entirely. She said, "Instead of salty, I suddenly crave something sweet."

"Looks like they have cotton candy, too."

"Cotton candy?" She said the words as though weighing their adequacy. "I haven't had that since I was a little girl."

He imagined her as a child, beating up all the boys because she could. *What I would give to have been one of those boys.* He laughed, thinking of how many beatings she'd given him since they'd met. *I am one of those boys.* He took his wallet from his pocket and approached the vendor.

Behind the cart, a large woman wearing pigtails said, "Popcorn's three dollars. Cotton candy's two for four."

Vixen pointed. "Blue cotton candy for me, please."

Chase laughed at her impish grin. "You're adorable."

"Why?"

"You just are."

"I long to return to simpler times," she said.

"Don't we all?" He took a ten-dollar bill out of his wallet. "Popcorn for me."

"Cotton candy is two for four. Otherwise, it's one for two-fifty."

"That's fine." He waved the bill at her.

The woman blinked slowly as if annoyed. As she reached for the money, another hand snapped it from his fingertips.

"Five-fifty, it is," a five-foot-four young man said. "I'm taking over this stand, Miss Piggy Longstocking."

"Pardon me?" The large woman tossed her pigtails when addressing the man. "I wasn't told I'd have a replacement."

"Mr. Burns said otherwise," he replied. "Said people were complaining about you sweating in the popcorn maker."

Chase noticed Vixen narrow her eyes. *Is this one of her brothers? Or is she simply measuring him as she does everyone else?* He decided to do the same, scanning the newcomer head to toe. Muscles rippled along the man's arms. He had short, red hair and his eyes blazed like green garnets. The more Chase studied him, the more he pieced together an image of a leprechaun.

"I'll not tolerate this," the woman growled as she marched away.

"Take it up with Mr. Burns," the young man said, laughing before turning to them. "Popcorn for my main man and blue dryer lint for the lady."

Not exactly the picture I'd paint of a cold-blooded killer. But Vixen wasn't exactly a portrait of death either. Chase would keep this one on his list of suspects. So far, the believable possibilities had three faces: the man before him; a tattooed guy with a knife at his hip two carts down; and a woman near the bounce house not paying attention to the playing children.

"Can you add a twist of pink?" Vixen said.

"For you, my dear." A pink strand was twirled around the blue. "Anything." He handed it to Vixen.

Chase reached for a premade popcorn bag.

The man behind the cart smacked it, and every other bag, to the ground.

Chase found himself in a fighting stance.

"Did you not hear me say the woman sweat in the popcorn, my brother?" He tsk-tsked and threw kernels into the machine. "I'll make a new batch." He made a show of wiping out the popcorn maker, then added spice to the kernels.

Chase felt foolish for jumping into the stance, but Vixen looked pleased. He stood straight and cleared his throat. "Sorry."

"No apologies needed," the young man said, glancing back at Chase. "But you know what *is* needed? Something to make this corn pop like no other."

"Yeah?" Chase asked. "What's that?"

"Some good old imported walnut salt," said the young man. "Are you allergic to walnuts, my good and friendly giant?"

"Not at all, but popcorn doesn't have to be fancy."

"But if it can be—" The young man ducked behind the cart. "I say let it put on a dress and dance about." He reappeared with a black salt shaker.

Chase smiled, appreciating the man's jovial nature. "Are you joining the Police Academy?"

"I'm more a scientist than a uniform-wearing, trigger-happy Eagle Scout."

"Not all cops are that way," argued Chase.

The young man tapped the side of his nose with a finger. "The news says otherwise."

The popcorn started pop-pop-popping.

Chase eyed the man. "If you don't approve of law enforcement, why work the barbecue?"

"My friend got me the gig. Dropped me off and everything. Said I should get out more. See the people. Salt some popcorn."

Chase glanced at the black salt shaker, frowning. *If this man is an assassin, then ...* "I'm good without salt."

"I'll not stand you getting second-best," the young man said, waiting for the final pops. He scooped the popcorn into a bag and waved the shaker over it before handing the popcorn to Chase. "Enjoy."

"Sir, can you step away from the cart?"

Chase slowly turned to see "Miss Piggy Longstocking" standing behind him with an officer at each side.

"Prank's over, I suppose," the scoundrel said, laughing and pointing at Chase and Vixen. "You two lovebirds have a fine day now, ya hear?" The leprechaun ran away, zigging and zagging as though avoiding gunfire.

Chase glanced back at the officer. "I take it there is no Mr. Burns?"

"What gave it away?" "Miss Piggy Longstocking" scoffed as she bent to retrieve the bags of popcorn from the ground.

Chase shrugged and backed away from the cart. "Sorry you had to deal with that."

She rolled her eyes.

Vixen walked away, eating her cotton candy. He followed. "Is that guy going to reappear and stab me in the kidney seven times?"

"Perhaps," she said. "I couldn't tell you if I knew."

He tried to pinch off some cotton candy.

"Hey." She slapped his hand away. "You have popcorn."

"If you think I'm eating this, you're insane." He dropped it in a trash bin. "The skate park looks empty. And it's far enough away, the officers at the barbecue wouldn't hear a fight."

"Wait." Vixen looked at him as though he were daft. "You'd face him instead of run?"

"What's your point?"

"Your whole house is rigged for capturing or slowing my people."

"We're too far from my house," Chase reasoned. "Probably too far from my car. If I try to run, he will pursue, possibly taking me off guard. I stand a better chance if it's on my terms."

"What if I said you *need* to get to your car?"

"I'd trust you."

"Then." She sighed. "Do what you think is best." She looked beyond him.

Chase turned to see the leprechaun leaning against a tree, staring back and wearing an enigmatic smile. *Maybe I should run.* Instead, he walked right up to him. "I'm Chase."

"Nightshade's the name, poison's my game. Only you're not in distress, so I assume you realized that what I sprinkled over the popcorn wasn't salt."

"Something felt off about you insisting I take my popcorn fancy."

"I would usually applaud your cunning and say you passed. Only, I promised to kill you." He shifted off the tree and reached behind his back, hands returning with black knives.

Chase stood his ground. "I already fought a man with blades."

"His weren't coated in golden poison frog alkaloid toxins."

"You raise frogs?"

"Nah." Nightshade shook his head. "You can't get the same toxicity from captive animals. I get my poison shipped directly from Columbia, where boys scavenge the forests for the perfect specimens."

"That's cool," Chase said, reaching into his jacket pocket to pull out the gas mask concealed within. It was a smaller version than the full helmet he owned, fitting over only his mouth and nose.

Nightshade raised an eyebrow. "If I hadn't misplaced my gas canister in your car, that might have proved beneficial."

Glad I didn't run as Vixen suggested. He shrugged. "We need to get further away from the barbecue," he said, voice muffled.

"I say let 'em watch." Nightshade swung a blade in a wide arc.

Chase bounced back and took off running for the skate park. He could hear Nightshade and Vixen close behind. *Yes, follow little man.* Once he reached the lip of the down-curved concrete, he slid to the bottom, rolled, and faced his opponent.

Nightshade ran down the steep incline, barreling into Chase with both knives forward. They sank into the vest's chest. A white mist sprayed out around the blades.

Chase grabbed the little man and pulled him into a bear hug.

"Fuck, you're clever," Nightshade growled, struggling to pull away. Soon he stopped fighting altogether, falling slack in Chase's arms.

Vixen stood at the top of the skate park pit and smiled proudly. Then she shook her head as though disappointed.

What is her deal?

Chase waited for the remaining mist to stop before

kneeling to lay Nightshade on the concrete. He sat next to the unconscious leprechaun while staring up at Vixen. "Your ankle going to let you get down here?"

"I'll just sit," she said, doing exactly that at the lip of the pit. "He wasn't kidding, Hunter. That was stupid clever."

"This doesn't last long, so ..." He took a syringe out of his pocket, bit off the cover, and stuck the needle into Nightshade's neck.

As the plunger pressed down, the little man stirred and opened an eye to look at Chase. "Hi," he said weakly.

Chase laughed. "Sweet dreams."

"Nighty, night," Nightshade whispered, his eyes drifting toward Vixen. "Love you."

Chase glanced up at Vixen and pulled off the gas mask. "Can you have Officer Clark bring my Cavalier closer so we can get Nightshade out of this pit?"

Nodding, she rose to her feet.

"Vixen," Chase said, realizing he'd almost led Trevor to his death, "better find the gas canister hidden inside my car before he jumps in."

She nodded, frowning. "Will do."

Chapter Nineteen

Follow Me

THE royals believed God put them on this earth to rule. Thus, the Cloaks killing royals was against God's plan. Those caught using the Cloaks to kill off a royal-faced card in the game would themselves be put to death. The Cloak cards soon disappeared entirely. The people responded by utilizing the lowest card to kill off the king. French royalty erased the number from the One card, leaving only the image of the suit at its center. They renamed the card "Ace," a term that stood for bad luck. They believed this would halt its use as the king killer. Other royal families adopted this practice for their people and the Ace rapidly spread across Europe. However, instead of dissuading people from using the card, it came to represent the play that would kill off those unlucky enough to get in its way. Thus, the Cloak card was reincarnated in the body of the Ace. This, too, was reflected in the Guild as the Cloaks began calling themselves the "Four Aces."

June 8, 2016
03:10 PM CDT
Oklahoma City, Oklahoma

~ **Four of Spades** ~

ALAN stormed into Jim's office and slammed the door so hard it failed to latch.

This was Jim's favorite part. He couldn't help but smile at the mix of desperation, befuddlement, and fury creasing every wrinkle on Alan's face.

"You promised an increase in profits, Mr. Vancent." Alan threw financial documents at Jim's desk. "Now the money is gone! All of it."

The paper pushers outside the glass walls of Jim's office had been desperate to appear deeply focused on their work, but that statement made everyone stand to attention.

"They're all listening," Jim said. "Tell them why you did this. Tell them why they'll no longer be employed, due to your actions."

Jim was like the magician who disappears a helicopter from a stage. Alan and the onlooking wage slaves were his audience, staring dumbfounded at the successful execution of his illusion. Only, it wasn't a helicopter that vanished. It was every penny, from every account, all at once. At least, it appeared to be all at once. He'd spent months preparing for it to look that way.

"My actions?" Alan loosened his tie. "Jim, how in the hell did you pull this off?"

A magician never reveals his tricks. "I'm not sure why you're trying to blame this one on me. I would never. But I understand your reaction, Alan. It's how I felt when I saw the accounts this morning. How could you? And to your father's company, no less?"

Alan grabbed a stapler.

Showtime.

The stapler flew.

Jim let it catch him at the center of his chest. "Please, stop! Don't hurt me." He curled into a ball and threw a hand out to deflect the next assault. "We shouldn't all have to pay for your crimes because you got caught."

"The FBI is at my house, Jim." Alan grabbed a pen holder and chucked it at Jim's hand. "They're in my kitchen." He threw Jim's nameplate. "My wife made them coffee." A stone coaster took flight.

Jim let the coaster hit his shoulder before crawling out of the chair. He clasped his hands together as though in prayer as Alan approached. "I'm so sorry. I called them." He let Alan pull him up by the collar. "When I discovered your deception, I panicked. I don't usually associate with criminals. I didn't know what to do. I screwed up. How can I make it up to you?"

Alan balled up a fist and stared down at Jim with contempt. His eyes shifted to take in the rest of the office. Jim's gaze followed.

Most of the employees were still watching, some were packing up their things, and a few were on their phones, trying to explain to their spouses why the mortgage wouldn't get paid.

Alan dropped Jim and backed away. "They know me. They know I wouldn't do this."

"I saw your search history," said Jim. "Non-extradition

countries. Smart. Was Montenegro your choice? If you left now, you might get away. Go now before they catch you. I'll do my best to slow their pursuit when they arrive to look over the books."

Alan laughed derisively. "Go to hell."

They all say some version of that.

Alan walked over to the fire alarm pull station. "Burn in Hell!" He triggered the fire alarm and walked out of the office. Even though most of the workers watched him pull it, they followed him out as though there were an actual fire.

"Childish prick." Jim laughed, returning to his desk. He rubbed his chest where the stapler had connected, stretched his shoulder where the coaster would leave a bruise, and smiled. *Much better than last time.* He scratched the scar where a bullet had caught him in his last vanishing coins trick.

The six-story office building was a buzz of panicked sheep rushing down flights of stairs. Jim spent that time pouring himself a snifter of brandy and took a seat. The brandy burnt his throat as he downed it in one gulp. He poured another. The blaring alarm made his head throb, but they'd turn it off once someone informed the building manager that it was sparked out of anger.

The smell of smoke tripped over the hairs in his nose. He sneezed.

"That petty fucker set the building on fire." He stood to better see. Smoke poured in through the stairwell. "Oh shit." Jim grabbed his laptop and suitcoat and ran to the window. Gazing down, he could see smoke escaping the building several stories below. "Fuck, fuck, fuck, fuck." He twirled around to see a firefighter step through the smoke at the stairs.

The firefighter's voice was muffled as he called out.

Jim was sure he heard Vancent. "That's me." Jim ran to him. "I'm not surprised they sent you to find me. A horrible wrong has been committed."

The man said something Jim couldn't quite make out. "What was that?"

The firefighter pulled off his mask. His face was rough with burn scars.

"We can't go down," the man said. "Fire is spreading. We'll need to go to the roof." He started up the steps.

"Are you insane?" Jim yelled. "I'm not going up a level."

The firefighter turned. "We have a special lift outside the roof access that will get you to the ground quicker than you can spit." He snapped two fingers to emphasize his promise of a swift return to safety.

Now that's more like it. Jim chased after him.

The firefighter escorted him up one flight to a metal ladder that led to a ceiling hatch. "Through there, Mr. Vancent."

Jim climbed up and out. He reveled at the sight of the blue sky. *I'm almost free of this nightmare.* Jim ran to the edge of the gravel roof and looked around. "Where's the lift?" He turned in time to see his savior disappear down the ladder, the hatch closing behind him. "I don't understand." *Maybe he's checking on the lift.*

He looked down again, but failed to see a lift, let alone a fire engine of any sort. "No, no, no, no." He ran to the other side of the building. Still nothing. No firefighter in sight. Not one hose flooding the building with water. All he could see was smoke billowing out of his blazing building.

Jim tried the roof access, but it was locked from inside. He pounded on the hatch. "If this is about money, I have plenty! Get me down from here and I'll make you rich. I'll give you a million dollars."

No reply.

"Two!"

Nothing.

He ran to the roof's edge, searching for any form of deliverance. "Help!" he yelled.

"Someone is on the roof!" a woman yelled from below.

Fire engines could finally be heard rushing to the scene. They were close, but not nearly close enough.

This cannot be happening. Jim tried the roof access again. He jerked his hand away. "Fuck!" The handle was hot.

He ran to the edge and screamed repeatedly, waving his hands over his head as fire engines raced up the road.

Something buckled under him and loose bits of gravel rattled along the roof. The whole building was shifting.

"They're too late!" He turned and his shoe smeared gravel across the melting tar beneath.

I must get down! In a panic, he ran about the roof. *Nobody is going to get to me in time.* He ran to the roof access and grabbed it again, fighting through the pain as he tugged. "Open, you motherfucker!" He couldn't stand it any longer and jerked his hands away. Skin stuck in strands like glue to the metal. He stared at the bloody bubbles on his palms. A gruesome image of scalded flesh covering his body erupted at the forefront of his vision. "Nope!" *I'm not going out that way.*

Part of the roof crumpled.

There were trees on one side of the building. If he could leap far enough, he might land in the branches. He'd be broken by the time he met the ground, certainly. But alive.

He darted toward them. *Five more lunges and I'm there.* "Five." His foot slammed down. "Four." Hot tar splattered his calf. "Three." Something gave. "Two." The roof opened under his weight.

He slapped out his arms to catch his fall. Boiling tar oozed through spread fingers. Fire spewed up around him as it sought new oxygen. All Jim heard was a thunderous sound as it devoured him.

With the firefighter's final trick, he made Jim Vancent disappear.

Chapter Twenty

Cookies

June 8, 2016
06:45 PM CDT
Kansas City, Missouri

WHEN Nightshade stirred, Vixen stroked his cheek. "Why did you fall for Chase's ruse?" She smiled as she thought of the gas erupting from Chase's vest. *Who am I kidding?* "I would have, too."

Nightshade's eyes shot open. "Where? Owww ... Headache. I gotta piss."

"I'll help you up," Vixen said, reaching for him.

"I'm fine." He pushed her hand away. He tried to stand but crumpled to the floor. "Ouuuch."

Chase appeared at the top of the steps. "You might want to avoid standing for thirty minutes."

"Cool. I'm pissing on your floor."

Sure enough, he did exactly that.

"No, Mica." Vixen closed her eyes and pinched the bridge of her nose.

Nightshade chuckled.

"He's fine," Chase said, laughing. "If all I get for knocking him out is urine on my floor, I consider that a win."

"See?" Nightshade glanced at her. "Perfectly acceptable."

She rubbed her forehead. "Of course, you two would get along."

Chase leaned over the couch to look at Nightshade. "Would you rather we not?"

Nightshade gave Vixen a knowing look. A sympathetic smile crossed his lips before he plastered on a joyful one. He rose to his knees to face Chase. "She's rejoicing on the inside."

"You need fluids." Chase went to the fridge and returned with a water. "How are you feeling?"

"Groggy with a side of migraine."

"That good, eh?" Chase looked at Vixen. "You okay?"

Standing, she limped to the window to avoid his questioning gaze. She parted the curtain with her little finger and stared out at nothing in particular. "I should probably go."

"Really?" Chase said. "I made cookies."

"Grew bored of eating nuts out of a cookie jar?"

"Didn't miss 'em as much as I'd thought."

Vixen smiled, knowing he'd baked cookies because she'd mentioned a craving. Curious, she asked, "Chocolate chip?"

"None other."

She heard him open the lid and turned to see. *I probably told Nightshade to kill him minutes after he filled that jar for me.* A lump grew in her throat. She blinked rapidly.

"What's wrong?" Chase said, replacing the cover.

"Give them here," Nightshade said, breaking the tension. He opened and closed his hands over and over as a child would when wanting to be held. "I'll eat them all."

Chase grinned. "You can have just one, then to bed with you."

Nightshade's face caved into wrinkles. "What?"

Chase handed the jar to him. "I've always wanted to tell an adult that to see their reaction."

Nightshade already had one cookie in his mouth with another in hand to follow.

Chase shot Vixen a concerned look. Before he could go to her, Nightshade began coughing.

"Wrong—" He choked, pointing at his throat. "Wrong pipe."

"There's a cure for that," Chase said. "I believe it's called chewing."

Nightshade coughed hard a few times and cleared his throat. "My lungs were jealous of my stomach." He held the jar out for Vixen. "Here."

She shook her head, turning to look out the window. This time her eyes did catch something. A Ford F-150 crept slowly up the street. The driver wore a bomb suit and a gas mask. Backing away from the window, she snapped her fingers at Nightshade.

"What?" he said, the words barely discernible due to his mouth being full of yet another cookie.

"Powder Keg."

The moment the name tripped across her lips, she heard the jar drag across the floor. Out of her peripheral, she saw Nightshade crawl to the kitchen window with the jar in tow. Cookie crumbs dotted his lips.

Grabbing another cookie, Nightshade rose on one knee and glanced out. He bit off a bite and chewed while contemplating. "My legs aren't working enough to subdue him and your ankle's blown, chica." He took another bite and looked Chase up and down. "He could, though."

"I could what?"

Vixen shook her head. "Nothing." She limped to the front door and swung it open.

The F-150 had stopped outside the driveway. Powder Keg remained inside.

She shook her head.

The driver nodded, then drove off.

"What was that?" Nightshade said from beside her, stuffing the last of the cookie in his mouth.

"We have an understanding."

Crumbs sprayed from his lips as he spat, "An understanding?" He wiped his mouth. "We're ordered to bring him in if we see him. We just saw him. That's my understanding."

"Trust me on this."

"You know I trust you, but this could get you thrown in the hole. This could get me thrown in for being here."

"What's the hole?" Chase asked.

Nightshade turned on his knee. "It's what it sounds like: A place you get dumped for days without food or water. You have to do something pretty bad to find yourself there." He gestured at Vixen. "I believe this would apply."

"Have you been thrown in before?" asked Chase.

"No," said Nightshade. "It's not exactly on my bucket list of exotic places to go."

Vixen rolled her eyes. "We're the only two who saw him. Chase isn't telling anyone. Don't freak out over nothing."

Nightshade waved wildly at the door. "That man dropped a ceiling on Noose and you're telling me to let it go? What if this house explodes? What then?"

"Yeah," Chase said. "Could we please avoid blowing up my home?"

Vixen shut the door. "I told you, we have an understanding. He doesn't want to kill Chase. He's protecting him."

"Protecting him?" Nightshade echoed. "Why?"

"I don't know," she admitted. "He said it had something to do with Ace sending two assassins at once to test him."

"Why would he care?" Chase said. "I mean, I'm thankful and all, but why put his life on the line for me over a principle? How does what happens to me affect him?"

She shrugged. "I'm really not sure. I've been trying to piece that together myself. All I've come up with is he really dislikes Ace and the way he runs things."

Nightshade furrowed his brow. "You think he nearly killed Noose and Pockets over a difference of opinion?"

"Oh, I know," said Vixen. "It doesn't make sense."

Chase sat at the table. "I take it he doesn't usually take a special interest in the recruits?"

"He doesn't participate in testing at all," Nightshade said. "So, why would he?"

"I couldn't say," Chase said. "I don't know him."

"Know him?" Nightshade laughed. "Nobody *knows* him."

Vixen pulled out a chair and sat. "Nobody's seen him without the mask on."

Nightshade slid the cookie jar onto the table and sat as well. "As far as we know, he showers in it."

The only true conversation Vixen had with Powder Keg had been in her room, and it wasn't terribly enlightening. "Whatever his intention, I'm sure it doesn't involve blowing up your house with you inside."

Chase shrugged. "I doubt I'll stop worrying about that until all of this is over. When I'm either dead or part of the Guild."

She smirked. "That's fair."

"Now eat a damn cookie," Chase said to her, pointing at the jar. "I made them for you and he's eating them all."

She glanced at Nightshade. "Are there any left?"

Nightshade rolled his eyes exaggeratedly and stared at the ceiling. "No promises."

Chase chuckled. "If not, I'll make more."

Nightshade looked in the jar, then handed it to Vixen. "Looks like five."

"Thank you for leaving a few," Vixen said and smiled at Chase. "And to you for baking them. Even if I was high on laughing gas when I wanted them."

"What now?" Nightshade laughed. "Tell me everything."

She ignored him and bit into a cookie. It was the best she'd ever tasted. Her mouth salivated for more. She took another bite and chewed slowly to savor it.

Nightshade slapped the table. "Right?!"

"These are heaven," cooed Vixen.

Beaming, Chase sat back down. "I'm glad you like them."

"Like them?" she said, mid-chew. "Love them!"

"It's my mother's recipe. One of the only things I have that's hers."

Vixen brushed Nightshade's hand away when he reached for another. "He made them for me."

Nightshade patted his belly. "You're right. I've had enough. Gots to keeps my beautiful figures."

"I'll make more tonight."

Nightshade drummed his fingers on the table. "Funny thing is, after a good five minutes, you're left with a nutty aftertaste."

"It'll be worth it for the *now*taste," she said.

"I didn't think about that until after I'd dumped out the nuts and replaced them with cookies," said Chase. He watched adoringly as she ate the next one.

She loved the way he looked at her. *He wouldn't if he knew I'd asked Nightshade to kill him.* She closed her eyes to block him from view. She felt his eyes on her all the same.

"Just one more," Nightshade pleaded.

"Quiet," said Vixen. "You're interrupting my ability to savor them."

"Whatever. Gimme."

"You two seem close," Chase said.

Her eyes drifted open to see Chase smiling at them. "He and I joined the Guild around the same time. We became fast friends."

"I wanted more than friendship," Nightshade admitted. "As I'm sure you relate. Just about lost it when I first saw her."

She smiled, wiping crumbs from her lip. "That's sweet."

Nightshade pointed his thumb at her. "She started saying things like that before I realized I'd lost my chance. I'm forever broken because of her."

Chase leaned back in his chair. "You seem fine to me."

Nightshade put the back of his hand to his forehead theatrically. "It's all an act, my good man."

Chase nodded at her. "You want some milk?"

"Yes, please and thank you." She saved the next cookie to dip.

Chase returned with a glass, then excused himself, saying, "I need to go to the bathroom." He made it to the steps before glancing back. "Speaking of which, I'd like to return to find the urine cleaned off the floor and the seat you're sitting in wiped clean."

Nightshade chuckled. "No promises."

"Yes, promises." Chase started up. "Our future friendship depends on it. The cleaners are in the cabinet under the sink."

Vixen dipped the cookie in the milk and chewed while watching Chase go. She found his walk profoundly attractive. She didn't know a walk could be found attractive.

"I hate him." Nightshade laughed.

"I know. He's the worst." She glanced to see Nightshade's eyebrow raised at her.

"I'd like him if I weren't jealous."

"Of what?" asked Vixen, dipping the cookie.

"Of what?" Nightshade laughed. "Be careful, Vix."

"Don't call me Vix. I can't be rubbed on your chest." The cookie fell apart in the milk.

"That reminds me of a dream I had once. You were naked and we were—"

"I'm going to tell your future wife you dream of me."

He waved dismissively. "My future wife will be all cool and say, 'That's my crazy, little man.' Then I'll kiss her, and say, 'You know it.'"

She dropped the rest of the cookie in. "I hope you find her."

"Where was I before you distracted me?" Nightshade slapped the table. "I *remember*. Be careful with this one," he said, uncharacteristically serious. "You're getting attached. Something's not right with his testing. Ace told me to go out of my way to kill him. 'Do everything you can,' he said." Vixen must have made a face because Nightshade felt the need to add, "Twice, he said this." He held up two fingers. "Twice."

She frowned. "I know."

Nightshade shook his head. "I don't think you do. The words 'do everything you can' have never left his lips before, even for an actual contract. But he says it while staring at me with those cold, dark eyes of his."

"I don't understand Ace's obsession." Vixen swirled the crumbled, soggy cookie around in the milk. "Either he wants to bring in a god of assassins or he wants Chase dead."

Nightshade got up and walked to the sink for the rag dangling from the faucet. "If Chase were a target, you think he'd be in the bathroom, clearly shitting?" He ran the rag under the water and rung it out. "He'd be dead already."

She shook her head. "But Chase isn't a god of assassins either. In fact, he's never killed anyone."

Nightshade disappeared below the counter and returned with a bucket of cleaning supplies. "You'd know better than I." He upended the supplies into the sink and began filling the bucket with soapy water. "I fought him for approximately three seconds before lights went out." He bent to clean his piddle puddle.

"He's lucky, clever, and a fast learner," Vixen said. "But his inexperience alone should have killed him by now." She watched the top of the stairs. "I don't want him to die, but I definitely don't want to be the one to kill him."

"Hey, I tried," Nightshade said. "My sister told me to kill him and I did my best to carry out her wishes."

"You said earlier you wanted to rub me on your chest. Not very brotherly of you."

"What can I say?" chuckled Nightshade. "Taboo is my voodoo."

"You don't make any sense," said Vixen, smirking.

He shrugged. "Agree to disagree."

She heard the toilet flush. "I can't kill him."

Nightshade came around to the chair and wiped it down. "He's survived worse than you."

"He trusts too easily."

"Your testing him will teach him not to."

"Or he won't see me coming." She nibbled at the inside of her cheek. "If that day comes, I'll wish you succeeded today."

He began to reply, but stopped when the bathroom door opened upstairs.

Chase appeared at the top of the stairs. "What do you want to do?"

Nightshade thumped the bucket of soapy water on the table. "I actually have a chick to kill in Oregon. I need to quite literally jet."

"I'm your ride," remembered Vixen.

"I can walk."

"The airport's twenty miles."

"Then, yes, I'd appreciate that."

"One sec," said Chase. "I'll grab you some clean underwear and shorts." He ducked into his room.

"Perfect," Nightshade belted out, dropping his soiled

pants and boxers to his ankles. He stepped out of them and ran to the bottom of the stairs.

Chase reappeared and covered his eyes.

"They're just genitals." Nightshade guffawed. "Throw them down and deliver me from nudity."

"Gladly." Chase tossed them blindly.

Vixen remembered fondly tossing clothing to Chase the day she met him.

Nightshade bent to pick them up.

It was Vixen's turn to cover her eyes. "You'll have to forgive him, Chase. He's not of this planet."

"Hey," Nightshade said, glaring. "You promised never to reveal my secrets."

"You're not hiding your inability to grasp social norms. You pissed on his floor and flashed your privates."

"That's not the point." Nightshade pulled the underwear on and jumped into the shorts. "If I decide to tell people I'm from a universe far, far away, that's my decision."

"Hush and get in the car." Vixen smiled at Chase. "I need to do an inventory at the safe houses we have here, so I'll be back a little late. Feel free to head to bed without me."

"Sounds good," Chase said.

"Wait." Nightshade twirled. "You're sleeping together?"

"Key word is 'sleeping,'" she insisted. "That's all."

"Uh-huh." Nightshade walked to the door and swung it open. "You are most definitely telling me about this in the car."

"That's all there is to tell, ya nut job."

"Sure, it is." Nightshade looked around. "Where's my bag of tricks?"

Chase pointed at the fireplace where a backpack rested.

"It's there. Your knives are inside with all the vials, shakers, and canisters I found on you."

"Perfect." Nightshade scooped it up. "It was a pleasure being incapacitated by you."

"I enjoyed this awkward encounter as well." Chase made his way down the stairs. "Be safe on your flight."

"One more thing," Nightshade said, one foot outside the door. "Do you trust Vixen?"

Chase glanced between Nightshade and Vixen before he replied, "Implicitly."

Vixen shook her head. "Wrong answer, Hunter."

Nightshade anticipated what came next, speaking in sync with her: "Trust people to your detriment."

"First rule during testing," Vixen said. "Don't trust anyone. Until you are officially a card holder of our Guild, I could turn on you at any moment."

Nightshade slung the pack over his shoulder. "She'll kiss ya today, kill ya tomorrow." He turned and whispered to her. "He's been warned."

"At least I'll get a kiss first." Chase walked to the couch. "The coroner will find a smiling corpse."

Vixen felt her lip perk in a half smile, but quickly removed it.

Nightshade's head drooped. "Never mind, he's an idiot." He then skipped away while singing, "Off to force-feed a lady mushrooms. Mushrooms? Yes, deadly musharoooms."

"You passed your third test," Vixen said, trying to smile proudly. "I'll be back shortly."

Chase stood a little taller and smiled. "I'll look forward to seeing you."

She closed the front door behind her when she left and waited to unlock the car until she neared it. "How's your roommate situation?"

Nightshade got in, laughing. "Yeah, that didn't work out. He dead."

"What?!" Vixen yelled while getting in the driver's seat. "Did you poison your roommate?"

"Maybe ... sorta ... mighta, maybe ... sorta, kinda ..." He nodded. "Maybe sorta did."

She felt her eyes widen involuntarily. "What?"

"Mighta kinda did."

"You can't *kill anyone* unless you have a contract. Without it, Ace could have you cut from the deck."

"I did."

"Wait." She was confused. "You took a target as your roommate? That gets them close enough to kill, but leaves ample evidence of your connection."

Nightshade put his seatbelt on. "He wasn't a hit when I took him as a roommate."

"That bites. Do you know who wanted him dead?"

"Well, that would be me," he said matter-of-fact. "I hired myself."

Vixen put her head in her hands, sighing heavily. "What am I going to do with you?"

"Could start with getting me to the airport."

She turned the key and started up the street. "Why?"

"Why did I kill him? Or are you asking 'why' in general annoyance?"

She narrowed her eyes. "Both."

"He was bringing drugged women into my home and

raping them."

"Why didn't you turn him into the police?"

"You know my birth was a result of rape. Felt like I was poisoning my dad." He placed his "bag of tricks" between his legs. "It was downright therapeutic."

She sighed. "Sorry I encouraged you to get a roommate."

"All this could have been avoided had you simply moved in."

She laughed. "You never asked."

"Would you have?"

She laughed harder.

"That's what I thought," he said before shifting in his seat.

He stared at her for nearly a minute before she glanced at him.

"What?"

"You're really not screwing him?"

"I swear."

"The looks he gave you suggest otherwise. What else can a woman do to make someone fall so hard for them?"

"Imagine that," she said, returning her eyes to the road. "A man who falls in love with a woman when sex isn't on the table."

"Sex is on the table," Nightshade said, then danced in his seat. "Or on the floor, in a bed, or in the shower. He just hasn't asked for it yet."

"I practically gave myself to him on a silver platter and he turned me down." She pulled onto the highway. "I finally find a man I could fall in love with and I'm ordered to kill him."

"You mean to say the love of my life could be the person I must kill?" He thought on that. "This girl in Oregon could be the one for me."

Vixen grinned. "What happened to being broken by my rejection?"

"I am. Absolutely shattered in fact." He combed his fingers through his hair. "But she could be the woman to put all these pieces back together."

"Good luck with that," Vixen said. "Why did you accept the contract to kill her?"

"She cut a baby out of a woman's womb."

"Not ideal for the love of your life."

Nightshade shook his head. "Love's tricky like that."

"Please don't marry this girl."

Nightshade grew mockingly serious, and said, "How else am I going to make you jelly?"

"You've got a point," she conceded mockingly, then frowned. "I wish he'd fuck me and get it over with."

"The anticipation that bad?"

"It's not that."

"Why, then?" asked Nightshade.

"He's distracted."

"Everyone's distracted by you, Laura. How would having sex with him change that?"

"When I give my body to someone, they stop wanting it," Vixen said. "They desire what they see, get their hands on it, and don't care if they drop it."

"Damn." Nightshade's expression turned to anger. "Someone dropped you hard."

She glared at him.

He drew back. "I know you well enough to see this discussion's over." He scrunched his nose. "However, it's clear

Chase hasn't stopped holding onto what you've given him. And if you gave more, that boy wouldn't drop you." He took a deep breath. "Unfortunately, my advice in this case is to refrain from giving him more to hold onto. Because when he keeps holding you after, the knife will slip from your fingertips and bury itself in the floor at your feet." He turned and looked out his window, being true to his word and letting the conversation end.

Vixen bit the inside of her cheek. *I'm going to have to kill the one person who wants to hold onto me.* This time, when tears formed, she did not blink them away. She forced herself to endure each slow streak and taste their salt as they caught the corners of her lips.

Chapter Twenty-One

גֹּלֶם

THE royalty put people to death for using Aces as a substitution for the Cloaks, deeming it a treasonable offense. The Guild stepped forward and fought back for the people. The Guild members began carrying a card on their person, that number or face becoming part of their identity. The royalty quickly backed down when nobles began dying in the night. A loss so significant against such a small faction was unheard of. As history is written by those in power, their war with the Guild of Four became forgotten lore.

June 8, 2016
07:11 PM CDT
Irving, Texas

~ Nine of Spades ~

"WE'RE sorry. We are unable to complete your call as dialed.

Please check the number and dial again."

Veronica frantically put her phone in her pocket and ran to her desk. *If I didn't stay late, this wouldn't be happening.* She pulled the Kel Tec P11 from the desk drawer. *Bullets, bullets, bullets ...* She found the clip full of 9MMs and pushed it into place. "What the fuck was that thing?" She finally took a moment to breathe. *Wasn't human.* She pushed her chair away to gain more room. *Looked like a stone gargoyle from castle-tops.* She laughed nervously. *My new antidepressants are messing with me. I'm going insane. It's not real. It's all in my ...*

The thumping of its feet cut off her thoughts. They were coming up the hallway outside her office.

She ducked behind her desk and brought the rear sight of the gun to her forehead. *It's all in your mind, Veronica. It's not real.* She dialed security again.

The recorded intercept message she'd heard twice before replied, "We're sorry. We are unable to complete your call as dialed. Please check the number and dial again."

She dialed 911.

"We're sorry. We are unable to complete your call as dialed. Please check the number and dial again"

Veronica screamed at the phone and threw it against the wall.

The thumping came to a stop outside her door.

"You're not real," her voice quaked. *It can't be real. It's not.*

The thumping entered her office and stopped again.

Shit, oh shit, oh shit ... She pressed her back against the desk and held her breath. There was a mechanical humming, then silence. She peeked. The monster's red eyes stared back from across the desk. She let out a surprised shout that transitioned into the loudest, highest pitched scream she'd ever made.

It roared back at her. It stood ten feet tall and three feet wide. Steam snaked up from its nostrils. Up close, it looked like a gorilla made entirely of stone. *Almost* entirely. Its teeth looked to be of metal as did the razor-sharp claws of its hands. She couldn't see its feet, but assumed metal claws were there as well.

She nearly pissed herself. *Pull it together, Veronica.* Her eyes met the awards for excellence hanging on the wall. The gold paperweight in the shape of an oil well she'd been given for 20 years of service. She was always the strong woman, the one who got it done, no matter how dirty or wrong the deed. She pointed the gun at the monster and squeezed two shots into its face.

If the bullets had any effect, the creature didn't show it. It leaned forward against the desk and roared again, the metal claws digging into the walnut wood.

She retreated until her back met the wall. Her hands trembled as she squeezed off another two bullets, this time into the monster's chest. It rose and straightened, the red eyes glaring.

She took another breath to calm herself. "What are you?"

Symbols Veronica didn't recognize lit up red upon its chest:

$$\text{גֹּלֶם}$$

WHAT is that? "I don't understand," she said, squinting as the symbols faded. "Are you of this planet?" *Maybe he's just scared.* She pointed at the ceiling. "Are you from out there?"

There was the sound of something snapping within the belly of the beast. The creature dropped and pushed.

She threw her hands against the desk as it pinned her to

the wall.

The monster brought its head close to hers and opened its mouth. Beyond the metallic teeth, she could see more symbols glowing red:

עֶלְיוֹנִין

THE air became heavy and moist. A smell all too familiar to those in her profession clung to the back of her throat.

Petrol! Veronica pushed the desk with all her might. *Come on.* The back of the monster's throat sparked. "Fuck!" By some miracle, the desk budged slightly and she dropped to hide beneath it.

Fire spread down the crack between the wall and desk. The back of her shirt grew warm, then hot. She could feel parts of it burning against her skin. She screamed and turned to fall upon her back.

The flames came to an abrupt stop. A loud roar shook the desk from all sides. There were two loud thuds against the frame, then a pounding atop it. She put down the gun and threw her hands up to support the top of the desk.

"Leave me alone!" she yelled.

Another thud sent a crack splintering down the middle of the desk. The desk that had survived thirty moves to satellite offices all over the world. She pushed harder against the wood, grunting with the effort. *I'm fucking dead.* Another thud came, this one softer than the last.

The desk stopped shaking. The thumping of the monster's feet could be heard walking away.

She raised her eyebrows. Though she managed to

extinguish the flame on her back, she could feel a burning sensation along her bra strap. She reached back to undo the bra and pull it off, but it pinched at her skin when she unhooked it. *It's melted to my flesh.* She imagined ripping off the bra and the pain that would come with it. *Better leave that to the professionals.* She returned the hooks to their eyes. *If I can get out of here alive, that is.*

There was a glimmer of yellow and red coming from the crack between the desk and wall. She could no longer hear the thumping of the monster's feet. Veronica dropped, setting her head on the ground. Cautiously, she peered through the small gap between the desk's wooden frame and the floor. Besides herself, the office appeared vacant.

She sat and placed her back against the frame. She took two long breaths, then pushed her feet against the wall. The desk moved enough for her to get free. She scooped up the gun and crawled out. Her beautiful desk was smoldering. It had been with her family for generations. *I'm going to kill that motherfucker.* She reloaded the gun.

"Helloooo?" she said, knowing she'd be safer under the desk if that thing were to return. When it didn't come thundering back, she stole across the room. She glanced out in one direction, then the other. *Where would a hell beast of that size hide?*

A thumping and rattling startled her. It came from down the hall. She gripped her gun tightly before stepping out. *I'd like to see it survive the entire clip being emptied into its face.* She gathered her resolve, nodded, and crept down the hall. She passed the kitchenette and bathrooms before coming to the employee lounge. The thumping and rattling came from further down. *It's in the cubicles.*

There was a landline phone on the wall near the kitchenette. Veronica picked it up and dialed security. A busy tone replied. But there was more. Someone clearly sighed. She narrowed her eyes and said, "Who's there?"

The busy tone cut off and a woman's voice said, "Lady, just die so my Golem can come home. You've done enough evil in this world. Just go to hell, knowing the demons there will welcome you in as their own."

"Who the fuck do you think you—?"

The busy tone cut back in.

Veronica smashed the phone against its mount until it fell to pieces in her hand.

She gripped the gun tightly in her palm and started marching down the hallway. "Where are you, you motherfucker?"

She closed the remaining distance and pressed her back against the wall. *Keep it together, Veronica.* She closed her eyes and took another long breath. *Keep it together.*

The gun went first, her face following close behind. Nothing greeted her, but the thumping and rattling was definitely coming from within.

Veronica stepped in the room, nervously looking around at the cubicles. They were tall enough to hide the monster. She took it slow. One cubicle after another, she poked in the gun, then followed. Gun, then follow. Gun, then follow. Gun, then follow. The thumping and rattling sounded three cubicles down.

She took a deep breath, held it, and let it slowly out as she continued. "Talked to your girlfriend on the phone." Gun, follow. "She sounds cute." Gun, follow. "Too bad I'll have to hunt her down and cut her pretty little face off when I'm through with you." Gun, follow. "What the fuck?"

Two thick, rubber ovals were spinning and thumping against the ground, a metal rod connecting them to one another. It gyrated and bounced noisily against the ground, office chair, and cubicle. "You're behind me, aren't you?"

Several cold sharp somethings sank into her mid-back. She was jerked backward. Something popped along her spine. There was an instant of pain, then nothing below her shoulders. The gun fell from her fingertips, clattering against the floor. Her eyes glanced over to see the smoldering eyes of the monster. "Don't."

The monster's head came close. The smell of Petrol enveloped her.

She coughed. "Please."

It roared before throwing her against the wall.

She collapsed and tried to catch herself. Only her left arm heeded the call for support. Her left ankle landed wrong, making a sick crack as it bent backward. She fell in a heap, her right leg bending awkwardly at the knee. It was strange. She should have been in agony sprawled out as she was. Yet, no pain from those injuries followed.

Her eyes rose to see the monster standing beside her.

Before this moment she swore she could escape, but that belief was held within a glass bubble of self-confidence that now lay shattered at her feet, fragmented and impossible to put back together. She was dying. There was no escaping that. But she was determined to drag this monster to hell with her.

The gun wasn't far off, if she could only move to retrieve it. She tested her body for what still worked. The left side of her face down to the fingers of her left hand remained responsive; the rest had abandoned her.

She pushed against the wall and fell on her side. The gun was still out of reach. Her palm pressed against the floor and scooted her forward. The sound of the monster taking a step sent adrenaline coursing through her body. She slapped her palm down again and pushed until her face landed within an inch of the gun. She scooped it up, realizing she'd never held the gun in her left hand before. It felt out of place.

The monster took another step.

She went to twirl and shoot the beast, only to find again that her body wasn't up to the once simple request. "Damn you." Her voice sounded distorted escaping only from the left side of her mouth. She pushed the tip of the gun against the ground until she was lying on her side. The effort seemed to take everything out of her. Raising the gun was a chore.

The monster stepped forward, blood dripping from its metallic claws.

My blood. It enraged her. She pulled the trigger. The gun went off in the monster's face. At the same moment, part of her finger slipped between the trigger and trigger guard. It pinched her so badly, she dropped the gun. *Fuck, fuck!* She grabbed it, raising it in time to see the monster nearly on top of her.

Yet again it was clear bullets had no visible effect.

A tear ran down her cheek as she glared at the monster. "Why—are you—" She choked. "Here?"

Symbols lit on a different part of the monster's chest than before:

רָצַח

I don't know what that means! She wanted to scream in its face, but her voice came out a whisper. "What?" She swallowed. Even that was a challenge. "Why—do this?"

The creature stood straighter, one of its clawed hands glistening crimson. The same symbols lit:

$$\text{רָצַח}$$

SHE coughed and tasted blood. "Fine—then." She pulled the trigger, managing this time not to pinch herself in the process. "Eat—me." She squeezed off two more shots.

The monster opened its mouth and the air grew thick.

She emptied the rest of the clip into its face. Flame spewed forth. The gun clicked as though apologizing for failing her. She took a breath to scream but only succeeded at inhaling fire.

Chapter Twenty-Two

Widower

June 8, 2016
08:47 PM CDT
Kansas City, Missouri

LYING in bed, Chase heard footsteps coming from behind. "I'm sorry I dropped my guard with Nightshade. I shouldn't have assumed my time was up."

Something pinched his neck.

He swatted at it only to feel something metallic. *No!* He snapped his other hand back to grab someone's wrist and spun around.

The person he held was darker than the room.

He grabbed his phone and lit up the screen. Through blurred vision, he could see the light reflecting off what appeared to be a syringe and sparkling in a diamond earring.

He felt numb, but managed the words, "What did you do?"

"Shhh ..." A woman hushed. "We'll talk soon."

He tried to get a better grip on her wrist, but his fingers

tingled. *I have to fight.* He hadn't expected to be tested twice in one day. But why not? He'd taken two at once before. He tried to leave the bed. *Why did I ... let my guard ... dowwwn I go.*

His toes found no purchase on the floor. His knees buckled, dropping the rest of him to splash against a murky pool of lumbering slumber.

HE jolted awake to the sound of thunder. He heard himself say, "I made more cookies."

"I smell them," a woman replied. "If you're fine with it, I'll have some later."

He blinked away the blur and found himself sitting at his dining room table. It was raining outside. He looked over to see the assassin perched on the arm of his couch. She wore a black hooded sweatshirt with black tights. Her skin was darker than both, her eyes twinkling brighter than the diamonds in her earrings and her wedding ring.

"You don't look terribly concerned," the woman said, pulling the hood back. Long black hair spilled out around her shoulders. She crossed her arms. She was at least twenty years his senior and she was beautiful.

"I'm happy to be alive. I let my guard down and I shouldn't be sitting here." He tried to move only to realize he was restrained. *I thought I'd felt something gripping my ankles and wrists.* He blinked a few more times to clear his vision and glanced down.

He wore gloves. Black wires fed from a laptop to his

fingertips. A bar separated his hands, a wrist shackled to each end. His eyes followed a wire that slipped out of the center of the bar, trailing down to a long glass container. Inside, he wiggled his cold toes. "Couldn't have given me socks?"

"I brought you down as you were. You're a big man, so I might have thumped your head a few times on the way down."

"Yeah, I feel that." He wanted to rub his head, but quickly realized that was impossible in his current predicament. He wiggled his fingers. "How's this work?"

"Do you see them yet?" She pointed at his feet as she made her way to the laptop. "If not, keep looking."

"See who?" He studied his feet further, seeing that each had been put through a separate hole. Inflated padding trapped his feet inside. He could feel metal bracelets around his ankles. He shifted his feet and, sure enough, heard chain links rub against one another. He noticed the wire from before went through to the bottom of the container. It split in half and ran in both directions, the smaller wires breaking away to feed in where black walls cut the case into sections. *What are those for?* His eyes caught the answer the moment lightning illuminated every window. "Spiders!" Thunder boomed. *I hate this. I've faced knives, poison, and a rhinoceros of a man, and yet this right here takes the cake.* A cold sweat threaded beads across his brow. "Please let me out."

"I'm Widow," the assassin said, taking a seat.

"Hi," Chase said, taking quick breaths. "I'm terrified."

She laughed softly. "Know that with every move you make, you come one step closer to death's door. A fly struggling to survive in a web only attracts the spider's attention."

"That's not helpful." Chase thought looking away from the

spiders would take his mind off them. It did not.

"I have a few baseline questions," said Widow.

"If they'll get me out of this, be quick with the asking."

Widow looked confused. "You're not going to attempt to break free by kicking or stomping?"

He swallowed hard, squeezed his eyes shut, and said, "Nothing is simple with the Guild. I thought the whole 'fly struggling' bit was to warn me against that nonsense."

"Very good," she said. "What color is the wall?"

He opened his eyes slightly to glare at her. "Why?"

"Baseline question."

"Sorry. This whole spider situation is—Ahhh! You know."

"I adore them."

"You're insane."

"Color?" she said, eyes directed at the computer.

He jumped when thunder clapped outdoors. "Ask me something else."

"Why?"

He ran his gloved hands over the table, and cleared his throat. "Because I'm looking at the wall and I live here and still, I cannot tell you. That's how freaked out I am."

"Okay," she said, eying him curiously. "First name?"

"Chase."

"Lie about your last name, please."

"Argenbright." He dug his fingernails into the fingers of the gloves. "I hated that guy."

Another clap of thunder.

He made fists.

"Careful with the gloves. If you squeeze too tightly, they'll—" A *thathump* interrupted her. "Never mind."

The thumps jolted his ankles. His eyes dropped to see the spiders claiming a greater amount of territory at each side of the glass container. He flattened his palms out on the table, raising his gaze to look at the wires strung between his fingers and the laptop. He took a deep breath and said, "Neeext question."

"I have a list I was given actually." She took out an envelope and opened it. "Okay, first question. Is Vixen still training you?"

I can't get her in more trouble. "No."

Widow's eyes narrowed and she gazed into his eyes. "Say again."

"No, she's not."

Her thumb tapped a key.

Chase's eyes went wide as his ankles felt the pop-pop. "Mother of—" He shook it off. "Screw you!"

"Is that a yes?"

He glared at her. "Next question."

"We'll come back to it." She eyed the paper. "Are you fucking Vix—" Her mouth shut and her eyes read on alone. Head shaking slightly, she put down the paper. "I'm sorry, these aren't the questions I'd expected." She rubbed her temples. "Let me rephrase: Are you having intercourse with Vixen?"

"That's seriously a question on there?"

"Are you having—?"

"No," Chase interrupted.

She dropped a finger to hover over the enter key.

He squeezed his eyes shut. "I swear, I swear, I swear!" Thunder crackled slow and long.

"Has she offered?"

He opened one eye when he realized his ankles hadn't felt

the thumping. *That would certainly get her in trouble.* "I'm not sure how to answer that."

"Yes or no works."

Something occurred to him. "Do I have to answer?"

"This won't take long. If you answer fully and accurately, you'll be free of the box."

He raised an eyebrow at her.

"I'll ask again," said Widow. "Has she offered to have intercourse with you?"

Chase watched lightning flash outside. The wind blew rain hard against the window.

Widow's fingers slipped away from the keys. "You want to sit here in silence?"

He nodded. *Not answering is the only answer keeping spiders off my ankles.*

"In all my years, nobody ever shuts up," Widow said. "They squirm at silence and have a compulsion to speak when questioned." She pushed her chair back and crossed one leg over the other. "You are the first to simply stop answering."

"Do you like silence?" asked Chase.

"I don't mind it."

"Nor do I, but if you want, you could answer a few questions for me."

"Sure," she agreed. "If you answer one final, crucial question for me."

He shook his head.

"I promise the answer won't betray Vixen's trust." She hovered a finger over the keys. "Do those cookies have nuts in them?"

"No, they're chocolate chip."

"My favorite." She removed her finger from the keyboard. "I'll take one, thank you."

"I'm sort of stuck," he said. "Otherwise, I'd get them for you."

"My legs are free and work just fine." She went and returned with the jar. She cradled it in one arm as her hand fished out the first cookie. "Ask away." She took a bite.

"Why go by Widow?"

She looked at the cookie while chewing. "These are good."

"My mother's recipe."

"Mothers are wonderful," she said, taking another bite.

"I didn't really know mine."

"I never had children." She frowned. "I wanted to, but my Thomas died before we could conceive."

"How'd he die?"

She stuffed the rest of the cookie in her mouth as though to keep from answering.

"Sorry," Chase said. "That's personal."

Widow chewed for a long while before shrugging and swallowing. "No, it's fine." A sad smile twisted her lip. "He fired his lab assistant because she tried to seduce him. When she came in for her final check, she proclaimed her love for him and shot him ten times in the chest."

"That's fucked."

"What's worse is I had come in to have lunch with him. I watched all this happen and blackout lost it." Deep in thought, she took out another cookie and bit into it.

"As you should have." Chase adjusted the manacles so he could lean forward. "Did you drop her down an elevator shaft?"

She coughed. "Sorry." She coughed harder. "I swallowed

wrong or something." She cleared her throat. "My husband was an arachnologist, researching how to use spider venom in breast cancer treatments." She scratched her throat. "Researchers in Australia were using Hadronyche modesta venom, but my husband thought Phoneutria fera venom was better suited to the job." Clearing her throat harder, she looked at the last of the cookie in her hand. "That amazing spider is one of the most poisonous out there. When I locked my husband's killer in the ten-by-eleven-foot habitat, they made quick work of her."

"Oh, shit!" He sat back. "That where your tag comes from? Killing a woman with black widows?"

"Not black widows." She stood and stretched her neck. "Brazilian wandering spiders."

Pointing at his feet, he asked, "Is that what these are?"

The cookie jar slipped from her arm and shattered at her feet.

"You lied," she choked out.

"Pardon?"

"You said no nuts."

"There aren't any."

"There's definitely—" She coughed and stretched her neck. "An aftertaste." Swallowing hard, she looked around in panic. "Where's my bag?"

"Oh, god!" He'd seen that look on his uncle's face. "You're allergic, aren't you?"

She cleared her throat hard. "Deadly aller—" Wheezing cut her off.

Lightning flooded the windows, giving her an eerie halo.

Chase tried to stand, but only succeeded in jarring the manacles.

Thump, thump. Lightning crackled. *Kabooom.*

"Nooo." He'd freed up more space for the hideous crawlies. "This is not happening." He looked to see Widow scrambling through her laptop bag. "Find it?"

"I think ..." She doubled over the table, coughing harder to clear her airway. "Purse in—the ca—" When she turned for the door, her knees buckled and she collapsed, fingers clutching at her throat.

Chase examined the wires, the manacles, everything. *I have to get out.* He couldn't watch her die. He remembered duct taping a cloropicrin vial under the counter behind him. It was meant to be a substitute for mace, but his research mentioned it being used in pesticides. With all the strength he could muster, he swung his arms up and back. The cable that ran from his hands to the container caging his feet snapped at the middle. There came a *thuthump, thump thump, thuthump* as every divider opened. His body bent backward over the chair, grabbed under the counter for the vial of cloropicrin, and freed it of the duct tape. He stuck it through the padding around his left ankle.

The spiders fought with one another, growing ever closer to his feet.

This'll suck. With a sharp twist, the vial shattered, its oily, yellow contents spilling over his foot.

The spiders continued fighting, this time in a scramble to get away from the fumes. Those closest to his ankle struggled to stay upright for barely a second before crumpling.

Widow was fading fast.

No, no, no. "This cannot be happening." He lifted his feet and shook the container back and forth to spread the fumes faster. A limp spider struck his ankle. He nearly bit off the end of his tongue for fear it may still be alive.

Where the liquid splashed against his feet, he felt a desire to itch, but the worst came from the fumes. His eyes burned and breath caught in his throat. He stood and waddled around to the counter where he found the meat tenderizer beside the knives. He brought it down against the glass.

It barely left a scratch.

Come on. He hit the container along the edge. A small crack appeared. "Thank you!" Focusing the blows on the edges near his ankles, he thwack-thwack-thwacked until the cracks became long and wide. He brought the mallet above his head and ... THCRACK!

The house lit bright and thunder rumbled long and hard as if cheering for him.

Feet free of the container, but still cuffed, he shuffled to the stairs. He jumped two at a time and rounded the corner at the top. After several quick breaths, he bounced down the hall and burst into his uncle's room. It was nearly impossible to rummage through a drawer with hands bound and separated by a pole, but he managed to find two epinephrine pens.

Hopping for the door, he prayed, "Please be alive, please be alive, please be alive." He reached the steps and jumped down half before lunging into a front flip to reach the bottom. Not quite sticking the landing, he careened sideways, crushing another human-size hole in the dry wall. Still mostly upright, he bounced to the assassin.

"Widow?" He dropped to his knees and placed one EpiPen on the floor. "Stay with me." With his teeth, he snapped away the safety cap to the other. "Who keeps spiders as pets?"

He felt her thigh to make sure she wasn't wearing armor. When he found none, he brought the pen out at an angle. "Something wrong with cats?" He slammed the tip hard into her thigh and heard a click. "They're happy to wait until you die before eating your face." He held it there for what felt like forever. "Come on, Widow."

Thunder rolled. She let out a moan.

"Thank you, Lord." He choked on his relief. "Dogs are great companions." He placed his mouth against hers and blew to open the passageway.

She coughed and Chase felt spittle dot his face.

"Birds are beautiful," he said.

Grabbing his leg, she squeezed hard and searched his face with wild eyes.

I don't think one's going to do. He grabbed the second pen and bit the cap off. "Whatever animal floats your boat, really." He stabbed the other thigh.

Click.

He held it there. "As long as the water floating the boat isn't made up entirely of spiders." After fifteen seconds, he threw the pen aside. "Come on." He dropped his mouth to hers and blew.

Widow coughed long and hard before drawing a thin, prolonged breath. As oxygen filled her lungs, she shook and dug fingernails into his flesh.

He took the pain without complaint.

When she had taken three breaths, her hand drew back bloody.

"You'll be all right." He helped her sit.

She leaned her weight against him, resting her head upon

his shoulder.

Chase could hear whispering. He lowered his ear.

"Forgive me, Thomas," she said. "Please, forgive me."

He lifted his arms and threaded her body through the space given by the pole. "Stop apologizing." He hugged her as best as he could. "You have nothing to apologize for. You aren't the one who killed him."

"I was late for," she gasped in a breath, "our lunch date."

He shook his head. "This isn't on you."

"I should have been there."

"Destiny is a bitch," he said, realizing how much that applied to his own feelings about Frank. "If only we could assassinate that bitch." He winked.

She stared at the ceiling and let out a broken sigh.

"Sorry I killed your spiders."

"You did what you had to." Her voice was stronger now. "As I lay there dying ..." She coughed, rubbed her puffy eyes, and cleared her throat. "I found peace knowing I'd see Thomas soon." A tear ran down her cheek. "I'll forgive you for killing my spiders. I may not forgive you for keeping me from him."

"That's fair." Trying to wipe the tear from her face, he accidentally bopped her nose with the bar. "Can you get this off me?"

She pointed at her laptop bag a short way from them.

"Scoot with me," he said.

Her weakened state made it a laborious task.

Chase noticed something move out of the corner of his eye when they reached the bag.

A spider, quite clearly dead, was moving.

I cannot handle zombie spiders.

It fell aside, freeing the larger spider underneath to crawl out of the container. It was apparently shielded from the chloropicrin by the bodies of its brethren.

Chase shifted faster with Widow.

Another spider struggled to follow, its hind legs not quite working. It used the stacked bodies of its expired friends to finally slip over the broken edge.

"Faster!"

"I'm looking," she said, digging through the bag.

The first spider stopped a few inches from his feet.

"Shit, shit, shit."

"What?" She looked at him before following his gaze. "Do not move."

"Is it like a T-Rex?"

"What? No."

Swallowing ever so carefully, he asked, "Are they aggressive?"

"Other names for them are 'murderess' and 'armed spider.'"

When lightning flashed, both spiders shot up their front four legs. The weaker of the two toppled over when its hind legs failed to support it.

Chase pulled his feet back to further distance himself from the nightmarish creatures. The first scurried closer on hind legs, stopping again inches from his feet.

"I told you not to move," she chided.

The other spider began dragging its back legs behind it.

"I'm sorry," he said, shaking his head. "I *hate* spiders."

The house lit, casting disjointed shadows of the spiders across the wood floor. The healthiest monster raised its front four legs and scurried backward on its back legs. The thunder rumbled with each step it took, making the spectacle all the scarier. It reminded Chase of a missile launcher he'd seen on television: The back four legs serving as the wheels; the front four, the missiles aimed and ready to decimate a target.

He shook his head. "That's a scary-ass pose."

To make matters worse, the spider scurried sideways around his feet while flicking its front feet several times in the air.

Widow pushed his arms over her head. "When he gets close enough, crush him with your feet."

"I'm not crushing *him* with any part of me."

The front door began to open. "When it rains, people drive like shit." Vixen stopped in the doorway, drenched from head to toe. "Widow?"

"Shut the door," Widow demanded. "You don't want these loose in the neighborhood."

"Want what loose?" Then she obviously saw the spiders because she yelled, "Fuck me, those are big."

The one circumnavigating Chase's feet went for her instead, its creepy legs tap-tap-tapping on the wood floor.

Chase twisted, shot his feet out, and felt the spider crunch under his heel. "Gaaauuugh ..." he groaned when it began to squirm. His feet rose and slammed down again and again and again and ...

Vixen yelled. "You're hurting yourself."

"I have to kill it, kill it, kill it."

"It's dead." Vixen ran over. "It's dead." Her cold, wet fingers gripped his feet, holding them still. "Chase, it's dead."

His eyes found the final spider. "Get that one."

It was walking in circles.

"No," Widow said, unlocking Chase's ankles and hands. "Let me." She approached the spider on hands and feet. "I'm so sorry, Edward." There was a whistling to her breathing.

Chase looked to Vixen. "Call the doctor."

"Why?" said Vixen, squeezing water from her hair. Her eyes went to his feet. "Were you bit?"

"No, but Widow had a severe allergic reaction to the cookies."

Vixen twisted her hair. A small pool of water grew on the floor around her. "She looks fine to me."

"Call Allison anyway."

"Where's Zetta's gadget?" Vixen asked. "Because I'm not going back out in that downpour."

"It's in my room."

Vixen kissed his cheek. "Be right back."

Chase looked at his feet. Blisters were forming where the chloropicrin doused them. Especially bad were the cuts on his ankle where the vial shattered. The desire to vomit returned. He emptied his stomach into the puddle of water Vixen had created. "What a day." He spit and rubbed his burning eyes.

"Goodbye, love," Widow said.

Chase looked to see her petting the dying arachnid. "What a long, long … looonnng, fucking day."

Chapter Twenty-Three

Course Adjustment

Meanwhile
June 8, 2016
10:16 PM CDT
In-flight

NIGHTSHADE had fallen asleep on the flight. He woke to a message on his phone. He opened the text and read.

Love of My Life: Remind me later to tell you about tonight.

K!

We've only been in the air for like an hour
Thanatos said something was wrong with the
landing gear.

Love of My Life: Oh, I'm sorry.

It's alright.
I should still make it to my assignment in time.

Love of My Life: Good. I was about to ask.

Love of My Life: Wanted to say real quick that I'm sorry for being shut off earlier.

Love of My Life: I'm just frustrated beyond words right now.

> Don't be.
> If I we're you, I'd be far more angry with Ace.
> Were*

Love of My Life: Well, I'm not happy.

Love of My Life: Did I tell you he threatened me?

> What?!
> DO TELL!!!

Love of My Life: I don't have time to get into it right now.

Love of My Life: I really shouldn't say anymore as it is.

Love of My Life: It'll just piss you off.

> Damn straight!
> Ace is passing everyone off lately.
> Pissing* Stupid phone!

Love of My Life: True.

Love of My Life: I just don't want to feed that fire.

Love of My Life: Even with you. Please don't have me.

Love of My Life: Hate* Mine too, apparently.

Typical…
He threatens you and you protect him!

Love of My Life: What can I say? I have a problem.
Love of My Life: Especially when it comes to letting him down.

11:20 PM EDT

NIGHTSHADE noticed the time change on his phone. He wrinkled his forehead.

I think my phone's going insane.

Love of My Life: Why do you say that?

Because it just shot forward in time, not backward. I'm heading West, yet it changed to an hour ahead.

Love of My Life: Reset your phone maybe?

He looked at a television and saw the graphic of their jet heading quickly in the opposite direction of his assignment. *What is Thanatos doing?*

I'm heading East?!

Love of My Life: WTF?

What the Duck, indeed!
Duck*
FUCK*** DUCKING PHONE!!!

He threw it across the jet and marched to the cabin. Reaching for the handle, he yelled, "Thanatos, are you high or—?"

The door swung open. Ace stood within.

His phone chimed from the opposite end of the jet to alert him to a text.

Nightshade backed away, looking beyond him to see Thanatos piloting. "I need to be in Oregon in time to put mushrooms in a lady's omelet. Can't do that if we fly any further East."

There came another chime.

Thanatos shook his head slowly. "Bway, ya don' wanna know."

"Sit," Ace said.

Nightshade followed the order.

Ace sat across from him. "We're going to land shortly in Indianapolis and I'm going to get off then head back to Kansas City."

"And I'm going to do what exactly?"

The phone chimed again.

Ace looked in the direction of the phone and grinned wickedly.

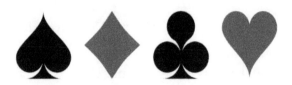

Chapter Twenty-Four

Fighting Fire with Fire

June 8, 2016
10:22 PM CDT
Kansas City, Missouri

CHASE trudged inside after helping Allison load Widow into the ambulance. He glanced at the floor where he'd killed the spider and shivered. "I can't sleep here."

"Why's that?" Vixen asked, typing into her phone.

"There are angry spider ghosts wandering about."

She appeared lost in thought. "You're crazy."

"Seriously. If we stay here, I'll feel them on me all night." He grabbed his keys. "We're staying at a hotel."

She glanced up from her phone. "How scandalous."

"You're welcome to stay here, but I'm not to blame when zombie spiders crawl into bed with you."

Tapping at her phone, she said, "I have a suite at the Ambassador Hotel if you'd like to stay there."

"Let's do that." After two steps toward the door, he turned. "Why have we been staying here when you had a *suite* at the *Ambassador*?"

Her forehead furrowed. She looked to be nibbling at the inside of her cheek.

"Something wrong?" he asked.

"Nightshade stopped texting."

"Is that strange?"

She nodded, glancing up from her phone. "Unless he's mid-kill, he always gets right back. I've sent five texts since his last one." She typed something else. "The last few texts may have led to him breaking his phone. He has a habit of doing that." She tapped her lip with the edge of her phone. "He mentioned going East, is all."

"I thought he sang about killing someone in Oregon."

"Exactly." She frowned. "I'm sure he's fine." She smiled, shaking her head. "What were you saying?"

"It's not important."

She squinted one eye for a second. "Staying at the Ambassador." She found her keys. "I'm driving."

The trip there was quiet. She was clearly worried about Nightshade, but Chase didn't have a clue what to say to make that better. It's not like he could charter a jet and go looking for her friend, no matter how badly he wanted to do that for her.

Once in their room, he collapsed onto the corner of the King bed. "I'm gonna sleep right here." He shut his eyes and feigned snoring.

There came the sound of her keys hitting the counter.

He hugged the covers. "You can have the rest of the bed, but I get this corner."

Her hand stroked his back. "Get undressed."

His eyes flew open. "What?" He turned his head to see her walking into the bathroom, blouse dangling from one hand while her bra hung from the other.

Eyes wide, he tried to look at anything but her. As always, when it came to her body, every effort was a complete and total failure.

She ducked inside.

Still, the same fear gripped him by the throat. *She could be my next test.* But, as he'd told Nightshade, he'd die a happy man. *I also told Nightshade I trusted her implicitly.* He nodded his head from side to side. *And they both said not to.* The struggle was real.

She poked her head out, her eyes narrowed. "Why aren't you naked?"

He groaned and buried his head in the covers. "I can't."

"I'm pretty sure I've felt you hard against me."

His face remained buried to hide the blood flushing into his cheeks. "I don't mean I can't perform. I'm pretty sure a touch from you would make eunuchs hard."

"I can't hear you, Chase," she said. "You're talking into the comforter."

He rose up to see her standing in the doorway, wearing nothing but fingernail polish. The hairs at the back of his neck lit on fire and in an instant, he was consumed in its blaze. He dropped his gaze to the floor.

"Look at me."

He shook his head. "Promise not to kill me?" Chase looked up to see her fingernails digging into the bathroom door frame.

She pressed her lips to one side and shrugged. "I'm not sure how I could."

He guffawed, then glared at her playfully. "Sure."

"With all that luck on your side, I don't know." She looked him up and down and sighed. Her thoughts were clearly wrestling one another.

"What's wrong?" he asked.

Her eyes met his. "I've never let myself get attached to the recruits. Just in case they ..."

Die. He nodded. "But with me?"

"I'm a little more than attached."

Long strides brought him to her. He cupped her chin in his hands as their lips became ... a little more than attached. Mid-kiss, he lifted her naked body in his arms and walked to the bed. Gently, he placed her down.

"Chase, wait," she said, pressing a hand to his chest.

"Too forward?"

"Not at all. Sexy as hell." She bit her lip for a long while before saying, "Why reject me the other day?"

"You'll think this is silly," he said, standing and running his hands through his hair. "I thought you'd kill me." It did sound stupid out loud. "That maybe you'd be my next test." He dropped his hands and shrugged. "How better to catch me off guard than to lure me into bed?"

Her face contorted as though hurt by this confession. "I—" The word hung in the air like a trail of smoke.

"I ruined it, didn't I?" He made a fist. "I'm stupid."

She shook her head. A tear fled from its prison at the corner of her eye. "You didn't ruin anything. And you're not stupid." Sitting up, she placed a hand on his fist and squeezed. She waited for him to open his hand before she placed hers inside his. "First rule during testing ..."

"Trust people to your detriment."

She squeezed his hand. "I'm people." She rose on her knees and kissed him repeatedly on the chin, cheeks, and lips.

Fingers working to unbutton and unzip his pants, she soon freed him of them. Those same fingers found him hard and waiting for her.

"Lie down," she whispered.

Chase took off his shirt and kissed her neck, shoulder, and breasts before lying on his back. "Vixen, I'll never reject you again."

She shook her head. More tears came. Crawling atop him, she ran her bottom lip through her teeth. "I want you to do something for me."

"Anything," he said, his eyes exploring her beauty.

Her eyes closed and she hummed in pleasure as she slid him inside of her.

His universe exploded as her heat enveloped him. "Oh, *dear Lord*, you are perfect!"

Her breasts melded to his chest and she pressed her lips to his ear. "Call me Laura."

June 9, 2016
07:09 AM CDT

CHASE woke the next morning to Laura straddling him and dotting his face with kisses.

Chuckling, he turned his face to the side. "This is why I don't have a dog."

She slapped his arm. "That's how we're going to start this glorious morning? You calling me a dog?"

He stretched his lips tight against his teeth, shaking his head vigorously.

She pinched his nipple. "That's what I thought." She

brought out her phone. "Let's instead begin the day by congratulating you for passing your next test."

Confused, he looked her up and down. "You had plenty of opportunities to stick a knife in me last night."

"Don't I know it." Laura laughed. "In fact, you spent most of it stabbing me." She winked and brought up her phone. "From Widow: Your boy passed another test without raising a finger. Radiant's flight had to land for repairs in Arkansas."

"They were going to throw another assassin at me this morning after two yesterday?"

"You're missing the point, sweetheart."

"Seriously?" He let her words sink in. "I can pass without ever seeing the opponent?"

"'Course."

He rolled his head back and forth along the pillow. "I'm two tests away from becoming an assassin."

"Could you look less pleased?"

"I don't know how to feel." He forced a smile. "I didn't expect to get this far."

Squeezing his arm, Laura said, "Feel proud." Her eyes went wide. "I've gotta pee!" She rolled sideways off him.

He barely noticed the sound of her perfect pink toes padding against blue carpet in rapid succession on her way to the bathroom. An increasing unease dominated his focus and his eyes shifted about the room. "I don't have my vest."

"Did you say something?" Her voice came muted behind the closed bathroom door.

"I'm not prepared." His entire body felt like a thumping heart. He stretched his jaw and felt a pop behind his ears. "I have to get home."

There was a muffled flushing of water followed by Laura washing her hands. "Let me get dressed, babe."

He barely registered her words as he got out of bed and walked to the door. He swung it open and started out.

"Chase," Laura said after him. "Chase!" She grabbed his arm and pulled him back into the room. "You're naked."

He looked down to see that was very much the case. "Oh."

"Are you all right?" Laura asked.

"Yeah."

She flicked his nose. "Look at me."

He did.

"You are going to be fine." Nodding, she added, "We'll get you home. Pants first."

He smiled at the reminder of when she'd thrown him a pair of jeans the day they'd met. It alleviated some of the panic enough for him to slow down and say, "Pants would help." He laughed nervously. "Thank you, Vixen?"

"I told you last night." She kissed him. "Call me Laura."

The memory of the night before crushed the remaining weight of his panic, replacing it with determination. *I must live to love this woman.* "Thank you, Laura. For everything." He pressed his lips to hers.

THEY arrived at his home half an hour later. He had begun to get out when she grabbed his arm.

"You're lucky," said Vixen. "If he'd shown up to find you not home, he'd have burned the house to the ground for fun."

"Happy to still have a house." He kissed her. "Happier to have you at my side." Noticing she hadn't turned off the car, he asked, "You're not coming in?"

"I did inventory at the safe houses yesterday. Now, I need to replace what's expired or empty." She took a phone out of the glovebox and handed it to him. "Every Guild member's number is in this, including mine under 'Queen of Spades.' The password to unlock it is GOF4. Only call me if you absolutely have to or I'll have a lot of explaining to do."

He nodded. "I'll see you later, then?"

She kissed him long and hard. When their lips parted, she placed her forehead to his and let out a happy sigh. "Give me a few hours and then we'll break in your bed."

"I can deal with that." He got out, then dropped his head to say, "Be safe."

She laughed. "Sure."

He closed the door and watched her go until she turned out of sight. He nearly skipped the distance to ... the slightly ajar front door. He looked at the phone she'd given him. *If she helps me through another test, she could get thrown in that hole she and Nightshade talked about.* He put his hand on the doorknob. *I've passed on my own before. I can do it again.* Dropping the phone in his pocket, he took a deep breath, flung the door open, and charged in. "Where are ya?"

"Right here, boy," said a man at the top of the stairs. A gloved hand rested on a firefighter's helmet and mask. His face was horribly scarred as if someone had thrown acid at him. He was eating one of Chase's bananas.

Chase noticed the man wore a large metal backpack. It looked heavy and cumbersome. "What's your name?" Chase took a seat at the table. "The firefighter?"

Rolling the banana peel, the man stood and answered, "Radiant."

"Thought you had flight trouble."

Radiant wrinkled his nose. "That answers whether or not Vixen is feeding you information."

I should have kept my mouth shut. "I don't see how my passing a test isn't crucial information for me to know."

Radiant sneered. "Perhaps."

Chase thought about the many times he'd started a fight on those stairs. More specifically how many of those he'd lost. "Did you come to congratulate me?"

"No." Radiant dropped the banana peel at his feet and began pulling on the mask. He started down the stairs. "I'm here to kill you," his voice came, muffled and low.

Chase launched forward, reaching the stairwell and grabbing Radiant's foot. He pulled.

Gravity did the rest.

Radiant rolled down the remaining steps with a metallic *clunka-clunka-clunk.* He groaned before rising on one leg.

Chase dropped into his fighting stance. "That metal backpack looks heavy."

Radiant stood and reached for the pack.

Chase sped forward, his foot meeting the side of the lower step and his body becoming airborne. His legs wrapped around Radiant's neck and he twirled.

Radiant spun about and fell hard to the ground.

When his body met the floor, Chase ducked, rolled, and sprung back up. "If you intend to pin me in, you'll need to get rid of the cumbersome thing."

Radiant found the wall and rose slowly. The front of the mask and helmet were askew. He took his time putting them back in place.

Or he's not fast because he doesn't have to be. That thought sent chills running down Chase's spine. "Come on, hot stuff."

"The others said you were acrobatic." Radiant popped his neck one way, then the other. "It's annoying." He reached over his back and pulled out a long tube with a nozzle. "My orders were to do all in my power to kill you. I feel compelled to do so."

That's what all the gear's for. Chase turned and ran for the door. The hairs on the back of his head singed as fire spewed forth behind him. He redirected, dropping and rolling toward the couch. He popped up, flipped over the top of it, and ducked down on the other side. There was a growing warmth at his back. He tore off his shirt and threw it away. *This fight turned ugly fast.*

The couch wouldn't last much longer than a hay bale ablaze during a drought. The putrid smell of fabric, wood, and glue stung his nostrils.

Chase's eyes narrowed when he remembered what was in the couch. He reached into the cushions and pulled out a stun grenade. He pulled the pin and kicked the couch as hard as he could with both feet, sending it sliding toward Radiant. The flash grenade followed, flying through the air. Chase covered his ears, and squeezed his eyes shut. There was an explosion and Chase could see the veins in his eyelids as a bright light erupted in the room. He opened his eyes to see Radiant stumbling about. The flashbang had clearly disoriented him.

The big man roared in anger. The flame splashed against the ceiling and then the wall as he tried to circumnavigate the couch in a daze.

I have to get out. Chase eyed the doorway. *If I stay here, I'm barbecue.* If he ran, Radiant would see the blur of him and redirect the flame. *Badly burnt, but alive.* He pulled out the phone that Laura gave him and input the code GOF4. He dropped to his stomach when a fount of flame painted the fireplace behind him. Scrolling through the contacts to find "Queen of Spades," he hit dial.

It rang twice before she picked up. "Told you not to call unless it's an emergency."

Chase rolled out of the way as fire consumed the wood to his right. His eyes went wide as the flame shifted to engulf his uncle's recliner. "Radiant, nooo!" He rose and put a hand out as though Frank's ghost were being exorcised from his life. "Stop!"

"Chase?" Vixen's voice yelled over the phone. "What's going on?"

The recliner popped. Springs shot out its front. Frank once said that if the house burnt down, he'd be happy as long as Chase and that recliner survived. Tears welled in Chase's eyes. But the recliner's sacrifice would be his saving grace. It meant the fire was far enough away to give him an opening to escape.

Chase ran for the door. Someone big and billowy ran into him, knocking him to the floor. The phone went spiraling out of his grip and skipped across the floor. Chase rolled under the table. When he looked up, he saw a white bomb disposal uniform. He backed further under the table. The last time he'd seen this person, a bomb went off overhead.

The spout of flame ended in a short *pifft* sound. Radiant's muffled voice yelled, "Get out, Powder Keg. I'll deal with you after."

The person standing in the doorway looked down at Chase through the glass lenses of a gas mask. "Stay there." His voice wasn't muffled like Radiant's. "Why are you here?" In fact, the mask didn't muffle his voice at all. "I heard engine trouble forced you to land your jet." That was clearly the voice of—

"Frank!" Chase belted out, unbelieving.

"Who's informing you of all this?" Radiant said. "Vixen? Traitorous bitch."

Powder Keg's protecting Chase suddenly made sense. *But Frank, an assassin?* That thought was preposterous.

Powder Keg pointed at the ground. "You're breaking our laws by violating your time."

Radiant limped forward. "You're no longer one of us after what you did, so why do you care?"

Powder Keg gestured at Chase. "Two people tested him at the same time. Then Ace tried to convince our snipers to test him." He slapped his chest. "That sits wrong with me. That's not a fair test."

"You believe Vixen and you helping him is fair? Maybe Ace knew you'd protect the boy, so he made survival more of a challenge."

"Try impossible," Powder Keg yelled. "Let me guess, you were commanded to do all in your power to kill him?"

Radiant nodded. "Those were my orders."

Powder Keg threw up his arms. "When you see promise, you test a recruit to the best of their ability to defend themselves. To emphasize killing the recruit whether or not they prove promising is against our laws."

Radiant shrugged. "Laws change."

"These laws do not."

"Not your laws anymore." Radiant brought the nozzle up. "We were told to bring you in alive or dead if you showed your face. Not that you ever do, hiding behind a mask twenty-four seven. So, be a good boy and let me discard you."

"I'll gladly lay down my life if you let him leave. Go for him, and I'll blow you to kingdom come."

Radiant pointed the hose at Powder Keg. "You're welcome to try. But I'll be taking both of you with me."

"Fuck that," Chase said, grabbing the smoke bomb taped to the underside of the table. He threw it as flame spewed forward.

Powder Keg stepped in front of the blaze just as a cloud of smoke filled the room.

Chase grabbed the back of the bomb disposal uniform and pulled his uncle toward the door.

Frank grabbed something from a pocket and hurled it into the fumes. There was a concussive blast to the air and the fire tripled in a cone from within the smoke.

The air grew thicker, hotter, less bearable. Chase found it hard to breathe. He pulled harder and they both fell outside onto the porch.

"Go!" Powder Keg bellowed.

Chase rolled off the porch and into the grass.

Something else exploded. Glass erupted out into the lawn as the windows shattered.

After putting several yards between he and the house, Chase jumped and ran for the pair of trees at the end of the yard. It wasn't until he was safely behind one that he looked back.

Powder Keg was rolling on the grass to extinguish the suit that was engulfed in flames. Part of the gas mask had melted away. He crawled out of the decimated suit and stood, wearing jeans and a white shirt. Rising, he tore off the mask and cradled it under his arm.

All doubt left as to who was in the uniform. "Frank!" said Chase. "You son of a bitch."

"Watch your tongue, young man," Frank said sternly. "Your grandmother was a sweet and wonderful woman." He ran for the tree opposite Chase and placed the mask on the ground at his feet. "Why isn't he following?"

"Hell, if I know," Chase yelled. "Might have something to do with the bombs you threw at him." He wanted to strangle his uncle. "You let me think you were dead."

Frank pressed his back against the tree. "Not now." He looked back at the house. "Seriously, where is he?"

"Likely dead," Chase barked. "Now answer the damn—"

"No, his suit is well armored. No, he's still coming."

"Armored against two explosives?"

"There he is," announced Frank.

Chase looked to see the doorway rimmed in fire. Radiant stepped through with a bazooka perched on his shoulder.

Frank sighed loudly. "Of course, he would."

Radiant pulled off his shattered mask and dropped it. "I never did like you much, Powder Keg." Blood covered half the man's face.

Frank nodded. "Feeling's mutual, bud."

Chase shook his head. "How about we not antagonize the guy with a rocket launcher."

Radiant aimed the bazooka at the tree in front of Frank. "Shall I kill you first?" The bazooka shifted toward Chase's tree. "Or force you to watch the recruit collect splinters?"

Frank knelt and pressed on the back of the mask. A hidden door popped open, revealing a pocket. With two fingers, he took from it a small house. It looked to be a miniature copy of their own. "This guest is no longer welcome in our home."

Chase was confused. "How's a toy house going to help?"

Frank turned the roof on the house once right, thrice left, twice right. "Radiant," he yelled as the roof of the toy house came away, revealing a button. "Stop this or die." The button blinked five times then became solid red.

Radiant laughed. "Splinter-riddled recruit, it is." He shifted the weight of the bazooka on his shoulder and lined up the sights.

Frank's thumb smashed the red button.

The earth shook as Chase's home exploded from the inside out. Chase pressed his body flat against the tree and closed his eyes. Heat encompassed him as though he stood at the center of a furnace. The sound punched through the tree and entered him violently. His organs shuddered and a concussive bass tone clapped his ears.

Things began crashing all around him. He pressed his back harder against the tree, wishing it were thicker. Something tore a hole in his shirt. His eyes flew open just in time to see their toilet smash into the roof of the car directly in front of him. The ringing in his ears threatened to bore a hole through to his brain. Debris fell like rain. Car alarms must have been going off because he could see brake lights flashing. As his hearing returned, more cars took up the siren call as pipes and bars crashed through windows, tore holes through convertible hoods, and took off side mirrors.

His Cavalier was on fire, crumpled and upside down in

the neighbor's yard across the street.

Doubt Officer Clark can salvage that.

It wasn't until the heavy debris was replaced by floating ash that Chase turned to look at the pillar of flame that was once his house.

He looked at his uncle who stared ahead as though nothing significant had occurred. The tree at his uncle's back was a testament to the explosion, for it was a pincushion of large, smoldering splinters. Among those splinters, Chase could see the nozzle of Radiant's flame thrower protruding at a sixty-degree angle.

Frank knelt to pick up the mask and smiled at Chase. "You good?"

A violent shiver shook Chase as he realized the man standing there wasn't an apparition nor was this a dream. His uncle was alive and part of the Guild of Four.

"You're dead," was all Chase could find the words to say.

Frank frowned, cradling the mask again under his arm. "I know."

Chase put a hand against his forehead and let out a breath through puckered lips. He took another breath and walked from one half-burnt tree to the other. He grabbed his uncle by the shoulders and shook. "You've got to be *FUCKING* kidding me!"

Frank placed a palm on Chase's cheek. "I know you have questions, but I have to go."

"Go?" Chase laughed. He released Frank. "Go where?"

"You know where Trevor Clark lives?"

"The extra water heater in the basement." Chase slapped his forehead. "That was a bomb, wasn't it? There was a freaking nuke in our basement."

"Not a nuke," Frank said. "That's not what's important right now. Do you know where Officer Clark lives?"

"I can get that information."

"I'll meet you there tomorrow morning at seven."

Chase furrowed his brow. "Be ready for a fight."

Frank smiled. "Of course." He squeezed Chase's shoulder. "We'll talk tomorrow." And then, he walked away.

Chase began to follow when someone grabbed his arm and jerked him around. He saw a furious, red-faced neighbor. He knew him from three houses down.

"What happened?" the neighbor yelled.

"I don't know," Chase said, shaking his head. "Call the police."

"Don't think I haven't."

"Good," Chase said, pushing past him on his way to an approaching Mustang.

Laura pulled over when she could no longer circumnavigate the debris. She got out and ran her fingers through her hair, staring at the blazing fire. He could tell she had been crying.

"I'm fine."

She ran to him, embracing and kissing him wildly.

He laughed, pulling away from the barrage. "I'm fine, I'm fine."

Laura planted a final, long kiss upon his lips. "I thought Scizzors was next, but this isn't his M.O. at all."

The neighbor from before marched up to him. "You'll be hearing from my lawyer."

"Whatever," Chase said, waving dismissively. He turned back to Laura. "This was Radiant."

"I heard you yell his name," she said. "His time had already ..." She shut her mouth while her eyes locked on something beyond him.

"What now?" Chase sighed and turned.

A large, hunched-over man dressed from head to toe in a cloak approached them. The cloak jutted out along his head and back.

Chase tilted his head to make out the man's face. What he could see struck him as odd. The man's lower jaw stuck out and looked to be lined with sharp, pointed teeth. "What are you?"

"Scizzors with two Zs," the man said with surprising clarity. "It appears I'm late to the party."

Chase nodded, but couldn't bring himself to say anything else. He ducked his head down to see what was jutting along the top sides of the man's head.

The creature lifted his head slightly, revealing reptilian eyes. "You going to gawk at me all day?"

"I'll gawk a minute longer," Chase confessed. "Are you evidence there's life on other planets?"

The man belted out a loud, deep belly laugh. "Thank you for the compliment, son." He pointed at Chase with a gauntleted hand. "That's exactly what I was going for."

"It gets better," said Laura.

"I'm sorry," the neighbor interrupted. He had been joined by a few other people. "I need to talk to you right now, young man."

Scizzors pulled back the hood and growled. Ram horns came into view.

The people backed up as one.

Scizzors made a guttural roar, then yelled, "I'll burn all yer houses down if ya don't run far, far from here."

They all stood, quivering.

"I said get!" Scizzors roared.

They scattered.

The gauntlet swiped again to slap Chase's shoulder. "They all think I belong in a circus," the monster said as his head and ram horns bobbed. "I've been there, done that."

Chase cleared his throat, his voice cracking when he said, "Are you my—next opponent?"

"I am." Scizzors clapped his left hand against the gauntlet. "I have the perfect farmhouse in mind." His head bobbed. "Nice and private."

Chase glanced at Laura.

She shrugged. "I'd go, unless you want to do it out here with all manner of emergency vehicles on approach."

Scizzors looked around. "I don't feel like a beast needing to be caged." He smiled widely.

At least, Chase thought it was a smile. The sharp, wicked teeth made it hard to tell.

Scizzors looked at Laura. "I hear you like to tag along on his tests." He shook his head. "That won't be happening."

"I know," she said, then met Chase's eyes. "You've got this."

Chase nodded.

"That-a-boy." Scizzors howled excitedly, clapping Chase on the shoulder a third time. "This is gonna be fun." Scizzors walked off, whistling a happy tune through his twisted teeth.

"The whistling makes it worse," said Chase.

Laura kissed him.

Chase pointed the direction his uncle had gone. "Powder Keg went that way. And he's my uncle Frank."

Laura nodded slowly. "That makes a lot more sense." She was still nodding as though the pieces of a puzzle were fitting together. "I'll try to catch up with him."

Chase kissed her. "I'm one step closer to finishing this."

"As I said." She kissed him again. "You've got this."

"He's huge." Admitting his fear made it all the more real. "How do you hurt someone who's endured that much surgery to look the way he does?"

"You don't have to hurt him," she said. "Just avoid him." She smiled. "He's really a big softy. Imagine a huge-ass teddy bear."

He forced a laugh before turning to see Scizzors with two Zs jumping into an SUV. "A big-ass teddy bear that can maul me to death. Can't say that's a better picture to conjure."

Chapter Twenty-Five

Triggered

June 9, 2016
07:43 AM CDT
Kansas City, Missouri

ACE stared at the dancing flame before lighting his clove. He snapped the metal lid shut. He sucked on the cigarette as though it were his lover's tit. *Maybe Powder Keg blew himself up.* The thought brought a smile to his lips. With how loud the explosion was, he wouldn't be surprised if Chase's entire block went up.

A man wearing blue jeans and a white undershirt came into view down the street.

Who's this, now?

The man stopped at a black F-150.

Couldn't be.

The man wore no bomb suit, but Powder Keg's gas mask was cradled under an arm.

Ace tried to make out the man's face. *If that's him, this'll be like seeing a whale out of water.* He dropped the lighter in his pocket and approached. "You know how to pinpoint one asshole out of six billion?"

The man had the truck door open and one leg inside. "If I were hiding, I would have torn the GPS tracker from the truck."

It is him. Ace's smile widened. "That kills the big reveal about how I found you." He slapped the man's back. "Care to *face me* for your crimes committed against the Guild?"

"Sure," Powder Keg replied. "If you face the Guild for crimes you've committed." He turned fast and grabbed Ace by the shirt.

When Ace saw the man's face, he choked smoke down the wrong pipe. His cigarette fell from his lips to burn a trail down his shirt. "You're—" Coughing, he backed away. "What in—?" He coughed some more. "How the fuck did you—?" More coughing. He jerked out of Powder Keg's grip and placed his hands on his knees, Ace coughed hard to clear his throat. He shook his head, bewildered. "This isn't possible."

Powder Keg shook his head. "You think every plan you hatch goes off without a hitch. That nobody sees through your bullshit. Half your so-called *traps* end in explosions." He took a step forward. "That's not a trap, you dumbass ape. That's called blowing shit up."

Ace barked a coughing laugh. "All this time, I thought you wore that mask to hide a hideous scar. I thought you were missing half your face or something." He pointed at the man. "You were Frank Douglas, best bomb disposal officer in America. Mentor to all the greatest and brightest in your field." His finger twirled. "Couldn't risk your face being caught on camera while blowing up a drug den. I can't believe I never saw past it. Not once did you take it off around me."

"You never asked," Frank said, seemingly unworried about his identity being blown.

"Would you, had I?"

"We'll never know. You never grew the balls to make the request."

Ace picked up the cigarette he'd dropped and blew an ant off it. Small rocks crunched between his teeth when he put it in his mouth. He took a long drag, smoke curling from his nostrils. "I have the right to kill you for attacking another card holder. In this case, many." He twirled the cigarette in the air between two fingers, the smoke spiraling around his fist. "I could kill you now and never have to answer for it."

Frank gently placed his mask on the ground between them and went to the bed of the truck. Retrieving a tire iron, he said, "You're welcome to try."

"As Frank Douglas, you should already be dead." Ace put the cigarette to his lips and breathed in until his fingers grew hot. "I fucking blew you up." Smoke spilled out around his lips and rose between their faces.

"You were sloppy," Frank said. "I saw it coming."

"Whose body parts did they find?"

"The city buries John Does on the second Sunday of every month. You killed me the Monday after."

Ace put the cigarette to his lips and drew in a long breath. "Why not turn me in for the unsanctioned kill of Frank Douglas?"

"When an Ace is accused of breaking our rules, all four Aces must be in attendance for the review. Masks are not permitted during testimony. I would have been protected by my Guild. Yet, somehow I knew you'd go after Chase to get to me." His lip twisted. "How was I supposed to know killing me was to get to him?"

Wait. He was the King when I was recruited. "As the King, you chose me to be recruited and tested."

"True, I was King at the time, but—"

"I get it. You recruited me knowing I killed your sister." Ace shook his head, smoke trailing in zigzags. "You wanted me to die during testing just as I want Chase to."

"No, I didn't realize at the time that you killed my sister." Frank took a step forward. "It wasn't until you bypassed Thanatos to recruit a young man who had no experience whatsoever in our field. You always brag about how you only missed once. Why else would you tell everyone to do all in their power to kill him if Chase wasn't that one?"

"I wanted him to die by the most elaborate trap yet." Ace itched his bottom lip. "Him surviving my bomb wedged a thorn in my spine."

"I'm your second miss." Frank pointed the tire iron at Ace. "How's that feel?"

Ace's smile trembled and drooped. "Even if he survives Scizzors, I still have an ace up my sleeve." The smile returned. "As for my second, you'll be taken care of tonight."

"You're pathetic," said Frank.

"Me? It's your fault your sister's dead."

"I'm sure that makes sense somehow in your twisted world."

Ace tossed the spent cigarette aside. "I thought they'd call on you to investigate the bombing in Chicago."

"They did."

"Yeah." He put another clove to his lips. "Why didn't you go?"

Frank shook his head. "My sister's funeral."

"Exactly." He lit the end, took a puff, and blew the smoke at Frank. "Your fault." A shorter drag. "You were out of commission for a year while adjusting to parenthood."

Frank's knuckles grew white. "For that, you killed her?" He advanced, swinging the tire iron wide.

Ace jumped backward to avoid the first swing and dropped to the ground, barely missing the second. "Couldn't kill you. The whole nation would have been looking for the cop killer." He got up and skipped backward. "Kill just her and you're the only one who cares."

Frank's lip quivered and he advanced faster.

Ace managed to dodge two hits before his legs met a car hood. As he crawled backward over it, the iron caught him in the ankle. He rolled off the back and bounced on his good leg. "Stop!"

"What's the incentive to stop?" Frank yelled, rounding the car. "How'd you put it? You have the right to kill me? That you could kill me right now and never have to answer for it?"

"What if there's a way for you to get revenge and be exonerated of all your crimes against the Guild?"

Frank eyed him suspiciously. "We both know you're not going to absolve me. And there's not a chance you'll sit happily by while being pummeled to death." He started forward again.

"Hear me out," Ace said, bouncing backward. "You don't kill me until I've tried all the remotes."

"Remotes?"

Ace pulled one of Powder Keg's remotes from his pocket. "Found these in your locker."

Frank raised an eyebrow. "You think there's a bomb nearby to which I do not hold the remote?" He raised the iron over his head.

Ace pushed the button. "Apparently not with this one." Tossing it aside, he tried another to no avail. "Are these even on?" He shook the remote and threw it at Frank.

The tire iron obliterated the remote out of the air.

Ace put his hand out with a remote tucked into each palm. "If you're right and none of these blow you to hell ..." He pocketed a remote and made a scribbling gesture in the air. "I'll write myself up as a hit and let you strap a bomb to my chest." His head bobbed in a nod. "Fair?"

"Bombs are too quick for what I want to do to you."

"I was wondering why you chose that." Ace pointed at the tire iron. "No deal unless it's a bomb."

"Fine," Frank said, grabbing the remote out of Ace's hand and pressing the button himself with no adverse consequences. He walked back to the truck. "I suppose decorating the neighborhood with your body parts could be quite therapeutic." He tossed the tire iron inside with a *clunka-clunk-clunk*.

Ace tried another and dropped the remote. "When you recruited me—"

"I didn't."

"You were the King."

"As you bypassed Thanatos to recruit Chase, my Ace bypassed me to recruit you."

"What?" Ace was completely blown away. "I thought I was the first Ace of Spades to pull that stunt."

"From the very beginning, something always rubbed me wrong about you. I wanted to go with a high-ranking member of the Zapatistas to gain influence in Mexico."

"That's rich," Ace said, pulling out the next remote. "Did

you even fight him on it or did you simply follow his orders like the sheep you all are?"

"We argued," Frank said. "He assured me if we recruited a member of the Zapatistas, the man's priority would have leaned heavily toward the EZLN. Ultimately, because of those mixed loyalties, we would have ended up discarding him. To recruit him would have been to kill him." He opened the door to the truck, reached in, and returned with a vest. Wires stuck out from the pockets. "Speaking of discarding members of the Guild, this'll look pretty on you."

Ace didn't balk at seeing the bomb vest. "You can revel in the fact that he regretted my recruitment in the end."

Frank didn't appear to revel in anything. "You took the name 'Ace' as your tag. From day one, he regretted your recruitment. He knew you had every intention of stabbing him in the back when you had enough support to rise to his position." He unbuckled the clasps on the vest. "Years of your lies being whispered into people's ears to secure your position when he died. And faster than any other card member you did rise."

Ace pushed the button on the next remote and tossed it over his shoulder. "I killed him, you know."

Nothing.

"I had my suspicions," Frank said, clearly unsurprised. "But that's all they were until now."

"You're not going to ask how?" Ace tossed the remote over his shoulder and found another.

"As if you're going to be silent after such a proclamation."

Ace grew excited. He'd never gotten to tell this particular story. "I paid all the money I had to one of our clients. I told him

to take out a hit and pay triple to guarantee the Ace's attention."
Laughing, Ace clapped his hands. "Here's where it gets good.
The hit was taken out on an infamous heroin dealer, known also
for human trafficking."

"I remember," Frank conceded. "The former Ace despised
traffickers. And heroin had a hand in his daughter's suicide.
Truly, a kill too good to be true." Frank stretched his arms along
the truck bed. "I take it you tipped off the heroin dealer."

Ace simply smiled in reply.

Frank nodded his head slowly. "But you still hadn't
gained enough support to rise to Ace. When he died, you
followed through with the hit, knowing your target wouldn't
expect the man who tipped him off to kill him."

"You have to admit that's a good trap."

Frank rolled his eyes.

"No?" Ace pressed the button to the next remote and
threw it aside when nothing happened.

"Running out?" Frank said. "Nervous?"

"You think you're perfect," Ace said, waving the next
remote around in the air. "That you'd never mistakenly leave a
bomb in your truck or on your person to which you do not have
the remote. Blah blah blah." He pressed the button. "Damn my
luck." He dropped it. "Just one left."

Frank dropped his arms from the side of the truck and
clutched the vest in both hands.

"You're so cocky." Ace growled dramatically, reaching
into his pocket and pulling out another cigarette. "As I'm about
to die, may I have one last smoke?"

Frank raised an eyebrow, but shrugged.

Ace put the clove cigarette to his mouth and pulled out his

lighter. "I'm also going to put some distance between us in case this one goes off."

The wrinkles next to Frank's eyes deepened. "You run and I'll find you."

"I expect you would." He lit the clove and limped behind a car. His hand dipped into his pocket to stroke the final remote. "Any last questions, Frank?"

"You should have killed me all those years ago and left my family alone."

Ace let the smoke flood out of his mouth. "That's more of a statement than a question, but whatever." He glared at Frank and scratched his lip. "Still can't believe Chase survived that."

"His car seat was of my own design," said Frank. "Built to withstand far more than a head-on collision."

"It was damn near all that was left." Ace felt the hairs on his neck rise as heat flooded through him. "And now he's fucking the woman I love."

"Vixen is half your age," said Frank. "You should never have set your sights on her."

"I'm the Ace. There are no sights too high." He ran his bottom teeth over his top lip. "Besides, I killed her father for her."

Frank's eyes narrowed. "Did she ask you to?"

"No," he admitted. "But when she couldn't pull the trigger, I did."

"Her complete loyalty was her thanks." Frank shook his head. "Not that you deserve it. Has it ever occurred to you that she may not have pulled the trigger because she realized she didn't want to?"

"Her loyalty is evidence of the opposite," said Ace.

"Not if you shot him before her mind could process why she hadn't," said Frank.

"Then I'm glad I did."

"If Vixen never comes around to loving you as you want her to, then what?"

The corner of Ace's lip twitched. "I'll take her like I've taken everything else."

Frank's mouth fell agape. "You wouldn't dare rape Vixen."

"I'd rape her until she bled out her eyes. Then I'd make her disappear for forcing me to."

Frank gripped the vest so tightly, his knuckles popped. "Good thing you die tonight." He nodded at Ace's pocket. "Push the next *goddamn* button."

Ace nibbled at his bottom lip. "You know—"

"Push the *fucking* button!"

Ace retrieved the final remote. "This button?" He held out the remote.

Frank's eyes went wide when he realized it wasn't one of his.

Ace dropped his finger.

The F-150 became a ball of fire.

Ace's eyes slammed shut as his body was thrown into the driveway behind him. He raised his head from the cement, vision blurry, ears ringing. *I didn't even use that much C-4.* A pain in his lower abdomen demanded attention. He looked to see a piece of metal sticking from the fabric of his shirt. A stain of red grew around it. "For fuck's sake." His vision cleared enough to see a screw jutting from his bicep as well. He pulled it from the muscle. "Fuuuck," he yelled at the sky.

People were coming out of their homes. *Let them watch.*

He was still dizzy, but he needed to know whether Frank was alive or dead. He stood, his fingers probing around the metal sticking from his abdomen. *I think I'll live.* Despite the pain, and plenty of it, he stumbled down the driveway. *Bar none, this was the stupidest stunt I've ever pulled.*

Frank was smashed against a car. Part of the F-150's bed had cut him in half.

"That'll 'bout do it," Ace said, groaning as his finger traced his stomach wound.

"Is that Powder Keg?" came Vixen's voice.

Ace looked to see her running toward them.

She dropped next to the old man's body. "What did you do?"

"Carried out my duty as the Ace."

"Why this way?"

"Call it poetic justice." He shook his head at her and limped away. "Why do you care? He was a traitor." When she didn't respond, he turned to see her picking up Powder Keg's shattered mask. "What do you want with that?"

She jolted as a child would when caught stealing candy. "I'm just looking at it."

"Bring it home." He laughed. "We'll mount it on my office wall or something."

"No."

"Do as you're told." Pain radiated, turning his stomach. "I need treatment." He bent, squeezing his eyes shut. "Tell the doctor to meet us at the airport."

"Us?"

"You clearly need more of an incentive to hold up your

side of the bargain." He glared at her. "I ordered Thanatos to drop one in a hole for you."

Chapter Twenty-Six

Mauled by a Giant Teddy Bear

June 9, 2016
07:51 AM CDT
Kansas City, Missouri

CHASE looked out the window of the Cadillac Escalade. The reassurance he'd felt from Vixen faded with every mile. He sighed deeply, thinking about how much he'd endured in less than twenty-four hours. Now, he sat in an SUV with a monster of a man, far scarier than all the spiders from the night before. He didn't know why, but not having a shirt on made him feel awkwardly vulnerable.

Scizzors adjusted the mirror. "Nervous?" No time was left for reply before he smiled crazily and said, "Of course, you are. I'm terrifying."

"Sorry I said those things about you."

The large man laughed with his entire body. "Never take back a compliment. I put a lot of effort into the way I look."

Chase looked over at Scizzors and noticed the driver side seat was only a metal frame. A bulk within the back of the monster's cloak bulged through the opening.

Scizzors saw him looking and glanced at the back of the Escalade. "Problem?"

"Your seat is missing some cushion."

Scizzors chuckled, shifting his weight. "I have to pack a special chair so I can drive without damaging my children." The bulk bulging from the hole swayed with his laughter as though alive.

Children? I am fighting an alien. "You enjoy scaring people?"

"To cease terrorizing would be to cease living." The gauntlet left the steering wheel and grabbed the cloak at the back of his neck. He pulled up and the "children" appeared: long tentacles with a faint blue glow, extending from his flesh about three feet. "My children scare the bejesus out of everyone."

That's what Laura meant by his having a tail. "They're glowing."

He grinned. "I think you'll find them quite stimulating."

"That doesn't sound ominous at all," Chase said sarcastically.

"Ominous it surely will be," Scizzors said, clearly amused. "Luckily for you, they were acting up earlier. Most of the first hour went into fixing them and now we're using part of the final hour driving."

"'Lucky.' That word has been tossed around a lot." Chase stared at his hands. "I'm just waiting for my luck to run out. If it doesn't run out and I live through luck alone, do I truly belong among you all?"

"Don't you worry yourself," Scizzors said, placing the gauntlet on Chase's shoulder. "Luck won't save you from me." The gauntlet clanked in several places when he punched Chase's shoulder. "Surviving me leaves no question. You belong."

"Thanks, I guess." Chase rubbed his arm. "Honestly, I feared fighting you even when I believed I'd be armored up. I was told you wouldn't blink if I Tasered you. Not that we'll find out. All my Tasers were blown to shit. Along with my gun, protective vest, and bombs." He rubbed his bare chest. "I feel naked. I'd say any remaining luck I had on reserve burnt up with my house."

"You'll stand before me unarmed." Scizzors honked at someone as they ran a red light. "You'll fight me taserless, gunless, vestless, bombless ..." He trailed off and sucked air through the mangled teeth. "Hands down, you'd deserve to sit at our table."

Chase nodded his head side to side. "I guess I'll just have to kick your ass."

Scizzors erupted in deep-toned laughter and slapped Chase's knee. "That's the spirit."

Chase rubbed his knee that was now throbbing. *Just have to kick his ass before the semi-truck of a man runs me over.* He did appreciate the fact that he wouldn't have to fight the monster right away. The road on the GPS screen turned gray like the ash left behind from the burning of a fuse. *When I step out of here a bomb of another type will blow up in my face.*

Scizzors adjusted the gauntlet and gave Chase a wide smile. The way his bottom jaw jutted out with teeth filed to points brought to mind a mutated angler fish.

He's going to rip my limbs off and beat me with them. I'd be less torn apart if I jumped from the car at seventy miles an hour. He needed desperately to think about something besides dismemberment. "Why an Escalade?"

Scizzors pointed a thumb over his shoulder. "Spacious as

Hades with enough room to conceal bodies and weapons."

I'll be the next body concealed. Chase stared out the window instead of focusing on the nightmare driving. "Do you know Kansas City well?"

"Not really," Scizzors admitted. "But Pockets told me of a place he brings people when he doesn't want their screams to be heard."

"Ah." Chase decided silence was better.

Ten minutes passed. They left the city and entered farm country. "Are we going to fight in a field?"

"Up to you," Scizzors said, cresting the top of a hill.

Behind a windbreak a mile down the road, Chase could glimpse faintly a two-story house.

"I like it," Scizzors said. "We can fight in peace there."

Pockets was right. *Nobody will hear my screams when he rips my spinal cord through my mouth.* Chase shivered at the grotesquely conjured image. "When you eat me, leave my pancreas for last. I hear it's sweet and makes the perfect dessert."

The wind was nearly knocked from Chase's lungs when Scizzors slapped him in the chest with the gauntlet.

"You're twisted." Scizzors guffawed. "I like you!" He shook his head, chuckling deeply. "If you survive, we'll be friends. But I'll keep that in mind if you don't."

Chase caught his breath. "Not okay."

"We're here, kid." Scizzors pulled into the driveway. "I'll meet you inside."

"You go on. I need a quick nap."

"We can fight in here, if you prefer." Scizzors smiled that horrifying, shark-toothed smile. "I'd advise against it, of course. You do not want to be stuck in a tight space with me."

Chase imagined a teacup pig trapped in a glass box with a tiger. "I'll be right in."

Scizzors nodded. "Good man." He turned the vehicle off and took the keys with him as he got out.

Chase remained seated as Scizzors walked toward the house. "He's not so big," he said aloud to pump himself up. Taking a deep breath, he nodded. "You've got this." He redirected his thoughts to Laura and Frank. *I need to return to them.* He closed his eyes and took in a deeper breath. "You can do this." He let the breath out slowly. *Scizzors spent most of his time getting his tentacles in place and driving here. I only have to survive the final stretch.* He opened his eyes and nodded again. "I can do this." Nodding fervently, he jumped out of the Escalade. "I've got this."

The sun was bright enough for him to believe the house would be mostly lit inside. An old barn had collapsed in on itself to his right and a small shed was to the left of the house. *The shed could be a place to hide.* The pig and tiger returned to mind. Oddly, he knew facing Scizzors head-on was his only option. Otherwise, he'd never feel like he belonged. His attention returned to the farmhouse. The front door was open, but he didn't dare go running in where Scizzors waited.

A tree had fallen against the house. He thought of Vixen coming through his window using the wood shed to get the drop on him. If he scaled it, there may be a way into the house that Scizzors wouldn't expect. He pondered taking off his shoes to make scaling the tree less difficult but didn't know what waited for him in the rundown farmhouse.

He ran and clambered up the termite-ridden tree. Bark broke away under foot. He regained his balance, took a breath, and continued on. There was a window on either side of where the tree had hit. The one on the left was broken. All he saw inside were a few two-by-four boards and a rusty toolbox. The other window was intact, but caked in dirt.

Hope he's still on the main level.

As if in answer, Scizzors called out from the front of the house. "Don't make me come looking for you." There was a smile he couldn't see wrapped around that threat.

Chase extended a foot to kick away what remained of the glass in the broken window. Once the path was clear, he perched on the windowsill. His foot tipped over a small two-by-four leaning against the window. It dropped with a thud.

"Tricky devil," Scizzors yelled before laughing maniacally. The thumping of heavy feet on stairs followed.

Chase returned to the tree, scaling it the final distance, and stalked quietly across the roof. Tile slipped under his feet, but he managed to keep his footing. Continuing slower, he found a hole in the roof on the far side and stared through it. Roof debris littered the floor. However, a clear spot could be seen between two fallen beams. The landing should be quiet because the floor was carpeted.

He dropped to his belly, swung his legs over, and hung down by his fingertips. Extending the tips of his toes to land quietly, he let go. His feet hit wet carpet. There came a crunching sound followed by tearing as the floor beneath gave way. His arms shot out reflexively and he found himself holding on for dear life. From his chest down, he was wrapped like a caterpillar in a fabric cocoon. He tried to look through the hole he'd created, but the carpet was bunched together, making it impossible. In trying to pull himself up, he felt nails, splinters, or both penetrating the carpet, needling him. He was thankful Allison had insisted on a tetanus shot after the whole Pockets and Noose debacle.

Heavy feet approached. Scizzors appeared in the doorway. The man looked completely bewildered, then began laughing raucously.

Chase glared at him. "You laugh a lot."

"I haven't laughed like this in a long time." Scizzors knelt in the doorway. "Thank you for that."

"I suppose this would look rather comical from where you're standing."

"Yes," Scizzors said, nodding enthusiastically. "Yes, it does."

"Well, come on in," said Chase. "Get busy caving in my skull."

"We'll both fall if I enter." Scizzors itched his upper lip with the sharp teeth as if considering what to do next. "I'll settle for throwing barbs at you."

Barbs?

The monster reached a hand into his cloak and retrieved three metal darts. "Hold still." He put two between his teeth and threw the third.

Chase winced, anticipating a pinch. Instead, the weapon sank into the floor inches from his nose. The dart was barbed.

Why miss?

Scizzors took a dart in each hand. "I know what you're thinking. Do I fall? Or stay as he staples my hands to the floor?"

"Those are equally bad options." Chase tapped the floor with a finger. "I don't know what's under me." The finger shifted to the dart. "Being riddled with those would be unpleasant."

"Be wiser about your approach, kid." Scizzors twirled the barbed dart around his fingers. "This room's been exposed to the elements. And that carpet soaked up and held water to better decay the wood it covered."

"Lesson learned," Chase said.

"Too bad it's your last." Scizzors snapped his hand forward.

Chase threw his arms up and fell through. The carpet caught on something and he twirled. His body twisted round and, face first, he plummeted. He threw his hands out to protect himself and met what could have been a table. Whatever it was collapsed under his weight. He laid staring up at the hole he'd made.

There came a cracking sound and the ceiling bowed. Roof debris shifted and slid into the hole.

He threw his arms over his face. "Not like this."

When nothing happened, he removed his arms. The room was a murky dark. Dust hung in the air as though gravity forgot to show up for its shift. Above him, the hole was plugged. A beam must have slid into just the right place to keep the rest from collapsing and crushing him. *Bad luck, followed by good.*

Pulse racing, he stood. *Glad Vixen isn't here to witness this.*

He took a moment to center himself in his surroundings. There were two other sources of light besides what little came from above. A thin laser beam of white streamed from a hole to his right. And to his left, a loose board let a narrow wall of light squeeze through.

He shook off the hit as best he could and stood. The dust in the air made him cough.

Footsteps came from above, then *thump-thump-thumped* down the stairs.

He went to the hole at his right and peered into a little girl's room. At least, he assumed it was a girl's room. What wallpaper remained was pink with unicorns and fairies. Chase didn't want to think further on why a hole in the wall would grant vision to a child's room.

His right wrist hurt. He pressed against it with his thumb. *Possibly sprained, not broken, definitely bruised.* Pain also blossomed on the left side of his head. He ran a finger along it, feeling blood matting his hair. *All this damage has been self-inflicted.*

The sound of wood splintering came from the other side of the hole. He peered through to see a door hanging off its hinges and Scizzors looking at the unbroken ceiling. His opponent's eyes fell on the wall Chase was behind and narrowed.

"Hmmm," Scizzors hummed, leaving the room.

I need to find a weapon. Chase felt around and confirmed the thing he'd landed on was a table. He found one of the legs and twisted at it. Sharp pains forked across his chest. His right leg radiated with a stabbing pain. He ran a hand gently along his ribs and pressed. *One ... maybe two of my ribs are damaged.* He couldn't feel any jagged protrusions or indentations in the bone. *Not broken.* There was heavy swelling. It clearly wasn't happy. *Cracked?* He felt at his leg and found more blood. His fingers traced a cut that ran from ankle to knee. *A nail must have cut me when I fell.* One thing was clear: *Fight's as good as over if that monster finds me.*

The steps passed by the room he was in and shadows interrupted the light bleeding in. Murmured speech followed.

Chase wound his way around the fallen table and put his eye to the light coming through the loose board.

Scizzors paced like a tiger searching for prey, all the while facing Chase.

There's clearly no door to this room. Not an obvious one. That made him worry further about the hole in the wall. Secret rooms are rarely ... kosher.

Scizzors walked right up to the loose board and put his eye against it.

Chase doubted he could be seen, but leaned sideways regardless.

"He should be ..." Scizzors paused as though thinking. "... right ..." Another pause followed by a loud BANG. "... here."

Chase stumbled backward.

BANG!

Chase licked his lips and spit the dust collected in his mouth.

The wall took another impact.

He breathed in and brought up his fists. *Let's do this.* He breathed out.

Silence.

Chase waited a little longer.

Nothing.

He neared the slit in the wall and peeked through.

Scizzors was at the far wall, rolling his shoulders.

Of course, he would.

Scizzors charged like a speared bull.

Chase jumped out of the way.

With a crunch and a crash, light flooded into the room along with the raging monster. Scizzors caught the crushed table with his ankle, stumbled, and fell. A wooden shelf covered in dusty jars took his full force. The wood buckled, jars shattered, and the beast on the floor roared in frustration.

The air grew dense with the smell of alcohol. It filled Chase's throat, choking him. He put the crook of his arm over his mouth and nose, and ran through the exit Scizzors had kindly made for him. At the sound of wood crunching and jars breaking, he turned back.

Scizzors rose, cloak dripping with old booze and covered in splinters. He turned to face Chase, the laughter and mirth from before a distant memory.

Chase regained his fighting stance.

Scizzors reached over his head, gripped the cloak, and pulled it over his head. When he let go, it thumped to the ground as loudly as a dead body would. The alcohol on the ram horns glistened in the light. The creature was all muscle. This became all the clearer when he hunched over, put both hands out like a bear, and roared, "Raaauuuhhh!" His teeth slipped out from under wetted lips as a sinister smile snuck free. The jagged angler fish look was rapidly replaced with the terrifying visage of a lion determined to maim a whole herd of antelope.

"Hope you're not an alcoholic," Chase said, ruefully.

Scizzors reached to the back of his neck. The room throbbed with a blue glow as the tentacles pulsed brightly. A few flickered, as if damaged by the shelf. At the monster's hip, the blue light reflected off what looked to be a metal whip.

Not good. Chase ran for the front door.

Heavy footsteps boomed in pursuit.

As Chase reached the door, something shattered against the back of his leg. He lost his footing, dropped, and smelled alcohol.

Another bottle flew past him and shattered on the porch.

Shit, shit, shit. He crawled for the door.

Scizzors grabbed him from behind and lifted.

Chase twisted in midair as Scizzors spun and threw him back into the room. The ribs already on fire caught his fall. Gasping, he put an arm around his chest. Slowly, he rolled over onto his back and lifted his head.

Scizzors was there, reaching down.

In his mind, Vixen screamed for him to MOVE.

He gritted his teeth and rolled. Fingernails scratched his skin, but he managed to escape being snatched up again. He kick-flipped and regained his feet while blindly swinging a fist.

Scizzors took the full punch to his jaw and staggered.

Chase laughed. "That'll work."

Scizzors backed up. His lip bled from a split likely put there by one of his shark teeth. He smiled wider and blood dripped onto his pearly whites.

That's so much worse. Chase resumed his fighting stance.

Scizzors stomped forward and threw a straight punch.

Chase shifted left and caught Scizzors by the wrist. When Scizzors pulled back, Chase held and swung his fist, using both his momentum and that of his opponent's to land another strong blow to the jaw.

Scizzors blinked and his knees nearly gave.

One of Vixen's attacks burst into mind. Chase wrapped his left leg around the outside of his opponent's left leg and put his palm to the monster's throat. In the same movement, his foot planted firmly to the ground and he pushed.

Scizzors toppled, twisting as he dropped.

Chase landed atop him and struck him twice in the jaw with each fist. This would have continued had he not recoiled due to the pain ricocheting between the nerves of his sprained wrist. He might as well have plunged the hand into boiling water. Breaking into a cold sweat, he cupped his wrist in his good hand. *At least he's out cold,* Chase thought.

If true, it wasn't for long. Scizzors opened his eyes and worked his jaw in a circle.

Chase channeled the pain from his wrist into rage and brought his head down.

Scizzors put chin to sternum, successfully lining a ram horn with Chase's forehead.

Vision blurred. Chase rolled off the monster. He rolled and rolled and rolled until he felt far enough away to stand. Rising, he shook on wobbling knees. Blinking away the gloomy shadows invading the corners of his eyes, he could see Scizzors getting up. *Fighting stance.* His hands came up. *You've got this.*

Scizzors strode forward.

Chase punched with his good fist. There was a flash of metal as the gauntlet blocked the hit. Two of Chase's fingers crunched out of place. "Mother fffuuu—" He vomited while cradling both hands against his stomach. He spit on the floor. *How does one fight without hands?*

Scizzors licked blood from his split lip. "That can't be pleasant," he said, pointing at Chase's fingers. "Pull them out and up."

"My other hand is sprained."

"I'll do it for you," said Scizzors.

"You're not supposed to help me."

"Who cares as long as I'm inflicting pain?" He held out the hand missing a gauntlet. "Give me your fingers."

Begrudgingly, Chase held out his hand.

Scizzors took the fingers and counted, "One ... two ..."

Chase took four quick breaths and held the fifth.

"Three."

Sharp bolts of pain shot through the dislocated fingers.

"Holy mother of—" Chase bounced on the foot missing a bloody gash. The room blurred and appeared to spin. He dropped to his knees. A breath caught in his throat and he choked on bile. *Not again ...* He threw up whatever remained in his stomach.

Scizzors grabbed hold of Chase's feet and began dragging him across the floor.

Chase kicked until he broke free. As he stood, Scizzors grabbed him by the arm, twirled him around, and let go. Chase hit the wall with his side and crumpled to the ground. He was surprised by how much the wall absorbed his impact. It would have looked worse than it was, though.

He remembered his first test. Pockets had feigned immense pain to lure him in close.

Chase pretended to have trouble standing and collapsed to a kneel. He wrapped one arm around his knees and put out a hand. "Please." He gasped. "I need ... I need a minute."

Scizzors rushed forward. "This isn't a schoolyard brawl, kid." He grabbed the extended hand.

Chase burst into an aerial flip. As he passed over Scizzors, he wrapped his arms around the beast's neck. His chest met the tentacles.

Something wasn't right.

Along the pulsing blue tubes, what felt like a hundred needles poked into his skin. A strange tingling came in waves, raising the hairs on his arms.

Scizzors reached back, but instead of grabbing Chase, he put a finger against a bulge at the back of his neck. "What a beautiful move you'll regret."

Chase didn't like the sound of that.

Scizzors pushed and the bulge in his neck popped.

The blue glow of the tentacles grew brighter and Chase could hear a slight humming.

I need to get off him. He tried to let go so he could drop, but Scizzors grabbed his arms and held. The sensation of being shocked by a light switch tickled Chase everywhere his body had contact with the tentacles. That sensation rapidly went from minor annoyance to body-convulsing electrocution. He didn't know how long he endured it, only that he somehow ended up on the ground.

He lay there until the full body shivers dissipated. The feeling was like none he'd ever had. He felt it in his teeth, fingernails, chest, and ears. Everything hurt. He didn't want to move, but realized he wasn't being attacked. Lifting his head, he saw Scizzors kneeling and popping his neck from left to right.

"What's—" Chase jolted. "wrong with you?"

"Got a little blowback." Scizzors regained his feet and turned. "That was stronger than I'm used to. The shelves must have damaged the pack."

"Still took it better than me." Chase crawled backward on hands and feet, struggling to recover his breath. "Let's not do that again."

"Agreed," Scizzors said, a vicious smile unzipping. "Let's play another game." The gauntlet unhooked the metal whip from the belt. "Pin the tail on the acrobat." The metal links unraveled. The whip looked to be as long as the monster was tall.

So, that's his tail. He thought back to his fight with Pockets and prepared to catch the chain whip. Then he saw the barbed hooks lining the final foot of its length. He needed to find a way around it. *Or run for the stairs?* They were too far away. *Door? Too far. Get in close to make the length of it worthless?* He bolted forward.

Scizzors snapped the whip back and flipped it forward.

Chase dropped into a roll. The whip popped somewhere behind him as he jumped up.

Scizzors kicked Chase backward and brought the whip up again.

Chase repeated the stunt. This time, as he came up, Scizzors punched him square in the face with his free hand. Chase fell backward and sprawled on the ground.

The whip went up.

"Shit!" Faster than should be humanly possible, Chase pulled off his pants and flung them up. They were torn from his grip.

Scizzors guffawed. "You crafty fuck." He began working to get the pants free of the barbs.

Chase got up and charged with his shoulder forward.

Scizzors dropped the whip, scooped Chase into a bear hug, and brought them face to face. He squeezed.

Air rushed from Chase's lungs. The damaged ribs began singing a tune of intense pain. His other ribs joined in the chorus. Pops ran the length of his spine. He gasped for air, unable to draw any. He went to headbutt Scizzors.

Scizzors turned his head and took the impact along his cheek. Overall, he seemed unperturbed. As unperturbed as a man can look while squeezing the life out of someone.

As Chase began to blackout, Laura's face appeared in his mind's eye. He recalled what she'd done to throw him off the first day of training.

Chase planted a kiss against his opponent's bottom lip. Sharp teeth raked against his mouth as Scizzors flung his head away.

Chase was thrown to the floor. Gasping painfully, he forced air back into his lungs. He heard spitting and shook off the dark filter from his eyes.

Scizzors wiped his mouth with a sleeve. "That's a first." He crouched and picked up the whip. Fingers made quick work of unhooking the fabric.

Chase stood, teetered, and backed up until he found a wall to lean against. "A Vixen special."

"She's a clever minx." Scizzors tugged at the pants until the rest tore away. Bits of blue jean remained on a few of the barbs. "Let's get back to it."

Chase swallowed. He weaved a wavering step, weakly awaiting his opponent's next move. "Don't think I won't use my underwear. I'm not shy."

"Go ahead." Scizzors walked a few steps forward, flipped the whip back, and snapped it forward.

Chase darted to the side as the whip popped the air a few inches from his face.

The whip whirled around its father's head and came again. Clink-clink-clink. POW!

Chase blinked this time, feeling a small cut open in his cheek. *Too close.*

This time, when it swung back, he darted forward.

Scizzors made it sing as it flashed.

Chase jumped, grabbed the whip at the middle, and

landed to slide on his knees. His palm slid up the length of it until he found the first barb, which he jammed into the monster's calf.

"Raaauuuh!" Scizzors clocked Chase across the side of the face with the back of the gauntlet, sending him sprawling.

Chase put a hand to his cheek and ran. *I have to get out of here.* When he was nearly to the door, he heard the clink-clink-clinking of the whip. Chase prepared to feel a gash open along his back. Instead, he felt the whip wrap around his throat, felt each barb bite and ensnare his flesh. He stopped in his tracks, knowing if he kept running, his throat would be torn open. *If it doesn't decapitate me altogether.* Slowly, cautiously, he turned to face the monster.

"Sorry, kid," Scizzors said. "I really liked you."

Chase closed his eyes, thinking of Laura and how much he loved her. He thought of his uncle being alive. There was so much unspoken there. So much to remain unspoken. He opened his eyes and ran at Scizzors.

Scizzors threw his head forward, clocking Chase with both horns. Chase crashed to the floor and felt the whip tighten around his neck. He scrambled in an attempt to get up.

"Auf wiedersehen," said Scizzors as he put a foot forward, gave the whip some slack, and threw all of his weight back.

Chase slammed his eyes shut when the barbs tightened and ...

The whip loosened and dropped as though Scizzors had let go.

Wait. Chase opened his eyes. *What?* Scizzors had done exactly that. "Why?" He put a hand to the barbs still puncturing his throat.

"Whew," Scizzors hollered. He clapped the gauntlet to his

mouth, saying through metal fingers, "That was so close."

"I'm confused," Chase said, bewildered. "I was dead. Why am I not dead?" *Has he spared me out of pity?*

Scizzors fished around in his pocket and took out a phone. "I must have turned the sound off. Boy, are you lucky it's on vibrate."

Chase cried tears of relief. "Time's up." His body was mangled and broken, but he'd survived this hulk of a man. "I survived."

"You survived," Scizzors echoed as he disappeared into the hidden room.

Chase prayed the next challenger wouldn't come for a month. The significant damage done by this creature was too much. Not to mention the self-inflicted bullshit. He took a deep breath, felt the pain vibrate in his ribs, and let it out. He sat up and began unraveling the whip from his throat. It went quickly until he came to the first barb. He tested the hook. Pain nearly doubled him over.

Scizzors appeared beside him. "Leave those for the doctor to look at," he said, adjusting the cloak over his tentacles. It smelled overwhelmingly of booze. "You ended this test surprisingly well considering the way it started."

"Sure," Chase said, standing. Pain played his ribs like a xylophone. Chase thought of all the places that hurt: contact burns where the tentacles tased him, a sprained wrist, two fingers turning purple, and cracked ribs. That, and the blood caked along his leg and head from the gashes accumulated by his own stupidity. *Not to mention this stupid thing.* He held onto the tail to limit its movements.

Chase thought of Vixen and his uncle waiting for him. *Let no more be unspoken.* He gritted his teeth when a barb shifted.

"Damn, this hurts."

"Tell that to my calf."

"I put one, maybe two, in you."

Scizzors smiled wickedly. "How many barbs did you get in your neck?"

"All of them."

"That's right." Scizzors held out his hand. "You were particularly unlucky today. You have a red necklace to prove it. Yet, you survived me." Scizzors smiled in as friendly a way as his face could manage. "Your final test is next. I hope you live because you'll make one hell of an assassin if you do."

"Oh, right." Chase's mind began to swim with doubts about his future career path. "That."

Chapter Twenty-Seven

Vignette

IN the 1860s, the four suits split up for the first time in a thousand years and spread out from Europe. The Hearts took the North, absorbing Europe where the Catholic Church had become divided over how to answer the rise of science and scholarship. The Diamonds took the East where they were already known for their dealings in Asian trade. The Clubs took the South, keeping a keen eye on starving countries as Africa fell into an economic depression. And the Spades boarded a boat headed West as the American Civil War had left the country's soldiers drowning in darkness. In their split, The Guild of Four regained their anonymity.

June 9, 2016
08:33 AM CDT
Kansas City, Missouri

VIXEN waited outside the operating room. Nightshade hadn't returned her calls, nor had he replied to her texts, and there was no word on Chase. Oddly, not hearing from one was significantly better than not hearing from the other. In Chase's case, up to this point, no news meant he was alive. Soon, though, word would come, determining whether or not she'd be his final test. Part of her wanted him to survive. The other part feared what came next if he did.

She put a hand on her overnight bag. She'd had to lose some clothing to fit Powder Keg's partially-melted mask inside. *How am I going to tell Chase he's gone?*

"Thank you, Allison." Ace's voice came from the other side of the door. "Can I keep it as a memento?"

Allison's voice followed. "I'd rather not explain to the staff where it came from. So, please do."

"I really appreciate it." He came through, looking pale and weary. In his hand was the metal shard from his abdomen "Let's go, Vixen."

Allison walked out behind him and smiled at her. "You know, I'd sleep a lot better if you'd all stop blowing each other up."

Vixen returned the smile. "Well, I think—" Her text tone went off. "Sorry." She brought up the screen and read the message:

Scizzors: Chase passed wearing a pretty necklace.

The phone should have burst to pieces with how tightly she squeezed. *Oh, thank heaven.*

She typed back:

Thank you for informing me.

Scizzors: Heading to the hospital now.

She closed her eyes and shook her head. *I'm the final test.*

"What's wrong?" Allison asked. The doctor's phone vibrated.

Vixen stared straight ahead. *What am I going to do?*

Allison made a grave expression. "Are you people trying to kill him?"

"What?" asked Vixen.

Allison turned the phone to show pictures of Chase's wounds.

That explains the necklace comment. The tail was still wrapped around Chase's throat. *How did you manage to—?*

"Vixen!" Ace had returned. "I thought you were following. Let's go."

"I'm coming," Vixen said. "Take care of him, Allison."

"You know I will."

"I do." She gathered up her overnight bag and went to Ace. "Feeling better?"

"She gave me these." He rattled a medicine bottle. "I don't feel much at all."

"That's good."

They began down the hall. "Did he pass?"

"He did."

Ace took a long breath and let it strain through tense teeth. "Good for him."

"I'll wait here for him to arrive," she said, stopping. "Scizzors did a number on him. They're coming to patch him up."

"No."

"You told me to build trust with him."

Ace shook his head, glaring at her. "You've done that. Now I need to convince you."

"Convince me of what?"

He hit a panel on the wall and two doors parted to the rear parking lot. He failed to clarify, continuing to the car.

"Seriously, what's going on?" said Vixen.

Ace remained silent until they boarded the jet twenty minutes later.

"Get us in the air," Ace said as he closed the clamshell airstair.

Noose came out of the cockpit. "Hey, Vixen."

"Noose," she said, smiling. "You look better."

"Back in black."

"As opposed to pale and buried under rubble."

Ace sat and pointed at the cockpit. "I said, in the air."

Noose's eyebrows knit together. "What's his problem?"

She shook her head.

Ace glowered.

"I'm going," Noose said. "Join me in the front if you need company, Vixen. He seems to be the opposite of chatty."

"I might take you up on that."

Noose went back to the cockpit. Within minutes, they were moving.

Vixen always loved the takeoff and landing, even with the ear popping. Something about it made her feel supernatural. All of the assassins in the Guild were encouraged to learn how to fly. She looked forward to learning if she ever got the chance.

Ace leaned his chair back and began rifling through the pages of a weapons catalog.

"Buying something?" Vixen said, trying to spark conversation.

Ignoring her, he turned the page.

She rolled her eyes. Sitting in her own recliner, she placed the overnight bag in her lap and opened the cabinet. Inside was the same reading material Ace had found. She turned pages until she came to the knives. *What am I doing? I don't care about any of this right now.* She threw the magazine back in the cabinet and closed her eyes. Chase's wounds appeared and her eyes opened.

"Hmmm," Ace hummed.

"Are you going to talk to me?"

He licked a finger and turned the page. "Hmmm, hmmm, hmmm," he hummed again, taking a pen out of the cabinet and circling something on the page. "That'll do nicely."

She fell back into her chair to stare at the television and let out a sigh. The weather played across the bottom of the screen. She glanced at Ace and saw the pen between his teeth.

Their eyes met.

He winked.

"What are you playing at?" said Vixen.

Ace looked back down at his magazine, pulled the pen from his lips, and circled something else. He capped the pen and dropped it and the catalog into the cabinet before reclining further. With a press of a button, the LEDs on his side of the cabin went dark.

"Fine," she said, smacking the button on her side.

The televisions at the front and back of the cabin dimmed.

She hadn't meant to fall asleep, but was glad when sleep came.

June 9, 2016
01:47 PM EDT
New York City, New York

IT wasn't until the jet touched down that she woke. After setting her seat up, she rubbed her eyes and stretched her back.

Ace came out of the cockpit. "Drop us off at headquarters before going home. And come in tomorrow around 9:30."

"I have a guy to kill tomorrow morning," Noose said, following him out.

"It's mandatory," Ace said, dropping the airstair and stepping out.

Noose shook his head but turned to Vixen. "Sleep well?"

She nodded. "Amazingly, actually."

"I'm the smoothest pilot we have."

"Zetta might disagree." Vixen put the backpack on and noted the extra weight of Powder Keg's mask.

"Yeah, don't tell her I said that," Noose laughed. "She scares me."

Ace glared at the both of them. "Are you two finished?"

"That depends," Vixen said, adjusting the straps of the bag to account for the mask pressing against her spine. "Are you done ignoring me?"

Ace walked away.

"Apparently not." She followed to find nearly all of their Hawker Beechcraft 900XP jets missing. *Why would he send them all out?*

Noose looked around as well.

Their Bell 429 helicopters were mostly accounted for,

however. *He's calling everybody home.*

She yelled at the back of Ace's head, "What's going on?" She followed him to one of the black helicopters. "Ace?"

"Still not chatty?" Noose said, walking beside her.

"Still an asshole, you mean?" She took off her backpack and crawled into the back of the helicopter with Ace.

Noose took up the pilot's seat.

Ace put on one of the headsets and brought the seatbelt across his chest. He closed his eyes and relaxed.

The four blades turned slowly at first, but soon sped until she couldn't tell one from another.

Vixen put on her own headset and cradled her overnight bag against her stomach. She stared out the window as they rose. Within minutes, New York City stretched out below them. She loved this city with all her heart. She believed it loved her, too.

Before long, they landed atop the bank that held their headquarters in its depths. Vixen was the first to jump out. The overnight bag returned to her back.

The helipads atop the surrounding buildings were all bare. *He cleared them for landing.*

Ace walked past her and entered the building through the roof access door.

By the time she caught up to him, he was at the elevator holding the door open.

She stepped in and rested her elbows on the banister.

He smiled. "I have a surprise for you."

Vixen raised her eyebrows. "We're talking now."

Ace put a key in at the base of the number pad and turned it. He pressed and held the thirteen button until it turned red.

The screen displaying what floor they were on changed to the image of a padlock. The elevator descended rapidly. Ace stood silently the entire way down.

I guess not. The elevator opened to their parking garage. The accounted for cars were Ace's black Jaguar XK Coup, Widow's black Alfa Romeo 4C Spider, Golem's heavily-modified Pontiac Bandit Firebird, Nightshade's blue Audi R8, and hers. There was a sixth vehicle as well, one alien to the garage: a beautiful red Ferrari 458 Italia, parked in a spot reserved for visiting Hearts. The Diamonds and Clubs visitor parking spots were empty, so the four Aces couldn't be gathering. *Or they are and that's why the jets are missing and the helicopters are waiting.* Could someone have called the four Aces to New York?

Ace headed through the sliding doors to their offices.

Vixen hurried after him. "Why is someone from the Hearts here?"

He had returned to ignoring her.

Annoyance boiled up her throat and erupted. "You called me home. Now tell me what the *fuck* is going on."

Ace pivoted on one foot and stomped toward her, his face the very definition of anger. He put a finger to his lips and pointed at an open door.

She glanced over to see Widow and another woman she'd never met staring back. The stranger wore all white, which highlighted her bronze skin and long brunette hair.

Vixen waved. "Sorry for interrupting."

"You're fine, love," Widow said.

The other woman walked to her and extended a hand. "I'm Vignette." Her voice purred with the slightest French accent. "Ace of Hearts."

Vixen took her hand and kissed it. When Vignette looked confused, Vixen said, "Was I not supposed to do that?"

Vignette's smile grew, causing smaller smiles to appear in the form of dimples. "We'll talk later, I hope."

"I'd like that." She kissed the woman's hand again. "Why do I keep doing that?"

Vignette laughed. "It happens."

"Does it?" Vixen said.

"No, but it's flattering you think I'm royalty."

"I'm a queen, sooo ..."

"Well, in that case." Vignette brought Vixen's hand up and kissed it.

Ace took Vixen's arm. "I'm sorry, but we have pressing business. You can kiss each other later."

"Of course," Vignette said, letting go of Vixen's hand. "You and I should talk as well, Ace."

"We'll see." He pulled Vixen along and turned down a hallway.

Vixen kept her eyes on the woman until she no longer could. "I like her."

When they were a ways down the hall, Ace turned and slapped Vixen across the face. "Why would you embarrass me like that?"

She cupped a hand over her cheek, her mouth agape. *What in the ... ?* Flashbacks of her father striking her mother blotted the canvas of her vision. Her younger self looked in panic for a bed to hide under. *I'm not that girl.* Ace was out of his mind if he thought hitting her was appropriate.

Apparently, she'd taken too long to answer, because he

raised his hand as though to strike her a second time.

She stood taller, glaring defiantly. "If you think I'll forgive a second strike, you're mistaken."

"I apologize," Ace said, clearly not sorry at all. Yet, he dropped his hand, regained his composure, and started down the hall. "Don't ever raise your voice to me again."

"Avoid hitting me and we've got a deal." Suddenly it occurred to her what hall they had turned down. *The hole.* "Nightshade better not be in there."

He opened the door and gestured for her to enter.

"I'm serious, Ace."

He raised an eyebrow at her. "After you."

She narrowed her eyes and went inside. "Nightshade?"

"Hey, Vix," he replied from beneath a grated, metal hatch.

Vixen dropped to her stomach and extended a hand into the hole.

Nightshade took it and squeezed. "Is Chase alive?"

"He is," said Vixen.

"Are you good?"

She shook her head. "Not with you in there."

"That's enough," Ace said, pulling a metal stool over to sit on.

Vixen glared at him. "What did he do?"

"Nothing, really," Ace admitted.

"You don't throw people in the hole for nothing," said Vixen.

"I'd like to second that," Nightshade agreed.

Ace sat, ignoring their complaints. "Do as I say and he's free to crawl out. He's been down there a while. He's probably famished. But I had a feeling Chase would get lucky again, because that's his specialty. He survives against all odds due to sheer *fucking* luck."

Vixen was confused. "What does Chase have to do with Nightshade?"

"I needed you to take this seriously. I told you to test him and—"

"I would be testing him. Right now. But you brought me here. And for what? To threaten me again?"

"When did I threaten you?" asked Ace.

"You know full well your comment in the car the other day was a threat." Vixen looked at Nightshade. "Apparently, he decided to threaten your life to really get my attention."

"Not cool, dude," said Nightshade.

Ace kicked the padlock on the grated hatch. "The adults are talking."

"I'm pretty sure I get it," Vixen said. "You're not asking me to test him, are you? This isn't about him proving himself to be a great assassin. You're asking me to—"

"Kill him," Ace said bluntly. "You don't and I'll leave Nightshade down there indefinitely." He pointed at the cement beside the hole. "I'll have another hole cut so you two can be neighbors."

He thinks he can get away with all this. "That's not something you can ask."

"I'm your Ace," said Ace. "I can ask anything I want. Before all this, you were loyal to me."

"I've been loyal to you because of what you did for me." She shook her head. "Up until this recruit shit, I thought you made sense. But I won't follow you blindly, just because you're my Ace. I'm not Radiant."

Ace's eye twitched and his lip quivered. "Radiant deserves respect for his sacrifice."

"Sacrifice?" Nightshade said. "What happened to Radiant?"

Vixen met his eyes. "He was sent after his testing time was up to kill Chase, only Powder Keg showed up and—"

"Powder Keg murdered him," Ace corrected. "That's what happened. So, I dealt with Powder Keg."

"Yeah, let's talk about that," Vixen said. "When did you become judge, jury, and executioner? All Aces are to be consulted if discarding one of our own is even remotely a question."

"I did consult them."

"Did you?" Vixen became painfully aware of Powder Keg's mask pressed against her back. No amount of adjusting the straps had helped. It was determined to remind her every second of Powder Keg's demise. "Did you also tell them of your mishandling of Chase's recruitment?"

Ace backhanded her across the cheek.

"The fuck!" Nightshade let go of Vixen's hand and grabbed onto the grates to pull himself up.

She rose on her knees. "I warned you not to hit me a second time."

"When I climb out of here, so help me god, Ace, you're a dead man." It sounded like Nightshade was attempting to do just that. "My poisoned blades will make love to your kidneys."

Ace reached over and turned a knob.

Nightshade screamed in pain.

Vixen dropped, reaching for him. She immediately yanked her hand back when something burnt her fingertips. "Stop it!"

she yelled, grabbing Ace's ankle.

Ace turned the knob back. "It's just a little boiling water that they use to clean out the hole." He looked at Nightshade. "I thought he'd appreciate a shower."

Vixen grabbed Ace's leg and bit him.

Ace grabbed her hair and twisted until she unlocked her jaws. "Have you lost your *fucking* mind?"

She grabbed his hand, trying to loosen his fingers from her hair.

He sat atop her back and pressed her head to the grate.

"Let her go!" Nightshade yelled. He was shaking and gazing back in horror. The water had already disappeared down a drain.

"You two keep making demands of your Ace." He grabbed her by the chin, pulling her face up to look at him. "Do again and see what happens."

It was hard to draw air, partially due to the angle of her throat and partially due to his full weight crushing the mask into her spine. "Stop. I—can't—breathe."

"That's another demand." He pulled harder.

He's going to break my neck.

Ace held.

Darkness swept through her vision.

He applied more pressure.

VIXEN woke to Nightshade tapping her cheek. She coughed and

put a hand over her throat.

Nightshade's eyes were so wide, they looked to be escaping their sockets. "You all right?" he asked.

She smiled poorly. "How bad does it hurt?"

"It's fine," he lied, his skin red and blistering. "I've always wanted a little color."

Vixen felt her jaw quiver.

Ace's foot appeared in front of her.

She glared up the length of it at him. "I'm telling Vignette everything."

He lifted her chin with the toe of his shoe. "Do, and I'll tell her you conspired with Powder Keg to kill me. I'll tell her you slept with the recruit and helped him pass his tests." He tapped his foot on the grate. "Before I tell her all that, I'll come in here and make the knob disappear. Continuous flow would boil Nightshade like a chicken. If he doesn't pass out, it'll be ten minutes of pure pain." He knelt. "And after I'm done with him, I'm coming for you. I'll say you attacked me. And, like Powder Keg, that I was forced to put you down."

She stared back defiantly. "Why are you being like this?"

"It's not my actions I'm concerned about." He stood and put his hand on the knob. "Do we understand each other?"

Nodding, Vixen said, "Chase was a distraction. Nothing more." She glanced at Nightshade. "Letting him live would only serve to prolong that distraction."

"Good," Ace said. "I don't believe you're sincere. I don't really care as long as it's done."

"I'll kill him tomorrow."

Ace crossed his arms. "I want it done here in New York. We have a meeting at 9:30 tomorrow morning. Bring his body to me beforehand."

She narrowed her eyes. "Between now and tomorrow morning? I'd have to fly him in, kill him, and get him to the meeting. Doesn't leave a lot of room for sleep."

"Then don't sleep," he said. "Zettabyte will bring him when she's done with her assignment. That gives you time to prepare."

"How do you want him to die?"

"I don't care if you stab him while he's inside of you. All I want is for his body to be here before 9:30. Or Nightshade boils." He walked past her to the door. "I'll ask again: Do we understand one another?"

Nightshade shook his head at her.

"We do," she said.

"Glad you came to your senses," Ace said and closed the door behind him.

Vixen let the tears flow. She gripped Nightshade's hand. "I'm sorry."

He squeezed her hand with both of his. "I should have killed Chase so you wouldn't have to."

"You tried." She placed her other hand down to cup his cheek. "He doesn't want to do this job anyway, so killing him might be a kindness."

"If he doesn't want to join us, then why has he fought so hard to survive?"

"I don't think he wants to die," Vixen admitted. "But if he survives, he's really, really not going to want to kill anyone. And if he doesn't pick up assignments, he will be discarded." She shook her head. "Killing him now in my own way will spare him a worse death down the road."

"This isn't on you," said Nightshade.

"It is, though." She frowned. "I said I'd test Chase when I believed Ace wanted the recruit to prove himself. Once you've agreed to a testing, you can't back out."

"We can't let Ace get away with this," Nightshade said, gripping her hand harder. "He can't walk away from this."

"He won't," she promised, pulling away from him. "I'm going to get you out." She started for the door.

"Laura?"

She stopped.

"If you want Chase to pass, test him to the best of his ability to survive. Push those limits, but don't kill him for me."

"Mica, you know as well as I he won't see me coming."

"You don't have to do this."

"Yes, I do."

She left the room.

He called after her, "Don't do this." He yelled louder when she closed the door. "Don't do anything for that devil!"

He is the devil, she thought. *How was I so blind after surviving my father?* She felt the many places Ace had hurt her. *He's out of his mind.* She walked to the end of the hall and turned for Ace's office. *But if I try anything, Nightshade or Chase or I die.* She knew it would likely be all of them together.

"Vixen." The French voice purred behind her.

Slowly, she turned to see Vignette and Widow. "I can't talk right now."

Widow narrowed her eyes. "Your face and throat weren't red before."

"Did Ace beat you?" Vignette asked, concern emanating from every pore.

"I got this training Chase."

Widow eyed her suspiciously.

"My father was abusive." Vignette placed a gentle hand to Vixen's cheek. "I have an eye for wounds like this. They were not there before."

She brushed away Vignette's hand. "What do you want?"

Widow nodded toward her door. "Come into my office."

Vixen stared down the length of the hall at Ace's office. *I'll deal with you later.* She nodded and followed them into the room. Widow's room was more or less empty. It contained a black, leather couch and a coffee table. On the wall was a portrait identical to her parking space.

Vignette sat on the couch and patted the cushion beside her. "I need the Queen of Spades to offer up her perspective."

Widow held out a hand. "I'll hang up your pack."

Vixen jerked away as though struck. "I'm fine standing." The mask pinched at her again. *Not now, Frank!*

Widow's eyes scanned Vixen over before she shut the door. "What's going on, love?"

Vixen changed the subject. "If this is a more thorough review of Powder Keg, Ace already discarded him."

Widow glared at Vixen. "PK is dead?"

"Yeah."

Vignette glanced between the two of them. "I was not consulted on that at all."

"Ace said you were," Vixen said.

"No." Vignette shook her head slowly. "I was not."

He's such a fucking liar. Vixen began shaking. *An abusive, motherfucking liar.*

Vignette threw a hand up. "That gets added to the list of

complaints." She leaned forward and pointed at Widow. "Thanatos and Widow have been reaching out to the other Aces about the conduct of your leader. I'm here for his review, not Powder Keg's. If I believe there are grounds, I'll reach out to the other Aces and request we gather."

"You have no idea," said Vixen. "His recent conduct has me questioning everything." She looked to Widow. "Is this in regard to the new recruit?"

Vignette answered, "There have been many things, most of which are not at all recent."

"Those being?"

"Truth is, the list is extensive." Vignette sat back and crossed one leg over the other.

"Then knock him from his high horse," Vixen pleaded, gesturing in the direction of the hole. "Nightshade's being punished over nothing. If you ask Ace what the offense is, he won't be able to answer."

Widow put up a finger. "I asked and was told he carried out an unsanctioned kill against his roommate."

That's the excuse Ace is going with? Vixen clamped her mouth shut and returned to lean against the wall. *He's already covering his bases.* He had warned her not to say anything. *Our word against his.*

"Whatever the reason," Vignette said. "Jokers don't belong to any suit. In fact, their job is to liaison between suits. I'll make sure he's released until all four Aces are consulted and it's decided he be returned to the hole."

Vixen hated herself for what she was about to say, but felt it necessary for the safety of all involved. "Ace will attack me and Nightshade for embarrassing him." She pointed at the wounds she'd already accumulated. "He's lost his fucking mind. If you let Nightshade out, he and I both will pay for that embarrassment. You have to leave him down there until something can be done about Ace."

Vignette shook her head. "I can't just leave the Joker in the hole."

Vixen adjusted the straps again. "Nightshade would side with me on this. I have a plan to get him out. Just give me the opportunity."

Vignette narrowed her eyes at Widow. "You think Nightshade would offer to stay in the hole?"

Widow glanced up at the ceiling. "He'd slit his wrists for Vixen."

"Give me time to deal with Ace," Vixen said.

"The man beats her," Vignette said, "and she believes he'll listen?"

Widow shrugged. "I don't know why she's loyal to him. Then again, I was fooled by him once."

"I'm in the room," Vixen said. "Talk to me, but not about me as though I'm not here. My parents did that when I was a child. I don't put up with it as an adult." She slapped her chest. "I pissed him off and he hit me."

Vignette stared long and hard at Vixen before saying, "Do not make any excuses for his abuses."

"I'm not," said Vixen. "I'm saying he's dangerous and he's made that clear in more ways than one. I'll deal with him."

"You can't kill him." Vignette sighed. "Not without being discarded yourself for acting outside the consent of the Aces. You'll have to get every card member of the Spades to vote him out. Can you do that?"

Vixen looked to Widow for that answer.

Widow looked uncertain.

"If we fail at the full vote," Vixen said, "he'll rain down fire on all who voted against him."

"It may not matter soon, anyway. His station as Ace is under review. It's a slow process, but in a week or two, he may cease to be your problem."

Vixen shook her head. "I don't have weeks."

Vignette frowned. "The other Aces and I have always hated Ace for his arrogance. When he was elected, we thought it was because most of you are Americans. You're accustomed to pompous leadership."

Vixen had expected Widow to defend the decision. Instead, she said, "It was a mistake to make him Ace. He charmed his way to the top. We didn't realize he'd abuse his power until it was too late."

Vixen rubbed her neck. "I'm just now figuring that out."

Vignette looked at her. "All I'm saying is, it might be sooner. A few days even."

Vixen shrugged. "That's still too slow."

"Slow is what we have," Widow said.

Play along. Vixen nodded, straightening. "How soon can you get the Aces here?"

Vignette shrugged. "Bringing us all together takes time, even when highly motivated."

"Then we wait," Widow said.

Vignette looked at her wristwatch. "That's the time I have for now." She stood. "Thank you both for speaking with me. You'll hear from me soon."

"We'll take what we get." Widow opened the door. "I'll

continue sending you what I find."

There was a question that still needed answering. "Why does Ace think you're here?" asked Vixen.

Vignette turned. "To request that Widow fill a vacancy among the Hearts. When I leave, I'll say she refused because the vacancy was for the three, not the eight."

Widow smirked. "He ordered me to tell her to fuck off, but to do so politely."

"Here's me fucking off politely," Vignette said before kissing them both on each cheek. "À la prochaine," she said and left the two of them standing in the doorway.

Widow turned to Vixen. "Be patient, love." She brushed Vixen's hair out of her face. "He'll get what's coming for doing this to you."

Vixen forced a smile. "Let me worry about me." She walked away from Widow, rolling everything over in her mind. His striking her, his strangling her, his throwing Nightshade in a hole to get to her. *You have my attention, asshole.* How had she not seen it all these years? His controlling everything about her. Choosing her car, the way her parking space was painted, the location of her office. Her father did the same with her mother, controlling their money and all her choices. When her mother finally got sick of it and called him out, he punished her physically until she remained silent. Until she finally gave in and put a bullet in her head.

Vixen shook uncontrollably.

She adjusted the bag at her back. Ace had forgotten to take the mask from her. It needled painfully. *Shut up, Powder Keg!* It was a constant reminder that she had to tell Chase. *Shut up!* Tell him his uncle was dead ... again. *Shut up!* Then would have to kill him. *Shut up! Shut up! Shut—* Her eyes caught Powder Keg's door. She was suddenly reminded of when he'd broken into her home. *Don't shut up.* She looked at Golem's workshop a few doors down. *Don't ever shut up.*

She ran to Golem's door and burst inside. "I need your help."

Being only two-and-half-feet tall, the primordial dwarf was hard to find among the massive stuff surrounding him in the workshop. He stood on a risen platform, wearing a welder's mask. Sparks showered down as he repaired a part on the ten-foot-tall monster suit he piloted.

She realized he hadn't heard her so she turned off the gas to the torch.

He lifted the mask and turned to look inquisitively at her.

"You up for a challenge?"

He hung up the torch and crossed his arms.

She took Powder Keg's mask from her backpack and set it on the platform at his feet.

He picked up the mask and looked it over. After several minutes, his eyes met hers.

She bit the inside of her lip. "Can it be fixed?"

He nodded.

Chapter Twenty-Eight

A to Zetta

THE Guild of Four kept their own history and continued to hold cards on their persons. No two assassins held the same card.

June 9, 2016
10:02 PM CDT
Kansas City, Missouri

~ Two of Spades and Three of Spades ~

IT'S as cold as a witch's tit up here, Tayla thought while cleaning her guns. She glanced up to see Zettabyte glaring at her. It was hard to take the redhead seriously when she looked barely seventeen. Freckles dotted her complexion. The girl was maybe four-foot-eleven and wore her fiery hair back in a ponytail.

Zettabyte's green eyes flashed with irritation.

Tayla finally gave in and asked, "Did I do something?"

A long sigh was followed by, "It's what you're not doing that is upsetting me."

Tayla began putting one of the guns back together. "I'm not a computery person. None of what you're telling me is sticking."

"Then why come?"

"Thanatos said I needed to shadow as many of our members as possible."

Zettabyte wrinkled her nose. "Does anything I've said make sense?"

"The delete key does the thing, and there's lots of ones and zeros."

Zettabyte narrowed her eyes. "I didn't say any of that. You're making shit up. Stop being such a bagbiter and get over here."

"That's another term I don't know," Tayla confessed, inching closer.

"Don't turn away from things you don't understand." Zettabyte began tapping away at her laptop. "If we avoid that which we do not know, we avoid growth altogether."

Maybe if I play along, we can get off this damn roof and go home. "First and only question I really have is why are we up here?"

Zettabyte stopped typing. "We're atop the Power and Light Building because I love the view of Kansas City from up here." She looked around and smiled. "I wanted to share it with you."

"We could have done all this from the airport? I thought we were here so your IP address couldn't be traced to the hanger or something."

"'IP' is a pretty computery term for someone who knows nothing." Zettabyte stretched her fingers over the keyboard. "But don't worry. By the time we leave, I'll have erased every digital footprint." Her eyes dropped to the screen. "To answer your question, we did everything but the final bit after touching down here."

Tayla finished the first gun by snapping the clip into place. "Explain what we did? Because I was lost through most of it."

"Airports check out everyone coming in by car, but pilots come in with barely a question asked. That is, if you've already gone through the proper channels, set the schedule, and sent the appropriate documentation when needed."

Tayla started putting the second gun back together. "We cleared all security by flying in."

"Exactly. Gaining full access to the hangers and my target's Cessna TTx." Zettabyte pressed some more keys and a map loaded on the screen followed by a glowing red dot. "I approached the pilot as an FAA inspector and requested access to the plane for testing. The guy argued for a half-hour because he'd only had to present maintenance and inspection paperwork in the past."

He was pissed.

Zettabyte turned the computer so Tayla could better see the screen. "I uploaded my program to override his autopilot."

"You can do that?" Tayla said, fearing all future flights. "With a push of a button, you can take over?"

"Yes, I'll delicately do just that." She adjusted the screen tilt. "They can override the autopilot with ease, but before they realize they're off course, I'll have moved them far enough to limit fallout." She looked at Tayla. "Ergo, when I ignite what I put behind their console, they won't crash into this beautiful city or any other city for that matter."

Tayla raised an eyebrow. "How will you know when they takeoff?"

"I've tapped into airport security." She brought up live camera feeds.

"What if they suspect something and don't takeoff?"

Zettabyte shrugged. "If they catch on and stay grounded, then you, my frustratingly frustrated student, are up."

A surge of pride flooded Tayla's chest with warmth. *They're beginning to trust me.* She finished assembling the second gun and holstered both. *I'm not simply shadowing.* "I'm in the field?"

"Unofficially." Zettabyte took the tie out of her hair and let the red splay over her shoulders. She pointed at the guns in Tayla's lap. "Not that I think you'll need those today."

Tayla holstered her Fangs. "You have my full attention now."

Zettabyte tapped the screen when the Cessna TTx came into view. "Here we go." She hit a few keys, switching the screen back to the map.

As the map moved with the red dot at its center, Zettabyte tapped a few times at her keyboard and another window popped up. The screen changed, then changed again.

"What's happening?" asked Tayla. "Did they hack you back?" *What if they're tracking us?* "Do we need to leave?" She ran her fingers along her belt to find the guns. "Zetta?"

"Calm down, spaz." Zettabyte pressed two keys together and all the screens appeared side by side. "It's a mirror that allows us to see what they see." When she took her finger off the keys, it became an aviation screen.

"That's too cool," Tayla said, watching over Zettabyte's shoulder. "How'd you do that?"

"If you'd been paying attention during the setup rather

than playing with your toys, you'd know already."

"Toys?" Tayla placed a hand on one of the holsters. "My Fangs are weapons." She pointed at the computer. "That's a frickin' toy."

Zettabyte ran her fingers across the keyboard, leaning to whisper to her monitor. "What's that?" She glanced up at Viper. "That's naughty. There would be questions if I pushed her off the building. Too many questions."

"I know you're threatening me, but the scariest part is you talking to a computer as if it's alive."

"She is alive." Zettabyte beamed with pride. "Let's show her what you can do, babe." She hit a few keys and brought up a black command screen. Her fingers danced across the keyboard.

"I'm not saying it's not powerful," Tayla assured her. "I'm saying—"

The building they were on went dark.

Tayla's eyes widened. "That is *not* cool, Zetta."

The computer screen was the only light atop the building, causing Zettabyte's red hair to glow like a fiery halo in the night.

"Seriously," Tayla pleaded. "Stop."

"If I can wink out a building called Power and Light, you know I could just as easily plunge the entire city into darkness." Zettabyte ran her hand along the screen. "Automated cars ... mine to control. Office buildings ... mine to control. Bank accounts ... mine to control. Damn near everything in this modern world ... mine to control." She tapped another button and the building lit back up.

Tayla clapped her hands. "Your tag should be God."

"That's blasphemous," Zettabyte said, stroking the side of the laptop as though it were a lover. "But I'm happy you're

grasping the sheer power bottled up in such a little package."
She put her fiery hair back into a ponytail and sat up. With a few
taps, Zettabyte brought back the aviation mirror.

Tayla laughed. "I feel like I'm the third wheel on this
date." She stood, popped her back, and stretched side to side.
"Would you like some time alone?"

Zettabyte was no longer listening. She was zeroed in on
the laptop screen, fingers busy at the keys.

Tayla dropped back down to watch, but nothing appeared
to be happening. *I think that's the point. If I can't see what's going on
while literally witnessing it, then they surely can't either.*

Tayla began reading the screen and said, "ETA is
estimated time of arrival, but what's ETE?"

"Estimated Time Enroute," Zettabyte said. "Quiet now."

Tayla pursed her lips together for barely a second before
asking, "Why have both?"

Zettabyte swatted at Tayla as she would an irritating fly.

Tayla pressed her lips into a thin line.

Zettabyte tapped the arrow key every three to four
seconds for ten minutes.

Bored, Tayla pointed. "What does LCL mean?"

Zettabyte's elbow shot back, catching the bridge of Tayla's
nose.

Although it hurt, Tayla grinned while rubbing at it.

"There we go," the redhead said, changing windows. This
one showed more of the map. She ran her finger along the screen
and tapped. "I'll detonate over a field here and ..." Zettabyte
switched back to the mirror and hit the arrow key a few more
times. "Shit." She tapped a few more times. "They know they're
off course."

Tayla narrowed her eyes. "I'm going in?"

"Not unless you can fly." Zettabyte put her thumb and middle finger together over the delete key. "Means we're done here." She snapped her fingers together, the middle finger striking DELETE.

The mirror went black and the screen returned to a map vacant a red dot.

Zettabyte popped her fingers against her cheeks and closed the laptop. "Since I blacked out the building earlier, we may want to be stealthy leaving. They might have sent someone to investigate the power failure."

"That was anticlimactic," said Tayla. "We didn't get to see or hear it blow up."

"I'm sorry," Zettabyte said, putting the computer in the laptop bag. "Let me fix that for you." Crouching down, she hugged her knees and made a humming noise. Zettabyte's body burst upward, her arms and legs flailing in the air as she yelled, "BOOM!"

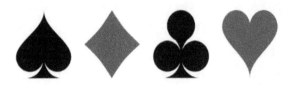

Chapter Twenty-Nine

Flight Plan

June 10, 2016
01:39 AM CDT
Kansas City, Missouri

WITH the injuries Chase accumulated from the fight, Allison demanded he stay for twenty-four-hour observation. She had hidden him in a wing of the hospital that was being renovated. For ten hours she sat with him. Once she started her shift, she made an appearance every hour or so. Scizzors wasn't happy about the delay, but managed to fall asleep during most of it. Chase was beyond exhausted, but Allison warned him not to drift off due to the head wound. It was driving him crazy. Thankfully, on one of her visits, she'd brought him trail mix to snack on.

"I'll be back in a while," said Allison. "If you need me, text me. I'll try to sneak back over here."

"I'll be fine," said Chase. "I really should go."

"Just seven more hours, I promise. It's for your own good." She backed toward the door. "I really have to go."

Chase raised his eyebrows. "I'm not stopping you."

She was nearly bowled over by Scizzors in the door. He had left some time before, muttering something about waiting tasting better with ice cream.

"Sorry, little lady," he said, a half-eaten ice cream cone in hand.

"It's fine." Allison sidestepped to give him a wide berth. Once out the door, she could be heard running down the hallway.

Scizzors eating ice cream was a strange thing to witness. He'd scoop it up with his bottom jaw and tilt his head back to swallow.

"I can't do seven more hours of this," said Chase. "I'm going insane."

Scizzors grabbed the keys to the Escalade. "If you want to go, let's go. I'm bored as fuck."

Chase rose on his elbows. "Seriously?"

"What's she gonna do?" asked Scizzors. "Tell her superiors she can't find the man she hid in their abandoned wing?"

"Good point." Chase crawled out of the hospital bed and limped to the door. He peeked out. "We're good."

Even with the medication Allison had given him, Chase could feel sharp criticisms from his ribs. It didn't help that Scizzors slapped him whenever something remotely funny came up.

Speaking of which ...

"Not sure why she's worried about you," Scizzors said, clapping Chase in the chest and belly laughing. "It's not like you fell through the top floor of a house."

Chase rubbed his chest. "I feel like you're criticizing me, but you went through a wall."

Scizzors sniffed at his shirt. "I still smell like an alcoholic's wet dream."

Chase closed his eyes when he got in the Escalade.

Scizzors kept randomly poking him with a sharp fingernail.

"Would you stop that?" Chase complained after twenty minutes of being prodded.

"Don't fall asleep," said Scizzors. "You're concussed."

"Fine." Chase opened his eyes. "Where are we?" They had pulled up to a small airport. The strip was brightly lit. Chase glanced around curiously. "What are we doing here?"

"Did you want to go home?" Scizzors asked. "Because sleeping on rubble can't be good for your back."

"No," Chase said. "But I need to meet someone and a plane won't take me to him."

"Jet," Scizzors corrected. "Ace is requesting you come to New York."

Chase looked out the window as a small puddle jumper landed. "How do I know you're not setting me up for the next opponent?"

"You don't," Scizzors admitted.

Chase took out the phone Laura had given him and started typing a message. This was made considerably harder due to the many fingers bound in splints.

Frank is waiting for me.

Do I have to get on this jet?

Scizzors parked the Escalade and got out.

Chase opened the door, stuck a foot outside, and waited for her reply.

"Technically," Scizzors began, "you don't have to follow Ace's orders yet. You're not a Guild member until you pass the next test." He came around to Chase's door. "But I have been ordered to return. So, if you're staying, you can use the car for a bit longer." He handed Chase the keys. "Just leave it here when you're done."

> *Queen of Spades: Your uncle left word with me.*
> *Queen of Spades: I need you in New York.*
> *On my way.*

"No, I'm coming," Chase said, handing the keys back to Scizzors.

"You sure?" Scizzors threw the keys on the driver seat. "Because I've never heard of them requesting a recruit come early."

Chase shrugged, causing ants to nibble furiously at his neck. "Vixen says she needs me."

Scizzors looked at the phone. "Why do you have one of our cells?"

Don't get her in more trouble. "I stole it off Nightshade."

Scizzors cocked an eyebrow, but turned and started toward a gate without raising further questions.

Chase winced when he dropped the short distance from

the Escalade to the gravel parking lot. "Is it cool if I hate you for a while?"

"I'd hate me for a while, too," Scizzors said, chuckling. "Sorry for messing you up so bad."

Chase shook his head. "That would be more convincing without the laughter."

"One test left," Scizzors said, glancing back. "Soon, you'll be the one messing people up."

"That doesn't sound appealing to me." Chase stopped, realizing how true the statement was. *I don't want to hurt people.* Even if they deserved it, he couldn't see himself pulling the trigger. He took a step back. *Unless the person was a pedophile.* "Do you have to kill everyone they tell you to?"

"Not at all," Scizzors said, walking to a black box with a cable bar running into the gravel. "If nobody wants to take an assignment, it's declined by the Guild." He opened an access panel and a keypad lit blue.

"If I only wanted to kill pedophiles, would that be fine?"

"Get in line." Scizzors laughed as he typed in 1352. The gate clicked and parted wide enough to let a car through. "You'll need to broaden your scope a little. You must assassinate two people a month, minimum. When pedos appear on our list, they tend to be snatched up quick."

Two a month? How will I even manage two a year?

They stepped through the gate. Most of what could be seen were smaller craft for dusting crops or recreational flight.

Scizzors pointed to the west and said, "We're this way."

Chase jolted when the gate latched behind them.

"You look a tad peaked," Scizzors said, walking backward.

Chase stopped under a light pole. His shadow gazed back

accusingly. "I don't know."

Scizzors stopped. "Did I say something wrong?"

Chase shook his head. "I was so determined to survive, I forgot to focus on what it means to live."

"That'll pass once you've killed a few baddies."

"I'm not so sure." It could have been the medicine wearing off, but Chase was definitely having a harder time breathing. "What if I can't kill the first few?"

Scizzors walked back to Chase and placed the gauntlet on his shoulder. There was still a smear of Chase's blood on it. "One of us will be there with you starting off. You'll shadow us while we take out our hits and when we believe you're ready, you'll begin. Not before."

"I'm just saying, what if I'm never ready?"

"I don't know," Scizzors conceded. "I heard you'd never killed anyone, which gave me pause to test you. But I also heard you were different in a good way. I had to see for myself."

"My ribs thank you for that."

A wicked grin spread from ear to ear. "I'll send them a welcome basket once you've joined."

Chase sighed. "Did you worry you wouldn't be able to kill when you began?"

"Not at all," Scizzors said, proudly. "Truth is, I knew some things could only be achieved in shadow. Once they set me loose, I took out twelve people my first month. Each person made the world a little less evil."

"Why, then, are there so many politicians still walking around?"

Scizzors popped him in the chest and laughed loudly.

Chase bent, cradling his chest and groaning. *I deserved that.*

"Sorry," Scizzors said. "I keep forgetting you're dying right now. Stop making me laugh."

"Yeah, that one's on me."

"If cleaning up the world doesn't get you hard, the money will."

Chase shook his head and straightened as best he could. "I don't care about that, either."

"That's a relief because those who do are *the* worst."

"If neither *gets me hard,* do I have the option of leaving once I pass?"

"You're in the Guild 'til you're dead."

"Back at square one."

"I'm confused." Scizzors adjusted the chain whip at his hip. "You had the choice to turn us down before testing. Too late for cold feet getting ya out of this union."

"Too many people approached me," said Chase. "I didn't have the option to leave."

Scizzors dropped his head. Under the lighting, the ram horns cast eerie shadows across his already terrifying face. "Who told you that?"

"Ace told Vixen."

His head rose, shaking slowly. "I'd heard some strange things had gone on with you. But that takes the maggot-ridden cake."

Chase backed toward the gate.

Scizzors put out a hand as though to stop him. "That's truly fucked up. But we'll make it work, kid. I promise. If you can't kill, we'll find a way around it."

"How?"

Scizzors shrugged. "Don't know. But when ya pass your

final test, we'll all be invested in finding you an alternative to pulling a trigger."

"What if I don't care to be part of any of this?" His eyes darted about for an escape.

"I've seen a lot of people with that look on their face right before they run from me," Scizzors said. "I won't chase you, but your final test will come. Maybe you'll hide and they won't be able to find you, but if so, you'll pass due to that. Eventually, we'll find you and bring you home. If you still run, we'll discard you and start over."

"I know 'discard' doesn't mean I go free."

"No, it does not," said Scizzors. "I'm not saying this isn't fucked. But Chase, you'd make a good Guild member. You'd be picky with your assignments, is all. And I know it's hard to imagine, but pedos aren't the only monsters out there." Scizzors tilted his head and locked eyes with Chase. "And that's coming from a monster." He nodded, horns bobbing in the light. "Our Guild does good work. I don't know why it's treated you poorly, but you'll come to see we're needed." The gauntlet clamped down on Chase's shoulder. "You're needed."

"I don't know how I'll—"

"You're with me, Chase." A female's voice came from his right.

Chase glanced to see a short young woman, seventeen or eighteen years old. A ponytail of bright red hair brought out the sparkling green of her eyes. Freckles speckled her cheeks, congregating in the deep dimples of her smile.

Chase realized he hadn't responded. "Sorry. That's me."

"I know. I'm Zettabyte." She scowled at Scizzors. "It's two in the morning. I thought you'd be here hours ago."

"Doctor's orders." Scizzors shrugged. "It's a three-hour flight. We'll get there with time to sleep a bit before Ace's meeting."

"Hope so," she said. "Tayla will go back with you."

Scizzors nodded. "That's what I heard."

"All right, then." Zettabyte tapped Chase's arm. "Let's go." She twirled on one foot, returning the way she'd come.

Chase followed, confused. "He's not coming with us?"

"Two jets are here and he'll need to pilot one home."

A sharp pain skipped rocks across Chase's chest. *I can't FUCKING BREATHE!* Deciding to focus on something else, he asked, "You're on my flight?"

"Do you have a license?" She walked as though she owned the airstrip.

"No."

"Then, yeah." She turned left at a hanger. "You'll sort of need me there."

Chase slowed, eyeing her. "You're the pilot?"

She laughed and pulled on a pair of black leather gloves. "Problem?"

"Nah," he lied, questioning in his mind how old one had to be to fly. *Maybe she's nineteen?*

They walked until they were beyond the reach of the lighting. She stopped beside a jet. It was dark black. If it weren't for the lit windows and the stairs lowered to splash light across his path, he could have missed it entirely in the midnight. The size and luxury of the jet made the other aircraft on the strip look like playthings. They didn't belong in its presence. Cold air tickled his cheeks and made him want to breathe deep. He feared too much his rib's reply to act on the urge.

He'd flown before, but on passenger planes—never in anything this luxurious. Despite his fear of a future unknown, the curiosity drove him forward. He ascended the steps with Zettabyte following.

The inside was more beautiful than the outside. Three black, leather, reclining loveseats and a seven-foot divan made for plenty of seating. Two cherry wood desks alluded to the plotting of assassinations. A television at the front of the large living space and one in the back displayed a jet stationary at the center of a map. The current weather trailed across the bottom of each screen.

Zettabyte pulled a bulky remote from a compartment and handed it to Chase. "Master control. Temperature, audio, video, XM radio, and television. You can do everything with this, besides fly the jet." She pointed at the back. "Bathroom's there." Her freckles shifted when she smiled. She stroked the divan. "I get better sleep on this than my bed. The other chairs swivel so you can use the desks. They recline if you prefer them over the divan."

Chase's mouth grew dry before he realized it was open in awe of the jet's opulence. "How much did this cost?"

"Twelve million." She leaned on a loveseat. "Would have been fifteen if we'd bought it alone, but we got a really good deal from one of our clients."

Words tripped and fell from his lips before he could right them: "They let a child fly it?"

Her eyebrows drew down slightly. "How old do you think I am?"

He feared offending her, so joked, "Five?"

She smiled in response. "Try twenty-two."

"Really?" Disbelief dripped from the word.

"Let's see," she said, counting her fingers and mumbling. "I was a baby, then grade school, followed by high school, carry the five, and yeah." She straightened. "Twenty-two."

Chase laughed, then grabbed his chest. "You probably get that a lot."

Zettabyte nodded. "I'm four-eleven with freckles. If I buy a movie with sex or violence in it, the cashier looks around for my parents." She went to the back and opened a storage space. "If you need to hide anything from faeries, put it here."

She's trying to put me at ease. He smiled. "Thank you for not hating me."

"There's still time." She winked. "Drinks are in this fridge drawer, snacks in the cupboard above." She glanced around, nodding slightly before meeting his eyes. "Anything else, I'll be up front."

"Question," said Chase. "How'd you become a pilot for the Guild?"

She passed him and opened the cockpit door. "Many of us train to be pilots. But I've been flying since I can remember. It's in my blood."

He felt the color drain from his face. "You're ..."

"A killer," she said, eyes stone-cold in their seriousness.

"Yeah." He felt stupid. If she was old enough to fly a jet, she was old enough to get paid to kill people. "I was going to say assassin, but—"

"Not technically," Zettabyte said, an ornery half-smile hooked at the corner of her lip. "I crash planes and people just happen to be inside them." She winked. "Enjoy the flight." With that, she entered the cockpit and closed the door behind her.

He furrowed his brow and stared at the cockpit door for a long while before sitting on the divan. *Is this my final test? Because I don't think I can survive a plane crash.* Then he noticed how soft and inviting the leather was. *At least, I'll die in comfort.* He lay down with the remote in hand and thought of starting a movie. Before he could stop himself, his eyes drew shut with lids full of lead.

He slapped the side of his head. Pain wove acidic threads through the joints of his braced fingers. *Where's Scizzors when I need to be poked and prodded?* He blinked them open and scolded himself. "Stay. Awake. You're. Concussed." He started scrolling through the movies.

CHASE wasn't sure how long he'd slept or when he fell asleep, but he was jarred awake by rocking and rolling. Last thing he remembered was scrolling through action movies. *At least, I'm alive.* Lightning flashed outside and the raucous boom of thunder shook the jet. *For now.*

He rose from the divan and knocked on the cockpit door. "Is everything all right?"

No answer.

He tried the door, but it was locked. He threw his weight against it, slamming it open to reveal empty seats inside. "Zettabyte?" He twisted to look at an empty bathroom. *They can't actually expect me to survive a fucking plane crash?*

The windows grew white as lightning struck the jet. He threw his hands over his eyes as glass shattered. Thunder rocked him from all sides. He was thrown against the pilot's chair as the jet slumped into a nosedive.

Chapter Thirty

Trust Implicit

June 10, 2016
06:13 AM EDT
New York City, New York

A million thoughts spiraled through Vixen's mind as she jogged toward the jet. Desperately, she continued to seek an alternative to the only plan she knew had a chance.

Golem had fixed Powder Keg's helmet. She knew most of the Spades weren't happy with Ace. If she revealed the recording at the meeting, it wouldn't matter whether he had a few people in his pocket; those few couldn't stop the many. She'd be able to turn the tables on Ace before he had a chance to retaliate. Especially now that Radiant, Ace's greatest supporter, was dead, thanks to Powder Keg.

She didn't know if she could pull this off. The only other option, as she saw it, was to run away with Chase and hand over the recording to the Eight of Spades. There was no doubt in her mind that Widow would do the right thing. But if Ace discovered what was going on before Widow could get that recording to the other Aces, he would kill her as well. *And then he'd never stop hunting us down.*

No. This crazy-ass plan was the only way to throw Ace off for just long enough to corner and dismantle him. She sighed heavily. Now to do the impossible: Explain to Chase why he had to sacrifice himself to pull it off.

Vixen boarded the jet and stopped cold. A hand leaped to her mouth. Chase already looked dead, lying there painted in bruises head to toe. A bandage was wrapped around his head and several fingers were hidden behind metal and cloth. He was covered in sweat, but still as concrete.

"Chase?" she said, approaching him slowly.

If he'd heard her, no movement betrayed that fact.

Vixen touched his shoulder gently.

He jolted upright, catching her wrist and pulling her to him. His other hand caught hold of her hair.

"Ow, ow, ow," Vixen complained, trying to pry his grip from her head.

His fingers tightened.

Why is he fighting me? "Chase." She punched a nasty bruise on his arm.

"We're going down," he yelled. "Crashing!" His eyes opened and darted about. "We're—" He blinked quickly, then focused in on her. "Hi." Longer breaths were taken and he finally settled, unhinging his grip from her hair. He reclined slowly. A heavy groan escaped him. Wrapping an arm around his chest, he settled back into the divan. He glanced at the top of her head. "Forgive me."

"It's okay." Vixen sat on the edge of the recliner nearest him. Her fingers combed through the knots he'd put in her hair.

"What was that about?"

"A dream," Chase said before wincing terribly. "Several, actually. All with similar conclusions." He took a sharp breath, stood, and walked to the refrigerator drawer. Once a water was in hand, he fished around in his pocket. His hand returned with a white pill tucked between two fingers. With a toss, it flew to the back of his throat. He drank, taking short sips followed by short breaths. "Why did I have to fall asleep?" He threw the bottle in the trash.

She frowned, remembering the text Scizzors had sent about the wounds accrued. The text failed to cover the extent of damage inflicted upon Chase's person. "He did a real number on you, didn't he?"

"We weren't exactly cuddling." Chase took another water from the drawer and poured it over his hands. "Scizzors wasn't the teddy bear you promised him to be." He splashed the water in his face. "Is my uncle with you?" He repeated the process and flexed his dripping jaw.

"Not exactly," she said.

He blew water from his lips. "What's that mean?"

She thought about telling him about Frank, but she wasn't prepared to see him break down. "What did you dream about?"

"The pilot always disappeared." He paused to take in a long, slow breath. "The jet was being torn apart by lightning in one dream and shot down in another. The last left me careening toward a skyscraper."

Zettabyte came out of the cockpit. "What's this about skyscrapers and lightning?"

Vixen gestured at Chase. "He dreamt you left him to die in the middle of a storm."

"I could get used to people thinking me a god." Zettabyte grinned. "Alas, lightning is a bit out of my wheelhouse."

Vixen walked to the airstairs. "We should go so you can get some sleep before the meeting, Zetta."

Zettabyte looked Chase over. "He appears to need a few minutes, yet. I'll get the helicopter warmed up." She started out, then turned. "Maybe this time I'll summon a hurricane or tsunami." She winked and left.

Vixen smiled. "Isn't she adorable?"

Chase winced and took a shallow breath as he sat on the divan. "I thought she was seventeen and said as much."

"No wonder you thought she'd kill you."

He shook his head. "That came after she told me she doesn't kill people; she crashes planes and people happen to be onboard."

"Sounds like her." Vixen took his hands in hers. She gently turned them, trying to assess the full extent of the abuse they'd withstood. "How bad is it?"

"Looks worse than it feels," he said, examining the wounds with her. "Embarrassingly enough, much of this was self-inflicted." Chase brought her up to speed on the extent of his injuries. He then smiled, "But I survived."

"You always do," she said, forcing a smile.

He nodded slowly. "I'll be quite pathetic until my meds kick in."

"I'm proud of you." *Although not excited I'll have to convince you to die.* She kissed his bruised cheek.

He pulled away from her.

That's not a good sign. For her plan to work, he needed to trust her implicitly. "What's wrong?"

"We need to talk," he said. "But I'm afraid to say."

That makes two of us. "What is it, sweetheart?"

He stared at his hands. "I don't know how I'll do this job when I can't stomach the idea of killing anyone. I told Scizzors I could possibly kill pedophiles, but even that seems out of reach." He looked around the jet at everything but her. "Are you disappointed?"

"I didn't think I could either," she confessed.

This brought his focus back to her, his brows knitted together. "Seriously?"

"My recruitment wasn't quite as strange as yours, but I didn't believe I was built for this either. Just kind of fell into it and then found out I was." Her hand met his knee. "Built for it, that is."

"You make this look like a lifelong passion."

"Far from it," Laura confided. "I wanted to be a nurse so I could save people." She gently stroked the brace on his fingers. "Then I saw how this work does exactly that. We kill those who are intent on destroying the lives of innocent people."

"What made you realize that?" he asked. "Specifically."

"A small terrorist cell planned to bomb the Turkey Point Nuclear Generating Station. Their aim was then to wait for the hospitals in Homestead, Florida, to fill up with the wounded before bombing those locations." She squeezed his knee. "The man they approached for the firepower was a contact of Powder Keg's. Your uncle buried them under seven stories of smoldering concrete." She stood. "Powder Keg conserved thousands of innocent lives by terminating thirteen extremist assholes."

Chase nodded and stared at his hands. "I get it. If Frank can do this, I guess ..." He trailed off.

"You don't look convinced."

"I get what you do is for the good of all," he said. "I just don't know if I can deliver that type of justice."

"You might be worrying over nothing."

He coughed a laugh. "Promise me this: If I pass, you'll help me find my way. You and Frank." He looked up at her and smiled weakly. "I never imagined my uncle was an assassin. So, if he, the most loving man I know, can do something like that, then there's hope for me. With both of you guiding me, I believe I'll find a way to balance being an assassin and a family man."

Vixen nodded, not sure how to respond. *He wants a family.* That made this so much harder.

Chase finished the second water, took a shallow breath, and stood. "I'll do my best not to disappoint."

"You haven't so far." And suddenly, Vixen realized how true that was. She knew him. Knew what his answer would be, because he was a man who constantly put himself in danger to save others. Even strangers. His actions to save Widow had proven that. *There's never going to be a good time for this.* She wrapped him in a gentle hug. "I love you."

Chase returned the hug as best he could in his condition. "And I, you."

He went to pull away, but she held.

She breathed in deeply. "No matter how badly you want to, do not break away from me until you've heard me out."

"What's wrong?"

"Just listen." Her chin quivered. "Frank will not be here to teach you how to live that life. I won't be either if you pass."

"What are you saying?" He tried to break away.

She held him tighter, fearing the words she must whisper

next.

Chase winced. "You're hurting me."

"Frank is dead."

His body dropped like a gym bag full of bricks. Her arms had been under his, so she crumpled with him. Together, they collapsed to the jet's carpeted floor. She stared at his face. His eyes stared back without focus, as though he saw through and beyond her.

She furrowed her brow. "Chase?"

"I just got him back."

"He was killed by a man I once trusted. That man is going to kill Nightshade, too." She cupped a hand over his cheek. "And me, if you pass." Her pinky stroked the curve of his jaw. "But I have a plan—"

The focus of Chase's eyes came back violently with a darkness she'd never seen in them. "Scizzors was right," he said, resolute. "Pedos aren't the only monsters out there." Rage swayed like a fire dancer behind those eyes. "What's rule number one?"

Vixen bit at her bottom lip. "I know, but—"

Chase's voice cracked as he uttered, "Say it."

"Trust people to your detriment." She bit the inside of her lip until it drew blood. "I'm so sorry. I know I've done you harm by trusting this man. And I'm going to ask you before the end of this conversation to let me harm you further. And to break the rule I keep bashing you over the head with." She tasted the blood on her tongue. "Trust me."

He closed his eyes long and hard. His breath was held and finally rushed from his nostrils. Placing his forehead to hers, he opened his eyes and gazed at her. "Tell me you love me again, and I'll follow you wherever you go."

"I won't use that word to lure you into danger."

His eyes scanned hers. "That's an 'I love you' if I've ever heard one."

She shifted her body along the carpet and hugged him softly. Despite whatever pain he felt, he squeezed her tightly.

When they separated, he was the first to stand.

He teetered and fell to sit on the divan.

She rose on a knee and took the back of his hands in her palms.

He took as deep a breath as he could, closed his eyes, and let it back out with a pained moan.

"Chase, I need you to look at me," said Vixen.

One of his eyes fluttered open.

"I need to tell you something," Vixen began. "Let me finish without interruption."

His other eye opened.

Vixen placed her hands on his knees. "It's a lot."

He nodded, solemnly. "I'm listening."

"Okay," Vixen said. "Here we go." She put a hand to her mouth as though to block the words she whispered next. "You have to die." She paused, expecting him to break the rule of silence.

His eyebrows furrowed, but he remained silent.

Dropping her hand, she went on. "I know that sounds crazy. But hear me out." She straightened. "Ace killed your uncle with an explosive."

His eyes widened a little, his lips pursing.

"Ace threatened me." She cleared her throat. "Even told your uncle he'd rape me before killing me. Then he put Nightshade in the hole. If I don't kill you, my best friend will be boiled alive."

Chase opened his mouth, then closed it and raised an eyebrow as his nostrils flared.

"I cannot kill Ace without dying myself as punishment, for a card member cannot kill another without being discarded."

He clearly didn't understand what she was getting at. She explained: "I have to get everyone at the meeting to vote for Ace to be discarded. The reason everyone is coming is because of you. He wants to present your body to them because you're the only target he's ever failed to kill." She let that sink in. When his eyes narrowed, she realized it had. "Feel free to talk now."

"That motherfucker killed my parents?"

"I'm relieved you caught that so I wouldn't have to say it."

He closed his eyes and began shaking. "Then he killed my uncle." His eyelids squeezed tight together. "Why are you convincing me to die? You should be pointing me in his direction." His eyelids snapped open. "I'm not a cardholder. There's nothing stopping me from gutting him."

Vixen shook her head. "He's expecting something like that, Chase. Ace is paranoid as hell. He wouldn't have told me his plan if he weren't prepared to take both of us out the moment we darkened his door." She squeezed his knees. "I have to take him off guard. The only way I can is for him to believe he's won. For him to see you dead, presented to him on a glass table."

Chase put his hands over hers. "No."

He has to. "You have to," she said. "I know you want vengeance, but if we don't do this my way, you'll end up dead anyway. We all will."

His hands felt warm and sweaty. She could feel his pulse

pounding.

"My plan will work," she assured. "He will die by the end of it."

He let out a heavy sigh and looked away.

Why am I doing this? "You have to die," she said, a tear running down her cheek. "I love you, but you have to. Because if you don't, by morning, you will anyway. Nightshade will die. I will die. And, knowing him, he'll get away with all of it."

He breathed in deep and shook his head.

I can't do this. She reached up and put a hand against his face.

He looked at her, eyes brimming with angry tears.

"I can't," she said. "I'm sorry, I—" Her chest rocked as a sob broke up the words. "You're right. I can't." She sat on the divan and pulled him into a hug. "I'm stupid for thinking it." Vixen stood and started away from him. Her wrist was pulled back and she came to a halt. Turning, she saw him standing behind her.

He nodded and pulled her into a kiss.

She cried as she returned it. Her arms encircled him and she pulled him against her. She felt her breasts press against the muscles of his chest. *He completes me. What happens if I kill the only love I've ever had?* She kissed him harder.

"I'm sorry," came Zettabyte's voice. "I didn't realize you two ..." She walked away. "Helicopter's ready."

Vixen kissed Chase's neck and whispered in his ear, "We really need to go."

He nodded against the side of her face. "I know."

"Forget I said anything," she said. "I can't go through with it."

Chase pulled away, gripped her shoulders, and kissed the tip of her nose. "Laura, I love you. If you say I must die to save you, with an added bonus of Ace getting what's coming to him, then ..." He smiled sadly. "Then, I believe you."

"But I can't do it," Vixen admitted.

"Whatever you choose," said Chase, "I will follow."

She shook her head, dumbfounded. "How did I get you?"

"You crawled through my window." Chase laughed. His hand leapt to his chest. "Ouch." He took a short breath. "I've loved you since the moment you first kissed me."

She smirked. "I think Allison's drugs are talking."

"No," said Chase. "It's all me." His eyes explored her face.

I adore the way he looks at me. She wrapped her arms around him and placed her lips to his. She didn't know how long they remained there, kissing passionately in the jet. She didn't care. In his arms was where she wanted to be. She shuddered. Even in his condition, she felt him grow hard against her. Her body was hot with anticipation, yet she found herself shivering. She broke the kiss to say, "I love you, too, Chase."

He smiled and kissed her nose. "We should probably go before she comes back to find us naked and writhing on the divan."

She sighed and placed her forehead to his. "I don't wanna. Once we step outside the jet, this gets real all too fast."

"We'll face it together."

She met his eyes. "Together."

He kissed the tip of her nose. "Always."

They exited the jet and started for the helicopter.

Vixen noted nearly all their jets were back at the airstrip. Everyone had to be present for this to work. A helicopter was taking off and she could see Scizzors piloting it.

Zettabyte watched Vixen and Chase from the helicopter window, clearly confused.

Vixen wiped the tears from her face and smiled back. *Why am I proud of this?* The love of my life will sacrifice himself before the day is through. She forced the thought to the back of her mind and boarded the helicopter.

Chase followed, shutting the door behind him.

Vixen checked her reflection in the window and fixed her hair where the helicopter winds had thrown each strand astray. She sat back and placed her headset on.

Chase slipped on his headset, too, and put his hand upon her knee. "Is it all right if I can't keep my hands off you?" The words came through the headset.

Vixen smiled.

"A few things," Zettabyte said, twisting 'round to look at the two of them. "I can hear everything you say through these. And ..." She pointed at the hand hiding Vixen's knee. "What is all this?"

When Chase tried to pull away, clearly fearing he'd gotten Vixen in some sort of trouble, Vixen took his hand and returned it.

"It's a long story," Vixen said. "One I don't have time to tell right now."

Zettabyte nodded and turned her attention back to the controls. "Fair enough." The helicopter lifted.

Another of the Guild's jets landed behind them.

Chase smiled at Vixen, but there was concern in those eyes mixed with a pinch of wrath. She could tell he wanted to talk about it. She glanced at Zettabyte and shook her head.

He nodded and wince-sighed.

It wasn't until they were entering lower Manhattan that he broke the silence. "It's beautiful." He shifted to get a better look. "That's the Brooklyn Bridge."

She got up, looked, and nodded. She took his finger in her hand and moved it to point at a ten-story building on the waterfront. "And that's where I live," she said, then moved his finger to point at a tall building nearby. "And that's where we land."

He brought his finger back to point at the ten-story building. "You live there?"

She sat back. "Widow is a few doors over and one story up."

Chase kept looking as they passed over the building. "It's really nice."

"Should be," Zettabyte said. "It's a couple million for a two-bedroom."

"Dollars?" Chase choked out as if the word had caught in his throat.

"Toenail clippings." Zettabyte laughed, glancing back at Vixen. "Should have seen when I told him how much the jet cost."

"I'm glad you didn't," said Chase, still marveling at the building. "That was embarrassing." When they were too far for him to see it, he looked at Vixen with eyebrows high. "How much are the payments on something like that?"

Zettabyte cracked up and turned to look at him. "Oh, honey," she began, then broke into hysterics again.

"What?" Chase looked back and forth between the two of them.

Zettabyte got a handle on her laughter. "She wrote them a check for the place."

Vixen smiled proudly. "Bought and paid for, thank you very much."

Chase went to say something, then swallowed whatever it was. He slumped and stared blankly at the empty seat across from him.

"Really?" Vixen said, surprised by his surprise. "How much do you think we make?"

He shook his head, his eyes glazed over.

"It's definitely not paid in toenails," Zettabyte said, before returning her focus to the top of the approaching building.

He grew quiet, glancing at Vixen as darkness seeped slowly back into his eyes.

This day might kill me. Vixen forced a smile and nodded.

"Here we be," Zettabyte said as the helicopter tilted to the side. "Lady and gentleman, we are about to begin our final descent. Currently, the weather is shitty as always in this godforsaken city." The helicopter jolted slightly when it met the helipad atop the bank. "I have certainly enjoyed having you onboard today. We hope to see you again real soon and thank you for flying the Guild of Four Airlines."

A chuckle shattered Chase's intensity, but was quickly stifled by his wrapping an arm around his chest. He groaned and undid his seatbelt. "It was nice to meet you, Zettabyte."

"It's been a pleasure." Zettabyte put her thumb up. "Pass and I'll terrify you more with my flying skills." She saluted him. "Signed, Yours Truly, Thorress, Goddess of Lightning."

Vixen smiled. "Thanks for bringing us in." She reached over the seat to squeeze Zettabyte's shoulder. "See you at the meeting."

Vixen and Chase took off their headsets and climbed out of the helicopter. They went through the roof access door and entered the elevator.

Vixen put her key in at the base of the number pad. She turned the key and pressed the thirteen until it turned red. The padlock appeared and the elevator plunged.

Chase braced himself against the banister as they plummeted. He took another pill from his pocket and swallowed it dry. "What does the lock mean?"

She leaned against the wall across from him. "Keeps it from stopping at any of the other floors and letting people on. It'll take us all the way to headquarters without interruption."

"Wait," he said, eyes widening. "This is it?" He gestured at the elevator floor. "Like, we're here, here."

Vixen nodded in affirmation. *Soon, I'll have to put his body on a table.*

The elevator slowed at the last moment and drifted to a stop. The doors opened. "Go ahead."

He stepped out, stopping at the first parking space. "Who painted these? They're gorgeous."

A man in a hole. "Nightshade," she said, walking beside him to look at the painting of a bear trap. The teeth of the trap were all upside-down As. She now hated the painting, purely because of who the parking space belonged to.

Chase walked around the lot, taking time to appreciate every space. Here and there, he'd point and guess who owned which one. "Widow," he said, pointing at the eight.

Vixen nodded, then stood on a space with a chain blade curled in a ball at its center. Three knives above and three below radiated out from it. The rest of the space was painted to look like a cutting board. A seven appeared to be carved into the wood, one at the top left and the other at the bottom right. "And this one?"

"Pockets," he said before pointing at a space with a cut-off noose shaped like a five. "Noose." A splatter of red was painted along the two corners that were empty of the number 5.

Vixen smiled at Chase's excitement. It was as though he'd completely forgotten about his rage. Up until he said ...

"Frank." He pointed at a space with a round, black bomb painted at its center. A fuse came out of it and curled up to create the illusion of a six. Radiating from the bomb, the painting made the space look like a crater in the ground. "That's about what our house looks like right now."

Vixen rubbed his back with the palm of her hand. "I knew a lot was going to happen to you, as it does to all of us during testing. But I didn't expect your house to be blown to bits." She gazed at the parking space. "Wrecked, maybe. Turned to ash, not so much." Her hand paused at the center of his back. "And Frank—"

Chase pulled away to walk to another spot. "This one definitely belongs to Scizzors." The space was painted with a giant squid at its center. It had ten tentacles, each with a ram's head tattooed upon it. "Can't believe I survived that monster."

To then fall victim to me. Vixen felt sick to her stomach. She forced a smile. "Want to see my car?"

Chase whistled as they approached her GT500. "It's beautiful."

She ran her fingers along the hood. "I call her 'Isis.'"

"Nice to meet you, Isis," he said, placing a hand against

the hood. "My name's Chase." He sat quietly for a bit. "She must be shy."

"Nah," Vixen said, getting in. She turned Isis on and pressed against the pedal. The Mustang roared to life.

Chase smiled and got in. "I think she likes me."

"I don't blame her." Vixen leaned toward him. "You're an easy man to like."

He kissed her passionately. When their lips parted, he kissed the tip of her nose.

She sighed, sadly. "I missed you."

"I missed you, too," he said. "Thought you'd abandoned me yesterday after Scizzors took me away."

She placed her forehead against his. "Never." She met his eyes. "You might wish I had by the time all of this is over."

"Never. No matter what the circumstance, I'll always need you." He locked eyes with her and kissed her nose again. "Being near you, smelling you, ..." His eyes dropped to look at her lips. "Tasting you." He kissed her. "Getting to know you better."

Not if I end up killing you. Vixen pulled away and looked out the front window. "I'll speak on your uncle's behalf today. I'll make sure everyone knows the truth about what happened."

Chase swallowed and joined her in looking out the window at a concrete wall. "He died because of me, didn't he?"

"This isn't on you." Laura turned off the GT500. "With your help, I'll punish the one responsible."

"Whatever you need," Chase said. He waited until she met his eyes. "Seriously."

I still don't know if I can do this. She nodded.

"Can I admit something?" asked Chase.

"Of course."

"I'm trying to stay calm, but I'm boiling inside."

She nodded. "You can hide it on your face all you want, Chase. But I feel it radiating from you."

He leaned his chair back. "Is it all right if we sit together a bit longer before going in?"

"We have plenty of time," she said.

"Distract me with stories of this city. Tell me what you love about it."

"Why?" She laughed. "That's boring."

"Nothing about you is boring," said Chase. "I want to hear your beautiful voice. If it's the last thing I hear before I die, then I'll die happy."

Chapter Thirty-One

Hangman

TO this day, the Guild of Four consists of fifty-four assassins, all working together to make the world a better place. They are made up of the people, for the people. A strict book of Guild laws governs them.

June 10, 2016
08:31 AM EDT
New York City, New York

~ Five of Spades ~

NOOSE parked his motorcycle and pulled off his helmet. His eyes rose to the flowers at the top of a twenty-four-story apartment building. *Each story's approximately ten feet. If I give myself seventy-eight yards ...* He took the heavy backpack off and thumped it to the ground. *I should be good to drop the final two or three.* He opened the bag and looked at the machine inside. *Better work or I'm going to drop you on your creator's toes.* Golem had made him the tow-line feeder because he was worried about descending a building in his weakened state. He could still feel where the rod had pierced him, and his wrist popped every time he rolled it. He hated how long it had taken before he was allowed to pick up his kids. *We're not doing that again any time soon.*

Upon pressing a button with a noose symbol, the display read: YARDS TO FINAL LOCK, then changed to 000.00. He typed in 07500 and hit ENTER. The machine whirred and clicked twice before the numbers appeared 075.00. He pulled about four feet of rope from it and the number dropped to 073.77. *Seems to be working.* If the machine did fail, he wouldn't be able to beat Golem upside the head with it after. He'd be a broken clump of flesh, bones, and organs on shattered concrete.

In the apartment building, the elevator was out of commission. Stairs had been his worst enemy after Powder Keg dropped a ceiling on him. He checked his watch. He was running short on time if he planned to get back for Ace's mandatory meeting. "Who has a meeting at 9:30 in the A fucking M?"

A sign beside the stairwell read: Freeman Celebration Through Roof Access Door.

By the time he'd ascended twenty flights, he was more than ready to kill the asshole who held a party in a roof garden. He finished the trek and opened the door to see balloons lining a walkway. A whole lot of people cheered and clapped before falling silent.

"Sorry," he apologized. "I'm not who you're waiting for."

A tall man walked over. "I don't recognize you." He held out a hand. "I'm Cain. You here for Jamaad's party?"

I'm here for you, Noose thought, taking the man's hand and shaking. "I was supposed to fix the railing before the party, but ran late."

The man's smile was charming, but oozed with fake. "Don't let us stop you."

"I won't," Noose said, brushing past the man. He walked, counting his steps to the metal railing framing the flat roof. He dropped the backpack on the ground. Breaking his strides into yards, he started pulling out the amount of rope needed. He passed it through the railing bars.

He checked his watch, then sighed in exasperation. *If traffic's bad, I'm not getting back in time.* Then again, he'd brought his bike. Not that he cared to get back. Ace rambled on about stuff they were already aware of because he adored the sound of his own voice. *Sometimes I really hate my job.*

He reached in the backpack and pushed the button with a padlock symbol. The display read: DISTANCE (1) JOLT (2)

He pressed the 2 key.

The display then read: TIME FOR LOCK 00:00.

He typed in 0010.

The display returned to the amount of rope remaining before the final lock.

There came an eruption of cheering and clapping.

Noose zipped up the bag and turned to see a young black man laughing and accepting hugs.

"The man of the hour, everybody," Cain announced. "Welcome home, Jamaad."

Noose tied a noose knot in the rope and studied Cain. *Inflated ego, big head.* Adjusting the rope, he made the hole bigger. *There we go.*

"If everyone could sit," Cain said, gesturing at the front row of chairs, "I'd like to get started by thanking you for coming.

They said he was guilty." He pointed at Jamaad. "But you stood up for him. You proved he couldn't have committed the murder and after two appeals ..." The man gestured at the sky. "Jamaad Freeman is, pardon the pun, a free—"

"Who names their child Cain?" Noose interrupted.

The tall man turned. "Beg your pardon?"

"Biblically speaking, it's a man who killed his brother." Noose tightened his hold on the knot. "In your case, it's a brother not by blood, but by friendship. You didn't kill him, but ..." He paused to glare at a man pulling a gun on him. "You're going to want to put that down, Urick."

Urick kept the gun on Noose. "If you think knowing our names will stop us from killing you, you'll be sorely disappointed."

"I know more than names." Noose took a hand off the rope and put a finger to his forehead. "You think I'd approach you alone? I have a sniper in the building across from us." *If only that were true.*

The gun lowered, but only slightly. Urick scanned the building opposite them.

Cain approached. "He won't be able to kill all of us before we throw him off the roof."

"If you let me finish, I'll throw myself off."

Cain kept coming. "State your business and get jumping."

"The police were beginning to link you to the murder of a Marine. You planted the gun in Jamaad's room and tipped them off."

Cain pulled a gun of his own. "That business is slanderous and has no place here. Let me walk you to the edge."

"Fine," Noose said. "Let's go." He lunged forward and

pushed the gun aside.

It went off. The bullet tore into a flowerbed, spraying dirt and petals into the air.

They struggled before Noose kneed Cain in the groin, knocked the gun to the ground, and looped the noose over the man's head.

Someone in the audience got off a shot.

Cain cried in pain.

Noose laughed, thankful it wasn't he who took the bullet. "I'm not sure that was intended for me." He grabbed Cain's arms, bringing him up to use as a human shield.

Everyone in the audience was standing, their expressions a mixture of confusion, anger, and nervousness. Everyone, that is, but one man. He was seated with arms crossed, smiling.

Noose snapped two fingers together beside Cain's ear. "You paid the only man who knew the truth for his silence. Turns out, he bought himself enough rope to hang you with."

Cain threw his head back.

Noose avoided the blow easily and pushed Cain hard before dashing for the railing. He reached down, scooped up the backpack, and dove over the side. Noose plummeted until the rope resisted, then fell slower. He could feel more than hear Cain being dragged across the rooftop. After falling another story, Noose came to an abrupt stop.

The backpack began beeping every second.

Noose looked up, not quite able to see what he knew was there. Cain would be pinned against the bars of the railing, his neck broken.

The backpack chimed a total of ten seconds before letting Noose plunge the remaining twenty stories.

Noose closed his eyes and gritted his teeth, fearing the final lock wouldn't break his fall. His eyes drifted open when his descent slowed for the final ten yards and stopped six feet from the ground. "I'm going to kiss Golem on the mouth." The machine whirred, then there came a sawing sound as it clipped the rope for him. He dropped the final few feet to the ground.

The people on the sidewalk gave him suspicious looks.

"I'm a street performer," Noose said, pointing at the severed rope. "New trick I'm trying out."

Quickly, he got on his motorcycle and glanced up to see several people from the party leaning over the railing and pointing.

One yelled, "Stop him!"

Nobody tried.

"I love this city." Noose put on his helmet and looked at his watch. *And I'm going to be late.*

Chapter Thirty-Two

Death

WHEN someone joins the brotherhood, they do so for life. If an assassin dies, either of old age or from the hazards of the job, a new recruit is chosen.

June 10, 2016
08:44 AM EDT
New York City, New York
Guild of Four Spade Suit Headquarters

CHASE smiled at Laura, adoring her every word. *If only I could listen to her voice for a thousand years.* The time had sped by as they talked.

"And if you've never had avocado on toast, the place to go is Two Hands. It's strange, but amazing. You're served by Australians, which sounds crazy, but it's crazy in an interesting way." She laughed. "I'm sorry, I've been rambling." She looked outside the car. "People have been coming in and I've ignored all of it."

"Don't be sorry," said Chase. "I'm happy." He smiled. "You said your favorite place to eat was Vinegar House. What's your favorite meal there?"

"Vinegar Hill House," she corrected. "Their red wattle country chop is to die for." Her smile faded at the word "die."

Might as well ask since it's on her mind. "When does my test start?" asked Chase.

"An hour ago," Laura spat as though the words tasted foul on her tongue.

"This has been the easiest of my tests for sure."

She forced a smile. "Right?"

Chase smiled, sadly. "How are you going to do it?"

She shook her head. "Stop thinking about it." She got out of the car and shut her door.

He joined her. "Hard not to."

Scizzors waved when he stepped out of an Escalade. "Good to see you, Vixen."

"Good flight home, I hope," she replied.

Scizzors grabbed a duffel bag from the back seat and hoisted it over his shoulder. "Painfully long after the day I had." He looked at Chase as he walked toward a sliding door. "You look like hell."

"You'd know," said Chase. "You're from there, aren't you?"

"Yup." Scizzors guffawed and disappeared inside.

Laura took a deep breath. "Let's do this." They went through the sliding doors.

Scizzors was turning a corner when Chase heard the big man yell, "There had better be bagels."

Widow came out of an office reading something from a

folder.

Chase greeted her. "I see you've caught your breath."

"Well, look at you," Widow said, clearly excited to see him. "I see Scizzors got his hands on you."

"His hands, his feet, his tail ..." Chase let that speak for itself.

"I take it you passed all your tests," said Widow.

He pointed with a splinted finger at the largest bruise on his face. "Passed that last one with flying colors."

"I'm pleased to hear it." Widow closed the folder and looked him over. "I want to hug you, but you're likely that shade of purple everywhere."

"I really am quite pretty."

"Well, I'm happy for you," Widow said, then nodded at Laura. "Vixen." She dipped back into the office.

She's in for a shock.

Ahead, Pockets talked to a black man wearing a black suit with a silver tie. The man had dreads pulled back and bound by a hair tie.

Chase turned to Laura. "I can't keep being congratulated. I'll crack and they'll know something's up."

"Come with me," she said, opening the door to another office.

The smell of smoke wafted out.

"Radiant's office?"

"No." She frowned.

Chase immediately knew whose office it was when he saw the recliner sitting in the corner. *He had his favorite chair here as well.* He felt sick.

Laura gestured at the recliner. "Take a seat."

Chase stared at it. "I can't."

"Why not?" She closed the door.

"That was his chair," said Chase. *I'm not worthy.* "I'll never get the chance to fill his shoes."

She closed the door and hugged him gently. "I'm sorry for the hand I played in this."

"It's okay," Chase said, stroking her back. "I mean, it's not great." He kissed her neck. "But I love you."

"I love you, too." She ran her fingers through his hair and placed her lips to his.

Chase planted a soft kiss on the tip of her nose. *I need something answered before I die.* Placing his forehead to hers, he asked, "I was never supposed to survive the others, was I?"

"No," she confessed.

He pulled away slightly. "Did they all know?"

"I don't think so. I *believe* I was the only one threatened. And I'm reasonably sure Radiant was the only one who knew out of those who tested you since he was ordered to show up anyway."

He stroked her cheek. "Do you think this will work?"

She raised her eyebrows and nibbled at her bottom lip.

"That confident, eh?" He sighed. "Why not?"

Laura pulled away from him and sat on the floor with her back to the wall. "Because I can't do this. If I can't promise the plan will work, how can I sacrifice you for it?"

He knelt, winced, and took her hand. "Is there a plan B?"

She had thought of spreading the recording to everyone, but that risked Ace getting wind of her plan. "Not without more time to plan. I learned too late what was going on." She thumped the back of her head against the wall a few times. "Ace is a master of manipulation. Everything else I can think of has too many loopholes for him to slither through."

"And everything else ends with you being hurt?"

She nodded. "Me, you, and others."

"I'm not risking your life." Chase took a deep breath and let it out. "You're not getting yourself killed over me. I love you too much to let you throw away your life."

"I feel the same way about you." A tear barely escaped her eye before she swept it away. She slapped him hard, then kissed his reddened cheek. "That's for making it impossible not to love you. If this doesn't work, you'll be dead."

He rubbed his cheek. "Isn't that the idea?"

"Needlessly dead, I mean," said Laura. She looked at the floor. "Ace has to see you breathless on a table."

He put a knuckle under her chin so she'd look at him.

Her eyes met his. Another tear ran down her cheek. "I've never done anything like this before, Chase. It could fail."

"You won't fail," he assured her. "You're too amazing to fail." He sat beside her and put an arm around her.

She cried for a moment against his neck.

"Look," he said, "if I passed your test, I'd kill this dude and be killed anyway. You said a cardholder can't kill another without being discarded." He ran a finger down her arm. "If I didn't die and I became one of you, I wouldn't live long, for one of two reasons: One, Ace would find a way to kill me as he's threatened to do to you and Nightshade. Or, I wouldn't kill anybody but pedophiles and would then be discarded for not contributing."

She shuddered and let out a choked, "Yeah."

"When you talk of alternatives," he said, rubbing her back,

"you sound insecure and full of doubt." He pulled away and gazed deep into her eyes. "When you told me I had to die this morning, you did so with conviction. I don't like it, but if my death secures your life, then I choose option A."

She shook her head. "But—"

"But nothing," he interrupted. "You are the best thing that ever happened to me. Ace was the worst. If my death saves you and kills him, then I choose death every time. The hours spent with you have been out of this world, phenomenal."

Laura wiped at her tears, bobbing a nod in response. She took his hand in hers and kissed his wounded fingers.

Chase smiled and drew an infinity symbol on her leg with his finger. "My only regret is that I won't see Ace's face when he realizes he's fucked."

"So fucked." Her body calmed. "You'll be there," she said. "I know you will be."

In spirit, maybe. "I'll haunt his ass all the way into the next world," Chase said, smiling. "You're all that matters to me, Laura." He kissed the tip of her nose. "I love you."

"I love you, too," she said, standing. "Get up."

He rose and kissed her.

She took his hand and raised it in front of his face. "Do you trust me?"

Chase smiled. "To my detriment."

Vixen choke-laughed and wiped a sleeve across her eyes. "Then stare right here at the center of your wrist." She returned the sleeve to wipe her nose. "Right here," she said, tapping where she wanted him to look. Her eyes glazed over as she, too, looked at the wrist. She paused for a good minute, staring.

"You've got this," said Chase. "Stop doubting yourself."

He pulled her into a hug and kissed her.

She took a deep breath, shook it off, and reset, holding Chase's wrist in front of his face. "I want you to stare right here." Her voice had changed slightly. It was lower, a calming monotone. "Hold your hand there and gaze into your wrist as if you could see to the bone. I'm the love of your life, so you can trust me."

This is how she kills? Chase shook his head, breathed in, then out, and did as she said. "You're the love of my life, and I trust you." He submitted himself to the inevitable. "I'm ready."

Laura continued, "Gaze through your wrist and into the bone. I'm the love of your life, so you can trust me." She brought her free hand up between his wrist and face. "I'm putting my hand right here and you are slowly closing your eyes." She began to drop her hand.

Chase's vision blurred as his eyelids began to settle. He imagined he could see the bones in his wrist until their outlines appeared.

"Focus on your wrist," she continued. "As you look at your wrist, you will notice a force is pulling your hand to your face. It is magnetized to your face, and you can't stop it as it is slowly pulled to your face."

She had slowed her speech. That, or it felt like she had. He felt as though he were drifting into space, further and further out into the cosmos with her every word.

She went on: "As your hand comes toward you, you'll notice your eyes begin to lose focus. Your eyes will begin to lose focus, and when your fingers brush your face, you will sleep." The moment Chase's hand touched his face, she said, "Now sleep and let me lead you."

His world went black. There came muffled noises and he felt her hand upon his. He was walking. At least, he believed he was walking. There was a snap. He opened his eyes and heard the final word of a statement.

"... wake," she said. "But you will be cemented to the floor. So, now you are cemented right where you stand." She snapped her fingers. "You will notice your surroundings but they will not scare you. This will feel to you like the place you were meant to be all your life. It will feel like your heaven."

There was a glass table with cards etched into the glass. Chase loved the table, as though it had been in his family for generations. He longed to sit in the leather chairs, but couldn't move.

"I love you," Laura said. "Do you know I love you?"

"I do," Chase answered. "I love you, too."

"You trust me because you know I love you. If you trust me, nod up and down." She tilted her head and repeated it in a slightly different way: "I'm the love of your life, and for this reason, you trust me. Nod if you understand."

He nodded.

She quirked her lips in a half smile. "I want you to now focus inward on your heartbeat. Feel it and tap your finger against your leg for every beat you feel."

His finger tapped as though she had taken control of his body.

Laura breathed in slowly and let it out through her nose. A tear ran down her cheek and she said, "You are relaxed and have complete control over your heartbeat. Your finger taps along with your heartbeat, and you gain control over how fast or how slow your heart will beat." She stepped closer and pointed at her forehead. "I want you to face me now and look at my forehead. Your finger will continue to tap with your heartbeat, and you will look at me. Look right here at my forehead."

Chase looked where she was pointing as his finger tap-tap-tapped against his pant leg.

Laura went on: "You can see right through my head. Right through to the brain and to the back of my skull. I'm going to take your free arm and it's going to feel wet and heavy like a moist towel." She did, and it did. "And when I drop it, you are going to sleep," she said, then snapped and dropped his arm. "Sleep."

Darkness took him again. He could feel the thoughts going through his mind as if they were commands. *Everything she says will make me go deeper. Down, deeper into sleep. I will focus deeper on her voice, and everything she says will instantly* (snap) *and completely become my reality* (snap). *On the count of three* (snap). *And on that number alone I will wake* (snap). *One, two, three* (snap). Chase opened his eyes and looked deep into her eyes. He felt rested, as though he'd slept for days.

"Do not fear the darkness," she said. "I will be there in that darkness. Submit to it when it takes you. The snapping of my fingers will take over for the tapping of yours. As I snap my fingers, your heartbeat will slow. I'm the love your life. You know all I say is truth," she said. "Nod your head if you agree."

She's the love of my life. Chase nodded. *All she says is truth.*

"As I snap my fingers, your heart will beat with them. When the snapping of my fingers slows, so, too, will the beating of your heart," Laura said. "I will now slow the snapping of my fingers. I'm the love your life. You know all I say is truth," she said. "Nod your head if you agree."

He nodded.

"Nod if you feel your heartbeat slowing," she said.

Chase nodded.

His heart felt as though it were in his head, the throbbing putting pressure on his temples. She snapped her fingers slower and the throbbing, in turn, slowed.

"As it slows, you feel a sense of wonder," she continued. "You know by slowing your heartbeat, you are closer to saving the love of your life. You know you will get vengeance for your family. No longer will there be a need for concern that I shall die, for by your heartbeat slowing, I will be safe from harm." She paused before saying, "You know by slowing your heartbeat, you will take vengeance upon the man who threatened to rape and kill me. You know by slowing your heartbeat, you will take vengeance on the man who killed your family. If you believe this, nod your head."

By me slowing my heartbeat, she will live on and vengeance will be carried out against a man who threatens to rape and kill her. He nodded his head.

"You feel a sense of foreboding," she went on. "You feel this sense of foreboding that if your heartbeat does not slow with the snapping of my fingers, Ace will come in here and rape me. You feel this sense of foreboding that if your heartbeat does not slow with the snapping of my fingers, Ace will kill the love of your life. You feel this sense of foreboding that if your heartbeat does not slow with the snapping of my fingers, your family's murderer will go free. This fear scares you down to your core. Nod your head if you agree."

If my heartbeat does not slow with the snapping of her fingers, she will be raped and murdered, and the man who killed my family will go free. He nodded. *Nothing scares me more.*

"You know your heartbeat must slow in order to save me."

My heartbeat must slow to save her.

The pauses between her snaps grew longer and longer.

Nothing scares me more. He felt himself drifting further into darkness. *Nothing scares me more.*

"Your heartbeat is slowing," she said. "Your heartbeat is slowing further and further with every slow snap of my fingers."

My heartbeat is—Nothing scares me more …

She further slowed her snapping. "Nod your head if you agree."

My heartbeat— Chase went to nod. Instead, darkness took him.

Chapter Thirty-Three

And

EACH Guild member has the right to choose which assignments he or she carries out. If none take the assignment, the request, along with the money paid, is returned to the client.

June 10, 2016
09:17 AM EDT
New York City, New York
Guild of Four Spade Suit Headquarters

ACE watched Vixen walk up to his door via the monitor on his desk. *I half-expected her to run away with him.* Before she could knock, he said, "It's open."

Vixen stepped in.

Ace pressed a button. The door slammed shut and two machine gun turrets mounted above the door clicked as they locked on her.

She pivoted on one foot to look at them. "Fancy." She leaned to the right, then back, and to the left. They followed her every movement.

Ace fingered the tip of the bowie knife he held in his lap under the desk. "Is it done?"

Vixen twirled, then raised an eyebrow. "I'm here, aren't I?"

"I want to hear how."

"I told him I loved him. I didn't have to convince him to love me. That was already firmly established."

"I'm confused." There was no blood on her. "How did you kill him, *exactly*?"

"As I always do." She crossed her arms. "I told him you threatened my life." She glared at him. "Which you did. That boy was ready to kill you, but I told him I had a better plan. I told him if he came after you, we'd all end up dead."

Ace glanced at the turrets. "That's no lie." He placed his foot on the desk and tucked the knife's eight inches of steel into the sheath bound at his ankle.

Vixen eyed the blade. "I told him if he trusted me and died, I'd get vengeance for him. That I'd wait until you weren't paying attention and kill you."

Why do I feel she plans to do exactly that? "Did you, now?" Ace stood and rounded the desk. "What did he say?"

"He told me to do what I needed to." Vixen walked to him. "And I hypnotized him, told him to trust me, and commanded his heart to stop." She pressed in close and ran a finger along Ace's earlobe. "And like that—" She snapped her fingers next to his ear. "His heart ceased."

He reached for one of her breasts, but stopped himself. "Vixen," he said. "I've never been more turned on by you."

"Go ahead." She nodded at her breast. "Take it like you've

done everything else."

Why does that sound familiar? Ace focused on her eyes and saw there was still anger behind them. *I might have gone overboard throwing Nightshade in the hole.* Ace backed away from her. "So, you made him your puppet, then cut his strings."

Vixen shrugged. "By far, my best performance," she said. "I even believed it. I think I had to in order to sell it."

I knew she couldn't love him.

She backed away until she met the door. "The meeting is starting soon. Chase's body is waiting on your table beside Powder Keg's helmet."

A thrill ran the length of his spine. "They're in the conference room?"

"Was that not where you wanted them?"

He threw the door open and walked briskly down the hall to peek inside the conference room.

Chase was laid flat on the glass table in front of Ace's chair. The helmet rested a few inches from the dead man's head.

Ace put a hand against the wall to steady himself. Pleasure washed over him. "This is better than sex."

"Really?" said Vixen. "I don't think you're doing it right."

"You can prove me wrong someday." Ace grabbed the back of her head and kissed her hard.

Vixen broke the kiss. "Nightshade," she reminded.

"Right," he turned and pointed at the first person he saw. "Widow."

She looked up from a folder. "I'm coming to the meeting."

He held out a key. "I appreciate that, but I need you to let Nightshade out of the hole."

"Gladly," she said, taking the key and sprinting down the hall to do so.

Ace flung the conference door wide open. "Got the son of a bitch! The one who got away. My one and only miss."

Vixen followed him in and closed the door.

He stood next to Chase's body and put a finger to the dead man's throat. No pulse. *This is the best day of my life.* He pulled his hand away and took a bow. "That'll 'bout do it." He laughed. "I'm sorry for my behavior over the past few months."

"I knew you had your reasons." Vixen walked up and glanced down at Chase. "I laid him over your card on the table to show this was your kill." She smiled sweetly. "Thought you'd appreciate that."

It is my kill. He nodded. "I do." It was hard to contain his excitement, but he wanted to wait until everyone was present. He pointed at the summon button on the wall.

Vixen pressed it and it lit green.

Within minutes, everyone began filtering into the room. Most eyed the body with confusion as they sat at their seats.

"Why is there a body on the table?" Scizzors said, walking in with a pair of reading glasses balanced on the tip of his nose. He sat in the chair with a hollow back, took off his glasses, and pointed them at the body. "That's Chase."

"It is," Ace said, joyfully. "This is the one who got away. My one and only miss." He ran a hand along Chase's arm. "A miss no longer."

Thanatos glared. "Yu bumbohole."

"I'm with Thanatos. You asshole," Scizzors yelled, slapping a hand to the table. "Chase was a recruit, not a hit."

Ace crossed his arms. "He was both."

Eagle sat in her chair. "You're going to stand there and admit you used Guild recruitment to kill someone?"

Maybe this wasn't such a good idea. "I thought you'd be impressed," he said. "It was the perfect trap."

"Impressed?" Pockets laughed and put the tip of a knife against the table. "Why would we be—impressed with you? You wasted valuable time—and finances."

"On a trap, no less," Beast added.

Ace's excitement was waning. He looked at Chase's body. "But he's the one who got away."

Golem appeared and was helped into his seat by Zettabyte. He signed something to her upon seeing the body.

"You don't want to know," she said, glaring.

Widow walked in. "Ace, what the fuck is wrong with you?" She then saw Chase and threw a hand to her mouth, gasping. "But he passed."

"Why'd you enter cursing if it wasn't about Chase?" asked Zettabyte.

Nightshade entered behind her. The very appearance of him answered the question. Those who were sitting immediately stood upon seeing his burns. Where visible, Nightshade's flesh was red and blistered. Second-degree burns split the skin along his face, neck, arms, and feet.

Vixen's hands balled into fists.

It'll take her a while to forgive me for that.

"What in the—actual fuck!" said Pockets.

"There was an accident," Ace said. "If I'd known the severity of the burns, I would have gotten him medical atten—"

"You knew he'd been burnt?" interrupted Widow. "And you left him there?"

Scizzors started for the door. "Let's get you to a hospital."

Nightshade put out a hand and everyone stopped. "Is that

Chase?" he said, voice weak.

"It is," said Pockets. "Ace wanted his one—and only miss splayed out dead—for all of us to see."

Nightshade shot Vixen an empathetic look.

"Don't look at her like that." Ace ran fingers through his hair and took a step back. "Him being dead means I haven't missed one kill. My record is *flawless*. Pardon me for wanting to share that with you all."

"It's an unsanctioned kill," said Eagle.

Beast reached over and took her hand. "How can you justify this after throwing Nightshade in the hole for doing the same? And then burning him?"

Everything was unraveling. *They're all fucking idiots.* "That was an accident." He pointed at Vixen. "She'll tell you."

"Where's Noose?" Vixen said, instead. She looked around as though counting heads. "He needs to be here. Everyone needs to be here for this."

She gets it.

People were talking amongst one another.

Ace slapped the table. "Listen up!"

"We're all ears," Nightshade said, as though daring Ace to say another word.

"I sanction the kills," Ace said, believing he'd found the perfect answer. "Therefore, I sanctioned this one. But even if I hadn't, I wasn't the one who killed him."

"No," Vixen said. "You just threatened Nightshade and me, demanding I kill Chase during the test. And when I refused, you turned the boiling water on."

"*Accidentally,*" Nightshade reiterated.

I shouldn't have to— "I shouldn't have to threaten you," he yelled, realizing Vixen's act had been for him, not for Chase. "You're supposed to try to kill him. That's the point of the testing period. To test their ability to survive."

"Still," Scizzors said. "You sanctioned a kill on a recruit."

They're not listening. "Technically, he could have survived and joined the Guild. Then my one miss would have been forever out of reach." He placed his hand against Chase's leg. "But he died and that's a win. If not for you, it most definitely is for me." He pointed at Vixen. "Did you actually believe he'd make a good assassin?"

"Not at first," Vixen admitted, narrowing her eyes at him. "But Chase proved himself."

"Yeah." Ace stuttered a laugh. "Surprised the living fuck out of me, too."

Noose walked in with his motorcycle helmet under his arm.

"Oh, thank god, you're here," Vixen declared.

"Okay." Noose laughed. "I know I'm late, but not that ..." He dropped his helmet when he saw Nightshade. "What the fuck happened to you?"

"Shut up and take a seat," demanded Nightshade.

"Sorry I asked." Noose picked up his helmet and walked around the table. "Why's everyone standing?"

Everyone ignored him.

Scizzors placed a hand against the table. "He survived me. That's saying something."

"Who did what?" Noose said before he finally saw Chase. "Who managed to kill the slippery bastard?"

Nightshade glared at Ace, his usual mirth a distant memory.

Noose thumped his helmet down on the table. "Pardon me for being late to the party."

"Here's the skinny," said Nightshade as he gestured at Ace. "Ace demanded Vixen kill the recruit during testing." His hand spiraled around his face. "I'm perma-blushing because he scalded me when she refused. He threatened my life and hers, thus forcing her to do *everything* in her power," he said, pointing at the dead recruit, "to kill Chase."

Noose gestured at Pockets. "And here I thought our testing him together was twisted."

The expressions around the room made it clear not everyone was aware of this fact.

Ace pinched the bridge of his nose and sighed loudly. "That was a scheduling error."

"Another accident," said Widow. "Like Nightshade's burnt flesh?"

Eagle shook her head. "Was it an *accident* when you demanded I test Chase, even though it's against Guild law for a sniper to do so?"

"No," said Ace. "That wasn't an accident. If I make a demand of you, you should follow it. I'm your Ace."

"Eh sniper is notta test," Thanatos said. "Tiz only death."

"We know," Ace yelled, slapping the table again. "I know a sniper is only death. You've only said it a million times. In fact, it's the only *fucking* thing you say that I truly understand."

"And yet, you called on us," said Eagle.

"Oh, my god!" *I'm going to kill everyone in this room.* "None of you get it." Ace threw his hands in the air. "I'd rejoice with any of you over a perfect score."

Noose pushed his helmet further onto the table, sat, and

placed his feet on the glass. "You are aware two of our suit are dead because of this bullshit?"

"Powder Keg betrayed us," Ace said and pointed at Radiant's vacant seat. "He killed Radiant. I killed him."

"Radiant missed his time to test Chase," Vixen said. "Missed it entirely. Yet, arrived anyway by Ace's order. Making Chase an actual hit." She pressed something at the front of Powder Keg's mask. "As far as him discarding Powder Keg, this should clear up any questions you might have."

Ace reached for the mask. "What are you doing?"

Vixen pushed it across the table to Scizzors.

Ace backhanded her across the face.

She clearly saw it coming, but didn't move to block him. When her colleagues jumped to her aid, she put out a hand to stop them.

His eyes went wide. *I played right into her hand.*

Vixen grinned through a broken lip. "Let's all sit down and have a listen."

Everyone took their seats.

"This is ridiculous." Ace tried to round the table to get Powder Keg's mask. "Give it here, Scizzors."

Viper pointed both her guns at him.

Ace backed away with his hands up.

The guns were holstered.

Ace gestured at Vixen. "She was in love with the recruit and is now trying to poison you against me."

Scizzors laughed. "You're doing a good job of that yourself." He nodded to Vixen. "You good?"

"I will be," she said, nodding at the mask. "Play current bookmark."

~ RECORDING ~

Ace's voice was the first thing they heard, soft as though from a distance. "You know how to pinpoint one asshole out of six billion?"

"If I were hiding," Powder Keg's voice replied, much closer, "I would have torn the GPS tracker from the truck."

"That kills the big reveal about how I found you." Short pause. "Care to *face me* for your crimes committed against the Guild?"

"Sure. If you face the Guild for crimes you've committed."

There was the sound of a scuffle followed by choking and heavy breathing.

Ace said, "You're—" Coughing. "What in—?" More coughing. "How the fuck did you—?" Heavy coughing and a short pause. "This isn't possible."

"You think every plan you hatch goes off without a hitch. That nobody sees through your bullshit. Half your so-called *traps* end in explosions. That's not a trap, you dumbass ape. That's called blowing shit up."

Ace laughed hoarsely. "All this time, I thought you wore that mask to hide a hideous scar. I thought you were missing half your face or something." Short pause. "You were Frank Douglas, best bomb disposal officer in America. Mentor to all the greatest and brightest in your field." Short pause. "Couldn't risk your face being caught on camera while blowing up a drug den. I can't believe I never saw past it. Not once did you take it off around me."

"You never asked."

"Would you, had I?"

"We'll never know," said Powder Keg. "You never grew the balls to make the request."

~ CONFERENCE ROOM ~

Noose laughed, putting his feet on the floor. "Sounds about right."

Scizzors paused the recording.

"This is stupid," Ace said, stepping forward. "Scizzors, give it here."

"I think we'll continue listening," Scizzors said. "If that's all right with everyone else."

The Guild members nodded.

Whatever. Powder Keg betrayed us. "It doesn't matter. You'll see I was justified." Perfect timing delivered his next line in the recording.

~ RECORDING ~

"I have the right to kill you for attacking another card holder," came Ace's voice. "In this case, many."

~ CONFERENCE ROOM ~

"Exactly," Ace spat.

~ RECORDING ~

Ace went on, "I could kill you now and never have to

answer for it."

There was some rustling, a clunking, and the sound of metal scraping on metal. "You're welcome to try."

"As Frank Douglas, you should already be dead." Short pause. "I fucking blew you up."

~ CONFERENCE ROOM ~

All eyes hit Ace at once.

"I can explain that," Ace said. "I sanctioned my kill of Frank Douglas."

"Funny," said Nightshade. He had remained standing, likely because it hurt to sit. "You sure are sanctioning a lot of questionable kills. I'd be interested to see if they're on the books."

Zettabyte took her laptop out of her bag and placed it on the table. "Give me a sec."

"My files are encrypted," Ace said. "You can't get into them."

Beast looked over Zettabyte's shoulder. "She just did."

"No." Ace started around the table.

Scizzors rolled into Ace's path. "Viper."

Her guns left their holsters again.

I should rip your fucking horns off. Ace glared at Scizzors, then at Viper. "This is mutiny."

Zettabyte shook her head. "No mention of Frank Douglas anywhere. But there is this other file labeled 'Personal Marks.' I say we open that."

Nightshade walked over to watch her work. "Yes, please."

"Shhh," Widow hushed everyone. "He just admitted it.

Rewind a little."

"Admitted what?" Ace growled.

Vixen leaned against the table. "Reverse ten seconds."

~ RECORDING ~

"... the Monday after," Powder Keg said.

Short pause before Ace could be heard saying, "Why not turn me in for the unsanctioned kill of Frank Douglas?"

"When an Ace is accused of breaking ..."

~ CONFERENCE ROOM ~

"Interesting." Scizzors laughed. "You were saying?"

Dear god! "That's out of context, and you know it. Besides, we've gone over this already. I sanction the kills."

"Sounds directly from context," Widow said. "And a sanctioned kill is paid for. Who paid for it?"

"I did," Ace said.

Nightshade looked up from the laptop. "As did I. You sanctioned me killing my roommate over the phone. So, if that's the story you sold everyone about why I was in the hole, I have a feeling they're about to return the receipt."

"Shut it," Ace said, placing his hand against the table. "Or I'll throw you back in."

"I'd like to see you try," said Vixen. "An Ace is not allowed to drop a Joker in the hole without the approval of the other Aces. They are liaisons, not suit members."

Ace leveled a glare at her. "After what you've done, you'll be in there soon enough."

"You did this to yourself," she scoffed. "And what's crazy is you think you're still going to come out on top."

I always do.

"I'm curious," Widow said, turning to Zettabyte. "Have you found a money trail into the Guild's coffers for these so-called sanctioned kills?"

"No," Zettabyte said. "But I am finding hits where he pocketed every dime. Assassinations our Guild would never take. One is titled, 'Rich Bitch's Secret Lover'?"

"I command you to stop," Ace demanded.

"Take your own advice," Scizzors yelled. "Since when do we get involved with scandals and affairs?"

Ace laughed. "We throw away good money because it might make us look bad. That rule has never made sense."

Scizzors shook his head. "Why join the Guild if you thought we were foolish and narrow-minded? You could have turned us down and went with the Ghosts."

"Or Legion," Beast suggested.

Ace looked from Scizzors to Beast. "Those guilds make half of what we do."

"Right," Scizzors said. "Because we have a reputation we uphold. Killing outside it lowers our standing with our more influential clientele."

They're all fucking blind. "We could make three times the amount we are."

"No," said Widow. "You're missing the point entirely. For a few years, we could get away with that. Then we'd lose all respect and be no better than the Brotherhood of Havoc."

"With me at your helm," Ace said, "you'd never drop so low."

"With you?" Widow laughed. "We've reached out to the other Aces because your actions have already decayed the very foundation of our established prestige."

"Wait," Ace said. "Go back to the part where you stabbed me in the back."

"You left us no other option."

Traitors. All of them. "Fine." Ace walked to his chair and fell into it. "I'll take the profits I made from my personal marks and funnel them back into the Guild."

"We don't—want them," Pockets said. "For us to accept them would be—to stamp them with our approval."

"Wait," Noose said. "Did you just pull remotes out on Powder Keg?"

"What?" Several people, including Ace, said together.

Noose gestured with a backward rolling finger.

Vixen leaned in. "Reverse ten seconds."

~ RECORDING ~

"... in your locker," Ace said.

"You think there's a bomb nearby to which I do not hold the remote?" Powder Keg said.

"Apparently not with this one," Ace said. There came a clattering. "Are these even on?"

There was a cracking sound.

"If you're right and none of these blow you to hell," Ace said, "I'll write myself up as a hit and let you strap a bomb to my chest. Fair?"

"Bombs are too quick for what I want to do to you."

~ CONFERENCE ROOM ~

"Sorry to interrupt," said Zettabyte. "But why do you have files on all of us?"

"I'm your Ace," he said. "Of course, I keep files on you."

"If this information fell into the wrong hands, we'd be screwed." Zettabyte looked around at everyone. "If I can hack into his computer, others can and may have already." She focused on the screen and tapped another key. "I mean, there's a financial folder and an assets folder." Her eyes went wide. "And an 'Outside Guild Personnel Folder'? Ace, these people trust us to keep their names anonymous. They should not exist in any of our digital records nor should we exist digitally."

Ace stood and slapped the table. "That's enough!" he yelled. His fingers throbbed from the impact. "I am your Ace and I demand respect!"

"You have none of mine," Scizzors said, rising.

"Quiet," Vixen interrupted. "This is the part I think you should hear."

What is she talking about?

They all grew silent.

~ RECORDING ~

"From the very beginning, something always rubbed me wrong about you," Powder Keg said. "I wanted to go with a high-ranking—"

~ CONFERENCE ROOM ~

"There's nothing on this stupid recording," said Ace. "Turn it off."

Vixen held up a finger. "Right here."

~ RECORDING ~

Ace was mid-reply: "—fight him on it or did you simply follow his orders like the sheep you all are?"

~ CONFERENCE ROOM ~

Eagle laughed. "Good to know what you think of us." Contempt was all that remained in her expression.

She wasn't the only one who looked on the verge of gutting Ace where he stood.

That's what you are. "I was trying to get under his skin," Ace swore. "Nothing more."

Scizzors quoted from their laws: "Aces should be humble and know every assassin under them serves a purpose. They should be aware of how each should be used, and manage them accordingly."

"I did nothing wrong," Ace said defiantly. "I'm your Ace. I used you as I saw fit."

"Yet, you sent me to test Chase," said Widow. "It's clear now, with the questions you sent with me, you hoped for insight into his and Vixen's relationship."

"That's your skillset," Ace pointed out.

"Hey!" Vixen yelled at nobody in particular. "You don't want to miss this."

Silence replied.

~ RECORDING ~

"—tag. From day one, he regretted your recruitment," Powder Keg said. "He knew you had every intention of stabbing him in the back when you had enough support to rise—"

~ CONFERENCE ROOM ~

"This is fucking ridiculous," Ace said. "Vixen is trying to—"

A BANG sent bells ringing in his skull. He ducked and looked around.

Everyone had their hands to their ears. Everyone, that is, but Viper.

Ace turned and saw a hole in the wall. "You almost killed me."

"Trust me," Scizzors said. "She missed on purpose." He pointed at Ace's chair. "Take a seat and shut up."

"You can't tell me what to do," Ace yelled back.

Scizzors rose from his chair and pointed. "Sit."

Ace wanted to dive for the chair, but forced himself to descend slowly. He had to appear calm. *What does Vixen think is on that tape? What have I forgotten?* He sat and raised an eyebrow. "Better?"

"Much." Scizzors looked at Vixen. "Did we miss anything?"

Vixen leaned against the wall. "Reverse twenty seconds."

~ RECORDING ~

Powder Keg could be heard saying, "—lies being whispered into people's ears to secure your position when he died. And faster than any other card member you did rise."

~ CONFERENCE ROOM ~

"Fuck!" Ace realized too late what came next.

~ RECORDING ~

"I killed him, you know," Ace's voice confessed.

~ CONFERENCE ROOM ~

Scizzors stood with a fury Ace had never before seen on a face. The monstrous man reached his hand out and snapped his thumb and middle finger together.

Two others snapped their fingers as well.

"Turn that off," Widow said. "We've heard enough."

"Pause playback," said Vixen.

The recording stopped.

I'm so fucked. Ace pulled the bowie knife from the sheath secured to his ankle. He bolted from the chair toward Vixen.

Apparently, she believed she was safe with everyone present. He had a fistful of her hair and the knife pressed to her throat before she could respond. Hiding behind her, he glared at the others. "I'll kill her if you don't let me leave."

Viper scratched the side of her head with the barrel of a

gun, then pointed it at him. "Or I split your melon in half right now."

Vixen slapped back at Ace.

He let her hit him and pressed the knife harder to her throat.

She went still and let him hold her against his chest.

More people snapped their fingers.

"Stop it with the snapping," Ace demanded. "It's giving me a headache."

"Open your eyes," Vixen said, snapping two fingers together. "Ace, do you actually think you can get out of here alive?"

Viper smiled. "Give the word and I'll paint the wall with him."

Ace ducked his head behind Vixen's. The side of his leg rubbed against the table.

"Let Vixen go!" Scizzors roared in rage. "Face us like a man."

"Come at me and she dies," Ace said, running the knife's edge against Vixen's neck to open a small cut.

She yelped.

Eagle rounded the other side of the table with a Nighthawk T4 9MM. "Do you believe we would agree to any of your demands after hearing that?"

"I guess not," Ace said, pointing the knife at Eagle. A droplet of blood fell from the blade's tip. "But come near me and she dies."

Vixen slapped her hand against the table. "Playback bookmark 827!"

~ RECORDING ~

"You wouldn't dare rape Vixen," said Powder Keg.

"I'd rape her until she bled out her eyes," Ace said. "Then I'd make her disappear for forcing me to."

"Good thing you die tonight."

~ CONFERENCE ROOM ~

Snaps erupted from around the table as those who hadn't yet decided Ace's fate did so.

"That's it," Ace growled. "If I'm going to die, you're going to Hell with me." He raised the knife in preparation to stab Vixen in the stomach.

"One, two, three, *wake*!" Vixen screamed, snapping her fingers together.

Ace brought the knife down, but something took his wrist and diverted the blade into his own side. Excruciating pain exploded as eight inches of steel scraped against the bone of his rib. "What the fuck?" he yelled in shock, his heart skirting around his chest like a deflating balloon. The knife sank to its hilt inside him. Chase's hand was wrapped around the handle.

The dead man took in a deep breath and jolted upright, a dot of red blood upon his forehead.

"Fucking asshole!" Ace brought his head forward to get a better look at Chase.

Vixen threw her head back, catching Ace in the bridge of the nose. She escaped and took a gun from Viper.

Ace faltered backward, the knife coming free of his body. He shook his head. Blood splattered from his nostrils.

Chase flew up and grabbed him by the front of the shirt.

Ace's left arm felt as though it had been torn off as he spun around. Chase's face blurred in his vision before Ace felt his spine crunch against the glass table. When his head hit it, he heard a crack. Whether it was his skull, the table, or both, he couldn't say. Pain blossomed at the back of his head.

What's happening? Chase was dead. *I checked his pulse.* "You're dead!"

Chapter Thirty-Four

Consequences

DURING recruitment, seven Guild members have two hours each to assess a chosen recruit's ability to survive. One hour is generally used for preparation; the final is spent carrying out a fatal assault. The recruit must avoid death by any means necessary. If the seven Guild members fail to kill the recruit in their allotted time, then a new card member is accepted into the fold of the Guild of Four.

June 10, 2016
09:53 AM EDT
New York City, New York
Guild of Four Spade Suit Headquarters

A finger snapped.

    ... Must slow to save her.

    More snapping.

    The throbbing in Chase's head came rushing back, putting

pressure against his temples. *I'm still alive?* His body felt like it had been submerged in warm jelly. He tried to shake the feeling, but it wasn't lifting. He could hear a voice. His uncle's voice. *He's not alive.* No, it couldn't be Frank's voice. *But it is.* The voice was slightly distorted, as though it might be coming from a television. *No, not a television.*

His uncle kept a recorder and would often listen to case files in the living room. For the particularly gruesome cases, he would only listen to them when he thought Chase was asleep. Frank would listen all the way through then speak if something occurred to him while reviewing the case. He did this religiously, playing recordings over and over to make sure he hadn't missed anything. That's what Chase heard: *Frank's recorder.*

But someone else's voice came from it as well. And there were other voices all around. *A fight?*

Chase's heartbeat was slow, but strong. With every thump, he felt like his heart would explode in his chest. He tried to get his eyes open, but they wouldn't budge. He couldn't move anything but the finger tapping his leg along with more snapping.

A man complained about having a headache.

"Open your eyes," Laura's voice came, followed by her snapping fingers.

Chase's eyes flew open.

A man in his forties was holding a knife to Laura's throat.

She looked at Chase. "Ace, do you actually think you can get out of here alive?"

"Give the word," a woman spoke up, "and I'll paint the

wall with him." The voice was unfamiliar.

Ace was using Laura as a shield. The side of the man's leg came close.

Chase glared at the man holding the knife. *You're responsible for all of the pain in my life.* He tried to bite the man's leg, but his body wouldn't respond to any of his commands. *I'm in a hypnotic state. That's why I couldn't open my eyes until she said the words.* Frustration gripped his heart and squeezed. *Give me the command to strike, Laura.*

"Let Vixen go!" a voice bellowed. "Face us like a man."

Now, that was Scizzors. He could barely see a ram horn in his peripheral.

"Come at me and she dies," said Ace. He opened a small gash in Laura's throat to prove his seriousness.

Laura let out a short scream.

Chase's eyes widened when he saw a droplet of blood run down the metal of the blade. *Give the command, give the command, give me the fucking command ...*

"Do you believe we would agree to any of your demands after hearing that?" a female's voice said.

Chase vaguely recognized the voice. It was the woman from the pair of assassins who first approached him. *Falcon? No ... Eagle. Eagle and Beast, together they are Griffin.*

"I guess not." Ace pointed the knife in the direction of Eagle's voice. Blood dripped from the blade onto Chase's forehead. "But come near me and she dies."

GIVE THE COMMAND!

Laura slapped the table next to Chase's head and yelled, "Playback bookmark 827."

A bolt of lightning shot through Chase's brain, but still, he could not move.

Frank's voice came from the recorder: "You wouldn't dare rape Vixen."

Ace's voice followed: "I'd rape her until she bled out her eyes. Then I'd make her disappear for forcing me to."

Despite his rage, Chase's heartbeat continued to throb painfully slow against his temples.

"Good thing you die tonight," said Frank.

YES, HE NEEDS TO DIE! I NEED THE COMMAND!

Snapping erupted from all around him. Chase's heartbeat *thump-thump-thumped* along with them.

"That's it," Ace said. "If I'm going to die, you're going to Hell with me." The knife rose.

Laura's eyes went wide and she yelled, "One, two, three, WAKE!" Two of her fingers snapped together. It was like a gun went off in his head, only he was the bullet.

The knife swung down.

Before it could sink into Laura's stomach, Chase grabbed the wrist holding it. He wrenched it around and plunged it into Ace's liver. There was a crunch when the knife went as far as it could go.

"What the fuck?" Ace was obviously startled to see Chase alive.

Chase's lungs filled with air. He bolted upward.

"Fucking asshole," Ace yelled, squinting at Chase.

Laura threw her head back and broke the man's nose. He lost control of her and she escaped a few paces to stand beside a woman Chase didn't recognize. The woman gave her a gun.

Ace stumbled away, blood leaking from his nose onto his upper lip.

Chase still held the knife.

Ace retreated until the blade slid free of his gut.

Blood gushed hot over Chase's hand. He let it fuel his rage. Knowing Laura was out of harm's way, Chase lunged. He grabbed Ace by the front of the shirt with his left hand, plunged the knife into the man's upper arm with his right, and lifted him while twirling around. With all his strength, Chase slammed Ace down onto the glass table.

There was a sickening crack when Ace's head met the table. A spiderweb splintered out along the glass. Blood immediately began filling the cracks.

Ace looked back, an expression of terror and confusion on his face. "You're dead!"

"End playback!" Laura yelled.

The recording stopped abruptly.

Chase pinned Ace with one hand and twisted the knife.

"Hooo, fuck," Ace cried out in pain. "Stop!"

Chase took a moment to glance around the room, but none of the other assassins moved to stop him. His heart was pounding so hard, he could hear it pump blood in and out.

"Don't kill me," Ace pleaded.

Chase returned to glare at the man. "By the looks on their faces, you're already dead."

He pulled the knife out and, with it in hand, punched Ace in the face. The small pool of blood that had collected at the back of the man's head splattered outward. Chase's rage and adrenaline fought past the pain he felt from the damage accrued from his fight with Scizzors.

Ace groaned.

Chase popped his neck from side to side. The throbbing at

his temples was unbearable. "Why do you want to kill everyone I love?" He punched Ace hard in the face. Blood spurted out of the man's nose and mouth.

Ace lay still, his eyes open. They gazed glassy at the ceiling.

I think I killed him. Chase shook Ace to be sure.

The bloodied man coughed, then took a deep breath. "You hit like a fucking anvil."

Chase heard words of agreement come from others around the table. He didn't look up to see from who.

"You can't kill me." Ace laughed. "None of you can."

Chase pulled the man in close. "You expect me to show mercy?"

"If you kill me, I'll haunt every last one of you." He laughed a little louder. "Don't test me on this."

Chase placed the knife against the man's throat as had been done to Laura earlier. It was meant to cut a small hole, but he managed to carve out a deep four inches. It bled worse than Chase expected. He clamped a hand over it to staunch the dark flow.

"Spades fall," Ace choked in terror, "if I die."

"Haunt away," Scizzors said.

"You can't," Ace insisted. He grabbed Chase's wrist with his right hand. "You're no killer."

Chase looked at the knife. *What am I doing?* He lifted off Ace slightly. "You're right." Frank's words from the recording returned to Chase. *Good thing you die tonight.* "I wasn't." Chase jerked his hand out of Ace's grip and plunged the knife down into the man's chest.

"No, no!" Ace yelled. "Don't, please!" He grabbed Chase's

wrist again.

Chase turned the blade.

Ace's grip grew weak. A gargled groan escaped.

Chase left the knife embedded in Ace's chest and lifted him with both hands. He screamed in the man's face, lifted higher, then slammed him down. The glass tabletop burst into a thousand shards.

"My computer!" Zettabyte's voice called in a world far, far away.

Ace gurgled a few final breaths, staring up at Chase.

He's trying to say something. "I don't want to hear it!" Chase yelled, pulling the knife free. "This is for father." He stabbed Ace in the stomach. "Mother." This time, in the side. "Frank." In the throat. "And Laura." He rammed the knife as hard as he could into Ace's groin. He left it embedded between the man's legs.

What am I? Chase rose, his heart still beating wildly in his ears. Seeing his hands covered in blood, he began to swoon. The world spun out from under him and he stumbled backward. The seat of a chair brushed the back of his legs and he fell into it.

Laura ran to him and snapped in his ear, once every second and a half. She did this for half a minute until the throbbing in his chest, neck, and temples slowed. She raised both hands and snapped her fingers in his face.

He sucked in air as though breathing had been a challenge before. His ribs complained angrily, but he tried to ignore them as he took another long breath. The throbbing against his temples was replaced with a headache threatening to cripple him. He squinted his eyes and pulled Laura onto his lap and into a hug. "I thought you killed me." He fought the migraine. "I thought I was—" He swallowed. "—dead."

"I thought I might have," she said, pulling him in tighter. "I've never done that before. I didn't know for certain it would work."

"I'm glad it did." He let out a relieved sigh. "I thought you told me I had to die?"

She pulled away, placing her hand against his cheek. Tears glistened at the corners of her eyes. "It only worked because you believed you had to. Otherwise, you would have fought your heart slowing." She planted her lips against his.

Someone cleared their throat.

"Need us to leave?" Scizzors said.

Their lips parted and Chase looked past Laura at everyone. "Um." He smiled. *I may yet die if I don't say the right thing.* "Am I a dead man for killing your Ace?" *That probably wasn't it.*

"He was already dead," said Noose. "He was too blind to see that."

"Their snapping sped my pulse," Chase said, realizing Laura's plan. "How did you know they'd snap?"

Scizzors sat in his chair. "Because she knew Ace deserved to die." Scizzors parted his lips in that horrific smile of his. "When we take an assignment, we can decide at any time to not kill the person." He leaned back in the hollow-back chair, his tentacles splaying out behind him. "However, during each assignment, there is a time we make up our mind to do so."

"A time of no turning back," Eagle said.

Widow leaned forward. "It's when we've seen enough and heard enough from them to prove beyond a shadow of a doubt that they deserve to die."

"As per our Guild's custom," Scizzors went on, "we snap our fingers to prove our body is in congress with our mind."

"Well, then, thank you," said Chase, leaning back in the

chair. "That saved my life."

"And," Laura said, looking down at her watch, "time."

Everyone was looking at her strangely. Chase was sure he wore a similar expression.

She looked up and tapped her watch. "You survived your final test," she said. "If you had stayed out cold for the remainder of your testing, you'd likely be dead."

Scizzors clapped. "You survived everything Ace threw at you."

"Welcome," Widow said, "to the Guild of Four."

Chase felt pride well up inside him. He was about to say something when Zettabyte yelped as though in pain. She was on the glass-covered floor looking at her laptop screen.

A shard must have cut into her. Otherwise, why would she have made such a noise?

A really small person jumped down from a chair. Like, really small. The child—or not a child—reached out and put a hand on her arm.

She looked at the little man as though she were horrified.

"What's wrong?" Beast said.

"We're being haunted," she said, staring at Ace's body. "He wasn't lying."

"What?" Nightshade said. "You don't really believe in that, do you?"

Chase hadn't realized this before, but Nightshade's skin was burnt bad. Broken blisters fed into actual tears in the skin. *I couldn't save him from Ace.*

Zettabyte sat silently for a bit before saying, "I don't believe in ghosts. But being haunted is not always supernatural." She looked at Chase, then at Widow. "When I hacked into his computer earlier, there was a heart monitor at the top. It was strange, but I thought little of it." She lifted the laptop to show the dwarf. "It must have been a live feed, because it's flat-lined."

The little man let out a heavy sigh and nodded.

"What does this mean?" Laura said, walking over to look at the screen.

"It means," Zettabyte said, "we're royally fucked."

The man with the dreadlocks Chase had seen earlier talking to Pockets reached into his pocket and pulled out a phone. He put it to his ear. "Yo, whatta gwaan?" He listened for a minute, looked at Scizzors, and shook his head.

"What is it, Thanatos?" Scizzors asked.

The dark man came around the table and handed Scizzors the phone.

Scizzors put it to his ear. "Go for Scizzors." As he listened, his jaw dropped little by little. His face twisted and his eyes met Thanatos's. "You can't be serious. Check again."

Few expressions looked good on the monster's face, but this was the most terrifying of all. Chase never imagined he'd see Scizzors fearful of anything.

"How bad is it?" Scizzors kicked Ace's body. "That's what he meant by haunting us." He shook his head. "Never mind, we'll figure it out." He hung up and glanced around the room. "We have half an hour before this world swallows us whole."

"What's happening?" Noose said, his eyes moving from Scizzors to Zettabyte.

Zettabyte cleared her throat and turned the computer screen for all to see. Most of them couldn't read anything off it, being it was in her lap, but she explained so they wouldn't have to. "The heart monitor caused everything in the folders to lag when I opened them. I had only moved the financial and assets folders by the time he died." She looked apologetic. "I would have found a way to move it all faster, had I known."

"Known what, love?" Widow said, her own face growing sullen.

"The rest of the files," Zettabyte said, tapping the screen of the laptop. "There was a full dossier in there on each of us."

Scizzors nodded and lifted the phone. "That was my contact at the DoD." He sighed loudly. "The files were shared a few minutes ago."

"Shared?" Nightshade said. "Shared with who?"

Scizzors dropped the phone in his lap. "Law enforcement, both local and federal. A copy likely went out to every corporation, criminal outfit, terrorist cell, and god knows who all."

"To the helicopters," Widow said, standing. "Every government official and enemy of ours from across the world will know our names, our aliases, and the people we've killed." She pointed at the door. "We should split up and hide until we can create new names for ourselves."

How will I protect Laura from every government, criminal, terrorist, and corporation that wants her dead? He wasn't fully trained yet and they were about to take on the world.

Without realizing what he was doing, Chase said, "What do we do?"

"You're free to go," Widow said. "You're the only one he wouldn't have had a dossier on."

"If I turn down being a Guild member, I'm dead," he said. "If I accept, I'll be fighting to keep Laura alive."

"We'd let you go," Scizzors said, not glancing around for

confirmation from the others.

Noose stood. "If Ace had a jacket on us all, how'd he fail to realize Powder Keg was Chase's uncle?"

Widow shrugged. "Powder Keg kept to himself and came before Ace's time. Ace would have known who he'd killed and some of his aliases. But he wouldn't have the personal information needed for identification."

They'd strayed off-topic. Chase put fingers to his lips and whistled loudly.

All eyes gravitated to him.

"I accept," he said. "I'm here, if you like it or not." He pointed at Laura. "I'm not leaving her side if people are coming for her." He pointed at Scizzors. "Besides, you need assassins they don't know. And you promised to make me a hell of an assassin if I passed."

"We would have trained you," Scizzors said, frowning. "Having a few assassins they don't know won't cut it. We're no longer a chapter of the Guild that can operate in the dark."

"Okay," Chase said. "What do we do as a chapter that operates in the light? Now that you've risen to the top of everyone's most wanted list?"

"We get out of the country," Widow said. "Spread out and find shelter with those who aided us in the past."

"That won't work," Zettabyte said. "I removed the financial folder, so we're protected there. But our safe houses and those we trust are now public domain." She hit a key on the computer. "I'll send them a message warning them to change their names and go into hiding." She pointed at the computer. "We can't thank them for all they've done by leaving them out to hang." She looked around for support.

Chase was relieved to see everyone nod.

Widow walked to the door. "We'll contact the other suits. Call the Diamonds, Hearts, and Clubs. They'll have people who can hide us who weren't in those files."

"Each card suit is meant to operate within their area of the world." Scizzors argued. "We cannot operate while hiding in their safe houses. In time they'd feel the need to discard us and start the Spades from scratch." He sat back down and pushed his chair to the wall. "No, what we need to do is keep working or we'll have our own people to fight off. They'll kill us all, because that's what is best for the Guild as a whole."

"What if there's another way?" said Chase.

Noose laughed and threw up a hand. "Why does he keep talking?"

"Hear me out," Chase said, glaring at the man. "Zettabyte sends out a similar message. But instead of your allies fending for themselves, have them pool their resources and congregate at your most fortified safe houses."

"Everyone gather at one place?" Noose laughed. "Are you suggesting group suicide? Because I'm not really into drinking the Kool-Aid."

"Chase, if you have a point," warned Scizzors, "I'd get to it."

"We can't run." Chase looked to Laura for support. "We can't hide."

She nodded and picked up the directive. "We can't fight by ourselves. Not with what's coming." She looked to Widow. "We unite."

"Bring in everyone you trust," Chase said, standing. "And give anyone that comes at us a fight for their life. It's one of the reasons you test your card members. We escape, we assess our situation, then we strike. The tests are what help you survive against all odds and come out on top."

Widow smiled. "We continue working, but do so in groups."

"Kill everyone who opposes us," Scizzors added. "Respond to every attack with ferocity. Scare the ever-loving shit out of everyone who wishes us harm."

Zettabyte stretched her fingers over the keyboard. "I'm game."

Chase, empowered by their approval, went on: "We know the fight is coming. They don't know we're prepared for it. They'll expect us to flee." He smiled at the faces around the room. "I've fought you. They don't have a clue who they're dealing with." He pointed at Pockets and Noose. "You'd never fought side by side before you fought me, correct?"

"That was—a learning experience," said Pockets.

Noose finally dropped his expression of annoyance. In fact, there was a look of respect previously vacant from his countenance that now flickered around the dark of his eyes.

"Yet, I survived only because of Powder Keg," Chase said. "If it weren't for the ceiling collapsing, I'd be dead." He pointed at Widow and Nightshade. "Poison, traps, and spiders. That's some scary lions, tigers, and bears shit right there." He pointed at Scizzors. "Don't get me started on how terrifying you are and Laura called you the Guild's 'teddy bear.'"

"You haven't seen Golem in action," Scizzors said, patting the dwarf on the back.

The room erupted in laughter.

The dwarf was nodding.

What's scary about that guy? Deciding it to be a joke, Chase moved on, gesturing at Zettabyte. "You can hack their systems, Vixen's a master of distraction, and the rest of you have talents I haven't witnessed because they're not *allowed* for testing. I don't know what that means, but it horrifies me." He paused, standing straighter. "Alone, you are beaten. In pairs, you are unstoppable." He gestured around the room at everyone together. "With all of you together, fighting the enemy as one ..." He let that speak for itself.

Scizzors thrummed a low hum in his throat. "The lack of anonymity will generate new business. That'll be especially true when we take out those hunting us." He smiled wickedly. "This'll be the hardest our suit has fought to stay alive in a long, long time."

"Stick together and fight?" Noose said, as though he were testing the taste of the words. "I can't do it."

Chase sighed, feeling defeated. "I know you don't like me. But—"

"You misunderstand," Noose said, head shaking. "I fully support the rest of you going. But I can't. Max and my gremlins don't know what I do. My husband thinks I'm a pilot. My children think I'm a kind and gentle giant."

"They'll come around," Vixen said. "This is the only way you'll all be safe."

"No," said Noose. "I know my husband. He's a pacifist and I adore his naivete about the world. But when he learns of what I have done time and time again ..." He ran his teeth over his bottom lip. "He'd learn of that at the same time I uproot our lives and force my family to live in a bunker. I will not, cannot, do that to him."

Vixen looked heartbroken as she said, "Anyone else not coming?"

"My wife knows about me," Scizzors said. "She loves that I'm a monster who devours the evil of this world." He looked around at bewildered faces. "Yes, someone married this." He gestured at his face. "And, no, she's not blind. She's the greatest person this world has to offer. You'll love her. You can't meet her and not love her. She is the beauty of this world, and that beauty adores this disfigured, twisted beast."

Realizing people were still somewhat stunned into silence by the Guild monster's revelation, Chase spoke up. "Where to, then?"

Widow raised a hand. "It's not big, but we can use the cave where I raise my spiders."

Pockets shook his head, "I don't—do spiders." He frowned. "Or dark places."

Beast leaned back in his seat. "If I joined without Eagle, my tag would have been Pluto."

Nightshade laughed. "Beast, as much as we'd like to be on another planet right now, none of us have a rocket ship."

"Pluto was the god of riches," Eagle said, shifting her expensive prosthetic through the split in her skirt.

Nightshade shook his head. "Like you'd know that if you weren't married to the guy."

"My real name is Alexander Seeke," Beast said. "My father, Eric Seeke, created the company known today as Tex Strong Industries."

Chase recognized the name as did others around the table. Scizzors, Eagle, and Thanatos were the only ones who didn't look surprised by the revelation.

"Wait," Noose said, pointing at Beast. "You're a rich son of a bitch?"

"Yeah." Beast shifted uneasily in his seat as though uncomfortable talking about it. "Tex Strong Industries works on more defense contracts than any other corporation." He shifted again. "When my father died, he left me everything."

Eagle placed a hand on his shoulder. "All this to say, you're free to live with us in a heavily-fortified mansion that sits at the center of a heavily-fortified military compound."

"It's in my father's name still," Beast said, looking around the room at everyone. "So, I doubt it was in my dossier. Won't take them long to find it, but it gives us time." He leaned forward and rested his elbows on his knees.

Eagle squeezed his shoulder. "There are already hundreds of people living there. You'll all blend in."

"Not likely," Beast laughed.

That brought smiles to the table.

Widow looked to Zettabyte. "Get the message out to those we trust. Send another to the other card suits. Tell them what happened here." She turned to Scizzors. "I was already working on getting Ace out. I've made a lot of friends among the Hearts and the Diamonds. They may not be able to help much, but they could divert some heat."

Laura reached into her pocket and took out something. She handed it to Chase.

He opened his palm to see the six of spades.

"It was Powder Keg's card," she said. "He'd want you to have it."

He ran his finger along its burnt edges. "Thank you." A tear threatened to fall from his eye. He was grateful to have a piece of his uncle to carry with him wherever he went. "Does this mean I'm the Six of Spades?"

"Looks like it," Widow said, wearing a supportive smile. She turned to Scizzors. "We need to vote on an Ace. I nominate Thanatos."

"And I nominate Scizzors," said the woman who gave Laura the gun.

"Viper, I'm a monster," Scizzors said. "An Ace should be able to kill without a trace. Not my style, I'm afraid." He looked at Widow. "I nominate you."

Widow smiled. "I'll not turn it down."

"Any others?" Scizzors said, looking around the room. "Then all in favor of Thanatos?" Three people raised their hand. "All in favor of Widow?" The rest of them, including Thanatos, raised their hands. Chase did as well. He didn't know Thanatos, so the decision was easy.

"That's it, then," Scizzors said, looking at Thanatos. "Sorry, friend."

Thanatos shrugged. "No badda mi."

Scizzors stepped forward. Glass crunched under his boots. "Chase is now the Six of Spades and Widow, our Ace." He leaned down next to Ace's body and dug through bloody pockets. He pulled out a card. It was stained a permanent red. "Sorry, Widow. We'll have to get you a new one."

"Can you see the Ace of Spades?" she said from across the room.

"Barely."

She went and took it. "Thanks, love." Upon further inspection, she smirked. "I like it this way."

Scizzors let her claim it, the tips of his fingers red with

Ace's blood. "For the Guild."

The voices of those around the room responded as one: "For the Guild."

"For the Guild," Chase said after.

The feeling of belonging flooded over him. He didn't know how he could ever fill his uncle's shoes. There was far more for him to learn. He hadn't thought he could kill. But to protect Laura, he had found the part of him willing to. Although danger lurked in every direction, he didn't care what happened as long as she was with him.

As the assassins discussed amongst themselves how better to move forward, Chase left the room and wandered to his uncle's office. He closed the door and stood staring at the six of spades card. "I love you, Frank. I'm sorry you died trying to protect me." He wiped a tear from his eye. "Because of you, I can live to love Laura. This isn't exactly what I meant when I said I wanted to follow in your footsteps." He laughed, then gripped his chest in pain. He dropped back and sat ... in his uncle's recliner.

Chase gripped the arms, preparing to hurl himself from it. Then he stopped, settled in, and looked at the six of spades. "I still have pieces of you. This card and a recliner."

A knock came at the door. Laura peeked inside. "We're about to leave." She pressed her lips to the side, then asked, "You all right?"

"That depends."

"On?"

He ran his hands along the armrests of the recliner. "Whether or not we can take this with us."

ACKNOWLEDGEMENTS

Thank you to my family, who supported me through the chaos of my childhood and adulthood. I'm sort of a mess, and they have never stopped loving me. To my parents, thank you for encouraging our passion for the arts. I'm grateful to all my brothers for surrounding me with their own special, creative energy.

Jordan, thank you for being the spark that ignited the fire for this book over 20 years ago. Stephen, I appreciate you lifting me out of the muck as I neared giving up on this book and for kicking my ass back onto the road. David and Jacob, your artistic, competitive spirit inspired me, and I know both of you took the time to read this book when it was rough. I'm talkin' road to hades rough!

Priscilla has read this book approximately 197,382,456 times and still enjoys the characters. Thank you for the gift of your sharp, editorial mind and for always pushing me to improve every sentence. You are truly the reason this book reached the quality needed for publication.

I want to express my heartfelt gratitude to my wife and daughters for understanding the long hours I spend scribbling and giving me the space I need to create something new. Morgan, my love, thank you for encouraging me to explore projects outside my comfort zone. Building this life with you and our daughters has been an incredible adventure, and the stories we've created together are far more meaningful than anything I could ever write.

quite matter-of-fact about it all and so do the characters in the story, who see nothing amazing in Stuart's acting like any other person. See if you notice, as you chuckle over this tale, how often strange things are made to seem real or even ordinary. To enjoy Stuart Little, don't say " Oh, come now! You don't expect me to believe *that.*" Whistle up your imagination and go soaring away on its wings for a joy ride in the realm of make believe.

WHEN Mrs. Frederick C. Little's second son was born, everybody noticed that he was not much bigger than a mouse. The truth of the matter was, the baby looked very much like a mouse in every way. He was only about two inches high; and he had a mouse's sharp nose, a mouse's tail, a mouse's whiskers, and the pleasant, shy manner of a mouse. Before he was many days old he was not only looking like a mouse but acting like one, too — wearing a gray hat and carrying a small cane. Mr. and Mrs. Little named him Stuart, and Mr. Little made him a tiny bed out of four clothespins and a cigarette box.

Unlike most babies, Stuart could walk as soon as he was born. When he was a week old he could climb lamps by shinnying up the cord. Mrs. Little saw right away that the infant clothes she had provided were unsuitable, and she set to work and made him a fine little blue worsted suit with patch pockets in which he could keep his handkerchief, his money, and his keys. Every morning, before Stuart dressed, Mrs. Little went into his room and weighed him on a small scale which was really meant for weighing letters. At birth Stuart could have been sent by first class mail for three cents, but his parents preferred to keep him rather than send him away; and when, at the age of a month, he had gained only a third of an ounce, his mother was so worried she sent for the doctor.

The doctor was delighted with Stuart and said that it was very unusual for an American family to have a mouse. He took Stuart's temperature and found that it was 98.6, which is normal for a mouse. He also examined Stuart's chest and heart and looked into his ears solemnly with a flashlight. (Not every doctor can look into a mouse's ear without laughing.) Everything seemed to be all right, and Mrs. Little was pleased to get such a good report.

" Feed him up! " said the doctor cheerfully, as he left.

One morning when the wind was from the west, Stuart put on his sailor suit and his sailor hat, took his spyglass down from the shelf, and set out for a walk, full of the joy of life and the fear of dogs. With a rolling gait he sauntered along toward Fifth Avenue, keeping a sharp lookout.

Whenever he spied a dog through his glass, Stuart would hurry to the nearest doorman, climb his trouserleg, and hide in the tails of his uniform. And once, when no doorman was handy, he had to crawl into a yesterday's paper and roll himself up in the second section till danger was past.

At the corner of Fifth Avenue there were several people waiting for the uptown bus, and Stuart joined them. Nobody noticed him, because he wasn't tall enough to be noticed.

"I'm not tall enough to be noticed," thought Stuart, "yet I'm tall enough to want to go to Seventy-second Street."

When the bus came into view, all the men waved their canes and brief cases at the driver, and Stuart waved his spyglass. Then, knowing that the step of the bus would be too high for him, Stuart seized hold of the cuff of a gentleman's pants and was swung aboard without any trouble or inconvenience whatever.

Stuart never paid any fare on busses, because he wasn't big enough to carry an ordinary dime. The only time he had ever attempted to carry a dime, he had rolled the coin along like a hoop while he raced along beside it; but it had got away from him on a hill and had been snatched up by an old woman with no teeth. After that experience Stuart contented himself with the tiny coins which his father made for him out of tin foil. They were handsome little things, although rather hard to see without putting on your spectacles.

When the conductor came around to collect the fares, Stuart fished in his purse and pulled out a coin no bigger than the eye of a grasshopper.

"What's that you're offering me?" asked the conductor.

"It's one of my dimes," said Stuart.

"Is it, now?" said the conductor. "Well, I'd have a fine time explaining that to the bus company. Why, you're no bigger than a dime yourself."

"Yes I am," replied Stuart angrily. "I'm more than twice as big as a dime. A dime only comes up to here on me." And Stuart pointed to his hip. "Furthermore," he added, "I didn't come on this bus to be insulted."

"I beg pardon," said the conductor. "You'll have to forgive me, for I had no idea that in all the world there was such a small sailor."

"Live and learn," muttered Stuart, tartly, putting his change purse back in his pocket.

When the bus stopped at Seventy-second Street, Stuart jumped out and hurried across to the sailboat pond in Central Park. Over the pond the west wind blew, and into the teeth of the west wind sailed the sloops and schooners, their rails well down, their wet decks gleaming. The owners, boys and grown men, raced around the cement shores hoping to arrive at the other side in time to keep the boats from bumping. Some of the toy boats were not as small as you might think, for when you got close to them you found that their mainmast was taller than a man's head, and they were beautifully made, with everything shipshape and ready for sea. To Stuart they seemed enormous, and he hoped he would be able to get aboard one of them and sail away to the far corners of the pond. (He was an adventurous little fellow and loved the feel of the breeze in his face and the cry of the gulls overhead and the heave of the great swell under him.)

As he sat cross-legged on the wall

that surrounds the pond, gazing out at the ships through his spyglass, Stuart noticed one boat that seemed to him finer and prouder than any other. Her name was *Wasp*. She was a big, black schooner flying the American flag. She had a clipper bow, and on her foredeck was mounted a three-inch cannon. She's the ship for me, thought Stuart. And the next time she sailed in, he ran over to where she was being turned around.

"Excuse me, sir," said Stuart to the man who was turning her, "but are you the owner of the schooner *Wasp*?"

"I am," replied the man, surprised to be addressed by a mouse in a sailor suit.

"I'm looking for a berth [1] in a good ship," continued Stuart, "and I thought perhaps you might sign me on. I'm strong and I'm quick."

"Are you sober?" asked the owner of the *Wasp*.

"I do my work," said Stuart, crisply.

The man looked sharply at him. He couldn't help admiring the trim appearance and bold manner of this diminutive seafaring character.

"Well," he said at length, pointing the prow of the *Wasp* out toward the center of the pond, "I'll tell you what I'll do with you. You see that big racing sloop out there?"

"I do," said Stuart.

"That's the *Lillian B. Womrath*," said the man, "and I hate her with all my heart."

"Then so do I," cried Stuart, loyally.

"I hate her because she is always bumping into my boat," continued the man, "and because her owner is a lazy boy who doesn't understand sailing and who hardly knows a squall from a squid." [2]

"Or a jib from a jibe," cried Stuart.

"Or a luff from a leech," bellowed the man.

"Or a deck from a dock," screamed Stuart.

"Or a mast from a mist," yelled the man. "But hold on, now, no more of this! I'll tell you what we'll do. The *Lillian B. Womrath* has always been able to beat the *Wasp* sailing, but I believe that if my schooner were properly handled it would be a different story. Nobody knows how I suffer, standing here on shore, helpless, watching the *Wasp* blunder along, when all she needs is a steady hand on her helm. So, my young friend, I'll let you sail the *Wasp* across the pond and back, and if you can beat that detestable sloop I'll give you a regular job."

"Aye, aye, sir!" said Stuart, swinging himself aboard the schooner and taking his place at the wheel. "Ready about!"

"One moment," said the man. "Do you mind telling me *how* you propose to beat the other boat?"

"I intend to crack on more sail,"

---

[1] **berth:** the seaman's term for a job aboard ship.

[2] **a squall from a squid:** A *squall* is a windstorm. A *squid* is an underwater creature with long arms that seize and hold its victims by means of suckers. The next remarks contain similar contrasts.

said Stuart.

"Not in *my* boat, thank you," replied the man quickly. "I don't want you capsizing in a squall."

"Well, then," said Stuart, "I'll catch the sloop broad on, and rake her with fire from my forward gun."

"Foul means!" said the man. "I want this to be a boat race, not a naval engagement."

"Well, then," said Stuart cheerfully, "I'll sail the *Wasp* straight and true, and let the *Lillian B. Womrath* go yawing [1] all over the pond."

"Bravo!" cried the man, "and good luck go with you!" And so saying, he let go of the *Wasp*'s prow. A puff of air bellied out the schooner's headsails and she paid off and filled away on the port tack,[2] heeling gracefully over to the breeze while Stuart twirled her wheel and braced himself against a deck cleat.

"By the by," yelled the man, "you haven't told me your name."

[1] **yawing:** steering wildly off the course.
[2] **port tack:** *Port* is the sea term for "left," and *tack* means to sail at an angle toward the direction from which the wind blows.

"Name is Stuart Little," called Stuart at the top of his lungs. "I'm the second son of Frederick C. Little, of this city."

"*Bon voyage*, Stuart," hollered his friend, "take care of yourself and bring the *Wasp* home safe."

"That I will," shouted Stuart. And he was so proud and happy, he let go of the wheel for a second and did a little dance on the sloping deck, never noticing how narrowly he escaped hitting a tramp steamer that was drifting in his path, with her engines disabled and her decks awash.

When the people in Central Park learned that one of the toy sailboats was being steered by a mouse in a sailor suit, they all came running. Soon the shores of the pond were so crowded that a policeman was sent from headquarters to announce that everybody would have to stop pushing, but nobody did. People in New York like to push each other. The most excited person of all was the boy who owned the *Lillian B. Womrath*. He was a fat, sulky boy of twelve, named LeRoy. He wore a blue serge suit and a white necktie stained with orange juice.

"Come back here!" he called to Stuart. "Come back here and get on *my* boat. I want you to steer *my* boat. I will pay you five dollars a week and you can have every Thursday afternoon off and a radio in your room."

"I thank you for your kind offer," replied Stuart, "but I am happy aboard the *Wasp* — happier than I have ever been before in all my life." And with that he spun the wheel over

smartly and headed his schooner
down toward the starting line, where
LeRoy was turning his boat around
by poking it with a long stick, ready
for the start of the race.

"I'll be the referee," said a man in
a bright green suit. "Is the *Wasp*
ready?"

"Ready, sir!" shouted Stuart,
touching his hat.

"Is the *Lillian B. Womrath*
ready?" asked the referee.

"Sure, I'm ready," said LeRoy.

"To the north end of the pond and
back again!" shouted the referee.
"On your mark, get set, GO!"

"Go!" cried the people along the
shore.

"Go!" cried the owner of the
Wasp.

"Go!" yelled the policeman.

And away went the two boats for
the north end of the pond, while the
sea gulls wheeled and cried overhead
and the taxicabs tooted and honked
from Seventy-second Street and the
west wind (which had come halfway
across America to get to Central Park)
sang and whistled in the rigging and
blew spray across the decks, stinging
Stuart's cheeks with tiny fragments

of flying peanut shell tossed up from
the foamy deep. "This is the life for
me!" Stuart murmured to himself.
"What a ship! What a day! What a
race!"

Before the two boats had gone
many feet, however, an accident happened on shore. The people were
pushing each other harder and harder
in their eagerness to see the sport, and
although they really didn't mean to,
they pushed the policeman so hard
they pushed him right off the concrete wall and into the pond. He hit
the water in a sitting position, and
got wet clear up to the third button
of his jacket. He was soaked.

This particular policeman was not
only a big, heavy man, but he had
just eaten a big, heavy meal, and the
wave he made went curling outward,
cresting and billowing, upsetting all
manner of small craft and causing
every owner of a boat on the pond to
scream with delight and consternation.

When Stuart saw the great wave
approaching he jumped for the rigging, but he was too late. Towering
above the *Wasp* like a mountain, the
wave came crashing and piling along
the deck, caught Stuart up and swept
him over the side and into the water,
where everybody supposed he would

drown. Stuart had no intention of drowning. He kicked hard with his feet, and thrashed hard with his tail, and in a minute or two he climbed back aboard the schooner, cold and wet but quite unharmed. As he took his place at the helm, he could hear people cheering for him and calling, "Atta mouse, Stuart! Atta mouse!" He looked over and saw that the wave had capsized the *Lillian B. Womrath* but that she had righted herself and was sailing on her course, close by. And she stayed close alongside till both boats reached the north end of the pond. Here Stuart put the *Wasp* about and LeRoy turned the *Lillian* around with his stick, and away the two boats went for the finish line.

"This race isn't over yet," thought Stuart.

The first warning he had that there was trouble ahead came when he glanced into the *Wasp*'s cabin and observed that the barometer had fallen sharply. That can mean only one thing at sea — dirty weather. Suddenly a dark cloud swept across the sun, blotting it out and leaving the earth in shadow. Stuart shivered in his wet clothes. He turned up his sailor blouse closer around his neck, and when he spied the *Wasp*'s owner among the crowd on shore he waved his hat and called out:

"Dirty weather ahead, sir! Wind backing into the southwest, seas confused, glass falling."

"Never mind the weather!" cried the owner. "Watch out for flotsam [1] dead ahead!"

Stuart peered ahead into the gathering storm, but saw nothing except gray waves with white crests. The world semed cold and ominous. Stuart glanced behind him. There came the sloop, boiling along fast, rolling up a bow wave [2] and gaining steadily.

"Look out, Stuart! Look out where you're going!"

Stuart strained his eyes, and suddenly, dead ahead, right in the path of the *Wasp*, he saw an enormous paper bag looming up on the surface of the pond. The bag was empty and riding high, its open end gaping wide like the mouth of a cave. Stuart spun the wheel over but it was too late: the *Wasp* drove her bowsprit straight into the bag and with a fearful *whooosh* the schooner slowed down and came up into the wind with all sails flapping. Just at this moment Stuart heard a splintering crash, saw the bow of the *Lillian* plow through his rigging, and felt the whole ship tremble from stem to stern with the force of the collision.

"A collision!" shouted the crowd on shore.

In a jiffy the two boats were in a terrible tangle. Little boys on shore screamed and danced up and down. Meanwhile the paper bag sprang a leak and began to fill.

The *Wasp* couldn't move because of the bag. The *Lillian B. Womrath* couldn't move because her nose was stuck in the *Wasp*'s rigging.

Waving his arms, Stuart ran forward and fired off his gun. Then he

---

[1] **flotsam**: trash floating on the water.

[2] **bow** (bou) **wave**: a wave thrown up at the bow, or front, of a ship.

heard, above the other voices on shore, the voice of the owner of the *Wasp* yelling directions and telling him what to do.

"Stuart! Stuart! Down jib! Down staysail!"

Stuart jumped for the halyards, and the jib and the forestaysail came rippling down.

"Cut away all paper bags!" roared the owner.

Stuart whipped out his pocketknife and slashed away bravely at the soggy bag until he had the deck cleared.

"Now back your foresail and give her a full!" screamed the owner of the *Wasp*.

Stuart grabbed the foresail boom and pulled with all his might. Slowly the schooner paid off and began to gather headway. And as she heeled over to the breeze she rolled her rail out from under the *Lillian*'s nose, shook herself free, and stood away to the southard. A loud cheer went up from the bank. Stuart sprang to the wheel and answered it. Then he looked back, and to his great joy he perceived that the *Lillian* had gone off in a wild direction and was yawing all over the pond.

Straight and true sailed the *Wasp*, with Stuart at the helm. After she had crossed the finish line, Stuart brought her alongside the wall, and was taken ashore and highly praised for his fine seamanship and daring. The owner was delighted and said it was the happiest day of his life. He introduced himself to Stuart, said that in private life he was Dr. Paul Carey, a surgeon-dentist. He said model boats were his hobby and that he would be delighted to have Stuart take command of his vessel at any time. Everybody shook hands with Stuart — everybody, that is, except the policeman, who was too wet and mad to shake hands with a mouse.

When Stuart got home that night, his brother George asked him where he had been all day.

"Oh, knocking around town," replied Stuart.

Accepting Impossible Happenings in Fantasy

1. What attitude did his family take toward Stuart? How did the people in the story behave when they met him around the city?

2. How did Stuart get the job of sailing the *Wasp*? What is funny about the *Wasp*'s owner asking Stuart, "Are you sober?"

3. What parts of the story sound exactly like a model sailboat race on a pond? What parts sound like a real sea adventure?

4. Describe Stuart Little's personality as it shows up in this incident. How does his answer to his brother's question at the end fit with your impression?

Seafaring Terms

Did you enjoy the sea flavor of this story? The author had a lot of fun imitating the salty talk you usually find in books of adventurous seafaring. Stuart Little, like the heroes in sea stories, "loved the feel of the breeze . . . and the heave of the great swell under him." See if you can match Stuart as a sailor, or at any rate, as a reader of sea tales. On page 253, the first two terms are explained in the footnote. Try to guess the meaning of the others and then check yourself by looking in a dictionary. Also check the meaning of *capsize*, *bon voyage* (be sure to give this phrase a French pronunciation!), and *barometer*.

The Ballad of the Harp-Weaver

EDNA ST. VINCENT MILLAY

Fantasy is not always humorous. Often it is grim and sorrowful, as in this poem by a famous modern writer. This is as strange a tale as you will ever hear. It is told in plain words, very simply and directly, but the effect is far from simple. In your mind it will create weird and shadowy pictures and you may find yourself puzzled by the meaning of the story. The first time you read the poem don't worry about the exact meaning; just follow your imagination wherever it goes.

"Son," said my mother,
   When I was knee-high,
"You've need of clothes to cover you,
   And not a rag have I."

"There's nothing in the house   5
   To make a boy breeches,
Nor shears to cut a cloth with
   Nor thread to take stitches.

"There's nothing in the house
   But a loaf-end of rye,   10
And a harp with a woman's head

Nobody will buy,"
   And she began to cry.

That was in the early fall.
   When came the late fall,   15
"Son," she said, "the sight of you
   Makes your mother's blood
     crawl —

"Little skinny shoulder blades
   Sticking through your clothes!
And where you'll get a jacket from   20
   God above knows.

"It's lucky for me, lad,
   Your daddy's in the ground,
And can't see the way I let
   His son go around!"   25
And she made a queer sound.

That was in the late fall.
   When the winter came,
I'd not a pair of breeches
   Nor a shirt to my name.   30

I couldn't go to school,
   Or out of doors to play.
And all the other little boys
   Passed our way.

"Son," said my mother,   35
  "Come, climb into my lap,
And I'll chafe your little bones
  While you take a nap."

And, oh, but we were silly
  For half an hour or more,   40
Me with my long legs
  Dragging on the floor,

A-rock-rock-rocking
  To a mother-goose rhyme!
Oh, but we were happy   45
  For half an hour's time!

But there was I, a great boy,
  And what would folks say
To hear my mother singing me
  To sleep all day,   50
  In such a daft way?

Men say the winter
  Was bad that year;
Fuel was scarce,
  And food was dear.   55

A wind with a wolf's head
  Howled about our door,
And we burned up the chairs
  And sat upon the floor.

All that was left us   60
  Was a chair we couldn't break,
And the harp with a woman's head
  Nobody would take,
  For song or pity's sake.

The night before Christmas   65
  I cried with the cold,
I cried myself to sleep
  Like a two-year-old.

And in the deep night
  I felt my mother rise,   70
And stare down upon me
  With love in her eyes.

I saw my mother sitting
  On the one good chair,
A light falling on her   75
  From I couldn't tell where,

Looking nineteen,
  And not a day older,
And the harp with a woman's head
  Leaned against her shoulder. 80

Her thin fingers, moving
  In the thin, tall strings,
Were weav-weav-weaving
  Wonderful things.

Many bright threads,   85
  From where I couldn't see,
Were running through the harp-
    strings
  Rapidly,

And gold threads whistling
  Through my mother's hand. 90
I saw the web grow,
  And the pattern expand.

She wove a child's jacket,
  And when it was done
She laid it on the floor   95
  And wove another one.

She wove a red cloak
  So regal to see,
"She's made it for a king's son,"
  I said, "and not for me." 100
  But I knew it was for me.

She wove a pair of breeches
   Quicker than that!
She wove a pair of boots
   And a little cocked hat.   105

She wove a pair of mittens,
   She wove a little blouse,
She wove all night
   In the still, cold house.

She sang as she worked,   110
   And the harp-strings spoke;
Her voice never faltered,
   And the thread never broke.
   And when I awoke —

There sat my mother   115
   With the harp against her shoulder,
Looking nineteen
   And not a day older,

A smile about her lips,
   And a light about her head,   120

And her hands in the harp-strings
   Frozen dead.

And piled up beside her
   And toppling to the skies,
Were the clothes of a king's son,   125
   Just my size.

A Strange Tale

1. Almost everyone asks, the first time he reads this poem: Did the mother actually weave clothes for her son? Read the poem a second time, and then discuss the answer with others in the class. Refer to particular lines to make clear how you arrived at an opinion.

2. How could a harp be used for weaving, even in an imaginary way?

3. The harp was the only expensive thing the mother owned. In what way do you think it proved valuable to her in the end?

4. Read aloud stanzas in the poem that you particularly like, either for the music of the words or the pictures they create in your mind. Some class members can join forces to give a group reading of the poem, after practicing with the teacher's help.

An Encounter
with an Interviewer

MARK TWAIN

If you have read the television play based on *Tom Sawyer,* on page 127, or better, if you have read that novel, you know something about Mark Twain's sense of humor. Would you like to interview him — on a morning when he felt like having a little fun? Then you must not be as serious as this reporter!

"An Encounter with an Interviewer," from *Tom Sawyer Abroad,* by Mark Twain. Reprinted by permission of Harper and Brothers.

THE nervous, dapper, "peart" young man took the chair I offered him, and said he was connected with the *Daily Thunderstorm,* and added:

"Hoping it's no harm, I've come to interview you."

"Come to what?"

"*Interview* you."

"Ah! I see. Yes — yes. Um! Yes — yes."

I was not feeling bright that morning. Indeed, my powers seemed a bit under a cloud. However, I went to the bookcase, and when I had been looking six or seven minutes, I found I was obliged to refer to the young man. I said:

"How do you spell it?"

"Spell what?"

"Interview."

"Oh, my goodness! What do you want to spell it for?"

"I don't want to spell it; I want to see what it means."

"Well, this is astonishing, I must say. I can tell you what it means, if you — if you —"

"Oh, all right! That will answer, and much obliged to you, too."

"In, *in,* ter, *ter, inter* —"

"Then you spell it with an *I?*"

"Why, certainly!"

"Oh, that is what took me so long."

"Why, my *dear* sir, what did *you* propose to spell it with?"

"Well, I — I — hardly know. I had the Unabridged, and I was ciphering around in the back end, hoping I might tree her among the pictures. But it's a very old edition."

"Why, my friend, they wouldn't have a *picture* of it in even the latest e — My dear sir, I beg your pardon, I mean no harm in the world, but you do not look as — as — intelligent as I had expected you would. No harm — I mean no harm at all."

"Oh, don't mention it! It has often been said, and by people who would not flatter and who could have no inducement to flatter, that I am quite remarkable in that way. Yes — yes, they always speak of it with rapture."

"I can easily imagine it. But about this interview. You know it is the custom, now, to interview any man who has become notorious."[1]

"Indeed, I had not heard of it before. It must be very interesting. What do you do it with?"

"Ah, well — well — well — this is disheartening. It *ought* to be done with a club in some cases; but customarily it consists in the interviewer asking questions and the interviewed answering them. It is all the rage now. Will you let me ask you certain questions calculated to bring out the salient[2] points of your public and private history?"

"Oh, with pleasure — with pleasure. I have a very bad memory but I hope you will not mind that. That is to say, it is an irregular memory — singularly irregular. Sometimes it goes in a gallop, and then again it will be as much as a fortnight passing a given point. This is a great grief to me."

[1] **notorious:** famous in an unpleasant way.
[2] **salient** (sā′lĭ·ĕnt): prominent.

"Oh, it is no matter, so you will try to do the best you can."

"I will. I will put my whole mind on it."

"Thanks. Are you ready to begin?"

"Ready."

Q. How old are you?

A. Nineteen, in June.

Q. Indeed? I would have taken you to be thirty-five or six. Where were you born?

A. In Missouri.

Q. When did you begin to write?

A. In 1836.

Q. Why, how could that be, if you are only nineteen now?

A. I don't know. It does seem curious, somehow.

Q. It does, indeed. Whom do you consider the most remarkable man you ever met?

A. Aaron Burr.

Q. But you never could have met Aaron Burr, if you are only nineteen years —

A. Now, if you know more about me than I do, what do you ask me for?

Q. Well, it was only a suggestion; nothing more. How did you happen to meet Burr?

A. Well, I happened to be at his funeral one day, and he asked me to make less noise, and —

Q. But, good heavens! If you were at his funeral, he must have been dead; and if he was dead, how could he care whether you made a noise or not?

A. I don't know. He was always a particular kind of a man that way.

Q. Still, I don't understand it at all. You say he spoke to you, and that he was dead.

A. I didn't say he was dead.

Q. But wasn't he dead?

A. Well, some said he was, some said he wasn't.

Q. What did you think?

A. Oh, it was none of my business! It wasn't any of my funeral.

Q. Did you — However, we can never get this matter straight. Let me ask about something else. What was the date of your birth?

A. Monday, October 31, 1693.

Q. What! Impossible! That would make you a hundred and eighty years old. How do you account for that?

A. I don't account for it at all.

Q. But you said at first you were only nineteen, and now you make yourself to be one hundred and eighty. It is an awful discrepancy.[1]

A. Why, have you noticed that? (*Shaking hands.*) Many a time it has seemed to me like a discrepancy, but somehow I couldn't make up my mind. How quick you notice a thing!

Q. Thank you for the compliment, as far as it goes. Had you, or have you, any brothers or sisters?

A. Eh! I — I — I think so — yes — but I don't remember.

Q. Well, that is the most extraordinary statement I ever heard!

A. Why, what makes you think that?

Q. How could I think otherwise? Why, look here! Who is this a picture of on the wall? Isn't that a brother of yours?

[1] **discrepancy** (dĭs·krĕp′ăn·sĭ) : failure to agree.

A. Oh! Yes, yes, yes! Now you remind me of it; that *was* a brother of mine. That's William — *Bill,* we called him. Poor old Bill!

Q. Why? Is he dead, then?

A. Ah! Well, I suppose so. We never could tell. There was a great mystery about it.

Q. That is sad, very sad. He disappeared, then?

A. Well, yes, in a sort of general way. We buried him.

Q. *Buried* him! *Buried* him, without knowing whether he was dead or not?

A. Oh, no! Not that. He was dead enough.

Q. Well, I confess that I can't understand this. If you buried him, and you knew he was dead —

A. No! No! We only thought he was.

Q. Oh, I see! He came to life again?

A. I bet he didn't.

Q. Well, I never heard anything like this. *Somebody* was dead. *Somebody* was buried. Now, where was the mystery?

A. Ah! that's just it! That's it exactly. You see, we were twins — defunct [1] and I — and we got mixed in the bathtub when we were only two weeks old, and one of us was drowned. But we didn't know which. Some think it was Bill. Some think it was me.

Q. Well, that *is* remarkable. What do *you* think?

A. Goodness knows! I would give whole worlds to know. This solemn,

[1] **defunct:** the dead one.

this awful mystery has cast a gloom over my whole life. But I will tell you a secret now, which I never revealed to any creature before. One of us had a peculiar mark — a large mole on the back of his left hand; that was *me.* *That child was the one that was drowned!*

Q. Very well, then, I don't see that there is any mystery about it, after all.

A. You don't? Well, *I* do. Anyway, I don't see how they could ever have been such a blundering lot as to go and bury the wrong child. But, 'sh! — don't mention it where the family can hear it. Heaven knows they have heartbreaking troubles enough without adding this.

Q. Well, I believe I have got material enough for the present, and I am very much obliged to you for the pains you have taken. But I was a good deal interested in that account of Aaron Burr's funeral. Would you mind telling me what particular circumstance it was that made you think Burr was such a remarkable man?

A. Oh! it was a mere trifle! Not one man in fifty would have noticed it at all. When the sermon was over, and the procession all ready to start for the cemetery, and the body all arranged nice in the hearse, he said he wanted to take a last look at the scenery, and so *he got up and rode with the driver.*

Then the young man reverently withdrew. He was very pleasant company, and I was sorry to see him go.

Questions and Answers

1. How did Mark Twain first upset the interviewer? How did he tangle up the reporter about his age?

2. What was odd about Aaron Burr's funeral, as Mark Twain tells it?

3. Why doesn't he know whether he is himself or his brother Bill?

4. Discuss whether you think interviews would be boring or interesting to famous people like Mark Twain. What is there in the reporter's manner that might have led Mark Twain to tell tall tales?

5. This yarn is mostly conversation and would make a good radio skit. Let two class members read the parts in play form. The reporter should speak in a serious tone, but let Mark Twain exaggerate his part by using a drawl and acting puzzled at times.

Putting Words in Reverse

Did you know that you can make familiar words lead a double life and work overtime for you? By adding three prefixes to words you can make them have an opposite meaning. Mark Twain used all three in his tall-tale interview. Everybody knows *un-*, meaning "not," as in *unabridged*. A trickier form is *in-*, which sometimes politely changes its *n* to match the first letter of the main word. This happens most often before *r*, as in *irregular*, and before *l*, as in *illegal*. The prefix *dis-* also has a negative meaning, "taking something away." *Disheartening* illustrates this meaning, and so does *disappear*.

Practice using these prefixes by combining them with the words in this list. Some of the words can be used with two of the prefixes, each resulting in a slightly different meaning.

fair	able
quiet	logical
like	rational
arm (ed)	loyal
literate	respect
courage (Careful! There's a booby trap in this one!)	

A Scientific Note

DON MARQUIS

The sharp eye of Don Marquis, a newspaperman who was also a poet, caught a little news item. His wonderful sense of humor played with it. His love of fancy rhymes embroidered it. You'll enjoy the result!

The transplanting of bones in the human body is entirely possible. — *News Story*

I fell from out an airy-o-plane
And hit a railway track,
And lay there thinking while a train
Ran up and down my back;
It shattered me, it battered me,   5
It made my hair turn gray,
It somewhat widely scattered me
Along the right of way;
It lifted me, it sifted me,
It flung me here and there,   10
It rather broadly drifted me;
It raveled me, it graveled me,
It sprayed me through the air —
In short, the well-known firm of Krupp°
By shooting cannon at a pup   15
Would scarcely more have used him up.

The docs inspected parts of me,
The docs collected parts of me,
The docs rejected parts of me,
And those selected parts of me   20
They scratched 'em up and patched 'em up —
(Except infected parts of me) —
And went to work and matched 'em up.

But bones of me and scruff of me
And soft of me and tough of me   25
They couldn't find enough of me,
And so they took much-shredded me,
Those surgeons, and they wedded me
Unto the remnants of a zoo,
And part of me is really me and part of me is kangaroo —   30
Is elephants and cormorants and dodo birds and skinks,°
Is gulls and whales and dolphins' tails and jaguars and minks —
And femurs°
Out of lemurs,

14. **Krupp**: German makers of guns and cannon. 31. **skinks**: small lizards. 33. **femurs** (fē′mĕrz): thighbones.

And eyelids from a lynx —   35
And bones and things and ribs and wings from simian° sort of ginks.

They welded 'em and melded 'em and wished 'em into me,
They lopped at 'em and chopped at 'em and swished 'em into me,
They toiled at them and boiled at them and dished 'em into me —
They fixed me up and mixed me up   40
And joined me with a zoo,
And part of me is really me —
But some is kangaroo!

And now when I go down the street
Strange instincts move my leaping feet   45
Of kangaroo and cockatoo and bear and parakeet,
And now and then I utter cries in strange outlandish tones;
Upon my soul, I can't control my yelps and jumps and moans,
Because the surgeons bungled me,
Because the surgeons jungled me,   50
And left the fires of wild desires a-burning in my bones!
For only part of me is me and part is something else,

For some of me is ostriches and some of me is smelts,°
And some of me is human hide and some of me is pelts!
And sometimes it's embarrassing,   55
Most awful so, and harassing,
But mostly I endeavor not to take it very sad —
The only thing that jolts me much,
The only way I get in Dutch,
The only time my spirits sag,   60
Is when I feel compelled to wag
A score or so of spectral° tails I never really had.

36. simian (sĭm′ĭ·ăn): an ape or monkey. 53. smelts: small fish. 62. spectral: ghostly.

Birth of a Tall Tale
1. How did the news item start the poet's imagination on this tall tale?
2. Why did he need to have such a terrible accident to begin his tale?
3. How many animals contributed parts to patch him up? Why do you think the author put in so many?
4. What sort of troubles does he have, now that he is in action again?
5. Why is this tale funnier in rhyme than it would be in prose?

The Legend
of Sleepy Hollow

WASHINGTON IRVING

Some places seem made for ghosts to haunt, and some people are always seeing ghosts in any dark spot. Put the two together and you get America's best-loved ghost story. It was told by Washington Irving, whom you already know as the author of " Rip Van Winkle."

Irving grew up in the Hudson Valley of New York, where the Dutch had settled before the English came. He loved to write of the quaint customs and tales he learned in his youth. He makes fun of the solid Dutch farmers in a gentle way, but it is easy to see, in the shortened version of the story that follows, that he was very fond of them.

IN THE bosom of one of those spacious coves which indent the eastern shore of the Hudson, there lies a small market town which by some is called Greensburgh, but which is more generally and properly known by the name of Tarrytown. This name was given by the good housewives of the adjacent country, from the tendency of their husbands to linger about the village tavern on market days. Not far from this village, perhaps about two miles, there is a little valley among high hills, which is one of the quietest places in the whole world. A small brook glides through it, with just murmur enough to lull one to repose; and the occasional whistle of a quail, or tapping of a woodpecker, is almost the only sound that ever breaks in upon the uniform tranquillity.

From the listless repose of the place, and the peculiar character of its inhabitants, who are descendants from the original Dutch settlers, this glen has long been known by the name of Sleepy Hollow, and its lads are called the Sleepy Hollow Boys throughout all the neighboring country. A drowsy, dreamy influence seems to hang over the land. The whole neighborhood abounds with local tales, haunted spots, and twilight superstitions; and the nightmare seems to make it the favorite scene of her gambols.

The dominant spirit, however, that haunts this enchanted region, and seems to be commander in chief of all the powers of the air, is the apparition of a figure on horseback without a head. It is said by some to be the ghost of a Hessian trooper [1] whose head had been carried away by a can-

---

[1] **Hessian** (hĕsh'ăn) **troopers** were German soldiers hired by the British to fight the Americans during the Revolution.

non ball, in some nameless battle during the Revolutionary War; and who is ever and anon seen by the country folk, hurrying along in the gloom of night, as if on the wings of the wind. His haunts are not confined to the valley, but extend at times to the adjacent roads, and especially to the vicinity of a church at no great distance. Certain historians of those parts claim that the body of the trooper having been buried in the churchyard, the ghost rides forth to the scene of battle in nightly quest of his head; and that the rushing speed with which he sometimes passes along the Hollow, like a midnight blast, is owing to his being late, and in a hurry to get back to the churchyard before daybreak. The specter is known, at all the country firesides, by the name of the Headless Horseman of Sleepy Hollow.

In this by-place of nature, there abode, some thirty years since, a worthy fellow of the name of Ichabod Crane; who sojourned, or, as he expressed it, "tarried," in Sleepy Hollow, for the purpose of instructing the children of the vicinity. The name of Crane was not inapplicable to his person. He was tall, but exceedingly lank, with narrow shoulders, long arms and legs, hands that dangled a mile out of his sleeves, feet that might have served for shovels, and his whole frame most loosely hung together. His head was small, and flat at top, with huge ears, large green glassy eyes, and a long snipe nose, so that it looked like a weathercock, perched upon his spindle neck, to tell which way the wind blew. To see him striding along the profile of a hill on a windy day, with his clothes bagging and fluttering about him, one might have mistaken him for the spirit of famine descending upon the earth, or some scarecrow eloped from a cornfield.

His schoolhouse was a low building of one large room, rudely constructed of logs; the windows partly glazed,[1] and partly patched with leaves of old copybooks. It stood in a rather lonely but pleasant situation, just at the foot of a woody hill, with a brook running close by, and a formidable birch tree growing at one end of it. From hence, the low murmur of his pupils' voices, conning over their lessons, might be heard in a drowsy summer's day, like the hum of a beehive; interrupted now and then by the authoritative voice of the master, in the tone of menace or command; or, perhaps by the appalling sound of the birch,[2] as he urged some tardy loiterer along the flowery path of knowledge. Truth to say, he was a conscientious man, and ever bore in mind the golden maxim, "Spare the rod and spoil the child." Ichabod Crane's scholars certainly were not spoiled.

I would not have it imagined, however, that he was one of those cruel tyrants of the school, who joy in the smart of their subjects. On the contrary, he administered justice with discrimination rather than severity,

[1] **glazed:** glassed.
[2] **birch:** the stick or rod with which he punished his pupils.

taking the burden off the backs of the weak and laying it on those of the strong. Your mere puny stripling, that winced at the least flourish of the rod, was passed by. The claims of justice were satisfied by inflicting a double portion on some little, tough, wrong-headed, broad-skirted Dutch urchin, who sulked and swelled and grew dogged and sullen beneath the birch. All this he called "doing his duty by their parents," and he never inflicted a chastisement without following it by the assurance, so consoling to the smarting urchin, that "he would remember it, and thank him for it the longest day he had to live."

When school hours were over, he was even the companion and playmate of the larger boys; and on holiday afternoons would convoy some of the smaller ones home who happened to have pretty sisters, or good housewives for mothers, noted for the comforts of the cupboard. Indeed it behooved him to keep on good terms with his pupils. The revenue arising from his school was small, and would have been scarcely sufficient to furnish him with daily bread, for he was a huge feeder. To help out his maintenance, he was, according to country custom in those parts, boarded and lodged at the houses of the farmers whose children he instructed. With these he lived successively a week at a time; thus going the rounds of the neighborhood, with all his worldly effects tied up in a cotton handkerchief.

That all this might not be too hard on the purses of his patrons, who are apt to consider the costs of schooling a grievous burden, and schoolmasters as mere drones, he had various ways of rendering himself both useful and agreeable. He assisted the farmers occasionally in the lighter labors of their farms; helped to make hay; mended the fences; took the horses to water; drove the cows from pasture; and cut wood for the winter fire. He found favor in the eyes of the mothers by petting the children, particularly the youngest. He would sit with a child on one knee, and rock a cradle with his foot for whole hours together.

In addition to his other vocations, he was the singing master of the neighborhood, and picked up many bright shillings by instructing the young folks in psalmody.[1] It was a matter of no little vanity to him, on Sundays, to take his station in front of the church gallery, with a band of chosen singers; where, in his own mind, he completely carried away the palm from the parson. Certain it is, his voice resounded far above all the rest of the congregation; and there are peculiar quavers still to be heard in that church, and even half a mile off, quite to the opposite side of the millpond, on a still Sunday morning, which are said to be descended from the nose of Ichabod Crane. Thus, by various little makeshifts, the worthy pedagogue [2] got on tolerably enough, and was thought, by all who understood nothing of the labor of headwork, to have a wonder-

---

[1] **psalmody** (säm'ŏ·dĭ): singing of psalms.
[2] **pedagogue** (pĕd'á·gŏg): a schoolteacher.

fully easy life of it.

The schoolmaster is generally a man of some importance in the female circle of a rural neighborhood, vastly superior to the rough country swains, and, indeed, inferior in learning only to the parson. Our man of letters, therefore, was peculiarly happy in the smiles of all the country damsels. How he would figure among them in the churchyard, between services on Sundays gathering grapes for them from the wild vines that overran the surrounding trees; reciting for their amusement all the epitaphs on the tombstones; or sauntering, with a whole bevy [1] of them, along the banks of the adjacent millpond; while the more bashful country bumpkins hung sheepishly back, envying his superior elegance and address. [2]

From his half-itinerant life, also, he was a kind of traveling gazette, carrying the whole budget of local gossip from house to house; so that his appearance was always greeted with satisfaction. He was, moreover, esteemed by the women as a man of great learning, for he had read several books quite through, and was a perfect master of Cotton Mather's *History of New England Witchcraft*, [3] in which, by the way, he most firmly believed.

He was, in fact, an odd mixture of small shrewdness and simple credulity. His appetite for the marvelous, and his powers of digesting it, were equally extraordinary; and both had been increased by his residence in this spellbound region. It was often his delight, after his school was dismissed in the afternoon, to stretch himself on the rich bed of clover bordering the little brook that whimpered by his schoolhouse, and there con over old Mather's direful tales, until the gathering dusk of the evening made the printed page a mere mist before his eyes. Then, as he took his way, by swamp and stream and awful woodland, to the farmhouse where he happened to be quartered, every sound of nature, at that witching hour, fluttered his excited imagination: the moan of the whippoorwill from the hillside; the boding cry of the tree toad; the dreary hooting of the screech owl, or the sudden rustling in the thicket of birds frightened from their roost. His only resource on such occasions, either to drown thought, or drive away evil spirits, was to sing psalm tunes; and the good people of Sleepy Hollow, as they sat by their doors of an evening, were often filled with awe, at hearing his nasal melody floating from the distant hill, or along the dusky road.

Another of his sources of fearful pleasure was to pass long winter evenings with the old Dutch wives, as they sat spinning by the fire, with a row of apples roasting and spluttering along the hearth, and listen to their marvelous tales of ghosts and goblins, and haunted fields, and haunted brooks, and haunted bridges,

[1] **bevy** (bĕv′ĭ): group.
[2] **address:** manner of speaking.
[3] In Cotton Mather's time, around 1700, witches were taken very seriously, and Mather, a preacher and a scholar, thoroughly believed in them.

What fearful shapes and shadows beset his path amidst the dim and ghastly glare of a snowy night! How often was he appalled by some shrub covered with snow, which, like a sheeted specter, beset his very path! How often did he shrink with curdling awe at the sound of his own steps on the frosty crust beneath his feet, and dread to look over his shoulder, lest he should behold some uncouth being tramping close behind him! And how often was he thrown into complete dismay by some rushing blast, howling among the trees, in the idea that it was the Galloping Hessian on one of his nightly scourings!

All these, however, were mere terrors of the night, phantoms of the mind that walk in darkness; and though he had seen many specters in his time, yet daylight put an end to all these evils. He would have passed a pleasant life of it, if his path had not been crossed by a being that causes more perplexity to mortal man than ghosts, goblins, and the whole race of witches put together, and that was — a woman.

and haunted houses, and particularly of the headless horseman, or Galloping Hessian of the Hollow, as they sometimes called him. He would delight them by his anecdotes of witchcraft, and would frighten them woefully with speculations upon comets and shooting stars, and with the alarming fact that the world did absolutely turn round, and that they were half the time topsy-turvy!

But if there was a pleasure in all this, while snugly cuddling in the chimney corner of a chamber that was all of a ruddy glow from the crackling wood fire, and where, of course, no specter dared to show his face, it was dearly purchased by the terrors of his walk homeward later.

Among the musical disciples who assembled, one evening in each week, to receive his instructions in psalmody was Katrina Van Tassel, the daughter and only child of a prosperous Dutch farmer. She was a blooming lass of fresh eighteen; plump as a partridge; ripe and melting and rosy-cheeked as one of her father's peaches; and universally famed, not merely as a beauty, but as an heiress. She was withal a little of a coquette, as might be perceived even in her dress, which was a mixture of ancient and modern fashions, as most suited to set off her charms. She wore the ornaments of pure yellow gold which her great-great-grandmother had brought over from Holland, the tempting stomacher of the olden time, and a provokingly short petticoat, to display the prettiest foot and ankle in the country round.

Ichabod Crane had a soft and foolish heart toward the sex; and it is not to be wondered at that so tempting a morsel soon found favor in his eyes, more especially after he had visited her in her paternal mansion. Old Baltus Van Tassel was a perfect picture of a thriving, contented, liberal-hearted farmer. He was satisfied with his wealth, but not proud of it, and prided himself upon the hearty abundance, rather than the style in which he lived. His stronghold was situated on the banks of the Hudson, in one of those green, sheltered, fertile nooks, in which the Dutch farmers are so fond of nestling. A great elm tree spread its broad branches over it, at the foot of which bubbled up a spring of the softest and sweetest water, in a little well formed of a barrel. Close by the farmhouse was a vast barn that might have served for a church, every window and crevice of which seemed bursting forth with the treasures of the farm. Rows of pigeons were enjoying the sunshine on the roof. Sleek unwieldy porkers were grunting in the repose and abundance of their pens. A stately squadron of snowy geese were riding in an adjoining pond, convoying whole fleets of ducks. Regiments of turkeys were gobbling through the farmyard, and guinea fowls fretting about it, like ill-tempered housewives, with their peevish, discontented cry. Before the barn door strutted the gallant cock, clapping his burnished wings, and crowing in the pride and gladness of his heart — sometimes tearing up the earth with his feet, and then generously calling his ever-hungry family of wives and children to enjoy the rich morsel which he had discovered.

The pedagogue's mouth watered as he looked upon this sumptuous promise of luxurious winter fare. In his devouring mind's eye he pictured to himself every roasting-pig running about with a pudding in his belly, and an apple in his mouth. The pigeons were snugly put to bed in a comfortable pie, and tucked in with a coverlet of crust; the geese were swimming in their own gravy; and the ducks pairing cozily in dishes with a decent competency of onion sauce. In the porkers he saw carved out the future sleek side of bacon, and juicy, relishing ham; not a turkey but he beheld daintily trussed up, with its giz-

zard under its wing, and perhaps a necklace of savory sausages; and even bright chanticleer [1] himself lay sprawling on his back, in a side dish, with uplifted claws. As the enraptured Ichabod fancied all this, and as he rolled his great green eyes over the fat meadowlands, the rich fields of wheat, of rye, of buckwheat, and Indian corn, and the orchards burdened with ruddy fruit which surrounded the warm tenement [2] of Van Tassel, his heart yearned after the damsel who was to inherit these domains.

When he entered the house the conquest of his heart was complete. It was one of those spacious farmhouses, with high-ridged but lowly-sloping roofs, built in the style handed down from the first Dutch settlers; the low, projecting eaves forming a piazza along the front, capable of being closed up in bad weather. Under this were hung flails, harness, various utensils of husbandry, and nets for fishing in the neighboring river. Benches were built along the sides for summer use; and a great spinning wheel at one end, and a churn at the other, showed the various uses to which this important porch might be devoted. From this piazza the wondering Ichabod entered the hall, which formed the center of the mansion and the place of usual residence. Here rows of resplendent pewter, ranged on a long dresser, dazzled his eyes. In one corner stood a huge bag of wool ready to be spun; in another

a quantity of linsey-woolsey just from the loom; ears of Indian corn and strings of dried apples and peaches hung in gay festoons along the walls, mingled with the gaud of red peppers; and a door left ajar gave him a peep into the best parlor, where the claw-footed chairs and dark mahogany tables shone like mirrors; andirons, with their accompanying shovel and tongs, glistened from their covert of asparagus tops; and a corner cupboard, knowingly left open, displayed immense treasures of old silver and well-mended china.

From the moment Ichabod laid his eyes upon these regions of delight, the peace of his mind was at an end, and his only study was how to gain the affections of the peerless daughter of Van Tassel. In this enterprise, however, he had more real difficulties than generally fell to the lot of a knight-errant of yore, who seldom had anything but giants, enchanters, fiery dragons, and such like easily-conquered adversaries, to contend with. Ichabod, on the contrary, had to win his way to the heart of a country coquette, beset with whims and caprices which were forever presenting new difficulties; and he had to encounter a host of fearful adversaries of real flesh and blood, the numerous admirers who beset every portal to her heart, keeping a watchful and angry eye upon each other, but ready to fly out in the common cause against any new competitor.

Among these the most formidable was a burly, roaring, roistering blade, of the name of Abraham, or, accord-

[1] **chanticleer** (chăn'tĭ·klēr): the rooster.
[2] **tenement** (tĕn'ĕ·mĕnt): here means "estate" or "dwelling."

ing to the Dutch abbreviation, Brom Van Brunt, the hero of the country round, which rang with his feats of strength and hardihood. He was broad-shouldered and double-jointed, with short, curly, black hair, and a bluff but not unpleasant countenance, having a mingled air of fun and arrogance. From his Herculean frame and great powers of limb, he had received the nickname of "Brom Bones," by which he was universally known. He was famed for great knowledge and skill in horsemanship. He was foremost at all races and cock-fights. He was always ready for either a fight or a frolic; but had more mischief than ill will in his composition; and, with all his overbearing roughness, there was a strong dash of waggish good humor at bottom. He had three or four boon companions, who regarded him as their model, and at the head of whom he scoured the country, attending every scene of feud or merriment for miles around. In cold weather he was distinguished by a fur cap, surmounted with a flaunting fox's tail; and when the folks at a country gathering spied this well-known crest at a distance, whisking about among a squad of hard riders, they always stood by for a squall.[1] Sometimes his crew would be heard dashing along past the farmhouses at midnight, with whoop and halloo, and the old dames, startled out of their sleep, would listen for a moment till the hurry-scurry had clattered by, and then exclaim, "Aye, there goes Brom Bones and his gang!" The neighbors looked upon him with a mixture of awe, admiration, and good will; and when any madcap prank or brawl occurred in the vicinity, always shook their heads, and warranted Brom Bones was at the bottom of it.

This harum-scarum hero had for some time singled out the blooming Katrina for the object of his gallant-ries, and it was whispered that she did not altogether discourage his hopes. Certain it is, his advances were signals for rival candidates to retire. When his horse was seen tied to Van Tassel's paling, on a Sunday night, a sure sign that his master was courting or, as it is termed, "sparking," within, all other suitors passed by in despair.

Such was the formidable rival with whom Ichabod Crane had to contend, and, considering all things, a stouter man than he would have shrunk from the competition, and a wiser man would have despaired. He had, however, a happy mixture of pliability and perseverance in his nature.

To have taken the field openly against his rival would have been madness. Ichabod, therefore, made his advances in a quiet and gently insinuating manner. Under cover of his character of singing master, he made frequent visits at the farmhouse; not that he had anything to fear from the meddlesome interference of parents, which is so often a stumbling-block in the path of lovers. Balt Van Tassel was an easy, indulgent soul; he loved his daughter better even than his

[1] **stood by for a squall:** a seaman's way of saying "got ready for trouble." A squall is a storm.

pipe, and, like a reasonable man and an excellent father, let her have her way in everything. His notable little wife, too, had enough to do to attend to her housekeeping and manage her poultry; for, as she sagely observed, ducks and geese are foolish things, and must be looked after, but girls can take care of themselves. Thus, while the busy dame bustled about the house, or plied her spinning wheel at one end of the piazza, honest Balt would sit smoking his evening pipe at the other. In the meantime, Ichabod would carry on his suit with the daughter by the side of the spring under the great elm, or sauntering along in the twilight, that hour so favorable to the lover's eloquence.

I profess not to know how women's hearts are wooed and won. To me they have always been matters of riddle and admiration. He who wins a thousand common hearts is entitled to some renown; but he who keeps undisputed sway over the heart of a coquette is indeed a hero. Certain it is, this was not the case with the redoubtable Brom Bones. From the moment Ichabod Crane made his advances, the interests of the former evidently declined. His horse was no longer seen tied at the palings on Sunday nights, and a deadly feud gradually arose between him and the schoolmaster of Sleepy Hollow.

Brom, who had a degree of rough chivalry in his nature, would have carried matters to open warfare, and have settled their pretensions to the lady according to the mode of the knights-errant of yore — by single combat; but Ichabod was too conscious of the superior might of his adversary to enter the lists against him. He had overheard a boast of Bones', that he would "double the schoolmaster up, and lay him on a shelf of his own schoolhouse"; and he was too wary to give him an opportunity. There was something extremely provoking in this obstinately pacific system; it left Brom no alternative but to play boorish practical jokes upon his rival. Ichabod became the object of whimsical persecution to Bones and his gang of rough riders. They harried his hitherto peaceful domains; smoked out his singing school, by stopping up the chimney; broke into the schoolhouse at night and turned everything topsy-turvy; so that the poor schoolmaster began to think all the witches of the country held their meetings there. But what was still more annoying, Brom took all opportunities of turning him into ridicule in the presence of his mistress, and had a scoundrel dog whom he taught to whine in the most ludicrous manner, and introduced as a rival of Ichabod's to instruct her in psalmody.

In this way matters went on for some time, without producing any material effect on the relative situation of the rivals. On a fine autumn afternoon, Ichabod, in pensive mood, sat enthroned on the lofty stool whence he usually watched all the concerns of his little literary realm. In his hand he swayed a ferule,[1] that

[1] **ferule** (fĕr′o͞ol): a ruler, to be used for punishment.

scepter of despotic power; the birch of justice reposed on three nails, behind the throne, a constant terror to evildoers. Apparently there had been some appalling act of justice recently inflicted, for his scholars were all busily intent upon their books, or slyly whispering behind them with one eye kept upon the master; and a kind of buzzing stillness reigned throughout the schoolroom. It was suddenly interrupted by the appearance of a Negro. He came clattering up to the school door with an invitation to Ichabod to attend a merrymaking, or " quilting frolic," to be held that evening at Mynheer Van Tassel's. Having delivered his message with an air of importance, he dashed over the brook, and was seen scampering away up the Hollow, full of the importance and hurry of his errand.

All was now bustle and hubbub in the late quiet schoolroom. The scholars were hurried through their lessons, without stopping at trifles; those who were nimble skipped over half with impunity, and those who were tardy had a smart application now and then in the rear to quicken their speed or help them over a tall word. Books were flung aside without being put away on the shelves, inkstands were overturned, benches thrown down, and the whole school was turned loose an hour before the usual time, bursting forth like a legion of young imps, yelping and racketing about the green, in joy of their early emancipation.

The gallant Ichabod now spent at least an extra half hour at his toilet, brushing up his best, and indeed only, suit of rusty black, and arranging his locks by a bit of broken looking glass that hung up in the schoolhouse. That he might make his appearance before his mistress in the true style of a cavalier he borrowed a horse from the farmer with whom he was living, a choleric old Dutchman of the name of Hans Van Ripper, and, thus gallantly mounted, issued forth, like a knight-errant in quest of adventures. But it is proper that I should, in the true spirit of romantic story, give some account of the looks and equipments of my hero and his steed. The animal he bestrode was a broken-down plow horse that had outlived almost everything but his viciousness. He was gaunt and shaggy, with a thin neck and a head like a hammer; his rusty mane and tail were tangled and knotted with burrs; one eye had lost its pupil and was glaring and spectral; but the other had the gleam of a genuine devil in it. Still, he must have had fire and mettle in his day, if we may judge from the name he bore of Gunpowder. Old and broken down as he looked, there was more of the lurking devil in him than in any young filly in the country.

Ichabod was a suitable figure for such a steed. He rode with short stirrups, which brought his knees nearly up to the pommel of the saddle; his sharp elbows stuck out like grasshoppers'. He carried his whip perpendicularly in his hand, like a scepter, and, as his horse jogged on, the motion of his arms was not unlike the flapping of a pair of wings. A small wool hat rested on the top of his nose, for so his scanty strip of forehead might be called; and the skirts of his black coat fluttered out almost to the horse's tail. Such was the appearance of Ichabod and his steed, as they shambled out of the gate of Hans Van Ripper, and it was altogether such an apparition as is seldom to be met with in broad daylight.

As Ichabod jogged slowly on his way, his eye ranged with delight over the treasures of jolly autumn. On all sides he beheld vast stores of apples; some hanging on the trees; some gathered into baskets and barrels for the market; others heaped up in rich piles for the cider press. Farther on he beheld great fields of Indian corn, with its golden ears peeping from their leafy coverts, and holding out the promise of cakes and hasty pudding; and the yellow pumpkins lying beneath them, turning up their fair round bellies to the sun, and giving ample prospects of the most luxurious of pies. Next he passed the fragrant buckwheat fields, breathing the odor of the beehive, and, as he beheld them, soft anticipations stole over his mind of dainty slapjacks, well buttered and garnished with honey by the delicate little dimpled hands of Katrina Van Tassel.

It was toward evening that Ichabod arrived at the castle of the Heer Van Tassel, which he found thronged with the pride and flower of the adjacent country. Old farmers, a spare, leathern-faced race, in homespun coats and breeches, blue stockings, huge shoes, and magnificent pewter buckles. Their brisk, withered little dames, in loose crimped caps, long-waisted gowns, homespun petticoats, with scissors and pincushions and gay calico pockets hanging on the outside. Buxom lasses, almost as old-fashioned as their mothers, except for a straw hat, a fine ribbon, or perhaps a white frock. The sons, in short square-skirted coats with rows of stupendous brass buttons, and their hair generally queued [1] in the fashion of the times.

Brom Bones, however, was a hero of the scene, having come to the gathering on his favorite steed, Daredevil, a creature, like himself, full of mettle and mischief, which no one but himself could manage. He held a tractable, well-broken horse as unworthy of a lad of spirit.

Fain would I pause to dwell upon the world of charms that burst upon the enraptured gaze of my hero, as he entered the state parlor of Van Tassel's mansion. Not those of the bevy of buxom lasses, with their luxurious display of red and white; but the ample charms of a genuine Dutch country tea table, in the sumptuous time of autumn. Such heaped-up platters of cakes of various and almost indescribable kinds, known only to experienced Dutch housewives! There was the doughty doughnut, the tenderer olykoek,[2] and the crisp and crumbling cruller; sweet cakes and short cakes, ginger cakes and honey cakes, and the whole family of cakes. And then there were apple pies and peach pies and pumpkin pies; besides slices of ham

---

[1] **queued** (kūd): gathered in a pigtail.
[2] **olykoek** (ŏl'ĭ·kōōk).

and smoked beef; and moreover delectable dishes of preserved plums, and peaches, and pears, and quinces, not to mention broiled shad and roasted chickens; together with bowls of milk and cream, all mingled higgledy-piggledy, pretty much as I have enumerated them, with the motherly teapot sending up its clouds of vapor from the mist.

I want breath and time to discuss this banquet as it deserves, and am too eager to get on with my story. Happily, Ichabod Crane was not in so great a hurry as his historian, but did ample justice to every dainty.

He was a kind and thankful creature, whose heart dilated in proportion as his skin was filled with good cheer; and whose spirits rose with eating as some men's do with drink. He could not help, too, rolling his large eyes round him as he ate, and chuckling with the possibility that he might one day be lord of all this scene of almost unimaginable luxury and splendor. Then, he thought, how soon he'd turn his back upon the old schoolhouse, snap his fingers in the face of Hans Van Ripper and every other niggardly patron, and kick any itinerant pedagogue out of doors that should dare to call him comrade.

Old Baltus Van Tassel moved about among his guests with a face dilated with content and good humor, round

and jolly as the harvest moon. His hospitable attentions were brief, but expressive, being confined to a shake of the hand, a slap on the shoulder, a loud laugh, and a pressing invitation to fall to and help themselves.

And now the sound of the music from the common room, or hall, summoned to the dance. Ichabod prided himself upon his dancing as much as upon his vocal powers. Not a limb, not a fiber about him was idle; and to have seen his loosely hung frame in full motion, and clattering about the room, you would have thought Saint Vitus himself, that blessed patron of the dance,[1] was figuring before you in person. How could the flogger of urchins be otherwise than animated and joyous? The lady of his heart was his partner in the dance, and smiling graciously in reply to all his tender looks; while Brom Bones, sorely smitten with love and jealousy, sat brooding by himself in one corner.

When the dance was at an end, Ichabod was attracted to a knot of the sager folks, who, with old Van Tassel, sat smoking at one end of the piazza, gossiping over former times, and drawing out long stories about the war. But all these were nothing to the tales of ghosts and apparitions that succeeded. The neighborhood is rich in legendary treasures of the kind. The immediate cause of the prevalence [2] of supernatural stories in these parts was doubtless owing to the vicinity of Sleepy Hollow. There was a contagion in the very air that blew from that haunted region; it breathed forth an atmosphere of dreams and fancies infecting all the land. Several of the Sleepy Hollow people were present at Van Tassel's, and, as usual, were doling out their wild and wonderful legends. Many dismal tales were told about funeral trains, and mourning cries and wailings heard and seen about the great tree where the unfortunate Major André [3] was taken, and which stood in the neighborhood. Some mention was made also of the woman in white that haunted the dark glen at Raven Rock, and was often heard to shriek on winter nights before a storm, having perished there in the snow. The chief part of the stories, however, turned upon the favorite specter of Sleepy Hollow, the headless horseman, who had been heard several times of late, patrolling the country; and, it was said, tethered his horse nightly among the graves in the churchyard.

The lonely situation of this church seems always to have made it a favorite haunt of troubled spirits. It stands on a knoll,[4] surrounded by locust trees and lofty elms, from among which its decent whitewashed walls shine modestly forth. A gentle slope descends from it to a silver sheet of water, bordered by high trees. To look upon its grass-grown yard, where the sunbeams seem to sleep so quietly, one would think that there at least

---

[1] **Saint Vitus'** (vī′tŭs) **dance** is the name of a disease that makes one shake and twitch.

[2] **prevalence** (prĕv′ȧ·lĕns): widespread acceptance.

[3] **Major André** (än′drå): a British officer who was hanged as a spy.

[4] **knoll** (nōl): a small, round-topped hill.

the dead might rest in peace. On one side of the church extends a wide woody dell, along which raves a large brook among broken rocks and trunks of fallen trees. Over a deep black part of the stream, not far from the church, was formerly thrown a wooden bridge. The road that led to it, and the bridge itself, were thickly shaded by overhanging trees, which cast a gloom about it, even in the daytime, but occasioned a fearful darkness at night. This was one of the favorite haunts of the headless horseman and the place where he was most frequently encountered. The tale was told of old Brouwer, a most heretical disbeliever in ghosts, how he met the horseman returning from his foray into Sleepy Hollow, and was obliged to get up behind him; how they galloped over bush and brake, over hill and swamp, until they reached the bridge, when the horseman suddenly turned into a skeleton, threw old Brouwer into a brook, and sprang away over the treetops with a clap of thunder.

This story was immediately matched by a thrice marvelous adventure of Brom Bones, who made light of the Galloping Hessian as an arrant jockey. He affirmed that, on returning one night from the neighboring village of Sing Sing, he had been overtaken by this midnight trooper; that he had offered to race with him for a bowl of punch, and should have won it, too, for Daredevil beat the goblin horse all hollow, but, just as they came to the church bridge, the Hessian bolted, and vanished in a flash of fire.

All these tales, told in that drowsy undertone with which men talk in the dark, the countenance of the listeners only now and then receiving a casual gleam from the glare of a pipe, sank deep in the mind of Ichabod. He repaid them in kind with large extracts from his invaluable author, Cotton Mather, and added many fearful sights which he had seen in his nightly walks about Sleepy Hollow.

The revel now gradually broke up. The old farmers gathered together their families in their wagons, and were heard for some time rattling along the hollow roads, and over the distant hills. The late scene of noise and frolic was all silent and deserted. Ichabod only lingered behind, according to the custom of country lovers, to have a tête-à-tête [1] with the heiress, fully convinced that he was now on the high road to success. What passed at this interview I will not pretend to say, for in fact I do not know. Something, however, must have gone wrong, for he certainly sallied forth, after no very great interval, with an air quite desolate and chopfallen — Oh, these women! these women! Could that girl have been playing off any of her coquettish tricks? Was her encouragement to the poor pedagogue all a mere sham to secure her conquest of his rival? Heaven only knows, not I! Let it suffice to say, Ichabod stole forth with the air of one who had been sacking [2]

[1] tête-à-tête (tāt′á·tāt′): a private conversation.

[2] sacking: stealing from.

a henroost rather than a fair lady's heart. Without looking to the right or left to notice the scene of rural wealth, on which he had so often gloated, he went straight to the stable, and with several hearty cuffs and kicks, roused his steed most uncourteously from the comfortable quarters in which he was soundly sleeping, dreaming of mountains of corn and oats, and whole valleys of timothy and clover.

It was the very witching time of night that Ichabod, heavy-hearted and crestfallen, pursued his travel homeward, along the sides of the lofty hills which rise above Tarrytown, and which he had traversed so cheerily in the afternoon. The hour was as dismal as himself. In the dead hush of midnight, he could even hear the barking of the watchdog from the opposite shore of the Hudson; but it was so vague and faint as only to give an idea of his distance from this faithful companion of man. Now and then, too, the long-drawn crowing of a cock would sound far, far off, from some farmhouse away among the hills — but it was like a dreaming sound in his ear. No signs of life occurred near him but occasionally the melancholy chirp of a cricket, or perhaps the guttural twang of a bullfrog, from a neighboring marsh, as if sleeping uncomfortably, and turning suddenly in his bed.

All the stories of ghosts and goblins that he had heard in the afternoon now came crowding upon his recollection. The night grew darker and darker; the stars seemed to sink deeper in the sky, and driving clouds occasionally hid them from his sight. He had never felt so lonely and dismal. He was, moreover, approaching the very place where many of the scenes of the ghost stories had been laid. In the center of the road stood an enormous tulip tree, which towered like a giant above all the other trees of the neighborhood, and formed a kind of landmark. Its limbs were gnarled and fantastic, large enough to form trunks for ordinary trees, twisting down almost to the earth, and rising again into the air. It was connected with the tragical story of the unfortunate André, who had been taken prisoner close by, and was universally known by the name of Major André's Tree. The common people regarded it with a mixture of respect and superstition, partly out of sympathy for the fate of its ill-starred namesake, and partly from the tales of strange sights and doleful lamentations told concerning it.

As Ichabod approached this fearful tree, he began to whistle; he thought his whistle was answered — it was but a blast sweeping sharply through the dry branches. As he approached a little nearer he thought he saw something white hanging in the midst of the tree — he paused and ceased whistling; but on looking more closely perceived that it was a place where the tree had been struck by lightning, and the white wood laid bare. Suddenly he heard a groan — his teeth chattered and his knees smote against the saddle; it was but the rubbing of one huge bough upon another, as they were swayed about by the breeze. He passed the tree in safety, but new perils lay before him.

About two hundred yards from the tree a small brook crossed the road and ran into a marshy and thickly wooded glen known by the name of Wiley's Swamp. A few rough logs, laid side by side, served for a bridge over this stream. On that side of the road where the brook entered the wood a group of oaks and chestnuts, matted thick with wild grapevines, threw a cavernous gloom over it. To pass this bridge was the severest trial. It was at this identical spot that the unfortunate André was captured, and under cover of those chestnuts and vines were the sturdy yeomen concealed who surprised him. This has ever since been considered a haunted stream, and fearful are the feelings of the schoolboy who has to pass it alone after dark.

As he approached the stream his heart began to thump. He summoned up, however, all his resolution, gave his horse half a score of kicks in the ribs, and attempted to dash briskly across the bridge. But instead of starting forward, the perverse old animal made a lateral movement, and ran broadside against the fence. Ichabod, whose fears increased with the delay, jerked the reins on the other side and kicked lustily with the opposite foot. It was all in vain. His steed started, it is true, but it was only to plunge to the opposite side of the road into a thicket of brambles and alder bushes. The schoolmaster now bestowed both whip and heel upon the starveling

ribs of old Gunpowder, who dashed forward, snuffing and snorting, but came to a stand just by the bridge, with a suddenness that had nearly sent his rider sprawling over his head. Just at this moment a splashing step by the side of the bridge caught the sensitive ear of Ichabod. In the dark shadow of the grove, on the margin of the brook, he beheld something huge, misshapen, black, and towering. It stirred not, but seemed gathered up in the gloom, like some gigantic monster ready to spring upon the traveler.

The hair of the affrighted pedagogue rose upon his head with terror. What was to be done? To turn and fly was now too late; and besides, what chance was there of escaping ghost or goblin, if such it was, which could ride upon the wings of the wind? Summoning up, therefore, a show of courage, he demanded in stammering accents, " Who are you? " He received no reply. He repeated his demand in a still more agitated voice. Still there was no answer. Once more he cudgeled the sides of the inflexible Gunpowder, and, shutting his eyes, broke forth with involuntary fervor into a psalm tune. Just then the shadowy object of alarm put itself in motion, and, with a scramble and a bound, stood at once in the middle of the road. Though the night was dark and dismal, yet the form of the unknown might now in some degree be made out. He appeared to be a horseman of large dimensions, and mounted on a black horse of powerful frame. He made no offer of harm or sociability, but kept aloof on one

side of the road, jogging along on the blind side of old Gunpowder, who had now got over his fright and waywardness.

Ichabod, who had no relish for this strange midnight companion, and bethought himself of the adventure of Brom Bones with the Galloping Hessian, now quickened his steed, in hopes of leaving him behind. The stranger, however, quickened his horse to an equal pace. Ichabod pulled up and fell into a walk, thinking to lag behind — the other did the same. His heart began to sink within him. He endeavored to resume his psalm tune, but his parched tongue clove to the roof of his mouth, and he could not utter a stave. There was something in the moody and dogged silence of this persistent companion that was mysterious and appalling. It was soon fearfully accounted for. On mounting a rising ground, which brought the figure of his fellow traveler in relief against the sky, gigantic in height, and muffled in a cloak, Ichabod was horror-struck, on perceiving that he was headless! — but his horror was still more increased, on observing that the head, which should have rested on his shoulders, was carried before him on the pommel of the saddle. His terror rose to desperation. He rained a shower of kicks and blows upon Gunpowder, hoping, by a sudden movement, to give his companion the slip — but the specter started full jump with him. Away then they dashed through thick and thin; stones flying, and sparks flashing at every bound. Ichabod's flimsy garments fluttered in the air, as he stretched his long lank body away over his horse's head, in the eagerness of his flight.

They had now reached the road which turns off to Sleepy Hollow; but Gunpowder, who seemed possessed with a demon, instead of keeping up when the saddle fell to the earth, and he heard it trampled under foot by his pursuer. For a moment the terror of Hans Van Ripper's wrath passed across his mind — for it was his Sunday saddle; but this was no time for petty fears. The goblin was hard on his haunches; and (unskillful rider that he was!) he had much ado to maintain his seat; sometimes slipping on one side, sometimes on another, and sometimes jolted on the high

it, made an opposite turn, and plunged headlong downhill to the left. This road leads through a sandy hollow, shaded by trees for about a quarter of a mile, where it crosses the bridge famous in goblin story, and just beyond swells the green knoll on which stands the whitewashed church.

As yet the panic of the steed had given his unskillful rider an apparent advantage in the chase; but just as he had got halfway through the hollow the girths of the saddle gave way, and he felt it slipping from under him. He seized it by the pommel, and endeavored to hold it firm, but in vain; and had just time to save himself by clasping old Gunpowder round the neck, ridge of his horse's backbone, with a violence that he feared would cleave him asunder.

An opening in the trees now cheered him with the hopes that the church bridge was at hand. He saw the walls of the church dimly glaring under the trees beyond. He recollected the place where Brom Bones's ghostly competitor had disappeared. "If I can but reach that bridge," thought Ichabod, "I am safe." Just then he heard the black steed panting and blowing close behind him; he even fancied that he felt his hot breath. Another convulsive kick in the ribs, and old Gunpowder sprang upon the bridge. He thundered over the resounding planks. He gained the opposite side; and now Ichabod cast a look behind to see if his pursuer should vanish, according to rule, in a flash of fire and brimstone. Just then he saw the goblin rising in his stirrups, and in the very act of hurling his head at him. Ichabod endeavored to dodge the horrible missile, but too late. It encountered his cranium with a tremendous crash — he was tumbled headlong into the dust, and Gunpowder, the black steed, and the goblin rider passed by like a whirlwind.

The next morning the old horse was found without his saddle, and with the bridle under his feet, soberly cropping the grass at his master's gate. Ichabod did not make his appearance at breakfast — dinner hour came, but no Ichabod. The boys assembled at the schoolhouse, and strolled idly about the banks of the brook, but no schoolmaster. Hans Van Ripper now began to feel some uneasiness about the fate of poor Ichabod and his saddle. An inquiry was set on foot, and after diligent investigation they came upon his traces. In one part of the road leading to the church was found the saddle trampled in the dirt. The tracks of horses' hoofs deeply dented in the road, and evidently at furious speed, were traced to the bridge, beyond which, on the bank of a broad part of the brook, where the water ran deep and black, was found the hat of the unfortunate Ichabod, and close beside it a shattered pumpkin.

The brook was searched, but the body of the schoolmaster was not to be discovered. The mysterious event caused much speculation at the church on the following Sunday. Knots of gazers and gossips were collected in the churchyard, at the bridge, and at the spot where the hat and pumpkin had been found. The stories of Brouwer, of Bones, and a whole budget of others, were called to mind; and when they had diligently considered them all, and compared them with the symptoms of the present case, they shook their heads, and came to the conclusion that Ichabod had been carried off by the Galloping Hessian. As he was a bachelor, and in nobody's debt, nobody troubled his head any more about him. The school was removed to a different quarter of the Hollow, and another pedagogue reigned in his stead.

It is true, an old farmer, who had been down to New York, on a visit several years after, and from whom this account of the ghostly adventure was received, brought home word that Ichabod Crane was still alive; that he had left the neighborhood, partly through fear of the goblin and Hans Van Ripper and partly in mortification at having been suddenly dismissed by the heiress; that he had changed his quarters to a distant part of the country; had kept school and studied law at the same time, had been admitted to the bar, turned politician, electioneered, written for the newspapers, and finally had been made a justice of the Ten Pound Court.[1] Brom Bones, too, who shortly after his rival's disappearance con-

---

[1] **Ten Pound Court** could handle cases involving not over ten pounds.

ducted the blooming Katrina in triumph to the altar, was observed to look exceedingly knowing whenever the story of Ichabod was related, and always burst into a hearty laugh at the mention of the pumpkin, which led some to suspect that he knew more about the matter than he chose to tell.

The old country wives, however, who are the best judges of these matters, maintain to this day that Ichabod was spirited away by supernatural means; and it is a favorite story often told about the neighborhood round the winter evening fire. The bridge became more than ever an object of superstitious awe, and that may be the reason why the road has been altered of late years, so as to approach the church by the border of the millpond. The schoolhouse, being deserted, soon fell to decay, and was reported to be haunted by the ghost of the unfortunate pedagogue; and the plowboy, loitering homeward of a still summer evening, has often fancied his voice at a distance, chanting a melancholy psalm tune among the tranquil solitudes of Sleepy Hollow.

The Ghost Won

1. Why were ghost stories so abundant in Sleepy Hollow?

2. What did Ichabod like best about Katrina Van Tassel?

3. Match the pictures on pages 272 and 284 with the description of Ichabod as he looked at various times. Do the drawings fit your impression of him? Perhaps some of you can draw Ichabod as he was dancing, or in his schoolroom.

4. Why was Ichabod looked up to by the women in the community?

5. Why did Katrina encourage Ichabod for a while? Was she a " coquette "?

6. What made Ichabod so ready to believe in ghosts on this particular night?

7. Tell what Ichabod thought was happening on the way home, and what *you* think happened.

8. Here are three good reasons why this story has been a great favorite for over a hundred years. Try to decide which is most important to you.

a. The writer's gentle way of joking.

b. The pleasant picture of life in a picturesque corner of our country.

c. The action of the story itself.

Pick out a short section of the story that illustrates each quality, then read one aloud to the class and see if they can tell which of the three it illustrates.

Synonyms for Ghosts

Many words you read or hear are alike in meaning. For example, *observe* and *watch* mean very nearly the same. But even among these *synonyms*, as such like words are called, there are little differences. The words Irving uses for all the spooky crew that plagued Ichabod Crane show how synonyms vary slightly in meaning.

Long ago, *ghost* meant simply the spirit in a living person, and it gradually came to mean the spirit without the body. So a *ghost* is the wandering spirit of a dead person, like Major André. *Apparition* contains a clue to its meaning. Do you see that the first part of the word looks much like *appear?* Other spooks may specialize in groaning or rattling chains, but an apparition *appears* before people. It is seen. A *specter* can also be a *ghost* or an *apparition*, but the word carries a special feeling of evil or danger. A *specter* rouses more fear than an ordinary ghost. A *phantom* is the vaguest of all the ghost family. It could be a mere trick of your imagination.

Which of these synonyms could not properly be used of the headless horseman that pursued Ichabod? Which one would Ichabod himself be most likely to use?

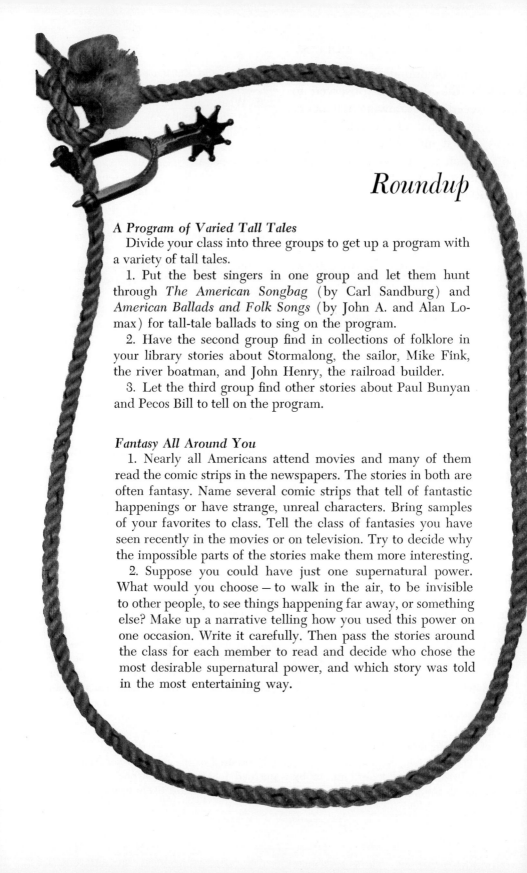

Roundup

A Program of Varied Tall Tales

Divide your class into three groups to get up a program with a variety of tall tales.

1. Put the best singers in one group and let them hunt through *The American Songbag* (by Carl Sandburg) and *American Ballads and Folk Songs* (by John A. and Alan Lomax) for tall-tale ballads to sing on the program.

2. Have the second group find in collections of folklore in your library stories about Stormalong, the sailor, Mike Fink, the river boatman, and John Henry, the railroad builder.

3. Let the third group find other stories about Paul Bunyan and Pecos Bill to tell on the program.

Fantasy All Around You

1. Nearly all Americans attend movies and many of them read the comic strips in the newspapers. The stories in both are often fantasy. Name several comic strips that tell of fantastic happenings or have strange, unreal characters. Bring samples of your favorites to class. Tell the class of fantasies you have seen recently in the movies or on television. Try to decide why the impossible parts of the stories make them more interesting.

2. Suppose you could have just one supernatural power. What would you choose — to walk in the air, to be invisible to other people, to see things happening far away, or something else? Make up a narrative telling how you used this power on one occasion. Write it carefully. Then pass the stories around the class for each member to read and decide who chose the most desirable supernatural power, and which story was told in the most entertaining way.

Your Bookshelf

Between Planets, by Robert A. Heinlein (Scribner, 1951)

Thrilling science-fiction of the future when space ships link the planets.

The Door in the Closet, by Josephine Daskam Bacon (Viking, 1940)

An imaginative girl finds that it opens into another world.

The Golden Flash, by Mary McNeer (Viking, 1947)

A fire engine goes on strange adventures of its own.

Grandfather Tales: American-English Folk Tales, selected and edited by Richard Chase (Houghton Mifflin, 1948)

A wealth of the best-loved tales and also ballads with music.

Gulliver's Travels, by Jonathan Swift, new ed. (World, 1948)

An all-time favorite about a seaman's adventures among tiny people and giants.

It Happens Every Spring, by Valentine Davis (Farrar, Straus, 1949)

A college professor gets hold of a magic baseball.

Joe Margarac and His USA Citizen Papers, by Irwin Shapiro (Messner, 1948)

The tall-tale hero of the steel mills could teach Americans how to appreciate their own country.

John Henry and His Hammer, by Harold W. Felton (Knopf, 1950)

He could lay railroads so fast that he was matched against a steam drill.

Knock at the Door, by Elizabeth Coatsworth (Macmillan, 1931)

A boy born among the fairies makes his way among ordinary men.

Lodestar: Rocket Ship to Mars, by Franklin Branley (Crowell, 1951)

Science-fiction by a science teacher — imaginary rocket flight to the red planet.

Magic Walking Stick, by John Buchan (Houghton Mifflin, 1932)

It transported its owner to strange adventures in faraway places.

Mister Stormalong, by Anne Malcolmson and Dell J. McCormick (Houghton Mifflin, 1952)

Amazing exploits of the tall-tale sailor.

Mr. Twigg's Mistake, by Robert Lawson (Little, Brown, 1947)

When Mr. Twigg fills a package of "Bities" with pure Vitamin X and a boy feeds it to a mole, the neighborhood is in for some surprises.

My Friend Mr. Leakey, by J. P. S. Haldane (Harper, 1938)

A modern magician has fun with the old tricks in present-day London.

Ol' Paul, the Mighty Logger, by Glen Rounds, rev. ed. (Holiday, 1949)

A rich store of Paul Bunyan tales.

Pecos Bill, by James Cloyd Bowman (Whitman, 1937)

The mighty cowboy who was raised by coyotes.

The Pirates in the Deep Green Sea, by Eric Linklater (Macmillan, 1949)

Modern Scottish boys are on easy terms with everything in the sea, including men who drowned long ago.

Sam Patch, the High, Wide, and Handsome Jumper, by Arna Bontemps and Jack Conroy (Houghton Mifflin, 1951)

The legends began with a real person, but how they grew!

The Twenty-One Balloons, by William Pène du Bois (Viking, 1947)

They carried an enterprising professor into incredible adventures.

Upstate, Downstate: Folk Stories of the Middle Atlantic States, by Moritz Adolf Jagendorf (Vanguard, 1949)

Ghosts, enchanted creatures, and pirates.

Voyage of the Luna I, by David Craigie (Messner, 1949)

Stowaways on a rocket ship to the moon.

Good Sport

The Surprise of His Life

E. C. JANES

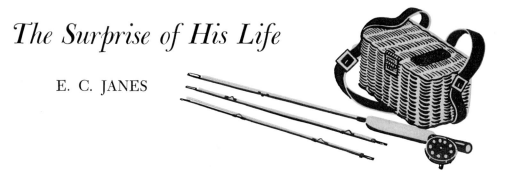

Not all sport is found at big games. A boy with a fishing rod in his hand and a clear stream before him can find plenty of sport. And even though fishing is not a " team " game, it can teach you some valuable lessons in good sportsmanship.

THE big trout thrashed to the surface, flurrying the dark surface of the pool to foam. Clinging grimly to his bent and straining rod, Kerry Johnson dared to think of the prize fly rod in Baker's store window. The fish had been on for ten minutes now and if there was a bigger squaretail trout in Warren County it must be mounted on someone's wall.

A sudden screech of his reel, as the trout surged downstream, sent Kerry's heart into his throat and he looked anxiously at the taped second ferrule [1] of his ancient rod. Cautiously he reeled in, groping his way over the slippery rocks, gaining back precious line until he felt the dogged shaking of the great fish throbbing through the bamboo.

At the pressure of the tip, it burst to the surface again, rolling, tumbling, slapping the water with its wide tail. He caught a glimpse of broad spotted flanks gleaming pink and scarlet in the afternoon sun. Then the trout lunged into the black depths so suddenly that the ma-

[1] ferrule (fĕr'ĭl): a metal ring put around a cane to prevent splitting.

"The Surprise of His Life" by E. C. Janes from Open Road, May 1949. Reprinted by permission of Open Road.

neuver caught Kerry unaware. A new, lithe rod would have taken the unexpected strain, but it proved too much for this dried and war-torn stick. A quick snap like a pistol shot echoed above the rushing waters as the rod broke at the ferrule. To Kerry's ears it was the crack of doom. An inch of slack was all the big trout needed and a second later he was free.

Mechanically, Kerry reeled in his limp line, swallowing the lump in his throat. His gray eyes stared dully at the quiet waters of the pool while the rod in Baker's window went glimmering away. So near and yet so far! A moment ago the prize had been almost within his grasp; now it was as remote as the pot of gold he used to believe lay at the end of the rainbow.

The old rod had played its last fish. What a time for it to fold up! Still, what else could he expect? It had been his father's rod in its prime and it was dusty when he had found it eight years ago. He was nine then and he had used it ever since. He had varnished it and rewound it, but even with the best of care bamboo can live only so long. Just a week ago he had noticed the crack in the middle joint above the ferrule and had carefully taped it. If only it had lasted another five minutes, he'd have been the owner of a shiny new thirty-five-dollar rod, first prize in the Junior Division of the Warren County Trout Fishing Contest. The trout he had just lost would go four pounds at least, maybe more. And now . . .

Bitterly he set off through the woods toward home. As he walked his spirits lightened somewhat. There was still a chance. The contest ran for another three days and no one would dream a big trout such as this lived in Carter Brook. The old cannibal must have come up from the river on the spring freshet and stayed there waxing fat on his small six- and seven-inch relatives. The veterans were all fishing the river, whipping the big still pools with dry flies at dawn and dusk.

Maybe he could fix the rod somehow; if not, he could always cut a pole in the woods. He still had a chance; and he *had* to win that prize — not only because he wanted that shiny rod more than anything in the world but also because the old fishermen around town expected him to win.

He did the chores and ate the supper which his mother had waiting for him and went downtown to Baker's store to look at the bulletin board and to admire the prize rod once more. The usual crowd of fishermen were there, ribbing one another and watching for any entries which might be brought in before closing time. A quick glance at the board showed Kerry that Tom Blake's two-and-a-half-pound square-tail still led the junior division of the brook trout class. Tom, standing beside the counter, looked anxious as Kerry came in and then seeing him empty-handed he taunted:

"I thought you were the champ. When you going to bring in your fish? "

Kerry's freckles stood out on his pale face but he forced a smile.

" I'm waiting for the last day," he said easily.

" Well, don't wait too long," Tom said, sauntering out the door.

As Tom left Kerry noticed the stranger who had come in and now stood talking to Mr. Baker. A little, stooped old man with a deeply wrinkled face and snow-white hair, he leaned against the counter and breathed heavily two or three times as though catching his breath. A moment later Mr. Baker led the old man up to Kerry, and as they came near he saw the smiling blue eyes in the old man's ruddy face.

" Here he is, sir," Mr. Baker said, grasping Kerry by the arm. " Kerry Johnson, the fishin'est kid in these parts. He'll show you the best spots."

The old man smiled and held out his hand.

" I've heard a lot about your trout up here, son, and before I pass on to the Happy Hunting Grounds, I want to catch a few of them. Think you could lead me to 'em? "

Kerry hesitated. He had the farm chores and he had some serious fishing to do during the next three days. He had no time to waste on this old fellow.

" I shouldn't stay out long," the old man said. " A couple of hours a day is all I can take now. I'd expect to pay you."

That did it. Money was scarce in Kerry's life.

" O.K." he said and gave directions for finding his home. " Be there at eight. Mr. — "

The old man laid a hand across Kerry's shoulder. " Thanks a lot, son," he said. " Just call me Uncle Jim. Everybody does."

Earning his money wasn't as easy as Kerry had expected. He suggested several good places to fish next morning, and in each case Uncle Jim had asked questions concerning the spot and then shook his head.

" Too long a walk, my boy," or " Too swift water for me," or again, " I can't climb hills, son," he had said.

" That's the trouble with having a seventy-five-year-old body and the spirit of a kid," he added ruefully. " I ought to give up fishing, but I love it too much. Isn't there some place we can drive to? "

" Yes," Kerry said, " but the fishing isn't too good. It's all cleaned out."

" Well, it will have to do," Uncle Jim said. " And sometimes you'll find a big fish in those places that everyone has overlooked."

That was true, Kerry thought grimly, but there was one such fish the old man wouldn't see.

When they stood on the banks of Barry Brook, foaming down out of the hills along the highway, the old man's eyes sparkled. He took deep breaths of pine-scented air and looked approvingly at the stream.

" That's trout water, son! " he said. " It'll be fun to whip it even if there aren't any fish."

He began expertly to joint his rod and Kerry, watching him, felt his

the stream.

Kerry had seen good fishermen before, men like Hank Sabin and Roy Brown who could cast a fly ninety feet, but he'd never seen an angler with the grace, precision, and delicacy of this old man.

Suddenly, as Kerry watched in fascination, the water bulged beneath Uncle Jim's Coachman, floating far down the glassy run. Uncle Jim struck gently as the fly disappeared and a small native trout flashed gold against the green water. Uncle Jim chuckled and drew him in. Carefully, he released the tiny hook and returned the fish to the water. His eyes shone with pleasure.

In the next half hour he took four more small fish which he carefully released. He was breathing a bit heavily by now and they sat down to rest beneath a spreading pine.

While they rested, legs dangling in the running water, Uncle Jim looked about contentedly, watching the antics of a red squirrel in the branches above them, listening to the Indian drum of a grouse[3] from a nearby thicket.

"Time turns back," he told Kerry, "and I'm a boy again. There are no automobiles, no airplanes, and very few fishermen." And almost as though talking to himself he went on to tell of those long-gone days, fascinating tales of great trout swirling in the clear, wilderness waters of his boyhood. Stories, too, of salmon on

eyes start from their sockets. The rod which the old man caressed with loving hands was a *Kendall*. It wasn't like the prize rod in the store. Compared to this, the store rod was a crowbar. A Kendall was tops . . . like a Rolls Royce.[1] One like this three-and-a-half-ounce stick cost ninety dollars.

" That's a Kendall! " he blurted out.

" Yes," Uncle Jim said smiling. " It's a pretty good rod."

He threaded a tapered line through the guides and tied on a 5X leader and a number 20 Coachman.[2] Then he stepped gingerly into

---

[1] **Rolls Royce:** an expensive British-built car.
[2] A **leader** is a short piece of transparent line used to attach the end of a fishline to the lure; 5X indicates a small size. A **Coachman** is a brightly colored artificial fly used as a lure.

[3] A **grouse** is a large ground bird which makes a noise like the roll of drums by standing on a log and beating its wings against the air.

the Restigouche,[1] landlocks[2] of St. John, and squaretails from Kennebago — the adventures of sixty years of fishing.

Kerry listened wide-eyed, wondering in his heart if in days to come, life would bring him wonderful experiences such as these. The old man seemed to read his thoughts.

" If we all remember the folks that will come after us," he said, " there'll always be clean waters with fish in them. But too often we think only of ourselves. Men who own factories pollute the waters and men who fish take all they can catch and in the end there are no streams or no fish left."

The idea made Kerry think. Uncle Jim's fishing methods made him think, too. Uncle Jim never kept a fish; he didn't even carry a creel.

" We fish today for fun, not food," he said.

The two hours turned into six with frequent rest periods and the next day was the same. Kerry had no time to go after the prize trout of Carter's Creek. But that could wait. Uncle Jim proved a wonderful companion and he even let Kerry catch a fish on the Kendall rod, complimenting him on his prowess. It was almost like having a father to fish with, something of which Kerry had always dreamed. His father had been a great fisherman, too. His mother told him a little about his skill and Kerry often wished they might have waded

the streams together. This old man seemed almost like a father or a genial grandfather and from him Kerry learned much of trout lore and learned, too, the essentials of sportsmanship. He became strangely attached to Uncle Jim and hated to think of his leaving.

Then the last day came and during the morning, Uncle Jim caught a dozen trout in Barry Brook, the largest an eight-inch fish. At last he reeled in his line.

" Well, son," he said, " I guess this is it. I've had a wonderful time and I'll never forget it." A trace of sadness edged his words. " I guess we're not going to get the big boy."

" There aren't any here," Kerry said.

" You know," Uncle Jim went on, " I've fished all my life but I've never yet caught a truly large brook trout.

---

[1] **Restigouche** (rĕs′tĭ·gōōsh): a Canadian river famous for its salmon fishing.

[2] **landlocks:** fish cut off from the sea by some barrier.

Salmon, bass — yes, but never a squaretail to mount. I guess now I never will. At my age there isn't much time left. Well, so be it."

"I know where there's a big one!" Kerry's own words surprised him. They had just popped out. "It's easy to get there, too. Come on."

He didn't know what madness possessed him. He only knew that right now the most important thing in the world was to have this great old man achieve his life's ambition. They drove to the bridge over Carter Brook and Kerry led the way to the deep, dark pool. He showed Uncle Jim where the trout lay and, as he talked, the old man's eyes lighted and his breath came quick and fast.

"He's a really big one?" he asked and Kerry noticed that his fingers trembled as he tied on a number 14 Dun.

"He'll go over four pounds," Kerry said.

"H'm!" Carefully, the old man studied the pool, marking the drift of the water as it eddied around the granite ledge beneath the old hemlock. Kerry sensed that the climax of sixty years of fishing went into these preparations and into the cast that shot the fly out to land light as thistledown upon the purling water. Jauntily it floated down the current, caught the eddy and swept past the granite ledge. Again. Aga . . .

Swop! Deliberately, the big boy rose, engulfing the fly, and rolled his monstrous bulk back into the depths. The tiny rod doubled and the reel sent its screeching song ringing across the pool. Breathlessly, Kerry watched.

The old man stood planted firmly with water lapping belt-deep around his waders. He held the fish in on that gossamer strand of leader, exerting a continuous killing strain. The great fish bored and thrashed and foamed and flung himself in a somersault, but the little rod ducked and vibrated and held. Sixty years of fishing skill put on the pressure and released it as the emergency required. How long it lasted Kerry never knew.

Slowly the big trout tired, allowing himself to be drawn, bewildered and shaking doggedly, nearer and nearer the old man's outstretched net. A slow, deliberate sweep and the old warrior came up, glistening and flopping in its meshes. And Kerry knew he had stood in the presence of champions.

The old man stumbled ashore and sat down panting.

"You're right, my boy," he said weakly. "This is my mounting trout. After all these years." He drew a scale from his pocket and hooked it to the fish's jaw. "Four pounds, nine ounces," he breathed.

Then a troubled look crept into the blue eyes. Uncle Jim hesitated, holding the fish aloft. He shook his head and before Kerry knew what was happening, he walked to the bank and put the big fish gently into the water. It lay a second finning wearily; then it settled slowly into the depths.

Kerry gasped, and with that came

a realization of what he had done. He had lost his chance of winning the contest and the rod in Baker's window. And now Uncle Jim had released the fish he had said he wanted. Bitterness at himself and his friend choked Kerry as he stared at the old man.

Uncle Jim shook his head again slowly. "I just couldn't do it," he said wonderingly. "That old fellow belongs here in this pool, not over an old man's mantel." He paused. "Did you ever want something terribly, my boy, and then not be able to take it when you had a chance?"

Kerry nodded and tears stung his eyes. "Yes," he said sobbingly and he blurted out the story of his own encounter with the big trout, of his smashed rod and his hopes to win the prize.

"And you gave me this chance?" Uncle Jim said slowly. "Son, I want to shake hands with a real sportsman."

The old man left that night, and that night Tom Blake received the shiny rod in Baker's window which was first prize in the contest. It was a heavy disappointment but something in the old man's look and in his handclasp took some of the bitterness from the occasion. And the twenty-five dollars he had pressed upon Kerry would help out at home. And, somehow, it was comforting to know that the great trout still swam in the deep dark pool.

A week later a package came and with it a note. The package contained a new fly rod. The note was brief.

"Dear Kerry," it said, "I am sending you this rod in appreciation of all you did for me on my recent trip to Warren County. I know that it will be in good hands and I hope you catch our trout with it, as well as many others in the years to come."

His shining eyes drank in the lithe, slim beauty of the four-ounce rod and turned once more to the note. It was signed in a shaky hand but the signature was the same as the autograph on the butt joint of the rod.

"Sincerely yours,
James F. Kendall."

A Prize and a Surprise

1. How did Kerry first lose a chance to capture the big trout? Why was he particularly keen to win the contest?

2. How did Mr. Kendall show that he was an expert fisherman? Why was it hard for Kerry to find good fishing places for him?

3. "We fish today for fun, not food," said Mr. Kendall. How did the old fisherman prove that he fished for pure enjoyment of the sport? Discuss whether you think it is good sportsmanship to kill animals in fishing or hunting. There is no single answer to this question; so expect some class arguments!

4. What made Kerry change his mind about leading the old fisherman to his big trout? What was Mr. Kendall's reason for releasing the fish?

5. What is the surprise in the ending of the story? For what did Kerry finally win a prize?

Exact Meanings

Most of us, when we read an interesting story, sail along on the phrases and sentences without worrying too much about the exact meaning of each word. Occasionally, however, it is a good idea to look closely at particular words and make sure that you know their precise meaning. In that way you can add new words to your own vocabulary and use them correctly and confidently. Here are five passages from "The Surprise of His Life," with a word italicized in each. First write your own definition for the word. Then have someone write a dictionary definition for it on the board. Did you know the exact meaning?

1. Kerry sensed that the *climax* of sixty years of fishing went into these preparations . . .

2. He held the fish in on that *gossamer* strand of leader, exerting a continuous killing strain.

3. . . . he went on to tell of those long-gone days, *fascinating* tales of great trout . . .

4. Men who own factories *pollute* the waters . . .

5. . . . he even let Kerry catch a fish on the Kendall rod, complimenting him on his *prowess*.

Fisherman's Lack

RICHARD ARMOUR

Caught no fish;
  Tell you why:
Water too low,
  Wind too high,

Left dark glasses,
  Brought wrong bait,
Boots sprung leak,
  Started too late,   5

Too many people —
  Drat those boys!   10
Too many dogs,
  Too much noise,

Flies wouldn't float,
  Lost best hooks,
Owner of stream   15
  Gave dirty looks.

Could tell you more,
  Talk two seasons.
Got no fish,
  Plenty of reasons!   20

"Fisherman's Lack" by Richard Armour from *The Saturday Evening Post*, June 25, 1949. Reprinted by permission of the author.

Happy Daze

B. J. CHUTE

A basketball player dressed up like a valentine may be a funny sight, but it's a bad idea to make too much fun of him. The laughter did not drown out the thrills in this game. It just piled them up.

WHERE would America be," demanded "Happy" Holmes, "if Columbus hadn't been willing to try something different? "

The captain of the Trenton High basketball team gave him a dirty look. "We aren't discussing America," he pointed out. "We're discussing the loathsome possibility of putting red hearts all over my basketball pants, and just because you're manager of the team is no reason to — "

"Not your *pants*, Bill," Happy corrected him. "On your jersey, to hide the moth holes. My idea for your pants was a little red edging. Tatting, perhaps. Last time I noticed Tommy's they struck me as being very ragged at the seams."

Tommy Lewis, star Trenton guard, let out a howl that shook the locker room. "Red tatting! " yelped Tommy, opening and shutting his mouth like an embattled clam. "Red tatting! Happy, have you lost your mind? "

"Slim" Davidson, six-foot-one center, put in his oar. "What mind? " he wanted to know. "Look, my good idiot, even for you, this is one of the worst ideas that anyone has ever perpetrated on the face of this glorious continent."

"You see? " said Happy smugly to Bill. "I told you we were discussing America." He turned back to Slim, rather indignantly. "What's wrong with my idea? The team certainly needs new uniforms, doesn't it? "

There was a general grunt of acquiescence,[1] and Happy went on. "Well, we have to raise money, don't we? And how are we going to raise money unless we have some kind of a show or something? And what could be smarter than to combine the show with the big game against Carson on Valentine night? That way the whole school can see how badly we need the uniforms — "

"Me," said Bill, "in red hearts. Ha! "

"And," Happy continued, un-

[1] acquiescence (ăk·wĭ·ĕs′ĕns): agreement.

moved, "we will win the game, which will prove how much we deserve the uniforms — "

"Oh, we'll win the game too, will we?" said Slim sardonically.[1] "Won't that be just wonderful? You wouldn't have heard about Carson being undefeated all season, I suppose? You wouldn't know that the odds are about four to one against us?"

Happy brushed this aside with an airy wave of his hand. "I leave the winning part up to you fellows," he said broad-mindedly, and went on with his plans. "After the game we'll have a big Valentine party in the gym, and *that* way we'll get all those who don't usually go to the basketball games. A nifty way to make the whole school basketball-conscious, if ever I saw one. Everyone always goes to parties."

Bill tried to be reasonable. "I see all that," he conceded, "and heaven knows we need the uniforms. But why do we have to be decorated with hearts?"

"Because it's a novelty," Happy explained patiently, "and novelty is what counts in this world. Did you ever hear of a gym decorated with players to match?" There was a general and heartfelt No, and Happy nodded triumphantly. "Exactly. I'm now cutting hearts out of red cloth, and I'm going to spend the afternoon sewing them to your jerseys."

"Over my dead body," said Tommy, on principle.

"I have an extra thimble, if you want to help," Happy advised him.

[1] **sardonically** (sär·dŏn′ĭ·kǎl·ĭ): bitterly.

"And by the way, does anybody know anybody who tats? I still think tatting to hide the tatters would be awfully appropriate."

"*No* tatting," said five voices at once.

Happy smiled sweetly. "I think I know someone who has a great-aunt who tats," he said dreamily. "Seriously, fellows, wouldn't you rather have a little tatting than no new uniforms? Where's your pride?"

"Red hearts on our pants," said Bill oratorically, "and he has the nerve to ask us where our pride is."

"Not on your pants, my good man," said Happy. "I told you — on your jerseys. Here, *you* can have this."

Bill looked at Happy and heaved a magnificent sigh, but he took the thimble.

Suddenly wherever you went at Trenton High School, there were large heart-shaped signs, hand-printed on red cardboard.

> Valentine Basketball Party.
> Come One. Come All.
>
> Support Your Team. Help Buy
> New Uniforms.
>
> Your ticket entitles you to a
> Spine-Tingling Game, followed
> by a Magnificent Party.
> Surprises! Entertainment!
> THRILLS!

One of these signs hung in the gymnasium itself and, a few days before the game, Bill Endicott, with a basketball cuddled under his arm, stood contemplating it. He was wearing a bathing suit and a gloomy expression. The reason he was wearing the bathing suit was that the starry-eyed Happy, having sewed hearts on the team's uniforms, refused to risk them in a mere practice session.

The reason he was wearing the gloomy expression was that he had just been reading a sports writeup on the prowess of the Carson basketball team.

Rusty Miller, Bill's redheaded running mate, joined him.

Bill said, "Hi. Did you see that story on the Carson team in the *Herald* this morning?"

Rusty nodded. "They're good, all right."

"They took Central High 33 to 18," said Bill sadly, "and we were lucky to beat Central by two points."

"Carson's good," Rusty said again.

"So's Trenton," said a voice reassuringly, and Happy came prancing over, trailing yards of red cloth. "Look what I got. We'll use it to drape the baskets with. . . . Say, aren't you about due to start practice?"

"Coach isn't here yet," said Bill absently; then his mental gears began to mesh and he gave a startled yelp. "Drape the baskets! You can't *do* that!"

"I'll leave room for the ball to go through," Happy soothed him. "Ah! Here's the coach now. Hi, coach! Look what I've got."

Coach Bennett looked at the red material with an expression that was somewhere between amusement and pain. He said it was very beautiful and then added mildly, "Shall we be very much in your way if we practice a little basketball, Happy?"

"Oh, no, not at all," said Happy blandly. "I can work around you. Hi, fellows." He acknowledged the arrival of the rest of the squad, said suddenly, "I need a freshman," and vanished from the gym.

Coach Bennett's eyebrows rose gently. "What does he need a freshman for?"

"Happy always picks freshmen for his assistants," Slim Davidson said resignedly. "He says they're so meek and helpless." He broke off, as the teams lined up and practice got under way.

A few moments later Happy returned, beaming from ear to ear and with his freshman in tow. "This is Archie," he said to the room at large. "Archie's going to help me decorate. I found him in a study hall, trying to do an equation in algebra. Discouraged, he was, so I brought him here for some fresh air."

"Happy, the Charitable Institution," said the coach dryly. "All right, gang. Get going again."

The teams obediently got going, and Happy, after a moment's thought, sent Archie off for a stepladder, which he then set up near one of the baskets.

"It wobbles," he observed. "You hold it for me, Archibald, and I'll do my well-known Alpine act. Can you yodel?"

Archie, looking rather solemn, said he could not yodel.

"Never mind," said Happy forgivingly. "*I* will yodel." He proceeded to mount the ladder cautiously, yodeling in a restrained manner so as not to rock it, and began to drape the backboard with the red cloth.

At this moment, Slim aimed for the basket, rightly feeling that Happy, yodel and all, was no more than a technical obstruction. The shot was a little wide of its mark, and just at the critical moment Happy raised his head to speak to Archie.

The ball struck him accurately on the parting in his hair, ricocheted off, and popped through the basket.

From below, there was a startled round of applause. Happy looked on the upturned faces before him and rubbed his head gently.

"You guys," said Happy, "are in my way. Archie, I need more nails. Somebody hold this ladder, please, while Archie goes for nails. . . . And, look, while I'm here, can't you use the other basket?"

"Catch me," said Bill. "I feel faint."

"Take an aspirin," said Happy, doing some more draping. "Does anybody know where I can get red shoelaces?"

"Red *shoelaces!* Why red shoelaces?"

"For your shoes, naturally," said Happy. "Pass me up that ball, will you, please?"

Numbly Tommy passed up the ball. Happy held it over the basket and dropped it in. Owing to the wadding of extra red cloth, however, the ball failed to come out the other end.

"Oh, heck!" Happy mourned. "I suppose it has to come through while you're playing, doesn't it?"

Tommy sat down on the floor. "It's the usual thing," he said gently.

"Ah," said Happy, sagely nodding his head. "I was afraid of that. It makes things very awkward."

"Awkward?" said Tommy.

"Awkward," said Happy severely. "And, frankly, though I don't like to fuss, you fellows are in my way."

Tommy looked at Bill. Bill looked at Slim. Slim looked at Rusty. The look traveled around the room and came back to Tommy with compound interest. "Well," said Tommy, "what are we waiting for?"

Acting in that spirit of close cooperation which is so essential to a team, they descended suddenly upon Happy's ladder. Between them they picked it up with Happy still at the top, yelling like an outraged monkey on a stick, and carted it to the door. Happy, wailing, appealed to the coach, the team, Archie, the school as a whole, and finally to the lifelong friendship which he suddenly claimed to have had with all of them.

All in vain. They deposited him outside in the corridor, bade him a fond farewell, and went back, locking the door behind them, triumphantly sure that they had done a good job.

There was one flaw.

When they were ready to start practice again, it turned out that Happy, the forehanded, had taken the ball with him and, when they finally tracked him down, he had already sprinkled it artistically with gummed red-paper hearts.

"Spectacular" was an understatement in describing the gymnasium the evening of the Trenton-Carson game. Happy had really let himself go, and this, as he pointed out, in spite of the team's lack of co-operation.

"I don't mind being thrown out on my ear at ten-minute intervals," he said wistfully, "but I do resent being stuffed into a locker, along with the old shoes. By the way," he added, more cheerfully, "I couldn't find red shoelaces, so I dyed all yours. I hope you don't mind."

They said they were deeply touched at the thought that Happy would dye for them, and pointed out in self-defense that their only objection to his decorating campaign had been the way he persisted in working during practice. Didn't he want the team to make at least a decent showing against Carson?

"I expect you to beat them," said Happy with airy optimism, and went on admiring his handiwork.

It was really a remarkable achievement. The iron girders overhead were covered with twisted red crepe paper, from which hung red cardboard hearts on long streamers. The backboards were draped perilously in Happy's precious red cloth — "That stuff will fall down into the basket, you mark my words," was Bill's dire prophecy — red crepe paper was intricately wound through the meshes of the baskets themselves, the scorers' table was festooned with hearts, and all the light fixtures sported silvered-cardboard cupids.

With the teams about due on the court, Happy was rushing around in a small frenzy, seeing to it that everything was in order. His special concern was for a large packing box which stood near the court and which was carefully draped in dark cloth, with the hard-working Archie mounting guard over it.

Happy galloped up to Archie. "Are they all right?"

Archie raised a corner of the cloth. "You can see for yourself," he said. "They're perfectly contented. In fact, they're even cooing a little."

"I wish they wouldn't," Happy murmured. "I want them to be a complete surprise to everybody." He peered into the dim interior of the box where a dozen sleek white pigeons were moving restlessly about, their sharp beaks tapping at the seed that lay on the floor. Around the neck of each pigeon hung a tiny cardboard heart, which had been coated with phosphorescent paint and which gleamed in the dull interior.

"Boy!" said Happy excitedly. "Can't you just picture what it's going to look like when all the lights go out and we release the pigeons? It'll be sensational."

"You've got it all fixed about the lights, haven't you?" Archie demanded anxiously, smoothing the cloth down again.

"I'll check with the janitor right now," Happy decided. "Now, look,

don't forget — the moment the lights
go out, you release the pigeons."

Archie nodded solemnly, responsibility resting heavily on his shoul-

and he looked up without enthusiasm as Happy skittered to a stop beside him.

The janitor was a long, sad man
with a long, sad face. On seeing
Happy it became even longer and
sadder.

"Don't tell me again," said the
janitor. "I know all about it. When
the gun goes off at the end of the
game, I'm supposed to turn out all
the lights." He nodded toward the
control switch nearby. "Nothin' to
it. Just don't tell me again."

Happy promptly did tell him
again. "Bang, the gun," he said, trying to make it more graphic and
arouse the janitor to greater interest.

"Click, the lights. Flutter, flutter,
the pigeons. It's going to be beautiful."

"Mebbe," said the janitor, declin-
ing to commit himself.

Happy despaired of ever rousing
him to a true appreciation of the
beauties of his plan and, after one
last reminder, he tore himself away
and joined the Trenton supporters,
listening with pleasure to the admiring comments they were making
on his decorations.

"Wait till they see the team," said
Happy to himself, and at that moment the first team trotted out onto
the floor.

ders, and Happy, satisfied that his
sensational surprise was in good
hands, dashed off in search of the
school janitor. The janitor was standing near the door, studying a screw,

There was a moment's stunned silence from the stands, then a riotous burst of cheering, whistling, and stamping of feet.

Happy practically purred. The costuming was definitely a success, and no one could say that the result wasn't striking, because striking was an understatement.

The Trenton uniforms — white jerseys and blue pants — had lent themselves admirably to Valentine decorations, and while there might be those who would say that hearts stitched all over the top and red ribbon (it turned out that the great-aunt did knitting, not tatting) fluted around the bottom were a trifle extreme, still the general effect was both startling and novel. Red shoelaces added a note of brilliance to the footwear, and the final touch was given by long scarlet sashes wound around the players' waists, giving them a vaguely Spanish-toreador effect.

After a few moments the applause died down, then was taken up by the opposing stands as the Carson team ran out onto the floor. Their green and white uniforms looked very smart and were obviously new, but they were hardly in a class with Trenton's, and the Trenton players, in spite of their early objections to hearts on their clothes, felt for a moment decidedly superior even to this husky bunch of well-dressed skyscrapers.

The feeling of superiority lasted for perhaps two seconds, and then the Carson team, after one startled glance at their opponents, burst into howls of laughter.

"Great guns!" shouted the Carson captain, collapsing in simple hysterics on a teammate's shoulder. "Look what they've let in." He stuck a finger under his chin, did a pretty curtsy to Bill, and said to him coyly, "May I have the next waltz?"

Bill turned a bright and furious

purple. Happy had worked long and hard on their costumes, and no smart aleck from Carson was going to make wisecracks about them. Thought they were funny, did they? Them and their newspaper clippings! Them and their undefeated records!

He glanced at his teammates. Their jaws were sticking out, and Rusty's hair looked redder than usual.

A Carson guard, gazing upon his opponents with obvious delight, said suddenly, "Oh, mithter, won't you pleathe be my Valentine?" and the Carson stands rocked with laughter.

"Listen —" said Bill, taking a step forward.

"Are you ready?" said the referee calmly.

The stands decided to forget the clothes question and concentrate on the ball game. A sudden silence descended as the ball was centered, then the whistle shrilled and the players sprang into action.

Carson's Elliott had an inch height advantage over Slim, but Slim leaped into the air like a coiled spring and tipped the ball to Bill, who charged toward the basket and bounced a pass to Rusty. Rusty snared it from under the nose of a Carson guard, pivoted, and shot for the goal.

The ball dropped through cleanly, and the Trenton gallery let out a yell of triumph that shook the cupids on the light fixtures.

"How do you like that?" said Rusty, glaring at the Carson guard.

"A-tisket, a-tasket, he shot a little basket," said the guard. "Say, fellows, aren't their uniforms just too ducky?"

"Listen," said Rusty, "that's about enough of —"

Fortunately, at that moment, the ball was thrown in, and Carson's McBride, leading candidate for All-Conference, bagged it and streaked downcourt.

"Watch it, Tommy!"

The rangy Trenton guard watched it so thoroughly that he forced a pass. The Carson break had been fast but not quite fast enough, and Trenton was set defensively before the Green and White could get a shot at the basket. For a moment the rooters were treated to a brilliant exhibition of ball handling, culminating in a rush by McBride for the basket with the ball dribbled ahead of him.

"Out of my way, Cupid," yelled McBride.

Thus addressed, Bob Evans, Tommy's running mate at Trenton guard, crowded McBride to the sidelines in no uncertain manner. The Carson star, not to be thrown off balance, turned and shot instantly for the goal. The ball traveled briefly around the rim and slipped through the net.

Two to two.

Play speeded up to a blitzkrieg tempo, and the solid power of the Carson five began to make itself felt. Their comments were also making themselves felt, and Trenton tempers worked up rapidly to boiling point. Carson was riding them unmercifully, never missing a chance to make a crack at Happy's Valentine costumes.

"Is *that* the famous Bill Endicott?" said a Carson player in mock awe, as one of Bill's long shots from center floor circled the rim of the basket and bounced out. "That fellow in the pretty red sash?"

"You'll eat this red sash before we're through," Bill prophesied grimly, giving the adornment a hitch.

The Carson man gave a pitying laugh and glanced at the scoreboard. Carson, 22; Trenton, 14. "Looks like it, doesn't it?" he said. "Say, I know what you guys need — red bows in your hair."

"We've already got you in our hair, thanks," Rusty retorted, and got revenge by the swift interception of a pass intended for McBride. There was a shriek from the panting Trenton stands: "Yea, Rusty. Sock it to 'em."

Rusty raced down the floor, dribbling the ball at top speed, but was balked in a shot for the basket by the close guarding of a Carson man, who grinned and said, "What's the trouble, Kewpie? Lost your bow and arrow?"

Rusty charged him, the guard both charged and pushed. The referee said sharply, "Take it easy there," and hauled them apart, signaling a double foul. Carson made it good. Rusty, who was not as a rule any too steady on free throws, was too indignant to miss this one, and the ball swooped through the net — 23 to 15, in Carson's favor.

A moment later the gun signaled the half, and the players left the court to an accompaniment of cheers.

Happy followed the squad to the locker room and stood with his hands in his pockets, looking very miserable. "Gee, fellows," he said, "I'm sorry about your costumes. I didn't realize Carson would razz you so much. I'll take the hearts and stuff off right away."

Tommy, who had been the most vocal in his objections to the decorations, stuck his chin out dangerously. "Over my dead body," he said. "Before we get through with that bunch of guys, they'll wish they'd never

seen a heart. Stick another pin in my sash, will you, Happy? It's slipping."

Considerably reassured, Happy produced an enormous pin. "Wait till you see the surprise I've planned for after the game," he said. "Boy, is that something! . . . Bill, you need pinning?"

Bill gave his own sash a dubious jerk. "No, I guess not. All I'm interested in right now is taking those Carson fellows to pieces."

Coach Bennett, aware that his team was already playing over its head, said mildly, "You're doing all right."

"Did you notice what a turnout we've got, too?" Happy interrupted eagerly. "You're going to get decent uniforms out of this game anyway."

"We're going to get more than that," said Bob Evans sternly, and got to his feet as the timekeeper called them back to the court.

Carson's Elliott outjumped Slim on the tip-off and tapped the ball to the guard who whirled and back-passed to McBride. There was an anxious moment after the Carson ace's long-distance toss, while the ball circled the hoop, then a cheer from the Green and White stands as it dropped through.

Rusty retaliated by slanting the ball to Bill, who flashed downcourt, eluded his guard and caged an easy try. Carson, 25; Trenton, 17.

Bill, feeling his sash slipping, squirmed around in an effort to anchor the pin more safely. "Can I tie that for you, my little man?" said McBride kindly in passing, and a moment later was awarded a free throw on a personal as Bill undertook a bit of guarding that was more enthusiastic than it should have been.

McBride made it good, and Trenton took over the ball, with Bill leading the play. Carson covered for a pass; Bill feinted, then shot unexpectedly for the basket — a long try that rolled around once, wavered, then swished through the netting.

"Why, lookit what Kewpie did!" said the Carson center, clasping his hands in pretty surprise.

This remark proved to be an error in judgment. Kewpie, the next time he got his hands on the ball, promptly did it again.

Carson, 26; Trenton, 21.

Happy, on the sidelines, began to take deep breaths to quiet his nervous system. Trenton was putting on an unexpected show. Five points wasn't much of a lead for the Green and White. He leaped suddenly from his seat as a tense period of spectacular Carson ball-handling ended in a long try. Rusty appeared from nowhere to intercept, raced down the floor and caged a one-hand shot.

"Yea, Trenton! Come on!"

Carson replied in kind, as Carson's Brewster broke for the basket, snagged the ball on the run and whipped it to the net. Twenty-eight to twenty-three for the big Green — still a five-point lead, which shifted suddenly to seven points as McBride popped one in under the basket not more than a moment later.

Happy came out of his tranced attention to the game long enough to notice regretfully that the red draping behind the baskets was beginning to come untacked, owing to the way people kept missing baskets and hitting the backboard instead. Happy was opposed to this on principle. Also one of the silver cupids had fluttered down from a light fixture and landed on the referee's head during the course of play, and the referee had given it a murderous look.

Decorations, however, no longer seemed important. Happy wound his arms around his knees, parked his chin on top and tried to maintain some semblance of calm.

The fourth quarter, however, found Trenton still trailing seven points, and Happy's shoulders began to sag. They weren't going to be able to come from behind, not with the tight, expert guarding of the Carson defense.

No more cupids had floated from the ceiling, but it seemed to Happy that this was cold comfort, especially as the drapery behind one of the baskets was sagging perilously and Bill's sash was definitely coming undone. Happy glanced hastily over at Archie guarding the pigeons, then at the janitor. Everything was all right there anyway. Win or lose, the spectators were going to be treated to a genuine surprise.

"Only it's just got to be win," Happy told himself, feeling that even his pigeons would fail to comfort him if they lost now. He then leaped madly to his feet, as Tommy caged an under-the-basket shot on a long pass from Bill. Thirty to twenty-five. That was better.

"Come on, Trenton!"

Trenton came on.

Play tightened, speeded up mercilessly. Trenton players forgot their costumes; Carson forgot to make wisecracks. Spectators had no breath left for cheering; officials panted in pursuit of the dazzling play; the reporter from the *Trenton High Weekly* ran out of adjectives and broke his pencil point. Happy tugged madly at his hair with both hands and squirmed around on the bench like an electric eel.

Five more points, and it would be all even.

Trenton was bombing the basket now, trying to score at every opportunity. A lucky corner shot clicked, and Trenton trailed only three points. Then Bob Evans got the ball on an interception and glanced quickly around him. A brilliant ball-handler but conservative about long shots, he wanted someone in the open to pass to. Bill had the adhesive McBride practically wrapped around his shoulders. Rusty — There was a chance with Rusty.

McBride gave a yip of amusement. "He doesn't know whether he's a basketball player or a ballet dancer in that costume," he announced. "Look at him doing a hesitation waltz."

Stung, Bob smacked the ball unhesitatingly toward the goal by way of retort. It hit the backboard and

bounced through the basket.

"Yee-ow!" yelled Happy, along with the entire Trenton cheering section.

"Ballet dancer, huh?" said Bill to McBride with a satisfied grin, "Maybe *you* guys had better take up dancing."

The ball was thrown in again. Happy was on his feet, waving a stranger's hat and shouting hoarsely. Carson, 30; Trenton, 29. It was now or never.

Carson stalled.

The timer's gun was out. So, Happy noticed fleetingly, was the tail of Bill's sash, and Bill was quite unknowingly trailing clouds of glory.

Only it didn't matter now. It didn't matter if all the costumes and decorations and everything else folded up. "They've gotta win," Happy muttered, his hair wildly on end. "They've just gotta."

Seconds to go.

Tommy got the ball by a desperate but well-timed lunge, and the Trenton stands screamed approval. A reckless long shot crawled around the basket and skidded off the rim. A teammate flipped it back, and it jumped the basket maddeningly, seemingly headed for Carson possession again. Rusty leaped forward and batted the ball to Bill, just before McBride could get his fingers on it and settle the game forever.

The timekeeper raised his gun.

Bill jumped for the ball, and at that moment St. Valentine's Day took a hand in the proceedings. The fateful red sash tripped the forward and he stumbled, grabbing at the ball.

It went through his teammates' heads in that split second that Bill couldn't have shot for the basket anyway. He was covered by two men, and he might as well have been wrapped in barbed wire.

But something else went through Bill's head as he fell forward, hopelessly entangled in his sash. It was the fact that Rusty was now in the clear for an easy shot. Above Bill, the long-legged McBride controlled the situation. There would be no shooting a pass by those reaching arms.

But McBride had a trick of bracing himself solidly, his feet well apart. Bill, falling, remembered that, and he did the only thing he could do. He bounce-passed the ball between McBride's legs, yelled a warning to Rusty and then sprawled inelegantly on his nose.

Rusty scooped up the ball and shot instantly for the basket. The gun went off with the ball in mid-air.

And, at exactly the same moment, every light in the room went out.

There was an impassioned howl from the referee, frantic yells from the spectators, and a rising babble of voices, all demanding to know what had happened. "The ball!" they yelled. "Did it go through? Didn't *anybody* see?"

From Happy there came a despairing wail that drowned out all other sounds. Happy, alone, could fully appreciate the situation. The janitor, true to his promise, had snapped the light switch the moment the gun sounded. What was it to the janitor that the ball was still in the air? What did the janitor know about the

game of basketball? What, indeed, did he care?

Stricken dumb, after his single shriek, by unutterable woe, Happy heard rising around him in the darkness the flutter and beat of pigeons' wings. Overhead circled the little phosphorescent hearts, glowing beautifully.

It was a magnificent exhibition, but Happy was in no mood for it. He was enveloped in a gloom that was darker than the pitch-black gymnasium. Because now there was no way of knowing whether Rusty's shot had been good or not. And if Trenton had lost the game, just because he, Happy, had had a fool idea —

Desolation hit him amidships.

The referee shouted suddenly, "Hey! Get those lights on!" and evidently the janitor responded to the tone of authority, for a second later they winked on in full brilliance, illuminating a unique spectacle.

The air was full of pigeons. Two of them had fluttered down and settled confidingly on the referee, and the referee's expression was that of a man tried beyond human endurance. He permitted himself, however, one remark.

"Great jumping junipers," said the referee, torn between wrath and relief. "I thought they were bats!"

One pigeon was perched on Bill's head, but Bill, his hands dangling limply at his sides, was making no effort to do anything about anything. His teammates were grouped around him, played out and hopeless. The

end of the shot that might have won them the game had been lost in darkness among the pigeons. That was that.

Happy came out on the floor, his face tragic. "Gosh, fellows, I — I — It's all my fault. I told the janitor to put out the lights when the gun went off, so we could release the pigeons. But, gee, I didn't know the ball would be — Hey! Where is the ball?"

Everyone suddenly looked around. There was no ball. No ball on the playing court, no ball out of bounds, no ball flying away with a pigeon. All eyes turned involuntarily to the basket, and a hoarse yell rose from throats that were already sore with shouting.

Happy's red draperies had fallen forward, as Bill had feared they would, and wadded themselves neatly inside the netting. Caught there, resting on top of the scarlet cloth but obviously safely caged, was Rusty's triumphant last shot.

Trenton, 31; Carson, 30.

"Well!" said the referee, and got up enough strength to brush off the pigeons.

Hearts and Hoops

1. Why did Happy want to decorate the gym and the team for the Carson game?

2. How did the players like the plan for their "costumes"? What made them change their attitude later?

3. What effect did the rival team's razzing have on the Trenton boys?

4. Why was it important to Happy's plans to have the lights turned out when the final gun sounded?

5. How did the decorations lend a final thrill to the game?

6. Could you use a Happy in your school? What kind of job in the outside world could Happy fill very well?

Action Words

The lively action of a basketball game calls for lively words to describe it. Many of the terms you meet in talk of basketball can give as much vigor to other kinds of talk. Try putting *intercept, feint, lunge,* and *snare* in statements about other kinds of action. First make sure you know their exact meaning by fitting one of them into each blank in this narrative:

Sammy ....ed forward to .... the cat as it streaked for the open door. The cat tried to outwit him by making a .... at the open window and then tearing back toward the door. But Sammy made another .... and ....ed her.

Now use each one of the words in a new sentence of your own about another kind of action. Some of you may wish to demonstrate the meaning of these terms by "acting them out" in front of the class.

The Gallant Golfer

JOHN KIERAN

Please note the gallant golfer as from tee to green he hies;
For fun (or doctor's orders) he is taking exercise.
His head he carries (rather high), one club (that made the stroke).
He also carries matches just in case he wants a smoke.
And with the gallant golfer, as he wanders west and east,   5
There trudges forth a skinny kid who's burdened like a beast.
The lad who seeks no exercise but just his caddie fees,
Goes carting total tonnage that would spring a pack-mule's knees.
The golfer gay who goes his way a-whacking at the ball
May have the fun. But exercise? The caddie gets it all!   10

GOOD SPORT

Quick Kick

STEPHEN W. MEADER

Fall means football — fans cheering madly in the stands, bands blaring their fight songs from the side lines, teams struggling up and down the field. Everyone who enjoys this thrilling game knows it is teamwork that makes football good sport.

T HAT'S the new play. Like every good play in football, it takes eleven men — each doing his job."

Coach "Hike" Kilroy's steely eyes flashed around the darkening room. He picked up an eraser and swept it through the circles, crosses, and running lines of the blackboard diagram. Then he swung back to his audience.

"I've one more thing to say. Some of you hope for a conference championship. But if you keep on letting them block your punts you're going to get licked." For a few seconds he let the words sink in. "All right," he said shortly. "That's all for tonight."

The varsity squad rose and filed from the room in silence. Outside, their voices rose in laughter and fragments of song, but Barry Hughes, two-hundred-pound tackle and cap-

tain, stayed behind, his face serious. "Walking over, Coach?" he asked.

Kilroy nodded and they went slowly down the path. A fading October sunset shed golden light across the Cameron campus. There was a nip in the air — good football weather.

"This blocked punt business," Hughes began, "I think we can stop it, Coach. It's the left side of the line they break through. Hartley and Wiggins are strong enough but they need experience. Couldn't we work on that this week, and tighten up those holes?"

"We're going to," the coach replied. "But you know where the real trouble lies. It's Butch Davis. A grand punter, but slow. He has to take three steps to get the ball away, and I can't break him of it."

He paused a moment, and when he went on there was an edge of bitterness in his voice. "We've got the fastest pair of ends in the conference," he said. "I'd hoped to shoot in a quick kick play this year. It's one of the smartest tricks in the bag when it's done right. Boy, how we could use Jack Moran and Weasel Blake down the field, if we had a real quick-kicker! But I've combed the squad and there isn't a man in the lot that can boot one fast enough."

They said good night at a fork in the path, and Barry Hughes departed in the direction of the Commons. Kilroy's way led past the practice field toward his house on Faculty Circle. There was a thud of leather, over on his left. Four or five students were kicking up and down the field in the dusk. It was too dark to see much, but the coach stopped a moment to watch them, his mind still busy with team problems.

Suddenly he was all attention. The boys were playing one of those kicking games where, if you catch the ball, you can punt it at once, and if you miss you take three steps backward from the point where it is touched. A long, high spiral came down the field, and a boy ran sidewise to get under it. He caught the ball in his hands, took one brief step, and sent it whirling back with a low, hard-driven punt that angled to the right. There was frantic scurrying at the other end of the field. The ball took a high bounce, cleared the head of the nearest man, and rolled to within a yard of the goal line.

The boy who had kicked it laughed aloud. " Take yo' three steps in reverse," he shouted, " an' let's see what y'all can do! "

The receiver made a desperate effort. From deep in the end zone the pigskin sailed up and up, till Kilroy lost it in the darkness. Not so the boy he had been watching. Sprinting forward from mid-field, he was well inside the thirty-yard line when the soaring punt came down in his arms.

Again he wasted no time. " Look out — it's a drop kick! " cried one of his opponents, rushing to get behind the goal posts. But the ball beat him. From the ground in front of the kicker's toe it described a neat arc over the center of the bar, and bounced uncaught on the other side.

" Hi-yah! Another two bits! " crowed the winner, doing a war dance. " Yo' cain't deny that one! "

He was starting at a trot for the side line when Kilroy's gruff voice halted him.

" Hold on, son," he said. " Are you a student here? "

" Yes, suh."

" Freshman? "

" No, suh — sophomore."

" What's your name? "

" Warfill Jones. But they call me ' Waffle,' mostly."

" Ever play football? "

" In our little ol' high school, back home. Yes, suh."

" Where's that? "

" Warfill Co't House — in the Valley o' Virginia, suh! " He said those last words with a pride and reverence that conjured up pictures. Barefoot marchers in tattered gray, and Marse Robert himself, on Traveler.[1]

" Not very big, are you? " said the coach. " What do you weigh? "

[1] **Marse Robert** is General Robert E. Lee. **Traveler** was his famous horse.

"Hundred an' fifty-five, right about."

"You're not out for football here. Why not? Don't you like the game?"

"Sho' I like it. Trouble is, I jerk sodas fo' my keep, an' the busiest time o' day is from three o'clock till five-thirty. Only time I git fo' playin' is when other folks go home to supper."

Kilroy stroked his chin and thought. "How much do you make, at the soda fountain?" he asked.

"Six dollars a week an' bo'd. But I take in a little spendin' money from these spo'ts, yere. When I score a goal on 'em I make two bits."

"Yes, but don't you have to pay it when they score on you?"

Waffle Jones chuckled. "That's only 'bout once in a coon's age," he answered.

Kilroy made decisions fast, and stuck by them when they were made. He liked the Southern boy's trim build and alert grin.

"Listen," he said. "I want you on the squad. Tell you what we can do. There's a room over my garage, and I need someone to look after the car and tend the furnace. That'll cover your board. I think I can get three other faculty members to give you their furnace jobs at two dollars a week. You'll be kept busy about three hours a day, but it won't come in the afternoon. What do you say?"

"Gosh," stammered Waffle. "You — you mean I can try fo' the team?"

"Just that," nodded Kilroy. "It won't be easy, because the season's nearly half gone. But you'll have your chance. Now go down and tell that druggist he's got to find a new soda clerk. I'll come along in the car and pick up your clothes."

That was on a Monday night. Wednesday, as the squad jogged off the field after heavy scrimmage, Coach Kilroy stopped his captain at the edge of the running track.

"Left side of the line holding better today?" he asked.

Barry Hughes nodded. "Looked so to me. Anyhow, they ought to," he grinned. "I spent nearly an hour showing Hartley how to swing his hips on the charge, when we're punting. It'll take an eel to get through him if he keeps on improving. Wiggins, at guard, is clumsier, but he takes up plenty of room."

"By the way," said Kilroy abruptly, "how's this new kid, trying out for the backfield?"

Hughes laughed. "Waffle Jones?" he asked. "I don't know much about him but he seems to be a character. He's in dead earnest — a typical Southerner, with lots of fight. He tackled Butch Davis pretty hard this afternoon and Butch was sore. Called the boy 'po' white trash,' and Waffle came after him with both fists swinging. They'd have put on the Battle of Bull Run if I hadn't pacified 'em."

Kilroy frowned. "Hard tackling is all right," he said, "but we can't use hotheads. The scrub coach says Jones is a fair blocker and he handles the ball as if he knew how. He may be too light, though, to be much good to us."

"Wait a minute," put in Hughes. "Have you seen him boot one? He's got a hind leg like a mule and he gets 'em off in nothing flat. I thought — " he hesitated — " I just wondered if he wasn't the quick-kicker we were praying for."

In the gathering darkness Kilroy grinned. So Barry Hughes was impressed, too! But that near fight — it wouldn't do, to let a feud grow up between Butch and Waffle.

That evening, while Waffle was washing the car, his new employer strode into the garage. He looked on a while in silence. Then, " Jones," he said suddenly, " they tell me you've got a temper. Good. I wouldn't give two cents for a man that didn't. But if you can't control it, there's no point in your going out for a place on my team."

Waffle tossed the sponge into the bucket and stood up, looking him in the eye. " Thank you, suh," he answered, reddening. " I'll sho'ly try."

He did try, manfully, but it wasn't always easy. Butch Davis, the first-string fullback, kept his grudge, and whenever chance brought them together in scrimmage, the big line-plunger scowled and put extra steam into his attack. He had decided that Waffle Jones was showing off — trying to make an impression. And with the blunt, hardheaded fullback, that didn't go down.

Once, when Butch was charging in to make a tackle and Waffle cross-blocked him out of the play, the Virginia boy felt a heavy knee drive home to the pit of his stomach. He staggered to his feet, fists clenched, eyes blazing. But with his wind knocked out, the fighting words died in his throat in a wheezing moan. And by the time he could speak, he had himself in hand.

The first Saturday in November, Jones sat happily on the bench, a big new 68 gleaming on the back of his maroon jersey. He was part of the Cameron squad. Any minute, now, the coach might catch his eye and shoot him into the game.

It didn't happen, however. Cameron walked through the Harley team for thirteen points in the first half, and unleashed a beautiful passing attack to score three more touchdowns in the second. The line held on punts, and only once did Butch Davis fail to get his kick away. That was on third down and a Cameron man recovered the ball, so no harm was done.

The Harley victory gave Cameron a record of six straight wins and no defeats — a conference standing equaled only by the powerful State University team. And the school's championship hopes burst into a flame that swept the campus.

The only game of the year outside the conference was a contest with Harnell, to be played the following Saturday at Northville. Cameron had been scheduled as a breather for the Big Red team. Now, with the Maroon's impressive string of conquests in mind, the newspapers began to talk of a possible Cameron victory.

It was a hilarious crowd that gathered that Monday night after signal practice, for the weekly blackboard drill. But, as always, when Hike Kilroy held up his hand the chatter died instantly.

"I guess," he said deliberately, "you've all been reading the sport pages. Don't let it go to your heads. We've got two games ahead of us that aren't in our class — Harnell and State. I'm going to ask you a question. If you had your choice between beating Harnell, Saturday, and beating State for the title, which would it be?"

"State!" shouted thirty voices simultaneously.

Kilroy nodded. "I think we can win one of those two games," he said. "I'll tell you frankly it would mean more to my reputation to trim Harnell. We could shoot the works, and possibly catch them off their guard. I've got a new play to give you that's a giant killer. But State will be scouting us Saturday. Now get me right. We're going up to Northville and fight. We'll win if we can. But it'll be with straight football and plenty of substitutes. We're not going to cripple the team or give away our best plays. We're pointing for State!"

"Yea-a-ay, Hike!" bellowed someone in the back of the room, and the whole squad echoed the cheer.

Kilroy lifted his hand again. "All right," he said. "Let's get down to brass tacks. Here's that new play we're going to start work on tomorrow. We'll call it Number 91. It's a quick kick."

That week Waffle Jones found himself suddenly conspicuous. Out of the obscurity of the scrub, where he had been laboring without special distinction, he was elevated to the varsity squad. Every afternoon he and Butch Davis were taken aside by the head coach for a fifteen-minute kicking drill.

The situation irked Butch. He couldn't understand why a raw rookie who had come on the squad late in the season should receive special attention. Why didn't he take his chances with the rest? Why all this grooming of an unknown? Waffle, on the other hand, gazed in open-mouthed admiration at the fullback's high, graceful spirals. His own punts looked ragged by comparison. They had length and speed but the ball usually flew end over end and wobbled erratically.

"Gosh," he exclaimed, "I sho' would like to kick thataway! How is it you hold 'em?"

"Here, Jones," the coach interposed sharply. "Don't you go fooling with spirals. Kick your own way, and remember all I want is speed and direction."

He tossed the ball to Red Landis, the center, who crouched above it, awaiting the signal to pass.

"This time," said Kilroy, "I want you closer to the line and over here to the left — the Number 3 spot, in a double wing-back formation. Landis, you'll have to watch your pass. Keep it on his right, and waist high. I'm going to be the opposing tackle and block it if I can. All right — let her go!"

Waffle saw the ball shoot toward

him, caught it at arm's length, and swung his foot, all in the space of a second. Then Kilroy's charge knocked him flat. By the time he regained his feet, the scrub quarter, who had been elected to catch and return punts, was running after a bouncing oval, far over in the corner of the field.

"You'll do," puffed Kilroy, with one of his rare smiles. "They'll never get through on you any faster than I did. And you placed it just right. Take a couple more for practice and we'll start scrimmage."

Flushed with pleasure, the Virginia boy stole a look at Butch Davis. But the big fullback had turned on his heel and was walking away.

For ten thrilling minutes of the afternoon scrimmage, Waffle Jones was in the line-up of the varsity. And twice during that time Hal Decker, at quarter, called the 91 signal. The first time, a bad pass from center dribbled off the Southerner's finger tips and he was forced to fall on the ball beneath an avalanche of scrub linemen. But the second try worked.

The team had the ball on its own forty-yard line, second down and four to go. The scrub secondary was in close, expecting a running play. Waffle got his kick away fast and the varsity ends raced down the field under it. The scrub safety man was caught flat-footed. He turned, as the oval sailed over his head, and rushed back after it, but Moran touched it down five yards from the goal. Forced to punt, the scrubs lost

twenty yards on the exchange, and a few plays later the first team put over a score.

Heading for the gym at a trot, when practice was finished, Waffle felt a big hand slap him between the shoulder blades.

"Nice work, kid!" said a friendly voice, and Barry Hughes jogged up beside him. "Don't worry about that wide pass. You won't get one in fifty like that from Red Landis. He's steady as a rock."

Thirty-five men entrained for Northville on Friday night, and Waffle was undoubtedly the proudest member of the party. He spent an hour or two Saturday morning strolling up and down the famous hills of the Harnell campus. Then the squad had an early lunch and rested till game time. It was a gray day, overcast and cold. After the warm-up, Waffle pulled on his hooded maroon jacket and took his place on the bench.

The game started slowly. It took the big Harnell machine a few minutes to thaw out. Then, just as their power thrusts off tackle began to work, Decker recovered a fumble, and a brilliant forward from midfield took the Red defense by surprise. Weasel Blake, catching it on the run, squirmed past the safety man and ran for a touchdown.

Foley, the Maroon's left halfback and star placement kicker, converted the point. And at the end of the opening period the score was 7–0 in Cameron's favor.

After that the aroused Harnell

team gave them no more chances. Half a dozen times the Red attack swept down the field, only to be held by a fighting Cameron line in the shadow of the goal. Then one of Butch Davis's beautiful punts would take the ball back to mid-field and the steam roller would start again.

It couldn't go on forever. Five minutes before the half ended a smashing cross buck split the tiring Maroon forward wall, and Harnell scored. Promptly Kilroy took out the whole first line and sent them to the dressing room. And the reserves managed to avert another touchdown for the remainder of the period.

In the second half Cameron kept the offensive for a time, and even threatened the Red goal. Then the breaks went against the Maroon. A pass intended for Blake was intercepted and a Harnell back, running behind quick-forming interference, galloped to the Cameron five-yard stripe before he was downed. Two sledgehammer blows at the line took the ball over. Harnell was leading by a touchdown.

The next kick-off was short, and a good runback gave Cameron the ball on its own forty-five-yard line. Waffle Jones began to fidget on the bench. He looked at Kilroy expectantly. The Red backs were drawn in. It was just the time for the 91 play. The coach glanced toward him with a shake of the head that was barely perceptible.

Decker knifed through on a spinner for three yards. Butch Davis plowed off tackle for two, tried again

at center and made only inches. Then the big fullback dropped far to the rear and kicked a high spiral that fell neatly in the safety man's arms on the Harnell twenty-yard line. Waffle gave a little groan. The chance was gone.

Cameron fought gallantly through the last quarter, but always on the defensive. Kilroy began putting in substitutes. Waffle Jones saw the coach beckon and sprang to his feet. With a pounding heart he ran up and down the side line, then sprinted out on the field.

Those final minutes of the game were a nightmare of grueling punishment. Under the steady pounding, Cameron's reserves gave ground doggedly but inevitably. The young Virginian lost all track of yardage. All he knew was the desperate charge of the secondary to pile up a play that had pierced the line — the smash of his body across an interferer's legs — the clutch of his hands on a stained red jersey.

Once he saw a broad white stripe

on the ground when he picked himself up. There must have been a touchdown, he thought dully. But he was being pounded on the back and a voice yelled, " It's a penalty! Harnell offside! " And then came the faint crack of a gun. The game, Waffle realized, was over.

As he stumbled toward the side line, someone threw a blanket around his shoulders. He was trotting with the squad toward the showers. " Say," he panted, as a big figure pulled abreast of him, " what was the score? "

Barry Hughes peered at him and laughed. " Fourteen–seven," he answered. " You were sure in there fighting, kid! "

Fourteen–seven. Then they had really held them — stopped the Harnell attack with second stringers! He was proud of Cameron in defeat.

The whole squad got a rest on Monday. But Tuesday afternoon, in a drizzling rain, they went to work

in earnest. The field was guarded that final week. Forty stalwart undergraduates patrolled the running track, with suspicious eyes for anyone resembling a stranger. And inside the cordon, Hike Kilroy cracked the whip over his squad. There were brief daily drills in fundamentals, but the work was concentrated on two or three new deception plays and the quick kick.

Waffle Jones was in the varsity line-up most of the time, now. He tried to keep clear of Butch Davis, but the fullback's hostility was too open to be ignored. Once, when he was sent in at half in the middle of scrimmage, he saw Butch turn to Bill Ray, the right guard, and heard him say something about " — that po' white trash is in again!"

In a flash he stood before his enemy, fist drawn back and trembling. "When the season's over," he said, through clenched teeth, "I'll take that out o' yo' hide!"

Barry Hughes shouldered between them. "Shut up, kid," the captain growled, "and you too, Butch. Now get in there and play football!"

By Friday night the whole squad was down to a fine edge — not overtrained but restless and fidgety as a bunch of thoroughbreds at the barrier.[1] In his room over the garage, Waffle Jones tried to do some studying, gave it up, went to an early picture show, and turned in at nine-thirty. For half an hour he tossed on his pillow, signals racing through

[1] **thoroughbreds at the barrier:** race horses at the starting point of a race.

his head, his muscles twitching with eagerness for battle. Then he dropped into a sound sleep and didn't wake till it was time to tend furnaces in the morning.

The campus was astir early. Old grads and pretty girls began to appear, and excited students cut their morning classes. Waffle lunched with the team and took a walk until it was time to dress. The players were gruff and silent in the locker room. At just the right moment, Hike Kilroy strolled in.

"Hi, gang!" he called cheerily. "Last game! No more black-and-blue practices. Just a swell afternoon for football, and a chance to prove you're as good as I think you are. Let's get the jump on 'em and play 'em off their feet!"

The tension was gone in an instant. Waffle felt a surge of warlike joy, and jumped to his feet with the rest. The squad laughed and thumped one another on the back.

There was a big crowd in the stands, cheering mightily as the vanguard of maroon jerseys trotted on the field. Three blue-clad State elevens were already snapping through their signal drill. They were big, all right. They outweighed Cameron ten pounds to the man, and looked it.

Waffle went through the warm-up in a sort of trance and woke up to find himself on the bench, with Barry Hughes and the State captain shaking hands in mid-field. There was little wind. State won the toss and chose to receive.

And the kick-off! It went to the fifteen, and Blue interference seemed to form by magic. Downed by right halfback Judd on the thirty-five. The teams barely had time to crouch, when Craven, State's hard-running back, was racing around left end behind a flying cloud of blue. It took Decker, the safety man, to bring him down, and he was five yards past the center stripe.

Caught off balance, the Cameron team had hardly lined up before a crushing off-tackle thrust gained twenty yards more, and then a long forward settled in the arms of a State back for a touchdown.

The game was just a minute old and Cameron was six points behind. A moment later it was seven, as Craven converted the point with a placement.

Waffle sat stunned. The "jump," so important in a close game, had gone to the enemy. He wondered if it *would* be close.

State received again, and this time Jack Moran, downfield like an Irish whirlwind, slammed the great Craven in his tracks. The stands roared as Barry burst through on the first play to smother a runner behind the line. State fell back to kick and the game was under control once more.

The rest of the first period was a slam-bang battle. Cameron worked the ball into enemy territory twice, and on one occasion reached the blue twenty-yard line, but was held for downs by inches.

It was well along in the second period, and Coach Kilroy was beginning to steal glances at his watch, when Waffle heard Decker bark a signal, and watched, tense and breathless, as the play started. It was one of the new tricks. Cameron's ball on the State thirty-five.

The oval went to Decker, then to Foley, and deftly back to Butch on a fake reverse. Butch put back his long arm and threw a low, swift pass that traveled twenty yards like a bullet.

Weasel Blake was in the clear — out to the right. He took one quick look over his shoulder, reached upward, and snagged the ball without losing stride. Two defense men raced across to cut him down. The first he shook off with a sidewise leap. The second brought him to earth a step short of the goal.

There was no holding Cameron then. Barry and Ray tore a hole in the State line, and Butch Davis went through the gap like a moose through a thicket. The teams lined up in front of the goal posts. Decker knelt to catch the placement. And just as the half ended, Foley's toe smacked it cleanly over to tie the score.

Through the frenzied yelling from the stands, the subs raced for the gym. Waffle Jones was standing just inside the door when the Varsity came in. He waited till Davis had settled wearily on a bench, then stole toward him.

"Say, Butch," he muttered lamely, "I just wanted to tell you — well — you were swell!"

The big line-plunger looked up at

him without reply, frowned, and bent once more to retie his shoelaces. Reddening, the boy walked away. His eagerness was gone. He hardly cared whether Cameron won or lost. Then a hand slapped his shoulder and the friendy voice of Barry Hughes was asking how he felt.

" Going to pull old 91 on 'em, this half! " grinned the captain, as he lay back on the rubbing table.

" You bet! " said Waffle, and felt better.

Kilroy came in for the last three minutes. He talked quietly, without heroics, but there was an edge to his words. " All right," he finished. " Every man in every play. You've got the stuff to win this game."

It was obvious, as the second half started, that the State team had been given a tongue lashing. They tore in with a sullen ferocity that ruined Cameron's first two plays after the kick-off. Davis planted a long punt down the field. And then the bigger team's power attack started.

Smash, smash, smash at the line, and then a swinging end run behind interference that looked like a battery of tanks. First downs by inches — first downs by yards. Twice the Maroons stiffened to hold them and kick out of danger. But the third time State crashed over. On the try for point, Ray's headlong rush half checked the rising ball and it hit the crossbar to bounce back. No goal. State, 13; Cameron, 7.

That was still the score when they changed ends for the final quarter. There was swaggering confidence in every movement of the blue jerseys. They had a lead, and they had the Maroon ball carriers stopped.

Held on her own thirty-yard line, Cameron punted. The State runback brought the ball nearly to mid-field, and they started what looked like another touchdown march. Two downs and only a yard to go for first down. Then came a break — a little carelessness in the State backfield, and a fumble that rolled wide. Moran, the cruising ball hawk, was on it like a shot.

Even before the referee had untangled the pile, Waffle heard his name called, " Go in there, Jones, and do your stuff! " said Kilroy. " This is the spot."

Running across the field, jumping into the left halfback position, Waffle felt numb with excitement. The signal called for a buck. Judd went through right guard for three yards. The ball was just over the center line, ten yards in from the left side of the field.

" Fifty-seven — ninety-one — forty-six — nine — eleven — " Hal Decker was barking.

Waffle saw the square, close defense of the State backs, braced himself, and caught the pass, rifled true into his hands by Red Landis. With the quick thud of his toe came a looming wave of Blue linemen, but the ball was away. As he scrambled to his feet he saw Weasel Blake swooping after the rolling pigskin, deep in the far corner of the field. Then he gave a startled gasp. The flying end checked his speed, waited till the ball bounced over the goal line, and flung himself on it just as the blue-clad pursuers reached him.

"Gosh!" choked Waffle in dismay. "Now it'll have to come out twenty yards!"

Decker was whooping, pounding him on the back. "Come out nothing!" cried the hilarious quarter. "Their safety man had his hands on it, and that crazy end-over-end kick of yours got away from him. It's a touchdown!"

On the scoreboard new numbers were posted: "State, 13; Cameron, 13."

They lined up. With Foley out, Butch would attempt the placement. "We've got to make this point — *got to make it!*" Waffle was telling himself feverishly. "Got to protect Butch's toe! He's slow!"

Just behind him and to the right he heard Hal Decker, down on one knee, yelping the signal. And suddenly he knew something was wrong. Hartley, the left tackle was hurt. Crouched there in the line, his back swayed uncertainly. At the instant the ball was passed he toppled sidewise, and through the wide-open gap came a State guard like a runaway locomotive. Waffle didn't wait for the charge. He met it — hurled himself forward with all the strength in his wiry body. There was a sickening smash, and daylight went out abruptly.

When he came to, it was raining — raining bucketfuls, it seemed. The water boy stopped showering him and grinned.

"Collar bone," a bearded man said, in a matter-of-fact tone.

They supported him between them and carried him off through a lane of anxious, friendly faces — the team! It wasn't till they reached the bench that he recalled what had happened. Then he tried to turn to see the scoreboard and felt a knife stab his shoulder.

"Doctor, suh," he asked humbly, "could yo' tell me about that last placement?"

"We made it," smiled the medico. "And Hartley's all right. Just a bump on the head. Now lie still. I'm going to set this."

The next thing Waffle remembered was a tremendous sound of cheering and the beat of marching feet. Then Hike Kilroy's rugged face was bending over him.

"Good work, Jones," said the coach. "If any man saved that game, you did! Here's a chap wants to tell you so."

And with that the boy found himself looking up at Butch Davis.

"You win, kid," said the fullback huskily. "When you're feeling like it again you can kick me all over the campus if you want to."

"Huh!" chuckled Waffle. "Reckon I don't want to. But I'll play yo' a game o' kickin' up an' down the field — two bits a goal!"

Two Victories

1. What particularly interested the coach in Waffle's kicking? What was the chief weakness of the Cameron team? What were the two reasons for it?

2. Why was Waffle discouraged in his early days on the squad? What did he have to learn besides football? What do you think was the cause of Butch's treatment of Waffle?

3. Did Barry Hughes's activities help you to understand the job of a football captain? Why was he a good captain?

4. Why did the coach use only " straight football and plenty of substitutes " against Harnell?

5. How did Waffle save the game with State? What was his reward? What caused Butch to change his attitude?

Have a Forum on Football Terms

Every fall the air is full of football talk. Reading a story like " Quick Kick " gives meaning to many of these words, but it would be a good idea to get some of the ardent football players in your group to give detailed explanations of them. Select four of them to make up a panel of experts. Let each take one of these topics to explain to the class:

1. The overall plan of the game. This speaker should explain the *toss*, the significance of *downs*, and the special use of *converting*.

2. Formations. The *double wing-back* is used by the team in the story, but there are several others.

3. Types of plays. A number are mentioned in the story — *power thrusts off tackle, fake reverse, end run, cross buck, forward pass.*

4. Penalties. The only one in the story is for *offside*, but in nearly any game there will be others.

Good-by, Babe Ruth!

H. G. SALSINGER

CHIEF IMPRESSIONS OF THE BABE. There has never been anyone like Babe Ruth in the baseball world. In the sports columns of the newspapers, over radio and television, and in the casual chats of fans at games or on street corners, you will still hear his name mentioned. He was the idol of his day, the home-run king who sent a shiver of expectation through the crowd each time he stepped up to the plate. Babe Ruth was more than a great player. As you will discover in this short biographical sketch, he was also a great friend.

This sketch is like many articles and biographies that are popular in today's magazines. It puts before you information that is lively and interesting. Unlike a fiction story it does not tell of a series of happenings in any strict order. Rather, it groups facts and short anecdotes around a few main points the author is trying to get across to the reader. In order to make the main

"Good-by, Babe Ruth!" by H. G. Salsinger from *American Boy Magazine.* Reprinted by permission of J. A. Humberstone.

points stick in your mind the author supports each point with details that explain or illustrate it. As you read, notice how the various facts and little stories about Babe Ruth leave you with three or four main impressions about him.

O N THE day before New York and St. Louis started the World Series of 1926 the Yankees were having a final workout. Every player was nervous and tense, as players are before the start of the World Series. Near the close of practice one of the groundkeepers approached Babe Ruth and told him that a man who had been sitting in one of the field boxes wanted to speak to him. Ruth walked to the box and the man introduced himself and told Ruth:

"My name is John R. Remington and I'm an architect. I know you've never heard of me and I'm sorry to bother you, but I have a son, Johnny. He's very sick. He has been sick for two months. We have called specialist after specialist and they can't do much for the boy, they say, because he doesn't care about anything but you. I was talking to the doctors last night and they said if I could only get a note from you, a ball or a bat or something, with your autograph, it would probably do what all their sciences can't do. And unless something like that happens, I'm afraid we're going to lose Johnny."

"Where do you live?" asked Ruth.

The family lived in New Jersey. The architect gave Ruth a card with name and address.

"How far's this place from here?" asked Ruth.

It was eighty-three miles away.

"How do you get there?"

The architect explained how you got there.

"All right, I'll try to help you in some way," said Ruth and hurried off.

Late that afternoon there came a loud knock on the front door of the Remington home. The maid, answering the summons, was confronted by a giant of a man, round and ruddy of face. He looked enormous as he stood there, both arms filled with packages.

"I'm Babe Ruth and I want to see Johnny."

He was ushered into the sickroom. The pale face of the sick boy turned up to the great figure. He stared and was speechless. It really couldn't be true; he must be dreaming.

"What's the idea of you being sick, Johnny?" bellowed the mighty Ruth. "I've come to find out about it. Look, I've brought you a couple of souvenirs . . ."

Ruth dropped two bats, two gloves, several baseballs, a mask, and a chest protector on the sickbed.

"You know, Johnny, you've got to get going. I was talking to the doctor and he says you're coming along fine and that you'll be back in a few days with all the old pep. I thought maybe you'd need a few things, and so I brought these along. I hope you'll be hitting .400 and breaking windows two blocks away."

For an hour the great idol of the

baseball stadiums sat beside the sick-bed of a strange boy, discussing base-ball, sport in general, giving intimate pictures of some of the great players, telling inside stories of the game. Finally Ruth departed.

The following spring the New York Yankees, their training season

us can do for you, please let us know. We owe you Johnny's life."

"Gee! I'm glad to hear that Johnny's doing so well and I want you to give him my regards and tell him I'm happy to hear about him."

"I will surely do that."

The kindly gentleman bowed and

drawing to a close, were swinging north. They were playing an exhibition game at Memphis, Tennessee. Ruth sat in the lobby, talking to newspapermen. A kindly gentleman approached the group and asked if Mr. Ruth was present. Ruth walked over to meet him.

"I'm Mr. McLean," the man introduced himself, "and I'm Johnny's uncle. We feel so greatly indebted to you, Mr. Ruth, that I don't know what I can say or do to show my appreciation."

"That's fine," interrupted Ruth. "And how is Johnny?"

"Johnny's great. Just perfect. And we owe it all to you, Mr. Ruth. We had given Johnny up. He just kept getting weaker. You did what all the specialists couldn't do; you saved Johnny's life. And I want to tell you that if ever there is anything any of

left. Ruth returned to the group that he had deserted to talk to the stranger.

Ruth pondered for a few minutes before he remarked, "I wonder who that man is and who this Johnny is that he's talking about."

"And that," concluded the newspaper reporter who told me of the incident, "is the most typical Ruth story that I know and I've known Ruth ever since he broke into the big leagues and I saw him intimately, season after season. You see, he had no idea who the boy was; it was just a boy in need of help and Ruth answered the call, and he forgot his good deed as soon as it was done. He didn't even remember the incident."

That's Ruth. He has come closer to the heart of Boyville than any man who ever played baseball, and in conquering the heart of Boyville he has also conquered the grandstands and bleachers. Baseball never knew another player who so touched the heartstrings of the people, young and old, as Ruth touched them. There may never be another like him.

One day a New York newspaper-man interviewed ballplayers about their hobbies. What did they like best outside of baseball? What would they do if they had a million dollars and complete leisure? He approached Ruth and the Babe gave a sincere and honest answer:

" What I like best in the world, even better than baseball, is kids, and if I had a million dollars I'd use it to get a private home for every orphan in the country so none of them would have to go to the orphans' asylums."

Ruth may or may not have been the greatest ballplayer of all time. The matter is open to debate and will be argued for years to come. Some say that Tyrus Raymond Cobb was a greater ballplayer than Ruth. Some say that John (Honus or Hans) Wagner was greater than Ruth. A minority will pick this player or that, but be that as it may, one thing is certain: Ruth is the most popular man the game has ever known.

He became one of the immortals of sports. As long as baseball is played, Ruth will always be included in any all-time line-up. He was, to begin with, one of the greatest left-handed pitchers ever developed. He could probably have continued as one of baseball's immortal

portsiders [1] had it not been for his power at bat.

George Sisler was like that. He started out as a first-class left-handed pitcher and he promised to be an amazing one, but he had so much skill at bat that using him merely as a pitcher would have been stupidity. Sisler was taken off the pitching rubber and became one of the greatest batters of all time, and, incidentally, one of the greatest fielding first basemen.

George Herman Ruth could hit with such power that he was made into an outfielder so that he could play every day. As an outfielder he became one of the best. For a man of weight and bulk he was surprisingly fast. He never had ideal form at bat, but who cares for form in a man who

[1] **portsiders:** *port* is a sea term for "left."

can drive a ball as far as Ruth drove it? He was off balance when he swung and he looked ungraceful, but what of it? He became the super-slugger of all time, the King of Clout, the Big Bam of Swat, the Sultan of Wallop. Maybe he didn't have correct form, but he had rhythm and uncanny timing.

Here's something about Ruth that you've probably never realized, and it was Mickey Cochrane who called attention to the fact. Cochrane should know, because he has crouched behind the plate many times, reaching for a ball that never got as far as his glove because Ruth drove it out of the park. Cochrane told me that Ruth swung on and hit more breaking balls than any other batter in the game.

A breaking ball is almost anything but a fast ball. It's generally a curve ball, slow or fast, or a change of pace, or spit ball, or one of the freak deliveries. Many times in the newspapers you've read something like this: "Ruth swung on a fast ball and hit another home run." Well, Cochrane told me, the chances are three to one that Ruth did not swing on a fast ball because Ruth for years had seen very few fast balls.

When Ruth began making his reputation as a home-run hitter most of his home runs were hit off fast balls. Pitchers were the victims and pitchers, naturally, sought ways and means of stopping Ruth. They began pitching him curve balls and slow balls. They pitched them low and inside and outside the plate.

They had Ruth puzzled for a while but eventually he began hitting them. You see, looking at the various kinds of curves and slow balls the pitchers were serving him, he finally became as familiar with them as he was with fast balls.

Ralph Perkins, one-time coach of the New York Yankees, told me that he kept a record of the balls Ruth had hit over a stretch of weeks. He reported: "Ruth made forty-nine hits, and forty-one of those hits, including home runs, triples, doubles, and singles, were made off slow balls and curve balls. The other eight were made off fast balls."

When Mickey Cochrane broke into the major leagues with Philadelphia, Perkins was the Number One catcher of the Athletics. Connie Mack broke Cochrane in gradually. One day the Athletics were playing the Yankees, and the recruit Cochrane was nominated as catcher for Rube Walberg. Before the game started, Mr. Mack gave his new catcher a few words of warning. "When Ruth comes to bat signal only for low curve balls and slow ones. Whatever you do, don't give him a fast one."

The ninth inning arrived. Philadelphia was leading by two runs. The first batter got on base and the next two were retired. Ruth came to bat. Retire him and the game would be over with Philadelphia winning by two runs. Two strikes on Ruth. Cochrane got a grand idea. He would cross Ruth up by having Walberg pitch a fast ball. Ruth hadn't seen one pitched to him all day. Cochrane gave the fast-ball signal and Walberg pitched it but the ball never reached Cochrane's glove. Ruth drove it over the right-field fence and the score was tied.

Mr. Mack was very angry. He ordered Cochrane to the clubhouse and substituted Perkins, his veteran catcher.

In the twelfth inning, when New York came to bat, the score was still tied. New York got a man on base. Philadelphia retired the next two. Once more Ruth came to bat. Perkins, recalling what calamity had followed the fast ball Cochrane had ordered, decided that he would call for anything but a fast ball; he called for a curve, Walberg pitched, and the curve broke beautifully but Perkins never laid his hands on the ball. Ruth, with a full swing, sent the ball over the center-field fence.

" It was the longest drive I've ever seen in baseball," commented Perkins when he told me the story. " It won the game for the Yankees by two runs."

Ruth learned to hit curve balls as well as he ever had hit fast ones. He collected more than seven hundred home runs in American League competition and most of them were made off the kind of deliveries that are designed to fool batters — the breaking balls — curves of various kinds and slow balls.

He is the greatest slugger of the baseball ages, but he did more for baseball than pack extra-base hits into the record books; he brought the public to the ball parks and he

went in whole-heartedly for Young America. Ruth, as he has honestly confessed on numerous occasions, loves boys more than baseball. Committed to an orphan asylum as a boy, he knew the pangs of the homeless. Having met with rebuffs and lack of paternal care in his youth, his heart has always gone out to the young, especially to orphans.

More baseball lore is spun around Ruth than any man before him. Of giant proportions, he remains, and probably always will remain, the most heroic figure of our national game. He was built for an idol's throne. Nature fitted him physically and temperamentally for the role he has played. He is what he is because he has always been sincere, natural, honest. He has made mistakes, but they have endeared him all the more to the great public. He has always been so thoroughly human, so unaffected, so simple and sincere, that he has won the heart of a nation.

Stories? They will tell them about Ruth as long as baseball is played. He is the Robin Hood of American Boyville.

There was the time in Chicago when a little fellow who didn't have the price of elevated carfare climbed the bank that leads to the track so that he could steal a ride. He came in contact with the third rail, was badly burned and sent to a hospital. Ruth heard about him and hurried to the hospital.

There was the time in Iowa when a crippled boy in a hospital was forbidden to leave his bed and travel thirty miles to the ball park to see his idol in an exhibition game. Babe traveled thirty miles over country roads and in a driving rain and sat at the boy's bedside for half an hour.

There was the time in Nashville, Tennessee, when an old and ragged mountaineer came to the hotel and knocked on the door of Ruth's hotel room. Ruth had just gone to sleep. Awakened by the mountaineer's knock, he got up and admitted him. The mountaineer had a ten-cent ball that he asked Ruth to sign for his boy who was ill up in the mountains and who could not come to Nashville to see Ruth play. Ruth didn't sign the ball. Instead, he dressed, took the mountaineer by the arm, escorted him to the leading sporting goods store in town, bought a baseball uniform, six balls, a bat, a glove, and then climbed into a taxicab, pulling the mountaineer and his purchases after him.

"Now, tell the driver where you live and how to get there and we'll pay the kid a visit."

He did.

There was the time in Macon, Georgia, when Ruth left the park after an exhibition game and became surrounded by a mob of boys. They had all come to see him play, they lacked the necessary money, they could not crash the gate, and so they waited outside for their idol.

"Gee, Babe, we was just goin' to have a game and we ain't got enough pitchers for two teams. We need just one more. Won't you play?"

He played. He got back to the hotel just as the Yankees were leaving. He was dirty, his clothes were torn, he was perspiring, but he was happy.

"Listen, Hug!" he shouted to his manager, the late Miller Huggins. "We certainly had a swell game of ball. I made four hits. And say, Hug, you ought to scout the other team's third baseman. He made three hits and he made 'em all off me."

There was the time when he found a newsboy crying. He was a little fellow, and he had sold no papers because the bigger boys shouldered him aside. The Babe took his papers and peddled them and he got anywhere from a dime to a dollar per copy.

There was the time when he took the old apple woman's cart on a cold day and sold her apples for her.

There were hundreds of other times when the Babe made happy the lives of others, young and old. The hospitals and the orphanages know him well, and so do thousands and thousands of boys. The stories of his good deeds and his kindly acts will never be completely recorded. He was a great ballplayer and the greatest slugger of all time. Maybe he was also the greatest all-around player, but that doesn't matter. He is, as a million boys will tell you, "one grand guy," one of the grandest that baseball has known.

Getting the Main Points

1. What does the story about Johnny Remington tell you about Babe Ruth as a person? What do you learn about his

character from the fact that he later forgot who Johnny was?

2. What details about his playing does the author mention to prove that " as long as baseball is played, Ruth will always be included in any all-time line-up "?

3. How does the fact that Babe Ruth grew up in an orphan asylum help you to understand his beliefs and actions?

4. What is the author's conclusion at the end of the sketch about Babe Ruth as a person? What kind of stories does he tell in order to lead up to this conclusion?

5. As a way of telling the difference between *main points* and *details*, look back through the selection and find at least three *general* statements about Babe Ruth as a person or as a player. Discuss with your teacher how you can recognize a general statement, and why it is important that an author or speaker give details to support such statements.

Casey at the Bat

ERNEST LAWRENCE THAYER

As long as baseball is the great American game — as long as the fans like a laugh along with the thrills — this swinging ballad will be a favorite. It was written by a newspaperman but has already become a kind of modern folk tale, known to thousands of baseball fans.

The outlook wasn't brilliant for the Mudville nine that day;
The score stood four to two, with but one inning more to play;
And so, when Cooney died at first, and Burrows did the same,
A sickly silence fell upon the patrons of the game.

A straggling few got up to go in deep despair. The rest   5
Clung to the hope which springs eternal in the human breast;
They thought, if only Casey could but get a whack, at that,
They'd put up even money now, with Casey at the bat.

But Flynn preceded Casey, as did also Jimmy Blake,
And the former was a pudding and the latter was a fake;   10
So upon that stricken multitude grim melancholy sat,
For there seemed but little chance of Casey's getting to the bat.

But Flynn let drive a single, to the wonderment of all,
And Blake, the much-despised, tore the cover off the ball;
And when the dust had lifted, and they saw what had occurred,   15
There was Jimmy safe on second, and Flynn a-hugging third.

Then from the gladdened multitude went up a joyous yell;
It bounded from the mountaintop, and rattled in the dell;
It struck upon the hillside, and recoiled upon the flat;
For Casey, mighty Casey, was advancing to the bat.   20

There was ease in Casey's manner as he stepped into his place;
There was pride in Casey's bearing, and a smile on Casey's face;
And when, responding to the cheers, he lightly doffed his hat,
No stranger in the crowd could doubt 'twas Casey at the bat.

Ten thousand eyes were on him as he rubbed his hands with dirt;   25
Five thousand tongues applauded when he wiped them on his shirt;
Then while the writhing pitcher ground the ball into his hip,
Defiance gleamed in Casey's eye, a sneer curled Casey's lip.

And now the leather-covered sphere came hurtling through the air,
And Casey stood a-watching it in haughty grandeur there;   30
Close by the sturdy batsman the ball unheeded sped.
"That ain't my style," said Casey. "Strike one," the umpire said.

From the benches, black with people, there went up a muffled roar,
Like the beating of the storm waves on a stern and distant shore;
" Kill him! Kill the umpire! " shouted someone on the stand;   35
And it's likely they'd have killed him had not Casey raised his hand.

With a smile of Christian charity great Casey's visage shone;
He stilled the rising tumult; he bade the game go on;
He signaled to the pitcher, and once more the spheroid flew;
But Casey still ignored it, and the umpire said, " Strike two."   40

" Fraud! " cried the maddened thousands, and the echo answered, " Fraud! "
But a scornful look from Casey, and the audience was awed;
They saw his face grow stern and cold, they saw his muscles strain,
And they knew that Casey wouldn't let that ball go by again.

The sneer is gone from Casey's lips, his teeth are clenched in hate,   45
He pounds with cruel violence his bat upon the plate;
And now the pitcher holds the ball, and now he lets it go,
And now the air is shattered by the force of Casey's blow.

Oh! somewhere in this favored land the sun is shining bright;
The band is playing somewhere, and somewhere hearts are light;   50
And somewhere men are laughing, and somewhere children shout,
But there is no joy in Mudville — mighty Casey has struck out!

Fancy Words for Fun

Most of the time words are well used only when they fit in with the general tone of what you are saying. But when you want to stir a laugh, there's nothing more successful than putting in a big, dignified word that does not fit the tone at all. That is one way the poet amuses you with his story of Casey's downfall. First guess from context the literal meaning of *dell, visage,* and *spheroid.* Then check your guesses with the dictionary. What simple words could have been used in their places? Why is the effect better with the fancier terms?

Find other words or whole phrases in the poem that add to the humor by sounding poetic or dignified in contrast with the tone of the story.

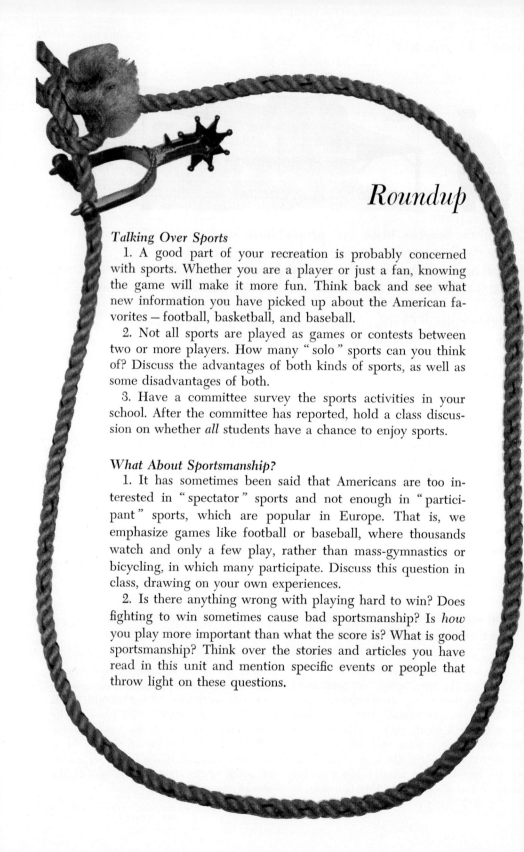

Roundup

Talking Over Sports

1. A good part of your recreation is probably concerned with sports. Whether you are a player or just a fan, knowing the game will make it more fun. Think back and see what new information you have picked up about the American favorites — football, basketball, and baseball.

2. Not all sports are played as games or contests between two or more players. How many "solo" sports can you think of? Discuss the advantages of both kinds of sports, as well as some disadvantages of both.

3. Have a committee survey the sports activities in your school. After the committee has reported, hold a class discussion on whether *all* students have a chance to enjoy sports.

What About Sportsmanship?

1. It has sometimes been said that Americans are too interested in "spectator" sports and not enough in "participant" sports, which are popular in Europe. That is, we emphasize games like football or baseball, where thousands watch and only a few play, rather than mass-gymnastics or bicycling, in which many participate. Discuss this question in class, drawing on your own experiences.

2. Is there anything wrong with playing hard to win? Does fighting to win sometimes cause bad sportsmanship? Is *how* you play more important than what the score is? What is good sportsmanship? Think over the stories and articles you have read in this unit and mention specific events or people that throw light on these questions.

Your Bookshelf

The American Boy's Omnibus, by Stanley Pashko (Greenberg, 1945)

Sports, hobbies, magic, and handicrafts.

Boating Is Fun, by Ruth Brindze (Dodd, Mead, 1949)

How to row, sail, or paddle small craft.

Boy's Guide to Fishing, by K. and E. E. Morton (Greenberg, 1947)

Tips on how and where to land the big ones.

Escape on Skis, by Arthur D. Stapp (Morrow, 1949)

The boys' sporting trip turned into a fight for life when they crossed the trail of dangerous criminals.

Fighting Southpaw, by Richard Flood (Houghton Mifflin, 1951)

Rough times for a piano-playing boy drafted to pitch for a baseball team.

Gridiron Challenge, by Jackson Scholz (Morrow, 1947)

Playing the game includes getting along with others. Another good sports novel by the same author is *Fielder from Nowhere* (1949).

Hickory Wings, by Clem Philbrook (Macmillan, 1951)

Keen rivalry among prep-school skiers.

Highpockets, by John R. Tunis (Morrow, 1948)

Team play shows the meaning of real democracy. Other good sports books by Tunis include *The Kid Comes Back* (1946) about a war cripple who came back in baseball, and *Yea! Wildcats!* (Harcourt, Brace, 1944) with fair play winning in basketball.

The Kid Who Batted 1.000, by Bob Allison and Frank Ernest Hill (Doubleday, 1951)

He wanted more than a place in the big leagues — and got it.

Knockout, by Philip Harkins (Holiday, 1950)

Up from the slums to a Golden Gloves championship. The same author tells a story of high school football and character-building in *Punt Formation* (Morrow, 1950)

Phantom Backfield, by Howard M. Brier (Random House, 1948)

Football and friendship and plenty of action.

The Purple Tide, by Leland Silliman (Winston, 1949)

High school baseball and football.

Rambling Halfback: A Bronc Burnett Story, by Wilfred McCormick (Putnam, 1950)

Another rousing sports story of the boys at Sonora High. Another book about the same gang is *Flying Tackle* (1949) by the same author.

Red Embers, by Dorothy Lyons (Harcourt, Brace, 1948)

A girl trains her own polo pony and makes the All-American team.

Skating Shoes, by Noel Streatfeild (Random House, 1951)

Story of an English girl who loves ice-skating.

Squeeze Play, by Colin Locklons (Crowell, 1950)

Baseball provides the chief activity in an immigrant boy's adjustment to school life.

Tournament Trail, by Tom Kock (Lothrop, 1950)

A whole series of tight basketball games.

Town and Country Games, by Robert North (Crowell, 1947)

Sport for the body, and for the wits, too.

Warrior Forward, by Dick Friendlich (Westminster, 1950)

Fireworks follow when a sophomore gets a former star's place in the basketball line-up.

The Will to Win, by Stephen W. Meader (Harcourt, Brace, 1936)

Short stories of many sports.

Gendreau

Animals

Wild Dog

RUTH ELIZABETH TANNER

Making friends with a wild dog seemed to the cowboy to be a slow job. Carefully he tried to overcome the dog's new fear of men. He never knew how well he had succeeded until the perilous night of the blizzard.

THE prairie grass was thick and soft beneath Tip's padding feet as he moved through the gathering dusk. Somewhere in the distance a mourning dove raised her voice in a sleepy *coo-coo;* now and then a grasshopper flew blindly up and away; the ceaseless throbbing of locusts filled the air.

A sudden *whirr* rose from a clump of sage as a prairie chicken shot up into the air. She floundered one-sidedly, came down again and, dragging one wing, flopped along on the ground. Tip paused to watch her for a moment, but he did not give chase, for he knew she was trying to lead him away from her nest.

Then he trotted over to the clump of sage and after a little searching found her nest cleverly hidden in the matted grass. Sorely tempted, he sniffed at the eggs. He was very hungry and, though he would never have considered eating an egg in the barn or hen house, these out on the open prairie did not seem quite the same. His hunting instinct told him to take them; they did not belong to his mas-

"Wild Dog" by Ruth Elizabeth Tanner. Reprinted by permission of the author.

ter. But from generations of shepherd and collie forebears he had inherited another instinct. That was to guard faithfully, no matter what the cost.

He licked his lips again, but with a quick shake of his head he turned and marched away without a single backward glance. His better instinct had won.

Two hours later, after dining on a fat prairie dog and a quail, he started for home. When he came to the top of a high hill he sat down, pointed his white nose to the full moon, and sent forth the long mournful howl of a lost or forsaken dog.

Sims, Tip's old master, had sold his ranch in New Mexico and returned to the East. As he could not take a half-grown dog to an apartment in a large city, he gave Tip to a friend in Belmont just before taking the train. But Tip did not understand. He slipped away and traveled the twenty miles back to the only home he had ever known. For a month he had been guarding the empty ranch, waiting for his owner's return.

At first he had gone hungry quite a lot. But the sand hills south of the house were full of cottontails, and the sage-covered prairie was alive with jack rabbits. He soon grew accustomed to finding his own meals. Still, he was lonely, and now he voiced all his uneasiness and his yearning for love and companionship in his mournful appeal to the moon.

To the north on the Flying M Ranch, old Mr. Marvin turned restlessly in his bed. " Bill! Dusty! " he called.

" Yeah," came a sleepy answer.

" Hear that dog? There are too blamed many dogs around here. From now on when you boys see a stray, shoot him. They'll be getting the calves next."

A few evenings later, Tip paused in his wandering to watch a couple of riders coming up the coulee.[1] He was about to make a friendly advance when — bang! — a shot rang out, and a bullet kicked sand into his face. Crack! A second shot grazed his shoulder like a hot iron.

For a moment he had been confused. Then he came to life, and fled like a tawny streak, dodging behind brush, skimming over the open places. A man on a long-legged black was pounding madly after him. Twice more the rider fired at a flash of yellow and brown, but both bullets went wild.

Finally the pursuer gave up and returned to his companion, a lanky, sunburned boy. " He got away! Why didn't you take a hand, Dusty? "

Dusty's gray eyes crinkled as he smiled. " I'm glad you didn't get him. That's a good dog, a collie. He looks like a pup that fellow Sims had."

" Anyway, I nipped him."

" Poor fellow. I'm sorry for that," Dusty said slowly.

" Boss's orders," the cowhand explained.

" The boss can shoot him if he wants to, but I won't," Dusty declared.

Twice more in the next week some of the Flying M men shot at Tip, but

[1] **coulee** (kōō′lĭ): a steep, trenchlike valley.

after that he saw them first and vanished.

Still they heard him serenading the moon. A dog whose ancestors have for generations lived with men and who has known a loved master cannot so easily break the tie that binds him to mankind. He was very lonely, but as there was no human for him to serve he spent his energy guarding the ranch buildings. Like a wild animal, he had formed the habit of sleeping days and roaming about at night. Perhaps the heat and his avoidance of chance riders started him doing this.

One evening he woke, stretched out, and, yawning like a sleepy child, came out from under the ranch house.

"*Woof!*" he yelped, dodging to one side in surprise. Stretched across the path beside the sagging step was a four-foot rattlesnake! Tip bristled. Ordinarily he would have gladly given the snake the right of way, but this was *his own* yard; he would not stand for the intrusion.

A snarl rose in his throat and like a flash he seized the snake before it could coil. He shook and shook it, then threw it down with all the strength he had. The snake landed with a thump and was coiled like a spring, ready for battle. Tip circled about. The snake was raging with fury. His rattles buzzed. His little eyes glittered with hate. The deadly rattler's head, balanced at least a foot from the ground, swung about, ever facing the dog as Tip minced about the snake.

Finally Tip pretended to step forward, and the rattler struck with every ounce of energy in his powerful coils. His head went fully three feet through the air. His fangs brushed Tip's whiskers as the collie dodged backward. Tip walked away feeling sick. The snake had struck much farther than he had expected him to. Death had missed him only by an inch, but he was not ready to give up.

After a moment he returned to the raging snake. Again he stepped forward, but with more caution this time. As before, the rattler struck, but when he landed on the ground Tip seized him and shook him long and hard. This performance was repeated time after time. The snake was a powerful and experienced fighter, and the battle was long and hard. But finally the snake failed to recoil.

Tip waited and watched him for a moment. Then, shaking his head distastefully, he trotted away toward the creek to wash that hateful taste from his mouth.

The dog gravely herded away stray cattle and horses from the ranch. But he welcomed Mollie and her calf with a friendly, wagging tail, although they wore the Flying M brand now. They had been sold when his old master left, but Tip still felt they belonged here the same as he did.

Autumn came with its yellow-brown grass and its chilly nights. Food was not so plentiful, yet Tip had grown in both size and cunning. He was a beauty. In color and marking, with the white ruff about his throat, he was like a collie. But he resembled his shepherd ancestors in his broad, powerful frame.

One evening as he scouted upwind several miles from his home, his keen nose caught the warm scent of freshly killed meat. A few moments later he found two coyotes feeding upon a dead calf.

Bristling with fury, he fell upon the killers and drove them away. Then, after hesitating for a little, he made a good meal of the tempting meat. Nothing would have induced him to kill a calf; all his instincts were against it. But the calf was dead so he ate his fill. Then, circling about the dead animal, leaving plenty of tracks, he went his way.

After that his reputation grew. A wild dog, crafty, powerful, cruel; alone he could kill a two-year-old cow! The boys at the Flying M had strict orders to " get that dog." Of all this Tip was unaware. He went his way as usual, glorying in his strength and in the art of matching his wits, both with the wild things and with men. To him it was a game.

His avoidance of men was even more than a game. He knew of their far-reaching guns and he played safe.

Then winter with its snowy blanket closed down. Dusty was to ride the upper branches of the Little Comanche Creek, keeping watch over the range cattle and sleeping in Sims's old ranch house.

" Don't let that wild dog eat you," one of the men warned him as he was getting ready to leave the main camp.

" Oh, he's no wilder'n I am. I'll have him eating out of my hand by Christmas."

" Two bits says you won't."

" Two bits. It's a bet." Gravely they called a third cowboy to witness the wager.

Tip's home was beneath the kitchen, and at first he resented Dusty's intrusion. He stayed away for two whole days, but the next night he returned. Two saddle horses were munching hay in the barn. He listened for a moment; it was such a friendly sound. Guardedly he approached the house. It seemed as before, but his sharp ears could hear the breathing of a man within. After a long, hesitating pause, he crawled under the house and curled up in his own bed.

When Dusty started for the barn the next morning, he stopped short and a slow smile spread over his face. Those fresh tracks in the snow told their story.

" I'll win that two bits yet," he said softly. After that it became a game for two. Dusty put out food every day. Tip daintily ate what he chose, though he always left Dusty's biscuits. This amused the cowboy. " If the boys knew this I'd never hear the last of it." Still he knew it was too good to keep. He would tell them sooner or later.

In turn, Tip guarded all of Dusty's things. Each morning found fresh tracks in the snow. But the month passed, and never once had the man seen his newly found friend. Then one day Dusty lost a glove. Next morning it was on the step just outside the door.

Dusty was delighted, so he dropped his old red muffler about a quarter of a mile up the trail where he knew he could find it if Tip didn't. The lost article was on the doorstep the following morning. " Old fellow, I'll bring you a rabbit today to pay for this," he promised, addressing the mouth of Tip's hole.

Staying alone in a cow camp, seeing no one for weeks at a time, is a lonely business at best. Dusty derived a great deal of amusement from Tip's actions. To some people, winning the love of a wild thing is a fascinating pastime. It was even more than that to the big, kindly cowboy. He felt that Tip had not received a square deal.

Tip had grown fond of Dusty, too. He longed to become real friends, to feel the caress of a hand on his head. Yet those burning shots could not be easily forgotten. Thus they lived until the latter part of November; each drawing a great deal of pleasure and satisfaction from his unseen comrade.

Then one cold, bitter night Dusty did not come home. As darkness fell Tip grew uneasy. He watched and listened. Dusty had never been so late before. Tip trotted to the top of the nearest hill, then back again. Time dragged, yet no Dusty. The dog grew more and more uneasy.

Some folks declare that dogs cannot reason. Perhaps they cannot, but something had brought an anxious light to Tip's eyes as he trotted restlessly about. Finally, as if he were unable to stand the suspense any longer, he picked up the trail Dusty's horse had left in the snow that morning and followed it at an easy lope. In and out among the rough, choppy hills, repeatedly doubling back to the creek, he wound. The stinging wind was rising. Sleet beat in his face and clung to his long shaggy coat.

On and on, farther into the flinty badlands, he traveled. He was running now, sure that something was wrong. The snow was coming fast, but the trail was still readable. Then suddenly on a steep sidehill he came to a big slide in the snow. His keen nose told him the story. The horse had fallen and, with his rider, had rolled to the bottom. Tip raced on a short distance to the only dark spot in the white expanse.

It was Dusty, stretched out unconscious in the snow. His hat was gone, his face was bared to the driving sleet. Tip whined softly. His fear for the moment was forgotten as he licked the boy's icy face with his red tongue.

Again he whined, but there was no answer. He poked his nose under Dusty's arm and moved it, but the arm was cold and unresponsive. Anxiously he walked about the quiet figure. He noted how one leg was stretched out in a helpless fashion. It had made a furrow in the snow. Dusty was no quitter. Battered and bruised, with a broken leg dragging painfully behind, he had pulled himself fully fifty yards before unconsciousness overcame him.

Tip sat up and howled his longest, most anguished notes. He trotted to the top of the hill and repeated them again and again, returning at intervals to try to arouse the unconscious cowboy. Once Dusty moved a little. A faint moan escaped his lips. Raising his hand, he inadvertently rubbed it against the quivering, eager dog.

In the meantime Dusty's horse, limping badly, with the bridle reins dragging and a stain of blood on the saddle, had returned to the main ranch ten miles away. Six men, grim and steady, started out into the rising storm on what they knew was an almost hopeless hunt. The back trail was dim, and snow was falling fast. Chances were ten to one they would not find Dusty until it was too late. He might be anywhere in an area ten miles one way by six the other. Even if they did find him, after lying out in this bitter cold for hours, he — they refused to think of that.

The men spread out in twos after agreeing that three shots fired in rapid succession would mean that Dusty was found.

After what seemed endless hours in the saddle, Mr. Marvin turned to Bob, his companion. "Hear that dog howl! I'd like to shoot him." Then a little later he added, "Funny, him howling on a night like this."

"Say!" Bob brought his horse to an abrupt halt. "Dusty bet me twenty-five cents he could tame that dog. Do you suppose . . ."

"There's a chance," the boss muttered. When hope is nearly dead, men will grasp at straws. Without another word they turned and urged their horses on at a faster pace.

The long eerie howls rose faintly again, but only once more. Then, in spite of straining their ears hopefully,

desperately, nothing but the crunching of their horses' feet and the swirling wind could be heard. Still they fought on blindly, refusing to give up that one faint glimmer of hope.

After wailing until his voice was hoarse, Tip gave up calling for help. He tried in vain again to rouse Dusty, then for a few moments he lay down with his warm body close beside the boy.

Presently, as if in answer to some call, he rose and trotted down-wind. At the slide he came to Dusty's hat, half buried in a drift. He hesitated a moment, then picking it up he loped away into the night.

The two men coming to a hill paused uncertainly. "Which way?" called Bob.

The boss drew rein and wiped the snow and frost from his mustache. "Say, what's that?" He pointed.

Dimly through the falling snow they saw a quick-moving shape. It hesitated, then drew near, and laid something on the ground at the feet of Bob's horse. Then it disappeared in a flash.

Bob was on the ground instantly. "Dusty's hat."

They looked anxiously about for the dog, but the gray curtain of the storm had closed. The dog had vanished. "Here, Pup! Come, Shep!" Mr. Marvin called.

From the right-hand trail came a sharp bark. They turned and followed. Bob whistled and Mr. Marvin kept on calling, "Here, Pup. Here, Shep!" Ahead came the sharp, imperative bark.

"And to think I ordered that dog shot," the boss muttered as he urged his weary horse on. "If he takes us to Dusty, I'll . . ." What could a fellow do to square himself with a dog? He couldn't think of any way just then, but he would later.

Thus they went on through the storm. The dog's yelping grew far away on several occasions. Then he would double back with anxious inquiries, to bound ahead again when he was sure they followed.

Suddenly the horses were floundering in the deep snow at the foot of the slide. In a glance the men read the grim story of the fall! Tip raced ahead to Dusty's side to lick his hand and tell him help was coming.

Three shots were fired into the air; the men were off their horses. Shoving aside the drifted snow, they began rubbing Dusty's numb arms and feet. A roll from behind the boss's saddle turned out to be a warm wool blanket and a thermos bottle of steaming coffee. The boss took his sheepskin coat, warm from his own body, and put it on the unconscious cowboy.

Soon two other men arrived. Tip hovered about, watching. At last he saw Dusty open his eyes, choke on the hot coffee, then speak. Tip's work was done. Dusty would be all right now, he was sure, so he turned his steps homeward.

There was a certain pride in his bearing as he went his rounds about the ranch in the days that followed. Again he was gallantly taking care of the place as he waited a loved one's return, and this time he did not wait in vain.

Man's Best Friend

1. What kept Tip from eating the prairie chicken's eggs?

2. How did he learn to be afraid of men?

3. Was Dusty friendly toward Tip from the first? How could he tell he was gradually winning the dog's confidence?

4. How did Tip find Dusty after his accident? How did he guide the rescuers?

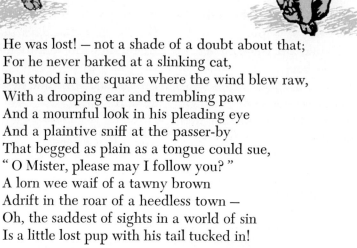

Little Lost Pup

ARTHUR GUITERMAN *

He was lost! — not a shade of a doubt about that;
For he never barked at a slinking cat,
But stood in the square where the wind blew raw,
With a drooping ear and trembling paw
And a mournful look in his pleading eye   5
And a plaintive sniff at the passer-by
That begged as plain as a tongue could sue,
" O Mister, please may I follow you? "
A lorn wee waif of a tawny brown
Adrift in the roar of a heedless town —   10
Oh, the saddest of sights in a world of sin
Is a little lost pup with his tail tucked in!

Well, he won my heart (for I set great store
On my own red Bute — who is here no more)
So I whistled clear, and he trotted up,   15
And who so glad as that small lost pup!
Now he shares my board, and he owns my bed,
And he fairly shouts when he hears my tread;
Then, if things go wrong, as they sometimes do,
And the world is cold and I'm feeling blue,   20
He asserts his right to assuage my woes
With a warm, red tongue and nice, cold nose
And a silky head on my arm or knee
And a paw as soft as a paw can be.

When we rove the woods for a league about   25
He's as full of pranks as a school let out;
For he romps and frisks like a three months' colt,
And he runs me down like a thunderbolt.
Oh, the blithest of sights in the world so fair
Is a gay little pup with his tail in the air!   30

* Guiterman (gĭt′ĕr·măn).

"Little Lost Pup" from *Death and General Putnam and 101 Other Poems* by Arthur Guiterman, published and copyright 1935, by E. P. Dutton and Company, Inc., New York. Reprinted by permission of the publisher.

Tail Down, Tail Up

1. How did the writer know the puppy was lost? How was the puppy's tail a sign of his feelings, then and later?

2. Pick out descriptions that show Mr. Guiterman really knew how puppies act.

3. Would you rather adopt a stray puppy or buy a fine one from a pet dealer? Why?

Words Have Neighbors

Have you discovered that often a word is not so difficult when you look closely at its neighbors — the other words and phrases surrounding it? In this poem the meaning of the word *plaintive* in line 6 may not seem clear at first glance, but look at its neighbors. The lost pup has a "drooping ear and trembling paw" and "a mournful look." His eye "pleads" for help. You can guess that his "plaintive sniff" at strangers is a sorrowful, sad, and complaining sound. Used as a noun, a *plaintiff* in a lawsuit is a person who brings a complaint against someone else. Why is the poet's use of *sue* in line 7 appropriate here?

By looking at their neighbors, try to get the meaning of *assuage* in line 21 and *bl'th-est* in line 29. Check your meaning against the definition in a dictionary, and look at the pronunciation, too.

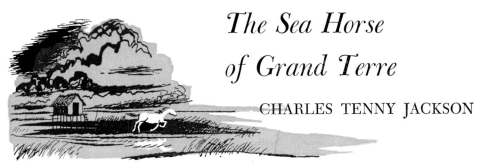

The Sea Horse
of Grand Terre

CHARLES TENNY JACKSON

WIND AND WATER. Have you ever seen the bayous and swamps of Louisiana? If not, this story will take you into strange and unusual country. At first you may lose your bearings in these surroundings, but as you read along you'll soon learn "the lay of the land." For instance, in the first paragraphs of the story several places and things are described — *seine, lugger, drying platforms, catch-flag* — that will be unfamiliar to anyone who has not lived near the lowlands by the sea. Don't try to understand each one of these terms at the start. Like any good traveler, keep your eyes open and enjoy the sights, even if they are strange. Soon enough you will discover that the story takes place during a storm on a marshy island, where a herd of cattle and some horses have been stocked. Look for the clues that tell you the people in the story make their living from shrimp-fishing and have platforms built above the swamp ground on which to dry out their catches.

Every story takes place *somewhere*. Often the setting, as the place of a story is called, is very important to notice. What happens to the characters may depend on their surroundings — their work, their neighborhood, their section of the country. That is why this writer plunges you into a strange setting at the beginning of his story, so that you will be prepared to meet the great "sea horse" who becomes the friend of two boys caught in a hurricane.

ALLESJANDRO, the seine captain,[1] first told the men at Chinese Platforms that the lightkeeper at Grand Terre Island was sick. One of the Zelie's crew had gone ashore for water, and reported that old Miller was "done beat out with fevah." The Zelie had two hundred dollars' worth of shrimp which a few hours' delay under the Louisiana sun would spoil, so the lugger sailed for the drying platforms, where Allesjandro told Mr. West, the camp boss.

And the camp boss turned with simple confidence to his sturdy sixteen-year-old son, who, that morning, was idling in the shade of the commissary with his chum, George Fernald.

"Better go see to the old man, Paul. The Two Sisters is flying the catch flag, and the launch is going to tow her in. Landry will put you ashore, and you can hike up the beach with some lemons and stuff. See if he needs the doctor."

And blazing hot as low-lying Grand Terre appeared in the September calm, the boys were eager to go. Miller was a friend of Paul's. In half an hour, they had the few delicacies and simple remedies which the camp possessed, and were on the launch speeding for the outlying reef. For a week, black majestic storm clouds had swung about Barataria[2] Bay, at intervals, for this was the time of the equinox,[3] when the south coast had been swept time and again by the West Indian hurricanes. Still the shrimp luggers went out, and when the boys landed in the salt marsh, they saw the Two Sisters, limp-sailed and far on the gulf, but flying the red flag that told of a successful catch. The launch went on through Four Bayou Pass to meet her, while the lads turned up the six-mile beach to the lighthouse.

"Dad said that Gaspar, who takes care of the oyster beds here and keeps an eye on our cattle, might round up a couple of horses for us," commented Paul. "But all the stock seems to be miles away, and Gaspar isn't around his shack."

They passed the tiny, palm-thatched hut perched on a ten-foot platform above the tides. The mud beneath was trampled where the stock sought refuge from the sun, and here Paul pointed out a great hoof-mark.

"That's Big King's, the stallion that Father turned loose here when he went into this experiment with stock on the salt marsh. He has never been able to recapture him since. Gaspar complains that the white stallion hates him, and chases him every time he goes ashore. The Zelie's crew say

[1] Allesjandro (ä'lĕs·hän'drō) was in charge of the crew that was hauling the big net called a seine (sān).

[2] Barataria (băr·à·târ'ĭ·à).

[3] equinox (ē'kwĭ·nŏks): the time when the sun's center crosses the equator, and day and night are of equal length everywhere. It is usually a time of unsettled weather.

that they saw Big King follow Gaspar in his skiff away out in deep water, and that the Cajun [1] was so scared that finally he dived over and swam to their boat. Gaspar sometimes declares he'll shoot the horse or quit his job! "

" Must be a regular old sea horse! " laughed George. " Is that him — that beautiful big white fellow over in the mangroves? " [2]

" Yes," Paul whispered cautiously. " And don't provoke him to charge us. There isn't a place to escape him if he does! "

Two hundred yards away, the splendid creature stood, his eyes warily on the invaders. He snorted menacingly, his mane erect and tail spread, but he let them pass, and then charged magnificently down the wet sands to turn and watch them, with the surf breaking about his legs.

" What a grand old fellow he is! " cried Paul. " Father ought not to put him in the charge of an oyster digger like Gaspar. Of course he'd hate him! "

It was dazzling noon when the weary lads reached the lighthouse. The oppressive calm made the heat in the marshy hollows intolerable, and they hailed with relief the sight of the keeper, whom they found lying on his airy platform. The keeper's eyes were feverish as he explained how, all the morning, he had watched them with his powerful glasses, which gave him the only diversion of his monotonous life. But he wasn't sick, he said — just a " touch o' sun," and he was chagrined to find the *Zelie* had reported him ill.

" Lighthouse folks ain't no business gettin' sick, ever," he declared.

All the same, he was glad to get the lemons and other things the boys brought, and when they tried to make him a cornstarch pudding, the ensuing hilarity seemed to hearten him wonderfully. When they came out on the gallery, he declared " all this cuttin' up " had made him " plumb well." But when the keeper gazed around, he fixed an intent look on the southeast.

" Your dad's goin' to have the launch at Four Bayou for you? " he asked. " Well, you boys better get off. The wind's scuddin' them clouds fast, over there, and this is the hurricane month, remember. There's a sea running now, and — feel that? The air's twitching! "

And in fifteen minutes it was more than twitching. Out of the strange, calm oasis with the black clouds rolling up all about the horizon, there suddenly shot a squall from the southeast that tore the sand from under the boys' feet when they went down Mr. Miller's ladder. But they didn't mind the blow. They laughed, and shook Miller's hand, and promised to come the next day with the launch and make another pudding, and with raisins in it.

[1] **Cajun** (kā′jŭn): A contraction of "Acadian," used in Louisiana to name the descendants of early French settlers who came from Nova Scotia. Longfellow's poem "Evangeline," which you will find in this book, tells how the exiled Acadians made their way to Louisiana.

[2] **mangroves** (măng′grōvz): shrubs and trees that grow along warm coasts, making dense thickets out into the water.

"Mebbe you will and mebbe you won't," shouted the old man. "It's time for a blow up from Cuby, and I reckon I'm better off here than you'll be on your dad's crazy platforms. You boys won't see old man Miller for a while, if a sou'east sea begins to pound over them marshes. In La Cheniere [1] storm, there wasn't a thing above water except this light, from here to upper Lafourche.[2] And your dad's platform villages — pooh! wasn't stick or stump left of any of 'em!"

As they tramped on the harder sand, as near to the water as they could, the boys talked of the dreaded gulf hurricanes. On their left, the sand was already blowing from the dunes, and when they reached a little bayou which they had crossed dry-shod in the morning, they found the water pounding half a mile inland, and had to go around it.

"The gulf is so shallow for miles out," explained Paul, "that the least little wind kicks up a quick sea."

But when they rounded the bayou and went over the low ridge, the wind was so fierce as to stagger them and whirl the loose sand around their feet.

"Whew!" cried George; "and just see how the water's rising, Paul! It's all through the grass there, and beyond — why, it's a lake!"

"Let's cut over on the bay side and see if the mangroves won't break the wind a bit," suggested Paul. "If it keeps on, we can't well walk against it." He reached a rise in the meadows and vainly stared at the pass which, two miles away, was hidden by the oncoming rain and scud.[3] There was no boat in sight, and, northward, Barataria Bay was whipped to as furious a sea as was the outside water to the south. "It's there, sure," Paul muttered, "but, if we *made* the launch, I don't think she'd live in that gale. But we can run to Grand Bank and put into that camp for the night."

He hastened on, not telling his friend all his fears. But from the highest dune they saw nothing except the oyster guard's thatched hut, and, far off, near the mangrove clumps, a few of the cattle wandering with the storm.

"Ticklish business if we have to spend the night in this shack," George declared half an hour later, when, wet and tired, they reached the hut on the edge of the marsh and climbed the ladder to the door. Indeed, the sight was an evil one. The oyster stakes had entirely disappeared, and the rising sea was pouring across the island in three places, back on the way they had come. The pounding water against the piles [4] made the shack reel, while every now and then portions of the thatched sides would be torn off, and go humming away in the gale. The boys went in and inspected the gaping roof; the sheets of rain reached every inch of the interior: they were as well off outside.

[1] La Cheniere (lă shĕn·yĕr').
[2] Lafourche ((lä·fōōrsh').

[3] scud: loose clouds driven swiftly by the wind.
[4] piles: heavy timbers driven deep into the ground for a foundation.

Where Gaspar had gone they did not know; they concluded that he had abandoned his job — "Scared off by the big horse," said Paul.

"If the water keeps on rising, you'll lose all your stock," observed George. "But the launch — where do you suppose it is?"

Though night and darkness were coming on, they could see the pass enough to know it held no boat. What had happened was that the launch, early in the afternoon, had broken its propeller in towing the *Two Sisters,* and had then drifted until both boats grounded in the marsh, where the crew clung, half drowned, to the lugger's rigging through the night of the hurricane. The boys, huddled in what should have been the lee [1] shelter of the thatch on the platform, noticed again how fast the shallow sea was rising. Grand Terre light was invisible in the storm, and it seemed that the whitecaps were speeding across the island everywhere except over the higher sand ridge near them. Watching this, they saw the backs of the cattle moving through the mangroves, and then Mr. West's old bay mare.

"The stock are coming back!" cried Paul. "The water's coming from the pass now, and it's turned them." He looked apprehensively at his companion's face. "George, if it rises high enough to get a sweep at this shack over the bars, the platform won't last half the night."

"Your cattle are coming here anyway. And look — the big horse is leading them!"

The stock had been accustomed to huddle in the shade of the platform hut, and now they were deserting the mangrove ridge to seek this bit of human companionship. The cows were mooing in a scared fashion as they waded, more than knee-deep, to the place. The two bay horses cast appealing looks up at the boys, and Paul called down encouragingly. Big King lunged about the piling and whinnied, watching off to the mainland. The frail structure trembled when the crowding cattle got under it.

"Better drive them out," George shouted above the wind. But this was impossible and presently, as the darkness fell, the animals were quieter in the fierce rain, though the waves pounded over their backs, and the calves could hardly keep their footing.

Paul crawled back on the platform after an inspection of the base of the timbers. The sands were washing up badly, and the tramping hoofs assisted at the slow settling of the platform. Paul could touch the horses' necks from the floor, and once his fingers went lightly along the rough mane of the white stallion. The big brute turned about, his fine, wary eyes on the boy. But he did not bite; he even seemed to crowd closer to his master's son.

"Get over there — you!" Paul yelled. "Don't crowd against that post!"

He reached down and slapped the great horse, and then dug him in the ribs ineffectually. King neither resent-

[1] **lee:** the side away from the wind.

ed it nor obeyed. The boys lay out full length on the boards to avoid the wind, and in the last light saw their dumb companions half buried in the waves. Although the rain was not cold, they were shivering with exhaustion from the pounding wind and water. For an hour, the dark was intense. Then it seemed as if the rising moon broke the gloom a trifle, though the storm did not abate.

"It's still rising!" commented Paul, after he had thrust a crab-net pole down by the piling; "and very fast, George. I wish it were daylight!"

Then, when he had crawled back to his wet comrade, there came a tremendous shock to the platform. They heard one of the calves bawl wildly, and felt a rush and stagger of the animals beneath them. Paul jumped up and ran to the other end of the reeling platform, where an entire side of the thatched wall fell out into the sea.

"It's a big tree!" he shouted back, as George groped for his hand. "I was afraid of that, whenever the tide got high enough to bring the drift off the gulf side. Now we're in for it! It tore out three of the piles, and it's dragging at another. Come, let's try to get it off!"

Thirty-five miles away, the Southwest Pass of the Mississippi poured all the flotsam [1] of the mighty river into the gulf, to be spread far along the sand dunes by the tides; and every southeaster sent this wreckage charging over the marshes. In every great blow the platform dwellers of Barataria dreaded this invasion. The lads

[1] **flotsam:** floating trash and wreckage.

vainly hunted for poles to fend off the tree pounding under their shelter. Some of the cattle had been knocked down and others were scattered, and Paul saw one of the mares go swimming off in the whitecaps to certain death. Above the wind they heard the frightened stock struggling for footholds in the sand, and the groaning of the timbers. There was nothing to do. The shack, trembling, twisting, finally settled slowly back; the big cypress tree had gone on, luckily. But presently a smaller one was battering at the piling, and more of the cattle were scattered.

"The other end of the platform is sinking!" George shouted. "Everything is gone there!"

They fought their way back just in time to see more than half the thatch hut tumble into the waves. Paul had saved a coil of half-inch rope from Gaspar's belongings, with the idea of tying fast some of the loose piles, but this was now useless.

"The rest of it will go, sure!" he muttered. "George, when it does, jump clear of the cattle and head southwest." He looked helplessly off in the dark. "If we can swim to the mangroves, maybe we can hold on a little longer."

But to reach the ridge, even if it was above the breakers, was an impossibility, for one would have to swim directly into the storm. And the boys had lost all sense of direction. The next big shock from the driftwood sent them to their feet in a wild effort to leap free of the animals, although how many of them there still were they did not know. The last log crashed through the midst of them and left the platform tilted at such an angle that the boys could no longer walk on it. Paul slipped, and went over the side to his waist, but he still clung to his rope. As he kicked to recover his footing, while George reached down to help him, he slowly became aware that his legs were over about the horse's neck when George was thrown into the water beside him. The stallion was plunging about with Paul firmly astride his back and George fighting to grasp the rope. Another instant and the wrecked platform slid down upon them, striking Paul in the side and dealing the horse a savage blow on the flank, driving him out from under the piles where

the wet, heaving back of Big King. His hold on the boards was slipping; the entire platform seemed to be coming after him.

"It's all sinking!" George yelled at him. "Don't let it pin you under the water!"

But Paul was motioning wildly for his friend to slide after him. He was reaching around the slipping boards to drag the rope about the big stallion's neck.

"If it goes," he shouted, "hang to the rope; maybe Big King will drag us free of the stuff."

He was working busily at the rope he had fought to the last against the sea. He plunged on madly, with the water breaking over his back, to which Paul clung while he tried to drag his friend up behind him. They never would have succeeded if King had been on dry land. But the water and the small drift impeded his struggles to shake off the rope and the burden, and now he dashed into a depression where his hoofs failed to find bottom, and the waves swept entirely over him.

The panting lads clung to the rope and to each other. Paul was dragged off the back of the swimming horse, and then they both were thrown against him and regained a hold on his tough and heavy mane. But the whitecaps were almost drowning them. Big King reached a ridge and drew himself up where the water was hardly to his breast; then he plunged on in the teeth of the storm, swimming again. He knew well enough where he was going. While the foolish cattle drifted with the waves out to the open bay, the lionhearted stallion fought his way seaward and to the mangrove ridge.

But before he gained it, the boys were all but washed off. Once, indeed, Paul felt his friend's hand slip from his. George went over the horse's flank and under the water, but he kept his grip on the rope. From his gasps, the rope was apparently all but strangling the stallion. When they reached another shallow, Paul leaned forward and loosened it.

"Hold up, old fellow!" he muttered; "hold up, and we'll make it yet!"

And the big wild horse actually twisted his shaggy neck knowingly under the boy's fingers as he eased the line! Paul got George on the animal's back again, as they reached the mangrove ridge. The bushes, beaten by the hurricane, cut and pounded their faces, and the choppy seas broke through, churning the sands about them. But the water here was not more than three feet deep, and Big King fought through it.

Paul was anxious to stop him now. They were on the highest point, and no other refuge was possible. He be-

gan patting the horse and murmuring to him as one would to a pet colt, and, after a quarter of a mile of fruitless tramping, Big King suddenly rounded the thickest clump of mangrove and stopped, with his tail pointing into the gale.

"He knows!" whispered Paul, weakly, to his comrade. "It's the only shelter to be found. Now if he only lets us stay on his back!"

But apart from nervous and resentful starts and shakings, the horse did not stir. He seemed badly exhausted, himself. The boys lay forward on his heaving back, Paul clinging to him, and George to Paul, and there the weary, dark hours passed. The sea was rising more slowly now. At times, King struggled deeper into the bushes as the sand washed from under his feet. And how the wind did blow! It was as if the air above them was full of salt water, and even with their backs to it, the boys could not speak without strangling. The lashing mangroves skinned their legs painfully, and the salt added to their suffering. But their chief fear was the rising water. They measured it time and again during the long night, but could never tell whether it was coming up or whether their live refuge was slowly sinking. The stallion changed his position whenever his legs went in too deep.

"Old boy," muttered Paul, "you can manage this much better than we can."

Somehow, in his heart, he felt a hot and almost tearful love and admiration for the dreaded horse of the

Grand Terre meadows.

"If we ever get out," Paul told George, "I'll take him back to New Orleans and ride him. He's the biggest, bravest horse in all the world!"

"*If* we get out!" retorted George. "And I do believe the rain *is* quitting!" And with the ceasing of the rain, a slow lightening came over the waters. Yet not for hours longer, while the long tugging swells surged through the mangroves and kept the tired boys ever struggling to retain their place, did it become light enough to be really day. And then they saw nothing in any direction but gray sky over the stormy sea. For two hundred yards the higher mangroves were above the flood. Of the palm-thatched hut and the platform not a stick remained; nor was a single one of the cattle or either of the two mares in sight.

"Nobody but Big King," muttered Paul, "and you and me, George! I'm going to get down and pet the old fellow!"

He swung off in water to his armpits and went about to King's head. The horse bared his teeth, and then slowly, with lessening pride, allowed the boy's hand to stroke his muzzle.

"Old man," whispered Paul, "you weathered the blow for us, didn't you!"

And the strangest thing was that, when the boys were tired of standing in the water, the great creature allowed them to climb again on his back. At last the wind died out, and when the first glint of sun broke through, it could be seen that the sea

was not rising farther. Big King began nibbling at the mangroves, while the exhausted lads half dozed and watched the waters to the north. It was two hours before they could see anything two miles distant, and knew that the "hurricane tide," so feared by the shrimpers, had turned again seaward. Drift and wreckage were going out through the flooded pass. And finally, almost at noon, Paul made out the little gas steamer that ran from camp to camp, headed down from the direction of the platforms.

"It's looking for us, George!" he cried. "But Dad — he'll never dream we lived through it all!"

With weak yells of jubilation they watched the boat. From a mile away Big King's white flanks caught the attention of the steamer men. Then they saw the boys, and fifteen minutes later Paul and George were shaking hands with Paul's father.

"Dad, your old sea horse did it!" cried the son. "I'm going to get him off this island, for he deserves better things. He ought to get a lifesaving medal!"

"I'll wager," laughed Mr. West, "you'll never lay hands on him again!"

And the boys never did, though they made three trips to Grand Terre after the sea went down, first to attend to old man Miller, and then to tame the great white horse. Big King did not molest them; he even let Paul come close enough to reach out a loving finger to his nervous muzzle. But that was all; at sight of a halter or the motion of a hand to his neck, he was off again, charging magnificently down the wet sands to turn and watch them, with the surf breaking about his legs. To the end of his days he was the lonely and wild sea horse of Grand Terre.

Locating the Story's Setting

1. How well did you find your bearings in the Gulf country of this story? See if you can spot the answers:

a. How did the boys get to the lighthouse?

b. If the shack and the lighthouse were on the same island, why was Miller safe during the storm while the boys were not?

c. Where did the horse seek refuge after the shack collapsed — toward the gulf or toward the bay? What was the difference?

2. Did the sea horse live up to his reputation the first time the boys saw him?

3. Were the boys pleased or alarmed when Big King first took shelter under the shack where they were? Why?

4. How did the storm destroy the shack? By what means did the boys get on the horse?

5. Did the horse recognize his companions when he saw them later? Did he change his way of life? Explain whether this ending pleases you or leaves you dissatisfied.

My Animal Friends

GEORGE AND
HELEN PAPASHVILY*

You will find many things new to you in this story of a boy who lived in the Russian province of Georgia back in the days when the Tsars ruled the country. The ways of living are different from ours but there, too, animals are important, as they are the world over.

U NLESS you've loved an animal — given one a corner of your heart to live in, then this story is not for you.

    * Papashvily (på·păsh′vĭ·lĭ).

Put it down and take up another. For this is about the friends I had in my life who happened to be animals — dogs and a bear, horses, geese, water buffalo, sheep, an elephant, and a few other ends and odds of species I got acquainted with here and there.

Now in our family already when I was born, besides naturally my father and my mother, was Bootsa, our shepherd dog.

When it was our sorrow to lose my mother before I even knew her face

Bootsa took me for her own. She watched beside me as I slept and brought my father in from the fields when I woke and cried. After I could walk she kept me from the woods and the pond, from the horse's feet and the beehives, from all the bright dangers that call to little children left alone.

The first I remember Bootsa she was a giant of a dog, higher than a table and wider than a bed, with a tail that raised a windstorm when she wagged it.

Little by little, as I got older Bootsa shrank and before long we met in the middle. For a while we were shoulder to shoulder, eye to eye, the same size, and then slowly I was taller.

But no matter how much I grew Bootsa was still in command. She was a strict dog and she didn't stand any nonsense from her own children or from me. Puppies, to her, were all the same, be they dog ones or human ones.

Though Bootsa had me for her responsibility she never took me for her friend. She was too old and important in our family, I guess, to bother with me who was so new to it and still on trial.

But her puppy Basar *was* my friend, my first friend and my best friend, for all the five years he lived.

We walked together in the days; we shared half and half the bread I had to eat; we slept side by side at night. When I was glad, he was glad, too, and he raced and barked and chased the wind. When I was sad, he — but I think I never was sad while I had him.

That was something I learned only when I lost him.

One low cloudy night wolves came after our sheep. Basar, dozing by my bed, heard them, ran out and alone himself fought the pack until he drove them off. He brought the sheep safe home and barked us out to get them. Only then did he feel free to lie down beside me and to die.

Gray, Basar was, marked with black, wide chested and his eyes were jewel stones flecked in gold. Still my hand remembers the curve of his rough head and sometimes, even yet, through the green fields of my dreaming he runs again to meet me.

After Basar died I didn't have a dog. I didn't want one that wasn't him. Yet the house needed company. The emptiness in it echoed back and forth against the walls until the whole room was bursting with the silence.

Oh, cats we had, and the meanest gander in all of Georgia.[1] He had outlived three tsars [2] and made as many enemies alone as they had altogether, and there was our pair of water buffalo and Challa, my own golden colt. I felt good friends to all of them and they to me, but they had business of their own in the field and barn.

I wanted somebody or something to stay with me in the house and walk with me on the road, to play ball with me, to wrestle and race, but not another dog. For it seemed as if Basar, when he went, had carried my heart

---

[1] This **Georgia** is a province in the U.S.S.R., bordering on the Black Sea.

[2] Rulers of the Russian Empire (until 1917) were called **tsars** (zärz).

away with him and hid it as so often he did his bones.

A few weeks before the Easter I was ten, a herder coming down our road from the ridge above stopped to give me word my Uncle Giorgi [1] who lived on the other side of the mountain wanted to see me.

Now my Uncle Giorgi was a near genius and if he wanted he could have made a great career for himself. There wasn't a faster, better stonemason in our district, or the next, than him. But he came down from his mountain and worked only when he needed cash for tobacco and salt. Then he went home again.

It wasn't that he had any real grudge against people. Oh, sometimes he complained they were dirty and destructive but still he was broadminded enough to admit human beings are all right in their place.

" God made them," he always said, " so I accept there must be a reason for them."

It was just my Uncle Giorgi's choice to live alone on his mountain and share his orchard and garden with all, animal or human, passing his way. A guest was guest for him — whatever was their species.

The birds in the trees and the fox in the den came at his call. The oldest eel slid from the deepest pool to eat cheese from his hand. The doe brought her new fawn for his good wish. The wild boars, most fierce and proud of all the animals, paid him the honor of ignoring him.

That was my Uncle Giorgi for you, and up the road I went to his house one new spring morning and all the way the woods were sad and still to see me pass alone where so often Basar and I walked happy together.

My Uncle Giorgi, when I came near, was talking with a quail but he broke off the conversation and took me into his house and gave me honey and loquats [2] and milk and corn bread. After we finished eating and I told him all the news about everybody at home he went to a basket beside the hearth, lifted something out, and brought it to me.

In that very minute I knew here was what I wanted most in all the world.

" Your Easter present," my Uncle Giorgi said.

" To be mine, really mine, to keep? "

" Yours to keep. Feed him and brush him and give him clean water to drink."

" I will, I will."

" Treat him always as you should wish — were he the master and you the animal."

" Oh, I will. Let me hold him."

" For by how you treat an animal you make your own luck. Remember it! "

" I will. Give him to me."

My Uncle Giorgi set him in my arms. Above my hand I could feel a heart beating. I touched the round, black button nose, the scraps of ears against his head. I ran my hand over his rough coat. He opened milk-blue

[1] The Russian name **Giorgi** is pronounced "zhorzhi."

[2] **loquats** (lō′kwŏts): plumlike fruit.

eyes to me, yawned, stuck out a tongue pink as watermelon, sneezed and went back to sleep.

"Where's his mother?" I said.

My Uncle Giorgi shook his head.

"Doesn't she care if I have him?"

"Not any more. She's dead. Shot to make a day's sport for someone and left. I found this little one beside her crying and cold. You must feed him milk for a little while."

"I will. I'll feed him and brush him and take care of him and keep him as long as I live."

"No," my Uncle Giorgi said, "for your sorrow you cannot. Accept it. None of the animals we love live as long as we do."

"Why not?"

"I don't know. Maybe to remind us how short time really is. What will you name him?"

"Kola."

So next day I took my Kola and started home. Now the whole forest was awake. Cuckoos calling and the hoopoe [1] birds chattering back and forth while the rabbits went rushing ahead from bush to bush with the news. From the highest rocks the mountain goats stopped and looked down to see me walking proud with my little bear beside me.

But when we got home Kola, I'm sorry to say, wasn't made very welcome. The cats ignored him. Challa, my own colt, rolled his eyes, ruffled his underlip, and stamped his feet. Loma and Mertskella, the water buffalo, only shook big ears at him and went back to their hay.

The first time Kola went outdoors alone the gander nipped his stub tail so hard that Kola hid under my bed and cried his heart dry to find the world so strange and cruel and full of geese. It took a whole comb of honey to coax him out again.

The neighbors were afraid of Kola, too, and warned my father to send him away before he ate us all up.

My father was a clever man and though he could not agree with them he listened to all they had to say, which satisfied them almost as much.

Only he told me, "Teach Kola to be a good bear and not to hurt or frighten anybody. For your sake and for his own."

I did. I taught him to be clean. I carved him a nice comb from mulberry wood, and sleeked him up every day with it, and I took him swimming with me in the river whenever I went.

I taught him to be friendly and not to eat what wasn't his or growl for nothing or bite even in play.

I taught him to bow and shake hands and wrestle and jump and play soldier and catch a ball and dance the Lezghinka. [2] I taught him all I knew myself — how to follow a bee at the flower home to the hive in the tree; the way to know a ripe apple from a sour one; the road through the thicket to the clearing where the big blue plums grew.

The only thing Kola wouldn't learn, no matter how many times I showed him, was to crack nuts with a stone. He preferred to use his teeth. And I

---

[1] hoopoe (hōō′pōō).

[2] Lezghinka (lĕz·hǐnk′à): a simple, lively dance.

couldn't keep
him from being curious.

Often when we were drilling
I went marching on in full parade
only to find my army had broken
ranks to investigate something — a
butterfly on a cedar, a rope tied to a
post, a basket set upside down, a bell
ringing on the road.

The whole world was a question for
Kola and each day he learned a little
piece more of the answer.

Often and often this got him into
trouble. Once workmen came from
the city to build a fine house for a
prince. After a few days passed I had
a complaint from the carpenter that
Kola had growled at him.

From then on I kept Kola at home
during the day. But nights he went
back there and climbed all over the
scaffold — not to hurt anything, but
just so he would know, too, the same
as the rest of us, how a prince's house
gets built.

The carpenter found out and so on
purpose he left a cross plank with the
far end resting on air. When Kola
stepped there it threw him to the
ground and bruised him so badly he
couldn't walk for a week.

After that Kola waited his chance
until one night the carpenter forgot
to put all of his tools away. The next
day the hammer was gone. While the
carpenter searched everywhere Kola
sat on it and watched, picking his
teeth with his long claws and laughing from the side of his muzzle as only
bears can.

Naturally I scolded Kola for dis-
gracing us with such actions. But
when the whole story came out and
the stonecutters on the job told Kola's
side, the carpenter was most to blame.
He started it by giving Kola the first
time he saw him tobacco soaked in
honey to tease him.

The best I could I tried to show
Kola not to be mean and pay back

bad with worse. Only it was hard when human beings set him such an example.

Another time Kola took my cousin's little boy and washed him in the brook. My cousin instead of appreciating the favor wrung her hands and called for the army and all the saints to come out of heaven and help her. But the baby, when I took him away,

It happened Kola and I were visiting my Uncle Giorgi at the time and a week of the soldiers had almost gone when coming back home in the half-dark of evening I saw some cadets walking toward me. One was playing a concertina, the rest singing. When we met, because I did not give them the road, they pounded and cursed me between them.

screamed so hard we had to give him back to Kola to laugh and splash some more.

After this Kola was in bad reputation, at least with all the mothers in our village, until late that fall when a regiment on special maneuvers [1] marched in. The Tsar's officers were quartered on us [2] and it was hard, for they were each for themselves little tsars over us. They used our road and left us the ditches to walk in. Our vegetable gardens were stolen bare. Our lambs disappeared and the women did not dare spread even a pocket handkerchief on the grass to dry.

[1] **maneuvers** (má·nōō′vĕrz): large-scale military exercises.
[2] **quartered on us**: lodged in our homes.

Kola was not with me but trailed a little way behind, for at the curve of the road he had stopped to see if anybody was home in a hollow tree. Now down on his four feet like a dog he came out from the shadows just in time to see the cadets snatch my cap and throw it into the ditch and push me after.

Well if they had their army, I had mine.

"Kola!" I called and whistled our "Charge."

The officers began singing again, the concertina with them. Then suddenly it stopped on a long thin half-note. Kola stood up on the road — taller and taller and still taller.

One swing of his paw tore the blouse from the nearest cadet. The second threw the concertina player into the ditch beside me where the fellow lay crying, " The Devil has risen from the ground. He struck me with his pitchfork." The rest took warning and without waiting for the same thing to happen to them ran away as fast as they could.

The concertina giving a last noisy breath on the ground interested Kola. With his forepaws he picked it up and pulled at the ends. It gave a loud whine for him. He pulled harder. It sounded again. But his next pull tore the bellows in half. He shook it a few times but the concertina was dead. He put the pieces around his neck. I got my cap and came out of the ditch.

We went home together — walking all the way on the path.

By morning the whole village knew what had happened. From then on soldiers walked with care. Fruit hung undisturbed on our trees. Bread cooled on the ovens without watching. Though I didn't know it until long long after, my Kola grew to be a legend in the Tsar's army. " In Mtsketa do as you please," veterans told recruits, " and in Dushet, too. But in Kobiankari [1] take care! There the men are so fierce the very children walk with wild beasts at heel for pets."

For our village Kola was a hero. The women gave him so much honey and fruit and chestnuts and white bread from their pantries he could have made himself a wedding party with it.

The very same neighbors who warned my father when first I got Kola were proud now to be living on such good terms with a bear. They showed him off to their visitors and laughed to see *them* afraid.

Finally the maneuvers were over and the soldiers went away and we were all living happy in our village until the summer of the next year when two things happened that never happened before.

War came, and so did a circus.

The circus was first. Up the great highway from Tiflis it rolled one hot day in three painted carts pulled by donkeys.

In the first sat some Syrians with a bunch of monkeys. In the next were golden-skinned men with almond eyes who juggled balls and whirled knives as they rode. The last wagon was covered with a cloth tucked and tied in on every side and painted on it: BEWARE — OF — LION — WITHIN. The whole village watching the circus pass caught a long breath when the cover rippled and belled in the still air.

Kola raised his head when the lion went by, sniffed, scrumpled his nose, sniffed again. He would have gone after the cage to investigate it some more but I kept him by my side to see the last part pass, a pair of goats, three small dogs, and a dusty man.

The circus made a camp in the meadow beside the stream. Three kopecks [2] for the performance, one more to see the lion, and still another to

---

[1] **Mtsketa** (mĕts·kēt′á). **Dushet** (dū·shĕt′). **Kobiankari** (kō·bĭ·ān·kär′ĭ).

[2] A kopek (kō′pĕk) is a coin worth 1/100 of a ruble (rōō′b'l), or less than our cent.

hear him roar. Kola and I were the first ones to take a ticket as soon as the whole troupe was dressed and ready to play their parts.

Donkeys wearing head plumes counted to ten and answered questions. Dogs with pleated ruffs around their necks walked a tightrope. Monkeys were sick in bed until the goats came, doctors in frock coats wagging their beards, to give them medicine. Then they jumped up cured and did a thousand tricks.

Oh, it was a beautiful sight when the whole thing was going at once. The Syrians tumbling over and under each other and up into the air, turning circles as they came down. The donkeys rolling barrels; the dogs waltzing to a flute; the monkeys plunging through hoops as they rode the goats around the ring.

The golden jugglers threw their knives, spun them up and stood in the rain of bright blades and caught them as they fell without a scratch. The flutes played louder; the pink flares burning at the corners lit it all as bright as day, and the lion from his generous heart treated us all to free roars.

Next morning early before the sun was up I went back again. Because of Kola, the man, the dusty one who owned the circus, let me help him and come in free.

I carried wood and water and combed the donkeys and fixed bread and sugared milk for the lion. He was getting old, poor fellow, and the few teeth he had left, the owner told me, hurt him too much for chewing. But his roar was still fine and prickled young hair to hear it.

"Often and often I had bears," the owner said. We were eating breakfast. "In fact I am called 'Vanno, The Bear Man.' This is the first time I ever took the road without a bear." He scratched Kola's head. "How old is he?"

"Six."

"It's hard to find a new bear. Not every bear suits me. My last bear grew old and died. I gave him a funeral many a prince might envy. Some people thought it was a scandal. I didn't. I wanted him to enter heaven in style."

"Do bears go to heaven?" I said. It was a question that had bothered me for a long time but I never had the courage to ask anybody before.

"If they don't," Vanno gave a threatening look at the sky, "better not expect *me* up there."

He rubbed Kola's hard head awhile. "Can he wrestle or dance?"

"Can he?" I said.

I gave Kola our signal. He went through all his tricks. There was nothing he enjoyed more than an appreciative audience.

"Too good to be wasted on a village," Vanno said when Kola finished and made his best bow. "Let him come with me and find a career for himself."

"No."

"Come, come. I'll pay you well. What will you take for him?"

"Nothing."

"Fifty rubles?"

"No."

" Seventy-five? "

" No."

" A hundred rubles? "

" No," I said, " but I will trade him to you."

" Even better. For what? "

" For your oldest son! "

Vanno laughed. " You are a good boy. And when I tell you your bear is the smartest one I've ever seen, remember, I speak as an expert. Keep him. I don't blame you. Were he mine I would do the same. But just in case you must ever part with him, and only God knows what is yet to be with all the talk of war, bring him to me in Tiflis. Rustaveli Prospect.[1] Ask anyone near the fountain. I am not — " he finished proudly, " — unknown."

After a few more shows, the jugglers packed their knives, the donkeys were harnessed and the circus creaked on. The last thing, at the top of the hill, Vanno, The Bear Man, stopped and called back to me, " Remember. Rustaveli Prospect near the fountain. I will make it a hundred and fifty rubles! "

A hundred and fifty rubles! That was a fortune. It could buy a farm. It could buy a tradesman a prince's title. It could buy a substitute to send to war.[2] It could not buy Kola.

Hardly had the circus gone when the war came. Whether we wanted or not, it took us all. It took our neighbor on the hill and my Cousin Wardo and the three sons of the Widow Jakeli

---

[1] **Prospect:** a long, straight street or avenue.
[2] In many European countries, when a man was drafted for the army he could hire someone else to go in his place.

---

and in the second year my father and then me.

Before I knew it I was a soldier, a Russian soldier with a gun and a uniform that didn't fit me.

And Kola? What would become of my Kola now? There was ten days left before I must leave the village and join the regiment, then eight days, then six.

No one was left in our village but the women and the children and a few old, old men. Food was getting scarce. Who could take care of Kola? So at last with a slow, sad heart I had to remember Vanno, The Bear Man.

Tiflis was thirty-nine miles away. Off we started and as we went I tried to explain to Kola the best I could what was happening to us.

Sometimes a farmer gave us a ride in a buffalo cart; sometimes we walked. Nights lying under haystacks, Kola asleep by my side, I tried to cheer myself thinking how well fed and happy Vanno, The Bear Man's, animals were — how they came with full trust at his call and gave their performances with pleasure. It seemed strange even to me that a soldier could still cry.

When we came to Tiflis I did not go through the bazaar to look at the booths full of woven carpets and bright brasses and carved daggers and new saddles. I did not stop for the vendors with baskets of pomegranates on their heads and strings of walnut candy in their hands. I went straight to the fountain.

" Vanno, The Bear Man? " I asked a boy filling his jug.

He pointed to the house opposite.

With Kola at my heels I climbed the outside stairs and knocked. Vanno opened the door.

"Well! Well!" he shouted. "May ever you be victorious. So you finally decided. Come in and eat breakfast with me. Later I will pay you as I said."

He put a piece of corn bread before me and some fruit. I cut them both in two, gave Kola his share, and ate mine. Then I spoke.

"No, Bear Man. I have not come to sell him." I told him I was taken for a soldier and how things were in the village.

He shook his head. "Wars are good for nobody, and still they have wars. Do you understand it?"

"No," I said, "all I know is I must do the best I can for Kola. I want you to keep him for me until I come back. You will treat him well, I know. With his tricks he can earn his own living and something over for you. And if I don't come home —"

"God forbid," Vanno crossed himself.

"Use that hundred and fifty rubles to see Kola lives in peace when he is old and cannot travel with you any longer."

"It shall be as you wish," Vanno said and shook my hand on it. He went to his desk and wrote the agreement on a paper and gave it to me.

"Rest easy, my son. Sometimes in my dealings with men I may be a little sharp, but I never in my life gave an animal less than its due."

Then was the worst. To tell Kola good-by. Vanno went to the window and looked out at the fountain. I sat beside Kola. I explained it all over to him again. I showed him the paper and though neither of us could read much it comforted us. I put his paw on Vanno's shoulder to show him he was a friend. I rubbed his shaggy head. At last Vanno caught a chain to his collar. Then I knelt down and kissed his muzzle and without daring to look back once I ran down the stairs.

The war was even worse than I expected. Mud and lice. Hunger and cold. Pain and waste. Whenever I think of it I remember especially the beautiful horses lifting their heads and feet high with life one minute, lying torn and bloody the next. Dying for what — for a quarrel they didn't make — for glory they didn't want — for prizes they wouldn't share?

When their tormented eyes asked us this question the only answer we could give them was a straight quick bullet.

For us men it wasn't much better.

After twenty months I had a furlough, two weeks. First was a bath; second, clean clothes; third, get Kola and go home.

I rode in a carriage to Vanno's house. Before I got out I could see it was empty, the door padlocked, the windows boarded up. I knocked and shook at the latch. No answer.

Once again someone at the fountain helped me, this time an old man.

Vanno. Yes, he knew him. At last Vanno, too, had been called for a soldier. Gone about two months. Where or what regiment, he couldn't say. The old lion died. Some Syrians, he thought, had come for the monkeys. But a bear, a smart bear, he smiled to think of that animal it was so smart, Vanno himself had taken it away. Where he could not say. Nor could anyone else in the neighborhood help me.

Tiflis was strange to me, but I searched everywhere I could think — through the markets, the Syrian quarter, all the theaters. I went home to my village hoping for some news there. My father was gone, of course, but I thought perhaps some of the neighbors had heard of Kola. No letter or message waited for me.

I went back to Tiflis and spent the days following the trail of some traveling shows into the country but no Kola was with them.

My furlough finished and I met the other soldiers who were going back to the front with me the next day. They had a carriage and they wanted to drive about five miles outside town to a little inn in the woods for a farewell celebration.

"Come on," they urged me. "There's music and a green lawn for dancing and all we can eat and drink for last time maybe until the war is over."

So I went along, and time did pass better in somebody's company than my own. When we came to the inn it was crowded but the host led us to a table under a little green arbor and laid a clean cloth and gave us fresh trout and cucumbers and salt cheese and pickled mushrooms and new bread.

"And wine! " I called out across the garden to the waiter. "Bring us wine to drink with it."

The answer to me was a great bellowing roar that sent everybody to their feet. Then we heard wood splinter and bricks crash. From the kitchen, the cook came screaming, "Run, run for your lives."

Something plunged after him. Men crowded back. A woman fainted. I stood on a chair and looked over the arbor. Long before my head understood my heart knew. I jumped across the table and pushed my way through the crowd.

"Kola," I cried, and he ran into my arms.

When I could make him stop hugging me I looked around. The proprietor stood ready with a gun aimed at us, the cook beside him with a cleaver. The women were still screaming, hands over their eyes so they wouldn't see me killed.

"Please everybody," I said, "be at ease. This is my bear and he doesn't hurt anybody. I lost him and he found me. He recognized my voice when I spoke and he's excited. But how," I said to the innkeeper, "did *you* get him? I left him with Vanno, The Bear Man."

"The young soldier tells the truth," the man spoke to the whole garden. "As I stand here, it *is* his bear, and no ordinary animal either. So my brother Vanno told me, and so I found out for myself. When Vanno was called to the army he came to me, ' I have arranged

ANIMALS

for the other animals but you must keep the bear and keep him well until I return or you will answer to me and to the bear's brother who is also a soldier.' Then to prove the rareness of this beast he showed me a bankbook. Ladies and gentlemen, it is true, may I lose heaven if I lie, to the account of Kola, a bear, is deposited one hundred fifty rubles in the Tiflis Government Bank. Now, young sir, let me chain him again."

"No," I said, "he will stay quietly beside me."

And he did. We made a place for him at our table. We ate and we drank and we danced and Kola crying with joy did all his tricks over and over and hugged me until I hardly had breath left in me.

I stayed until at last he fell asleep from so much food and wine and we could put him on the chain. Then I had to tell him good-by again.

"Keep him," I said to the innkeeper. "Send me news of him until I come for him." I gave him my address.

The next morning I was supposed to go direct to the troop train but I couldn't. I had to have one more glimpse of Kola first. I took a carriage back to the inn. When I drove in, the place was in an uproar. The proprietor ran here and there. The cook chattered. The waiters looked behind the doors. Finally the story came out. When they carried Kola's food to him that morning his post was splintered, his chain broken. Kola had run away.

"He's gone to find me," I said.

I looked until I found his tracks and we followed them half a mile up the mountain to where the deep forest began. There I told the others to wait. I walked in alone calling as I went. Far back in among the rocks I thought I heard a rustle — yes — and a low growl. I stood in the half-darkness and spoke.

"Kola? Kola, if that's you, don't come out. Go back into the woods and be your own bear. For you it's a better chance than tied on a chain. Wait for me there and the day wars are over I'll come for you again. Stay hidden and wait."

Then I turned and went back down the road to town alone. And in the forest my Kola still waits.

Animals in the Family

1. What made Uncle Giorgi different from most people? Tell things he said to show what kind of person he was. What advice did he give George about taking care of Kola?

2. What did the boy teach his bear to do? Do you know anyone who has trained a pet with such care? If so, tell what the pet has been taught, and how.

3. Which one of Kola's adventures did you enjoy most — washing the baby, getting even with the carpenter, or teaching the soldiers better manners? Why was that one more fun?

4. Describe the circus that came to George's village. How was it different from circuses you have seen? What was Vanno's attitude toward animals? Tell parts of the story to support your answer.

5. How did the war twice upset Kola's life? How well did Vanno live up to his bargain with George about taking care of Kola?

6. Tell why the ending of this story was both a sad and a happy one. Would you prefer a different ending? Why?

 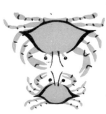 

Three Fables

We do not know who first thought of making fables, but there should be a statue to his memory, for we have no gayer combination of sense and fun than these little stories. In most fables animals act and talk like people, and there is a lesson, or moral, that is the important point of the story. Two of the fables that follow are modern ones; the third is an ancient one by Aesop.

THE LITTLE GIRL AND THE WOLF

JAMES THURBER

ONE afternoon a big wolf waited in a dark forest for a little girl to come along carrying a basket of food to her grandmother. Finally a little girl did come along and she was carrying a basket of food. "Are you carrying that basket to your grandmother?" asked the wolf. The little girl said yes, she was. So the wolf asked her where her grandmother lived and the little girl told him and he disappeared into the wood.

When the little girl opened the door of her grandmother's house she saw that there was somebody in bed with a nightcap and nightgown on. She had approached no nearer than twenty-five feet from the bed when she saw that it was not her grandmother but the wolf, for even in a nightcap a wolf does not look any more like your grandmother than the Metro-Goldwyn lion looks like Calvin Coolidge. So the little girl took an automatic out of her basket and shot the wolf dead.

MORAL: *It is not so easy to fool little girls nowadays as it used to be.*

THE SCOTTY WHO KNEW TOO MUCH

JAMES THURBER

SEVERAL summers ago there was a Scotty who went to the country for a visit. He decided that all the farm dogs were cowards, because they were afraid of a certain animal that had a white stripe down its back. "You are a pussycat and I can lick you," the Scotty said to the farm dog who lived in the house where the Scotty was visiting. "I can lick the little animal with the white stripe, too. Show him to me." "Don't you want to ask any questions about him?" said the farm dog. "Naw," said the Scotty. "*You* ask the questions."

So the farm dog took the Scotty into the woods and showed him the white-striped animal and the Scotty closed in on him, growling and slashing. It was all over in a moment and the Scotty lay on his back. When he came to, the farm dog said, "What happened?" "He threw vitriol,"[1] said the Scotty, "but he never laid a glove on me."[2]

A few days later the farm dog told the Scotty there was another animal all the farm dogs were afraid of. "Lead me to him," said the Scotty. "I can lick anything that doesn't wear horseshoes." "Don't you want to ask any questions about him?" said the farm dog. "Naw," said the Scotty. "Just show me where he hangs out." So the farm dog led him to a place in the woods and pointed out the little animal when he came along. "A clown," said the Scotty, "a pushover," and he closed in, leading with his left and exhibiting some mighty fancy footwork. In less than a second the Scotty was flat on his back, and when he woke up the farm dog was pulling quills out of him. "What happened?" said the farm dog. "He pulled a knife on me," said the Scotty, "but at least I have learned how you fight out here in the country, and now I am going to beat *you* up." So he closed in on the farm dog, holding his nose with one front paw to ward off the vitriol and covering his eyes with the other front paw to keep out the knives. The Scotty couldn't see his

opponent and he couldn't smell his opponent and he was so badly beaten that he had to be taken back to the city and put in a nursing home.

MORAL: *It is better to ask some of the questions than to know all the answers.*

THE YOUNG CRAB AND HIS MOTHER

AESOP

"WHY in the world do you walk sideways like that?" said a Mother Crab to her son. "You should always walk straight forward with your toes turned out."

"Show me how to walk, Mother dear," answered the little Crab obediently. "I want to learn."

So the old Crab tried and *tried* to walk straight forward. But she could only walk sideways, like her son. And when she tried to turn her toes out she tripped and fell on her nose.

MORAL: *Do not tell others how to act unless you can set a good example.*

Fables for Sense and Fun

1. Are all the "morals" true and sensible? Which one do you think is most amusing? Write a fable of your own using the same characters, or make drawings for your favorite one.

2. Telling fables aloud is fine practice in speaking, because you must not ramble and the details must be just right. The greatest collection of such stories in existence is *Aesop's Fables,* supposed to have been written by a Greek slave about twenty-five centuries ago. Select one of Aesop's fables to tell to the class.

---

[1] vitriol (vĭt′rĭ-ŭl): sulfuric acid.
[2] never laid a glove on me: never hit me. This is a phrase from the boxing ring.

The Vulture

HILAIRE BELLOC *

The vulture eats between his meals,
    And that's the reason why
He very, very rarely feels
    As well as you and I.

His eye is dull, his head is bald,
    His neck is growing thinner.
Oh! What a lesson for us all
    To only eat at dinner!

* Hilaire Belloc (hĭ·lâr′ bĕl′ŏk).

Moti Guj—Mutineer

RUDYARD KIPLING

TOLD WITH A CHUCKLE. Rudyard Kipling gave the world scores of fascinating stories about India, where he was born and lived part of his life. Many of the stories are about animals. You probably know Rikki-Tikki-Tavi, the mongoose, and you surely know Mowgli and his wild animal cronies of *The Jungle Book.* In Moti Guj [1] you meet the most impor-

¹ Moti Guj (mō′tĭ gōōj).

tant animal in India, the elephant. The heavy work that is done in other lands by horses and oxen and bulldozers is done in India by elephants.

A story about an elephant can be told in several different ways. Kipling may give you an exciting thriller, or make you chuckle over an amusing prank, or stir your sympathy for the hard-working animal. Whatever his purpose, it will be reflected promptly in the *mood* of his writing. If his mood is honestly solemn, give him a serious hearing. If there is a twinkle in his eye (and his words), get ready to enjoy his little jokes.

Once upon a time there was a coffee-planter in India who wished to clear some forest land for coffee-planting. When he had cut down all the trees and burned the underwood, the stumps still remained. Dynamite is expensive and slow fire slow. The happy medium for stump-clearing is the lord of all beasts, which is the elephant. He will either push the stump out of the ground with his tusks, if he has any, or drag it out with ropes. The planter, therefore, hired elephants by ones and twos and threes, and fell to work. The very best of all the elephants belonged to the very worst of all the drivers or mahouts [1]; and this superior beast's name was Moti Guj. He was the absolute property of his mahout, which would never have been the case under native rule; for Moti Guj was a creature to be desired by kings, and his name, being translated, meant the Pearl Elephant. Because the British government was in the land, Deesa, the mahout, enjoyed his property undisturbed. He was dissipated. When he had made much money through the strength of his elephant, he would get extremely drunk and give Moti Guj a beating with a tent peg over the tender nails of the forefeet. Moti Guj

never trampled the life out of Deesa on these occasions, for he knew that after the beating was over, Deesa would embrace his trunk and weep and call him his love and his life and the liver of his soul, and give him some liquor. Moti Guj was very fond of liquor — arrack [2] for choice, though he would drink palm-tree toddy [3] if nothing better offered. Then Deesa would go to sleep between Moti Guj's forefeet, and, as Deesa generally chose the middle of the public road, and, as Moti Guj mounted guard over him, and would not permit horse, foot, or cart to pass by, traffic was congested till Deesa saw fit to wake up.

There was no sleeping in the daytime on the planter's clearing; the wages were too high to risk. Deesa sat on Moti Guj's neck and gave him orders, while Moti Guj rooted up the stumps — for he owned a magnificent pair of tusks; or pulled at the end of a rope — for he had a magnificent pair of shoulders — while Deesa kicked him behind the ears and said he was the king of elephants. At evening time Moti Guj would wash down his three hundred pounds' weight of green food with a quart of arrack, and Deesa would take a share, and sing songs between Moti Guj's legs till it was time to go to bed. Once a week Deesa led Moti Guj down to the river, and Moti Guj lay on his side luxuriously in the shallows, while Deesa

---

[1] mahout (má·hout').

[2] arrack (ăr'ăk): a liquor that is distilled from rum.

[3] palm-tree toddy: a drink made from fermented sap of the palm tree.

went over him with a coir-swab [1] and a brick. Moti Guj never mistook the pounding blow of the latter for the smack of the former that warned him to get up and turn over on the other side. Then Deesa would look at his feet and examine his eyes, and turn up the fringes of his mighty ears in case of sores or budding ophthalmia.[2] After inspection the two would " come up with a song from the sea," Moti Guj, all black and shining, waving a torn tree branch twelve feet long in his trunk, and Deesa knotting up his own long wet hair.

It was a peaceful, well-paid life till Deesa felt the return of the desire to drink deep. He wished for an orgy. The little draughts that led nowhere were taking the manhood out of him.

He went to the planter, and, " My mother's dead," said he, weeping.

" She died on the last plantation two months ago, and she died once before that when you were working for me last year," said the planter, who knew something of the ways of nativedom.

" Then it's my aunt, and she was just the same as a mother to me," said Deesa, weeping more than ever. " She has left eighteen small children entirely without bread, and it is I who must fill their little stomachs," said Deesa, beating his head on the floor.

" Who brought you the news? " said the planter.

" The post," [3] said Deesa.

" There hasn't been a post here for the past week. Get back to your lines! "

" A devastating sickness has fallen on my village, and all my wives are dying," yelled Deesa, really in tears this time.

" Call Chihun,[4] who comes from Deesa's village," said the planter. " Chihun, has this man got a wife? "

" He? " said Chihun. " No. Not a woman of our village would look at him. They'd sooner marry the elephant."

Chihun snorted. Deesa wept and bellowed.

" You will get into difficulty in a minute," said the planter. " Go back to your work! "

" Now I will speak heaven's truth," gulped Deesa, with an inspiration. " I haven't been drunk for two months. I desire to depart in order to get properly drunk afar off and distant from this heavenly plantation. Thus I shall cause no trouble."

A flickering smile crossed the planter's face. " Deesa," said he, " you've spoken the truth, and I'd give you leave on the spot if anything could be done with Moti Guj while you're away. You know that he will only obey your orders."

" May the light of the heavens live forty thousand years. I shall be absent but ten little days. After that, upon my faith and honor and soul, I return. As to the inconsiderable interval, have I the gracious permission of the heaven-born to call up Moti Guj? "

Permission was granted, and in an-

---

[1] **coir-swab** (koir'swŏb′): a mop of coarse coconut fiber.
[2] **ophthalmia** (ŏf·thăl′mĭ·à): an inflammation of the eyes.
[3] **post**: mail.
[4] **Chihun** (chē′ŭn).

swer to Deesa's shrill yell, the mighty tusker swung out of the shade of a clump of trees where he had been squirting dust over himself till his master should return.

"Light of my heart, protector of the drunken, mountain of might, give ear!" said Deesa, standing in front of him.

Moti Guj gave ear, and saluted with his trunk. "I am going away," said Deesa.

Moti Guj's eyes twinkled. He liked jaunts as well as his master. One could snatch all manner of nice things from the roadside then.

"But you, you fussy old pig, must stay behind and work."

The twinkle died out as Moti Guj tried to looked delighted. He hated stump-hauling on the plantation. It hurt his teeth.

"I shall be gone for ten days, O delectable[1] one! Hold up your near forefoot and I'll impress the fact upon it, warty toad of a dried mud puddle." Deesa took a tent peg and banged Moti Guj ten times on the nails. Moti Guj grunted and shuffled from foot to foot.

"Ten days," said Deesa, "you will work and haul and root the trees as Chihun here shall order you. Take up Chihun and set him on your neck!" Moti Guj curled the tip of his trunk, Chihun put his foot there, and was swung onto the neck. Deesa handed Chihun the heavy *ankus* — the iron elephant goad.

Chihun thumped Moti Guj's bald head as a paver thumps a curbstone. Moti Guj trumpeted.

"Be still, hog of the backwoods! Chihun's your mahout for ten days. And now bid me good-by, beast after mine own heart. O my lord, my king! Jewel of all created elephants, lily of the herd, preserve your honored health; be virtuous. Adieu!"

Moti Guj lapped his trunk round Deesa and swung him into the air twice. That was his way of bidding him good-by.

"He'll work now," said Deesa to the planter. "Have I leave to go?"

The planter nodded, and Deesa dived into the woods. Moti Guj went back to haul stumps.

Chihun was very kind to him, but he felt unhappy and forlorn for all that. Chihun gave him a ball of spices and tickled him under the chin, and Chihun's little baby cooed to him after work was over, and Chihun's wife called him a darling; but Moti Guj was a bachelor by instinct, as Deesa was. He did not understand the domestic emotions. He wanted the light of his universe back again — the drink and the drunken slumber, the savage beatings and the savage caresses.

Nonetheless he worked well, and the planter wondered. Deesa had wandered along the roads till he met a marriage procession of his own caste,[2] and, drinking, dancing, and tippling, had drifted with it past all knowledge of the lapse of time.

The morning of the eleventh day

---

[1] **delectable** (dê-lĕk′tȧ-b'l): delightful, very pleasing.

[2] **caste** (kăst): Among the Hindus in India people are divided into classes, or castes, which are not allowed to mix.

dawned, and there returned no Deesa. Moti Guj was loosed from his ropes for the daily stint. He swung clear, looked round, shrugged his shoulders, and began to walk away, as one having business elsewhere.

" Hi! ho! Come back, you! " shouted Chihun. " Come back and put me on your neck, misborn mountain! Return, splendor of the hillsides! Adornment of all India, heave to, or I'll bang every toe off your fat forefoot! "

Moti Guj gurgled gently, but did not obey. Chihun ran after him with a rope and caught him up. Moti Guj put his ears forward, and Chihun knew what that meant, though he tried to carry it off with high words.

" None of your nonsense with me," said he. " To your pickets, devil-son! "

" Hrrump! " said Moti Guj, and that was all — that and the forebent ears.

Moti Guj put his hands in his pockets, chewed a branch for a toothpick, and strolled about the clearing, making fun of the other elephants who had just set to work.

Chihun reported the state of affairs to the planter, who came out with a dog whip and cracked it furiously. Moti Guj paid the white man the compliment of charging him nearly a quarter of a mile across the clearing and " Hrrumping " him into his veranda. Then he stood outside the house, chuckling to himself and shaking all over with the fun of it as an elephant will.

" We'll thrash him," said the planter. " He shall have the finest thrashing ever elephant received. Give Kala Nag and Nazim twelve foot of chain apiece, and tell them to lay on twenty."

Kala Nag — which means Black Snake — and Nazim were two of the biggest elephants in the lines, and one of their duties was to administer the graver punishment, since no man

can beat an elephant properly.

They took the whipping-chains and rattled them in their trunks as they sidled up to Moti Guj, meaning to hustle him between them. Moti Guj had never, in all his life of thirty-nine years, been whipped, and he did not intend to begin a new experience. So he waited, waving his head from right to left, and measuring the precise spot in Kala Nag's fat side where a blunt tusk could sink deepest. Kala Nag had no tusks; the chain was the badge of his authority; but for all that, he swung wide of Moti Guj at the last minute, and tried to appear as if he had brought the chain out for amusement. Nazim turned round and went home early. He did not feel fighting fit that morning and so Moti Guj was left standing alone with his ears cocked.

That decided the planter to argue no more and Moti Guj rolled back to his amateur inspection of the clearing. An elephant who will not work and is not tied up is about as manageable as an eighty-one-ton gun loose in a heavy seaway.[1] He slapped old friends on the back and asked them if the stumps were coming away easily; he talked nonsense concerning labor and the inalienable rights[2] of elephants to a long "nooning";[3] and, wandering to and fro, he thoroughly demoralized the garden till sundown,

---

[1] **heavy seaway:** high waves caused by rough weather at sea.

[2] **inalienable** (ĭn·āl′yĕn·á·b'l) **rights:** a favorite phrase for describing the natural rights of men. It means rights that are not to be given up at any price.

[3] **nooning:** a rest period at noontime.

when he returned to his picket[4] for food.

"If you won't work, you shan't eat," said Chihun, angrily. "You're a wild elephant, and no educated animal at all. Go back to your jungle."

Chihun's little brown baby was rolling on the floor of the hut and stretching out its fat arms to the huge shadow in the doorway. Moti Guj knew well that it was the dearest thing on earth to Chihun. He swung out his trunk with a fascinating crook at the end, and the brown baby threw itself, shouting, upon it. Moti Guj made fast and pulled up till the brown baby was crowing in the air twelve feet above his father's head.

"Great lord!" said Chihun, "flour cakes of the best, twelve in number, two feet across and soaked in rum, shall be yours on the instant, and two hundred pounds weight of fresh-cut young sugar cane therewith. Deign only to put down safely that insignificant brat who is my heart and my life to me!"

Moti Guj tucked the brown baby comfortably between his forefeet, that could have knocked into tooth-picks all Chihun's hut, and waited for his food. He ate it, and the brown baby crawled away. Moti Guj dozed and thought of Deesa. One of many mysteries connected with the elephant is that his huge body needs sleep less than anything else that lives. Four or five hours in the night suffice — two just before midnight, lying down on one side; two just after

---

[4] **picket:** the place where he was usually tied to a stake when not at work.

one o'clock, lying down on the other. The rest of the silent hours are filled with eating and fidgeting, and long grumbling soliloquies.[1]

At midnight, therefore, Moti Guj strode out of his picket, for a thought had come to him that Deesa might be lying drunk somewhere in the dark forest with none to look after him. So all that night he chased through the undergrowth, blowing and trumpeting and shaking his ears. He went down to the river and blared across the shallows where Deesa used to wash him, but there was no answer. He could not find Deesa, but he disturbed all the other elephants in the lines, and nearly frightened to death some gypsies in the woods.

At dawn Deesa returned to the plantation. He had been very drunk indeed, and he expected to get into trouble for outstaying his leave. He drew a long breath when he saw that the bungalow and the plantation were still uninjured, for he knew something of Moti Guj's temper, and reported himself with many lies and salaams.[2] Moti Guj had gone to his picket for breakfast. The night exercise had made him hungry.

"Call up your beast," said the planter; and Deesa shouted in the mysterious elephant language that some mahouts believe came from China at the birth of the world, when elephants and not men were masters. Moti Guj heard and came. Elephants do not gallop. They move from places at varying rates of speed. If an elephant wished to catch an express train he could not gallop, but he could catch the train. So Moti Guj was at the planter's door almost before Chihun noticed that he had left his picket. He fell into Deesa's arms, trumpeting with joy, and the man and beast wept and slobbered over each other, and handled each other from head to heel to see that no harm had befallen.

"Now we will get to work," said Deesa. "Lift me up, my son and my joy!"

Moti Guj swung him up, and the two went to the coffee-clearing to look for difficult stumps.

The planter was too astonished to be very angry.

Sensing the Author's Mood

1. In your reading of the story, how soon could you tell that Kipling intended to amuse you? What first made you think so?

2. Tell some of the names Deesa called Moti Guj. Why are they funny?

3. What excuses failed to get Deesa time off for a spree? Why did the planter finally let him go?

4. How did the planter and Chihun try to make Moti Guj work the eleventh day? Why were they unsuccessful?

5. What makes Kipling's account of Moti Guj's behavior on his day off especially funny? Did Kipling want you to think that elephants do things that only men can do?

6. Do you think elephants can understand their masters and remember promises as well as Moti Guj did? Select two committees to report to the class, after they do library reading, on these subjects: (1) fact and fable about elephants' memories, (2) elephants as intelligent workers.

---

[1] **soliloquies** (sŏ·lĭl'ŏ·kwĭz): speeches made to oneself.

[2] **salaams** (sȧ·lämz'): low bows.

Roundup

How Do You Like Your Animals?

1. Do you like best the stories about animals you know well, or those about stranger ones? Can you tell why?

2. Do you believe that animals can actually think, as Moti Guj and Tip appeared to do? Tell incidents from your own experience or from your reading that will support your answer.

3. If you could have one of these animals to keep, which one would you want? Why?

Animals and People

1. List the many relationships between animals and men — animals as pets, as servants, and so on. How many more can you think of? What animals have men always regarded as enemies? Don't forget the little ones.

2. What animals are " big business " in America? How many products of these businesses do you use regularly?

3. Many popular movies feature animal actors. Tell of one you have seen. How was the animal an important character in the plot?

Writing About Animals

1. If you have had pets, write an account of " The Pet I Loved Best," or " The Oddest Pet I Ever Had."

2. If you have not had pets of your own, write about " The Most Amusing Animal I Ever Knew," or the most intelligent, or the luckiest. Describe the animal in detail so that your reader will be able to see it. Tell incidents to prove that it deserves the title you give it.

Your Bookshelf

Aesop's Fables, translated by Thomas James and George Taylor Townsend (Lippincott, 1950)

The classic tales of animals who talk and think like people.

Amik, the Life Story of a Beaver, by Luis M. Henderson (Morrow, 1948)

Realistic narrative about an interesting animal.

Cedar's Boy, by Stephen W. Meader (Harcourt, Brace, 1949)

A boy and a colt in a sequel to the popular *Red Horse Hill* (1930).

Chip, the Dam Builder, by Jim Kjelgaard (Holiday, 1950)

Adventures of a beaver, told by the writer of the fine dog stories *Big Red* (1945) and *Irish Red* (1951).

Farm Animals, by Dorothy Hogner (Oxford, 1945)

This tells you more about them, even if you know them well already.

Favorite Dog Stories, edited by Marguerite Bloch (World, 1950)

The Golden Stallion, by Theodore J. Waldeck (Viking, 1947)

Pursuit of a beautiful wild horse. Waldeck is also the author of *Treks Across the Veldt* (1944), about capturing wild animals in Africa.

High Courage, by Clarence W. Anderson (Macmillan, 1941)

A girl's faith in her race horse defies discouragement from others.

Hill Ranch, by Rutherford Montgomery (Doubleday, 1951)

Many animals, tame and wild.

The Jungle Book, by Rudyard Kipling, new ed. (Grosset, 1950)

Imaginative stories about a boy who was adopted by wolves, and had a bear for a friend and a tiger for a mortal enemy.

Let Them Live, by Dorothy P. Lathrop (Macmillan, 1951)

The case for protection of wildlife.

Palomino and Other Horses, edited by Wesley Dennis (World, 1950)

Short stories about all kinds of horses.

Smoking Hoof, by Gertrude Robinson (Oxford, 1951)

An action-packed story of a boy and his horse during the Revolution.

Smoky Ridge, by Fredric Doyle (Longmans, 1944)

Wild animals of the Great Smoky Mountains and the constant perils to their lives.

Son of the Black Stallion, by Walter Farley (Random House, 1950)

The taming of a magnificent horse with a wild temper.

South Pole Husky, by Charles Strong (Longmans, 1950)

A Norwegian boy and his dog win places in Amundsen's expedition and take part in the race to the pole.

The Sun-Dog Trail and Other Stories, by Jack London (World, 1951)

Twelve vivid stories by a master storyteller.

This Fascinating Animal World, by Alan Devoe (McGraw-Hill, 1951)

Answers all your questions about the odd behavior of animals.

Wild Animals of the Five Rivers Country, by George Corey Franklin (Houghton Mifflin, 1947)

Eighteen stories about little-known animals of the Southwestern mountains. The series is continued in *Wild Animals of the Southwest* (1950).

Wild Horse, by Glenn Balch (Crowell, 1948)

The ranch boy was determined to put his brand on the wild horse. Another good boy-and-horse story by Balch is *Lost Horse* (1950).

Windy Foot at the County Fair, by Frances Frost (Whittlesey, 1947)

A horse and some delightful people.

Americans All

Buffalo Dusk

CARL SANDBURG

Indians — and the buffaloes! They shared the wild, free life of the open prairies. As the prairies were fenced in and plowed, both faded into the dusk at the end of their day. Carl Sandburg remembers them quietly, in a few simple words. But his lines bring back the ghosts of the Indians and the buffaloes for one vivid moment before the shadows close in again.

The buffaloes are gone.
    And those who saw the buffaloes are gone.
Those who saw the buffaloes by thousands and how they pawed the prairie
        sod into dust with their hoofs, their great heads down pawing on in a
        great pageant of dusk,
Those who saw the buffaloes are gone.
And the buffaloes are gone.

A *Glimpse of the Past*

1. What words make you see the great herds of buffaloes?

2. What repeated words give the poem its melancholy tone?

3. Why is free verse (unrhymed lines of uneven length) better than verse with regular rhythm and rhyme for this poem? Can you find other poems in this book that are written in this form? Compare " Buffalo Dusk " with another poem that has regular rhythm and rhyme.

Buffalo Grass

ALICE MARRIOTT

We love our American countryside and think it is beautiful now. But to an Indian who remembers the early days, it was more beautiful when the buffalo roamed the wind-swept prairies. In this story a young girl has a chance to see what it was like long ago, before the land and the people changed.

For Hannah the south porch of the big house was the best part of home. Here you could sit and watch sunrise or sunset; watch the shapes of the earth change and move as the sun moved. Then you knew, when you sat out there, that the earth was alive itself.

Grandmother sat beside her and thought that the earth had gone dead. Lights played and moved and cloud shadows came and went, but the earth itself had somehow died. It all seemed one color now; not like the old days when its shapes really changed and flickered like flames under the wind. She stirred and sighed, and spoke in Kiowa:[1]

" When the buffalo moved across

[1] **Kiowa** (kī′ô·wä): the language of her Indian tribe.

it, there were other colors and other lights."

The thought was near enough to Hannah's own to startle her. " There are lots of colors there now."

Her father spoke from behind them. " Not like there used to be. In the days that even I remember, there was one color when the wind was from the north and another when it was from the south. One from the east and another from the west. Now the grass is all one color on each side and it doesn't change with the wind."

" Sometimes the colors change. Down near Lawton, they say, there's a prairie where the grass takes different colors."

" In Buffalo Park. Government made it to be like the old days."

" Is it, Father? "

" Pretty much. Grandmother would know better than I do. The buffalo were already gone when I was a young man."

" Is it, Grandmother? Is that Buffalo Park like the old days? "

Grandmother shook her head. " How do I know? I've never seen it. A buffalo park . . . Are there buffalo there? "

"Buffalo Grass" by Alice Marriott from *Southwest Review*, Autumn 1942, Volume XXVIII — 1. Reprinted by permission of *Southwest Review* and the author.

Father nodded. " Lots of buffalo. They were there last autumn when I went with the army officers, looking for old battlefields. We saw the buffalo then. They came close."

Grandmother was sitting straight now, like a young woman. " Lots of buffalo and they came close? I wish I could see them. I want to see them."

Hannah stared. Grandmother often said " I wish," but never " I want."

" Do you want to see them, Grandmother? "

" I need to see them. When the buffalo were first gone, there was a man. He made a ceremony to bring them back. I was one of those he called to help him. He was going to bring the buffalo out of the earth. Then his power failed. No buffalo. I was the one that kept them from coming back. I was too scared. I thought them back into the ground. Maybe some are out now. I want to see them. I want to tell them how sorry I am, to keep them shut up down there. I'm a pretty old woman, and soon it will be too late. I want to see the buffalo."

Father nodded. " I guess you'd better. Daughter, can you take your grandmother? "

Hannah said in English, " Casings [1] pretty bad."

" You make it. Just one day trip. Leave here early in the morning, be back that night. You don't got to hurry."

Hannah thought a while. " All right. I never saw a whole lot of buffalo myself. Just two, one time, in a circus." She changed back to Kiowa.

" When do you want to go, Grandmother? "

Grandmother thought, too. " You can't hurry these things. Buffalo don't hurry. Got to plan buffalo hunt a while ahead. I guess we go four sleeps from now."

" All right." Her son rose slowly. " I fix the car; Hannah make a lunch. Then you can go."

It didn't sound like a lot, just to fix the car and a lunch, but Grandmother kept them at it the whole four days. Everything had to be just right. " You owe respect to buffalo. They keep us alive," she said when Hannah suggested the upholstery of the car didn't really need scrubbing. Even Father went so far as to suggest tying a rawhide saddle on the engine hood, so Grandma could ride the car like a horse.

" In the old days, you wouldn't make fun of the buffalo — wouldn't make fun of your mother. You'd know you needed them both."

But by the next morning she had got over her hurt feelings. Even after four days of getting ready, she still had things to see to at the last minute. She brought out her best Pendleton blanket from the trunk and spread it over the seat. She put on her best clothes, and she painted her face. [2] Hannah — already thinking of fifty miles of dusty road each way, of the crowds of white people that hang around government parks, of all the things that could happen to a car with bad casings with two women in it — wished the paint had been left off.

---

[1] **casings:** automobile tires.

[2] **painted her face:** in the old Indian style.

384

But Grandmother would have to show respect for the buffalo.

The sun was low in the morning, and the shadows of the little hills were on the grass, changing its color for Hannah's eyes. Grandmother looked at it and said, " All brown," and got into the car. She arranged her dress carefully, and set her moccasins firm on the floor of the car, as if they were in stirrups. Then she said, " All ready." Hannah let out the clutch and they started.

They took the back road, down through Cut Throat Gap and around Saddle Mountain. It was longer than the highway, but it was pretty. Grandmother pointed out places as they went along.

" That big bend there, by the river. Buffalo River. That's where they held the Sun Dance the year I was born. The Year That the Horses Ate the Ashes.[1] That little butte over there. That's where the two boys froze to death, the time they ran away from the first government school. See where that hole is, where the ground kind of dips down? That's where the old trading post stood. It burned down The Year the Kiowa Ran Away to Texas."

On and on. Every little dip, every bend and curve, the spring where

[1] Indians identified years by important events, not by numbers, as we do.

they stopped to drink and to fill the radiator, even the beds of water cress below it, all had their histories and their names. It was all alive, this country; people walked across it that Hannah could not see, but Grandmother could. She did not call their names, for they were dead, but she told to whom they were related, and how that made them kin to her and to Hannah. Some places were happy; there had been Sun Dances and ceremonies. Other places were unhappy; people had died there and had been mourned. Hannah could feel the mourning even now. On, with the sun rising higher, and the shadows drawing up under the things that cast them, on and on they drove.

Two lines of high, tight fence ran across the prairie from a gate, and Grandmother sat stiff, suddenly. " What is that? It looks like grass in the old days. Real grass. All different colors."

It was, too. It was like changeable silk, the kind the Caddos [2] used to trim their blankets. Yellow as the wind struck it, rose color as it died away, then a sort of in-between color, with patterns that moved like the patterns in silk when you folded it.

[2] Caddos: another tribe of Plains Indians.

"That's the Buffalo Park. Buffalo ought to be here. I don't see them."

Grandmother glanced quickly overhead. "Not now. It's nearly noon. Sun's too high. Now's the time when the buffalo lie down by the creeks and rest. They're wise. They don't run around in the sun like we do."

Hannah nodded, "I guess you're right. We'll find some shade, too. Lie down ourselves."

All these last four days she had been in a hurry. Her plans had been pushing her. It had been the most important thing in the world to get here quickly, to find the buffalo and look at them, and to be gone. That the buffalo might not be there to be seen had not come into her thoughts. Now the hurry had rushed itself away; she was no more pushed for time than her grandmother or the buffalo themselves. She could find shade and lie down and sleep. It would take all night to get home. That was all right. They could sleep again when they were there.

Shade was not even in sight, and when they had driven through the gates, with the lines of fence on either hand, it was still not easy to find. Grandmother didn't care. She sat and watched the grass turn over in the sun, flickering and bending and straightening like little campfire flames, and was happy. It was the old kind of grass; the old, rippling, running prairies, even if there were fences. She was glad her eyes were going, because she didn't always see the fences and could forget about them. It was all peaceful and alive again.

There was a creek, with a pebble bank, shelving down to clear shallow water. Grandmother took her Pendleton from the seat of the car and spread it on the ground for them to lie on. Hannah brought the lunch from the car, to find that her grandmother had gathered up little sticks and twigs and boughs and built a fire. " Long ago I camped here. I had forgotten. Your grandfather and I were hunting for some horses that had run off. We stopped and ate here, and built a little clear fire like this."

They didn't really need the fire, for coffee would stay warm a long time in the thermos bottle, but it was nice to heat it in tin cups. They let the coffee get stone cold to cool the handles, and sipped it; they slipped into sleep as if eating and drinking and sleeping and being were all one thing.

Shadows were running away from the things that cast them, and there was blue light in the wonderful rose color of the prairies when Hannah wakened. Grandmother was sitting still beside her, just watching the wind walk across the grass. Hannah stretched, and Grandmother nodded at her. " You had a sleep. That's good. Now, we'll go and see the buffalo."

It had taken so long to put things in the car this morning, and it seemed to take only a minute now. The fire was out, everything packed away, and the blanket spread on the car seat almost without their moving. They started back along the fence.

There was a little draw ahead of them across the blueing prairie, and there was something dark moving

along it. Grandmother saw it before Hannah did. " There they are. You'd better stop. I'll call them this way."

She stood up in the car and lifted her voice out of her throat. Not loud, but clear and high and true. It ran across the grass to stop the herd and turn them, and Hannah understood why women went on the hunts in the old days. It was to draw with their voices the herds to them. No man had a voice that could do that.

The buffalo had changed their course and were moving jerkily along up the draw. They were coming nearer, and Grandmother called to them again. They actually began to hurry then.

Grandmother stood in the car beside her granddaughter. Tears were running down her face and her mouth tasted salt, but she was singing; she had never made a song before, but now she found words in her heart and sang them aloud.

Once we were all free on the prairies together.
Blue and rose and yellow prairies like this one.
We ran and chased and hunted.
You were good to us;
You gave us food and clothes and houses.
Now we are all old, we are tied,
But our minds are not tied.
We can remember the old days.
We can say to each other, Those times were good.

Something had happened to the buffalo. They were near to the fence, now, but they had stopped. The clear, high call they had obeyed; the song puzzled them. The herd broke apart, shuffling and snorting against the wire, and Grandmother, dropped from her song, stared at them.

Then she saw. They were yearlings; little more than calves. And she had been singing to them about the old days. The tears were still on her cheeks, but she began to laugh. She laughed and laughed, and Hannah stared at her in wonder and fright.

"Of course you don't understand my singing," Grandmother said. "Of course you don't know what it's about when I sing about the old days. You don't remember. You're just calves. You were born inside the fence, like my own grandchildren."

Then she sat down in the car, and waited to be driven home.

The Old and the New

1. Grandmother belongs to a different world from that of her family. How would you describe the granddaughter's attitude toward the old woman? In what way might her attitude change after this trip?

2. Why was it important for the Grandmother to see the buffalo? Find the line in her song that explains what she meant by saying the buffaloes "keep us alive."

3. What do you think was the granddaughter's view of the buffalo *before* and *after* she took the trip?

4. What memories did the ride through the countryside bring back to the Grandmother? Why is the mention of "grass" so important in the story? How would the grass show that the land and people had changed?

5. What meaning do you get from the old woman's last remark, "You were born inside the fence, like my own grandchildren"?

The Kiskis

MAY VONTVER

THE BIG QUESTION. It would be a dull world if people were the same from day to day or from year to year. Fortunately, people *do* change constantly. At times each of us changes his attitudes, his ideas, and his manner. In this story you will meet three young members of the Kiski [1] family who undergo a drastic change in the course of the school year. It is easy enough to see that they are different, but the thing for you to dis-

[1] Kiski (kĭs′kĭ).

"The Kiskis" by May Vontver. Reprinted by permission of the author and H. G. Merriam.

cover is *why* the change comes about.

That word "why" is a good tool for any reader to carry with him as he settles down with a story about people. If you ask yourself *why* things happen in a story, and *why* the characters act as they do, you will come up with answers that tell you the story's theme or main idea. In the following story keep in mind two questions: Why are the Kiskis shy and unsociable with their classmates, and Why do they finally change their ways? Your answers will give you the idea behind the story and may leave you with a new understanding of people.

H ADN'T you better eat in the house today? It is cold outside," the teacher suggested.

Pretending not to hear her, the three Kiskis slipped silently through the door with their double-handled Bull Durham tin can. They stood in a knot on the south side of the schoolhouse and ate from the one tin. From her desk Miss Smith observed that they now and then put one bare foot over the other to warm it. This was the second time they had disregarded her invitation to eat in the house with the others. The rest of the children had drawn their seats into a circle about the stove and began to eat.

Teddy Kirk at last decided to enlighten the teacher. " They have only bread in their lunch pail. That's why they won't eat with us."

Miss Smith made no reply. She suspected that the lunches of the group around the stove weren't very sumptuous either. She knew hers wasn't. The people with whom she boarded

were homesteaders,[1] too.

" What about these Kiskis? Who are they? " she asked Mr. Clark that evening at supper.

" The Kiskis? Oh, they took up their claim here last fall. They are pretty hard up. They have only one horse. Kiski hauled out all the lumber for his shack and barn with it. Thirty miles it is to Hilger. I was hauling wheat then, and I used to pass him on the road walking beside the load and pushing when it was uphill."

Miss Smith smiled crookedly. One horse in a country where four- or six-horse teams were the rule was somewhat ludicrous. It was pathetic, too.

" Now, now! you needn't look that way! Kiski broke ten acres with that horse of his last spring. Got the ground in shape and got it seeded, too. The horse pulled, and the old man pushed, and, by golly, they got it in." There was respect, even admiration, in his voice.

" They have eight children, though," Mrs. Clark broke in. " The two oldest girls are doing housework in Lewistown."

Eight children. That meant three at home younger than the ones at school.

" Have they any cows? "

" One, but she's dry now. It's pretty hard for them."

Miss Smith decided not to urge the Kiskis again to eat in the schoolhouse.

The Kiskis in school were painfully shy. Rudolph, the oldest, going on eleven, hid his timidity under a sullen

[1] **Homesteaders** were people, usually poor people, who took up government land to make a home. The land they settled on was their *claim* until they lived on it long enough to own it.

demeanor. Once in a while, however he could be beguiled to join in a game of " Pum-Pum-Pull-Away " or horse-shoe-pitching. He was a good pitcher. Margaret, next in age, expressed her shyness in wistfulness. Johnny, barely six, refused to speak. Never would he answer a question in class. Never a word did he utter to the children on the playground. He might, now and then, have made remarks to his sister and brother in Bohemian,[1] but, if so, he wasn't ever caught making them. Yet, he was by nature a happy child. When anything comical happened in school or something funny was said he would laugh out loud with an especially merry, infectious laugh. It was plain that he observed and understood more than his usual behavior indicated. The teacher, mindful of her psychology texts, tried vainly again and again to utilize these occasions of self-forgetfulness by surprising him into speech.

At the beginning of the term in September every child had come to school barefoot. As the season advanced the other pupils, family by family, donned their footwear, but the Kiskis continued to arrive barefoot, although it was now late in October and getting cold.

" Why don't you wear your shoes? " " Aren't your feet cold? " " Haven't you got any shoes? "

With their bare goose-fleshed feet Rudolph, Margaret, and Johnny picked their way between the prickly-pear cactus without answering. But it was plainly to be seen that more and more the continued questioning and the curious staring at their bare legs and feet embarrassed them.

Gradually the weather grew colder. the cracked gumbo [2] froze to cement. Still the Kiskis came barefoot to school.

Then the first snow fell. It was but a thin film. Disks of cactus and tufts of bunch grass stuck through. Yet it was heavy enough to show plainly the tracks of the Kiski children's naked feet.

One day when John and Margaret had planned to reach school just as the bell rang, to escape the inevitable and dreaded comments of the others, they miscalculated the time. All the children were on the porch watching as the Kiskis walked, heads down, toward the schoolhouse.

" I don't see how you can stand it! "

It was the irrepressible Teddy Kirk speaking. The others left their remarks unspoken, for this time Margaret answered, and there was defiance in her indistinct mumble.

"We like to go to school barefooted. We get there quicker that way."

She did not tell them that they had not come barefoot all the way; that at the hill nearest the schoolhouse they had stopped and undone the gunny sacks wrapped about their feet and legs and hidden them under a rock. When they went home, they would put them on again, for no one else went their way.

But little Johnny wasn't so good at

---

[1] **Bohemian** (bṓ·hḗ′·mĭ·ȧn): the Czech language, spoken by people from Czechoslovakia.

[2] **gumbo:** soil that makes sticky mud.

keeping his mouth shut at home as he was at school. He didn't know better than to tell that none of them had worn the gunny sacks *all* the day. Fortunately or unfortunately for the children, a little Old World discipline [1] was exercised upon them. The next day they wore the gunny sacks *all* the way to school. They wore them all day, too.

Their schoolmates and their teacher after a while grew used to seeing the coarse string-bound sacks, but the Kiskis never became used to wearing them. No longer did Rudolph take part in the games. Margaret grew sullen and unapproachable like him. On pleasant days when the girls strolled by twos and threes with their arms about each other Margaret stood alone in a corner against the wall. Sometimes they invited her to come with them; but she never answered. All recess she would stand there just looking at the ground. At last the girls quit asking her. Margaret made believe that she did not notice either them or their neglect. No longer did Johnny's laughter ring out in unexpected places. All three were creeping farther and farther into their shells of silence. Finally Rudolph ran away. After two days his father located him in a barn, where he had been hiding in the hayloft. Unless he had milked the cows in that barn he had had nothing to eat during his absence. He was brought home and made to go back to school.

---

[1] **Old World discipline:** the elder Kiskis came from Europe, the "Old World," where parents are stricter with children than in America.

In November the threshers came to Kiski's place. Because the field there was so small, they made that threshing their last job before pulling out of the country. Mr. Kiski hauled the wheat to Hilger and bought shoes and stockings for the children who attended school.

Other school children, the smaller ones especially, always proudly displayed their new shoes at school the first day they wore them. Several times that fall the teacher had been asked to admire the pretty perforations on the toes, the shiny buttons, or the colored tassels on the strings. But the Kiskis were almost as painfully conscious of their new footwear as they had been of the gunny sacks. They arrived with faces darkly flushed, sat down immediately, and pushed their feet far back under their seats. The teacher had hoped that to be shod like others would gradually restore their former morale. She was mistaken.

Kiski's cow had come fresh. The children had butter on their bread now. Miss Smith heard about it. She had occasion to pass by the children as they stood eating, and she saw that it was really true about the butter. Yet the Kiskis would not eat with the others. They continued to go out at noontime. If the weather was severely cold or stormy they ate in the hall, quickly. Then they would come in, without looking at anyone, and go to their seats.

As the four-month term drew to a close, Miss Smith's heart ached for the Kiskis. They had not learned a great deal from their books; she had been unable to supply them with the many bare necessities they lacked; and their own keen realization of being different had made their attendance a torture. They were so unapproachable, too, that she had found little opportunity to show them her love and sympathy. She had had but one chance that she knew of to do so, and she was grateful for that one occasion, though it had not affected the Kiskis' silence nor changed in the least their subsequent conduct.

It came about in this way. Miss Smith had been late to school. There had been a heavy snowfall in the night, and she had not had previous experience in breaking trail. If she had not been new in the country she would have known that wading three miles through knee-deep snow takes considerable time. When at length she reached the schoolhouse the Kiskis were there standing about the cold stove. All were crying — even Rudolph! They had been too miserably cold and numb to attempt building a fire for themselves. As soon as Miss Smith had the fire crackling merrily she took Johnny in her lap, undid the new shoes and stockings, and began to chafe the cold little feet. And when his crying still persisted she began telling " The Tar Baby." She had noticed early in the term that he particularly relished this tale. And sure enough, at the very first " Bim " of Brother Rabbit's paw on the tar baby's cheek Johnny laughed through his tears right out loud — something he had not done for a month. Miss Smith decided to tell stories all day.

She felt justified in entertaining the Kiskis this way, for they were the only pupils who braved the roads that morning. She had a great fund of fairy tales and folk tales and a gift for telling them; also she had that day an audience whom professional entertainers might well have envied her. Johnny leaned against her knee. She put one arm about Margaret, who stood on one side, and would have put the other about Rudolph on the opposite side had she dared. He was a boy and eleven. With shining eyes and open mouths they drank in " Cinderella," " Hansel and Gretel," " Snow White," " The Hag and the Bag," " Jack and the Beanstalk," " Colter's Race for His Life," and " Mowgli."

Only to replenish the fire and melt snow for drinking water did Miss Smith stop. Her audience was too timid and self-effacing to make any spoken requests, but after each happy ending their eyes clamored, " More, more! "

At noon the water on the top of the stove was boiling. Miss Smith put condensed milk and a little sugar in it and brought the hot drink to the Kiskis in the hall. For out there they had gone as soon as she announced that it was dinnertime. They accepted with smiles and drank every drop, but without a word. Miss Smith, too, stayed in the hall to drink her tea with them. Then the storytelling went on again, until three o'clock in the afternoon, when the teacher bundled them up in some of her own wraps and sent them home.

Going back to her boarding-place, stepping carefully in the tracks she had made in the morning, Miss Smith reflected that should the county superintendent ever learn of her program for the day she would be in for a reprimand. In such a case, she thought, she would defend herself on the grounds that since formalized education had failed noticeably to benefit the Kiskis, it was not altogether unreasonable to try a little informality. Anyhow, she was fiercely glad that the Kiskis' school term would include one happy day.

It was with sorrow and regret that Miss Smith made her way to the schoolhouse on the last day of the session. With the other pupils she had accomplished something in the way of progress, but the Kiskis she would leave embittered, shyer, and more isolated than she had found them.

She had just reached the shack and barely had time to pile the kindling into the stove when she was aware of subdued noises in the hall. She thought absently that it was unusually early for the children to be arriving. When the door opened a crack to allow someone to peer in, she began to wonder what was going on. Then with a rush the three Kiskis were at the stove.

With her unmittened purple hands Margaret was thrusting something toward her. It was a small, square candy box of pristine [1] whiteness. A wide pink silk ribbon ran obliquely across

---

[1] **pristine** (prĭs′tēn): here means "unmarked," "unsoiled."

---

the top and was looped into a generous bow in the center.

"We brought you a present, Teacher," Margaret began breathlessly.

This time, however, Rudolph did not want his sister to be the chief spokesman. "There are fourteen pieces, Teacher. Two have something shiny around them. We looked."

And before Miss Smith had time to recover from this surprise a miracle came to pass. Johnny spoke, and he spoke in English!

"It is to eat, Teacher. It is candy."

Miss Smith said, "Thank you, children. It was very good of you to give me this."

She shook the stove grate vigorously. The ashes flew into her eyes. She had to wipe them.

"Open it, Teacher. Open it now."

The teacher took the box to her desk. The Kiskis followed and stood about her watching. There really were fourteen pieces. Johnny pointed out the two with tin foil. Each of the fourteen reposed daintily in a little cup of pleated paper. It was a wonderful box and Miss Smith was lavish with praises of it.

She held the opened box out to them. "Take one," she invited; and as they made no motion, "Please, do."

The three black heads shook vigorously. Johnny's hands flew behind him.

"They are for you, Teacher," they protested. "You eat."

But Miss Smith couldn't eat just then. More than anything else she wanted to see the Kiskis enjoy the contents of that box themselves. She felt small and unworthy to accept their astounding offering. But again, how could she refuse to accept it and kill cruelly their joy in giving? It was a gift not to be lightly disposed of. An inspiration came.

"Would you care if I shared it? There is enough so that every child in school can have a piece. Johnny could pass it around when they all get here. Would you like that?"

"Yes, yes, yes." Their black eyes shone.

Johnny carried the box to his seat and sat down with it. Rudolph and Margaret hovered about the teacher, happy, eager, excited. Rudolph explained how it all came about.

"Anna came home from Lewistown last night. Margaret and I wrote her a letter once and told her to buy us a present for you. We were afraid she'd forget, but she didn't."

Teddy Kirk was coming. Rudolph and Margaret saw him and ran out on the porch.

"We brought candy for Teacher. You are going to get some, too. Johnny has it. Come and see!"

Teddy was too taken aback to say anything. They led him in easily. The pieces were counted again.

Other children came. Rudolph and Margaret met each new arrival before he got to the door. To each in turn Johnny exhibited the box and its contents. He did not mind being the center of attraction now. He made use of his new-found speech, too.

"I am going to pass it around," he told them. "When the bell rings I am going to pass it."

Rudolph and Margaret talked. They chattered. The other children kept still. They had to get used to these new Kiskis.

When the bell rang, a few minutes before time, everybody was in his seat. Johnny got up and passed the candy. Teacher saw to it that he got one of the shiny pieces.

Candy — candy of any kind — was a rare treat to everybody. These chocolates were very fresh. They had soft creamy centers. Some had cherries in them. The children had not known that sweets like these existed.

They took their time about the licking and nibbling. Delights such as these had to be given their just dues. There was no needless or premature swallowing. And to think that the Kiskis had provided it! The Kiskis were assuming importance.

The Kiskis ate candy, too. They beamed on everybody. They had had something to give and everybody thought their gift wonderful.

The sun shone. At recess the girls again walked about by twos and threes. Margaret walked with them. Teddy presented Rudolph with one of his horseshoes, and Rudolph began to pitch it. Edward, the other first-grader, found a string in his overall pocket and promptly invited Johnny to be his horse. Johnny accepted.

He trotted; he paced; he neighed surprisingly like a horse. Then he kicked at the traces awhile.

"You should say, 'Cut it out,'" he instructed his driver.

That noon the Kiskis ate lunch in the schoolhouse.

Seeing the Idea Behind the Story

1. Let's take the first of the two big questions raised by this story: *Why were the Kiskis shy and unsociable?* Discuss the following points and see what answers your class arrives at:

a. Why did the Kiskis eat lunch in the hall? Why wouldn't they play with the other children?

b. After the Kiskis got butter on their bread and shoes on their feet, why did they still feel ill at ease with the other children?

2. Now for the second big question: *Why did the Kiskis change?* Here are some guides to that answer:

a. Why did the Kiskis want to give the teacher a present? How did they get it for her?

b. In what ways did their behavior change on the day they brought the present to her?

c. Why did bringing the gift for the teacher cure the Kiskis' shyness? Let several class members state their ideas of the explanation and then discuss some of the best ones.

3. Do you think the Kiski parents did the best they could for the children? Tell how you arrive at your opinion.

4. Try to explain the difference between the pleasure of receiving a gift and the pleasure of giving one. What feelings do you have on each occasion?

"Yes, Your Honesty!"

GEORGE AND HELEN PAPASHVILY *

A young immigrant not too sure of the English language can easily provoke laughter in his first tangle with the law. But his faith in American justice soon changes our laughter to admiration. In the following pages he tells his own story, and since he leaves out nearly all the little words, you may find his way of talking strange at first. But not for long!

Six months in America and already I was a jailbird. Happened this way.

* Papashvily (på·påsh′vĭ·lĭ).

The weeks seemed extra long that first half year I was in New York. No holidays, no feast days, no celebrations to break up the time, and then when Saturday came around I had only twelve dollars, at most fourteen dollars in my pay envelope.

The man I met in Central Park on my first day in America gave me a job in his garage like he promised. But after I was there about two months his wife's mother got sick and they closed up and moved to the country.

"Yes, Your Honesty!" from *Anything Can Happen*, by George and Helen Papashvily. Reprinted by permission of Harper and Brothers.

With my poor language, wasn't easy to find another place.

I tried silk mill and, after that, factory where they made statues — ugly ones — from plaster. I stayed there until head artist gave camel to cast, only looked like a cow, this camel. I was ashamed to make such a monstrosity animal so I changed shape little bit here and there to give some camel personality to it.

But when artist saw he got mad and told me how many schools he was in — London, Paris, Dresden — (just my point, no camels living in any of those places, certainly) and I'm fired again.

Then I went for house painter but somehow the boss and me didn't suit each other. Finally I met a Georgian,[1] there were only two, three of us in New York this time, who worked in a cleaning factory, and he took me for his assistant. It was awful place. I dipped the clothes to take away spots. The gas we used came up in my head and through my throat and out my ears. My every piece of meat whole week long was spiced with that gas.

But no matter how the week went the Sundays were good, because then we made all day the holiday and took ourselves in Van Cortlandt Park where there was country and trees and flowers. We could make fires and roast cubed lamb *shashliks*[2] and walk on the grass and forget the factory. For one day anyway we could enjoy to live like human beings.

From six o'clock on, every Sunday morning, subway was packed full. Russians, Syrians, Greeks, Armenians, all kinds of peoples, carrying their grampas and babys and gallon jugs and folding chairs and charcoal sacks and hammocks and samovars[3] and lunch baskets and rugs. Everyone hurrying to their regular place in the park so they could start tea and lay out the lunch to make the day last a long, long time.

Well, this particular Sunday when all my trouble began was in the late spring. Bright blue day with a high sky and white lamb clouds. The kind of day that's for adventures.

I had my first American-bought suit on and a purple striped tie with a handkerchief to match and a real Yankee Doodle hat from straw. I felt happy and full of prance.

Five or six other fellows and me were visiting around the park. We went from family to family we knew and drank a glass of wine here, tried two pieces of cake there, met an uncle just in from Buffalo, saw a new baby first time out, and so on.

While we were making shortcut down a quiet path to get on other side of the park we came to a beautiful tree foaming over with white blossoms, how they call in English, dogswood.

"Flowers. Flowers," one Russian fellow, name of Cyrille,[4] said. "I gonna pick. Take bouquet to my lady

---

[1] Georgian: a fellow countryman of the writer, from the republic of Georgia in the Union of Soviet Socialist Republics.

[2] *shashliks:* cubes of lamb placed on a sharp stick with slices of tomato and red pepper, and roasted over a fire.

[3] samovars (săm′ŏ·värz): Russian urns for tea-making.

[4] Cyrille (sĭr′ĭl).

friend." I don't know who he was, this fellow; he joined us some place we stopped.

"Pick! Pick!" Everybody got the idea. "Pick flowers, take a bouquet to all the lady friends."

"Why spoil a tree?" I said. "Use your brains better. If you want to make friends with a nice young lady, ask her to take a walk. Tell her you gonna show her a bouquet bigger than a house, a bouquet growing right out of the ground. Something interesting. That way you get a chance to be acquainted while you're walking. Maybe you know so good on the way back you can invite for ice cream."

No, no, won't listen. They have to break the tree down. Tear his arms and legs off like wolves. Jumping. Jumping. Who's gonna get the biggest branch? Makes me sick.

"Personally," I said, "I would be ashamed to give a lady flowers that I got for nothing. That I stole. I prefer better to buy. Shows more respect. Or else don't give."

All of a sudden that fellow, Cyrille, who had now the biggest bunch climbed down from the top branches and said to me, "I have to tie my shoelace. Hold my bouquet for a minute, I'll be back." So I held. In that minute a policeman was there.

"Awright. Awright," he said. "Defacing public property. Awright." He asked us our names and started writing them down on a piece of paper.

"What he does?" I asked Sergei.[1]

"Gives us a summons."

"Summons?"

"We have to go in court."

"We're arrested?"

"Something like that. If we pay the fine, everything be O.K. But if we ignore, throw away the summons, they chase us; lock us up."

"What's your name, buddy?" policeman asked me.

I explain the best I can I'm not picking, I'm only holding for the other fellow.

But he doesn't believe me. "Don't argue," he said. "Don't argue or I'll run you in right now."

I explained again. "Boys will tell you," I said. "I wasn't picking."

No, he doesn't believe them neither. "Don't alibi him," he said.

I'd be sorry to be a man like that policeman, suspicious that everybody is a liar. What's the use for a person to live if he can't trust nobody?

So he wrote a ticket for me, too, and went away. And still tying his shoe, that fellow Cyrille wasn't back yet.

"This is an awful, awful thing," I said.

"It's nothing." Sergei could laugh.

"Nothing! I lived my whole life at home and I was never in trouble. Now I'm six months in America and I'm a crook. Nothing, you think? How my father likes to hear such kind of news? Arrested. What will our village say? The first man from Kobiankari [2] ever comes in the U.S.A. — for what? To go in prison!"

---

[1] Sergei (sĕr·gyā′ĭ).

[2] Kobiankari (kŏb·yän·kä′rĭ).

" Look," Sergei said, " You don't even have to go in court. Send the money. Plead guilty."

" But I'm not."

" You only say you are. Saves time."

" Then the policeman's right never to believe anybody. Say first, I didn't. Then, next time, change around, say I did."

" If you won't plead guilty, you'll have to go in court and have a trial."

" Then I'll go."

" Lose a day's pay."

" I lose."

" How about we find the policeman," Arkady [1] suggested, " and try once more? "

" No use," Sergei said. " For myself I'm gonna plead guilty, but the best thing we can do for Giorgi Ivanitch,[2] let's we go back in New York and see a fixer."

" What means vixer? " I said. " Vixer? Kind of a fox, isn't it? "

" *Ef.* Fixer. It's a man. People pays him for fixing things. He knows how to manage all kinds of permits; he fills out income-tax blanks; tears up traffic tickets. Suppose you're refused a license for something, you give the Fixer the money, he finds some way around to get it anyway for you."

" Still sounds like a fox."

" That's vixen," Sergei said. " Keep straight the words in your head. You get everybody mixed up. Fixers has big connections. Influences."

So we went and Fixer had big rooms to show up he's a Somebody,

¹ Arkady (är′kă·dĭ).
² Giorgi Ivanitch (zhôr′zhĭ ē·vä′nĭch).

but the floor was imitation marbles, the stand lamps some kind of cast-metal golded over to look real, and on a veneer table sits a big plated vase full with paper roses. Is plank mahogany, the panels in the wall? I felt them. Nope. Plyboard.

" If he matches his office," I told the boys, " he's not even gonna be a real man. Gonna be a dummy stuffed with straw and a victrola in his mouth."

" Shut up or you'll be twice in jail."

" So what can I do for you, my boys? " Fixer came in. " In trouble? "

I showed the summons.

" Trouble with the police? " The Fixer shook his head very sad. " Trouble with the police is serious business. No doubt you're a foreigner? "

" In the U.S.A. I am, yes," I said.

" Well, give me a retaining fee. Ten dollars is customary, but I'll make you for five and we see what we can do."

I paid him the money over.

" Now let's hear."

My committee explained the whole story.

Fixer thought. Looked through his papers. Made a few notes on a pad. Thought again. "I tell you," he said finally, "only one solution. You go in court tomorrow, plead guilty, is about a two-dollar fine and it's all over. I use my connections on the side to fix everything for you."

"Look," I told him, "I didn't pick flowers. So I'm not gonna say I did. Hang me in chains but nobody can make me say I did do what I didn't do."

So that ends that. No more help from the Fixer. He's mad.

Sergei suggested how about we go to see old Mr. Cohen, he was years and years in the U.S.A. Maybe he can think of something.

"Listen," Mr. Cohen said, when we told him everything. "Fixer Mixer leave alone all. Take my advices. I been a citizen for forty-seven years with full papers. When they ask you the first question say, 'Not guilty, Your Honor.'"

"Not guilty, Your Honor. What means 'Your Honor'?"

"Means the judge. All judges in the U.S.A. named Your Honor."

"Not guilty, Your Honor. Then?"

"Just tell your story nice way."

"With my broken words?"

"Say the best way you can. Probably judge gonna listen and try to understand you. Of course it can happen you get a mean judge, one that's too tired to pay attention, that don't like foreigners to bother him. But very few those kind. If you get such a one,

pay your fine, don't argue. But don't be disgusted with the U.S.A. Just come and tell me."

"What you gonna do?"

"Why, next time, I vote against him, naturally. We don't keep him in office no more, if he don't act nice."

So next morning I went in court. Called the other names, Igor,[1] Arkady, Sergei, Philip. Guilty. Guilty. Guilty. All sent money to pay their fines.

Now my name. I couldn't understand a word they asked me. I was nervous. My English was running out of my head like sand through a sieve. How they told me to call a judge? Your Honorable? No. Your Highness? No, that's Russian. Your? — They were asking me something. I had to answer. I took my courage in my two little hands and spoke out. "Not guilty, Your Honesty."

Courtroom went wild. Laughing and laughing. Laughing like hyenas. The judge pounded with the hammer. Bang. Bang. Bang! His face was red like a turkey's. What I done? I was sure I was going in Sing Sing and be thrown in the deepest-down dungeon.

But the judge was giving the audience bawling-out first. "Word honesty — applied by this — cause such mirth — contempt of court."

"Young man." Now he was through with them, it be my turn. "Address the Court as Sir."

"Yes, sir."

"Did I understand you to plead not guilty?"

"Yes, sir. Not guilty."

"This officer says you and your

[1] Igor (ē′gŏr).

friends were violating an ordinance, destroying a tree. Breaking the limbs."

"Yes, sir. Some was picking. I wasn't."

"Have you any proof of this?"

"No, sir. Friends were with me, but they can't come today. They all pleaded guilty, sent you a fine. Cheaper than to lose a day's pay."

"Why didn't you do that?"

"Because if I'm guilty I admit it, but if I'm not guilty, no man gonna make me say I am. Just as much a lie to say you guilty when you not as to say you innocent if you did wrong."

"Yes, that's correct. How long are you in the United States?"

"Six months."

"In court here before?"

"No, sir."

"Ever in trouble at home? Assault or kill a man?"

"Yes, sir."

"How many?"

"Hundreds. After the first year, I never counted them any more."

"Where was this?"

"In the War. I'm a sniper. It's my job to shoot all the Germans I see. Sometimes Bulgarians, too, but mostly they didn't have much interest to show themselves, poor fellows."

"I see. I mean in civil life. When you were not a soldier, not in the army. Ever hurt or strike anybody?"

"Yes, sir. Once."

"What?"

"Knocked a man's teeths out. Few."

"Why?"

"Catched him giving poisoned meat to my dog to eat."

"Understandable. Only time?"

"Yes, sir."

"Sure?"

"Yes, sir."

"Did you actually see this man," His Honesty asked the policeman, "breaking the tree?"

"No, sir. Not exactly, but all the others admitted guilt and he was with them, holding a bunch of flowers."

"I believe he's a truthful man, Officer, and this time you were probably mistaken. Case dismissed."

And then His Honesty, big American judge, leaned over. And what do you think he said to me, ignorant, no speaking language, six months off a boat, greenhorn foreigner? "Young man, I like to shake hands with you."

And in front of that whole courtroom, he did.

Honesty Won!

1. What do you find amusing in George's descriptions of his first jobs? Why did he like the Sundays in the park?

2. How did the dogwood-picking start? Why did George refuse to join the pickers? How did he get mixed up in it?

3. Why did George dislike the Fixer? Discuss the idea that "fixing" or buying special privileges is a smart thing to do. Have you a right to complain about "bad government" if you think it is all right to have a traffic ticket fixed?

4. Look again at Mr. Cohen's conversation with George (p. 398). What specific things does he say that show the American way of living?

5. Why did the judge believe George? Find remarks in the court scene you particularly like and tell why you like them.

6. Which men in the story make you ashamed of Americans? Which ones make you proud of them?

Citizens in the Round

ROBERT P. TRISTRAM COFFIN

INVITATION TO REMEMBER. One way poets get much said in little space is by using references that touch off thoughts in the reader's mind. Naturally, talk about seafaring brings in bits of geography. How well can your memory guide you on the voyages? Talk about New England contains references that call back what you learned about the first Thanksgiving. Can you do your part in filling in the poet's pictures?

New England was tall clippers
Leaning around the globe;
New England was small pumpkins
And boys called Seth and Job.

New England was white steeples,   5
The white-haired hired man,
A hundred schooners blossoming out
Of the Mediterranean.

Small farms had feet in water,
The front yard curved a bit,   10
And Table Rock, Sumatra,
Got taken into it.

New England wives made piecrust
All over the Celebes
And hung the Monday wash
     between   15
The legs of Hercules.

Farm babies teethed off Chile,
In China Sea slept sound;
They crept on decks and grew up
Citizens in the round.   20

They thought in tea and teakwood,
Volcanoes, longitudes,
But thought in one-horse haying,
Rhode Island hens and broods.

They never sailed so far   25
But church bells called them back,
Sharp crabapples to gather,
New-mown hay to stack.

And when, white-haired and quiet,
They hoed small plots of corn,   30
They lived by wind and weather
As once off bleak Cape Horn.

Teaming Up with the Poet
1. Where did the New England skippers sail their ships? Which places can you locate from memory? Look up the others to round out the voyages.

2. How does the poet remind you that New Englanders were religious people?

3. Find three passages that prove the poet was thinking of sailing ships.

4. What references give a picture of New England farm life?

"Citizens in the Round" from *Primer for America* by Robert P. Tristram Coffin. Copyright, 1943, by The Macmillan Company and used with their permission.

AMERICANS ALL

Spelling Bee

LAURENE C. CHINN

Sadness dwells in many immigrant homes because the parents cling to the familiar ways of their former land while the children want to be like other young Americans. Only love and courage can bridge the gap between the old ways and the new.

WITH the closing of the door, Ellen left one of her lives behind and entered upon the other. She moved slowly down the long flight of stairs that flanked the restaurant, and turned left toward the hotel.

"No use eating dinner there," Mama had protested. "You can eat at home and go later."

"We are supposed to have dinner at the hotel, Mama." Ellen spoke the word "Mama" in the Cantonese [1] way, as if it were two words, with a quick, light stress on the second half. "When you are American, you do as Americans do."

"No harm being Chinese," Mama said.

[1] Cantonese (kăn'tŏn·ēz'): the dialect spoken in Canton, China.

Mama wasn't going to the high school with her tonight. Mama never went with her. On the street, Ellen shut out the world of home. This is easy when you speak Cantonese in one world and American in the other. Still, when you have won the county spelling bee, you can't help wanting your mother to watch you in the regional match. . . .

A big bus carried the thirty-five county champions from the dinner at the hotel to the high school. At eight o'clock the curtains parted, revealing the audience to the boys and girls on stage. Thirty-five boys and girls on stage, thought Ellen, feeling a little bit sad, and thirty-four mothers in the audience. Henry was there, with his girl friend, Dorothy. Now that Father was gone, Henry was head of the family. It ought to be enough that her brother was in the audience.

The teacher said, "botany," and smiled at Ellen. They had finished with the sixth-grade spelling books and were starting on the seventh. Twenty-eight girls and boys were still on stage.

"Physician," said the teacher. Henry was a physician. Less than a year ago he had been an intern. He worked hard. It isn't easy to establish confidence when you wear an alien face.

"Intense," Miss Kinsman said. If Mama had learned to speak English, maybe she wouldn't be so intensely shy. Mama had wrapped herself in her black sateen Chinese coat and trousers, wrapped herself also in her cloak of language, and refused to leave her kitchen even to buy groceries or a hat. Did Mama own a hat? Yes, Henry had bought one for her to wear to Father's funeral.

"Tragedy," said Miss Kinsman. They were in eighth-grade spelling now, and nineteen contestants remained.

"Tragedy," said Ellen, smiling at Miss Kinsman. "T-r-a-g-e-d-y."

Mrs. Dillard had begun helping her after school when she became school champion, and they redoubled their labor after she won the county spelling bee. Mrs. Dillard had said, "Barring accidents, you might even win and represent our region at the national spelling bee in Washington."

Now, after an hour in the eighth-grade speller, with fewer than a dozen champions still on stage, Ellen was beginning to think Mrs. Dillard might be right. Ellen might win. Only a nitwit would want not to win. Well, then, she was a nitwit.

One of the judges rose. "Perhaps it is time to go into the old Blueback," he suggested.[1]

A sigh rippled up among the contestants. Mrs. Dillard had taken Ellen all the way through the Blueback. "Trust your hunches," Mrs. Dillard had said, and her eyes had grown dreamy. "My goodness, I'd be proud to see a pupil of mine win the national spelling bee!"

But Ellen didn't want to go to Washington!

The teacher was smiling at Ellen. "Deign."

The girl next to Ellen had just spelled "reign." Ellen recalled the section, a group of words with silent g's. Ellen spelled, "D-a-n-e." She turned blindly to leave the stage. She had betrayed her talent for spelling, and she had betrayed Mrs. Dillard, and she had betrayed Henry.

"Just a minute," said Miss Kinsman. "I wanted you to spell d-e-i-g-n, meaning *condescend*, but you have correctly spelled its homonym, and capital letters aren't necessary by the rules of the contest."

"O-o-o-h," wailed Ellen. It's a fine thing when you try to miss a word and can't. "Could I — could I have a drink, please?" she gulped.

The judge said, "We will have intermission until the bell rings."

With a whoop the champions scattered. Ellen hurried down the aisle toward Henry and Dorothy. Dorothy hugged her. "I had no idea you were so smart, little genius."

[1] The old **Blueback** spelling book, which was used in American schools for a long time, contained many long, difficult words.

Henry said, " I'd be very proud to see you win, Ellen."

" I don't want to win." Suddenly she knew why. She put the knowledge into a rush of words, speaking in Cantonese. " To go to Washington without my mother would advertise that she is old-fashioned and very shy and goes nowhere — not even here — with me."

Henry's face paled. His eyes turned from Ellen's and met Dorothy's. Ellen rushed into the hall. She wished the tears would quit coming in her eyes. She knew what she would do. She wouldn't win, but she would stay as long as she could without winning, and she would find out whether she could have won. . . .

After three rounds in the Blueback, six contestants remained. Miss Kinsman turned to the " Words Difficult to Spell " section at the back. " Abeyance," she said. Ellen was relaxed. She'd worked hard on this part.

Acerbity. Ache. Acquiesce. Amateur. Queer spellings remind you of other peoples in other times who have used these words in other ways. Language is a highway, linking all peoples and all ages. Mama was wrong to use language as a wall.

Caprice. Carouse. Catastrophe. . . .

Three contestants remained. Miss Kinsman turned to a page of words of seven and eight syllables. Henry was alone at the back now. Maybe Dorothy had got bored and gone home. Ellen thought of her mother. Thirty-four mothers had driven in from thirty-four neighboring counties, and Mama hadn't come six blocks to see the contest.

" Incomprehensibility," said Miss Kinsman. It was a lonely word. Things build up inside a person that other people don't comprehend. And people can't comprehend the shyness of a foreign-born mother unless they've had a foreign-born mother.

" Indestructibility," said Miss Kinsman. Ellen had risen, but she wasn't listening. Two people had come in at the back. One was Dorothy. The other was utterly familiar, yet, in the hat and dress, utterly strange. They went to sit beside Henry, and Mama was smi'ing at Ellen on the stage. Ellen had lived all her life with the familiar, loving smile.

" I'm sorry. I didn't hear the word." Turning to Miss Kinsman, Ellen raised her voice for the proud announcement, " My mother just came in."

" Indestructibility," said Miss Kinsman.

Ellen spelled the word clearly. Mama wouldn't understand, but this was a beginning. Mama had found the courage to come. Mama would find future courage — enough to become American. She had to win, now, and take Mama with her to the nation's capital. She and Mama would look at the buildings and the memorials. After such a trip, Mama would never hide away in her kitchen again.

If Mama could do what she had done tonight, Ellen could keep her wits about her for as long as it might take to be winner.

Mama Saved the Day

1. Why was Ellen more disappointed over her mother's absence than a girl with an English-speaking mother might have been?

2. How do you know that Henry and Ellen were willing to work hard? What was in Ellen's mind when she thought, " It isn't easy to establish confidence when you wear an alien face "?

3. Why did Ellen decide that she did not want to win? How did she try to juggle words so as to lose?

4. What do you think Dorothy said to Ellen's mother to make her go to the spelling bee?

5. Imagine that Ellen's mother makes the trip to Washington with her. What sights would make her proud to be an American? Would Ellen expect her mother to change *all* her old ways? Discuss whether you think it is necessary for all Americans to think and act alike.

A Spelling Bee for Everybody

There's a new kind of spelling bee that is a team sport for the whole class. Let two leaders choose sides for two teams and keep the teams seated in order. Two contestants representing the two teams go to the blackboard at the same time, starting with the leaders. Both write the word that the teacher gives out. When one is right and the other is wrong, the winner scores a point for his team. The whole class can check the spelling and judge the result. Then the next two replace the first pair at the board, and the game goes on. It's fast, and it's fun. And all the time you are learning to spell the natural way, in writing. It's fair, too, because a good speller can be matched against a good speller and a weak speller against another weak one. That way everybody has a good chance to make a point for his team. (Words in the glossary at the back of this book are good ones to use for this kind of spelling bee.)

The Man Without a Country

EDWARD EVERETT HALE

EYE-WITNESS REPORT. This is the story of a young hero-worshiper with a hot head and a quick tongue who made a rash wish. Many of us have done the same thing. But he made his wish while he was on trial before a military court and it smacked of treason. The court decided upon a strange sentence — to have his wish fulfilled.

Think of the ways this story could be

told. The author could pretend to be the main character, Philip Nolan, and tell of the things that only Nolan himself saw or heard or felt. Or he could write as if he knew *everything,* not only Nolan's thoughts and actions but those of all the other characters. But the author chose a third point of view. He tells the story through the eyes of a bystander, a person who knew Nolan but was with him only a short time. As you read, notice that this person often mentions letters or records concerning Nolan he has seen, as well as conversations with others who knew Nolan. In this way he is able to round out the complete life story of Philip Nolan. The author's trick of pretending he knew Nolan is so skillful that you will begin to wonder if it is a true story and if Philip Nolan was an actual person. A good story is like that. It seems as real as life itself.

I SUPPOSE that very few readers of the New York *Herald* of August 13, 1863, observed in an obscure corner, among the " Deaths," the announcement:

NOLAN. Died on board U.S. Corvette *Levant,*[1] Lat. 2° 11′ S., Long. 131° W., on the 11th of May, PHILIP NOLAN.

Hundreds of readers would have paused at that announcement, if it had read thus: " Died, May 11, THE MAN WITHOUT A COUNTRY." For it was as *The Man Without a Country* that poor Philip Nolan had generally been known by the officers who had

him in charge during some fifty years, as, indeed, by all the men who sailed under them.

There can now be no possible harm in telling this poor creature's story. Reason enough there has been till now for very strict secrecy, the secrecy of honor itself, among the gentlemen of the navy who have had Nolan in charge. And certainly it speaks well for the profession, and the personal honor of its members, that to the press this man's story has been wholly unknown — and I think, to the country at large also. This I do know, that no naval officer has mentioned Nolan in his report of a cruise.

But, there is no need for secrecy any longer. Now the poor creature is dead, it seems to me worth while to tell a little of his story, by way of showing young Americans of today what it is to be *A Man Without a Country.*

NOLAN'S FATAL WISH

Philip Nolan was as fine a young officer as there was in the " Legion of the West," as the Western division of our army was then called. When Aaron Burr[2] made his first dashing expedition down to New Orleans in 1805, he met this gay, bright young fellow. Burr marked him, talked to him, walked with him, took him a day or two's voyage in his flatboat, and, in short, fascinated him. For the next year, barrack life was very tame to

---

[1] **Corvette** *Levant* (kôr·vĕt′ lê·vănt′): a corvette in the navy of that day was a small fighting ship that occupied about the same place that the destoyer has in the modern navy.

[2] **Aaron Burr** was a prominent figure in his day, at one time vice-president of the United States. He later was suspected of plotting to set up an empire in the Southwest, and was tried for treason.

poor Nolan. He occasionally availed himself of the permission the great man had given him to write to him. Long, stilted letters the poor boy wrote and rewrote and copied. But never a line did he have in reply. The other boys in the garrison sneered at him, because he lost the fun which they found in shooting or rowing while he was working away on these grand letters to his grand friend. But before long the young fellow had his revenge. For this time His Excellency, Honorable Aaron Burr, appeared again under a very different aspect. There were rumors that he had an army behind him and an empire before him. At that time the youngsters all envied him. Burr had not been talking twenty minutes with the commander before he asked him to send for Lieutenant Nolan. Then after a little talk he asked Nolan if he could show him something of the great river and the plans for the new post. He asked Nolan to take him out in his skiff [1] to show him a canebrake [2] or a cottonwood tree, as he said — really to win him over; and by the time the sail was over, Nolan was enlisted body and soul. From that time, though he did not yet know it, he lived as a man without a country.

What Burr meant to do I know no more than you. It is none of our business just now. Only, when the grand catastrophe came, the great treason trial at Richmond,[3] Fort Adams got up a string of courts-martial [4] on the officers there. One and another of the colonels and majors were tried, and, to fill out the list, little Nolan, against whom there was evidence enough — that he was sick of the service, had been willing to be false to it, and would have obeyed any order to march anywhere had the order been signed, "By command of His Exc. A. Burr." The courts dragged on. The big flies [5] escaped — rightly for all I know. Nolan was proved guilty enough, yet you and I would never have heard of him but that, when the president of the court asked him at the close whether he wished to say anything to show that he had always been faithful to the United States, he cried out, in a fit of frenzy:

"Damn the United States! I wish I may never hear of the United States again!"

NOLAN'S PUNISHMENT

I suppose he did not know how the words shocked old Colonel Morgan, who was holding the court. Half the officers who sat in it had served through the Revolution, and their lives, not to say their necks, had been risked for the very idea which he cursed in his madness. He, on his part, had grown up in the West of those days. He had been educated on a plantation where the finest company was a Spanish officer or a French mer-

---

[1] **skiff**: a light boat.
[2] **canebrake**: a dense growth of tall canes, frequently found in wet creek bottoms in Louisiana.
[3] Burr was tried at **Richmond**, Virginia.

[4] **courts-martial** (kōrts mär'shǎl): military courts, which try men in the army or navy on any charges affecting their service or loyalty.
[5] **The big flies** were the important men who might really have plotted with Burr.

chant from Orleans. His education
had been perfected in commercial ex-
peditions to Veracruz,[1] and I think
he told me his father once hired an
Englishman to be a private tutor for
a winter on the plantation. He had
spent half his youth with an older
brother, hunting horses in Texas; and
to him *United States* was scarcely a
reality. Yet he had been fed by *United
States* for all the years since he had
been in the army. He had sworn on
his faith as a Christian to be true to
United States. It was *United States*
which gave him the uniform he wore,
and the sword by his side. I do not
excuse Nolan; I only explain to the
reader why he damned his country,
and wished he might never hear her
name again.

From that moment, September 23,
1807, till the day he died, May 11,
1863, he never heard her name again.
For that half-century and more he
was a man without a country.

Old Morgan, as I said, was terribly
shocked. If Nolan had compared
George Washington to Benedict Arnold,[2] or had cried, " God save King
George," Morgan would not have felt
worse. He called the court into his
private room, and returned in fifteen
minutes with a face like a sheet, to
say:

" Prisoner, hear the sentence of the
Court! The Court decides, subject to
the approval of the President, that
you never hear the name of the

United States again."

Nolan laughed. But nobody else
laughed. Old Morgan was too solemn,
and the whole room was hushed dead
as night for a minute. Even Nolan lost
his swagger in a moment. Then Morgan added:

" Mr. Marshal, take the prisoner to
Orleans, in an armed boat, and deliver
him to the naval commander there."

The marshal gave his orders and
the prisoner was taken out of court.

" Mr. Marshal," continued old Morgan, " see that no one mentions the
United States to the prisoner. Mr.
Marshal, make my respects to Lieutenant Mitchell at Orleans, and request him to order that no one shall
mention the United States to the prisoner while he is on board ship. You
will receive your written orders from
the officer on duty here this evening.
The Court is adjourned."

Before the *Nautilus*[3] got round
from New Orleans to the northern
Atlantic coast with the prisoner on
board, the sentence had been approved by the President, and he was
a man without a country.

The plan then adopted was substantially the same which was neces-
sarily followed ever after. The Secretary of the Navy was requested to put
Nolan on board a government vessel
bound on a long cruise, and to direct
that he should be only so far confined
there as to make it certain that he
never saw or heard of the country.
We had few long cruises then, and I
do not know certainly what his first

---

[1] **Veracruz** (vĕr′á·krōōz′) is a Gulf seaport in
Mexico.

[2] **Benedict Arnold** was a traitor to the American cause during the Revolution.

[3] *Nautilus* (nô′tĭ·lŭs): the naval ship to which
Nolan was delivered.

cruise was. But the commander to whom he was intrusted regulated the etiquette [1] and the precautions of the affair, and according to his scheme they were carried out till Nolan died.

When I was second officer of the *Intrepid,* some thirty years after, I saw the original paper of instructions. I have been sorry ever since that I did not copy the whole of it. It ran, however, much in this way:

WASHINGTON (with a date, which must have been late in 1807)

Sir, — You will receive from Lieutenant Neale the person of Philip Nolan, late a lieutenant in the United States Army.

This person on trial by court-martial expressed, with an oath, the wish that he might "never hear of the United States again."

The Court sentenced him to have his wish fulfilled.

For the present, the execution of the order is intrusted by the President to this Department.

You will take the prisoner on board your ship, and keep him there with such precautions as shall prevent his escape.

You will provide him with such quarters, rations,[2] and clothing as would be proper for an officer of his late rank, if he were a passenger on your vessel on the business of his Government.

The gentlemen on board will make any arrangements agreeable to themselves regarding his society. He is to be exposed to no indignity of any kind, nor is he ever unnecessarily to be reminded that he is a prisoner.

But under no circumstances is he ever to hear of his country or to see any information regarding it; and you will especially caution all the officers under your command to take care that this rule, in which his punishment is involved, shall not be broken.

It is the intention of the Government that he shall never again see the country which he has disowned. Before the end of your cruise you will receive orders which will give effect to this intention.

Respectfully yours,

W. SOUTHARD, for the
Secretary of the Navy.

The rule adopted on board the ships on which I have met The Man Without a Country was, I think, transmitted from the beginning. No mess [3] liked to have him permanently, because his presence cut off all talk of home or of the prospect of return, of politics or letters, of peace or of war — cut off more than half the talk men liked to have at sea. But it was always thought too hard that he should never meet the rest of us, except to touch hats, and we finally sank into one system. He was not permitted to talk with the men, unless an officer was by. With officers he had unrestrained intercourse, as far as they and he chose. But he grew shy, though he had favorites: I was one. Then the captain always asked him to dinner on Monday. Every mess in succession took up the invitation in its turn. According to the size of the ship, you had him at your mess more or less often at dinner. His breakfast he ate

---

[1] **etiquette** (ĕt′ĭ·kĕt): any formally approved way of dealing with a situation. It fits the handling of Nolan as well as social manners.

[2] **quarters** refers to living quarters, or rooms, and **rations** means food.

[3] In the navy the officers who eat in a group make up a mess.

in his own stateroom. Whatever else he ate or drank, he ate or drank alone. Sometimes, when the marines or sailors had any special jollification, they were permitted to invite " Plain-Buttons," as they called him. Then Nolan was sent with some officer, and the men were forbidden to speak of home while he was there. I believe the theory was that the sight of his punishment did them good. They called him " Plain-Buttons," because, while he always chose to wear a regulation army uniform, he was not permitted to wear the army button, for the reason that it bore either the initials or the insignia of the country he had disowned.

THE READING

I remember, soon after I joined the Navy, I was on shore with some of the older officers from our ship, and some of the gentlemen fell to talking about Nolan, and someone told the system which was adopted from the first about his books and other reading. As he was almost never permitted to go on shore, even though the vessel lay in port for months, his time at the best hung heavy. Everybody was permitted to lend him books, if they were not published in America and made no allusion to it. These were common enough in the old days. He had almost all the foreign papers that came into the ship, sooner or later; only somebody must go over them first, and cut out any advertisement or stray paragraph that referred to America. This was a little cruel sometimes, when the back of what was cut

out might be innocent. Right in the midst of one of Napoleon's battles, poor Nolan would find a great hole, because on the back of the page of that paper there had been an advertisement of a packet [1] for New York, or a scrap from the President's message. This was the first time I ever heard of this plan. I remember it, because poor Phillips, who was of the party, told a story of something which happened at the Cape of Good Hope on Nolan's first voyage. They had touched at the Cape, paid their respects to the English admiral and the fleet, and then Phillips had borrowed a lot of English books from an officer. Among them was *The Lay of the Last Minstrel*,[2] which they had all of them heard of, but which most of them had never seen. I think it could not have been published long. Well, nobody thought there could be any risk of anything national in that. So Nolan was permitted to join the circle one afternoon when a lot of them sat on deck smoking and reading aloud. In his turn Nolan took the book and read to the others; and he read very well, as I know. Nobody in the circle knew a line of the poem, only it was all magic and Border [3] chivalry, and was ten thousand years ago. Poor Nolan read steadily through the fifth canto,[4] stopped a minute

---

[1] **packet:** a ship carrying mail and goods as well as passengers.

[2] *The Lay of the Last Minstrel:* a poem by Sir Walter Scott.

[3] The **Border** between Scotland and England was the scene of many conflicts before the countries were united.

[4] **A canto** (kăn'tō) is one of the main divisions of a long poem.

and drank something, and then began, without a thought of what was coming:

Breathes there a man with soul so dead,
Who never to himself hath said —

It seems impossible to us that anybody ever heard this for the first time; but all these fellows did then, and poor Nolan himself went on, still unconsciously or mechanically:

This is my own, my native land!

Then they all saw that something was to pay; [1] but he expected to get through, I suppose, turned a little pale, but plunged on:

Whose heart hath ne'er within him
      burned,
As home his footsteps he hath turned
   From wandering on a foreign strand?
If such there breathe, go mark him
      well —

By this time the men were all beside themselves, wishing there was any way to make him turn over two pages; but he had not quite presence of mind for that; he gagged a little, colored crimson, and staggered on:

For him no minstrel raptures swell;
High though his titles, proud his name,
Boundless his wealth as wish can claim,
Despite these titles, power, and pelf,
The wretch, concentered all in self —

and here the poor fellow choked, could not go on, but started up, swung the book into the sea, vanished into his stateroom, "And by Jove," said Phillips, " we did not see him for two months again. And I had to make up some story to that English surgeon why I did not return his Walter Scott to him."

That story shows about the time when Nolan's braggadocio [2] must have broken down. At first, they said, he took a very high tone, considered his imprisonment a mere farce, af-

[1] **something was to pay:** trouble was coming.

[2] **braggadocio** (brăg′a·dō′shĭ·ō): a swaggering pose of not minding his punishment.

fected to enjoy the voyage, and all that; but Phillips said that after he came out of his stateroom he never was the same man again. He never read aloud again, unless it was the Bible or Shakespeare, or something else he was sure of. But it was not that merely. He never entered in with the other young men exactly as a companion again. He was always shy afterward, when I knew him — very seldom spoke unless he was spoken to, except to a very few friends. He lighted up occasionally, but generally he had the nervous, tired look of a heart-wounded man.

THE BALL

When Captain Shaw was coming home, rather to the surprise of everybody they made one of the Windward Islands,[1] and lay off and on for nearly a week. The boys said the officers were sick of salt-junk,[2] and meant to have turtle-soup before they came home. But after several days the *Warren* came to the same rendezvous;[3] they exchanged signals; she told them she was outward-bound, perhaps to the Mediterranean, and took poor Nolan and his traps on the boat back to try his second cruise. He looked very blank when he was told to get ready to join her. He had known enough of the signs of the sky to know that till that moment he was

going "home." But this was a distinct evidence of something he had not thought of, perhaps — that there was no going home for him, even to a prison. And this was the first of some twenty such transfers, which brought him sooner or later into half our best vessels, but which kept him all his life at least some hundred miles from the country he had hoped he might never hear of again.

It may have been on that second cruise — it was once when he was up the Mediterranean — that Mrs. Graff, the celebrated Southern beauty of those days, danced with him. They had been lying a long time in the Bay of Naples, and the officers were very intimate in the English fleet, and there had been great festivities, and our men thought they must give a great ball on board the ship. They wanted to use Nolan's stateroom for something, and they hated to do it without asking him to the ball; so the captain said they might ask him, if they would be responsible that he did not talk with the wrong people, " who would give him intelligence."[4] So the dance went on. For ladies they had the family of the American consul, one or two travelers who had adventured so far, and a nice bevy[5] of English girls and matrons.

Well, different officers relieved each other in standing and talking with Nolan in a friendly way, so as to be sure that nobody else spoke to him. The dancing went on with spirit,

[1] **Windward Islands:** a group in the West Indies.

[2] **salt-junk:** the kind of salted meat that would keep on shipboard.

[3] **rendezvous** (rän′dĕ·vōō): a place agreed upon for a meeting.

[4] **intelligence:** information, here, about his country.

[5] **bevy** (bĕv′ĭ): a group.

and after a while even the fellows who took this honorary guard of Nolan ceased to fear any trouble.

As the dancing went on, Nolan and our fellows all got at ease, as I said — so much, that it seemed quite natural for him to bow to that splendid Mrs. Graff, and say:

" I hope you have not forgotten me, Miss Rutledge. Shall I have the honor of dancing? "

He did it so quickly, that Fellows, who was with him, could not hinder him. She laughed and said:

" I am not Miss Rutledge any longer, Mr. Nolan; but I will dance all the same," just nodded to Fellows, as if to say he must leave Mr. Nolan to her, and led him off to the place where the dance was forming.

Nolan thought he had got his chance. He had known her at Philadelphia. He said boldly — a little pale, she said, as she told me the story years after —

" And what do you hear from home, Mrs. Graff? "

And that splendid creature looked *through* him. Jove! how she *must* have looked through him !

" Home! ! Mr. Nolan! ! ! I thought you were the man who never wanted to hear of home again! " — and she walked directly up the deck to her husband, and left poor Nolan alone. He did not dance again.

NOLAN'S COURAGE

A happier story than either of these I have told is of the war.[1] That came

along soon after. I have heard this affair told in three or four ways — and, indeed, it may have happened more than once. In one of the great frigate duels with the English, in which the navy was really baptized, it happened that a round-shot [2] from the enemy entered one of our ports [3] square, and took right down the officer of the gun himself, and almost every man of the gun's crew. Now you may say what you choose about courage, but that is not a nice thing to see. But, as the men who were not killed picked themselves up, and as they and the surgeon's people were carrying off the bodies, there appeared Nolan, in his shirtsleeves, with the rammer in his hand, and, just as if he had been the officer, told them off with authority — who should go to the cockpit [4] with the wounded men, who should stay with him — perfectly cheery, and with that way which makes men feel sure all is right and is going to be right. And he finished loading the gun with his own hands, aimed it, and bade the men fire. And there he stayed, captain of that gun, keeping those fellows in spirits, till the enemy struck [5] — sitting on the carriage while the gun was cooling, though he was exposed all the time — showing them easier ways to handle heavy shot — making the raw hands laugh at their

[2] **round-shot:** cannon ball.

[3] **ports:** openings in the side of the ship for the cannon.

[4] **cockpit:** a protected section inside a sailing vessel.

[5] **struck** comes from the phrase "struck their colors," that is, hauled down their flag to admit defeat.

[1] **the war:** the War of 1812, between the United States and England.

own blunders — and when the gun cooled again, getting it loaded and fired twice as often as any other gun on the ship. The captain walked forward by way of encouraging the men, and Nolan touched his hat and said:

"I am showing them how we do this in the artillery, sir."

And this is the part of the story where all the legends agree; the commodore said:

"I see you are, and I thank you, sir; and I shall never forget this day, sir, and you never shall, sir."

After the whole thing was over, and he had the Englishman's sword,[1] in the midst of the state and ceremony of the quarter-deck,[2] he said:

"Where is Mr. Nolan? Ask Mr. Nolan to come here."

And when Nolan came, he said:

"Mr. Nolan, we are all very grateful to you today; you are one of us today; you will be named in the dispatches."

And then the old man took off his own sword of ceremony, and gave it to Nolan and made him put it on. The man who told me this saw it. Nolan cried like a baby, and well he might. He had not worn a sword since that infernal day at Fort Adams. But always afterwards on occasions of ceremony, he wore that quaint old French sword.

The captain did mention him in the dispatches. It was always said he asked that he might be pardoned. He wrote a special letter to the Secretary of War. But nothing ever came of it.

All that was near fifty years ago. If Nolan was thirty then, he must have been near eighty when he died. He looked sixty when he was forty. But he never seemed to me to change a hair afterward. As I imagine his life, from what I have seen and heard of it, he must have been in every sea, and yet almost never on land. Till he grew very old, he went aloft[3] a great deal. He always kept up his exercise; and I never heard that he was ill. If any other man was ill, he was the kindest nurse in the world; and he knew more than half the surgeons do. Then if anybody was sick or died, or if the captain wanted him to, on any other occasion, he was always ready to read prayers. I have said that he read beautifully.

THE SLAVES

My own acquaintance with Philip Nolan began six or eight years after the English war, on my first voyage after I was appointed a midshipman.[4] From the time I joined, I believe I thought Nolan was a sort of lay chaplain[5] — a chaplain with a blue coat. I never asked about him. Everything in the ship was strange to me. I knew it was green to ask questions, and I suppose I thought there was a "Plain-Buttons" on every ship. We had him

---

[1] **Englishman's sword:** In those days a defeated commander gave up his sword to the victor.

[2] **quarter-deck:** the part of the upper deck behind the mainmast where all important ceremonies are held.

[3] **aloft:** up in the masts and rigging of the ship.

[4] **midshipman:** one in training to become a naval officer.

[5] **lay chaplain:** one who performs the services of a minister without being regularly ordained.

to dine in our mess once a week, and the caution was given that on that day nothing was to be said about home. But if they had told us not to say anything about the planet Mars or the Book of Deuteronomy, I should not have asked why; there were a great many things which seemed to me to have as little reason. I first came to understand anything about The Man Without a Country one day when we overhauled a dirty little schooner which had slaves on board. An officer named Vaughan was sent to take charge of her, and, after a few minutes, he sent back his boat to ask that someone might be sent who could speak Portuguese. None of the officers did; and just as the captain was sending forward to ask if any of the people could, Nolan stepped out and said he should be glad to interpret, if the captain wished, as he understood the language. The captain thanked him, fitted out another boat with him, and in this boat it was my luck to go.

When we got there, it was such a scene as you seldom see, and never want to. Nastiness beyond account, and chaos run loose in the midst of the nastiness. There were not a great many of the Negroes; but by way of making what there were understand that they were free, Vaughan had had their handcuffs and anklecuffs knocked off. The Negroes were, most of them, out of the hold, and swarming all around the dirty deck, with a central throng surrounding Vaughan and addressing him in every dialect.

As we came on deck, Vaughan looked down from a hogshead, on which he had mounted in desperation, and said:

"Is there anybody who can make these wretches understand something?"

Nolan said he could speak Portuguese, and one or two fine-looking Krumen [1] were dragged out, who had worked for the Portuguese on the coast.

"Tell them they are free," said Vaughan.

Nolan explained it in such Portuguese as the Krumen could understand, and they in turn to such of the Negroes as could understand them. Then there was such a yell of delight, clinching of fists, leaping and dancing, kissing of Nolan's feet, and a general rush made to the hogshead by way of spontaneous celebration of the occasion.

"Tell them," said Vaughan, well pleased, "that I will take them all to Cape Palmas."

This did not answer so well. Cape Palmas was practically as far from the homes of most of them as New Orleans or Rio de Janeiro was; that is, they would be eternally separated from home there. And their interpreters, as we could understand, instantly said, "*Ah, non Palmas!*" and began to protest loudly. Vaughan was rather disappointed at this result of his liberality, and asked Nolan eagerly what they said. The drops stood on poor Nolan's white forehead, as he hushed the men down, and said:

[1] **Krumen** (krōō′měn): members of a tribe living in northern Africa.

"He says, 'Not Palmas.' He says, 'Take us home, take us to our own country, take us to our own house, take us to our own children and our own women.' He says he has an old father and mother who will die if they do not see him. And this one says he left his people all sick, and paddled down to Fernando to beg the white doctor to come and help them, and that these devils [1] caught him in the bay just in sight of home, and that he has never seen anybody from home since then. And this one says," choked out Nolan, "that he has not heard a word from his home in six months."

Vaughan always said Nolan grew gray himself while he struggled through this interpretation. I, who did not understand anything of the passion involved in it, saw that the very elements were melting with fervent heat, and that something was to pay somewhere. Even the Negroes themselves stopped howling, as they saw Nolan's agony, and Vaughan's almost equal agony of sympathy. As quick as he could get words, he said:

"Tell them yes, yes, yes; tell them they shall go to the Mountains of the Moon, if they will. If I sail the schooner through the Great White Desert, they shall go home!"

And after some fashion Nolan said so. And then they all fell to kissing him again, and wanted to rub his nose [2] with theirs.

But he could not stand it long; and getting Vaughan to say he might go

[1] "these devils" were the slave traders.
[2] rub his nose: among some peoples, a way of showing affection.

back, he beckoned me down into our boat. As we started back he said to me: "Youngster, let that show you what it is to be without a family, without a home, and without a country. If you are ever tempted to say a word or to do a thing that shall put a bar between you and your family, your home, and your country, pray God in His mercy to take you that instant home to His own heaven. Think of your home, boy; write and send, and talk about it. Let it be nearer and nearer to your thought, the farther you have to travel from it; and rush back to it when you are free, as that poor slave is doing now. And for your country, boy," and the words rattled in his throat, "and for that flag," and he pointed to the ship, "never dream a dream but of serving her as she bids you, though the service carry you through a thousand hells. No matter what happens to you, no matter who flatters you or who abuses you, never look at another flag, never let a night pass but you pray God to bless the flag. Remember, boy, that behind all these men you have to do with, behind officers, and government, and people even, there is the Country herself, your Country, and that you belong to her as you belong to your own mother. Stand by her, boy, as you would stand by your mother!"

I was frightened to death by his calm, hard passion; but I blundered out that I would, by all that was holy, and that I had never thought of doing anything else. He hardly seemed to hear me; but he did, almost in a whisper, say, " Oh, if anybody had said so to me when I was of your age! "

I think it was this half-confidence of his, which I never abused, which afterward made us great friends. He was very kind to me. Often he sat up, or even got up, at night, to walk the deck with me, when it was my watch.[1] He explained to me a great deal of my mathematics and I owe him my taste for mathematics. He lent me books, and helped me about my reading. He never referred so directly to his story again; but from one and another officer I have learned, in thirty years, what I am telling.

NOLAN'S REPENTANCE

After that cruise I never saw Nolan again. The other men tell me that in those fifteen years he aged very fast, but that he was still the same gentle, uncomplaining, silent sufferer that he ever was, bearing as best he could his self-appointed punishment. And now it seems the dear old fellow is dead. He has found a home at last, and a country.

Since writing this, and while considering whether or no I would print it, as a warning to the young Nolans of today of what it is to throw away a country, I have received from Danforth, who is on board the *Levant*, a letter which gives an account of Nolan's last hours. It removes all my doubts about telling this story.

Here is the letter:

DEAR FRED: — I try to find heart and life to tell you that it is all over with dear old Nolan. I have been with him on this voyage more than I ever was, and I can understand wholly now the way in which you used to speak of the dear old fellow. I could see that he was not strong, but I had no idea the end was so near. The doctor has been watching him very carefully, and yesterday morning came to me and told me that Nolan was not so well, and had not left his stateroom — a thing I never remember before. He had let the doctor come and see him as he lay there — the first time the doctor had been in the stateroom — and he said he should like to see me. Do you remember the mysteries we boys used to invent about his room in the old *Intrepid* days?[2] Well, I went in, and there, to be sure, the poor fellow lay in his berth, smiling pleasantly as he gave me his hand, but looking very frail. I could not help a glance round, which showed me what a little shrine he had made of the box he was lying in. The stars and stripes were draped up above and around a picture of Washington, and he had painted a majestic eagle, with lightnings blazing from his beak and his foot just clasping the whole globe, which his wings overshadowed. The dear old boy saw my glance, and said, with a sad smile, " Here, you see, I have a country! " Then he pointed to the foot of his bed, where I had not seen before a great map of the United States, as he had drawn it from memory, and which he had there to look upon as he lay. Quaint, queer old names were on it, in large letters: " Indiana Territory," " Mississippi Territory," and " Louisiana Territory,"[3] as I suppose our fathers learned such things: but the old fellow

---

[1] **watch:** turn to stay on duty on deck.

[2] *Intrepid* **days:** when they were all aboard that ship.

[3] **Indiana . . . Territory:** not much of the country west of the Appalachian Mountains had been settled enough to become states at the time Nolan was sentenced.

had patched in Texas, too; he had carried his western boundary all the way to the Pacific, but on that shore he had defined nothing.

"O Captain," he said, "I know I am dying. I cannot get home. Surely you will tell me something now? — Stop! stop! Do not speak till I say what I am sure you know, that there is not in this ship, that there is not in America — God bless her! — a more loyal man than I. There cannot be a man who loves the old flag as I do, or prays for it as I do, or hopes for it as I do. There are thirty-four stars in it now, Danforth. I thank God for that, though I do not know what their names are. There has never been one taken away: I thank God for that. I know by that that there has never been any successful Burr. O Danforth, Danforth," he sighed out, "how like a wretched night's dream a boy's idea of personal fame or of separate sovereignty seems, when one looks back on it after such a life as mine! But tell me — tell me something — tell me everything, Danforth, before I die!"

I swear to you that I felt like a monster, that I had not told him everything before. "Mr. Nolan," said I, "I will tell you everything you ask about. Only, where shall I begin?"

Oh, the blessed smile that crept over his white face! and he pressed my hand and said, "God bless you! Tell me their names," he said, and he pointed to the stars on the flag. "The last I know is Ohio. My father lived in Kentucky. But I have guessed Michigan, and Indiana, and Mississippi — that was where Fort Adams is — they make twenty. But where are your other fourteen? You have not cut up any of the old ones, I hope?"

Well, that was not a bad text, and I told him the names in as good order as I could, and he bade me take down his beautiful map and draw them in as I best could with my pencil. He was wild with delight about Texas, told me how his cousin died there; he had marked a gold cross near where he supposed his grave was; and he had guessed at Texas. Then he was delighted as he saw California and Oregon — that, he said, he had suspected partly, because he had never been permitted to land on that shore, though the ships were there so much. Then he asked about the old war — told me the story of his serving the gun the day we took the *Java*. Then he settled

down more quietly, and very happily, to hear me tell in an hour the history of fifty years.

How I wish it had been somebody who knew something! But I did as well as I could. I told him of the English war.[1] I told him of Fulton and the steamboat beginning. I told him about old Scott,[2] and Jackson,[3] told him all I could think of about the Mississippi, and New Orleans, and Texas, and his own old Kentucky.

I tell you, it was a hard thing to condense the history of half a century into that talk with a sick man. And I do not now know what I told him — of emigration[4] and the means of it — of steamboats, and railroads, and telegraphs — of inventions, and books, and literature — of the colleges, and West Point, and the Naval School, but with the queerest interruptions that ever you heard. You see it was Robinson Crusoe asking all the accumulated questions of fifty-six years!

I remember he asked, all of a sudden, who was President now; and when I told him, he asked if Old Abe was General Benjamin Lincoln's son. He said he met old General Lincoln, when he was quite a boy himself, at some Indian treaty. I said no, that Old Abe was a Kentuckian like himself, but I could not tell him of what family; he had worked up from the ranks. " Good for him! " cried Nolan; " I am glad of that." Then I got talking about my visit to Washington. I told him

everything I could think of that would show the grandeur of his country and its prosperity.

And he drank it in and enjoyed it as I cannot tell you. He grew more and more silent, yet I never thought he was tired or faint. I gave him a glass of water, but he just wet his lips, and told me not to go away. Then he asked me to bring the Presbyterian *Book of Public Prayer* which lay there, and said, with a smile, that it would open at the right place — and so it did. There was his double red mark down the page; and I knelt down and read, and he repeated with me, *For ourselves and our country, O gracious God, we thank Thee, that, notwithstanding our manifold transgressions[5] of Thy Holy laws, Thou hast continued to us Thy marvelous kindness* — and so to the end of that thanksgiving. Then he turned to the end of the same book, and I read the words more familiar to me: *Most heartily we beseech Thee with Thy favor to behold and bless Thy servant, the President of the United States, and all others in authority.* " Danforth," said he, " I have repeated those prayers night and morning, it is now fifty-five years." And then he said he would go to sleep. He bent me down over him and kissed me: and he said, " Look in my Bible, Captain, when I am gone." And I went away.

But I had no thought it was the end. I thought he was tired and would sleep. I knew he was happy, and I wanted him to be alone.

But in an hour, when the doctor went in gently, he found Nolan had breathed his life away with a smile.

We looked in his Bible, and there was a slip of paper at the place where he had marked the text:

---

[1] **English war:** the War of 1812 against England.

[2] **Scott:** General Winfield Scott, who was in command in the War of 1812 and the Mexican War.

[3] **Andrew Jackson** won the battle of New Orleans and was later President.

[4] **emigration** (ĕm'ĭ-grā'shŭn): the steady stream of settlers moving westward and filling up the new land.

[5] **transgressions** (trăns·grĕsh'ŭnz): violations.

They desire a country, even a heavenly: where God is not ashamed to be called their God: for He hath prepared for them a city.

On this slip of paper he had written:

" Bury me in the sea; it has been my home, and I love it. But will not someone set up a stone for my memory, that my disgrace may not be more than I ought to bear? Say on it:

In Memory of
PHILIP NOLAN,
Lieutenant in the Army of the United States.

" He loved his country as no other man has loved her; but no man deserved less at her hands."

Noticing the Point of View

1. What do you know about the man who told the story of Philip Nolan? In order to tell the story why would he have to be a naval man? an officer?

2. What happenings did the storyteller actually witness himself? Explain why these happenings alone would not give you the life story of Nolan.

3. Mention the different kinds of information that the storyteller drew on in order to tell a complete story.

4. Discuss whether the story seems more real told in this way than it would be had the storyteller been Nolan himself. Compare the " bystander " point of view in telling a story with a " third person " point of view, in which the author writes as if he knew everything about all the characters and happenings.

A Lesson in Patriotism

1. What reasons are given for the fact that, when he was in the army, Nolan did not feel as much patriotism as some other officers? How did Burr draw him into his conspiracy?

2. The passage from *The Lay of the Last Minstrel* is a famous one. You may wish to memorize it.

3. Which of the incidents here — the ball, reading the poem, interpreting for the slaves — seems to you most terrible for Nolan to bear? Try to state what his feelings were in each incident.

4. Why did the captain of the *Levant* finally tell Nolan all he could about his country? Do you think he did right? Why?

5. Find the passages on pages 418–19 that tell how much of American history Nolan missed during his lifetime. What are the main events he never knew about? Imagine that this story of Nolan's imprisonment began in 1900 and ended in 1950 or even later. What would be the main events of history, the inventions and other changes in life, he would not know about? You may wish to put your answer in the form of a conversation with Nolan.

6. Could such a punishment be carried out in our times? What special difficulties can you think of?

Direction Words

After Philip Nolan received his sentence, the navy's ships put it into effect. The rule adopted on board the ships — was " *transmitted* from the beginning." Transmit means " to send or transfer from one person to another," so that the navy passed along the order about Nolan from ship to ship. Can you see how this definition might also fit the radio term *transmitter?*

There are many English words that use prefixes that indicate direction. Here are a few common prefixes:

trans: across or beyond
sub: under or beneath
inter: between
peri: around or about

Using these definitions, how would you explain the meaning of *transport, transform, subway, interview, interplanetary, periscope?* Make a list of words you know which include each prefix, and then let the class combine the lists on the board.

America the Beautiful

KATHARINE LEE BATES

O beautiful for spacious skies,
  For amber waves of grain,
For purple mountain majesties
  Above the fruited plain!
    America! America!   5
God shed His grace on thee
And crown thy good with brotherhood
  From sea to shining sea!

O beautiful for pilgrim° feet,
  Whose stern, impassioned stress 10
A thoroughfare for freedom beat
  Across the wilderness!
    America! America!
God mend thine every flaw,
Confirm thy soul in self-control, 15
  Thy liberty in law!

O beautiful for heroes proved
  In liberating strife,
Who more than self their country
  loved,
And mercy more than life!   20
  America! America!

9. A **pilgrim** is one who journeys far, seeking
something he holds dear or holy, as our American
"pilgrim fathers" did in coming to America.

May God thy gold refine,
Till all success be nobleness,
  And every gain divine!

O beautiful for patriot dream   25
  That sees beyond the years
Thine alabaster° cities gleam
  Undimmed by human tears!
    America! America!
God shed His grace on thee   30
And crown thy good with brotherhood
  From sea to shining sea!

27. **alabaster** (ăl′á·bás′tẽr): fine white stone,
finer than marble.

Beauty of Land and Spirit

1. Each stanza gives a different reason
for loving America. Tell what each one is.
Which reason seems to you to be the
strongest one?

2. What does the poet pray for America? What prayer is repeated in the last
stanza? What does she mean by " brotherhood "?

3. Can we do anything to help keep
America " undimmed by human tears "?
Mention some of the things you can think
of that would help.

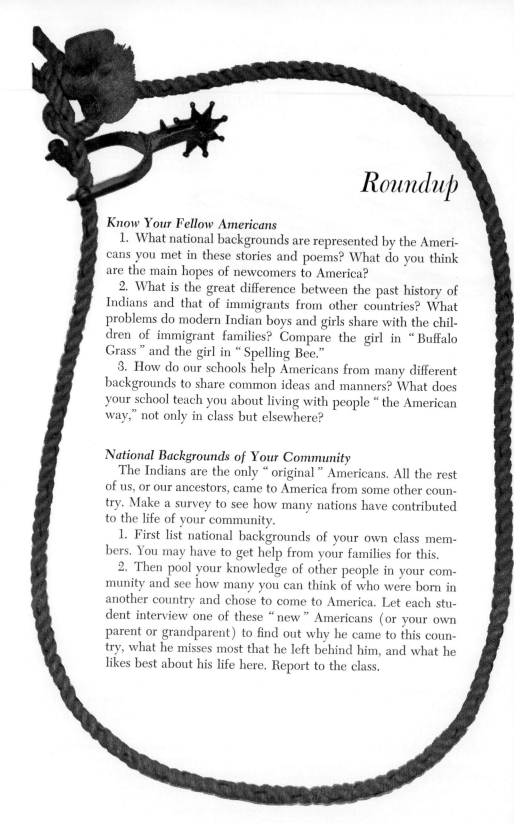

Roundup

Know Your Fellow Americans

1. What national backgrounds are represented by the Americans you met in these stories and poems? What do you think are the main hopes of newcomers to America?

2. What is the great difference between the past history of Indians and that of immigrants from other countries? What problems do modern Indian boys and girls share with the children of immigrant families? Compare the girl in "Buffalo Grass" and the girl in "Spelling Bee."

3. How do our schools help Americans from many different backgrounds to share common ideas and manners? What does your school teach you about living with people "the American way," not only in class but elsewhere?

National Backgrounds of Your Community

The Indians are the only "original" Americans. All the rest of us, or our ancestors, came to America from some other country. Make a survey to see how many nations have contributed to the life of your community.

1. First list national backgrounds of your own class members. You may have to get help from your families for this.

2. Then pool your knowledge of other people in your community and see how many you can think of who were born in another country and chose to come to America. Let each student interview one of these "new" Americans (or your own parent or grandparent) to find out why he came to this country, what he misses most that he left behind him, and what he likes best about his life here. Report to the class.

Your Bookshelf

Americans Every One, by Lavinia R. Davis (Doubleday, 1942)

Nine stories about new Americans from other lands.

Amos Fortune: Free Man, by Elizabeth Yates (Aladdin, 1951)

He was a prince in Africa, a slave in America, and then a free man on his own land.

Crazy Horse, Great Warrior of the Sioux, by Shannon Garst (Houghton Mifflin, 1950)

This heroic chief led his tribe's fight to hold their lands against the invading white men.

Dr. George Washington Carver, Scientist, by Shirley Graham and Paul D. Lipscomb (Messner, 1944)

Against terrific odds, this gentle Negro became one of our greatest and most helpful scientists.

The House Under the Hill, by Florence Crannel Means (Houghton Mifflin, 1950)

A Spanish-American girl in New Mexico. This author tells an interesting story of friendship between girls of varied backgrounds in *Assorted Sisters* (1947).

Indians on Horseback, by Alice Marriott (Crowell, 1948)

A full and accurate account of the life of the Plains Indians.

It Might Be You, by Ruth Adams Knight (Doubleday, 1949)

Serious stories of the heartbreak prejudice can cause.

Michael's Victory, by Clara Ingram Judson (Houghton Mifflin, 1946)

The great famine of 1845 drives an Irish boy to America and a life with both hard work and adventure.

New Friends for Susan, by Yoshiko Ochida (Scribner, 1951)

The life of a young Japanese-American in California.

Passage to America: the Story of the Great Migrations, by Katharine B. Shippen (Harper, 1950)

The stories behind the waves of immigrants.

Prairie School, by Lois Lenski (Lippincott, 1951)

Trials of the great blizzard of 1949. Other good books by this writer are *Judy's Journey* (1947), about the daughter of migrant harvest workers, and *Cotton in My Sack* (1949), about life on a small cotton farm.

Red Eagle: Buffalo Bill's Adopted Son, by M. O'Moran (Lippincott, 1948)

True story of an Indian boy who became a Texas Ranger after his foster father's death.

Something Old, Something New, by Dorothy Canfield Fisher (W. R. Scott, 1949)

Nine stories of " people who are America."

Song of the Pines, by Walter and Marion Havighurst (Winston, 1949)

A Norwegian boy fulfills his dream of success in America.

The Story of Phyllis Wheatley, by Shirley Graham (Messner, 1949)

Brought to America as a slave, she became one of our first women poets.

Willy Wong, American, by Vanya Oakes (Messner, 1951)

A boy finds it difficult to be both Chinese and American. The story of his grandfather, who helped to build the first transcontinental railroad is told in *Footprints of the Dragon,* (Winston, 1950)

You and Democracy, by Dorothy Gordon (Dutton, 1951)

Explains what democracy means in terms of everyday life.

Old Favorites

If

RUDYARD KIPLING

This poem probably hangs on the walls of more clubrooms and athletic dressing rooms than any other piece of writing in our language. In simple terms it explains how to make the finest possible person of yourself. Kipling speaks to "my son," but what he has to say fits girls just as well as boys.

If you can keep your head when all about you
    Are losing theirs and blaming it on you;
If you can trust yourself when all men doubt you,
    But make allowance for their doubting, too;
If you can wait and not be tired by waiting;   5
    Or, being lied about, don't deal in lies;
Or, being hated, don't give way to hating;
    And yet don't look too good, nor talk too wise;

If you can dream — and not make dreams your master;
   If you can think — and not make thoughts your aim;   10
If you can meet with Triumph and Disaster,
   And treat these two impostors just the same;
If you can bear to hear the truth you've spoken
   Twisted by knaves to make a trap for fools;
Or watch the things you gave your life to, broken,   15
   And stoop and build them up with worn-out tools;

If you can make one heap of all your winnings
   And risk it on the turn of pitch-and-toss,
And lose, and start again at your beginnings,
   And never breathe a word about your loss;   20
If you can force your heart and nerve and sinew
   To serve your turn long after they are gone,
And so hold on when there is nothing in you
   Except the will which says to them: " Hold on ";

If you can talk with crowds and keep your virtue,   25
   Or walk with kings — nor lose the common touch;
If neither foes nor loving friends can hurt you;
   If all men count with you, but none too much;
If you can fill the unforgiving minute
   With sixty seconds' worth of distance run,   30
Yours is the Earth and everything that's in it,
   And — which is more — you'll be a Man, my son.

One Code for Living

1. Which of the " if's " are hardest for most people? Which ones are easier? Of all these goals, explain which one you consider most important *for a young person in school.*

2. Reread lines 9 and 10. Some people do not agree with Kipling's statement in these lines. A class discussion will bring out interesting differences of opinion.

3. Why does Kipling call Triumph and Disaster " impostors," that is, deceivers who are not what they seem? How could you treat them " just the same "?

4. Can you think of definite incidents or situations that will explain the meaning of lines 25 and 26? Is Kipling talking about actual royalty when he says " kings "?

Word History

Have you ever wondered how words come into our language? Some are invented to name a new thing, as *television* was. Others, like *knave* in this poem, are words whose original meanings were changed over a long period of use. *Knave* comes from the German word *knabe* meaning " boy." In early times a knave was a servant boy, and probably because of repeated boyish pranks the word came to mean " a cheat or a deceiving person."

Two Favorite American Folk Songs

In the old days before radio and television began to fill up spare evenings, Americans used to gather in groups to talk and sing. Often they made up songs and passed them from group to group.

Here are two old favorites that have come down to us from the days when cowboys rejoiced in their life on the open range and Negro slaves found happiness in singing of the freedom that would be theirs in heaven. The best way to enjoy folk songs is to sing them.

HOME ON THE RANGE

COWBOY BALLAD

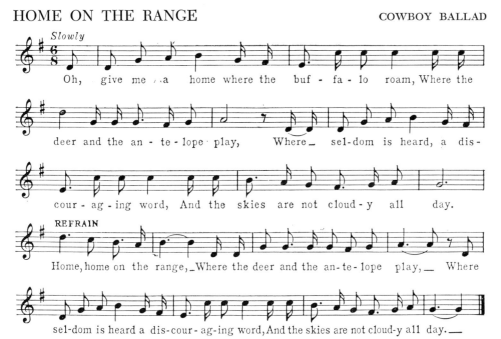

Oh, give me a home where the buf-fa-lo roam, Where the deer and the an-te-lope play, Where sel-dom is heard, a dis-cour-ag-ing word, And the skies are not cloud-y all day.

REFRAIN

Home, home on the range, Where the deer and the an-te-lope play, Where sel-dom is heard a dis-cour-ag-ing word, And the skies are not cloud-y all day.

2. How often at night when the heavens are bright
With the light of the glittering stars,
Have I stood there amazed and asked as I gazed
If their glory exceeds that of ours.

Refrain

3. Oh, give me a land where the bright diamond sand
   Flows leisurely down the stream;
   Where the graceful white swan goes gliding along
   Like a maid in a heavenly dream.
   Refrain

4. Then I would not exchange my home on the range,
   Where the deer and the antelope play,
   Where seldom is heard a discouraging word,
   And the skies are not cloudy all day.
   Refrain

ALL GOD'S CHILLUN GOT WINGS   NEGRO SPIRITUAL

2. I got wings, you got wings,
   All God's chillun got wings.
   When I get to heav'n I'm goin' to put on my wings,
   I'm goin' to fly all over God's heav'n,
           Heav'n, heav'n.
   Ev'rybody talkin' 'bout heav'n ain't goin' there,
           Heav'n, heav'n,
   I'm goin' to fly all over God's heav'n.

3. I got a harp, you got a harp,
   All God's chillun got a harp.
   When I get to heav'n I'm goin' to take up my harp,
   I'm goin' to play all over God's heav'n,
          Heav'n, heav'n.
   Ev'rybody talkin' 'bout heav'n ain't goin' there,
          Heav'n, heav'n,
   I'm goin' to play all over God's heav'n.

4. I got shoes, you got shoes,
   All God's chillun got shoes.
   When I get to heav'n I'm goin' to put on my shoes,
   I'm goin' to walk all over God's heav'n,
          Heav'n, heav'n.
   Ev'rybody talkin' 'bout heav'n ain't goin' there,
          Heav'n, heav'n,
   I'm goin' to walk all over God's heav'n.

Cargoes

JOHN MASEFIELD

PICTURES WITH SOUND EFFECTS. Imagine yourself looking at a row of three pictures. Each shows a ship from a different period of history and also reveals the cargo it carries. Now imagine that as you look at each picture you hear an orchestra playing a different piece of music for each. If the music matched the pictures, that would be an enjoyable way to look at pictures in an art gallery, wouldn't it? In this poem you will have exactly that pleasure. In each stanza the poet paints a picture of a ship with words, and those same words carry musical sounds that fit each picture. The poet does not tell you what he thinks about the pictures, but you should be able to decide for yourself.

"Cargoes" from *The Story of a Round House* by John Masefield. Copyright, 1912, by The Macmillan Company and used with their permission.

This poet, like most others, loves odd words that are both colorful and musical. An example is the word *quinquereme* (kwĭn'kwĕ·rēm), meaning an ancient ship rowed by five banks (*quin* means "five") of oarsmen. Another is *Ophir* (ō'fēr) the name of a country famous for its wealth in ancient times. Watch for other words that paint pictures and create music, as you pass from ship to ship.

Quinquereme of Nineveh from distant Ophir, | *Light voices*
Rowing home to haven in sunny Palestine,
With a cargo of ivory,
And apes and peacocks,
Sandalwood, cedarwood, and sweet white wine.   5

Stately Spanish galleon° coming from the Isthmus, | *Medium voices*
Dipping through the Tropics by the palm-green shores,
With a cargo of diamonds,
Emeralds, amethysts,
Topazes, and cinnamon, and gold moidores.°   10

Dirty British coaster with a salt-caked smokestack, | *Deep voices*
Butting through the Channel in the mad March days,
With a cargo of Tyne coal,
Road-rails, pig lead,
Firewood, ironware, and cheap tin trays.   15

6. A **galleon** (găl'ê·ŭn) was the type of heavy sailing ship used when the Spanish were carrying treasure from America to Spain. Much of the treasure was gathered in the Isthmus of Panama for shipping. 10. **moidores** (moi'dōrz): Portuguese gold coins.

Reading the Poet's Mind

1. Here are three ideas suggested by the poem. Which one do you think the poet had in mind? Why?

a. Cargoes used to be more valuable than they are today.

b. Old-time ships and their cargoes were more romantic than modern ones.

c. Modern ships toil through worse weather than earlier ones had to struggle against.

2. Describe in a few words the kind of cargo each ship carried. See how many other comparisons between the pictures of the three ships you can find.

3. The poet makes the *sounds* for each ship as different as the pictures. To bring this out, let the class read the poem aloud, using the suggestions in the margin. Change the timing and the tone of voice to fit the effect of each stanza (for the first, a light, rippling sound; for the second, a swelling, full-throated sound; for the third, a harsh, choppy sound). Or you might divide the class into teams of three, using a solo voice for each stanza. Does hearing the poem read aloud help you to picture the ships and their cargoes?

The House by the Side of the Road

SAM WALTER FOSS

A BROADER MEANING. When you see a picture of the Statue of Liberty what do you think of? No doubt you think about the whole idea of freedom and particularly the idea that the United States is a land of freedom. The Statue of Liberty is a *symbol*. It is a thing that stands for an idea; it suggests a broader meaning than itself.

You see or read or think of symbols almost every day — such common things as a beacon light (which can stand for help and guidance) or a skull-and-crossbones (which can stand for danger). Poets like to use symbols because they are a quick and interesting way to get across a point. In this poem, for instance, the poet speaks of living in a " house by the side of the road." He does not mean a *real* house near a *real* highway. Rather, he uses the house as a symbol for an idea. His idea is that he wants to be in the midst of life, seeing and understanding all kinds of people.

There are several other such symbols in the poem. See if you can match the things the poet mentions with the ideas they stand for.

> There are hermit souls that live withdrawn
>   In the place of their self-content;
> There are souls like stars, that dwell apart,
>   In a fellowless firmament;°
> There are pioneer souls that blaze their paths   5
>   Where highways never ran —
> But let me live by the side of the road
>   And be a friend to man.
>
> Let me live in a house by the side of the road
>   Where the race of men go by —   10
> The men who are good and the men who are bad,
>   As good and as bad as I.

4. firmament (fûr′mȧ·měnt): sky.

I would not sit in the scorner's seat
    Or hurl the cynic's ban° —
Let me live in a house by the side of the road   15
    And be a friend to man.

I see from my house by the side of the road,
    By the side of the highway of life,
The men who press with the ardor of hope,
    The men who are faint with the strife,   20
But I turn not away from their smiles nor their tears,
    Both parts of an infinite plan —
Let me live in a house by the side of the road
    And be a friend to man.

I know there are brook-gladdened meadows ahead,   25
    And mountains of wearisome height;
That the road passes on through the long afternoon
    And stretches away to the night.
And still I rejoice when the travelers rejoice,
    And weep with the strangers that moan,   30
Nor live in my house by the side of the road
    Like a man who dwells alone.

Let me live in my house by the side of the road
    Where the race of men go by —
They are good, they are bad, they are weak, they are strong,   35
    Wise, foolish — so am I.
Then why should I sit in the scorner's seat
    Or hurl the cynic's ban?
Let me live in my house by the side of the road
    And be a friend to man.   40

14. A **cynic** (sĭn′ĭk) is one who distrusts people and thinks they are usually selfish; a **ban** forbids or outlaws something.

Matching Things with Ideas

1. You remember that symbols are simple things that stand for ideas; they suggest a broader meaning. What ideas came to your mind as you read of these things in the poem:
    a. line 25: *meadows*
    b. line 26: *mountains*
    c. lines 27–28: *afternoon* and *night*
2. The poet speaks of people as travelers on a road. How are the " pioneer souls " in line 5 different from most people?

3. Does the poet expect all people to be good and fine? Find the lines that support your answer.

4. If you lived in a crowded city would you be better able to live as the poet suggests, or could you carry out his idea even in open farm country? What is *your* idea of being a good neighbor?

A Special Word

This poet refused to be a *cynic*. Look again at the footnote on page 432. Now look at a dictionary for a fuller meaning of the word. Did you discover that *cynic* is one of those special words that cannot easily be explained by another word? To explain the word you need to state the whole idea. For example, you can be a *doubter* (dout'ẽr) and still have faith in people's good intentions; you may simply doubt that a particular thing is right or accurate. But a cynic is suspicious of people's intentions no matter what the evidence is. He scorns the beliefs of other people.

What proof can you find in this poem that the poet is not *cynical?* Do you think that *cynicism* (sĭn'ĭ·sĭz'm) would be a difficult attitude to carry through life? Explain why or why not.

I Remember, I Remember

THOMAS HOOD

I remember, I remember,
　The house where I was born;
The little window where the sun
　Came peeping in at morn;
He never came a wink too soon,　5
　Nor brought too long a day;
But now I often wish the night
　Had borne my breath away!

I remember, I remember,
　The roses, red and white,　10
The violets, and the lily cups —
　Those flowers made of light!
The lilacs where the robin built,
　And where my brother set
The laburnum,° on his birthday —
　The tree is living yet!　16

15. Americans call this flowering tree lá·bûr'-
nŭm, but the English poet calls it lăb'ẽr·nŭm.

I remember, I remember,
　Where I was used to swing,
And thought the air must rush as
　　fresh
　To swallows on the wing;　20
My spirit flew in feathers then,
　That is so heavy now.
And summer pools could hardly cool
　The fever on my brow!

I remember, I remember,　25
　The fir trees dark and high;
I used to think their slender tops
　Were close against the sky;
It was a childish ignorance,
　But now 'tis little joy　30
To know I'm farther off from heaven
　Than when I was a boy.

Happy Memories

1. What particular scenes does the poet remember about his childhood? Why do you suppose he does not tell more about his family?

2. Find lines that reveal that the poet is not happy now.

3. When you are old, what do you think you will remember about your childhood days? Of course it is hard to know how you will feel many years from now, but you can get some clues from grownups. Compare your parents' and grandparents' best memories of childhood. Write a short poem or essay, pretending you are old and recalling the pleasures of earlier days.

Love Songs

Robert Burns was a poet who enjoyed the simple things in life — the sight of familiar places, the warmth of a family gathering. He was a simple man himself, a poor Scottish plowboy. Even after he became his country's most famous poet, he never lost touch with the countryside and its common folk. In the first poem, there is a bit of dialect that adds flavor to the words and is easy to pronounce when you read aloud. In the second, Burns tells of his sweetheart, Mary Campbell. The third poem is a famous song that expresses the faithfulness of a man to his love, in the present and in the future that he foresees.

JEAN   ROBERT BURNS

Of a' the airts° the wind can blaw,
   I dearly like the west,
For there the bonnie lassie lives,
   The lassie I lo'e best:
There wild woods grow, and rivers
    row,   5
   And mony a hill between;
But day and night my fancy's flight
   Is ever wi' my Jean.

1. **airts:** directions.

I see her in the dewy flowers
   I see her sweet and fair: 10
I hear her in the tunefu' birds,
   I hear her charm the air:
There's not a bonnie flower that
    springs
   By fountain, shaw, or green,°
There's not a bonnie bird that sings,
   But minds me o' my Jean.   16

14. **shaw:** grove; **green:** a grassy lawn.

SWEET AFTON

ROBERT BURNS

Flow gently, sweet Afton! among thy green braes,
Flow gently, I'll sing thee a song in thy praise;
My Mary's asleep by thy murmuring stream,
Flow gently, sweet Afton, disturb not her dream.

Thou stock dove whose echo resounds through the glen,   5
Ye wild whistling blackbirds, in yon thorny den,
Thou green-crested lapwing thy screaming forbear,
I charge you, disturb not my slumbering Fair.

How lofty, sweet Afton, thy neighboring hills,
Far marked with the courses of clear, winding rills;   10
There daily I wander as noon rises high,
My flocks and my Mary's sweet cot in my eye.

How pleasant thy banks and green valleys below,
Where, wild in the woodlands, the primroses blow;
There oft, as mild Ev'ning weeps over the lea,   15
The sweet-scented birk shades my Mary and me.

Thy crystal stream, Afton, how lovely it glides,
And winds by the cot where my Mary resides;
How wanton thy waters her snowy feet lave,
As, gathering sweet flowerets, she stems thy clear wave.   20

Flow gently, sweet Afton, among thy green braes,
Flow gently, sweet river, the theme of my lays;
My Mary's asleep by thy murmuring stream,
Flow gently, sweet Afton, disturb not her dream.

BELIEVE ME, IF ALL THOSE ENDEARING YOUNG CHARMS

THOMAS MOORE

Believe me, if all those endearing young charms,
    Which I gaze on so fondly today,
Were to change by tomorrow, and fleet in my arms,
    Like fairy gifts fading away,
Thou wouldst still be adored, as this moment thou art,   5
    Let thy loveliness fade as it will,
And around the dear ruin each wish of my heart
    Would entwine itself verdantly° still.

It is not while beauty and youth are thine own,
    And thy cheeks unprofaned° by a tear,   10
That the fervor and faith of a soul can be known,
    To which time will but make thee more dear;
No, the heart that has truly loved never forgets,
    But as truly loves on to the close,
As the sunflower turns on her god, when he sets,   15
    The same look which she turned when he rose.

8. **verdantly**: fresh and green, like a living vine. 10. **unprofaned** (ŭn·prō·fānd′): not touched wrongly or unsuitably.

Love Songs

JEAN

1. Why does Burns love the west wind? Is his love far away? How can you tell?

2. What things remind him of his Jean?

3. Burns liked to use the Scottish word " bonnie." Find three places in the poem where he uses it to describe something that he likes.

SWEET AFTON

1. Probably you sang " Sweet Afton " in your early school years without even thinking of it as a " poem." By now you know that most poems have a definite musical pattern. Try reading this poem aloud, giving it a musical lilt but not quite singing it. Then obtain a recording of the song, or ask your music teacher to furnish a musical score to sing in class as a group. How close-

ly does the music follow the sound of the words? Do you think that the words from any " hit " song of today would make a good poem? How can you find out?

2. Arrange a program of " Songs by Bobby Burns," including " Sweet Afton," " Auld Lang Syne," " Comin' Thro' the Rye," and others. Have a committee look up the main facts of Burns's life and write an introduction to the program, which you might wish to arrange with your music teacher to present before the school assembly.

BELIEVE ME, IF ALL THOSE ENDEARING YOUNG CHARMS

1. Are the lovers in this poem young or old?

2. How long does the poet think his love will last? What does he compare himself

to? Find the lines and read them aloud.

3. Would this poem please a sweetheart more than " Jean " would?

4. Moore wrote music for this poem. You can get good records of it. Play one of them in class.

Two Poems on Death

Through poetry a writer can often express his feelings in a sharper, more intense, way than he can in prose. In his poem about Abraham Lincoln's death, Walt Whitman reveals two feelings — rejoicing over the peaceful end of a terrible war, and grief over the death of a great leader. Both feelings are expressed in terms of a ship coming home safely after a stormy voyage — but with the captain dead.

The second poem was written by Robert Louis Stevenson, who all his life carried a gay and happy heart in a sick and suffering body. When he finally realized that death was coming he greeted it simply and serenely. These lines are carved over his grave on a mountaintop in the South Sea island of Samoa, where the Scottish poet spent his last years.

O CAPTAIN! MY CAPTAIN!

WALT WHITMAN

O Captain! my Captain, our fearful trip is done,
The ship has weathered every rack, the prize we sought is won,
The port is near, the bells I hear, the people all exulting,
While follow eyes the steady keel, the vessel grim and daring;
      But O heart! heart! heart!   5
         O the bleeding drops of red,
            Where on the deck my Captain lies,
              Fallen cold and dead.

O Captain! my Captain! rise up and hear the bells;
Rise up — for you the flag is flung — for you the bugle trills,   10
For you bouquets and ribboned wreaths — for you the shores a-crowding,
For you they call, the swaying mass, their eager faces turning;

Here Captain! dear father!
This arm beneath your head!
It is some dream that on the deck   15
You've fallen cold and dead.

My Captain does not answer, his lips are pale and still,
My father does not feel my arm, he has no pulse nor will,
The ship is anchored safe and sound, its voyage closed and done,
From fearful trip the victor ship comes in with object won;   20
Exult O shores! and ring O bells!
But I with mournful tread.
Walk the deck my Captain lies,
Fallen cold and dead.

REQUIEM   ROBERT LOUIS STEVENSON

Under the wide and starry sky
Dig the grave and let me lie:
Glad did I live and gladly die,
And I laid me down with a will.

This be the verse you 'grave for me:
Here he lies where he longed to be;
Home is the sailor, home from the sea,
And the hunter home from the hill.

Two Views of Death

O CAPTAIN! MY CAPTAIN!

1. What does the ship stand for? What is the port? What was the " fearful trip "?

2. If you haven't read " House by the Side of the Road " on page 431, look at the explanation of *symbols* at the beginning of that poem. Explain how this poem uses symbols, and tell why you think they are effective here.

3. Do you get the feeling that the poet knew Lincoln personally? Did many other people feel that way?

4. Which is the stronger feeling in this poem — the rejoicing or the grief?

REQUIEM

1. Requiem (look up its pronunciation) means rest, and it is also a name for any song about death. How does this poem fit both meanings?

2. Discuss whether you think the third line means the poet welcomes death because he has been painfully ill or for another reason. What other reason might he have had?

3. Was Stevenson's actual burial place the kind he asked for in the first two lines of the poem?

4. What do the lines about the hunter and the sailor mean to you? What is the " home " mentioned here?

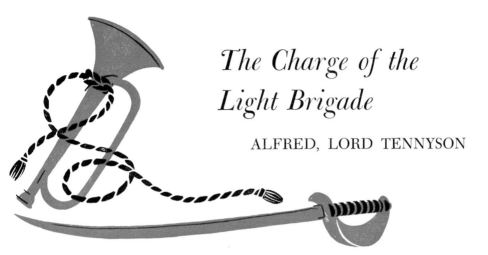

The Charge of the Light Brigade

ALFRED, LORD TENNYSON

As poet laureate (or "official poet") of England, Tennyson wrote verses on important national events. Many were triumphs, for he lived in the great days of the British Empire. But he wrote this poem about a disaster that revealed the courage and honor of English soldiers as no victory could do. During the Crimean War, in 1854, an English Light Brigade, through a mistake, was ordered to attack well-fortified Russian gun positions. Though they knew the charge was hopeless, they carried out the order. Most of the cavalrymen died before the Russian cannon, but the poet made them immortal.

> Half a league, half a league,° | *First group*
> Half a league onward,
> All in the valley of death
>   Rode the six hundred.
> "Forward, the Light Brigade!   5 | *Second group*
> Charge for the guns!" he said;
> Into the valley of death | *All*
>   Rode the six hundred.
>
> "Forward, the Light Brigade!" | *First group*
> Was there a man dismayed?   10
> Not though the soldier knew
>   Someone had blundered;
> Theirs not to make reply, | *Second group*
> Theirs not to reason why,
> Theirs but to do and die;   15
> Into the valley of death | *All*
>   Rode the six hundred.

1. **league:** a measure of distance (no longer used) equal to about three miles.

Cannon to right of them,   **|** *First group*
Cannon to left of them,
Cannon in front of them   20
   Volleyed and thundered;
Stormed at with shot and shell,   **|** *Second group*
Boldly they rode and well,
Into the jaws of death,   **|** *All*
Into the mouth of Hell   25
   Rode the six hundred.

Flashed all their sabers bare,   **|** *First group*
Flashed as they turned in air
Sabring the gunners there,
Charging an army, while   30
   All the world wondered.
Plunged in the battery smoke,   **|** *Second group*
Right through the line they broke;
Cossack and Russian
Reeled from the saber-stroke —   35
   Shattered and sundered
Then they rode back, but not —
   Not the six hundred.
                                            | *All*

Cannon to right of them,   **|** *First group*
Cannon to left of them,   40
Cannon behind them
   Volleyed and thundered;
Stormed at with shot and shell,   **|** *Second group*
While horse and hero fell,
They that had fought so well   45
Came through the jaws of death,
Back from the mouth of hell,
All that was left of them,
   Left of six hundred.
                                            | *All*

When can their glory fade?   50
Oh, the wild charge they made!
   All the world wondered.
Honor the charge they made,
Honor the Light Brigade,
   Noble six hundred!   55

A Salute to Valor

1. What was the attitude of the soldiers toward the order they received?

2. What weapon did the Light Brigade use? What weapon did the enemy use?

3. Was the outcome of the charge what the soldiers expected?

4. Why are these soldiers honored as heroes? Discuss whether you think soldiers must obey orders, even when there is no hope of success.

5. How does the sound of the poem give the effect of the hot battle? In reading it as a group — if you choose to do so — be sure to emphasize the contrast between the loud, strong parts and the slower, softer parts.

*How They Brought the Good News from Ghent to Aix**

ROBERT BROWNING

Robert Browning was one of the greatest of the English poets. Some of his poetry has deep thought and calls for the best attention of mature readers. But he also wrote many short poems like this one that are easy for anybody to read.

Before you begin it, think of the sound of a galloping horse's hoofbeats. Then read this poem in that rhythm, just the way you put words to music, and you'll get the right feeling of excitement for this famous ride.

I sprang to the stirrup, and Joris, and he;
I galloped, Dirck galloped, we galloped all three;
" Good speed! " cried the watch, as the gate bolts undrew;
" Speed! " echoed the wall to us galloping through;
Behind shut the postern,° the lights sank to rest,   5
And into the midnight we galloped abreast.

* **Aix** (āks). 5. **postern** (pōs'tērn): a city gate.

Not a word to each other; we kept the great pace
Neck by neck, stride by stride, never changing our place;
I turned in my saddle and made its girths tight,
Then shortened each stirrup, and set the pique° right,   10
Rebuckled the cheek strap, chained slacker the bit,
Nor galloped less steadily Roland a whit.

'Twas moonset at starting; but while we drew near
Lokeren,° the cocks crew and twilight dawned clear;
At Boom, a great yellow star came out to see;   15
At Düffeld, 'twas morning as plain as could be;
And from Mechelen church steeple we heard the half-chime,
So Joris broke silence with, " Yet there is time! "

At Aerschot, up leaped of a sudden the sun,
And against him the cattle stood black every one,   20
To stare thro' the mist at us galloping past,
And I saw my stout galloper Roland at last,
With resolute shoulders, each butting away
The haze, as some bluff river headland its spray.

And his low head and crest, just one sharp ear bent back   25
For my voice, and the other pricked out on his track;
And one eye's black intelligence — ever that glance
O'er its white edge at me, his own master, askance!
And the thick heavy spume-flakes which aye and anon
His fierce lips shook upward in galloping on.   30

By Hasselt, Dirck groaned; and cried Joris, " Stay spur!
Your Roos° galloped bravely, the fault's not in her,
We'll remember at Aix " — for one heard the quick wheeze
Of her chest, saw the stretched neck and staggering knees,
And sunk tail, and horrible heave of the flank,   35
As down on her haunches she shuddered and sank.

10. **pique** (pēk): part of the saddle. 14. Pronunciation of this place name and those that follow is
given in a footnote at the end of the poem. 32. **Roos** (rōs).

So we were left galloping, Joris and I,
Past Looz and past Tongres, no cloud in the sky;
The broad sun above laughed a pitiless laugh,
'Neath our feet broke the brittle bright stubble like chaff;   40
Till over by Dalhem a dome spire sprang white,
And " Gallop," gasped Joris, " for Aix is in sight!

" How they'll greet us! " and all in a moment his roan
Rolled neck and croup° over, lay dead as a stone;
And there was my Roland to bear the whole weight   45
Of the news which alone could save Aix from her fate,
With his nostrils like pits full of blood to the brim,
And with circles of red for his eye sockets' rim.

Then I cast loose my buffcoat, each holster let fall,
Shook off my jack boots, let go belt and all,   50
Stood up in the stirrup, leaned, patted his ear,
Called my Roland his pet name, my horse without peer;
Clapped my hands, laughed and sang, any noise, bad or good,
Till at length into Aix Roland galloped and stood.

And all I remember is, friends flocking round   55
As I sate with his head 'twixt my knees on the ground,
And no voice but was praising this Roland of mine,
As I poured down his throat our last measure of wine,
Which (the burgesses° voted by common consent)
Was no more than his due who brought good news from Ghent.   60

44. croup (kro͞op): the back part of a horse; the rump. 59. burgesses: the governing council of the city. 14. Lokeren (lō′kĕ·rĕn). 15. Boom (bōm). 16. Düffeld (dĕf′ĕlt). 17. Mechelen (mĕκ′ĕ·lĕn). 19. Aerschot (är′sκôt). 31. Hasselt (häs′ĕlt). 38. Looz (lōz). Tongres (tôɴ′gr′). 41. Dalhem (däl′ĕm).

The Rhythm of Riding

1. Is the swing of these lines different from the rhythm of a walk or a trot? In what way? What does poetry do for the story that prose could not have done?

2. How long did the ride last? How did the horses show the strain?

3. Is Roland the hero of this ride, or his master? What did the burgesses think?

4. Why doesn't the poet tell you what the good news was? What could it have been?

The Star-Spangled Banner

FRANCIS SCOTT KEY

And now, our national anthem!

Do you imagine, as you sing it, how Key felt when he wrote the words? He had gone aboard a British ship, during the War of 1812, to arrange for the exchange of prisoners. The battle on shore was still going on when night fell. He waited in terrific suspense for daybreak to show him whether the American flag still flew over the fort on shore.

O say, can you see, by the dawn's early light,
　　What so proudly we hailed at the twilight's last gleaming?
Whose broad stripes and bright stars, through the perilous fight,
　　O'er the ramparts we watched were so gallantly streaming;
And the rockets' red glare, the bombs bursting in air,　　　　　5
Gave proof through the night that our flag was still there:
　　O say, does the star-spangled banner yet wave
　　O'er the land of the free and the home of the brave?

On that shore dimly seen through the mist of the deep,
　　Where the foe's haughty host in dread silence reposes,　　　10
What is that which the breeze, o'er the towering steep,
　　As it fitfully blows, half conceals, half discloses?
Now it catches the gleam of the morning's first beam,
In full glory reflected now shines on the stream;
　　'Tis the star-spangled banner: O long may it wave　　　　15
　　O'er the land of the free and the home of the brave!

Oh, thus be it ever, when freemen shall stand
　　Between their loved homes and the war's desolation!
Blest with victory and peace, may the heaven-rescued land
　　Praise the Power that hath made and preserved us a nation.　　20
Then conquer we must, for our cause it is just,
And this be our motto, " In God is our trust."
　　And the star-spangled banner in triumph shall wave
　　O'er the land of the free and the home of the brave.

Old Favorites

Robert Burns

Evangeline

HENRY WADSWORTH LONGFELLOW

A TALE OF BYGONE DAYS. One of the best-loved of all American poets is Henry Wadsworth Longfellow. In his poems he liked to preserve the stories of great events in America's past, as he did in *Hiawatha* and *The Courtship of Miles Standish* — famous poems you have probably read. Some of Longfellow's stories tell of actual happenings, like " Paul Revere's Ride," but others, like *Evangeline,* are imaginary tales.

Evangeline grew out of a story told to Longfellow about the French settlers in Acadia (á·kā′dĭ·á), a district that is now Nova Scotia and New Brunswick. At the beginning of the French and Indian War, after the English had gained control of Acadia from the French, the Acadians were torn from their homes and scattered abroad. To make this event even more dramatic, Longfellow centered his poem on a youth and a girl, Gabriel and Evangeline. The result is a story so real that today, if you visit St. Martinsville in Louisiana, the natives will show you the " Evangeline Oak," where the heroine walked in the moonlight grieving for her lost lover.

The story will seem real to you, too, if you fall into its changing moods. The poem tells a simple tale — you can follow it easily with the help of the prose notes at the beginning of some stanzas — but there is much more to the poem than merely *what* happened and *how* it happened. With the magic of verse, Longfellow builds up a mood that fits each scene he presents. At times the mood is gay and happy, at other times threatening and fearful, at other times sad and thoughtful. You can see that mood in poetry is like any person's mood, and changes from time to time or from place to place.

Notice the descriptions of the people and places in the poem. When the poet describes one of the characters, try to see in your own mind how that character appears, and try to *feel* as he does. Notice too, that the description of a setting affects the story. The Acadian village, for example, is pictured in a way that fits the mood of the story at a certain point. You might think of *Evangeline* (printed here in a shortened version) as a movie while you read. It is a series of pictures of people and places, with appropriate mood music in the background.

PRELUDE

This is the forest primeval. The murmuring pines and the hemlocks,
Bearded with moss, and in garments green, indistinct in the twilight,
Stand like Druids of eld,° with voices sad and prophetic,
Stand like harpers hoar with beards that rest on their bosoms.
Loud from its rocky caverns, the deep-voiced neighboring ocean   5
Speaks, and in accents disconsolate answers the wail of the forest.

This is the forest primeval; but where are the hearts that beneath it
Leaped like the roe,° when he hears in the woodland the voice of the hunts-
    man?
Where is the thatch-roofed village, the home of Acadian farmers —
Men whose lives glided on like rivers that water the woodlands?   10
Waste are those pleasant farms, and the farmers forever departed!
Scattered like dust and leaves, when the mighty blasts of October
Seize them, and whirl them aloft, and sprinkle them far o'er the ocean.
Naught but tradition remains of the beautiful village of Grand Pré.°

Ye who believe in affection that hopes, and endures, and is patient,   15
Ye who believe in the beauty and strength of woman's devotion,
List to the mournful tradition still sung by the pines of the forest;
List to a Tale of Love in Acadie, home of the happy.

3. **Druids** (drōō′ĭdz): Celtic priests in ancient England, whose religious ceremonies took place
in forests. **Of eld** means of old times. 8. **roe** (rō): a deer. 14. **Grand Pré** (gräɴ prā): French for
"great meadow."

PART THE FIRST

In the Acadian land, on the shores of the Basin of Minas,°
Distant, secluded, still, the little village of Grand Pré   20
Lay in the fruitful valley. Vast meadows stretched to the eastward,
Giving the village its name, and pasture to flocks without number.
Dikes, that the hands of the farmers had raised with labor incessant,
Shut out the turbulent tides; but at stated seasons the floodgates
Opened, and welcomed the sea to wander at will o'er the meadows.   25
West and south there were fields of flax, and orchards and cornfields
Spreading afar and unfenced o'er the plain; and away to the northward
Blomidon° rose, and the forests old, and aloft on the mountains
Sea fogs pitched their tents, and mists from the mighty Atlantic
Looked on the happy valley, but ne'er from their station descended.   30

> The people of Grand Pré lived peacefully in the
> custom of their French ancestors.

There, in the midst of its farms, reposed the Acadian village.
Strongly built were the houses, with frames of oak and of hemlock
Such as the peasants of Normandy° built in the reign of the Henries.
Thatched were the roofs, with dormer windows;° and gables projecting
Over the basement below protected and shaded the doorway.   35
There in the tranquil evenings of summer, when brightly the sunset
Lighted the village street, and gilded the vanes on the chimneys,
Matrons and maidens sat in snow-white caps and in kirtles°
Scarlet and blue and green, with distaffs° spinning the golden
Flax for the gossiping looms, whose noisy shuttles within doors   40
Mingled their sound with the whir of the wheels and the songs of the
        maidens.
Solemnly down the street came the parish priest, and the children
Paused in their play to kiss the hand he extended to bless them.
Then came the laborers home from the field, and serenely the sun sank
Down to his rest, and twilight prevailed. Anon from the belfry   45
Softly the Angelus° sounded, and over the roofs of the village
Columns of pale blue smoke, like clouds of incense ascending,
Rose from a hundred hearths, the homes of peace and contentment.

    Somewhat apart from the village, and nearer the Basin of Minas,
Benedict Bellefontaine, the wealthiest farmer of Grand Pré,   50

---

19. **Minas** (mĭ'năs). 28. **Blomidon** (blŏm'ĭ·dŭn): a peak in the distance. 33. **Normandy:** a
province in France. 34. **dormer windows:** windows in little gables built out from the main roof.
38. **kirtles** (kûr't'lz): dresses. 39. **distaffs** (dĭs'tȧfs): instruments for holding flax or wool while
it is being spun to thread. 46. **Angelus** (ăn'jĕ·lŭs): the ringing of church bells for morning,
noon, and evening prayer.

Dwelt on his goodly acres; and with him, directing his household,
Gentle Evangeline lived, his child, and the pride of the village.

> *Fairest in the village was Evangeline, young daughter of the farmer Bellefontaine.*

Stalworth° and stately in form was the man of seventy winters;
Hearty and hale was he, an oak that is covered with snowflakes;
White as the snow were his locks, and his cheeks as brown as the oak leaves.
Fair was she to behold, that maiden of seventeen summers,   56
Black were her eyes as the berry that grows on the thorn by the wayside,
Black, yet how softly they gleamed beneath the brown shade of her tresses!
Sweet was her breath as the breath of kine° that fed in the meadows,
When in the harvest heat she bore to the reapers at noontide   60
Flagons of home-brewed ale, ah! fair in sooth was the maiden.
Fairer was she when, on Sunday morn, while the bell from its turret
Sprinkled with holy sounds the air, as the priest with his hyssop°
Sprinkles the congregation, and scatters blessings upon them,
Down the long street she passed, with her chaplet of beads and her missal,°
Wearing her Norman cap, and her kirtle of blue, and the earrings,   66
Brought in the olden time from France, and since, as an heirloom,
Handed down from mother to child, through long generations.
But a celestial brightness — a more ethereal beauty —
Shone on her face and encircled her form, when, after confession,   70
Homeward serenely she walked with God's benediction upon her.
When she had passed it seemed like the ceasing of exquisite music.

   Firmly builded with rafters of oak, the house of the farmer
Stood on the side of a hill commanding the sea; and a shady
Sycamore grew by the door, with a woodbine wreathing around it.   75
Rudely carved was the porch, with seats beneath; and a footpath
Led through an orchard wide, and disappeared in the meadow.
Farther down, on the slope of the hill, was the well with its moss-grown
Bucket, fastened with iron, and near it a trough for the horses.
Shielding the house from storms, on the north, were the barns, and the
    farmyard.   80
Bursting with hay were the barns, themselves a village. In each one
Far o'er the gable projected a roof of thatch; and a staircase,
Under the sheltering eaves, led up to the odorous cornloft.

   Thus at peace with God and the world, the farmer of Grand Pré
Lived on his sunny farm, and Evangeline governed his household.   85

---

53. **stalworth**: an old way of spelling *stalwart*. 59. **kine**: cattle. 63. **hyssop** (hĭs′ŭp): here, holy water. 65. **missal** (mĭs′ăl): prayer book.

Many a youth, as he knelt in the church and opened his missal,
Fixed his eyes upon her as the saint of his deepest devotion;
Happy was he who might touch her hand or the hem of her garment!
Many a suitor came to her door, by the darkness befriended,
And, as he knocked and waited to hear the sound of her footsteps,   90
Knew not which beat the louder, his heart or the knocker of iron.

> *Since their childhood days Evangeline had favored*
> *Gabriel, the blacksmith's son.*

But, among all who came, young Gabriel only was welcome;
Gabriel Lajeunesse,° the son of Basil° the blacksmith,
Who was a mighty man in the village, and honored of all men.
Basil was Benedict's friend. Their children from earliest childhood   95
Grew up together as brother and sister; and Father Felician,
Priest and pedagogue both in the village, had taught them their letters
Out of the selfsame book, with the hymns of the church and the plain song.°
But when the hymn was sung, and the daily lesson completed,
Swiftly they hurried away to the forge of Basil the blacksmith.   100
There at the door they stood, with wondering eyes to behold him
Take in his leathern lap the hoof of the horse as a plaything,
Nailing the shoe in its place; while near him the tire of the cartwheel
Lay like a fiery snake, coiled around in a circle of cinders.
Oft on autumnal eves when without in the gathering darkness   105
Bursting with light seemed the smithy, through every cranny and crevice,
Warm by the forge within they watched the laboring bellows.
Oft on sledges in winter, as swift as the swoop of the eagle,
Down the hillside bounding, they glided away o'er the meadow.

    Thus passed a few swift years and they no longer were children,   110
He was a valiant youth, and his face, like the face of the morning,
Gladdened the earth with its light, and ripened thought into action.
She was a woman now, with the heart and hopes of a woman.
She, too, would bring to her husband's house delight and abundance,
Filling it full of love and the ruddy faces of children.   115

II

Now had the season returned, when the nights grow colder and longer;
Birds of passage sailed through the leaden air from the icebound,
Desolate northern bays to the shores of tropical islands.
Harvests were gathered in; and wild with the winds of September
Wrestled the trees of the forest, as Jacob of old with the angel.   120

---

93. **Lajeunesse** (là′zhĕ·nĕs). **Basil** (băz′l). 98. **plain song**: a chant sung in church without music.

All the signs foretold a winter long and inclement.°
Bees, with prophetic instinct of want, had hoarded their honey
Till the hives overflowed; and the Indian hunters asserted
Cold would the winter be, for thick was the fur of the foxes.
Such was the advent of autumn. Then followed that beautiful season   125
Called by the pious Acadian peasants the Summer of All-Saints!

> *In the autumn the land yielded its harvest, and
> there was rest for the people.*

Filled was the air with a dreamy and magical light; and the landscape
Lay as if new-created in all the freshness of childhood.
Peace seemed to reign upon earth, and the restless heart of the ocean
Was for a moment consoled. All sounds were in harmony blended.   130
Voices of children at play, the crowing of cocks in the farmyards,
Whir of wings in the drowsy air, and the cooing of pigeons.

Now recommenced the reign of rest and affection and stillness.
Day with its burden and heat had departed, and twilight descending
Brought back the evening star to the sky, and the herds to the homestead.
Lowing of cattle and peals of laughter were heard in the farmyard,   136
Echoed back by the barns. Anon they sank into stillness;
Heavily closed, with a jarring sound, the valves of the barn doors,
Rattled the wooden bars, and all for a season was silent.

Indoors, warm by the wide-mouthed fireplace, idly the farmer   140
Sat in his elbowchair, and watched how the flames and the smoke wreaths
Struggled together like foes in a burning city. Behind him,
Nodding and mocking along the wall, with gestures fantastic,
Darted his own huge shadow, and vanished away into darkness.
Close at her father's side was the gentle Evangeline seated,   145
Spinning flax for the loom, that stood in the corner behind her,
While the monotonous drone of the wheel, like the drone of a bagpipe,
Followed the old man's song, and united the fragments together.

Thus as they sat, there were footsteps heard, and, suddenly lifted,
Sounded the wooden latch, and the door swung back on its hinges.   150
Benedict knew by the hobnailed shoes it was Basil the blacksmith,
And by her beating heart Evangeline knew who was with him.
"Welcome!" the farmer exclaimed as their footsteps paused on the thresh-
    old,
"Welcome, Basil, my friend! Come, take thy place on the settle°
Close by the chimney side, which is always empty without thee;   155

121. inclement (ĭn·klĕm′ĕnt): hard, severe. 154. settle: seat, bench.

Take from the shelf overhead thy pipe and the box of tobacco;
Never so much thyself art thou as when, through the curling
Smoke of the pipe or the forge, thy friendly and jovial face gleams
Round and red as the harvest moon through the mist of the marshes."
Then, with a smile of content, thus answered Basil the blacksmith,   160
Taking with easy air the accustomed seat by the fireside:
" Benedict Bellefontaine, thou hast ever thy jest and thy ballad!
Ever in cheerfulest mood art thou, when others are filled with
Gloomy forebodings of ill, and see only ruin before them.
Happy art thou, as if every day thou hadst picked up a horseshoe."   165

> *Basil warns that English warships threaten the Acadians, but Benedict is not fearful.*

Pausing a moment to take the pipe that Evangeline brought him,
And with a coal from the embers had lighted, he slowly continued —
" Four days now are passed since the English ships at their anchors
Ride in the Gaspereau's° mouth, with their cannon pointed against us.
What their design may be is unknown; but all are commanded   170
On the morrow to meet in the church, where his Majesty's mandate
Will be proclaimed as law in the land. Alas! in the meantime
Many surmises of evil alarm the hearts of the people."
Then made answer the farmer: " Perhaps some friendlier purpose
Brings these ships to our shores. Perhaps the harvests in England   175
By untimely rains or untimelier heat have been blighted,
And from our bursting barns they would feed their cattle and children."
" Not so thinketh the folk in the village," said, warmly, the blacksmith,
Shaking his head, as in doubt; then, heaving a sigh, he continued:
" Louisburg is not forgotten, nor Beau Séjour, nor Port Royal.°   180
Many already have fled to the forest, and lurk on its outskirts,
Waiting with anxious hearts the dubious fate of tomorrow.
Arms have been taken from us, and warlike weapons of all kinds;
Nothing is left but the blacksmith's sledge and the scythe of the mower."

Then with a pleasant smile made answer the jovial farmer: 185
" Safer are we unarmed, in the midst of our flocks and our cornfields,
Safer within these peaceful dikes, besieged by the ocean,
Than our fathers in forts, besieged by the enemy's cannon.
Fear no evil, my friend, and tonight may no shadow of sorrow
Fall on this house and hearth; for this is the night of the contract.   190
Built are the house and the barn. The merry lads of the village

---

169. **Gaspereau** (găs'pě·rō): a river whose mouth made the harbor. 180. **Louisburg, Beau Séjour** (bō sā·zhōōr'), and **Port Royal** were French ports in Canada that had been captured by the British.

Strongly have built them and well; and, breaking the glebe° round about
    them,
Filled the barn with hay, and the house with food for a twelvemonth.
René Leblanc° will be here anon, with his papers and inkhorn.
Shall we not then be glad, and rejoice in the joy of our children? "   195
As apart by the window she stood, with her hand in her lover's,
Blushing Evangeline heard the words that her father had spoken,
And as they died on his lips, the worthy notary° entered.

III

Then up rose from his seat by the fireside Basil the blacksmith,
Knocked from his pipe the ashes, and slowly extended his right hand,   200
" Father Leblanc," he exclaimed, " thou hast heard the talk in the village,
And, perchance, canst tell us some news of these ships and their errand."
Then with modest demeanor made answer the notary public:
" Gossip enough have I heard, in sooth, yet am never the wiser;
And what their errand may be I know not better than others,   205
Yet am I not of those who imagine some evil intention
Brings them here, for we are at peace; and why then molest us? "
" God's name! " shouted the hasty and somewhat irascible blacksmith;
" Must we in all things look for the how, and the why, and the wherefore?
Daily injustice is done, and might is the right of the strongest! "   210
But without heeding his warmth, continued the notary public:
" Man is unjust, but God is just; and finally justice
Triumphs: and well I remember a story, that often consoled me,
When as a captive I lay in the old French fort at Port Royal."

> *The notary points a moral with an old tale of how
> an unjustly accused girl is proved innocent.*

This was the old man's favorite tale, and he loved to repeat it   215
When his neighbors complained that any injustice was done them.
" Once in an ancient city, whose name I no longer remember,
Raised aloft on a column, a brazen statue of Justice
Stood in the public square, upholding the scales in its left hand,
And in its right a sword, as an emblem that justice presided   220
Over the laws of the land, and the hearts and homes of the people.
Even the birds had built their nests in the scales of the balance,
Having no fear of the sword that flashed in the sunshine above them.
But in the course of time the laws of the land were corrupted;
Might took the place of right, and the weak were oppressed, and the mighty

---

192. **glebe** (glēb): sod, turf. 194. **René Leblanc** (rĕn·ā′lĕ·bläṅ′). 198. **notary** (nō′tȧ·rĭ): an officer who certifies deeds and other documents to make them official.

Ruled with an iron rod. Then it chanced in a nobleman's palace   226
That a necklace of pearls was lost, and ere long a suspicion
Fell on an orphan girl who lived as maid in the household.
She, after form of trial condemned to die on the scaffold,
Patiently met her doom at the foot of the statue of Justice.   230
As to her Father in heaven her innocent spirit ascended,
Lo! o'er the city a tempest rose; and the bolts of the thunder
Smote the statue of bronze, and hurled in wrath from its left hand
Down on the pavement below the clattering scales of the balance,
And in the hollow thereof was found the nest of a magpie,   235
Into whose clay-built walls the necklace of pearls was inwoven."
Silenced, but not convinced, when the story was ended, the blacksmith
Stood like a man who fain would speak, but findeth no language;
All his thoughts were congealed into lines on his face, as the vapors
Freeze in fantastic shapes on the windowpanes in the winter.   240

   Then Evangeline lighted the brazen lamp on the table,
Filled, till it overflowed, the pewter tankard with home-brewed
Nut-brown ale, that was famed for its strength in the village of Grand Pré:
While from his pocket the notary drew his papers and inkhorn,
Wrote with a steady hand the date and the age of the parties,   245
Naming the dower of the bride in flocks of sheep and in cattle.
Orderly all things proceeded, and duly and well were completed,
And the great seal of the law was set like a sun on the margin.

> *The names of Evangeline and Gabriel, soon to be*
> *wed, are entered in the notary's record.*

Then from his leathern pouch the farmer threw on the table
Three times the old man's fee in solid pieces of silver;   250
And the notary rising, and blessing the bride and the bridegroom,
Lifted aloft the tankard of ale and drank to their welfare.
Wiping the foam from his lip, he solemnly bowed and departed,
While in silence the others sat and mused by the fireside,
Till Evangeline brought the draught board° out of its corner.   255
Soon was the game begun. In friendly contention the old men
Laughed at each lucky hit, or unsuccessful maneuver,
Laughed when a man was crowned, or a breach was made in the king row.
Meanwhile apart, in the twilight gloom of a window's embrasure,
Sat the lovers, and whispered together, beholding the moon rise   260
Over the pallid sea and the silvery mist of the meadows.
Silently one by one, in the infinite meadows of heaven,
Blossomed the lovely stars, the forget-me-nots of the angels.

       255. draught (dràft) board: checkerboard.

  Thus was the evening passed. Anon the bell from the belfry
Rang out the hour of nine, the village curfew, and straightway   265
Rose the guests and departed; and silence reigned in the household.
Many a farewell word and sweet good-night on the doorstep
Lingered long in Evangeline's heart, and filled it with gladness.

                                    IV

Pleasantly rose next morn the sun on the village of Grand Pré.
Pleasantly gleamed in the soft, sweet air the Basin of Minas,   270
Where the ships, with their wavering shadows, were riding at anchor.
Life had long been astir in the village, and clamorous labor
Knocked with its hundred hands at the golden gates of the morning.
Now from the country around, from the farms and neighboring hamlets,
Came in their holiday dresses, the blithe Acadian peasants;   275
Many a glad good-morrow and jocund laugh from the young folk
Made the bright air brighter, as up from the numerous meadows,
Group after group appeared, and joined, or passed on the highway.
Long ere noon, in the village all sounds of labor were silenced.
Thronged were the streets with people; and noisy groups at the house doors
Sat in the cheerful sun, and rejoiced and gossiped together.   281
Every house was an inn, where all were welcomed and feasted;
For with this simple people, who lived like brothers together,
All things were held in common, and what one had was another's.
Yet under Benedict's roof hospitality seemed more abundant;   285
For Evangeline stood among the guests of her father;
Bright was her face with smiles, and words of welcome and gladness
Fell from her beautiful lips and blessed the cup as she gave it.

  Under the open sky, in the odorous air of the orchard,
Stripped of its golden fruit, was spread the feast of betrothal.   290
There in the shade of the porch were the priest and the notary seated;
There good Benedict sat, and sturdy Basil the blacksmith.
Not far withdrawn from these, by the cider press and the beehives,
Michael the fiddler was placed, with the gayest of hearts and of waistcoats.
Gaily the old man sang to the vibrant sound of his fiddle,   295
And anon with his wooden shoes beat time to the music.
Merrily, merrily whirled the wheels of the dizzying dances
Under the orchard trees and down the path to the meadows;
Old folk and young together, and children mingled among them.
Fairest of all the maids was Evangeline, Benedict's daughter!   300
Noblest of all the youths was Gabriel, son of the blacksmith!

So passed the morning away. And lo! with a summons sonorous
Sounded the bell from its tower, and over the meadows a drum beat.
Thronged ere long was the church with men. Without, in the churchyard,
Waited the women. They stood by the graves and hung on the headstones
Garlands of autumn leaves and evergreens fresh from the forest.   306
Then came the guard from the ships, and marching proudly among them
Entered the sacred portal. With loud and dissonant clangor
Echoed the sound of their brazen drums from ceiling and casement —
Echoed a moment only, and slowly the ponderous portal   310
Closed, and in silence the crowd awaited the will of the soldiers.

> *The English commander proclaims the villagers un-*
> *der arrest, to be exiled from their homes.*

Then uprose their commander, and spake from the steps of the altar,
Holding aloft in his hands, with its seals, the royal commission.
" You are convened this day," he said, " by his Majesty's orders.
Clement and kind has he been; but how have you answered his kindness,
Let your own hearts reply! To my natural make and my temper   316
Painful the task is I do, which to you I know must be grievous.
Yet must I bow and obey, and deliver the will of our monarch;
Namely, that all your lands, and dwellings, and cattle of all kinds,
Forfeited be to the crown;° and that you yourselves from this province   320

320. **crown:** the king.

Be transported to other lands. God grant that you may dwell there
Ever as faithful subjects, a happy and peaceable people!
Prisoners now I declare you: for such is his Majesty's pleasure! "

    As, when the air is serene in the sultry solstice° of summer,
Suddenly gathers a storm, and the deadly sling of the hailstones   325
Beats down the farmer's corn in the fields and shatters his windows,
So on the hearts of the people descended the words of the speaker.
Silent a moment they stood in speechless wonder, and then rose
Louder and ever louder a wail of sorrow and anger,
And, by one impulse moved, they madly rushed to the doorway.   330
Vain was the hope of escape; and cries and fierce imprecations°
Rang through the house of prayer; and high o'er the heads of the others
Rose, with his arms uplifted, the figure of Basil the blacksmith,
As, on a stormy sea, a spar is tossed by the billows.   334
Flushed was his face and distorted with passion; and wildly he shouted:
" Down with the tyrants of England! we never have sworn them allegiance!
Death to these foreign soldiers, who seize on our homes and our harvest! "
More he fain would have said, but the merciless hand of a soldier
Smote him upon the mouth, and dragged him down to the pavement.

> Father Felician rebukes his people for their violence
> in church and prays that they be forgiven.

    In the midst of the strife and tumult of angry contention,   340
Lo, the door of the chancel opened, and Father Felician
Entered, with serious mien, and ascended the steps of the altar.
Raising his reverend hand, with a gesture he awed into silence
All that clamorous throng; and thus he spake to his people:
" What is this that ye do, my children? what madness has seized you?   345
Have you so soon forgotten all lessons of love and forgiveness?
This is the house of the Prince of Peace, and would you profane it
Thus with violent deeds and hearts overflowing with hatred?
Lo! where the crucified Christ from his cross is gazing upon you!
See! in those sorrowful eyes what meekness and holy compassion!   350
Hark! how those lips still repeat the prayer, ' O Father, forgive them! '
Let us repeat that prayer in the hour when the wicked assail us,
Let us repeat it now, ' O Father, forgive them! ' "
Few were his words of rebuke, but deep in the hearts of his people
Sank they, and sobs of contrition° succeeded the passionate outbreak,   355
While they repeated his prayer, and said, " O Father, forgive them! "

324. sultry solstice (sŭl′trĭ sŏl′stĭs) : the very height of summer (the solstice) is hot and sweltering, or sultry. **331. imprecations** (ĭm·prē·kā′shŭnz) : curses that wish evil to others. **355. contrition** (kŏn·trĭsh′ŭn) : sincere repentance.

Meanwhile had spread in the village the tidings of ill, and on all sides
Wandered, wailing, from house to house the women and children.
Long at her father's door Evangeline stood, with her right hand
Shielding her eyes from the level rays of the sun, that, descending,   360
Lighted the village street with mysterious splendor, and roofed each
Peasant's cottage with golden thatch, and emblazoned its windows.
Long within had been spread the snow-white cloth on the table;
There stood the wheaten loaf, and the honey fragrant with wild flowers;
There stood the tankard of ale, and the cheese fresh brought from the dairy;
And, at the head of the board, the great armchair of the farmer.   366
Smoldered the fire on the hearth, on the board was the supper untasted.
Empty and drear was each room, and haunted with phantoms of terror.
Sadly echoed her step on the stair and the floor of her chamber.
In the dead of the night she heard the disconsolate rain fall   370
Loud on the withered leaves of the sycamore tree by the window,
Keenly the lightning flashed; and the voice of the echoing thunder
Told her that God was in heaven, and governed the world he created!
Then she remembered the tale she had heard of the justice of Heaven;
Soothed was her troubled soul and she peacefully slumbered till morning.

v

Four times the sun had arisen and set; and now on the fifth day   376
Cheerily called the cock to the sleeping maids of the farmhouse.
Soon o'er the yellow fields, in silent and mournful procession,
Came from the neighboring hamlets and farms the Acadian women,
Driving in ponderous wains their household goods to the seashore,   380
Pausing and looking back to gaze once more on their dwellings,
Ere they were shut from sight by the winding road and the woodland.
Close at their sides their children ran and urged on the oxen.
While in their little hands they clasped some fragments of playthings.

> A procession of Acadians is led under guard to the
> beach and the waiting English ships.

Thus to the Gaspereau's mouth they hurried and there on the seabeach,
Piled in confusion, lay the household goods of the peasants.   386
All day long between the shore and the ships did the boats ply;
All day long the wains came laboring down from the village.
Late in the afternoon, when the sun was near to his setting,
Echoed far o'er the fields came the roll of drums from the churchyard.   390
Thither the women and children thronged. On a sudden the church doors
Opened, and forth came the guard, and marching in gloomy procession
Followed the long imprisoned, but patient, Acadian farmers.

Even as pilgrims, who journey afar from their homes and their country,
Sing as they go, and in singing forget they are weary and wayworn,   395
So with songs on their lips the Acadian peasants descended
Down from the church to the shore, amid their wives and their daughters.
Foremost the young men came; and raising together their voices,
Sang with tremulous lips a chant of the Catholic missions:
" Sacred heart of the Savior! Oh, inexhaustible fountain!   400
Fill our hearts this day with strength and submission and patience! "
Then the old men, as they marched, and the women that stood by the way-
    side
Joined in the sacred psalm, and the birds in the sunshine above them
Mingled their notes therewith, like voices of spirits departed.

    Halfway down to the shore Evangeline waited in silence,   405
Not overcome with grief, but strong in the hour of affliction —
Calmly and sadly she waited, until the procession approached her,
And she beheld the face of Gabriel pale with emotion.
Tears then filled her eyes, and, eagerly running to meet him,
Clasped she his hands, and laid her head on his shoulder, and whispered —
" Gabriel! be of good cheer! for if we love one another   411
Nothing, in truth, can harm us, whatever mischances may happen! "
Smiling she spake these words; then suddenly paused, for her father
Saw she slowly advancing. Alas! how changed was his aspect!
Gone was the glow from his cheek, and the fire from his eye, and his foot-
    step   415
Heavier seemed with the weight of the heavy heart in his bosom.
But with a smile and a sigh, she clasped his neck and embraced him,
Speaking words of endearment where words of comfort availed not.
Thus to the Gaspereau's mouth moved on that mournful procession.

> *Gabriel and Basil are carried into separate ships,
> leaving Evangeline behind them.*

    There disorder prevailed, and the tumult and stir of embarking;   420
Busily plied the freighted boats; and in the confusion
Wives were torn from their husbands, and mothers, too late, saw their chil-
    dren
Left on the land, extending their arms in wildest entreaties.
So unto separate ships were Basil and Gabriel carried,
While in despair on the shore Evangeline stood with her father.   425
Half the task was not done when the sun went down, and the twilight
Deepened and darkened around; and in haste the refluent° ocean

427. refluent (rĕf′lū·ĕnt): ebbing.

Fled away from the shore, and left the line of the sandbeach
Covered with waifs of the tide, with kelp° and the slippery seaweed.
Farther back in the midst of the household goods and the wagons,   430
Lay encamped for the night the houseless Acadian farmers.
Silence reigned in the streets; from the church no Angelus sounded,
Rose no smoke from the roofs, and gleamed no lights from the windows.

But on the shores meanwhile the evening fires had been kindled,
Built of the driftwood thrown on the sands from wrecks in the tempest. 435
Round them shapes of gloom and sorrowful faces were gathered,
Voices of women were heard, and of men, and the crying of children.
Onward from fire to fire, as from hearth to hearth in his parish,
Wandered the faithful priest, consoling and blessing and cheering.
Thus he approached the place where Evangeline sat with her father,   440
And in the flickering light beheld the face of the old man,
Haggard and hollow and wan, and without either thought or emotion.
Vainly Evangeline strove with words and caresses to cheer him,
Vainly offered him food; yet he moved not, he looked not, he spake not,
But, with a vacant stare, ever gazed at the flickering firelight.   445
"Benedicite!"° murmured the priest, in tones of compassion.
More he fain would have said, but his heart was full, and his accents
Faltered and paused on his lips, as the feet of a child on a threshold,
Hushed by the scene he beholds, and the awful presence of sorrow.
Silently, therefore, he laid his hand on the head of the maiden,   450
Raising his tearful eyes to the silent stars that above them
Moved on their way, unperturbed by the wrongs and sorrows of mortals.
Then sat he down at her side, and they wept together in silence.

> Grand Pré is set on fire, and the last exiles on the
> beach stare in horror at the red sky.

Suddenly rose from the south a light, as in autumn the blood-red
Moon climbs the crystal walls of heaven, and o'er the horizon   455
Titan-like° stretches its hundred hands upon mountain and meadow,
Seizing the rocks and the rivers, and piling huge shadows together.
Broader and ever broader it gleamed on the roofs of the village,
Gleamed on the sky and the sea, and the ships that lay in the roadstead.
Columns of shining smoke uprose, and flashes of flame were   460
Thrust through their folds and withdrawn like the quivering hands of a
    martyr.

429. **kelp**: a kind of large seaweed. 446. *Benedicite!* (bĕn′ĕ·dĭs′ĭ·tē): blessings on you. 456. The
Titans (tī′tănz) were giants in Greek mythology.

Then as the wind seized the gleeds° and the burning thatch, and, uplifting,
Whirled them aloft through the air, at once from a hundred housetops
Started the sheeted smoke with flashes of flame intermingled.
  These things beheld in dismay the crowd on the shore and on shipboard.
Speechless at first they stood, then cried aloud in their anguish,   466
" We shall behold no more our homes in the village of Grand Pré! "

> *With Evangeline and Father Felician at his side,*
> *Benedict dies, and is buried on the shore.*

  Overwhelmed with the sight, yet speechless, the priest and the maiden
Gazed on the scene of terror that reddened and widened before them;
And as they turned at length to speak to their silent companion,   470
Lo! from his seat he had fallen, and stretched abroad on the seashore
Motionless lay his form, from which the soul had departed.
Slowly the priest uplifted the lifeless head, and the maiden
Knelt at her father's side, and wailed aloud in her terror.
Then in a swoon she sank, and lay with her head on his bosom,   475
Through the long night she lay in deep, oblivious slumber;
And when she woke from the trance, she beheld a multitude near her.
Faces of friends she beheld, that were mournfully gazing upon her,
Pallid, with tearful eyes, and looks of saddest compassion.
Still the blaze of the burning village illumined the landscape,   480
Reddened the sky overhead, and beamed on the faces around her,
And like the day of doom it seemed to her wavering senses.
Then a familiar voice she heard, as it said to the people —
" Let us bury him here by the sea. When a happier season
Brings us again to our homes from the unknown land of our exile,   485
Then shall his sacred dust be piously laid in the churchyard."
Such were the words of the priest. And there in haste by the seaside,
Having the glare of the burning village for funeral torches,
But without bell or book, they buried the farmer of Grand Pré.
And as the voice of the priest repeated the service of sorrow,   490
Lo! with a mournful sound, like the voice of a vast congregation,
Solemnly answered the sea, and mingled its roar with the dirges.°
'Twas the returning tide, that afar from the waste of the ocean,
With the first dawn of the day, came heaving and hurrying landward.
Then recommenced once more the stir and noise of embarking;   495
And with the ebb of the tide the ships sailed out of the harbor,
Leaving behind them the dead on the shore, and the village in ruins.

---

462. **gleeds:** burning coals. 492. **dirges** (dûr′jĕz): songs of mourning.

PART THE SECOND

Many a weary year had passed since the burning of Grand Pré,
When on the falling tide the freighted vessels departed,
Bearing a nation, with all its household gods, into exile,   500
Exile without an end, and without an example in story.
Far asunder, on separate coasts, the Acadians landed;
Scattered were they, like flakes of snow, when the wind from the northeast
Strikes aslant through the fogs that darken the Banks of Newfoundland.
Friendless, homeless, hopeless, they wandered from city to city,   505
From the cold lakes of the North to sultry Southern savannahs —
From the bleak shores of the sea to the lands where the Father of Waters°
Seizes the hills in his hands, and drags them down to the ocean.
Friends they sought and homes; and many, despairing, heartbroken,
Asked of the earth but a grave, and no longer a friend nor a fireside.   510

> *Evangeline wanders among the scattered Acadians
> in search of her lover.*

Long among them was seen a maiden who waited and wandered,
Fair was she and young; but, alas! before her extended,
Dreary and vast and silent, the desert of life with its pathway
Marked by the graves of those who had sorrowed and suffered before her.
Sometimes she lingered in towns, till, urged by the fever within her,   515
Urged by a restless longing, the hunger and thirst of the spirit,
She would commence again her endless search and endeavor;
Sometimes in churchyards strayed, and gazed on the crosses and tombstones,
Sat by some nameless grave, and thought that perhaps in its bosom
He was already at rest, and she longed to slumber beside him.   520
Sometimes a rumor, a hearsay, an inarticulate whisper,
Came with its airy hand to point and beckon her forward.
Sometimes she spake with those who had seen her beloved and known him,

507. **Father of Waters:** the Mississippi River.

But it was long ago, in some far-off place or forgotten.
" Gabriel Lajeunesse! " said others; " Oh yes! we have seen him.   525
He was with Basil the blacksmith, and both have gone to the prairies;
Coureurs-des-Bois° are they, and famous hunters and trappers."
" Gabriel Lajeunesse! " said others; " Oh yes! we have seen him.
He is a voyageur° in the lowlands of Louisiana."
Then would they say, " Dear child! why dream and wait for him longer?
Are there not other youths as fair as Gabriel? others   531
Who have hearts as tender and true, and spirits as loyal? "
Then would Evangeline answer, serenely but sadly, " I cannot!
Whither my heart has gone, there follows my hand, and not elsewhere.
For when the heart goes before, like a lamp, and illumines the pathway,
Many things are made clear, that else lie hidden in darkness."   536

II

It was the month of May. Far down the Beautiful River,
Past the Ohio shore and past the mouth of the Wabash,
Into the golden stream of the broad and swift Mississippi,
Floated a cumbrous boat, that was rowed by Acadian boatmen.   540

*A band of Acadians, seeking their kin, float down
the Mississippi to the Louisiana bayous.*

It was a band of exiles; a raft, as it were, from the shipwrecked
Nation, scattered along the coast, now floating together,
Bound by the bonds of a common belief and a common misfortune;
Men and women and children, who, guided by hope or by hearsay,
Sought for their kith and their kin among the few-acred farmers   545
On the Acadian coast, and the prairies of fair Opelousas.°
With them Evangeline went, and her guide, the Father Felician.
Onward o'er sunken sands, through a wilderness somber with forests,
Day after day they glided adown the turbulent river;
Night after night, by their blazing fires encamped on its borders.   550
Level the landscape grew, and along the shores of the river,
Shaded by china trees, in the midst of luxuriant gardens,
Stood the houses of planters, with Negro cabins and dovecots.
They were approaching the region where reigns perpetual summer,
Where through the Golden Coast,° and groves of orange and citron,   555
Sweeps with majestic curve the river away to the eastward.

---

527. **Coureurs-des-Bois** (kōō·rûr′ dä bwä′): French for hunters and trappers. 529. **voyageur** (vwȧ·yȧ·zhûr′): in America, an agent of a fur company who transports supplies to the trappers and furs back to the markets. 546. **Opelousas** (ŏp·ĕ·lōō′sȧs). 555. **Golden Coast:** an old name for Louisiana, because of its citrus fruits.

They, too, swerved from their course; and, entering the Bayou of Plaque-
    mine,°
Soon were lost in a maze of sluggish and devious waters.
Over their heads the towering and tenebrous° boughs of the cypress
Met in a dusky arch, and trailing mosses in mid-air,   560
Waved like banners that hang on the walls of ancient cathedrals.
Deathlike the silence seemed, and unbroken, save by the herons
Home to their roosts in the cedar trees returning at sunset,
Or by the owl, as he greeted the moon with demoniac laughter.

Lovely the moonlight was as it glanced and gleamed on the water,   565
Gleamed on the columns of cypress and cedar sustaining the arches,
Down through whose broken vaults it fell as through chinks in a ruin.
Dreamlike, and indistinct, and strange were all things around them;
And o'er their spirits there came a feeling of wonder and sadness —
Strange forebodings of ill, unseen and that cannot be compassed.   570
But Evangeline's heart was sustained by a vision, that faintly
Floated before her eyes, and beckoned her on through the moonlight.
It was the thought of her brain that assumed the shape of a phantom.
Through those shadowy aisles had Gabriel wandered before her,
And every stroke of the oar now brought him nearer and nearer.   575
Then Evangeline slept; but the boatmen rowed through the midnight,
Silent at times, then singing familiar Canadian boat songs,
Such as they sang of old on their own Acadian rivers,
While through the night were heard the mysterious sounds of the desert,
Far off — indistinct — as of wave or of wind in the forest,   580
Mixed with the whoop of the crane and the roar of the grim alligator.

    Thus ere another moon they emerged from the shades; and before them
Lay, in the golden sun, the lakes of the Atchafalaya,°
Near to whose shores they glided along, invited to slumber.
Soon by the fairest of these their weary oars were suspended.   585
Under the boughs of Wachita° willows, that grew by the margin,

---

557. **Bayou of Plaquemine** (bĭ′o͞o of plăk·mĭn): A bayou is a sluggish creek. 559. **tenebrous**
(tĕn′ē·brŭs): dark, gloomy. 583. **Atchafalaya** (à·chăf′à·lī′à). 586. **Wachita** (wŏsh′ĭ·tô).

Safely their boat was moored; and scattered about on the greensward,
Tired with their midnight toil, the weary travelers slumbered.

Nearer, ever nearer, among the numberless islands,
Darted a light, swift boat, that sped away o'er the water,   590
Urged on its course by the sinewy arms of hunters and trappers.
Northward its prow was turned, to the land of the bison and beaver.
At the helm sat a youth, with countenance thoughtful and careworn.
Dark and neglected locks overshadowed his brow, and a sadness

Somewhat beyond his years on his face was legibly written.   595
Gabriel was it, who, weary with waiting, unhappy and restless,
Sought in the Western wilds oblivion of self and of sorrow.

*Gabriel passes by the boat where Evangeline sleeps
but neither knows the other is near.*

Swiftly they glided along, close under the lee of the island
But by the opposite bank, and behind a screen of palmettos,°
So that they saw not the boat, where it lay concealed in the willows;   600
All undisturbed by the dash of their oars, and unseen, were the sleepers.
Angel of God, was there none to waken the slumbering maiden!
Swiftly they glided away, like the shade of a cloud on the prairie.
After the sound of their oars on the tholes° had died in the distance,
As from a magic trance the sleepers awoke, and the maiden   605
Said with a sigh to the friendly priest, " O Father Felician!
Something says in my heart that near me Gabriel wanders.
Is it a foolish dream, an idle and vague superstition?
Or has an angel passed, and revealed the truth to my spirit? "
Then, with a blush, she added, " Alas for my credulous fancy!   610
Unto ears like thine such words as these have no meaning."
But made answer the reverend man, and he smiled as he answered:
" Daughter, thy words are not idle; nor are they to me without meaning.
Feeling is deep and still; and the word that floats on the surface
Is as the tossing buoy,° that betrays where the anchor is hidden.   615

---

599. **palmettos** (păl·mĕt′ōz): low palms. 604. **tholes:** the metal pins on the side of the boat that
brace the oars for the pull. 615. **buoy** (bōō′ĭ): a floating marker.

Therefore trust to thy heart, and to what the world calls illusions.
Gabriel truly is near thee; for not far away to the southward,
On the banks of the Têche,° are the towns of St. Maur° and St. Martin.
There the long-wandering bride shall be given again to her bridegroom."

    With these words of cheer they arose and continued their journey.   620
Softly the evening came. The sun from the western horizon
Like a magician extended his golden wand o'er the landscape;
Twinkling vapors arose; and sky and water and forest
Seemed all on fire at the touch, and melted and mingled together.
Hanging between two skies, a cloud with edges of silver,   625
Floated the boat, with its dripping oars, on the motionless water.
Filled was Evangeline's heart with inexpressible sweetness.
Then from a neighboring thicket the mockingbird, wildest of singers,
Swinging aloft on a willow spray that hung o'er the water,
Shook from his little throat such floods of delirious music   630
That the whole air and the woods and the waves seemed silent to listen.
With such a prelude as this, and hearts that throbbed with emotion,
Slowly they entered the Têche, where it flows through the green Opelousas,
And, through the amber air, above the crest of the woodland,
Saw the column of smoke that arose from a neighboring dwelling —   635
Sounds of a horn they heard and the distant lowing of cattle.

III

Near to the bank of the river, o'er-shadowed by oaks, from whose branches
Garlands of Spanish moss and of mystic mistletoe flaunted,
Stood, secluded and still, the house of the herdsman. A garden
Girded it round about with a belt of luxuriant blossoms,   640
Filling the air with fragrance. The house itself was of timbers
Hewn from the cypress trees, and carefully fitted together.
Large and low was the roof; and on slender columns supported,
Rose-wreathed, vine-encircled, a broad and spacious veranda,
Haunt of the hummingbird and the bee, extended around it.   645
Just where the woodlands met the flowery surf of the prairie,
Mounted upon his horse, with Spanish saddle and stirrups,
Sat a herdsman, arrayed in gaiters and doublet° of deerskin.
Broad and brown was the face that from under the Spanish sombrero°
Gazed on the peaceful scene, with the lordly look of its master.   650
Round about him were numberless herds of kine, that were grazing
Quietly in the meadows, and breathing the vapory freshness

---

    618. **Têche** (tĕsh): another bayou. **St. Maur** (săɴ môr). 648. **gaiters** (gā′tĕrz): leggings; **doub-**
let: a close-fitting jacket. 649. **sombrero** (sŏm·brâr′ō): a wide-brimmed hat.

That uprose from the river, and spread itself over the landscape.
Then, as the herdsman turned to the house, through the gate of the garden
Saw he the forms of the priest and the maiden advancing to meet him.   655
Suddenly down from his horse he sprang in amazement, and forward
Rushed with extended arms and exclamations of wonder;
When they beheld his face, they recognized Basil the blacksmith.

> *Evangeline finds Basil and is grieved to be told that*
> *Gabriel has gone on a long journey.*

Hearty his welcome was, as he led his guests to the garden.
There in an arbor of roses with endless question and answer   660
Gave they vent to their hearts, and renewed their friendly embraces,
Laughing and weeping by turns, or sitting silent and thoughtful.
Thoughtful, for Gabriel came not; and now dark doubts and misgivings
Stole o'er the maiden's heart; and Basil, somewhat embarrassed,
Broke the silence and said, " If you came by the Atchafalaya,   665
How have you nowhere encountered my Gabriel's boat on the bayous? "
Over Evangeline's face at the words of Basil a shade passed.
Tears came into her eyes, and she said with a tremulous accent,
" Gone? is Gabriel gone? " and, concealing her face on his shoulder,
All her o'erburdened heart gave way, and she wept and lamented.   670
Then the good Basil said — and his voice grew blithe as he said it —
" Be of good cheer, my child; it is only today he departed.
Foolish boy! he has left me alone with my herds and my horses.
Moody and restless grown, and tried and troubled, his spirit
Could no longer endure the calm of this quiet existence.   675
Thinking ever of thee, uncertain and sorrowful ever,
Ever silent, or speaking only of thee and his troubles,
He at length had become so tedious to men and to maidens,
Tedious even to me, that at length I bethought me, and sent him
Unto the town of Adayes° to trade for mules with the Spaniards.   680
Thence he will follow the Indian trails to the Ozark Mountains,
Hunting for furs in the forests, on rivers trapping the beaver.
Therefore be of good cheer; we will follow the fugitive lover;
He is not far on his way, and the fates and the streams are against him.
Up and away tomorrow, and through the red dew of the morning   685
We will follow him fast, and bring him back to his prison."

   Thus they ascended the steps, and crossing the breezy veranda,
Entered the hall of the house, where already the supper of Basil
Awaited his late return; and they rested and feasted together.

680. **Adayes** (à·dī′ĕz).

Over the joyous feast the sudden darkness descended.   690
All was silent without, and, illuming the landscape with silver,
Fair rose the dewy moon and the myriad stars; but within doors,
Brighter than these, shone the faces of friends in the glimmering lamplight.
Then from his station aloft, at the head of the table, the herdsman
Poured forth his heart and his wine together in endless profusion.   695

> *Basil, now a Louisiana herdsman, welcomes his*
> *countrymen to an abundant land.*

Lighting his pipe, that was filled with sweet Natchitoches° tobacco,
Thus he spake to his guests, who listened, and smiled as they listened:
" Welcome once more, my friends, who long have been friendless and home-
    less,
Welcome once more to a home, that is better perchance than the old one!
Here no hungry winter congeals our blood like the rivers;   700
Here no stony ground provokes the wrath of the farmer.
Smoothly the plowshare runs through the soil, as a keel through the water.
All the year round the orange groves are in blossom; and grass grows
More in a single night than a whole Canadian summer.
Here, too, numberless herds run wild and unclaimed in the prairies: 705
Here, too, lands may be had for the asking, and forests of timber
With a few blows of the ax are hewn and framed into houses.
After your houses are built and your fields are yellow with harvests,
No King George of England shall drive you away from your homesteads,
Burning your dwellings and barns, and stealing your farms and your cattle."
Speaking these words, he blew a wrathful cloud from his nostrils,   711
While his huge brown hand came thundering down on the table,
So that the guests all started; and Father Felician, astounded,
Suddenly paused, with a pinch of snuff halfway to his nostrils.
Then there were voices heard at the door, and footsteps approaching   715
Sounded upon the stairs and the floor of the breezy veranda.
It was the neighboring Creoles° and small Acadian planters,
Who had been summoned all to the house of Basil the herdsman.
Merry the meeting was of ancient comrades and neighbors:
Friend clasped friend in his arms; and they who before were as strangers,
Meeting in exile, became straightway as friends to each other,   721
Drawn by the gentle bond of common country together.

    Meanwhile, apart at the head of the hall, the priest and the herdsman
Sat, conversing together of past and present and future;

---

696. **Natchitoches** (năk′ĭ·tŏsh): an early French settlement, for which the tobacco is named.
717. **Creoles** (krē′ōlz): people descended from French or Spanish settlers in the Gulf states.

While Evangeline stood like one entranced, for within her   725
Olden memories rose, and loud in the midst of the music
Heard she the sound of the sea, and an irrepressible sadness
Came o'er her heart, and unseen she stole forth into the garden.
Passed she along the path to the edge of the measureless prairie.
Silent it lay, with a silvery haze upon it, and fireflies   730
Gleaming and floating away in mingled and infinite numbers.
And the soul of the maiden, between the stars and the fireflies,
Wandered alone, and she cried, " O Gabriel! O my beloved!
Art thou so near unto me, and yet I cannot behold thee?
Art thou so near unto me, and yet thy voice does not reach me?   735
Ah! how often thy feet have trod this path to the prairie:
Ah, how often thine eyes have looked on the woodlands around me!
Ah! how often beneath this oak, returning from labor,
Thou hast laid down to rest, and to dream of me in thy slumbers!
When shall these eyes behold, these arms be folded about thee! "   740
Loud and sudden and near the note of a whippoorwill sounded
Like a flute in the woods: and anon, through the neighboring thickets,
Farther and farther away it floated and dropped into silence.
" Patience! " whispered the oaks from oracular° caverns of darkness:
And, from the moonlit meadow, a sigh responded " Tomorrow! "   745

> *Evangeline departs with Basil to follow the course*
> *of Gabriel and to overtake him at last.*

   Bright rose the sun next day; and all the flowers in the garden
Bathed his shining feet with their tears, and anointed his tresses
With the delicious balm that they bore in their vases of crystal.
" Farewell! " said the priest, as he stood at the shadowy threshold;
" See that you bring us the Prodigal Son from his fasting and famine,   750
And, too, the Foolish Virgin who slept when the bridegroom was coming."
" Farewell! " answered the maiden, and, smiling, with Basil descended
Down to the river's brink, where the boatmen already were waiting.
Thus beginning their journey with morning, and sunshine, and gladness,
Swiftly they followed the flight of him who was speeding before them,   755
Blown by the blast of fate like a dead leaf over the desert.
Not that day, nor the next, nor yet the day that succeeded,
Found they trace of his course, in lake or forest or river,
Nor, after many days, had they found him; but vague and uncertain
Rumors alone were their guides through a wild and desolate country;   760
Till, at the little inn of the Spanish town of Adayes,
Weary and worn, they alighted, and learned from the garrulous landlord,

---

744. oracular (ŏ·răk′ū·lēr): In ancient times an *oracle* was supposed to be able to foretell the
future.

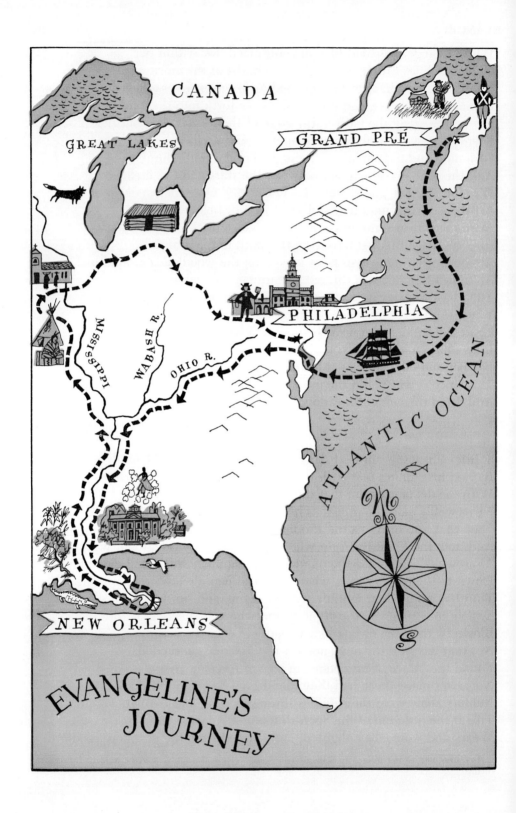

That on the day before, with horses and guides and companions,
Gabriel left the village, and took the road of the prairies.

IV

Far in the West there lies a desert land, where the mountains   765
Lift, through perpetual snows, their lofty and luminous summits.
Into this wonderful land, at the base of the Ozark Mountains,
Gabriel far had entered, with hunters and trappers behind him.
Day after day, with their Indian guides, the maiden and Basil
Followed his flying steps, and thought each day to o'ertake him.   770
Sometimes they saw, or thought they saw, the smoke of his campfire
Rise in the morning air from the distant plain; but at nightfall,
When they had reached the place, they found only embers and ashes.

    Once, as they sat by their evening fire, there silently entered
Into the little camp an Indian woman, whose features   775
Wore deep traces of sorrow, and patience as great as her sorrow.
She was a Shawnee° woman returning home to her people,
From the far-off hunting grounds of the cruel Comanches,°
Where her Canadian husband, a Coureur-des-Bois, had been murdered.
Touched were their hearts at her story, and warmest and friendliest welcome
Gave they, with words of cheer, and she sat and feasted among them   781
On the buffalo meat and the venison cooked on the embers.
But when her meal was done, and Basil and all his companions,
Worn with the long day's march and the chase of the deer and the bison,°
Stretched themselves on the ground, and slept where the quivering firelight
Flashed on their swarthy cheeks, and their forms wrapped up in their
      blankets,   786
Then at the door of Evangeline's tent she sat and repeated
Slowly, with soft, low voice, and the charm of her Indian accent,
All the tale of her love, with its pleasure, and pains, and reverses.

| *A Shawnee woman tells a tale of a lost maiden that*
| *fills Evangeline with fear.*

Told she the tale of the fair Lillinau,° who was wooed by a phantom,   790
That, through the pines o'er her father's lodge, in the hush of the twilight,
Breathed like the evening wind, and whispered love to the maiden,
Till she followed his green and waving plume through the forest,
And never more returned, nor was seen again by her people.
Silent with wonder and strange surprise, Evangeline listened   795

---

777. **Shawnee** (shô′nē): one of the more highly civilized tribes of Indians, who had been pushed
westward from the Atlantic coast. 778. **Comanches** (kō·măn′chēz): a tribe of Plains Indians.
784. **bison** (bī′s'n): buffalo. 790. **Lillinau** (lĭl′ĭ·nô).

To the soft flow of her magical words, till the region around her
Seemed like enchanted ground, and her swarthy guest the enchantress.
Slowly over the tops of the Ozark Mountains the moon rose,
Lighting the little tent, and with a mysterious splendor
Touching the somber leaves, and embracing and filling the woodland.   800
With a delicious sound the brook rushed by, and the branches
Swayed and sighed overhead in scarcely audible whispers.
Filled with the thoughts of love was Evangeline's heart, but a secret,
Subtle sense crept in of pain and indefinite terror,
As the cold poisonous snake creeps into the nest of the swallow.   805
It was no earthly fear. A breath from the region of spirits
Seemed to float in the air of night; and she felt for a moment
That, like the Indian maid, she, too, was pursuing a phantom.
With this thought she slept, and the fear and the phantom had vanished.

   Early upon the morrow the march was resumed; and the Shawnee   810
Said, as they journeyed along, " On the western slope of these mountains
Dwells in his little village the Black Robe chief of the Mission.
Much he teaches the people, and tells them of Mary and Jesus;
Loud laugh their hearts with joy, and weep with pain, as they hear him."
Then with a sudden and secret emotion, Evangeline answered,   815
" Let us go to the Mission, for there good tidings await us! "
Thither they turned their steeds; and behind a spur of the mountains,
Just as the sun went down, they heard a murmur of voices,
And in a meadow green and broad, by the bank of a river,
Saw the tents of the Christians, the tents of the Jesuit Mission.   820
Under a towering oak, that stood in the midst of the village,
Knelt the Black Robe chief with his children. A crucifix fastened
High on the trunk of the tree, and overshadowed by grapevines,
Looked with its agonized face on the multitude kneeling beneath it.
Silent, with heads uncovered, the travelers, nearer approaching,   825
Knelt on the swarded floor, and joined in the evening devotions.
But when the service was done, and the benediction had fallen
Forth from the hands of the priest, like seed from the hands of the sower,
Slowly the reverend man advanced to the strangers, and bade them
Welcome: and when they replied, he smiled with benignant expression,   830
Hearing the homelike sounds of his mother tongue in the forest,
And, with words of kindness, conducted them into his wigwam.

> *A Jesuit priest tells of Gabriel's travels, and Evange-*
> *line stays at the mission to await his return.*

There upon mats and skins they reposed, and on cakes of the maize ear
Feasted, and slaked their thirst from the water-gourd of the teacher.

Soon was their story told; and the priest with solemnity answered: 835
"Not six suns have risen and set since Gabriel, seated
On this mat by my side, where now the maiden reposes,
Told me this same sad tale; then arose and continued his journey!"
Soft was the voice of the priest, and he spake with an accent of kindness;
But on Evangeline's heart fell his words as in winter the snowflakes   840
Fall into some lone nest from which the birds have departed.
"Far to the north he has gone," continued the priest; "but in autumn,
When the chase is done, will return again to the Mission."
Then Evangeline said, and her voice was meek and submissive,
"Let me remain with thee, for my soul is sad and afflicted."   845
So seemed it wise and well unto all; and betimes on the morrow,
Mounting his Mexican steed, with his Indian guides and companions,
Homeward Basil returned, and Evangeline stayed at the Mission.

Slowly, slowly, slowly the days succeeded each other —   849
Days and weeks and months; and the fields of maize that were springing
Green from the ground when a stranger she came, now waving above her,
Lifted their slender shafts, with leaves interlacing and, forming
Cloisters for mendicant crows and granaries pillaged by squirrels.
Then in the golden weather the maize was husked, and the maidens
Blushed at each blood-red ear, for that betokened a lover,   855
But at the crooked laughed, and called it a thief in the cornfield.
Even the blood-red ear to Evangeline brought not her lover.
"Patience!" the priest would say; "have faith and thy prayer will be an-
    swered!"

| *Long after, Evangeline journeys to the Great Lakes and finds, once again, that her lover has departed.*

So came the autumn, and passed, and the winter — yet Gabriel came not;
Blossomed the opening spring, and the notes of the robin and bluebird   860
Sounded sweet upon wold° and in wood, yet Gabriel came not.
But on the breath of the summer winds a rumor was wafted
Sweeter than song of bird, or hue or odor of blossom.
Far to the north and east, it said, in the Michigan forests,
Gabriel had his lodge by the banks of the Saginaw River,   865
And, with returning guides, that sought the lakes of St. Lawrence,
Saying a sad farewell, Evangeline went from the Mission.
When over weary ways, by long and perilous marches,
She had attained at length the depths of the Michigan forests,
Found she the hunter's lodge deserted and fallen to ruin!   870

861. **wold** (wōld): a plain without woods.

Thus did the long sad years glide on, and in seasons and places
Divers and distant far was seen the wandering maiden —
Now in the Tents of Grace of the meek Moravian Missions,
Now in the noisy camps and the battlefields of the army,
Now in secluded hamlets, in towns and populous cities.   875
Like a phantom she came, and passed away unremembered.
Fair was she and young, when in hope began the long journey;
Faded was she and old, when in disappointment it ended.
Each succeeding year stole something away from her beauty,
Leaving behind it, broader and deeper, the gloom and the shadow.   880
Then there appeared and spread faint streaks of gray o'er the forehead,
Dawn of another life, that broke o'er her earthly horizon,
As in the eastern sky the first faint streaks of the morning.

v

In that delightful land which is washed by the Delaware's waters,
Guarding in sylvan shades the name of Penn the apostle,   885
Stands on the banks of its beautiful stream the city he founded.°
There from the troubled sea had Evangeline landed, an exile,
Finding among the children of Penn a home and a country.
There old René Leblanc had died; and when he departed,
Saw at his side only one of all his hundred descendants.   890
Something at least there was in the friendly streets of the city,
Something that spake to her heart, and made her no longer a stranger;
And her ears were pleased with the Thee and Thou of the Quakers,
For it recalled the past, the old Acadian country,
Where all men were equal, and all were brothers and sisters.   895
So, when the fruitless search, the disappointed endeavor,
Ended, to recommence no more upon earth, uncomplaining,
Thither, as leaves to the light, were turned her thoughts and her footsteps.

> Her long search at an end, Evangeline aids the sick
> and poor as a Sister of Mercy.

Gabriel was not forgotten. Within her heart was his image,
Clothed in the beauty of love and youth, as last she beheld him,   900
Only more beautiful made by his deathlike silence and absence,
Into her thoughts of him time entered not, for it was not.
He had become to her heart as one who is dead and not absent;
Patience and abnegation° of self, and devotion to others,
This was the lesson a life of trial and sorrow had taught her.   905
Other hope had she none, nor wish in life, but to follow

886. **Penn the apostle** was William Penn, founder of Philadelphia. 904. **abnegation** (ăb'nĕ·gā'-shŭn): self-denial.

Meekly, with reverent steps, the sacred feet of her Savior.
Thus many years she lived as a Sister of Mercy,° frequenting
Lonely and wretched roofs in the crowded lanes of the city,
Where distress and want concealed themselves from the sunlight,   910
Where disease and sorrow in garrets languished neglected.
Night after night when the world was asleep, as the watchman repeated
Loud, through the gusty streets, that all was well in the city,
High at some lonely window he saw the light of her taper.
Day after day, in the gray of the dawn, as slow through the suburbs   915
Plodded the German farmer, with flowers and fruits for the market,
Met he that meek, pale face, returning home from its watchings.

Then it came to pass that a pestilence fell on the city;
Wealth had no power to bribe, nor beauty to charm the oppressor;
But all perished alike beneath the scourge of his anger —   920
Only, alas! the poor, who had neither friends nor attendants,
Crept away to die in the almshouse, home of the homeless.
Thither, by night and by day, came the Sister of Mercy. The dying
Looked up into her face, and thought, indeed, to behold there
Gleams of celestial light encircle her forehead with splendor,   925
Such as the artist paints o'er the brows of saints and apostles.
Unto their eyes it seemed the lamps of the city celestial,
Into whose shining gates erelong their spirits would enter.

Thus on a Sabbath morn, through the streets, deserted and silent,
Wending her quiet way, she entered the door of the almshouse.   930
Sweet on the summer air was the odor of flowers in the garden;

908. **Sister of Mercy:** one of an order of nuns who devote their lives to helping those in distress.

And she paused on her way to gather the fairest among them,
That the dying once more might rejoice in their fragrance and beauty.
Then, as she mounted the stairs to the corridors, cooled by the east wind,
Distant and soft on her ear fell the chimes from the belfry of Christ Church,
Soft as descending wings fell the calm of the hour on her spirit;   936
Something within her said, " At length thy trials are ended ";
And, with light in her looks, she entered the chambers of sickness.
Noiselessly moved about the assiduous, careful attendants,
Moistening the feverish lip and the aching brow, and in silence   940
Closing the sightless eyes of the dead, and concealing their faces,
Where on their pallets they lay, like drifts of snow by the roadside.
Many a languid head, upraised as Evangeline entered,
Turned on its pillow of pain to gaze while she passed, for her presence
Fell on their hearts like a ray of the sun on the walls of a prison.   945
And as she looked around, she saw how Death, the consoler,
Laying his hand upon many a heart had healed it forever.
Many familiar forms had disappeared in the nighttime;
Vacant their places were, or filled already by strangers.

  Suddenly, as if arrested by fear or a feeling of wonder,   950
Still she stood, with her colorless lips apart, while a shudder
Ran through her frame, and, forgotten, the flowerets dropped from her
    fingers
And from her eyes and cheeks the light and bloom of the morning.
Then there escaped from her lips a cry of such terrible anguish,
That the dying heard it, and started up from their pillows.   955
On the pallet before her was stretched the form of an old man.
Long, and thin, and gray were the locks that shaded his temples;
But, as he lay in the morning light, his face for a moment
Seemed to assume once more the forms of its earlier manhood;
As are wont to be changed the faces of those who are dying.   960
Hot and red on his lips still burned the flush of the fever,
Motionless, senseless, dying, he lay, and his spirit exhausted
Seemed to be sinking down through infinite depths in the darkness,
Darkness of slumber and death, forever sinking and sinking.
Then through those realms of shade, in multiplied reverberations,°   965
Heard he that cry of pain, and through the hush that succeeded
Whispered a gentle voice, in accents tender and saintlike,
" Gabriel! O my beloved! " and died away into silence.
Then he beheld, in a dream, once more the home of his childhood;

---

965. **reverberations:** (rĕ·vûr′bĕr·ā′shŭnz) : long, rolling echoes.

Green Acadian meadows, with sylvan rivers among them,   970
Village, and mountain, and woodlands; and, walking under their shadow,
As in the days of her youth, Evangeline rose in his vision.
Tears came into his eyes; and as slowly he lifted his eyelids,
Vanished the vision away, but Evangeline knelt by his bedside.
Vainly he strove to whisper her name, for the accents unuttered   975
Died on his lips, and their motion revealed what his tongue would have
    spoken.
Vainly he strove to rise; and Evangeline kneeling beside him,
Kissed his dying lips, and laid his head on her bosom.
Sweet was the light of his eyes; but it suddenly sank into darkness,
As when a lamp is blown out by a gust of wind at a casement.   980

   All was ended now, the hope, and the fear, and the sorrow,
All the aching of heart, the restless unsatisfied longing,
All the dull, deep pain, and constant anguish of patience!
And as she pressed once more the lifeless head to her bosom,
Meekly she bowed her own, and murmured, " Father, I thank thee! "   985

   Still stands the forest primeval; but far away from its shadow,
Side by side, in their nameless graves, the lovers are sleeping.
Under the humble walls of a little Catholic churchyard,
In the heart of the city, they lie, unknown and unnoticed.
Daily the tides of life go ebbing and flowing beside them.   990
Thousands of throbbing hearts, where theirs are at rest and forever,
Thousands of aching brains, where theirs no longer are busy;
Thousands of toiling hands, where theirs have ceased from their labors,
Thousands of weary feet, where theirs have completed their journey!

   Still stands the forest primeval; but under the shade of its branches 995
Dwells another race, with other customs and language
Only along the shore of the mournful and misty Atlantic
Linger a few Acadian peasants, whose fathers from exile
Wandered back to their native land to die in its bosom.
In the fisherman's cot° the wheel and the loom are still busy;   1000
Maidens still wear their Norman caps and their kirtles of homespun,
And by the evening fire repeat Evangeline's story,
While from its rocky caverns the deep-voiced, neighboring ocean
Speaks, and in accents disconsolate answers the wail of the forest.

1000. **cot:** cottage.

The Long Search

PART THE FIRST

1. Why was Evangeline's and Gabriel's love so happy? What would their life have been like had the English not uprooted the Acadians?

2. The English ships came a short time before Evangeline and Gabriel were to be married. Does this fact make the story seem more tragic? Why?

3. What is the first sign of threatening danger in the story? Why do you suppose Longfellow included the notary's tale in the middle of the poem?

4. Why do you think the English destroyed the village and scattered the people?

5. How were Evangeline and Gabriel separated? What caused the death of Benedict?

6. Would the ending of Part the First have seemed so sad if the story had *begun* with the meeting in the church? Why?

PART THE SECOND

1. What route did Evangeline and Father Felician follow in going to Louisiana? Look at the pictorial map on page 470.

2. How near did Evangeline come to meeting Gabriel in Louisiana? Where had Gabriel gone?

3. How do you know that Gabriel finally devoted his life to searching for Evangeline? What did the Jesuit priest at the mission tell her (p. 473)?

4. How many years would you guess passed before Evangeline gave up her search?

5. Where did Evangeline spend the last years of her life? What work did she undertake?

6. How did Evangeline and Gabriel finally meet? Would you like the story better if Gabriel had lived? Discuss your feeling about this with others in the class who disagree.

THE WHOLE POEM

1. Look at the list of favorite subjects for poetry in the Roundup on page 480.

How many of them do you find in *Evangeline?* How does this explain in part why Evangeline is an old favorite?

2. During World War II, in Europe, many whole villages were moved away as the Acadians were. Could such a story as *Evangeline* have happened to the people of those villages, or would the same events be "impossible" now? Can you think of ways in which such a story might come about in the United States today? What things might change the story?

3. The dates of various events in this poem are not important to your understanding and enjoying it, but you should be able to apply some of your study of American history to the poem. Here are the chief dates: 1713 — Acadia passed from French to English rule; 1755 — Acadians exiled from their homes; 1754–1763 — French and Indian War (between the French and the English). How does the first event explain the friction between the Acadians and English? What connection do you see between the second and third events? After 1763, which nation was in possession of all of Canada? What evidence is there *today* of French settlement in Canada?

Capturing the Mood of a Verse Story

1. In the Prelude what is the mood or feeling that the poet tries to create? Why are phrases like "sad and prophetic" and "wail of the forest" effective, considering what the Prelude tells us about the Acadians?

2. What sort of feeling do you get from the opening description of Grand Pré and Evangeline's home and neighbors? Point out some of the details on pages 448–49 that help build up this feeling.

3. Reread the description on pages 450–51, lines 116–39. What time of year is the "Summer of All-Saints"? What do we usually call this time of year?

4. Compare the attitude of Basil with that of Benedict as they discuss the English ships. How do Benedict's statements

on page 452, lines 174–77 and 186–90, build up a feeling of safety?

5. Contrast the mood of the two scenes on pages 455 and 457, before and after the proclamation of the English commander. How did the people feel in these two scenes?

6. On page 464, does the description of the swamps match Evangeline's feelings? How?

7. Compare the feelings of the rest of the company at Basil's home with Evangeline's feeling. Why did she go out into the garden?

8. Why did the story told by the Shawnee woman impress Evangeline so deeply? Find the lines that seem to point toward a tragic ending.

Words Recall Old Stories

In the Middle Ages, rulers who feared that their subjects were plotting against them made a law that people must put out their fires early in the evening. That would keep people from gathering to plot rebellion. The French words for "cover up the fire," *couvre feu,* were shortened to *curfew* (kûr′fū). In those days before matches, fires were covered with ashes at night so that coals would be kept to start another fire in the morning. By Evangeline's time, a curfew was only a signal for bedtime. Some American towns still have curfews, a time for all people to be at home and off the streets. No one cares whether the fires are covered, but the old word lives on to remind us of long-ago days.

Roundup

Favorite Subjects of Poetry

Any collection of well-loved poems will probably have examples of all the favorite subjects of poets — love, death, nature, memories, home, heroes, patriotism. Name one poem from this group that is about each of these subjects. What nature poems do you remember best from the group in the Outdoors section, pages 81–89? Many of them are old favorites, too.

Favorites for Special Reasons

Think over the short poems and decide which one you would choose for each of these:

the best rhythm
the saddest mood
the happiest mood
the most musical sound
the clearest images (sights, sounds, feelings)
the most impressive idea
the best all-round poem

Take a poll and see which ones win the honors for the whole class.

Post a Note on Your Favorite Book

What is the very best book you ever read, the one you enjoyed most and remember most happily? Make a note about it on a card to post on your class bulletin board, where it can help your classmates to choose their reading. Give a brief description telling what the book is about (but *not* how it ends), and tell why it is your favorite.

Your Bookshelf

Collections of Poetry

All the Best Dog Poems, collected by Edwin Burtis (Crowell, 1946)

Bridled with Rainbows, collected by Sara and John E. Brewton (Macmillan, 1949)

Cowboy Jamboree: Western Songs and Lore, by Harold Felton (Knopf, 1951) Music with the songs.

I Hear America Singing, an Anthology of Folk Poetry, compiled by Ruth A. Barnes (Winston, 1937)

An Inheritance of Poetry, collected and arranged by Gladys L. Adshead and Annis Duff (Houghton Mifflin, 1948)

Magic Casements, compiled by George S. Carhart and Paul A. McGhee (Macmillan, 1926)

The Magic Circle, edited by Louis Untermeyer (Harcourt, Brace, 1952)

100 Story Poems, compiled by Elinor Parker (Crowell, 1951)

The Pocket Book of American Poems (Pocket Books, No. 529, 1948)

The Pocket Book of Story Poems, edited by Louis Untermeyer (Pocket Books, No. 342, 1945)

The Pocket Book of Verse, edited by M. E. Speare (Pocket Books, No. 62, 1940)

The Poet's Craft, edited by Helen F. Daringer and Anne Thaxter Eaton (World Book, 1935) Arranged to help you understand the varied charms of poetry and how they are achieved.

Rainbow in the Sky, collected by Louis Untermeyer (Harcourt, Brace, 1935)

Stars to Steer By, collected by Louis Untermeyer (Harcourt, Brace, 1941)

Stories in Verse, collected by Max T. Hohn (Odyssey, 1943)

This Singing World, collected by Louis Untermeyer (Harcourt, Brace, 1923)

Story Poems

" Annabel Lee," by Edgar Allan Poe

" The Ballad of East and West," by Rudyard Kipling

" The Courtin'," by James Russell Lowell

" The Glove and the Lions," by Leigh Hunt

" Gunga Din," by Rudyard Kipling

" The Highwayman," by Alfred Noyes

" The Inchcape Rock," by Robert Southey

" Kit Carson's Ride," by Joaquin Miller

" Maud Muller," by John Greenleaf Whittier

" Pershing at the Front," by Arthur Guiterman

" The Revenge," by Alfred, Lord Tennyson

" Spanish Waters," by John Masefield

Poems of Thought and Feeling

" Afternoon on a Hill," by Edna St. Vincent Millay

" Break, Break, Break," by Alfred, Lord Tennyson

" The Concord Hymn," by Ralph Waldo Emerson

" The Day Is Done," by Henry Wadsworth Longfellow

" Grass," by Carl Sandburg

" I Hear America Singing," by Walt Whitman

" I'll Tell You How the Sun Rose," by Emily Dickinson

" The Sea-Gypsy," by Robert Hovey

" Song " from " Pippa Passes," by Robert Browning

" A Time to Talk," by Robert Frost

" Travel," by Edna St. Vincent Millay

" A Vagabond Song," by Bliss Carman

" When Icicles Hang by the Wall," by William Shakespeare

Author Profiles

ROBERT BENCHLEY (1889–1945). It would be hard to find a writer or actor who has provided more gaiety than Robert Benchley. His books and short films have accounted for many a happy hour. Mr. Benchley, born in Worcester, Massachusetts, and educated at Harvard, had much experience in varied journalistic fields, having been associated with the New York *Tribune, Vanity Fair,* the New York *World, Life,* and *The New Yorker.* His death in 1945 brought a sense of loss to his large audience of readers and movie-goers.

ROBERT BROWNING (1812–1889), one of the greatest English poets, had an unusually happy life. His wealthy parents approved and helped his ambition to write poetry. After a romantic courtship, he eloped with Elizabeth Barrett, herself a popular poet. He enjoyed great fame during his lifetime. Many of his poems are good action tales.

WILLIAM CULLEN BRYANT (1794–1878) was the first American poet of major importance. He was born in a tiny village in Massachusetts, of Puritan stock. Before he was twenty, he wrote his most famous poem, "Thanatopsis." Trained as a lawyer, Bryant later became a newspaperman in New York. For nearly half a century he remained one of the leading figures in American literature and journalism. His poetry is characterized by a love of nature and by religious feeling.

ROBERT BURNS (1759–1796) was born in Ayrshire, Scotland, and was educated by his father. He worked at farming with his brother, and began to write. When he was twenty-seven he published a collection of his poems and became famous. For a time he lived in Edinburgh, where he was very popular; later he married and settled on a small farm.

J. FRANK DOBIE (1888–) became a university professor and folklore collector, after a happy outdoor boyhood in the ranch country in Texas. His time in the classroom was sandwiched in between trips around the ranch and mining country gathering tales of early days, which he has put into the following interesting books: *A Vaquero of the Brush Country, Coronado's Children, The Longhorns,* and *The Mustangs.*

WILLIAM O. DOUGLAS (1898–) grew up in the Northwest. As a child, he had infantile paralysis, but he recovered so completely that he has been able to lead an active life ever since, combining mountain-climbing, riding, and traveling with his law career. He was appointed to the United States Supreme Court in 1939 and has served on it ever since. He has written a book about his experiences in mountain-climbing, *Of Men and Mountains.*

ROBERT FROST (1875–) is the poet of New England, where he has lived most of his life. His poems are full of the customs, the countryside, and the people. Quiet humor and simple language mark his writings. Some of his collections of poems are *North of Boston, A Boy's Will, New Hampshire.*

ARTHUR GUITERMAN (1871–1943) was born in Vienna of American parents, was educated in New York, and worked on magazines there. A popular lecturer and poet, he is best known for humorous poems, though he also wrote serious ones. Some of his poems are collected in *The Laughing Muse, The Mirthful Lyre,* and *Ballads of Old New York.*

EDWARD EVERETT HALE (1822–1909) was born in Boston and educated at Harvard. He became a minister, and was pastor of churches in Boston and Worcester, Massachusetts. He is best known for his classic, " The Man Without a Country," but two other stories, " Ten Times One Is Ten " and " In His Name," started the Lend-a-Hand societies which have helped thousands of people.

OLIVER WENDELL HOLMES (1809–1894) had a distinguished career as professor of medicine at Harvard, besides writing some of America's best-loved humorous and serious poems, a number of novels, and brilliant essays. His father was a minister, and his son was a famous Supreme Court Justice. " The Chambered Nautilus " and " The Height of the Ridiculous " are two of his most popular poems.

WASHINGTON IRVING (1783–1859), the first great American writer recognized by Europeans, wrote both of his native New York and of the foreign countries where he traveled. Along with his humor he had a style so graceful and polished that Europeans claimed he could not be an American! Some of his most popular books are *The Knickerbocker History of New York, The Sketch Book,* and *The Alhambra.*

JOHN KIERAN (1892–   ) is famous as a sports columnist, participant in the radio program " Information Please," and author of books on nature and sports. He was born and educated in New York City. There he worked on the sports staffs of the *Times* and the *Sun.* He is recognized as an authority in the fields of sports and natural history.

RUDYARD KIPLING (1865–1936) was born in India, went to school in England, and returned to India as a young man to go into newspaper work. India is the setting for many of his poems and stories — *Barrack-Room Ballads, Plain Tales from the Hills, Kim.* One of his most popular works, *The Jungle Book,* was written at the suggestion of his publisher's eleven-year-old son.

JACK LONDON (1876–1916) spent much of his boyhood on the waterfronts of California cities, working at odd jobs to supplement the family income. For part of his adventurous life he tried gold mining in the Klondike, and later he was a war correspondent during the Russo-Japanese War. He traveled a great deal, and his short stories and novels are full of action and excitement. He wrote often of the wilds of Alaska and the Pacific islands and of the sea.

HENRY WADSWORTH LONGFELLOW (1807–1882) spent his boyhood in Maine, and after college and foreign travel he became a professor at Bowdoin and Harvard. He is called " The Children's Poet " because so much of his work appeals to young readers, especially his story-poems of America's past. But he is also one of our finest poets for any age. Two of his story-poems are *The Song of Hiawatha* and *The Courtship of Miles Standish.*

J. PAUL LOOMIS is the author of a book about horses, *Salto: A Horse of the Canadian Mounties.* He was born in Juneau, Alaska, and has traveled in the United States, Canada, and Siberia. He once took a two months' canoe trip through the Rocky Mountain region. His experiences as a rancher, his work as carpenter and boatbuilder, all enriched his background for writing short stories of the North.

JOHN G. MAGEE, JR. (1922–1941) was born in China of missionary parents. He attended school in England and joined the Royal Canadian Air Force in 1940. He was killed a year later while on maneuvers over England. Three months before his death he composed the sonnet " High Flight," while flying in a Spitfire at a height of 30,000 feet.

JOHN MASEFIELD (1878–   ) was born in England. While he was very young he went to sea and wandered about the world for several years. His early works, both prose and poetry, were devoted to the sea and the lives of sailors. It was not until he published *The Everlasting Mercy,* a long poem, in 1911, that he was recognized as a writer of importance. His poetry is more popular than his prose, for its vitality and intense feeling make a deep impression on the reader. Mr. Masefield is Poet Laureate of England, and now lives quietly in the country near Oxford University.

EDNA ST. VINCENT MILLAY (1892–1950) was one of the major poets of the United States. At the age of nineteen, while still a student at Vassar College, she wrote a remarkable poem called " Renascence." Miss Millay fulfilled the promise of her early days in *A Few Figs from Thistles* and *Second April. The Harp-Weaver and Other Poems* won the Pulitzer Prize for poetry in 1923. In addition to rhythmic beauty, her poetry has a deep emotional appeal. In 1927 she wrote the libretto for *The King's Henchman,* an opera which was produced by the Metropolitan Opera Company in New York.

JOHN MUIR (1838–1914) was born in Scotland and came to America when he was eleven years old, spending six weeks crossing the Atlantic in an old-fashioned sailing vessel. He became a naturalist and traveled extensively in the United States, keeping journals during his trips. He helped found Yosemite National Park and was a leader in the national movement to create forest reserves.

HELEN and GEORGE PAPASHVILY are an interesting couple. George Papashvily came to the United States as a penniless immigrant from Georgia, in the southern part of the U.S.S.R. His wife, a native American, manages the Moby Dick Bookshop in Allentown, Pennsylvania, and has helped put his experiences into several humorous books. They live on a farm nearby and raise a variety of crops and livestock, including a large number of animal pets.

CARL SANDBURG (1878–   ) was born in Illinois, of Swedish descent. At thirteen he began earning his own living, at first by a variety of hard jobs. Later he was a newspaper reporter in Chicago. He writes free verse in " the American language" about the common people of America. Some of his poems are collected in *Chicago Poems, Smoke and Steel,* and *The People, Yes.* He has also written a great biography of Abraham Lincoln and has collected ballads in *The American Songbag.* As a modern minstrel, he has traveled throughout the country, singing and playing his guitar before thousands of people.

SIR WALTER SCOTT (1771–1832) was born in Edinburgh, Scotland, and grew up hearing the tales of the Scotch Border that fill his novels and poems. The romantic descriptions of old castles, wandering minstrels, and beautiful ladies in his novels make the past live again and are still favorite reading for thousands. His poems capture the dash of old ballads in fresh musical beauty. Of his novels, you may enjoy *Ivanhoe* and *Rob Roy;* and *The Lady of the Lake* is one of his most popular poems.

ROBERT W. SERVICE (1874–   ) was born in England and lived in Scotland until he was twenty-one. Then he went to Canada and on to Alaska during the gold rush. His poems of the far North won him great popularity in America. Some collections of his poems are *The Spell of the Yu-*

kon, and *Ballads of a Cheechako.* He has also written novels.

WILLIAM SHAKESPEARE (1564–1616), the greatest poet and dramatist of the English language, was born at Stratford-on-Avon and grew up loving the open country better than school. In London his fellow dramatists were all better educated, but his rich human understanding, his imagination, and his gift of poetry lifted his work far above theirs. A poet of that day wrote that " he was not of an age but for all time," and the whole world has agreed. You will read his plays later — *Julius Caesar, As You Like It, Macbeth, Hamlet, The Tempest* — but you can enjoy many of the songs from the plays now.

ROBERT LOUIS STEVENSON (1850–1894) was a sickly boy, and he spent his life in search of a healthy climate. Leaving his native Scotland for travel in Europe and America, he finally settled on the South Sea island of Samoa. His novels and poems, gay and full of action, show his high spirit that could not be conquered by physical suffering. Two of his most popular adventure books are *Treasure Island* and *Kidnapped.*

ALFRED, LORD TENNYSON (1809–1892), began his life quietly in an English village where his father was rector. After schooling at Cambridge University, he devoted himself to writing poetry and in 1850 was given a government pension and made Poet Laureate. In 1884 he was made a baron and became Lord Tennyson. He wrote a wide variety of poems. The best for young readers are lyrics like " The Brook " and " Crossing the Bar " and narratives like *Idylls of the King* and *Enoch Arden.*

JAMES THURBER (1894–   ) was born and educated in Ohio, worked for various newspapers, and for a while was managing editor of *The New Yorker.* He is equally noted as a cartoonist and as a writer. *The Thurber Carnival* contains a collection of his stories and cartoons. You will like his modern fairy tales, *The White Deer, Many Moons,* and *The Thirteen Clocks.*

MARK TWAIN was the pen name of Samuel Langhorne Clemens (1835–1910). This world-famous writer spent his boyhood in the Mississippi River town of Hannibal, Missouri, tried his hand at being a river steamboat pilot, and then went west, finally becoming a reporter. His stories won rapid success and he was soon writing books, many about his own experiences. His keen observation, his winning humor, and his matchless style put him at the top of American writers. Some of his books are *Roughing It, The Innocents Abroad,* and *Life on the Mississippi.*

E. B. WHITE (1899–   ) was born in Mt. Vernon, New York, and graduated from Cornell University. He has been a reporter, a free-lance writer, and an editor. He writes both prose and poetry, and has earned a reputation for keen observation, subtle humor, and a fine style. Two of his books are *Stuart Little,* a fantasy, and *Here Is New York,* a descriptive essay about that city.

WALT WHITMAN (1819–1892) was a literary pioneer. After boyhood on Long Island he worked at many jobs — printer, teacher, editor — before he selected writing. Nearly all his poetry is what we now call free verse, without rhyme or a formal pattern. Recognition came slowly, but now he is honored as a great poet for his honesty, his expression of human feelings, and his understanding of America. He wrote and rewrote one book all his life — *Leaves of Grass.*

WILLIAM WORDSWORTH (1770–1850) was born in Cumberland, not far from the beautiful Lake Country of northwestern England. Left an orphan at the age of thirteen, he received a good education through the kindness of two uncles, and was graduated from St. John's College, Cambridge, in 1791. He spent a year in France and was greatly influenced by the revolutionary movement there. The love of nature and the spiritual insight shown in his poetry make him one of the greatest English poets. Especially in his sonnets, he shows the poetical power that made him immortal. In 1843 he was made Poet Laureate of England, one of the greatest honors that can be conferred on a poet.

WRITERS FOR YOUNG PEOPLE

DOROTHY CANFIELD (1879–   ) who is also known by her married name, Dorothy Canfield Fisher, has made her mark in the world as novelist and short-story writer. She was born in Kansas, the daughter of a prominent educator and an artist mother, and was educated in this country and in France. In 1907 she married John R. Fisher, and settled on a farm in Vermont, where she lives now. Two of her popular books are *Understood Betsy* and *Four-Square* (a collection of short stories).

GLADYS HASTY CARROLL (1904–   ), novelist and short-story writer, was born in Rochester, New Hampshire. She spent her childhood on a farm in South Berwick, Maine. After graduating from Bates College, she married Herbert A. Carroll, and they settled in South Berwick. Mrs. Carroll believes that New England is a living and growing community, full of material for the observant writer.

BEATRICE JOY CHUTE, writer of sport stories, is a pretty young woman now living in New York. She was born in Minneapolis and attended the University of Minnesota. She has written short stories for several magazines, and is represented in many anthologies of literature for young people. Her book, *Shift to the Right,* is a collection of sport stories.

ELIZABETH COATSWORTH (1893–   ), whose married name is Mrs. Henry Beston, was born in Buffalo, New York. She has written many types of literature, poetry, novels, essays, and she has won awards in the juvenile book field. *Fox Footprints* is one of her books of verse and *The Cat Who Went to Heaven* one of her stories for children. Mrs. Beston now lives on Chimney Farm in Maine.

ELLIS CREDLE, author and artist, comes from North Carolina. She knows the life of the mountaineers in her state and tells about it with enthusiasm in her books. Her vigorous crayon sketches in blues and browns have action and humor. Her books for young people include *Down Down the Mountain* and *The Flop-Eared Hound.*

STEPHEN W. MEADER (1892–   ) was a dreamy, book-loving boy, then a sports and outdoor-life fan. After he became a social worker he helped start the Big Brother movement. Now he writes adventure stories for young readers. Some of them are: *The Black Buccaneer, Away to Sea, Lumberjack, Clear for Action,* and *The Fish Hawk's Nest.*

GLEN ROUNDS was born in the Black Hills of South Dakota and grew up on a Montana ranch, listening to horse and cattle talk and swapping yarns with the range hands. He is an artist, and illustrated books before he began writing them. Legends and folklore are his main interests. Suggested reading: *Pay Dirt, Lumbercamp, The Blind Colt.*

Classification of Contents by Types

STORIES

NARRATIVE AND DESCRIPTIVE POEMS

LYRIC POEMS

HUMOROUS POEMS

A Reading Rate Improvement Program

Many teachers are keenly interested in helping their students to read more rapidly without loss of comprehension. The chart on the following page will enable the teacher more readily to utilize materials in the text for reading rate improvement. It gives word counts for selections (largely nonfiction) and assigns an approximate evaluation of student word rates within certain ranges. The evaluation of student rates is not intended to indicate scientifically established reading rate norms. Since reading rate will vary in accordance with the purpose of the reader and the type of material he is reading, our purpose is simply to indicate broad ranges of student achievement.

Valuable aids may be found in *Reading Tests* for *Adventures for Readers: Book II*. Part One of that manual contains objective tests on selections in the text; these may be used, in their present form or slightly expanded, for comprehension testing in conjunction with the testing and practice on reading rate. Part Two of the manual contains an extended unit on the improvement of speed in reading and varied exercises designed to develop basic reading skills. A copy of the *Reading Tests* may be obtained on request from the publisher.

SELECTIONS FOR TIMED READING

SELECTION	Number of Words	SUPERIOR		AVERAGE		BELOW AVERAGE	
		Time in Minutes	Words per Minute	Time in Minutes	Words per Minute	Time in Minutes	Words per Minute
Knowing the Flowers, p. 70	923	2–3	462–308	3½–4½	264–205	5–7½	185–123
On a Wisconsin Farm, p. 64	1888	3½–6	568–315	6½–9	290–210	9½–15	199–126
Mr. Chairman, p. 104	1443	3–4½	481–321	5–6½	289–222	7–11½	206–125
Inside a Hurricane, p. 145	1617	3–5	539–323	5½–7½	294–216	8–13	202–124
That Mysterious Stuff Called Snow, p. 164	1627	3–5	542–325	5½–7½	296–217	8–13	203–125
First of the Menfish, p. 169	1982	3½–6½	566–305	7–9½	283–209	10–16	198–124
An Encounter with an Interviewer, p. 260	1428	3–5	476–317	5–6½	286–220	7–11½	204–124
Can We Survive in Space? p. 174	2470	4½–8	549–309	8½–11½	291–215	12–20	206–124
Good-by, Babe Ruth! p. 326	2753	5½–9	501–306	9½–13	290–212	13½–22	204–125
"Yes, Your Honesty!" p. 394	2206	4½–7	490–315	7½–10½	294–210	11–17½	201–126
When I Was a Boy on the Ranch, p. 56	3420	6½–11	521–311	11½–16½	297–207	17–27½	201–125
Climb to Victory, p. 73	3598	7–12	514–300	12½–17½	288–206	18–28½	200–126
Out of Knee Pants, p. 118	3836	7½–12½	511–307	13–18½	295–207	19–30½	202–126
Quest for the Lost City, p. 180	3931	7½–13	524–302	13½–19	291–207	19½–31½	202–125
The Old Soldier, p. 210	3248	6½–10½	500–309	11–15½	295–210	16–26	203–125
Betsy Dowdy's Ride, p. 198	4391	9–14½	488–302	15–21½	293–204	22–35	200–125
The Pony Express Rider, p. 220	4616	9–15	513–308	15½–22½	298–205	23–37	201–125
The Voyage of the Raft Kon-Tiki, p. 150	5294	10½–17½	504–303	18–26	294–204	26½–42½	200–125

Glossary

Words that are defined or pronounced in footnotes throughout the text are not usually included in the glossary. Some glossary entries give several common meanings for a word; there is always one definition that will fit the context in this book. Many of the words that have been discussed in the various vocabulary sections throughout the text are included in this glossary. For study sections pertaining to these words, refer to the specific pages indicated by the page numbers.

A

adamant (ăd′*a*·mănt). Unyielding, very hard, inflexible.

adequately (ăd′ē·kwĭt·lĭ). Sufficiently.

adjacent (*a*·jā′sĕnt). Near, adjoining, next to.

adobe (*a*·dō′bĭ). **1.** An unburnt brick dried in the sun. **2.** A structure made of such bricks.

advent (ăd′vĕnt). Arrival, approach.

adversaries (ăd′vēr·sà·rĭz). Foes, opponents.

affirmed (*a*·fûrmd′). Declared to be true.

alien (āl′yĕn). Strange, foreign.

allusion (ă·lū′zhŭn). A casual reference, a mention of something.

almshouse (ämz′hous′). A house for the use of the poor.

aloof (*a*·loof′). **1.** Away from, but within view. **2.** Distant in feeling.

anguished (ăng′gwĭsht). Suffering extreme pain, either of body or mind; very distressed.

anticipated (ăn·tĭs′*i*·pāt·ĕd). Expected, looked forward to.

antiquated (ăn′tĭ·kwāt′ĕd). Old, outmoded, old-fashioned.

apostles (*a*·pŏs″lz). **1.** The twelve disciples sent forth by Christ to preach the Gospel. **2.** Those who urge the adoption of a certain plan.

apparition (ăp′*a*·rĭsh′ŭn). *See page 287.*

appraising (*a*·prāz′ĭng). Evaluating, judging.

apprehensive (ăp′rē·hĕn′sĭv). Uneasy about what will happen, fearful.

aptitude (ăp′tĭ·tūd). **1.** Natural ability or capacity. **2.** Readiness in learning.

aquamarine (ăk·wà·mà·rēn′). *See page 126.*

ardor (är′dēr). Enthusiasm, warmth of emotion.

arrant (ăr′ănt). **1.** Wandering, vagrant. **2.** Thorough, out-and-out.

arrogance (ăr′ō·găns). Haughtiness, lordliness, insolence.

artificially (är′tĭ·fĭsh′ăl·lĭ). Synthetically, not naturally.

askance (*a*·skăns′). Sideways, with distrust or envy.

aspect (ăs′pĕkt). **1.** Situation or condition. **2.** Look, appearance.

assail (ă·sāl′). To assault, to attack.

assassin (ă·săs′ĭn). A murderer.

assiduous (ă·sĭd′û·ŭs). Devoted and attentive in giving service.

asunder (*a*·sŭn′dēr). Apart, separated.

avert (*a*·vûrt′). To prevent.

B

balked (bôkt). Stopped short, prevented (from doing something).

bantered (băn′tērd). Ridiculed lightly and good-naturedly.

barren (băr′ĕn). **1.** Unprofitable. **2.** Without interest or charm, as *barren* writing. **3.** Stupid, dull.

bayou (bī′oo). A creek or small river. (The term is used in the lower Mississippi River basin and around the Gulf Coast.)

benignant (bē·nĭg′nănt). Gracious, kindly.

biologist (bī·ŏl′ō·jĭst). One who studies the science of living things.

brackish (brăk′ĭsh). Slightly salty; hence, distasteful.

buoyancy (boo′yăn·sĭ). **1.** The quality of being able to float on water or in air. **2.** Sprightliness of spirit.

burnished (bûr′nĭsht). Polished, bright.

buxom (bŭk′sŭm). Plump, pretty.

C

calculated (kăl′kû·lāt·ĕd). **1.** Determined by mathematics. **2.** Designed or planned for a certain purpose.

cantankerous (kăn·tăng′kēr·ŭs). Showing ill-temper, unreasonable, of a quarrelsome spirit.

canter (kăn′tēr). A gait resembling a gallop, with easy bounds.

āpe, chăotic, bâre, ăt, ăttend, ärt, flăsk, *a*top; ēke, mĕrely, ĕlect, ĕcho, prudĕnt, doēr; ītem, ĭnn, rarĭty; ōde, ŏpaque, fôr, dŏt, lôft, cŏnfide; soon, took; sour, toil; tūbe, ûnique, tûrn, sŭp, ŭntil.

491

carnivorous (kär·nĭv′ŏ·rŭs). Feeding on animals.

casualty (kăzh′ū·ăl·tĭ). 1. A person injured by an accident. 2. An unfortunate occurrence.

catapulted (kăt′a·pŭlt·ĕd). Hurled into the air, as from a slingshot.

cavernous (kăv′ẽr·nŭs). Like a cavern or cave; hence, dark and hollow.

cayuse (kī·ūs′). A small hardy horse of western North America.

celestial (sē·lĕs′chăl). 1. Heavenly, divine. 2. Of the sky.

chagrined (shà·grĭnd′). Mortified, angered.

chaos (kā′ŏs). Complete disorder.

choleric (kŏl′ẽr·ĭk). Angry, hot-tempered.

chronometer (krō·nŏm′ē·tẽr). *See page 150.*

cleat (klēt). A device with two arms, attached to the deck of a ship, used to secure a line.

colleague (kŏl′ēg). An associate.

colloquialism (kŏ·lō′kwĭ·ăl·ĭzm). *See page 168.*

commissary (kŏm′ĭ·sẽr·ĭ). A department or store supplying equipment and provisions, as in a lumber camp.

commotion (kŏ·mō′shŭn). A disturbance, an agitation.

compassion (kŏm·păsh′ŭn). Pity, sympathy.

competent (kŏm′pē·tĕnt). Capable, fit, able.

component (kŏm·pō′nĕnt). Part, ingredient.

compromised (kŏm′prŏ·mīzd). Agreed, settled by each side giving up something.

compulsory (kŏm·pŭl′sŏ·rĭ). Required by law or rule.

confided (kŏn·fīd′ĕd). Told confidentially, entrusted a secret.

confirmed (kŏn·fûrmd′). 1. Established, strengthened by evidence. 2. Ratified by approval, as a treaty between nations.

confronted (kŏn·frŭnt′ĕd). Faced in a hostile way, met.

congeals (kŏn·jēlz′). Freezes, makes hard as if by freezing.

congested (kŏn·jĕst′ĕd). Blocked, overcrowded.

conjectures (kŏn·jĕk′tūrz). Opinions based on incomplete evidence, guesses.

conjured (kŭn′jẽrd). Recalled, brought to mind, evoked.

consistently (kŏn·sĭs′tĕnt·lĭ). Regularly, steadily.

consoled (kŏn·sōld′). Comforted.

consternation (kŏn′stẽr·nā′shŭn). Mingled amazement and alarm.

contagion (kŏn·tā′jŭn). 1. Spreading of a disease by contact. 2. Spreading of an idea or feeling to the mind.

cordon (kôr′dŏn). 1. A line or circle of persons around any person or place. 2. A ribbon or cord worn as an ornament.

cormorants (kôr′mŏ·rănts). Sea birds of the pelican family.

cosmic (kŏz′mĭk). 1. Of or relating to the universe. 2. Vast.

countenance (koun′tē·năns). 1. Face. 2. The expression of the face.

counterbalanced (koun′tẽr·băl′ănst). Offset.

courier (kōor′ĭ·ẽr). 1. A special, swift messenger. 2. An attendant with travelers, who looks out for their hotels and comforts.

cowling (koul′ĭng). The hood over an engine.

cranium (krā′nĭ·ŭm). The skull.

craven (krā′vĕn). 1. A coward. 2. Afraid.

credulity (krē·dū′lĭ·tĭ). Belief, readiness to believe.

creel (krēl). A basket for fish that are caught.

crematorium (krĕm′a·tō′rĭ·ŭm). A furnace for burning corpses or rubbish.

croup (krōōp). The rump of a horse.

cudgeled (kŭj′ĕld). Beat or struck.

culminating (kŭl′mĭ·nāt′ĭng). Reaching a climax, or highest point.

curfew (kûr′fū). *See page 479.*

currying (kûr′ĭ·ĭng). Dressing the hair or coat of a horse with a metal-tooth comb.

cynic (sĭn′ĭk). *See page 433.*

D

daft (dȧft). 1. Foolishly enthusiastic. 2. Insane.

dastard (dăs′tẽrd). A coward, one who does sneaking, evil deeds.

dauntless (dônt′lĕs). Bold, fearless.

debris (dĕ·brē′). Rubbish.

deducting (dē·dŭkt′ĭng). Subtracting or taking away from the total.

deftly (dĕft′lĭ). Skillfully.

deign (dān). Condescend, do as a kindness.

delectable (dē·lĕk′ta·b'l). Delightful, pleasing to the taste.

delirious (dē·lĭr′ĭ·ŭs). 1. Wildly excited. 2. Out of one's head, raving.

demeanor (dē·mēn′ẽr). Outward bearing or behavior.

demented (dē·mĕnt′ĕd). Insane, mad.

demobilized (dē·mō′bĭ·līzd). Disbanded.

demoniac (dē·mō′nĭ·ăk). Devilish.

demoralized (dē·mŏr′ăl·īzd). 1. Put into disorder. 2. Corrupted.

depicts (dē·pĭkts′). Portrays, pictures.

depleted (dē·plēt′ĕd). Drained, exhausted, used up.

derelict (dĕr′ē·lĭkt). An abandoned ship.

derisively (dē·rī′sĭv·lĭ). Scornfully.

derived (dē·rīvd′). Received.

designate (dĕz′ĭg·nāt). 1. Indicate, make known. 2. To name, to identify.

---

bar; church; dog; ardŭous; fat; go; hear; jail; key; lame; meat; not; ring; pay; ran; see; shell; ten; there, thick; pastŭre; vast; wind; yes; zoo, zh = z in azure.

destination (dĕs′tĭ·nā′shŭn). Place set for the end of a journey.

detachment (dē·tăch′mĕnt). **1.** A body of troops sent on special service. **2.** Isolation, separation from worldly concerns.

detonate (dĕt′ō·nāt). Explode.

devastating (dĕv′ăs·tāt·ĭng). Ravaging, destroying.

devious (dē′vĭ·ŭs). Varying from a straight line, winding.

dialect (dī′á·lĕkt). **1.** Language. **2.** Local or provincial form of a language.

dilated (dī·lāt′ĕd). Expanded, enlarged.

diligently (dĭl′ĭ·jĕnt·lĭ). Busily, industriously.

dimensions (dĭ·mĕn′shŭnz). **1.** Size. **2.** Measurements of length, breadth, or thickness.

diminutive (dĭ·mĭn′û·tĭv). Very small.

dire (dīr). Extremely fearful, terrible.

disconsolate (dĭs·kŏn′sō·lĭt). Sad, deeply dejected.

dissipated (dĭs′ĭ·pāt·ĕd). **1.** Wasteful in the pursuit of pleasure. **2.** Scattered foolishly.

dissonant (dĭs′ō·nănt). **1.** Harsh in sound. **2.** Disagreeing in opinion.

distorted (dĭs·tôrt′ĕd). Twisted.

distracted (dĭs·trăkt′ĕd). **1.** Diverted, turned away. **2.** Confused. **3.** Driven almost mad.

divers (dī′vẽrz). Several.

doleful (dōl′fŏŏl). Sad, gloomy.

domain (dō·mān′). **1.** The lands belonging to a ruler. **2.** A field of thought or action.

dominant (dŏm′ĭ·nănt). Outstanding, ruling or controlling, chief.

drone (drōn). **1.** A lazy fellow. **2.** The male of the honeybees.

drought (drout). Dryness, want of rain or water.

dubious (dū′bĭ·ŭs). Uncertain, questioning, doubtful.

dunes (dūnz). Hills or ridges of sand piled up by the wind.

dwindled (dwĭn′d′ld). Became less and less, grew smaller.

E

edible (ĕd′ĭ·b′l). Fit to be eaten.

eject (ē·jĕkt′). To throw out, emit.

elation (ē·lā′shŭn). High spirits, joy.

eluded (ē·lūd′ĕd). Escaped, avoided, got away.

emancipation (ē·măn·sĭ·pā′shŭn). Freedom, liberation, release.

emblem (ĕm′blĕm). **1.** A symbol, a visible sign of an idea. **2.** A sign used for identification.

embrasure (ĕm·brā′zhẽr). **1.** An opening in a wall for a gun. **2.** A space made by setting a door or window farther forward than the wall.

encumbered (ĕn·kŭm′bẽrd). **1.** Obstructed, blocked up. **2.** Loaded down, burdened.

endeavor (ĕn·dĕv′ẽr). **1.** An effort, an attempt. **2.** To try.

engrossed (ĕn·grōst′). Absorbed, interested in and occupied with.

entranced (ĕn·trănst′). Carried away with delight, wonder, and interest.

environment (ĕn·vī′rŭn·mĕnt). *See page 103.*

erratically (ĕ·răt′ĭ·kăl·ĭ). **1.** Queerly, strangely. **2.** Unevenly, in a wandering manner.

ethereal (ē·thēr′ē·ăl). Delicate, spiritual.

eventualities (ē·vĕn′tū·ăl′ĭ·tĭz). Outcomes.

evolve (ē·vŏlv′). To develop, to produce.

excessive (ĕk·sĕs′ĭv). Extreme, immoderate, extravagant.

exile (ĕk′sīl). **1.** Banishment, forced removal to a foreign country. **2.** One who is expelled from his country.

exulting (ĕg·zült′ĭng). Rejoicing.

F

fantastic (făn·tăs′tĭk). **1.** Quaint, fanciful, whimsical. **2.** Imaginary, unreal.

farce (färs). An empty show or mockery, a ridiculous action.

feat (fēt). A notable deed.

ferocity (fē·rŏs′ĭ·tĭ). Fierceness, savageness.

fervent (fûr′vĕnt). Ardent, impassioned, zealous, burning with spirit.

festered (fĕs′tẽrd). **1.** Became sore or inflamed. **2.** Caused pain in the mind, rankled.

filly (fĭl′ĭ). A young female of the horse family.

flagons (flăg′ŭnz). Vessels for liquors, large bulging bottles.

flails (flālz). **1.** Instruments for threshing grain by hand. **2.** Beats with a whip.

flax (flăks). Linen fiber.

flexible (flĕk′sĭ·b′l). Not rigid, elastic, pliable.

flimsily (flĭm′zĭ·lĭ). In a frail fashion, insubstantially.

flinched (flĭncht). Drew back, as from pain or danger; winced.

flotillas (flō·tĭl′áz). Small fleets of vessels.

floundered (floun′dẽrd). Struggled clumsily.

fluency (flōō′ĕn·sĭ). Ready flow of words, ease in speaking.

forebears (fōr′bârz). Ancestors.

foreboding (fōr·bōd′ĭng). A feeling that evil is coming upon one, misgiving.

formidable (fôr′mĭ·dá·b′l). Alarming.

fortnight (fôrt′nīt). Two weeks.

forum (fō′rŭm). A public meeting place for open discussion.

frenzy (frĕn′zĭ). Wild emotional excitement.

frustration (frŭs·trā′shŭn). Defeat; also, disappointment due to defeat.

functioning (fŭngk′shŭn·ĭng). Working.

āpe, chãotic, bâre, ăt, ăttend, ärt, flăsk, átop; ēke, mẽrely, ēlect, ĕcho, prudént, doẽr; ītem, ĭnn, rarĭty; ōde, ōpaque, fôr, dŏt, lôft, cŏnfide; sōōn, tŏŏk; sour, toil; tūbe, ûnique, tûrn, sŭp, ŭntil.

G

gala (gā′lȧ). Festive, in a spirit of celebration.
gambols (găm′bŭlz). Frolics.
garrulous (găr′ṵ·lŭs). Talkative.
germinating (jûr′mĭ·nāt·ĭng). Beginning to grow, sprouting.
ghost (gōst). *See page 287.*
gingerly (jĭn′jẽr·lĭ). Carefully, very cautiously.
glens (glĕnz). Narrow valleys.
gloated (glōt′ĕd). Gazed upon with desire or satisfaction.
glowering (glou′ẽr·ĭng). Frowning, staring angrily.
gossamer (gŏs′ȧ·mẽr). **1.** Thin and delicate in appearance. **2.** A film of cobwebs.
granule (grăn′ūl). A small grain or grainlike particle.
graphic (grăf′ĭk). Vividly described.
grisly (grĭz′lĭ). Horrifying, ghastly.
grotesque (grō·tĕsk′). Distorted, fantastic.
guttural (gŭt′ẽr·ȧl). Produced in the throat, harsh, as a *guttural* sound.

H

halyard (hăl′yẽrd). A rope for moving the sails on a ship.
harassing (hăr′ȧs·ĭng). Annoying, worrying.
hazard (hăz′ẽrd). Risk, danger.
heirloom (âr′lōōm′). Any piece of personal property owned by a family for several generations.
helm (hĕlm). The apparatus by which a ship is steered, the tiller or wheel of a ship.
hemorrhage (hĕm′ŏ·rĭj). A discharge of blood from the blood vessels, caused by injury.
Herculean (hẽr·kū′lē·ȧn). Having the strength and size of Hercules, a hero of mythology famous for his strength.
heretical (hē·rĕt′ĭ·kăl). Strongly opposed to beliefs commonly held by others.
heritage (hĕr′ĭ·tĭj). That which is inherited.
hilarious (hĭ·lâr′ĭ·ŭs). Merry, boisterous.
hoary (hōr′ĭ). Gray or white with age, venerable, old.
homonyms (hŏm′ō·nĭmz). *See page 230.*
hysterics (hĭs·tĕr′ĭks). Outbreaks of wild emotion.

I

illusions (ĭ·lū′zhŭnz). False impressions, beliefs based on faulty or unreal conditions.
immersion (ĭ·mûr′shŭn). State of being under water.
imminent (ĭm′ĭ·nĕnt). Threatening to happen immediately.
impaled (ĭm·pāld′). **1.** Pierced by a sharp stake. **2.** Hemmed in by pales, or stakes, in a fence.

impeded (ĭm·pēd′ĕd). Hindered, obstructed.
imperative (ĭm·pĕr′ȧ·tĭv). Commanding.
impetuous (ĭm·pĕt′ṵ·ŭs). Impatient, hasty in thought or action.
implicitly (ĭm·plĭs′ĭt·lĭ). Completely, unquestioningly.
impunity (ĭm·pū′nĭ·tĭ). Excuse from punishment.
inadvertent (ĭn′ăd·vûr′tĕnt). Unintentional.
inapplicable (ĭn·ăp′lĭ·kȧ·b'l). Not suitable.
inarticulate (ĭn′är·tĭk′ṵ·lāt). **1.** Not distinct in speech, mumbling. **2.** Dumb, unable to speak.
incessant (ĭn·sĕs′ănt). Continual, unceasing.
incredulous (ĭn·krĕd′ṵ·lŭs). Finding it difficult to believe.
indentured (ĭn·dĕn′tûrd). Bound by a contract to serve a master for a number of years.
inducement (ĭn·dūs′mĕnt). A promise of gain, something that persuades.
inestimable (ĭn·ĕs′tĭ·mȧ·b'l). Valuable beyond measure.
inevitable (ĭn·ĕv′ĭ·tȧ·b'l). Certain to happen, beyond prevention.
infinite (ĭn′fĭ·nĭt). Without limits of any kind, vast, immense.
insignificant (ĭn′sĭg·nĭf′ĭ·kănt). Unimportant, little.
insurmountable (ĭn′sûr·moun′tȧ·b'l). Incapable of being avoided or conquered.
intact (ĭn·tăkt′). Untouched, uninjured.
intercourse (ĭn′tẽr·kōrs). Dealings between persons or nations, communication.
intermediate (ĭn′tẽr·mē′dĭ·ĭt). Being in the middle place, coming between.
interposed (ĭn′tẽr·pōzd′). Interrupted, broke in with words.
intimate (ĭn′tĭ·mĭt). Close, personal, private.
intimidated (ĭn·tĭm′ĭ·dāt·ĕd). Frightened.
intrepid (ĭn·trĕp′ĭd). Brave, undaunted.
intricacies (ĭn′trĭ·kȧ·sĭz). Complexities, entanglements.
intrusion (ĭn·trōō′zhŭn). The forcing of oneself into a place without right or invitation, unwelcome entry.
invisible (ĭn·vĭz′ĭ·b'l). Incapable of being seen.
irked (ûrkt). Annoyed, angered.
irrational (ĭr·răsh′ŭn·ȧl). **1.** Showing signs of loss of mind or reasoning. **2.** Absurd and unreasonable.
irrepressible (ĭr′rĕ·prĕs′ĭ·b'l). Not capable of being subdued or controlled.
itinerant (ī·tĭn′ẽr·ȧnt). Traveling from place to place.

J

jargon (jär′gŏn). Confused language, speech that cannot be understood.
jib (jĭb). A triangular sail on a vessel.

---

bar; church; dog; ardúous; fat; go; hear; jail; key; lame; meat; not; ring; pay; ran; see; shell; ten; there, thick; pastûre; vast; wind; yes; zoo, zh = z in azure.

jovial (jō′vǐ·ǎl). Merry, jolly.
jubilation (jōō′bǐ·lā′shǔn). A triumphant shouting, rejoicing.
judicial (jōō·dǐsh′ǎl). Like a judge, fair and balanced in action.

L

laggard (lăg′ērd). **1.** Slow and sluggish. **2.** A person slow in taking action.
languished (lăng′gwǐsht). **1.** Lost strength. **2.** Faded, withered.
leech (lēch). **1.** Either end of a square sail on a sailing vessel. **2.** A bloodsucking worm. **3.** A person who clings to another to get help from him.
legibly (lĕj′ǐ·blǐ). In a manner that is easy to read.
legitimate (lĕ·jǐt′ǐ·mǐt). Lawful.
lemur (lē′mēr). A mammal of the monkey family, found chiefly in Madagascar.
liberality (lǐb′ēr·ǎl′ǐ·tǐ). Generosity, quality of being generous.
linsey-woolsey (lǐn′zǐ-wŏŏl′zǐ). Coarse cloth of linen and wool.
listless (lǐst′lĕs). Spiritless, lacking energy.
lithe (līth). Flexible, pliant, capable of being easily bent.
lode (lōd). An ore deposit.
luminous (lū′mǐ·nǔs). Bright, shining.
lurid (lū′rǐd). **1.** Appearing like glowing fire. **2.** Violent or terrible.
lush (lǔsh). Rich, luxurious in growth.

M

maneuver (mả·nōō′vēr). **1.** Clever move. **2.** Swift and skillful move in military or naval plans.
manifold (măn′ǐ·fōld). Numerous and varied, many.
mariners (măr′ǐ·nērz). Sailors.
martyr (mär′tēr). A person who sacrifices his life or position for a cause or principle.
menace (mĕn′ǐs). Threat.
mendicant (mĕn′dǐ·kǎnt). **1.** Practicing beggary. **2.** A beggar.
meridian (mě·rǐd′ǐ·ǎn). An imaginary circle around the earth passing through the North and South poles and any given place on the earth's surface.
meteor (mē′tĕ·ēr). A heavenly body that moves with great speed.
metropolis (mě·trŏp′ō·lǐs). City.
mettle (mĕt″l). Quality of spirit, ardor, courage.
mien (mēn). The manner, looks, air of a person.
missile (mǐs′ǐl). A weapon thrown or shot out, as a bullet, spear, or arrow.

molesting (mỏ·lĕst′ǐng). Disturbing or interfering with.
momentarily (mō′mĕn·tả′rǐ·lǐ). *See page 141.*
murk (mûrk). Darkness, gloom.
myriad (mǐr′ǐ·ǎd). Great number.
mythical (mǐth′ǐ·kǎl). Imaginary, invented, based on a myth.

N

niggardly (nǐg′ảrd·lǐ). Stingy, miserly.
noncommittally (nŏn′kŏ·mǐt′ǎl·lǐ). Indicating neither agreement nor disagreement.

O

oasis (ỏ·ā′sǐs). A green spot in a desert.
oblivious (ŏb·lǐv′ǐ·ǔs). Forgetful, not mindful.
obscure (ŏb·skūr′). **1.** Remote or hidden. **2.** Dark, gloomy. **3.** Not distinct, faint.
ominous (ŏm′ǐ·nǔs). Threatening, foreboding evil.
oppressed (ŏ·prĕst′). Downtrodden, treated cruelly.
optimistic (ŏp′tǐ·mǐs′tǐk). Hopeful.
oratorical (ŏr′ả·tŏr′ǐ·kǎl). Pertaining to eloquent public speaking.
ordeal (ôr·dēl′). A severe trial or experience.
ordinance (ôr′dǐ·nǎns). A local law or regulation.
orgy (ôr′jǐ). **1.** A wild revel. **2.** Overindulgence in some activity.

P

pacified (păs′ǐ·fīd). Soothed, calmed.
pallid (păl′ǐd). Pale, wan, white in color.
parley (pär′lǐ). **1.** A formally arranged discussion between enemies. **2.** An informal talk to discuss terms.
paternal (pả·tûr′nǎl). Pertaining to a father, fatherly.
peerless (pēr′lĕs). Having no equal, matchless.
pelagic (pê·lăj′ǐk). Pertaining to the ocean.
perceptible (pēr·sĕp′tǐ·b′l). Capable of being seen, noticeable.
perfunctory (pēr·fŭngk′tỏ·rǐ). Indifferent, without interest.
perpendicular (pûr′pĕn·dǐk′ủ·lēr). **1.** Exactly upright or vertical. **2.** Extremely steep.
persistent (pēr·sǐs′tĕnt). **1.** Tenacious, going on resolutely in spite of opposition, persevering. **2.** Enduring or lasting.
pessimistic (pĕs′ǐ·mǐs′tǐk). Gloomy, unhopeful.
pestilence (pĕs′tǐ·lĕns). A plague, an epidemic of illness.
petrol (pĕt′rŏl). Gasoline. *British.*
phantom (făn′tǔm). *See page 287.*

āpe, chảotic, bâre, ăt, ảttend, ärt, flăsk, ảtop; ēke, mẽrely, ẽlect, ĕcho, prudĕnt, doēr; ītem, ǐnn, rarǐty; ōde, ŏpaque, fôr, dŏt, lŏft, cŏnfide; sōōn, tŏŏk; sour, toil; tūbe, ûnique, tûrn, sŭp, ŭntil.

phosphorescent (fŏs'fō·rĕs'ĕnt). Having the quality of shining in the dark.

pillaged (pĭl'ĭjd). Plundered, robbed openly.

pistil (pĭs'tĭl). The seed-bearing part of a flower.

plaintiff (plān'tĭf). *See page 347.*

plaintive (plān'tĭv). *See page 347.*

pliability (plī'á·bĭl'ĭ·tĭ). 1. Quality of being easily influenced or persuaded. 2. Flexibility, ease in bending.

poise (poiz). Balance, steadiness.

ponderous (pŏn'dẽr·ŭs). 1. Heavy. 2. Dull, lacking lightness of spirit.

porous (pō'rŭs). Full of small openings, like a sieve or sponge.

portal (pōr'tăl). Door, gate, entrance.

potentially (pō·tĕn'shăl·lĭ). Possibly but not actually.

preceded (prē·sēd'ĕd). Went before.

precise (prē·sīs'). Carefully exact, correct, accurate.

predecessors (prĕd'ē·sĕs'ẽrz). 1. Those who go before. 2. Ancestors.

prehistoric (prē'hĭs·tŏr'ĭk). Belonging to periods before history was written.

primeval (prī·mē'văl). Primitive, pertaining to the earliest age.

primitive (prĭm'ĭ·tĭv). 1. Ancient, of early times. 2. Very simple.

profusion (prŏ·fū'zhŭn). Abundance, lavish supply.

proprietor (prŏ·prī'ĕ·tẽr). Owner.

protruding (prŏ·trōōd'ĭng). Thrust out, projecting.

prowess (prou'ĕs). 1. Bravery, daring. 2. Unusual skill or ability.

psychologist (sī·kŏl'ō·jĭst). One who studies the human mind.

Q

quenched (kwĕncht). 1. Extinguished, put out. 2. Stopped.

quest (kwĕst). A seeking, search.

R

radiate (rā'dĭ·āt). 1. To spread or give out, as to *radiate* good humor. 2. To proceed in direct lines from a central spot.

random (răn'dŭm). In a haphazard way, without definite direction or method.

raptures (răp'tŭrz). Ecstasies, strong enthusiasms, expressions of intense joy and delight.

realm (rĕlm). Kingdom, domain.

reassuringly (rē'á·shōor'ĭng·lĭ). In a fashion to restore confidence.

rebuffs (rē·bŭfs'). Snubs, sharp repulses.

rebuke (rē·būk'). A short scolding, a reproof.

recoiled (rē·koild'). Sprang back.

reconnaissance (rē·kŏn'ĭ·săns). A survey, an examination of a region.

recurrence (rē·kûr'ĕns). Reappearance, repetition.

redoubtable (rē·dout'á·b'l). Dreaded, worthy of respect.

rejected (rē·jĕkt'ĕd). Turned down, refused.

reluctance (rē·lŭk'tăns). Unwillingness.

remote (rē·mōt'). Far away, situated at a far distance.

replenish (rē·plĕn'ĭsh). Refill, replace with a new supply.

replica (rĕp'lĭ·ká). A copy, a reproduction.

repose (rē·pōz'). Rest, ease, relaxation, sleep.

resolute (rĕz'ō·lūt). Steady, firm, determined.

retaliated (rē·tăl'ĭ·āt·ĕd). Returned like for like, paid back for wrong or injury.

retort (rē·tôrt'). 1. Sharp reply. 2. To answer quickly or sharply.

retrieve (rē·trēv'). 1. To bring back. 2. To regain or recover.

revenue (rĕv'ē·nū). Income, money received.

reverently (rĕv'ẽr·ĕnt·lĭ). Respectfully, worshipfully.

rhetoric (rĕt'ō·rĭk). Skillful speech, the art of expressive speech or writing.

ricocheted (rĭk'ō·shād'). Skipped with glancing rebounds along a flat surface, as a stone along the surface of water.

roistering (rois'tẽr·ĭng). Blustering, swaggering, celebrating noisily.

ruefully (rōō'fool·ĭ). Sorrowfully, regretfully.

S

salvage (săl'vĭj). 1. Act of saving a vessel or goods from loss at sea. 2. To save, to rescue.

sauntering (sôn'tẽr·ĭng). Walking slowly, strolling.

schooner (skōōn'ẽr). 1. A sailing vessel with two masts. 2. A large glass for beer.

scrimmage (skrĭm'ĭj). In football, the play that takes place when two teams are lined up and the ball is snapped back.

scrutiny (skrōō'tĭ·nĭ). Close examination, minute inspection.

scudding (skŭd'ĭng). 1. Moving swiftly. 2. Being driven by the wind.

scuttle (skŭt''l). To sink a vessel deliberately.

scythe (sīth). An instrument with a long, curved blade for mowing grass, grain, etc., by hand.

seaworthy (sē'wûr'thĭ). Fit for a sea voyage, able to stand stormy weather.

secluded (sē·klōōd'ĕd). Withdrawn, isolated, remote in location.

---

bar; **church**; **d**og; ar**d**ŭous; fat; go; hear; jail; key; lame; meat; not; ring; pay; ran; see; shell; ten; **th**ere, **th**ick; pas**t**ūre; vast; wind; yes; zoo, zh = z in azure.

secured (sē·kūrd′). 1. Made fast, fastened. 2. Obtained, got possession of.

semblance (sĕm′blăns). Appearance, likeness.

sequence (sē′kwĕns). A series.

sextant (sĕks′tănt). An instrument for measuring angular distances, especially at sea.

shrine (shrīn). 1. A place hallowed for its associations. 2. An object regarded with worship or respect.

sideburns (sīd′bûrnz′). *See page 33.*

sidled (sī′d′ld). Moved sidewise.

silhouettes (sĭl′ōō·ĕts′). *See page 33.*

simultaneously (sī′mŭl·tā′nē·ŭs·lĭ). Happening at the same time.

sinew (sĭn′ū). 1. A tough cord that joins the muscles to the bone. 2. Strength, energy.

sinister (sĭn′ĭs·tēr). 1. Threatening evil or harm. 2. On or toward the left.

sloop (slōōp). A sailing vessel with one mast.

sluggish (slŭg′ĭsh). Extremely slow in movement.

sluiced (slōōst). Drew off water through a trough or an artificial passage.

smelt (smĕlt). Any of certain small food fishes which closely resemble the trout.

sojourned (sō·jûrnd′). Dwelt for a time, stayed temporarily.

solicitously (sō·lĭs′ĭ·tŭs·lĭ). Carefully.

spacious (spā′shŭs). Of wide expanse, roomy.

spectacular (spĕk·tăk′ū·lēr). Wonderful, marked by grand display.

specter (spĕk′tēr). *See page 287.*

speculation (spĕk′ū·lā′shŭn). 1. Thought, guessing, inquiring consideration. 2. In commerce, the buying and selling of stocks or goods with expectation of profit.

splicing (splīs′ĭng). Joining two ropes by interweaving the strands.

spontaneous (spŏn·tā′nē·ŭs). Proceeding from natural impulse or desire, without plan or prompting.

sprightly (sprīt′lĭ). Lively, gay.

spume (spūm). Foam, froth.

squids (skwĭds). Sea animals with ten arms.

stalwart (stôl′wērt). Stout, sturdy, strong and brave.

stamen (stā′mĕn). The part of a flower that carries the pollen.

stipulated (stĭp′ū·lāt′ĕd). Plainly stated as part of an agreement.

stockade (stŏk·ād′). An enclosure or pen made of wooden posts and tall stakes.

stomacher (stŭm′ăk·ēr). An ornamental piece of clothing worn at the waist.

stooge (stōōj). Any person who plays a subordinate role to any more important person.

stress (strĕs). 1. Strain, force. 2. To emphasize.

stupendous (stū·pĕn′dŭs). Astonishing in size, amazing, immense.

substantially (sŭb·stăn′shăl·ĭ). 1. Really. 2. For the most part, mainly.

succession (sŭk·sĕsh′ŭn). 1. A following in order, a sequence. 2. The act or right of succeeding to the throne.

successive (sŭk·sĕs′ĭv). Following in order, consecutive.

sufficed (sŭ·fīst′). Was enough or sufficient.

sumptuous (sŭmp′tū·ŭs). Lavish, costly, luxurious.

surmises (sûr·mīz′ĕz). Guesses, thoughts based upon little evidence.

survive (sēr·vīv′). To live past or through an event.

suspension (sŭs·pĕn′shŭn). State of being held up in air or water.

swains (swānz). Country youths, especially those who go courting.

swarded (swôrd′ĕd). Grassy.

swarthy (swôr′thĭ). Dark in complexion, dusky.

swerved (swûrvd). Turned aside from a course or road.

sylvan (sĭl′văn). Characteristic of a forest or trees.

synonyms (sĭn′ō·nĭmz). *See page 287.*

synthetic (sĭn·thĕt′ĭk). Artificially made, not natural.

T

tally (tăl′ĭ). A score, a reckoning, an account.

tamarack (tăm′a·răk). An American tree.

tankard (tăngk′ērd). A tall drinking vessel.

taper (tā′pēr). A candle.

tapered (tā′pērd). Narrowed toward a point.

taunted (tônt′ĕd). Ridiculed and mocked.

taut (tôt). Tight.

tedious (tē′dĭ·ŭs). Tiresome, wearisome.

temperamental (tĕm′pēr·a·mĕn′tăl). Sensitive, easily excited.

tendril (tĕn′drĭl). A slender, coiling part of a climbing plant that attaches itself to something.

tension (tĕn′shŭn). Strain, anxiety.

terminal (tûr′mĭ·năl). 1. A town or place at the end of a railroad, busline, etc. 2. The end.

tethered (tĕth′ērd). Fastened by a rope or chain, tied.

thatch (thăch). Roof made of straw, reeds, or the like.

thermometer (thēr·mŏm′ē·tēr). *See page 150.*

toreador (tŏr′ē·a·dôr′). A bullfighter.

torrid (tŏr′ĭd). Arid and hot, burning.

āpe, chāotic, bâre, ăt, ăttend, ärt, flăsk, átop; ēke, mẹrely, ĕlect, ĕcho, prudĕnt, doēr; ītem, ĭnn, rarĭty; ōde, ōpaque, fôr, dŏt, lŏft, cŏnfide; sōōn, tōōk; sour, toil; tūbe, ūnique, tûrn, sŭp, ŭntil.

tortillas (tôr·tē'yäs). Round, thin cakes made from maize and baked on hot stones. *Mexican.*

tradition (trȧ·dĭsh'ŭn). Belief, custom, or story handed down from the past.

trance (trȧns). A daze due to surprise or shock, a spellbound condition.

tranquil (trăng'kwĭl). Peaceful, calm, quiet.

transmitted (trăns·mĭt'ĕd). *See page 420.*

transverse (trăns·vûrs'). **1.** A crosswise piece or course. **2.** The road that cuts through Central Park in New York City.

traversed (trăv'ẽrst). Traveled across, crossed.

treks (trĕks). Journeys.

trudge (trŭj). Walk wearily along.

turbid (tûr'bĭd). Disturbed, clouded.

turbulence (tûr'bṷ·lĕns). Disturbance, commotion, violent agitation.

U

ultimately (ŭl'tĭ·mĭt·lĭ). Finally.

unaffected (ŭn'ȧ·fĕk'tĕd). **1.** Natural, genuine. **2.** Feeling no effect, not influenced.

uncanny (ŭn·kăn'ĭ). Almost unearthly in quality, weird, mysterious.

undertow (ŭn'dẽr·tō'). The current beneath the surface of the ocean that pulls away from the shore.

undulating (ŭn'dṷ·lāt'ĭng). Moving backward and forward or up and down.

uniform (ū'nĭ·fôrm). **1.** Even, not varying, alike. **2.** Clothes that are alike in style.

unintelligible (ŭn'ĭn·tĕl'ĭ·jĭ·b'l). Not understandable.

unique (ū·nēk'). Without like or equal, matchless.

unmolested (ŭn'mȯ·lĕst'ĕd). Not interfered with or disturbed, let alone.

unperturbed (ŭn'pẽr·tûrbd'). Undisturbed, not troubled.

unresponsive (ŭn'rē·spŏn'sĭv). Not reacting readily, not answering.

unrestrained (ŭn'rē·strānd'). Free from control, interruption, or interference.

utilizes (ū'tĭ·līz·ĕz). Uses, makes use of.

V

vanguard (văn'gärd'). Those at the front of a group.

vehement (vē'ĕ·mĕnt). Acting with great force, eager.

vengeance (vĕn'jȧns). Punishment in return for an offense, revenge, retribution.

veritable (vĕr'ĭ·tȧ·b'l). Real, true, actual.

vibrating (vī'brāt·ĭng). Throbbing, moving to and fro.

vicinity (vĭ·sĭn'ĭ·tĭ). Neighborhood.

virtually (vûr'tṷ·ȧl·ĭ). Practically.

vocal (vō'kȧl). **1.** Clamorous, noisy. **2.** Related to the voice and speech.

vocation (vȯ·kā'shŭn). A line of work or employment in which one is engaged.

void (void). Emptiness, vacuum.

volition (vȯ·lĭsh'ŭn). Willingness.

W

waif (wāf). A stray person or beast.

wains (wānz). Wagons or carts.

warily (wâr'ĭ·lĭ). Watchfully, cautiously.

whet (hwĕt). To excite, to stimulate, to sharpen.

winced (wĭnst). Shrank, drew back, flinched.

writhing (rīth'ĭng). Twisting violently, as in pain.

Y

yam (yăm). The sweet potato.

---

bar; church; dog; ardŭous; fat; go; hear; jail; key; lame; meat; not; ring; pay; ran; see; shell; ten; there, thick; pastṷre; vast; wind; yes; zoo, zh = z in azure.

Index of Authors and Titles

499